LOVE AND UNITY

DISCLAIMER

The ten authors involved in this anthology have all gotten together because they wanted to do something to help Ukraine and those fighting for its people's freedom.

So, they've decided to donate all of the anthology's proceeds to the Ukrainian Defense Fund. The fund was put together by Alina Smolyar and Volodymyr Pielikh to help buy protective equipment for those fighting the senseless war against Russia's tyranny.

100% of the royalties the authors involved in this anthology get will be donated directly to the Ukraine Defense Fund.

If you'd like to learn more about this fund, or if you'd like to donate more to it, please visit the link below.

Ukrainian Defensive Territory Fund

https://www.spotfund.com/story/3b444b04-0678-4c5a-b73c-d5dcedb1d556?SFID=UkrainianDefensiveTerritory

The authors would like to collectively thank Mr. Pielikh, who is from Odessa, Ukraine, for assisting them and helping them to promote the anthology. They'd also like to thank him for generously donating his image, which has been used for the cover.

You can follow him on Instagram by visiting the link below.

Volodymyr Pielikh

https://www.instagram.com/volodymyrpielikh/

PARTICIPATING AUTHORS

Anneke Boshoff

Ayana Lisbet

D.L. Howe

Darley Collins

Havana Wilder

Kindra White

Lorelei Johnson

Louise Murchie

Melony Ann

Samantha Michaels

COPYRIGHT

First Edition, February 2022
Copyright © 2022 by Carxander Publishing

Copyright notice: All rights reserved under the International and Pan-American Copyright Conventions. No part of this book may be reproduced or transmitted in any form or by any means, electronic or mechanical, including photocopying, recording, or by any information storage and retrieval system, without permission in writing from the author or the publisher.

This book is a work of fiction. Names, places, characters, and incidents either are product of the author's imagination or are used fictitiously. Any resemblance to actual persons, living or dead, organizations, events, or locales is entirely coincidental.

Warning: The unauthorized reproduction of distribution of this copyrighted work is illegal. Criminal copyright infringement, including infringement without monetary gain, is investigated by the Federal Bureau of Investigations (FBI) and is punishable by up to five years in prison and a fine of up to $250,000.

Printed in the United States of America

ISBN: 9798827003724

Published by: Carxander Publishing
Florida

LOVE ALWAYS WINS

by Anneke Boshoff

CHAPTER 1

The Start of a Nightmare

    Prince Alexander looked at his reflection in his floor-length mirror. He's dressed in his royal attire like the good prince he is, ready to begin his search for a bride as expected from him, only downside is that Prince Alexander will be entering this year's season with a little secret of his own. His gaze landed on the photo on his bedside table, he smiled as he remembered that day.

    The thing is, Prince Alexander of Castleberry was the spare up until a few days ago. When his brother abruptly decided to abdicate the throne for reasons still unknown to them. For all Alexander cared, his brother could just as well drop dead.

    After Prince Joseph decided to abdicate, Prince Alexander was informed that he needed to return to the palace for this year's season. He will also have to find a bride, or rather, a queen in this year's season.

    Alexander didn't think highly of this as he didn't want to marry for anything other than love. He was away at college. He was set on getting married for love. Well, all plans change, as they say. And Alexander is definitely taking his life back.

    Alex stared at the photo once more, thinking about *HER*. "*Alex, this is way too high for me.*" *She laughed as Alexander held her close. She has always been afraid of heights, but she would do anything with Alexander. She was scared, yet she felt safe with him.*

    "*Do you trust me?*" *He looked at her as she smiled. She trusted him with her life, she trusted him more than she trusted herself.*

"Yes, I do. But this is high." Her hold on Alexander tightens as the instructor gives them the signal to jump. They both jumped, or rather, Alex pulled her after him. She was screaming as they went down until they came to a stop. She's still holding on to Alex as he laughed, he pulled her into a deep kiss.

"You were amazing, love. You did it! We Bungee jumped together." He laughed as he gave her another kiss.

"You are the amazing one. Thanks for doing this." She leaned into him, still hanging upside down, waiting to be taken down. This was a day they will never forget.

"Earth to Alexander!" Christian, Alexander's best friend, tried to get him out of the trance he was in. Christian being his long-time friend, they have known each other since they were little kids. Christian, being a diplomat's son, didn't care too much about all those things. He didn't even care if he had money or not.

"My apologies, Christian, were you saying something?" Alexander blushed as Christian chuckled. This is going to be a long season, he thought to himself.

"Um, I asked if you're ready?" Christian shook his head, he had never seen Alexander like this, he had always been the prime and proper prince. The one everyone could count on. Alexander only nodded as he walked toward the door. "Uh Um, Alexander..." Alexander turned, giving Christian a questioning look. "The ring." Christian motions to the ring.

"Shit, thanks, Christian." Alexander placed the ring in his breast pocket, patting it for good luck before heading out with Christian on his heels.

As Alexander stood on the pedestal with his father, he greeted each suitor that was in the season to be married. Either to him or any Duke that would want to get married. His eyes scanned the room until they landed on a beautiful girl in a pink dress standing with Christian. He would be able to know that laugh and smile out anywhere, even if there were millions of people around him.

"Your highness, it is such a pleasure to be here. May this season be fruitful for the monarch." The lady says as she holds out her hand for Alexander to kiss.

"Lady Clara, it's a pleasure to have you here as always. Please save a dance for me." Alexander kissed the back of her hand, his eyes never leaving the brunette beauty as she made her way to the line.

Alexander spoke to Kristen, another of the courtesans there to win his hand, and as she walked away, he turned to take a sip of his drink. After talking to almost all the ladies, he needed something strong. As he turned back to the receiving line, he was met with the most daring blue eyes as she smiled at him.

"Your Highness. I am honored to be here." She gave him a low curtsy, her eyes never leaving Alexander's.

"My Lady, it is my honor to have you as one of my suitors." He took her hand, kissing the back of it. He did not miss the spark as his lips met her skin, how could he, he knew that this is what was going to happen, he just needed to play it safe. He took in all her features, she was the most beautiful lady he had ever seen. Her blue eyes sparkled as she looked at him. He leaned a bit forward to whisper to her. "Jazmine!!" Alexander voiced as he looked around to make sure no one had seen him. He steps closer. "It's good to see you."

"It's good to see you as well, your Highness." She smiled at how happy Alexander seemed to see her. She knows she made the right choice to join the suitors.

"You have to understand that things here are different than back in Los Angeles." He stood up straight. He hated that he even had to mention it to her. He knew what would happen if one suitor got more attention than the others.

"I know, and it won't make me regret being here." She looked at him with a genuine smile, hoping that he would see that she wanted to be here no matter what. She just wanted to get this over with. For things to turn back to normal.

"I hope you never regret coming here." He took her hand just as his guard cleared his throat.

"I'm sorry, sir, time to move on." Alexander nodded, looking back at Jazmine.

"I'm sorry, our time has come to an end. Please save me a dance?" He didn't want to let her go, but he also knew he needed to keep it fair. This year's season will be tough on everyone.

"We really aren't in Los Angeles anymore." She gave him a sad smile. "I will see you on the dance floor." She turns towards Christian, the only other person she knows here.

Alexander watched as she walked away from him. He felt this burning fire deep inside his heart, knowing full well what he would be putting her through. She didn't deserve it. He turned back towards the first lady he had to dance with.

***

"How did it go with Alexander? Was he happy to see you?" Christian asked as he handed Jazmine a drink. He wanted Alexander to be able to find love and happiness and not just marry for political reasons.

"He did seem happy. He kept telling me things were different here. I hope he is happy." Jazmine took a sip of the Champagne. She knows coming here was the right thing to do, she just wanted more time with Alexander.

"Jaz, Alexander has a point. These noble bitches all have one thing in mind. They want to get the crown." Jazmine looked at Christian with fear in her eyes.

"Christian, that was a little too much. Alexander is just looking out for you" Jordan, one of the other noblemen, eyes Christian with a warning. Jordan is not eligible to get married yet. His older brother first needs to find a wife, which might never happen.

Jordan, Christian, and Jazmine get something to eat, talking and laughing as they share stories. Jazmine looked over and saw Alexander dancing with all the suitors, she knew this was what he should do, but still, she felt a little jealous.

As the evening came close to an end, Jazmine finally had her dance with the prince. As they swayed over the floor together, she couldn't help but notice how the light caught his eyes when he smiled at her, or how every time he saw her, his eyes shone.

They wished each other a good night as Jordan came to take her up to her room, and Alexander had other things he was obliged to do. His father requested his presence in his office, though Alexander only wanted to head to his room.

***

Alexander met his father in his office to talk about the suitors. Alexander wanted to do this, even if he already knew what he was going to do.

"Alexander, my son, have a seat." King Charles motioned for Alexander to sit on the sofa as he closed the door.

"Father, you wanted to discuss the suitors. I'm tired and would like to head to my room." Alexander was irritated, he didn't see the need for him to join the year's season, but his father demanded he did. He only hoped he would not find out what he had done before the end of the season.

"Yes, how do you feel about the ladies? Is there anyone who made the first impression on you?" Charles asked, sitting down behind his desk.

"Father, I know all the ladies. I, however, did find Lady Jazmine intriguing." He smiled as he thought about her coming all the way here for him.

"Yes, the sponsored suitor is quite a suitable suitor. Though I think she is hiding something. We were not able to get all the information on her with the background check." Charles tapped his finger against his lips for a bit before turning to Alexander.

"Father, how would she be able to hide anything for us? We have the best investigators. And if she is, we will find out" Alexander glared at his father, of course, he would find the only woman he thought was suitable to be hiding something.

"Very well, then. We will have another meeting after the Royal Regatta. By then, I want to know who your top three ladies are. You can go and rest now." Charles said before turning his attention to the files in front of him.

Alexander heads up to his room, hoping to have a quiet night and not have to deal with anyone. He saw Christian coming from his room, and he smiled. Christian nodded, walking further. Alexander grinned, picking up the pace to his room.

As he enters the room, he sees her. Her hair was down, and she had jeans on with a tank top.

"Finally, I thought they would keep you in that office all night." She smiled as she walked over to him, swaying her hips from side to side. He chuckled as he stared at her. He knows she is only trying to lighten the mood.

"No one could keep you away from me." He pulled her into his embrace. "I've missed you, my love" He lifts her face before kissing her sweetly. Her arms go around his neck, pulling him closer as she deepens the kiss.

He walks her over to the bed, and they both fall onto the mattress. "I have been waiting for this all night." He captured her lips again as she moaned, feeling him against her. They enjoy each other into the early morning before falling asleep.

Alexander woke up to a knock at the door. He looks to his side, her naked body curled up against him. He pulled her closer, kissing the top of her head. "Baby, I have to get the door. I will be right back," He got out of the bed, trying not to wake her, slipping on some sweatpants, before heading to the door.

Alexander goes to open the door to find his head guard, Brian, on the other side.

"I'm sorry for the interruption, sir. We might have a problem," Brian bows, handing a file to Alexander. Alexander looked at the papers in the file as his eyes grew wide, he looked up at Brian with a worried look.

"Does my father know?" Alexander started pacing in front of the door.

"No sir, I will keep it silent for as long as I can. I have sealed all these files." Brian wants Alexander to be happy, and keeping this information from King Charles was for the best. It would give Alexander the time that he needs.

CHAPTER 2

Off to the Derby

Alexander walked down the hall on his way to the dining room for breakfast. Today was the Derby, and he wasn't sure how it would go. After the Derby, they would be able to just relax for the rest of the day. Alexander's mind went to Jazmine, he was concerned about how the others would be treating her.

"Hey, how are you feeling about this?" Christian asked as he joined Alexander on his way to breakfast. Christian knew that Alexander wasn't dealing with this very well.

"I think it's a waste of time. You know this isn't what I want." Alexander looked down, trying to gather his strength, before looking up again, opening the door to the dining room and heading in. He was not going to see the suitors after breakfast, he didn't want to spend his breakfast with them either, but that's what a proper prince does.

Alexander walked in, greeting all the suitors before taking his seat at the front of the table. On his left, Christian was seated, and on his right, Clara had taken a seat, much to Alexander's dislike. Clara is one of the ladies that tried a little too hard. She feels they have been destined to be together since they were kids. He, on the other hand, does not see her that way.

"Your highness, it's so good to be able to have breakfast with you," Clara said as she took a sip of her coffee, batting her lashes at Alexander. He smiled at her, and looked around the room, not finding who he was looking for.

"Christian, where is she?" Alexander whispered as Christian pulled up his shoulders. He was not sure why she wasn't there yet, but he would find out.

"I don't know. Let me go check on her." He got up, heading to the door, before he could leave the room, Brian pulled him to the side.

"The King has asked to see her. Apparently, he wants to interview all the suitors before the Derby." Brian shared this information with Christian knowing fully well that he would tell Alexander. Christian nodded in understanding before heading back to the prince.

Christian stopped next to Alexander as he leaned in. "Your father asked to see her; he will be interviewing all the suitors," Christian said in half a whisper. He knew Alexander was going to flip over this. His father is trying to make things harder for Alexander.

Alexander wiped his mouth as he stared at Christian. "What the hell? I need to choose a wife, and he treats it like a job interview." Alexander was furious, his father was taking this too far. He got up and headed to his father's office.

***

Jazmine played with her fingers, feeling a little nervous before she knocked on King Charles's office door, she wasn't sure why he wanted to see her. The first thought that ran through her mind was that he had found out about her, and she was in trouble. Not having Alexander here scared her more; she wasn't even allowed to let anyone know that she was called to his office. She waited a few seconds before she heard the king calling for her to enter.

"Your Majesty, you wanted to see me." She knew how to keep him from seeing how worried she was. She had researched royalty 101.

"Yes, lady Jazmine please take a seat. We need to talk." King Charles demanded as he wanted to know what she was hiding. Her background profile was full of holes, and Alexander didn't seem to care. There was no way he would let someone like her be in the season to be chosen. "Lady Jazmine, tell me about yourself."

"There isn't much to tell, I'm from Los Angeles, and I love your country. I'm honored to be here." She wasn't sure how much she could tell him. She also didn't feel comfortable talking to him when she had no one else around her.

King Charles tapped his fingers on his desk as he stared at her with disgust. She thought she was being clever, but in reality, she was just pissing him off. "I need to know if there is anything, and I mean anything, that I should know which might cause a scandal and affect Prince Alexander's reign should he choose you." Charles hoped that he could find something out that would make her leave. He was not about to let her be with his son. He had his choice in who he wanted as queen.

"Not that I know off. I don't have a criminal record, I was an A student." She wasn't lying, the secret she had wasn't a scandal, was it? Charles narrowed his eyes at her. He could see she was hiding something, and he would find out what it was.

"Now, Lady Jazmine, you know it's an offense to lie to the king. I can have you arrested for treason." He smirked at her.

She lowered her gaze, feeling her heart racing. "Your Majesty, I……." She's interrupted by Alexander barging into the king's office.

"Father, what do you think you're doing?" Alexander asked, clearly annoyed with his father. He looked over at Jazmine, giving her a wink without his father noticing.

"Alexander, I'm interviewing the suitors to make sure you choose the right one to be queen."

"This is not a job interview, this is my life, my future." Alexander glares at his father before he turns his gaze towards Jazmine. He smiles softly at her. "I'm sorry for how my father is behaving, Lady Jazmine. You are free to go and have breakfast." She gets up, curtsying to the both of them before heading to the dining room.

As soon as Alexander heard the click of the door, he turned his fiery gaze on his father; he had so much rage that he felt like he could just blow up right there. "How could you do this? You told me I could choose. Now let this be, and let me make my own choice." Alexander was about to leave when Charles spoke.

Charles lets out a dry laugh. "You may choose anyone except Lady Jazmine. She is not suited to be queen." Charles narrowed his eyes at Alexander. He would do anything to make sure he did not choose her. Alexander doesn't turn back to his father as he returns to the dining room.

***

After breakfast, everyone headed to the race tracks, and all the suitors went through the questions from the press. Jazmine was loved by everyone, and she finally felt at ease as she walked off toward the area where they all had to meet.

As she stepped into the area, one of the ladies pushed her to the side, which caused her to almost fall. Thankfully, Christian was right there to catch her.

"Jaz, are you sure you're alright? Alexander would kill me if anything happens to you." Christian tried to see if she was hurt, and she couldn't help but chuckle a little bit.

"I'm fine, Thanks for saving me." She glared at the lady that stood there with a smirk on her face. "What are you doing here?" She turned her attention back to Christian. The guys were not going to be with them today. They would spend time together as suitors. She smiled, thinking of the time Alexander had to save her when she got lost on campus.

"Alexander, you need to help me. I have no idea where I am, and I'm scared." Her lip was quivering as she tried to keep herself from breaking down. Her phone trembled against her ear as she waited for Alexander to say something.

"Hey, I will be there in a few. Just stay where you are and keep your phone on." Alexander felt his heart racing; it was past midnight, she had to work, and he had an early class which made it impossible for him to walk her back to her dorm. And with her sense of direction, no wonder she got lost.

"Please hurry, I don't think it's safe." She tried to stop the tears from running down her face. She was so scared. She should have asked one of the other waiters to walk with her.

"Baby, I'm on my way. We know where you are. Please try and stay out of sight, we will be there in about 15 minutes." Alexander wanted to go faster, but they were still going to be a while before they would be by her side.

She stood against a wall near a light just so she could see who was approaching her. She felt her heart sinking when she saw three guys walking her way. Guys walking around this time of the night didn't mean anything good. She would never be able to take them all. Just as they got near her, a black SUV stopped. Before the car came to a complete stop, Alexander jumped out and ran towards her. She felt relieved that he was there.

"Alexander!" She cried, running to him. He pulled her to him, wrapping his arms around her to keep her safe.

"You're safe, love. I've got you!" He kissed the top of her head, leading her to the waiting SUV. "Now, let's get you home." He smiled at her while she rested her head on his shoulder. He will always come running when she needs him.

"Hey Jaz, are you still with me?" She snapped out of her memory when Christian shook her. She forgot that he was there.

"Yes, sorry. What are you doing here again?" She narrowed her eyes at him.

He wiggled his eyebrows at her as he threw his arm over her shoulders. Christian wasn't your average stuck-up Duke, he was more laid back and treated everyone the same. "I was sent to come to steal you." He starts to lead her away.

She laughed as she covered her heart with her hands. "Yes, please, that would be so much better." She smiled just thinking about being taken to Alexander. Christian led her towards the royal tent, he knew it would only be him and Alexander in the tent. Alexander might not have asked him to come to get her, but he knows Alexander would want to see her.

"You go in, I will get us some drinks." He smiled, handing her his card. She walked in, seeing Alexander looking out over the track, and she walked up to him wrapping her arms around him from the back. He tensed until he heard her sweet voice.

"Penny for your thoughts, your highness" She smirked, knowing how he feels when she calls him that.

He grabbed her hands, holding them to his chest. "I was just thinking of this beautiful lady and when I would see her again." He pulled her to his front, looking deep into her eyes. She wrapped her arms around his neck as he pulled her flush against him. This is all he wanted, to have her against him like this. He leaned down, and just before their lips met, Christian walked into the tent.

"Shit, sorry guys." He looked away, blushing. Alexander looked up, laughing at him. He turned to him, still holding on to Jazmine.

"It's fine, you always had a tendency to enter at the worst possible times." He chuckled as Christian gave him a smirk.

They spend the moment talking and just relaxing. Prince Alexander felt that he could be himself with Christian and Jazmine, and not the prim and proper prince everyone expected him to be.

"You should head to the other suitors." Alexander held her, not wanting to let her go, though he knew he had to.

"Will I see you again today?" She didn't want to leave him, she wanted to spend her time with him, but she knew they had to be careful and that she could only see him when he saw all the suitors.

"I will see you tonight." He leaned down, giving her a gentle, lusting kiss. When they broke apart, she smiled at him, wishing this didn't have to end. She walks out, giving him one last longing look.

Christian leads her to the other suitors, and as soon as she arrives, she wishes she was anywhere but there. "And where have you been?" Clara asked in an annoyed tone. Lady Clara had a dislike for Jazmine, and Jazmine knew exactly why. Clara didn't like anyone but herself.

"I got lost, but here I am now." She tried to walk away from their discussion.

"Getting lost, and it's only the second day. You will never make it till the end." Clara laughed, pushing her to the side.

Jazmine was sick of being pushed around. "Don't be so sure about that. I'm here for the prince and not to make friends with you." Jazmine felt the anger building in her, and she wanted to get out of there.

"Now, you listen to me. The prince and I will be together, it is how it always has been. We will be married, and no one will take that from me." Clara glared at her.

"It's such a shame the prince doesn't know that." Jazmine turned around and saw the driver that had to take her back to the palace approaching her. She was ready to leave and head to the lunch the queen wanted with all the suitors.

"Clara, you might want to see this," Kamilla, one of the foreign dignitaries' daughters, handed Clara her phone. Clara's eyes grow wide as she takes in the article.

"That bitch!" She said under her breath.

CHAPTER 3

Lunch With The Queen

Clara smirked as she looked at the phone, this might be just what she needed to make sure Alexander will be hers. "Kamilla, not a word of this to anyone. Do you understand?" Clara didn't want to risk anyone knowing this before she could use it to her benefit, and the event in Prince Alexander's winter home will be the perfect time to do it.

Clara and Kamilla watched as Jazmine got in the car before heading to their vehicles. They were heading to the palace for lunch with the queen, and Clara felt confident in the time she was going to spend with Alexander. She was going to make it a point to see him as much as she could.

***

"So, Jazmine, how did you like the Derby?" Jordan asked as Jazmine got comfortable in the car. She didn't know that Jordan would be in the car with her, not until she got in.

Jazmine smiled at Jordan. "It was great." She didn't know Jordan that well. He is one of Alexander's friends, but not one that Alexander trusted to be near her.

They arrive at the palace, where Jordan takes it upon himself to escort Lady Jazmine over to the other suitors. She felt nervous as all the ladies spoke of a surprise suitor, one that was a trusted friend of the queen. Jasmine knew she had nothing to be worried about, but a few said it was a princess from some small country that had her sights set on Prince Alexander.

"How are you always late?" Clara scoffed at Jazmine as she stood next to her.

"I'm not late." Jazmine didn't even look at her. She has had enough of Clara for one day. They were all standing in the dining hall waiting for the queen to come before they were allowed to take their seats.

They saw the Queen arrive with a Blond petit lady next to her. All the suitors gasped as they saw her. She wasn't supposed to be in this season. She's too old for Prince Alexander. Jazmine watched the lady as she walked with the queen to inspect all the suitors. She wasn't sure what made this lady so special.

"I thought I would only have to deal with one bitch then another joins us." Clara was fuming, she wanted them gone. Prince Alexander was hers, he has always been hers.

The longer Jazmine watched the lady walk, the more she tried to remember who she was. She suddenly gasps when she remembers what Alexander told her about Meredith, the one suitor that went crazy on Alexander's brother. This blond girl must be Meredith, and Jazmine doesn't want her near Alexander. Unfortunately, she knew she couldn't do anything about it as he had to be fair to all the suitors. She shook her head as she straightened up when the queen motioned for them all to take their seats.

Meredith narrows her eyes at Jazmine before she leans closer to the queen. "That's the one I told you about, she thinks the prince will choose her," Meredith whispers to the queen. The queen trained her eyes on Jazmine, watching her. She couldn't see anything wrong with the girl if she was being honest. The girl seemed well taken care of and good-mannered.

The queen asked Jazmine and the other suitors a few questions as they waited for the lunch to be served. Jazmine answered everything as truthfully as she could, there were things she couldn't disclose, and she was fine with it.

Clara made it a point to try to embarrass Jazmine, but she was able to remain calm and lady-like even though she wanted to strangle Clara at the first available chance she would get. The Queen, however, didn't seem to pay any attention to Clara at all. She was mostly conversing with Meredith and one of the other ladies that Jazmine hadn't met yet.

After they said their goodbyes to the queen, they all made their way over to their rooms. Jazmine was about to enter her suite when the lady she had not met yet walked up to her.

"Lady Jazmine, I don't think I have had the pleasure of meeting you." She held out her hand. "I'm Jolene Sung." She smiled as Jazmine took her hand, shaking it softly.

"It's a pleasure to meet you." Jazmine turned towards her door when she heard Alexander laugh, and then she heard Jolene speak.

"Your Highness, it's so good to see you. I didn't think we would be able to see you today." Jazmine internally rolled her eyes at the fake, sweet voice Jolene had put on. She could hear that Jolene was nervous but also flirty.

"I was just heading out to get some dessert with Christian and Jordan. Why don't you and Lady Jazmine join us?" Alexander winks at Jazmine without anyone noticing. He knows that if Jolene comes with them, he gets to spend a little time with Jazmine, even if they won't be able to touch each other. Just being near her will be perfect.

Jolene bit her lip as she stared at Alexander. "I would love to join you. I love ice cream."

"You know what we need." Alexander smiled at Jazmine as he wanted to do this just for her, but needed to be fair to all the ladies or at least as fair as possible.

"We need real food." Christian chirped in while Jolene laughed at his boldness.

"Christian, you always complain about the food. Let's hear what Alexander suggests." Jazmine smiles as Christian rolls his eyes. She knew him too well.

"Let's go out for some gelato instead." Alexander saw the excitement in Jazmine's eyes and the hope on Christian's face.

"That would be amazing, but do they have gelato here?" Jazmine couldn't believe that Alexander wanted to get some gelato. She was aware that it was not that big of a deal and that they probably had gelato everywhere in the world. It was her favorite dessert. She also knew that the guys didn't have it until she introduced it to them.

"Jaz, what do you mean this is the best thing I will ever eat?" Christian wasn't sure about this. He didn't like strange food, and this looked strange to him. It looked like ice cream, but it was different.

"Christian, just trust me. Alexander had some last week, and he's still alive. I really want one, but I want you to have one with me. Please..." She gave him her best puppy dog eyes. Christian had to stay with her, while Alexander had to head back to the palace to sort out some things with his family. They had only been dating for a month, but she already hated the fact that he was not with her. Christian offered to stay with her for the two weeks he was going to be away.

"Okay, Jaz, I will get one with you. But if I die, I'm haunting you for the rest of your life and your children's lives" Christian chuckled as she got up, getting them both one.

She sat the cherry gelato down in front of him. He looked up at her as she smiled at him, motioning for him to take a bite. He took his first bite, and it was as if the angels were dancing on his tongue, a smile forming on his face.

"Well?" she asked as she could barely contain her excitement.

"I have to hand it to you, Jaz. You made me speechless." Jazmine leaped forward, hugging Christian. She only wanted them to enjoy it as much as she did.

"So, we all meet just after sunset at the front of the palace?" Alexander spoke, bringing Jazmine out of her memory, this was his chance to spend some more time with Jazmine. He just didn't know if he could trust Jolene. Everyone nodded as they went to their separate rooms. Jazmine was the only one in front of her room already.

Alexander was heading to his room when Meredith stopped him. He didn't have time for her. He never wanted her to be one of his suitors in the first place, she was older than him, and he didn't like her at all. She just wants the crown and power.

"Alexander, what are you doing?" Meredith asked, tapping her foot on the floor, her arms crossed over her chest.

"Whatever are you talking about?" Alexander didn't have time for these games, he wanted to get ready to meet his friends for the night out. He also didn't know who made her his keeper.

"How could you bring her here? We both know what she did and how she ruined Joseph." Meredith was furious that Alexander didn't care what happened to Joseph. Joseph was supposed to be his brother. His family. He is supposed to protect his family.

"Meredith, you don't know what you are talking about. Jazmine is a suitor. I will treat all the suitors fairly." Alexander smirked. He had no idea what was going on, but he had to watch her carefully. She could ruin everything.

CHAPTER 4

When You Look Like That

Jazmine stood outside at the front of the palace, waiting for her friends and Alexander. She was so excited to spend some time with them outside of the castle. Even though no one knows that she knows them more than they think. She heard footsteps behind her, and when she turned around, she saw Brian walking her way.

"Lady Jazmine. It's not safe for you to be out here alone." He bowed to her before checking the area.

"Brian, it's good to see you. And I'm fine, I'm waiting for the others, we're heading to a bakery to have some gelato. I probably shouldn't have told you." She hangs her head, ever since Alexander told her who he was, Brian has always been there. He was assigned to Joseph, so the last few months before Alexander had to come back, he was around, and she grew fond of him. He always looked after them no matter where they went.

"Lady Jazmine, that's why I like you so much. You make my job so much easier. But if I must be honest, Alexander did tell me he plans on going out to the bakery tonight." He smiled at her, she was unlike any of the girls Alexander and Joseph used to hang out with. He could see why Alexander cared so much about her, and he would do everything to keep her safe.

They were standing around waiting for the others to come. Brian didn't want to leave her alone outside, Alexander had his other guard with him, and Brian would be following the group out for the evening.

"Lady Jazmine……. I'm so excited." Jolene squealed before she noticed Brian. She gave Jazmine a questioning look, not understanding what the head guard was doing with Jazmine.

"It's fine; Brian was just keeping me company while I was waiting for you all to come. Where are the others?" She gave Jolene a reassuring smile.

"Here we are, I'm so ready for this party to get started." Jordan came dancing around the corner in his goofy way.

"This is not a party, we are getting something to eat. That's it." Christian glared at Jordan, which made the ladies laugh a little. Christian greeted all of them before he noticed the look on Jolene's face. Jolene kept looking between Jazmine and Brian. "Jolene, is everything alright?"

"Yes, Christian, everything is fine." Jolene smiled, she didn't know Christian would pick up on her expression. Something was going on between Brian and Jazmine, and she wanted to find out. She had to impress her parents, and she would do what she had to do to get the prince.

"Sorry I'm late, I had a run-in with Meredith. Are we ready to head out?" Alexander greeted the group. When his eyes locked on Jazmine, he smiled; she looked perfect. Her hair was in a messy bun with a few strands hanging around her face, she had a pink flowing top on with a pair of skinny jeans. Jolene noticed the way Alexander looked at Jazmine, and she felt like she could push her from the steps. She knew that she was just one of the girls that might get the prince, but she didn't want him looking at others the way he looked at Jazmine.

"We weren't going to leave without you, we don't know what bakery has the gelatos," Jordan said, a little too excited.

They all laughed and headed to the waiting SUV. Alexander wanted this time with Jazmine, but now he had to share it with all the others, and he couldn't even get too close to her. They all pile into the car, with Jazmine, Alexander, and Jolene sitting in the middle while Christian and Jordan are in the back. When they got to the bakery, Jordan ran to the counter to order them all some Gelato. Christian told him it's not how it works as Alexander laughed, telling them he will order what they need while the others got a table. He headed to the counter as Jazmine walked with him.

"That was so sweet of you to invite everyone." She smiled as she ordered their drinks. Even though they were having dessert, they still needed some alcohol.

Alexander brushed his hand against her arm, making sure that no one was looking. "I would rather spend this time alone with you. Unfortunately, they were all there when I wanted to invite you. So, you see, my love, I was selfish." He whispered to her as she nibbled on her lip, beaming at him.

"You, Mr. Charming, are everything, but selfish." She grinned at him. He shook his head, he was not going to win. She had this way with him. She made him melt with just a look.

They got the order and walked over to the group. Alexander took a seat next to Christian, and before Jazmine could sit next to Alexander, Jolene stole the chair.

"You don't mind if I spend some time with Alexander? You went to order with him." Jolene smiled at Jazmine with a look of competition in her eyes.

"No, of course, I don't mind." Jazmine met Alexander's eyes, he could see the hurt in her irises, and he hated that. One thing he never wanted was for Jazmine to get hurt. He didn't want to be the cause of her tears. He knew at that moment they couldn't underestimate Jolene. Jazmine took the seat between Christian and Jordan.

"Jazmine, why don't we change seats?" Christian said in a low whisper; she nodded, and he got up, switching seats with her. Jolene glared at them; why does she need to be close to Alexander all the time?

They spend the evening talking and enjoying the gelato. Jordan kept saying how good it was, even though it was something simple. Alexander told them all about the things he and Christian did when they were younger. Jazmine understood more of the stuff they did now that she was seeing some of the places.

"Now, Prince Alexander, tell us how you feel about this year's season. Are there any front runners? Do you know if any of the nobles are interested in any of the ladies?" Jolene asked in her most innocent voice. Christian saw the way she eyed Jazmine anytime Alexander would say something to her. Alexander looked down before he spoke.

He reached his hand out and took Jazmine's one under the table, giving it a reassuring squeeze.

"I'm enjoying getting to know all the ladies. It's still early in the season for me to know how I feel. As for the other nobles, anything is possible." He smiled at Jolene, never letting go of Jazmine's hand. He knew this was going to be difficult, but he never wanted her to be in pain, and, at this moment, everything Jolene was doing was to hurt her. He, most of all, doesn't want Jazmine to doubt him. "I think it's time to head back to the palace. We don't want the guards to come looking for us." Alexander looked down at his watch, he wanted to head back, not because of the guards, but because he wanted to spend time alone with his girl.

They all got up before heading out. The group walked down the street with Brian not trailing far behind them. Jolene slowed down and fell into step next to Alexander. She had never done something like this, yet she wanted to be with Alexander so much more now that she had spent some time with him away from the other ladies. The way he spoke to her made her feel special.

Christian glanced over his shoulder at Alexander and Jolene before he turned his attention towards Jazmine. "Jaz, how are you holding up?" Christian asked as she walked between him and Jordan.

Jazmine shrugged her shoulders. "I'm alright, I think. Christian, this is harder than I thought. Every time I see him with one of the other ladies, I get jealous. I know he said I shouldn't worry and that he loves me. But I can't help it. I mean, here I am talking with you, and there Jolene is walking with him. It's just hard." She hung her head as she felt the tears starting to form in her eyes. Things were so much easier back in Los Angeles. Alexander saw that Jazmine didn't seem to look at Christian after she spoke, and he felt his heart breaking. He wanted to go to her, and take her in his arms, and never let her go, but he needed to play this safe, and with Jolene here, it wasn't safe. He couldn't let anyone know what was going on before the day of the coronation.

"Things will be alright. There are only a few more events, and then it's time for him to choose." Christian placed his arm around her shoulders, giving her a side hug. This was hard for both of his friends, and he would do what he could to help them through this.

"Thanks, Christian, I can always count on you to cheer me up." She laughed as he smiled at her. She could always count on Christian, that much she knew. Even after he and Joseph almost set the dorm on fire. She could still remember Christian running down the hall with nothing on but a cowboy hat and his boots. It was the talk of the dorm for at least a week.

Alexander and Jolene caught up with the group, much to Jolene's dislike. They walk to the SUV, get in, and head back to the palace. Once they arrived at the castle, everyone retreated to their rooms for the rest of the evening. The prince winked at his favorite woman, and she knew what that meant. He would send Christian or Brian over a bit later to help her sneak into his suite like he has done every night since they have been here.

***

Alexander sat on the sofa, going through some emails when the door to his quarters opened. He looked up and saw Jazmine waltzing in.

"Hey, Beautiful," he got up, striding over to her. He wrapped his arms around her and pulled her closer to him. "I've missed you." His lips fall on hers before he guides her to the sofa.

"Alexander. We need to talk." She looked at him with concern written all over her face. She loved him so much, and she was all for sneaking around to be with him, but this was getting too much for her. She never wanted to share him.

He looked at her and could see the emotions running through her eyes. He moved closer to her, pulling her as close as possible. He hated what this was doing to her. She has always been this free spirit, and he loved that about her.

"What's wrong, Love?" He moved a bit to be able to look her in the eyes.

"I don't like sharing you with the other ladies. I know you said that this would be hard, and we aren't in Los Angeles anymore, but the way the other girls are treating you gets me upset. You aren't a trophy to be won, you're you, the kindest, most loving person I know." She bit her lip, trying to keep her emotions intact. The last thing she wanted was for Alexander to feel bad about her having a terrible day.

He lifted his hand to her face, rubbing his thumb along her cheek. "Baby, you aren't sharing me with anyone. Yes, I have to indulge my father's request for this season, but you are the only one for me." He kissed her on the lips. She smiles into the kiss. He always knew just what to say. "And as for the other ladies; to them, I am just a trophy, but to you, I'm so much more. You see me as no one has ever seen me."

"You are my everything, Alexander." She giggled as he brought her to the bed. He sat down, pulling her on his lap. She rested her head on his shoulder as he wrapped his arms around her waist, holding her flush against him.

"Alexander, you never told me why you got a bakery to stock up on gelatos and have them add it to their menu." She tilted her head, staring at him. She wanted to hear the story, he would always do romantic things for her, but to have them keep gelatos in stock just for her was amazing.

Alexander smiled at her as he let her stand, moving further up on the bed. He sat with his back against the headboard before he motioned for her to sit with him. She curled up to his side, lying with her head on his chest as he rubbed her arm, holding her close.

"It was the first time I came back home. You and I had them the week before, and when I was out with Joseph doing a morning meeting in the capital, I missed you so much, I went from bakery to bakery trying to find something that would make me feel close to you, and when I got to this bakery, that baker asked me what he could do to make my day special. I told him how I wanted gelato as it reminded me of you. He agreed to make me some and promised he would always keep it for me, should I need some to remind me of you." The prince looked down at her as she wiped a tear from her cheek. He didn't think back then they would be where they are today, but he's happy that things happened as they did, and all he wanted to do was spend as much time with her as he could.

"Alexander, that was so thoughtful of the baker. He was not there this evening, I would have loved to meet him. I missed you just as much, by day three, Christian wanted to throw me off the cliff. You came back just in time." Jazmine ran her nails down Alexander's side, causing him to jump as she tickled him.

"You have asked for it." He pinned her down, bending over her with his knees on either side of her as he tickled her, causing her to scream as she tried to get away from him.

"Alex!" She wiggled under him, trying her best to stop him from his tickle attack. He laughed as he looked down at her, keeping her in place.

"Are you going to tickle me again?" Alexander asked as he stopped for a moment. She laughed, shaking her head no. She was breathless from laughing so much. He leaned down, kissing her softly as he let go of her hands, and she wrapped her hands around his neck, pulling him closer to her as she deepened the kiss. They break apart breathless, staring at each other, their foreheads and noses touching.

After a while, there is a knock on Alexander's door. He knew it was probably Brian or Christian to escort Jazmine back to her room.

Jazmine tightened her hold on Alexander. "Do I have to go? I will never be able to sleep without you." She pouted at him as he chuckled at the face she was making.

"I'm sorry, love, you can't stay tonight. I wish you could, I want you by my side always. Unfortunately, my father will be here early tomorrow morning, and we can't risk having him find you here." Alexander kissed her on the lips before he headed to the door as the knocking was more urgent.

Alexander opened the door, thinking Christian or Brian was on the other side. His eyes grew wide, taking in the persons on the other side.

"Father! Countess Meredith!" Alexander was shocked. What were they doing there?! Worst of all, they were going to see Jazmine in his bed, and that could be dangerous.

CHAPTER 5

Craving You

Alexander stood in his doorway; he had to get rid of them, he couldn't let them see Jazmine in his room.

"Alexander, we need to talk to you about your choice." Charles gave Alexander a look that let him know there wasn't any room for negotiations. He had to make sure Alexander would choose Meredith, they had an agreement with George, and he wasn't about to let his son ruin it. Joseph already ruined it by abdicating and leaving Meredith stranded in the states.

"Father, we have already discussed the choices I have. I will not be discussing it in front of Countess Meredith." Alexander glared at Meredith; his father will not force him to choose her. He pushed Joseph and looked at what had happened.

"Alexander! I know about Joseph and Jazmine and how she caused the break-up between Meredith and Joseph." Charles stated. He had a feeling Jazmine was up to no good, and now learning about her involvement with Joseph made sense. She jumped from one prince to the other.

"Father, it's not what you think. And even if it is, Meredith was involved with Joseph as well before now." Alexander felt his anger building up inside him.

Charles narrowed his eyes at Alexander but knew they weren't going to get anywhere tonight. "Alexander, we will continue this later. I can see that you are upset now." He nodded to Meredith as they left.

Alexander slammed his door closed, he knew his father would do anything to make this harder for him. Jazmine walked over to him, seeing the anger in his eyes, she knew something had happened. He pulled her to him before he roughly crashed his lips on hers in a bruising, demanding kiss. She was shocked at first; she had never seen Alexander like this. She threw her arms around his neck, deepening the kiss. Alexander picked her up in one swift motion, taking her over to the bed.

"Alexander..." She moaned as he tucked her close to his chest, and she could feel his hard cock throbbing against her. He grinded himself on her center a few times.

"Shhh.... I need you, Love." She could see the desire and need dancing in his eyes. She pulled him into her as they got lost in each other, forgetting about the world outside the four walls of his bedroom.

The first rays of sun came through the window when Alexander was woken up by a knock on the door. He glanced to his side, contemplating Jazmine as she was peacefully sleeping. She looked like an angel wrapped in his white sheet. Having her in his arms is all he ever wanted. He tried to move out of the bed without waking Jazmine up, covering her with the blanket, he put on some sweat pants and walked to the door, opening it to find Brian on the other side.

"Good morning, your highness. I'm sorry I couldn't come earlier. Countess Meredith was watching me, and she had someone following Christian." Brian bowed to Alexander. He hated that the prince had to go through this. Being the head guard made him know things that others didn't know.

Alexander waved his hand, dismissing Brian's concern. "It gave me a few more hours with her. The next event I won't be able to see her this much." Alexander smiled, he turned to get ready to leave.

After getting ready, he walked over to the bed, kissing Jazmine before waking her up. "Sweetheart, I need to go." He brushed his knuckles over her cheek as her eyes fluttered open.

"Do we have to?" She pouted as he let out a chuckle.

"Yes, we have to. Do you remember what I told you about this event? Please don't ever doubt my feelings for you. I love you so much." He leaned down, giving her another kiss. For the next event, he would have to give most of his attention to Dutchess Clara. Seeing as she would be hosting the event in Prince Alexander's winter house.

"I'm going to try. You will just have to make it up to me. And I love you as well, Alexander."

"I will see you soon." Alexander hugged her before heading out. He hated leaving her. All Alexander wanted to do was to tell everyone how he felt and what he wanted. He wanted all this to end right now.

***

Soon after Alexander left, Jordan and Christian came to get Jazmine to head to the winter home. Jazmine was staring out the window, Christian could see something was bothering her.

"What's on your mind?" Christian took her hand, squeezing it lightly.

"Christian, this is a whole week where I have to pretend to be alright with Alexander spending all his time with Clara. The one lady who told me I will not have him and that he will be hers." Jazmine didn't look at Christian, she couldn't let him see the tears forming behind her eyes. She was never this emotional, but then again, she never had to share Alexander.

Christian shared a look with Jordan. "Jaz, we will be there for you. And Alexander will be there. He hates this just as much as you do." Christian wished there was something more they could do. He wanted her to know how Alexander felt. Alexander wanted to stop this whole season, but with King Charles demanding it, Alexander couldn't go against the council or his father.

"Thanks, Christian, I will just have to be strong, I guess." There wasn't much she could do. She needed to be strong for them, as Alexander couldn't do anything. She also couldn't go home, that would mean she would lose Alexander forever, and this is something she didn't want.

They arrived at the winter home just as everyone was heading out to the lake to skate. Jazmine went to her assigned room; as she walked in, she found Brian waiting for her.

"Hey, Brian. Is everything alright?" She asked as she walked to her bed.

"Lady Jazmine, I was just securing your room as per Prince Alexander's orders. And I needed to make sure you were alright."

Brian gave her a reassuring smile. "Now, I do believe Prince Alexander has left you something." He nodded towards the closet as Jazmine went to it, seeing the outfit Alexander sent her.

"Brian, this is astonishing!" She smiled as she walked into the closet to get her dress.

Brian straightened himself as he watched her eyes sparkle. "He didn't want you to be cold. I will tell him you love it. Be safe, lady Jazmine, I will see you down there." Brian left the room, ensuring no one saw him. He knew this was the best for Alexander, he would do what he could to keep their secret. He would also do what he could to keep the two of them safe.

Jazmine got dressed in a pair of thighs and an oversized winter jersey before she met Jordan at the lake. While getting ready, she saw Clara talking to Alexander, and she felt her heart twitching at the sight of them. Clara had her hand in his and they were laughing. Every time Clara said something, she would put her hand on Alexander's chest.

"Jaz, come on, let's go skating." Jordan pulled her onto the lake as they went around talking. Jazmine lost her footing and fell on her ass. She sat on the frozen lake, laughing as Jordan tried to help her up.

Alexander looked over toward Jordan and Jazmine once he heard her laughter. Seeing her sitting on the ice, he wanted to go and help her, but he saw the way Clara was looking at him.

Clara didn't like the way Alexander's attention was divided. She saw the way he wanted to go to Jazmine, and she wasn't going to allow it. "Prince Alexander, there is something I need to tell you. Could we talk in private, please?" Clara pulled Alexander to the side, taking him to a bench. She made a point of it to sit as close to him as possible.

"What's going on, Clara?" Alexander's eyebrows furrowed as he looked at her. There was something in her eyes Alexander had never seen before.

"Alexander, I don't know how to say this. I know you are fond of Lady Jazmine. You should know that she has a secret relationship with Brian. She's been leading you on." Clara looked down; she didn't want Alexander to see the smirk on her face.

"What do you mean? How sure are you?" Alexander's jaw was set as he spoke through gritted teeth. He had to make it as if he was upset, but he also needed to know why she thought they were seeing each other.

"Yes, I have proof." Clara handed Alexander her phone, he saw a photo of Brian and Jazmine. It was raining, and Brian was holding an umbrella for her with his hand on the small of her back. Alexander could see why Clara would think that. It would be something people in a relationship would do, but it would also be something a father or brother would do for their sister. And he knew that is how Brian saw Jazmine. The daughter he never had. "And this is not all. I saw him leaving her room at the palace a few nights ago. I also saw him with her outside the palace the day of the lunch with the queen. Alexander, I just want you to be careful. She's here for the wrong reasons." Clara gave Alexander the best apologetic look she could. She was thankful for the information Lady Jolene had given her.

"Thank you, Clara. I will look into it." He got up to leave when she pulled him close. She got on her tiptoes, and before she could kiss him, he placed his hand on her mouth. "Lady Clara, we cannot be doing this. I need to be fair with all the ladies." He shook his head as he took a step away from her.

Jazmine sat on the side of the lake as she watched Clara and Alexander on a nearby bench. She didn't notice Jolene approaching her until she heard her talk. "It's so unfair that she has this advantage, don't you think? Just because she has known the royal family since they were kids, she gets to host an event." Jolene sat down next to Jazmine.

"We will all get that advantage, won't we?" She tried to look at Jolene, but the tears were forming in her eyes, and she didn't want Jolene to see them, she didn't know what was wrong with her. She needed to stop crying about everything.

"I won't. The court won't be visiting my home. I think Clara might be the front runner. Look at the way Prince Alexander is looking at her." Jolene smirked as she looked at the hurt on Jazmine's face.

"I'm sorry, Jolene, I need to go." Jazmine got up and looked in Alexander's direction just as Clara pulled him to her, ready to kiss him. She turned around and went back to the house. She felt the warmth of the tears threatening to spill as she tried to get to the house as soon as possible, not noticing Christian in front of her until it was too late.

"Jaz, where's the fire?" Christian asked, taking her in. His blood turned to ice as he saw the tears dancing in her eyes.

"Christian I just need to get out of here." She tried to pass around him, but he blocked her path.

"Jaz, what happened?" He pulled her to the side, knowing she was upset with something.

"He kissed Clara and that in front of everyone. Christian, why would he do that?" She felt the tears streaming down her cheeks. She has never been this hurt before. Couldn't they just go back to how it was? The two of them were far away from here and happy.

Christian glanced around, trying to see what she was talking about. Alexander would never do something like that. "Are you sure? Alexander would never do that!" Christian was confused as he knew Alexander, and this was not like him. He wouldn't put everything he and Jazmine worked in jeopardy just to kiss Clara.

She wasn't. The way it looked, they were about to kiss. "No, I left when she pulled him closer to her. I couldn't stand there and watch. And Lady Jolene says that Clara is the front runner, and this is only by the way Alexander looks at her." She wiped her tears from her face as she heard Clara telling everyone they were going skiing.

"Jaz, I don't think he kissed her. Let's go skiing and then I will talk to him. What do you say?" He held his hand out for her. She took it as they walked to the top together. After skiing, they all headed inside to warm up. Clara walked up to Jordan, Christian, and Jazmine, whining about why Christian didn't join them for ice skating. Jazmine had just about enough of Clara with all her down talking. Christian was her friend, and she wasn't going to have her speak to him like that.

"Clara, can you please just stop being such a bitch?" Jazmine felt her blood boil. She wanted to make sure Clara knew she was not going to sit around and watch her destroy her friends. She might think that she has the upper hand, but she does not.

"Aww... Does Cinderella have a soft spot for the bad boy duke?" Clara bats her eyes, laughing at Jazmine. "As much as I would like to stay here and chat with you, I promised Prince Alexander a private tour of the extension that was built while he was in America, and it might end in my quarters. I can't promise he would want any of you ladies when I'm done with him." She smirked, giving Jazmine a wink.

Jazmine watched Clara leave, feeling her heart falling to the floor. Clara was giving Alexander a private tour, and she planned on taking him to her quarters. She trusts Alexander, but she doesn't trust Clara.

Jazmine wiped her eyes before a tear could run down her cheeks. "I'm going to head to my room. See you all tomorrow" She got up, but Christian stopped her from leaving.

"Jaz, don't listen to Clara. You know Alexander will never go with her." Christian tried to reassure her, but he knew she would only feel better once she saw Alexander.

She shook her head as she hugged herself. She hated feeling like this. "I know, I'm just tired. I will see you in the morning." She smiled. She hugged Jordan before giving Christian one as well.

She walked to her room, thinking of what Clara had said. She needed to see Alexander, she hadn't spoken to him the whole day. She knew Alexander wouldn't be alone with Clara. Brian would be with him. She hoped.

As she walked into her room, she found a single red rose on her vanity with a note. She smiled as she read over the message.

To my Love,
I missed you so much today. Clara is making things difficult for me.
Thinking of you is the only thing that will get me through this time.
I love you more than anything.
A xxxx

She took the rose and added it to the flower arrangement; she felt better knowing Alexander was thinking of her. Even though he couldn't see her and she couldn't see him, she was still close to him.

She laid down on her bed, she hadn't realized how tired she was until she was on the bed. Just before she fell asleep, she heard Clara moan. She couldn't make out what was happening, so she got up and headed to the door when she heard it.

"Yes.... Alexander just like that," Clara moaned. Jazmine stopped instantly and felt as if the room was closing in on her. She felt like she couldn't breathe as she heard Clara's moans growing louder.

CHAPTER 6

Take It From Me

Jazmine dropped to her knees, hearing Clara scream Alexander's name over and over. She felt like someone had ripped her heart out, yet she never heard Alexander say anything. She has been with Alexander more than once, and every time she was with him, he wasn't quiet. Not if Clara was having that much fun. She should have heard Alexander at least once.

She walked over to her bed, taking her phone. If he were with Clara, he wouldn't be able to text her back. She typed out the text as Clara was moaning more and more.

Hey, are you done with your tour? Once she hit send, it wasn't long before she saw the three dots and got a reply.

A while ago. I wish I could see you. I missed you so much today. A smile grew on her face as she read the text. Before she could reply, her phone started ringing. She saw Christian's number and wondered what was going on.

"Hello," She said, a little unsure.

"Baby, it's me. Can you sneak out?" Alexander said half in a whisper.

"I can try. Where should I meet you?" She looked around the room, trying to find a way to get out of there unseen.

"Two doors from yours, there is a staircase, follow it to the top. I will be waiting for you there. Please say you will come," Alexander's voice was soft and gentle. All he wanted was to see her.

Since they arrived and Clara basically kidnapped him, they haven't seen each other at all.

"Alright, give me 10 minutes. Love you." She got dressed in thighs and a loose sweater. As she opened the door, the hall was empty and quiet. Even Clara wasn't making a sound anymore. She walked to the stairs, running up them, wanting to get to the top to see Alexander.

Alexander looked down just as she came into view, she looked breathtaking. How could he ever consider any of these women when he has her? She was perfect for him.

He walked up to her, wrapping his arms around her waist. All he wanted was to be with her. She leaned into him as his lips came crashing down on hers. They got lost in the kiss that they needed like they needed air. After a while, as they broke apart, Alexander looked at her. He could see something was bothering her. He took her hand, leading her through a door, and before she knew it, they were in his room.

"Baby, what's wrong? I can see there is something that's bothering you." He took her hands in his.

"Clara said some things to me, and then I heard her tonight and I really thought that was happening, but then you phoned me, and I knew that it wasn't. I think I'm just a little overwhelmed." She smiled at him weakly. He felt his anger boiling in him, Clara can be bitchy, he needed to know what she said to her.

"Love, what did she tell you, and what did you hear?"

Jazmine tangled her fingers together as she took a deep breath, letting it out slowly. "She told me that she was giving you a private tour that might end up at her quarters and that after she's done with you, you wouldn't want any of us. Then just as I was about to go to bed, I heard her moaning. She screamed your name, Alexander. It felt like I was punched in the gut listening to another woman screaming your name." She hung her head as the tears were about to form. She hated being this girl. She was never like this, she was strong and didn't let people get to her. But she loved Alexander so much, and the thought of losing him killed her.

Alexander pulled Jazmine against his chest. "Baby, I promise you I was not with her. She gave me a tour of the armory, and after that, I went to my room. Brian was with me the whole time. I hate seeing you like this. I'm going to tell everyone, I can't put you through this anymore." He got up walking to his door, he had enough of this. She was unhappy with all this that he had to do. Everyone was speculating about her, but no one knew the truth, except him, Christian, Joseph, and Brian.

"Alexander, no! You worked too hard for this. Your father won't accept it, and he will make things difficult for you. I will just have to weather the events. I love you." She pulled him back to the bed. She just wanted him to hold her, even if it was only for a moment. She couldn't let him give up what he worked so hard for just because she couldn't handle the touchy ladies.

"Alright, but I'm placing Christian by you for protection. And we will sort out your room situation. If Clara could do this, then anyone could be planning something." Alexander cupped her cheeks and smiled at her. He loved her so much and wanted this to be over. He wanted to be able to spend his life with her and only her.

***

The following evening was the winter ball. Everyone was excited about this ball; Jazmine, however, wondered what Clara had in store for her. She made her way down to the boutique to get ready. As she walked in, she saw Meredith, Clara, and Jolene; they were already dressed. Clara gave her a smirk, walking up to her.

"Prince Alexander was amazing last night." She whispered in her ear as she was about to leave, Jazmine locked eyes with her.

Jazmine bit her lip slightly to control her anger. "I'm sure he was. You know what, he is the best in the morning just after he wakes up and then in the shower all wet and slippery." She turned around, walking towards the racks to find a dress. Jordan entered with a shit-eating grin as he looked at the ladies. He walked over to Jazmine.

"You don't need a dress. This was delivered for you today." He handed her the gourmet bag she didn't even see in his hands. She took the bag and note with a smile as she walked into the changing room. As she opened the bag, she found 3 dresses inside, and her eyes landed straight on the light blue one. She wanted that one. She put it on before observing herself in the mirror. The dress fitted her flawlessly. It highlighted her curves and made her look like a goddess.

After getting ready, she and Jordan headed to the ballroom. Once she entered, she was amazed at how the ballroom looked. She loved every part of it, even if it was Clara's doing. Jordan came to her with a sad smile on his face telling her she was put in the back with Christian. She smiled and told him that she will be fine and that she will see him after. She didn't mind sitting with Christian. He was her friend and better company than half of the people here.

The ball went on without them getting food, Christian and Jazmine were chatting when Jolene sat down next to them, acting all friendly and telling them how she hated how they were treated. Just when the food arrived, Clara announced that it was time for them to open the dance floor. Jazmine got up seeing Alexander ask Clara to dance. He glanced at her, giving her a wink.

The dance went on with her laughing and having fun with Christian until it was time to change partners. As he twirled her, she found herself in Alexander's strong arms. He pulls her closer, taking in her familiar scent of cherries and vanilla.

"I've missed you so much," He whispered in her ear, causing her to blush.

"I've missed you too. Are you having fun?" She smiled warmly at him.

"I am now that I have you in my arms, even if it only is for a moment." He looked at her as the music changed, indicating another switch. His hand lingered on her waist as she looked up at him. He could see the desire in her eyes, and he was sure he was the same.

"Uh Um, I believe Alexander is my partner now." Clara pushed Jazmine out of the way. Alexander was shocked but still unable to say anything. Jazmine turned and walked towards Christian and Jordan, they were talking when she heard gasps and saw the look on Jordan's face. As she turned, she saw Alexander and Clara locked in a heated kiss. She stood there, unable to move. Christian took her arm, pulling her to the balcony door before anyone could see her break down.

Once they were outside, he pulled her to him. He knew what this was doing to her, he told Alexander this was a bad idea. He should have been forward with his father. There wasn't much his father could do; Alexander was the next in line for the throne, and it wasn't as if

Charles would tell him he couldn't be king. There was no one else that could take over.

"Jaz, everything will be alright." He looked down at her as she stepped back. Her makeup smudged from the tears.

Jazmine shook her head as she wiped her cheeks. "I can't... This isn't me... Clara is bringing the worst out in me, and Alexander is letting her." She felt her heart breaking with every word she said. She knows she was the one that told Alexander they should keep on doing it this way, but right now, she was regretting it.

"Do you want me to take you away from this?" Christian asks with uncertainty. He would do anything for her. In the time he has known her, she has become his best friend, and he wanted her to be happy.

She took another step back from Christian. "No, I just need to go to my room. I will talk to Alexander tomorrow when we are back at the palace." She kissed Christian on the cheek before slipping back to her room without anyone seeing her leave.

Alexander pushed Clara away, giving her a disgusted look. "What are you thinking?!" Alexander spat as he felt his heart sink when he saw Christian taking Jazmine out of the room. In that instant, he knew she saw the kiss. He also knew that it ripped her heart out. This was the one thing she asked him not to let happen, and Clara just did it.

"I'm just showing you what you are missing." She gave him a sly smile.

"Clara, I have to be fair to all the ladies here. Now, how will it look if I had to kiss all of them?" He felt his anger boiling inside him. He wanted to get to Christian and find out if Jazmine was alright. He turned and walked away from Clara, not giving her a chance to say anything. He didn't even want to see her right now.

Alexander made it to the balcony but didn't see Jazmine there, only Christian. "Christian, is she alright?" He felt his breath hitch as he saw the look on Christian's face.

"No, Alexander, she's not. How could you?" Christian felt upset with Alexander, but kind of still understood why he did it.

"Where is she? I will go and explain." He wanted to be with her. He didn't care who saw him at that moment. They have worked so hard to be with each other. He couldn't ruin that now.

Christian placed his hand on Alexander's shoulder. "She doesn't want to see you. She went to her room, and said she will talk to you when she gets back to the palace." Christian gave him a sad smile. He could see what it was doing to both his friends.

Alexander turned around. Walking to the door, he was stopped by Jolene. She talked to him about how his evening was going. He kept the conversation short and sweet. He wanted to get out of there. He wanted to get to Jazmine.

Brian noticed him, and how he tried to get away from everyone. Scanning the room, he could not see Jazmine. Panic took over, and he told one of the guards to get Alexander, so they could head out.

Alexander was relieved when the guard came to him, telling him Brian needed to see him. He apologized to Jolene before turning and heading for the door. Alexander and Brian headed for Jazmine's room and two guards were keeping guard at the entrance of the hall.

Jazmine was sitting on her bed, looking at the wall. She had just gotten out of the shower, getting dressed in warm nighties. She was lost in thought when there was a knock on her door. At first, she wanted to ignore it, but then the knock became more urgent. She wasn't in the mood for company, not even for Alexander. She got up to open the door, finding Alexander on the other side.

"Jaz... can I come in?" He gave her a pleading look. He needed to tell her how sorry he was. He needed her to know that the kiss was just Clara, he didn't kiss her back.

Jazmine tried to be strong, and she wanted him to leave, but she loved him. She wanted him with her. She moved to the side, letting Alexander in. She wasn't ready to talk to him, but she knew he wouldn't leave unless he could speak to her.

"Jaz.... I'm sorry. That kiss wasn't me. Clara kissed me, and I pushed her away. I told her to stop." He gave her an apologetic look. Trying to pull her to him, but she stepped out of his reach.

"I don't want to hear it, Alexander. Why don't you go back to her?" Jazmine pushed away from Alexander as he tried again to get near her. She opened the door, motioning for him to leave. She was just not ready to talk to him. He hung his head walking out the door. As soon as she closed the door, she sank to the floor, her head against the door, crying.

CHAPTER 7

Crazy Beautiful

It's been three days since Alexander spoke to Jazmine. He had tried a few times, she just didn't want to talk to him. He was feeling like he was losing her. He should never have even considered doing what his father wanted. He should have also told everyone when Clara started being too flirty and touchy with him. He couldn't lose Jazmine. Here he is sitting in his quarters getting ready for the Royal beach party when Christian comes walking in.

"Christian, is everything ready for today?" Alexander asked while putting his shoes on, not looking at his best friend. He knew why Christian was there; he just didn't want to talk to him about it, he wanted to speak with Jazmine.

"Yes, Jordan has the boat ready, and I have the food ready. She will love it." Christian walked over to the bar cart, pouring himself a drink.

"Thanks, now just to get her to talk to me. I know what happened hurt her. Even if I didn't want to kiss Clara, it still happened. I just need to talk to her. Christian, I can't lose her." Alexander hung his head; he felt defeated. All he wanted was to be with the woman he loves. He didn't care about any of the other women.

"Alexander, she won't walk away from you today. Maybe try and talk to her, make her see she's the one you love, even if it means not being fair to the ladies who are treating her like crap." Christian took a sip of his drink, looking at his friend. They needed this season to be over. Christian made it very clear from the start that he was not going to even entertain any ladies; he was not going to be choosing a wife like that even if it was tradition.

"I hope so. Let's get out of here. I need to see my girl." Alexander got up as they headed out to go to the pier.

***

Jazmine watched as they pulled up to the pier; Jordan was with her, going on about how she had been hiding the last few days and that it would not be in her favor to hide any longer. She wasn't paying attention to him, all she wanted was to be able to talk to Alexander without feeling the hurt she had been feeling for the past few days. She missed Alexander, but she couldn't look at him without feeling betrayed.

"Lady Jazmine, are you listening to me? You need to focus. This is a huge event for the royal family." Jordan scowled at her. He could see her mind was somewhere else.

They didn't notice that someone had opened the door. "Jordan! I believe that is no way to talk to a lady." Alexander glared at him, he hated the way Jordan spoke to Jazmine, this was not the first time he had heard him talk to her like that.

"Your highness, please forgive me. I was just trying to get her attention." Jordan gave his friend a slight bow. He knows that today none of them could put a foot wrong.

"You need to apologize to Lady Jazmine, not me." Alexander nodded in Jazmine's direction.

Jordan turned to Jazmine, telling her how sorry he was and that he would see her at the boat, and she should please try and be on time. Alexander gave him a nod as he walked away.

"Lady Jazmine. You look beautiful today." Alexander took her hand, kissing the back of it. All he wanted to do was pull her to him, but he knew the press was around and that it would not be proper of the prince to favor one of the suitors.

"Prince Alexander, it's good to see you." She smiled at him, and he could swear he felt his heart burst at the first smile he had gotten from her in the last few days. This gave him hope that not everything was lost.

They talked for a while about the event, Alexander telling her that he didn't like boats because he couldn't see the bottom of the ocean. He doesn't know what waits down there for him. Jazmine laughed at the thought of the strong prince being scared of the unknown.

They watched as King Charles came to give his speech. He tells them what the day is about and that he has an announcement to make. All the press gathers in front of the podium. Alexander looked around and saw that everyone was paying attention to the king. He moved closer to Jazmine, taking her hand in his, he wanted to be closer to her in any way he could right now. Christian saw it and moved to stand behind them to shield them from prying eyes. He wanted his friends to have this little bit of affection.

King Charles glanced around the crowd until his eyes landed on Alexander. He furrowed his brow when he saw that Jazmine was standing next to his son. "At the end of this season, I will be handing the throne over to Prince Alexander. He will have his coronation and then choose one of the suitors to be his queen. I will give a statement as to why as soon as I have spoken to my family." He smiled and told them it was almost time for the press to leave and the family to enjoy the beach.

Alexander watched as his father took his seat. He felt his heart racing, his father did tell him that at the end of this season he was stepping down, but why make an announcement right now? He looked toward Jazmine and he could see the shock in her eyes. He had not told her yet. She knew that he would eventually become king. Christian ran his hand down his face, this just got a hell of a lot more difficult.

As soon as Brian heard the announcement, he was on his radio, he wanted to make sure that the security was in place, and that Alexander would have what he needed.

"Alexander! How are you feeling?" Jazmine was concerned, she knew Alexander didn't know, if he did, he would have told her, Right?

"I'm shocked and not sure why he made the announcement. Jaz…" Alexander brushed a strand of hair out of her face. "Please know that this won't change the way I feel about you. You are the most important person in my life. I would give all this up for you."

Alexander rested his hand on her cheek as she leaned into his touch, she missed it so much.

"I'm here for you. This won't change anything. I know we need to talk, but just know that I'm here for you always." She moved towards him but stopped when she noticed the press coming their way.

They speak to the press, answering a few questions. Alexander was amazed by the way Jazmine handled the press, he felt proud of her, knowing she would be an amazing queen. Alexander told them he needed to get her to the festivities.

It was time for the beach party, everyone was excited to just have fun without the press and public around. As they got to the beach, Jazmine took it all in the white sand, and blue water, and then they had the food and drinks. Everything was perfect, she didn't think that this was something the Royal family would do.

Jordan and she walked over to the drinks when they saw Christian, he motioned for them to come over. He had all the food Jazmine loved as per Alexander's request.

"Christian, you are my hero." She smiled as she hugged him, taking in all the food.

"This wasn't me Jaz. Alexander did all this." He gave her a knowing look. He needed her to know that Alexander would do anything for her.

They all jumped when Jolene suddenly spoke behind them. "Why would Alexander do this for her?" Jolene gave them a questioning look.

"Alexander wanted to do something nice for all of you. He has the fancying food for you and then this for me and Jazmine." Christian winked at Jazmine. He loved good food. He didn't like the crap that the others liked to eat and he knew that Alexander also loved good food.

They all have lunch together. Jolene sat with them trying to find out how they felt about the whole announcement the king made. She was now more determined to prove to her parents that she could win the Prince's hand. She would be their favorite daughter if she was able to get him to choose her

After lunch, they all wanted to go for a swim. They all splashed around in the waves when Jolene motioned for Jazmine to meet her on the beach. They walked out and just as Jolene wanted to say something, she saw Alexander heading in their direction. She smiled at him as he got to them.

"Lady Jolene." He smiled, giving her a bow. "Lady Jazmine." Alexander racked his eyes over her body, taking in every detail, she looked so beautiful, her wet skin with the bright pink bikini, he felt the warmth inside of him. He wanted to spend some time with her alone and away from everyone.

"Prince Alexander, we haven't seen you much. Could I get a drink with you?" Jolene took his arm trying to pull him away from Jazmine. She and the other ladies have decided to try and keep Alexander from talking to Jazmine as much as they could. It has been easy the past few days seeing as Lady Jazmine was in hiding for some reason.

"I'm sorry, Lady Jolene. I have promised Lady Jazmine to have a short walk with her on the beach. Once we return, we can get that drink." He pulled his arm from Jolene's hands and turned to Jazmine, offering his arm to her. She smiled while taking it. They walked along the beach until Alexander led her towards a secluded spot on the beach.

He takes a seat before he pulls her down towards him. "Thank you." She leans into him as she sits between his legs looking out over the ocean.

He kisses the back of her head. "Baby, you don't have to thank me. I have just decided that from now on I will be putting you first no matter what. I don't care about being fair anymore." He placed his arm around her waist and pulled her closer to him. He wanted them to be like they were.

They sat there for a bit in silence as they just took in the special moment of being together. Alexander decided that he wanted them to jump off the cliff into the ocean. Jazmine was all for it until they climbed the cliff together. Alexander took her hand reassuring her that everything will be alright.

"One... Two... Three..." They jumped splashing in the water. Alexander swam over to Jazmine pulling her to him. He looked deep into her eyes, feeling the love they had for each other. They swam deeper into where they barely touched the bottom. She wrapped her legs around his waist pulling him to her.

He crashed his lips onto hers, running his tongue along her bottom lip asking for entrance, giving in to him she opened up for him and he slid his tongue in finding hers, and their kiss became more heated. Alexander moved his hands to her bikini bottom, never breaking the kiss, he pushed her bikini to the side, running his fingers through her folds. She moaned into the kiss feeling his touch for the first time in a few days.

"Alexander …. I need you" she arched her back pulling him closer. He bit his lip as he watched how he made her feel. He pulled down his swim trunks just enough to free his dick before lining himself up to her wanting entrance. He thrust into her feeling her walls stretch around him. They both moan at the sensation, he pulled out almost all the way before thrusting back into her. She moaned as he picked up the pace going faster and harder. "Alexander, this feels so good!" She found his lips again. She could feel the heat deep inside her core, she was close, and Alexander could feel it as well, he picked up the pace thrusting into her with more force. "That's it baby, cum for me!" That was all she needed as she came screaming his name. He didn't slow his pace thrusting through her climax until he found his own release moaning into her mouth.

She rested her head against his chest as they both tried catching their breath after their blissful moment. He looked up at her brushing his hand over her cheek. "I love you so much," He pulled her down, kissing her again. He would never be able to get enough of her. He wanted her all the time.

After they got out of the water and dried themselves off, Alexander pulled her against his chest again. "Baby, I'm sorry for what happened with Clara. I would never do something to hurt what we have. At my coronation, I'm telling everyone that I love you and always have. I wanted to do it so many times, but I understood that we needed to wait." She smiled at him, she felt her heart flutter at his words, she knew he was sorry and that he would not do anything to hurt her on purpose. She also knew that Clara was planning it the whole time.

She kissed his chest. "Alexander, I'm also sorry for doubting you. You have never given me a reason to doubt anything about you. I love you and am afraid of losing you." She looked down feeling ashamed for putting Alexander through all of this. This is just as hard for him as it is for her.

He placed his finger under her. "Baby, I'm yours. You will never lose me. I understand, all these ladies have been giving you a hard time. And they sometimes can be brutal and I will be having words with them all about how they treat you." He pulled her into his arms holding her close. "I hate to say it, but we need to get back." he took her hand as they walked back to the beach area where the party was being held, each going their separate way once they reached the beach.

***

King Charles was sitting in his office, he felt like he needed to do something about the way Alexander was acting. He could see that Alexander was favoring Jazmine and he needed to remind him that he should do what's best for the country and that was to choose Meredith as the queen. Charles was going over some papers when there was a knock on the door. He called for them to enter when Nicholas and Camilla came walking in. Nicholas was the most ruthless noble that they knew. He would be perfect for the plan.

"Your Majesty. You wanted to see us?" Nicholas bowed.

"Yes, I need you two to do something for me." Charles eyed them trying to see if he could trust them. They both nod waiting for the king to continue.

"It will be rewarding towards you." Charles handed them his offer and they both smiled. He told them what they need to do and that it should happen at the next event as the next event after that is the Coronation. He told them that he was still trying to find out what Lady Jazmine was hiding and that they should have a plan B if they weren't able to find out her secret.

CHAPTER 8

My Guiding Light

  Everyone has been in the country home for a few days, they had a country fair with all sorts of activities that Jazmine loved. She loved the country and hoped that once this was over, she would get to spend more time in the country. Alexander, Jazmine, and Christian had a private celebration for Christian's Birthday, since they have known each other they would make it a thing to do something together for each other's birthday.
  Being with all of them made her forget what was happening, she had a few run-ins with Clara and Jolene, but Meredith on the other hand was very quiet. She had thought that Jolene wanted to be friends with her, but Jolene was just as bad as Clara at times.
  It was the day of the Royal horseback picnic, Jazmine got dressed in her riding outfit before she headed down to meet with everyone. Before she made it to them, Christian found her telling her to meet Alexander at the stables, he would make sure Charles was distracted. Jazmine smiled heading towards the stables.
  As she walked in through the doors she saw Alexander standing by his horse feeding him an apple. That horse meant a lot to Alexander because his mom gave him the horse before she died. She smiled watching him with Blaze, he looked so happy at that moment. She walked over to him wrapping her arms around his waist. He smiled as soon as her cherry and vanilla scent infiltrated his nose.
  "Morning, love. How are you feeling today?" Alexander turned to look at her. He was concerned as she wasn't feeling well for

the past few days and he didn't want her to be sick while on the back of a horse.

She brushed the tips of her fingers along his day-old stubble. "I'm feeling much better. Just needed some rest." She smiled at him knowing he was worried. She just needed this to be over, she didn't want the stress anymore. Alexander smiled, feeling relieved that she was better, he was still concerned, he knew this is not easy for her and he never wanted her to be in this situation. If only his father had listened to him from the start none of this would have happened.

"Now why I called you here. I want you to ride Blaze today, he's the only horse I trust. I don't want anything to happen to you." Alexander gave her a knowing look. He wanted her safe and he wasn't sure what the other horses would do. He knew that Blaze would keep her safe while she was with him. She knew that there was no arguing, he wasn't taking no for an answer.

"Thank you. I don't mind taking Blaze, but what will the other suitors say?"

Alexander smirked. "I don't care what they have to say, I want you to be safe. You are the only one that's important to me and only your opinion matters to me." He leaned down, giving her a lingering kiss. He pulled away brushing his hand over her cheek before he turned to tell one of the stable hands that Jazmine was going to ride Blaze.

As they walked out king Charles came in to talk to Alexander, not noticing that Jazmine was walking out with Blaze. Jazmine made it to the group of suitors. Clara eyed Jazmine as she walked over with Blaze, knowing that it was Alexander's horse.

"What are you doing with Prince Alexander's horse?" She asked loud enough for all to hear. The ladies looked toward her waiting for an answer.

Before Jazmine could answer her, a guard told Jazmine that King Charles wants to see her in his office. She gave him a nod before following him to king Charles's office. She knew he was in the stables with Alexander and didn't know what this could be about. She didn't know what they spoke about. The guard opened the office door for her and she was met by King Charles, Countess Meredith, and Lady Jolene.

King Charles glared at her. "Lady Jazmine, it has come to my attention that you have been keeping information about yourself from us. Please sit as I want to discuss this matter with you right now." Charles motioned for her to take a seat in front of him.

Jazmine felt her stomach doing flips, did he find out? What would this mean for her and Alexander? Why was Brian or Alexander here as well? She took the seat and waited for him to continue.

"Now Lady Jazmine, tell me what your relationship is with my son, Joseph?" Charles gave her a demanding look.

"Joseph and I are good friends, we met when he was still engaged to Meredith, though he had other plans at the time. And we have stayed friends. It wasn't until recently that I found out he is Alexander's brother." She tried to keep her breathing even and to remember all the training she had gotten from Alexander, she didn't want them to pick up on her nerves. She wasn't lying to them, she just left out parts of the times she had with Joseph.

Jolene shook her head as Meredith opened her phone. "Then why was she at the Doctor's office with Joseph if they are only friends? And not any doctor but a gynecologist?" Meredith smirked at her showing the photo to everyone. She was not going to let Jazmine take the crown from her for a second time.

Jazmine looked at the photo as her eyes welled up. She remembered that day as if it was yesterday.

Jazmine sat in the reception area waiting for Joseph to come, she couldn't believe that she was the one that had to give him the news. He was so happy the day he found out he was going to be a dad. He went out and got the baby's first outfit, being so proud.

It wasn't long after the doctor gave her the news that Joseph came running into the waiting area, as soon as he saw her face, he knew something had happened. Walking over to her, he sank to his knees in front of her before taking her hands in his.

"Jaz.... What happened?" He asked with tears already in his eyes.

"Joseph, I'm so sorry. She wasn't feeling well, and I brought her in. It was different from morning sickness, I got scared. The doctor said that this happens often in early pregnancy, it can't always be explained." Jazmine wiped the tears that were running down her face, not only was her sister a mess in the doctor's room, she now had

Joseph breaking down in front of her. "She blames herself, she thinks that she did something wrong."

Joseph hung his head for a moment before he looked up at Jazmine again. "Where is she? I will never blame her. Yes, we lost our baby, but she is still my wife and I love her dearly." *Joseph got up and Jazmine told him where she was. She watched as he went in to see her.*

Amanda met Joseph when he was still engaged to Meredith, he told her about what he wanted to do, and he broke off his engagement to Meredith, shortly after that they started dating. Jazmine had met him when they got engaged and became friends, she was happy that he was going to be her brother-in-law.

It wasn't until after Joseph abdicated that Jazmine found out that he was Alexander's brother. They were never at her house at the same time. She was shocked to know that both sisters fell in love with the prince brothers.

She was brought back to reality when Charles again asked her why she was at the gynecologist with Joseph.

She swallowed the lump in her throat. "I'm sorry your majesty, I just don't feel that it is my place to share why we were there. All I can say is that I wasn't there for me and what Joseph went through was hard for him." She gave him an apologetic look.

"So, you are telling me that you did not have a romantic relationship with Joseph?" Meredith looked at her with disdain.

Jazmine scoffed. "I didn't have a romantic relationship with Joseph. He is married to my older sister." Jazmine felt like they were trying to get something on her. She didn't know where this was heading.

"Lady Jazmine, unfortunately, if you don't tell me what you were doing at the gynecologist with my eldest son. I'm going to have to ask you to leave. You will be withdrawn as a suitor and Prince Alexander will not choose you." Charles had a smile on his face giving her the news. This was one way to get rid of her, he knew her loyalty to them was strong and she wouldn't betray them.

She nodded her head. "Your Majesty, I understand, but it's not my story to tell you." She got up walking out of the office, as soon as she closed the door the tears came crashing down. How will she ever be able to tell Alexander the reason she left was that she couldn't tell his father that his brother and her sister lost their baby? That she felt it wasn't her place to tell them something like that. It was Joseph and Amanda's story to tell.

Walking towards her room, she bumped into Alexander. He gave her a look seeing her tear-stained face and the anger boiled up in him. He pulled her into his arms and he held her close. He didn't know what had caused her to be so unhappy, but he was going to find out and the person that did this will pay for hurting her.

"Baby what's wrong?" He wiped the tears from her cheeks. She looked down, she needed to tell him before his father got to him.

"I... I've been withdrawn as a suitor. Your father asked me about me and Joseph and the fact that we were at the gynecologist together, and I couldn't tell him. So, he told me to leave and that I will not be a suitor anymore." She cried covering her face with her hands. She was scared of losing Alexander. She wasn't sure how it would work now.

"Shhh... It's alright. It's a good thing you are more than a suitor to me. You are the woman I love, and no one will stop me from having you as my wife." He wrapped his arms around her stroking his hand over her hair and back. "I'm going to phone Joseph and tell him to phone my dad. He will clear this up quickly." Alexander tilts her face to look at him.

"That's just it, why is your father so against me? He has been digging into my life and wants to find something. Alexander what if he finds out before the coronation." Jazmine felt like this wasn't going to turn out as they wanted it to, she looked at him as her lip started trembling.

He leaned down, kissing her gently. "Then he finds out. There is nothing he can do. I have a surprise for you. I'm making the opening remarks at the country dinner and announcing the next event before the Coronation. It's a surprise event. I think you will love this event." He smiled as he could see how excited she was, only two more events before Alexander was choosing his bride.

"You know just how to cheer me up, Prince Alexander." She gave him a flirty smirk. Before breaking out in a fit of laughter. He shook his head, telling her he was going to phone Joseph.

Alexander spoke to Joseph, explaining what had happened and what their father said to Jazmine. Joseph was furious with his father for doing all of this just to make sure Alexander would choose Meredith.

Joseph told him he would make sure that this was sorted out before the end of the Dinner.

The next morning Jazmine was awoken by a knock on the door. Thinking that it was Christian or Jordan, she got up heading for the door. Opening it to see Brian on the other side with a wide smile on his face.

"Morning Lady Jazmine. I was sent by King Charles, he wanted me to inform you that you are welcome to stay and still be a suitor." Brian winked at her, the smile on his face never fading.

"Thank you, Brian. Have you told Alexander?" She knew that Joseph probably told his father what happened. She was still worried about what she was hiding. Bastien nods telling her that Charles told him.

Jazmine got ready for the country day and dinner, she was excited to find out what Alexander had planned for tonight. She was trying to wrap her mind around what it could be that he was planning on announcing.

They spend the day playing some games and hanging out. For the first time since she has been in Castleberry, she felt at ease. Not even Clara, Meredith, or Jolene could get to her. She and Alexander went to the garden maze just to get away from everyone for a little bit. They talked about what would happen after the Coronation and what he wanted to change for the country. The season was the first thing to go. As the bell ran, indicating the end of the games, they headed to the dinner where Alexander was about to make the opening remarks.

Jazmine found her way to where the other suitors were sitting only to be stopped by Nicholas, he wanted her to sit by them but she politely told him that she needed to be with the other suitors. She turned and walked away from him. He made her feel uncomfortable, something about his eyes scared her. He caught Meredith's eye winking at her as she gave him a discreet nod.

Jazmine took her seat just as Alexander stood up. "I would like to thank you all for being here. It is with great pleasure to inform you of our last event for this year's season." Alexander gave them a bright smile before locking his eyes with Jazmine. "It would have been at Duke Jordan's dutchy, but since Lady Jasmine has recently been named Duchess of Littleton, we will be attending the Lantern festival in Littleton next." Alexander could see the shock on everyone's faces, but all he cared about was the way Jazmine's eyes were sparkling knowing they were going to her duchy next. He was finally going to be able to show her, her dutchy.

"If he named her a duchess he's planning on choosing her. We need to act now." Meredith whispered to Camilla, both giving Nicholas a look saying they needed to act tonight. There was no more time to play around, they had to stop Alexander from choosing Jazmine.

Later that night Alexander and Jazmine were sitting in his room talking about the announcement. She still couldn't believe he had told the court that she was a duchess. He said that he was going to wait until the coronation.

"It's getting late, I should head to bed." Jazmine laid on Alexander's chest. She didn't want to move, even if she knew she had to. Being this close to him was all she wanted right now. She wanted to sleep in his arms.

Alexander kissed the top of her head. "Please stay with me tonight." Alexander tilted her face to look at him. She smiled as she nodded. He led her to the bed. They got ready for bed before both of them got in. She laid in his arms as he pulled her close, kissing the top of her head again. They fall asleep almost instantly in the warmth of each other's arms.

***

Nicholas walked into Jazmine's room just like Meredith told him to, looking around but he didn't see her. He heard the shower, thinking it was her that was in the shower. He sat in the chair making sure everything was ready for his plan. After tonight she wouldn't be able to be with Alexander and then he will take her.

He looked towards the bathroom door as it opened, shock on his face as he saw who walked out.

"Christian…. What are you doing here?" Nicholas took a step back. Trying to figure out what was going on. Did they give him the wrong room number? Fuck they are screwed now.

"This is my room. Get out!" Christian shouted pointing to the door. He was ready to punch Nicholas when he realized that Nicholas must be there looking for Jazmine. He shuddered just thinking about what he wanted to do to her.

Nicholas ran out of the room seeing Christian's face. He went back to Meredith as he tried to figure out what just happened. Walking into her room she saw the look on his face.

"Did you do it?" She asked. She wanted to let Charles know that it was done.

"No, give me the room assignments again, please. Where was Christian supposed to be?" Nicholas took the papers from her, looking them over. He pointed to a room and she looked at it. "Christian was in Jazmine's room. I think she's in his room. This must have been Alexander that moved her, he's helping her hide something. Whatever it is, it's big." Nicholas walked out of the room, frustrated that this plan didn't work. He wanted Jazmine now that he had the chance to see her up close.

Meredith walked over to Charles's room just as his guard Lucas was going in. She walked in with him. She had to tell him that it didn't work. That Alexander once again saved the day.

"Your Majesty, I have the information you needed on Lady Jazmine. This information will cause the scandal you need." Lucas handed over the folder to Charles.

Meredith let out a relieved sigh. "I hope so, we weren't successful. Lady Jazmine's room was changed but it wasn't on the room assignments." Meredith gave Charles an apologetic look. She hated letting him down, he was doing so much for her.

Charles opened the folder with a smile growing on his face. Meredith moved to read over his shoulder, she gasped when she read the contents.

"This is better than I thought. We will keep this and just before Alexander makes his choice this will be made public." Charles lets out an evil laugh. This will ruin Lady Jasmine and Alexander will have no other choice but to choose Meredith. Everything will work out as it should be. Meredith will control Alexander and King Charles will still rule the country indirectly.

CHAPTER 9

If I Ever Saw Heaven

Christian came barging into Alexander's room. He didn't have time to knock. He stopped when he saw Alexander sit up in bed, still disheveled from sleeping, Jazmine was still asleep next to him. Alexander slipped out of bed putting on a shirt, before walking over to Christian.

"Morning, what has gotten into you?" Alexander walked over to the coffee cart, putting on a pot of coffee.

"Jaz is in danger. I don't know what kind of danger. All I do know is that she's in danger." Christian sits down in the chair looking at Alexander as he froze at his words.

"What do you mean Christian? She's right there, safely sleeping." Alexander motioned to where Jazmine was laying.

Christian's eyes drifted to a sleeping Jazmine before he turned his gaze on Alexander again. "You know how you changed her room without changing it on the room assignments? Well last night when I got out of the shower, Nicholas was in my room. The room that would have been Jazmine's originally."

"Nicholas, why would he be in her room?" Alexander started pacing in front of Christian. What if he didn't change her room or if she was in her room and not with him? What would have happened to her? "Brian" Alexander's voice roared in the room. Brian came running into the room. Alexander told him what Christian told him.

"That's not all. He was shocked to see me, but he had a rope in his hands, and on his way out he dropped this." Christian handed a pack of pills to Brian and some condoms. Brian's eyes grew wide, knowing what the pills are and knowing what would have happened if Alexander didn't change her room.

Brain ran his hand down his face as he feared for Jazmine's safety. "Did you drink anything in the room?" Brian asked. Christian shook his head telling him that he didn't and that he left everything as is.

"Sir, where is Lady Jazmine? We need to make sure that she's safe." Brian placed the pills and condoms in a bag before placing them in his pocket. Alexander motioned to the bed where Jazmine was still sleeping even with all the commotion going on a few feet from her. Brian lets out a relieved sigh, knowing she was safe. He will be keeping a close eye on her. "I will get her security detail, ready sir. I will make sure she's safe when you are not around." Brian bowed before heading out the door. Christian told Alexander he would see him in Littleton before he followed Brian.

Later that day Jazmine was heading to Littleton, and for the first time since the season had started Alexander was driving with her. She and Alexander spoke about what was going to happen, and the fact that her being the host, meant that she got to spend most of Alexander's time with him, something he was not complaining about.

They arrived at Littleton and Jazmine's estate. Alexander watched as her eyes sparkled taking it in. She couldn't believe this was hers. "Alexander, this is amazing." She threw her arms around his neck pulling him into a hug. He was so thankful that the rest of the court had not arrived yet. Not that he cared anymore right now.

Alexander showed Jazmine around the estate, watching her take everything in. There wasn't a part of the estate she didn't love. She was amazing and to see her excited about this made his heart swell. He loved her so much and in only a week he could let Castleberry know what he has known from the start. That he was deeply in love with this angel in front of him.

The next evening was the Lantern festival as per tradition. The whole of Littleton was excited to see their new Dutchess. Everyone was excited to be there and as the night went on they all loved what Jazmine had brought to light. She gave the perfect speech even though Alexander helped her with it. She was still perfect.

As they stood there watching the lanterns, they couldn't help but be amazed by the sight of them. Alexander felt like his heart was going to burst to be this proud of what Jazmine had done. She was able to make the event special for everyone in such a short time.

Jazmine stood on the bridge leading to the front of the estate when Nicholas approached her. He looked around and saw she was alone walking up to her and resting his hand on her lower back. Jazmine felt his hand on her body and tensed up trying to move away, but he was holding on to her firmly. He let out a low growl that warned her not to move.

"It's been a beautiful ceremony. But what do you say we have a bit of private time?" He leaned closer to her, but before he could take in what was going on her fist connected with his jaw. She took a step back, narrowing her eyes at him.

"DON'T YOU EVER TOUCH ME AGAIN!" She yelled, feeling the adrenaline running through her veins. He walked up to her grabbing her arm, she tried to get away from him, but he was just too strong. She tried to get someone's attention but the music was just too loud.

"Listen here you bitch, you don't belong here. Now come with me or you will regret it!" He pulled her towards him before he felt a strong hand around his neck pulling him away from her.

Alexander rushed to Jazmine's side pulling her to him. Brian and Christian holding on to Nicholas. Alexander kissed her head before motioning for Christian to take Jazmine inside. Christian took Jazmine as he led her inside, knowing Alexander didn't want her to see what was about to happen. He just hoped Brian would keep Alexander from doing something stupid.

Alexander grabbed Nichols's shirt pulling his face only inches from him. "If you ever touch her again, I will personally kill you. Keep your hands off my Jazmine." Bastien gave Alexander a look knowing what he just said.

"Alexander, it's not like you will ever choose her. Your father won't allow that and then I will have her.." Before he could say anything more Alexander's fist connected with his jaw. Brian gave Alexander a warning, telling him not to cause a scene. Brian took a hold of Nicholas while Alexander tried to compose himself.

"Brian, take him to his room and make sure he has no contact with anyone until after the Coronation. I'm going to go see if Lady Jazmine's alright." Alexander narrowed his eyes at Nicholas. "You better hope she hasn't been hurt. If there is as much as one mark on her I will kill you." Alexander shook his head knowing full well what he could do to Nicholas, but only after the Coronation.

Alexander walked into the estate, seeing Christian with Jazmine as she cried into his chest. Christian was rubbing his hand up and down her back letting her cry all she wanted. He felt his heart break seeing her like this, knowing if they weren't around things could have been so much worse. Alexander walked up to them resting his hand on Christian's shoulder, Christian took a step back allowing Alexander to step up to Jazmine.

"I'm so sorry, love." He wrapped his arms around her holding her tight as a tear escaped his eye. All he wanted to do was keep her safe, and they were hurting her. The court was hurting her, he needed to fix this.

She lifted her head as she wiped her cheeks. "Thank you for saving me. I want to go lay down." She kissed him before heading to her room. She couldn't face anyone right now, she just wanted to take a shower and wash his hands off her. She knew that Alexander didn't do anything, but she felt dirty.

Later that night Alexander went to check on her, he was worried about her. She hasn't said anything and just went straight to bed. As he walked into her room, he saw her laying on the bed, she was asleep but still restless. He stripped down until he was only in his boxers before getting in bed next to her. He pulled her to him, and as soon as she felt his arms around her, she instantly calmed down. He loved that he was able to calm her down with just his touch.

***

The night of Alexander's Coronation had arrived. He was both anxious and excited. Anxious because he didn't know what his father had planned and excited because he could finally tell the world how he felt about Jazmine.

He stood in front of his floor-length mirror, making sure he looked his best. He only wanted to impress one woman tonight and that would be the one he makes his queen. Alexander heard a knock on his door and he called for them to enter. As he turned, he saw Christian entering.

"Hey, are you ready for this?" Christian smirked watching how Alexander's face lit up. Christian couldn't believe how far they have come. It's the end of the season and the day his best friends can finally be together.

"I am more than ready. After tonight nothing will be able to keep us apart." Alexander smiled as Christian handed him the ring. He took it and put it in his breast pocket, like with every event this past few weeks. The ring is his lucky charm.

Alexander and Christian headed down to the ballroom. Christian headed off to stand in the back like he always did. He was just here to support his friends, he watched Alexander at the door being greeted by all the ladies.

Jazmine just got out of the shower walking over to her closet to have a look at the dress her sister has sent her. Amanda wanted Jazmine to have a breathtaking dress, and seeing as Joseph was coming for the coronation, he brought it with him. Jazmine hasn't seen him yet but knew the dress was here so he should also be here.

As she walked in, she saw the most beautiful white and pink princess-style dress. The dress was full of little pink butterflies. She took the note to read it, smiling at her sister's words.

This is a dress fit for a princess or should I say a queen.
I love you, sis. Call me after. Joseph will be there for support as well.
Love
A xxxx

Jazmine got ready, putting on the dress she felt like a princess or rather a queen. She did her hair in a loose updo and her makeup was a natural look. Light and soft to fit her dress. There was a knock at the door. She called for them to enter and in came Jordan to tell her it was time to go.

They walked into the palace but not before the press stopped her to talk to her. Clara and Meredith were displeased with the press, loving Jazmine. Jolene gave her a look up and down, wondering how she got that dress. They all made sure that there were no decent dresses left in the palace boutique.

All the suitors had dinner together before heading to the ballroom to pay their good wishes to Alexander on his coronation. They each had to give him a gift for his coronation. Jazmine stood there waiting for her turn to see Alexander. She had a gift for him but it was not like any of the other suitor's gifts, she knew none of them would be able to give this gift to him.

She felt a hand on her arm that sent shivers down her spine. "Say goodbye to Alexander, because after tonight you won't see him ever again." Clara lets out an evil laugh before walking up to Alexander.

Jazmine stared at her with this satisfied look in her eyes. If only they knew. "Don't pay any mind to her. He won't choose her, he's choosing me, and I want you around to see what you could have had." Jolene smiled at Jazmine, pretending to be all innocent.

"Why don't we let Prince Alexander decide who he wants as his Queen," Jazmine smirked as walked up to Alexander. She had enough of these ladies who thought they were better than her. She will not let them ruin her night.

"Duchess Jazmine, how lovely it is to see you. And may I say that you look breathtaking tonight." Alexander locked eyes with her, kissing the back of her hand. She took his breath away in that dress. There was nothing more he wanted than to get her out of the dress.

"Prince Alexander, it's an honor to be here. Congratulations on becoming king. I'm sure you will be a wonderful king. I have a gift for you." Jazmine handed him a little black box. Alexander took it making sure his fingers brushed against hers, he opened the box and his eyes grew wide when he saw the keychain inside.

"Jaz... How did.." Before Alexander could finish Brian cleared his throat, Alexander shook his head, looking back at Jazmine. Of all the times they had to be interrupted right now. He needed to know about the gift. "Thank you for the lovely gift, you always know how to brighten my day." He kissed her cheek.

"And it's true…" She whispered only for him to hear. His smile grew even brighter. She just made his evening a thousand times better.

As the evening went on Alexander had to dance with all the suitors once again. Every time he would think that he could go to Jazmine so he could talk to her about the gift, one of the other suitors would ask him to dance.

"Now if it isn't lady Jazmine…" Jazmine's eyes grew wide when she heard the voice. She turned around, her smile beaming when she saw him.

"Joseph…" he walked up to her, hugging her. They spend some time catching up. She told him what had happened and how she and Alexander had to fight to be here tonight. He was furious with what his father was putting them through. His father promised to let Alexander choose if Alexander attended the season this year.

"Joseph, darling, what are you doing here?" Meredith walked over to them, giving Jazmine an evil smirk. Meredith knew what Charles had planned for her. And she couldn't wait to be the one on Alexander's arm at the end of the night. The one to get married to him.

"Countess Meredith. I'm here for my brother and my sister-in-law. I know you are aware that I'm married to Jazmine's sister." Joseph gave her a pointed look. He didn't have time for her. Not after what she did. She has been conniving and disrespectful towards Jazmine and he wasn't going to allow that.

"Your brother is lucky that you dare show up to something of his. Maybe you will be there for his wedding as well. You know the day that he marries me." Meredith shoots Jazmine an 'I won' look. Joseph spitting out his drink as he tried to stifle his laughter. Jazmine gave him a look, telling him to let it go. He turned his back on them not wanting her to see him laugh.

Meredith walked off, disgusted with Joseph's reaction. Both Joseph and Jazmine burst out in laughter as they watched her walk off. They then turned their attention towards the front of the ballroom where they watched as Charles and Alexander stood on the small stage placed in front. King Charles gave his speech, telling everyone how proud he was that Alexander was taking over from him. He handed the ring over to Alexander telling everyone that Alexander has to choose his bride. The Queen then thanked all the ladies for taking part in this year's season and that some of the nobles also made their choices.

"Alexander, it's time to choose your bride." The queen squeezed his arm. Alexander smiled widely, locking eyes with Jazmine as he took the ring from his pocket.

Before he could say anything, the phones went off. People were shocked by the headline flashing on their phones. Clara smirked knowing that she won't be able to be chosen. Brain walked up to King Charles and Alexander telling them what was going on.

"It appears that Lady Jazmine will withdraw as a suitor. Guards take her away." Alexander's eyes grew wide reading the headline. Brian ran to Jazmine's side, he needed to stop them from taking her. Joseph and Christian already keeping the guards from Jazmine.

"Christian, what's going on?" Christian handed his phone to her. Her eyes fill to the brim with tears as she reads the headline. *"PRINCE ALEXANDER BETRAYED BY SUITOR! LADY JAZMINE IS ALREADY MARRIED!"*

CHAPTER 10

Slow Dance With You

Her eyes filled to the brim with tears as she read the headline. **"PRINCE ALEXANDER BETRAYED BY SUITOR! LADY JAZMINE IS ALREADY MARRIED**!" She looked up at Alexander, seeing him and his father in an argument.

"Married, that bitch. How could she do this to Alexander?" Clara was ready to have a go at Jazmine when she saw the guards around her. Brian, Joseph, and Christian try to help her to keep the guards away from her. She immediately knew there was more to the story than what any of them knew. She looked over to Alexander, seeing that he was not at all shocked by the news. She felt ashamed of how she was reacting throughout the whole season. Clearly, Alexander knows Jazmine better than anyone else here. She thinks back to everything that happened over the past few months and it makes sense now. She should have trusted her friend and not been a bitch.

Lucas grabbed Jazmine's arm trying to pull her away from Christian and Joseph just as Brian got to them.

"Let her go!" Brian demanded as Lucas tried to get her to come with him. Jazmine tried to fight against Lucas's hold on her but he just tightened his hold on her. Brian grabbed his arm giving him a warning look.

Lucas didn't care what Brian did to him. He had his orders. "My orders are from the king. I have to remove her as she has been lying this whole season." Lucas smirked at Bastien. Charles told him to take her away, no matter who tried to stop him.

"No, please. Just let me explain. Alexander!" Jazmine shouted for Alexander but with all the noise he couldn't hear her. With the guards trying to get to her and Joseph, Christian, and Brian trying to keep them away from her, Alexander lost sight of her.

"Alexander, you need to make your choice now," Charles demanded. Alexander looked out over the crowd, his eyes first locked on Lady Jolene's, her blowing him a kiss, then on Duchess Clara's, her giving him a nod, as if to say do what you need to do, then on Countess Meredith's, her giving him a flirtatious smirk. Alexander toyed with the ring in his hand as he scanned the rest of the room until he saw her. His heart felt like it was shattering seeing the frightened look on her face. He looked at his father, knowing what he was about to do will have consequences.

"Jaz stayed behind me," Joseph said with his back towards Jazmine as he turned around he saw Lucas with a firm grip on her. Joseph walked up to him looking him square in the eyes. "Let my sister-in-law go and you won't leave here on a hospital bed." Joseph glared at him as Lucas started laughing.

"You can't do anything to me. King Charles has given me an order. And the sooner you all respect that the sooner we can all be done with this." Lucas pulled her to him, laughing at Joseph.

"Suit yourself. Just remember that my father isn't the king anymore and the king is on his way over here." Joseph chuckled as he motioned toward Alexander.

Alexander stood there watching as Lucas tried to take Jazmine away. He looked at the ring in his hand. He had to do it. He had to make up his own destiny. He slipped the ring on his fourth finger on his left hand before turning to make his choice.

"I'm ready to make my choice." Alexander smiled, locking eyes with Jazmine. "I choose...." Before he could say anything, Meredith ran to where he was standing.

"Alexander, you have to choose me. My father has an agreement with your father." She said in a hushed whisper. Alexander narrowed his eyes at her, squaring his shoulders as he turned back to the crowd.

"I chose Duchess Jazmine. I have always chosen her and always will choose her." Alexander lets out a breath he didn't know he was holding. He felt like a weight had been lifted off his shoulders.

"Alexander, you can't choose her. She's married, and it wouldn't be proper for the king to be the reason for a divorce of another couple." Charles gave him a warning pulling him to a more private side of the ballroom. He needed to make him see why he couldn't choose her.

"That's just it, father. I don't want her to get a divorce. If you listened to me from the start you would have known that long before Joseph abdicated, I met Lady Jazmine and fell in love with her after we were dating for a while. I asked her to marry me and she said yes." Alexander smiled remembering that day.

Alexander walked with Jazmine over to the peer they had their first kiss at. It was their second date and they were eating ice cream. Alexander tried to wipe some ice cream from the side of her mouth. He leaned in slowly with her looking up at him, pressing his lips to hers in a slow intimate kiss. She wrapped her arms around his neck deepening it.

Alexander wanted today to be just as special as that first kiss. Standing on the peer looking over the water, he could see the sparkle in Jazmine's eyes. He fell more and more in love with her every day they were spending together.

"Alexander, this is perfect. Thank you. I had an amazing day today." She rested her head on his shoulder.

"Jaz.... Today is not over yet." He smiled at her. "Baby, the first day I met you I knew that you were different. You liked me for me and cared about how I felt. You have been my biggest supporter, my best friend, and the woman I love." He brushed a strand of hair out of her face. Taking out the black velvet box from his pocket, still gazing into her eyes he sinks to one knee. "Jazmine Grey, I have loved you for so long. Will you make me the happiest man on earth and become my wife and princess? Jazmine, will you marry me?" Alexander opened the box showing the heart-shaped diamond engagement ring.

"Yes, Alexander ... A thousand times yes!!!!" She smiled through her tears. She loved him so much, but after learning that he was a prince she never thought they would be more and now he proposed. Alexander slipped the ring on her finger, before pulling her into a passionate kiss.

"What have you done Alexander?" Charles stared at him. He knew he couldn't do anything to Alexander anymore, he had already given him the crown.

"Father, eight months ago me and Lady Jazmine got married on a beach not too far from here. It was a week before Joseph abdicated, he had already told me he was abdicating and told me about the arrangement you had with Meredith's father. So, I got married to Jazmine with Joseph officiating the marriage. That means you have had two daughters-in-law for a while and you don't know about them. Because you don't care about your sons and their happiness." Alexander glared at him, taking out a document from his pocket and handing it to Charles.

"We will discuss this in the study." Charles turned, telling Lucas to take Jazmine to his office. He motioned for Alexander to go before he turned to Meredith motioning for her to follow them.

Lucas pulled Jazmine to the office with Christian, Joseph, and Brian right on their heels. Joseph was furious with the way he was treating Jazmine, but he didn't want to cause problems for Alexander by punching the guy.

As they entered the office, Lucas pushed Jazmine and the momentum caused her to trip and fall to the ground. Just as she fell Brian ran over to her, checking to see if she was alright. She was heartbroken at how things had turned out, the tears streaming down her face.

Brian walked up to Lucas getting right into his face. "You seem to forget that I'm the head of the king's guard. And as soon as this is done, so are you!" Brian growled at him. As they turned they saw Alexander standing at the door, his jaw clenched, and fist balled up. Brian could see the anger flashing in Alexander's eyes.

"Told you not to do it." Joseph smirked knowing full well what's about to happen. Christian went over to help Jazmine up.

"WHAT GIVES YOU THE RIGHT TO TREAT MY WIFE LIKE THAT!" Alexander shouted at Lucas. He wanted to kill him on the spot.

"Your Majesty…. I'm…. truly sorry for what I have done. I was just following orders." Lucas bowed, he didn't want to upset Alexander any further.

"Sorry won't cut it this time. Brian is over you and you did not want to follow his orders and he was following my orders. You still did not want to follow his orders after I was made king. I can't trust you to keep my family safe, you will be dismissed with immediate effect. And you better hope that the queen did not get hurt by you doing this to her." Alexander grabbed Lucas by the front of his shirt pushing him against the wall, glaring at him.

Alexander let him go before he turned towards Jazmine. "I'm sorry, King Alexander. King Charles will never let you stay with commoner trash like her."

Before Lucas could react, Alexander's fist connected with his jaw sending him back into the wall. Brian pulled Alexander back trying to get him to calm down when Joseph gave Lucas a blow to the jaw as he walked past him, sending him into the side wall.

Alexander walked over to Jazmine and pulled her into his arms. She wrapped her arms around his waist, resting her head on his chest. "How are you feeling? Are you alright, Love?" Alexander looked at her with concern in his eyes.

"I'm alright. How did your father take it? Are you alright?" Jazmine met his eyes. She could see he was concerned, knowing why he was concerned she tried to reassure him with her smile.

"We will find out shortly how my father feels. And I'm alright." He reached into his pocket taking out something. "I think this belongs to you." He slipped her wedding ring and engagement ring back on her finger kissing her hand after it was on.

"It's about time we get this back on my finger. Thank you." She got on her tiptoes kissing him. He led her over to the window, sitting down on the chair and pulling her on his lap.

"Now tell me about the gift you gave me." Alexander kissed the tip of her nose giving her a smirk.

"Is that what has been on your mind this whole time?" She giggled as he nodded. "Well, I found out about two days ago. And had the keychain made just for you." She smiled as he pulled her to him.

He peppered her cheek with light kisses. "Baby, that's amazing. I'm married to the love of my life and she's having my baby." He looked at her with so much love and adoration in his eyes. He can't stop thinking about how he got so lucky to have all of this.

Christian and Joseph walk over to Alexander and Jazmine as they sit by the window. Christian couldn't help the grin on his face as he watched his two friends clearly in love.

Everyone was standing around Alexander and Jazmine when Charles walked into the room, followed by George and Meredith. Alexander watched as Charles walked with papers in his hand sitting behind his desk.

"Christian and Joseph, I need you to wait outside. Brian, you will also not be needed." Charles motioned for them to leave. They gave Alexander an apologizing look before telling him they will be right outside.

"Father, I don't see why Meredith and her father need to be here. I am king now and you will not tell me how to do this." Alexander helped Jazmine up before getting up himself. He stood tall refusing to give in to his father. He made sure to shield Jazmine from his father as much as possible.

"Alexander, you are not thinking straight. I have brought annulment papers for you and her to sign." Charles pointed at Jazmine as he held out the papers.

CHAPTER 11

Reason To Stay

(8 Months Ago)

Alexander and Jazmine stood in front of Joseph, they were on a secluded beach in Castleberry. Joseph had to have Alexander get married in Castleberry for it to be legal. They could have obtained an international marriage license, but that would have required their father to approve it and they couldn't have him know what they were doing.

Joseph smiled at them after doing the ceremony. "I now pronounce you Husband and wife. You may kiss the bride." Joseph gave Alexander a smirk. Alexander pulled Jazmine to him, dipping her before capturing her in a passionate kiss.

Jazmine had her family there and their friends Christian and Brian were there. Joseph had told Alexander of his plans to abdicate, he also told Alexander about their father having an agreement with George, that the crown prince will marry Meredith and that she will be the next queen. Alexander decided to marry Jazmine before Joseph abdicated, he was not going to be stuck with Meredith. Brian helped to block all that information for as long as possible. He didn't want someone snooping around and finding out that the crown prince was married. Not even his father was supposed to find that out.

(Night of the Coronation)

"Alexander, you need to sign this annulment." Charles held it out to Alexander and Jazmine. Meredith moved closer to them, she was going to make sure Jazmine signed. She was not going to let some low-life commoner take her crown.

"I will not. I'm married to Jazmine and I will stay married to her." Alexander grabbed the documents from his father looking them over. He walked to the fireplace throwing it in, he smiled as he watched it burn. There was no way in hell he would ever leave the only woman he loves.

"I am your monarch, you will do as I say." Charles stepped right up to Alexander. He couldn't believe that Alexander would disrespect him like this. Alexander stared him down, he will not let his father do to him what he did to Joseph.

Alexander lets out a dry laugh. "You are mistaken. I'm the king and she is my queen." Alexander pulled Jazmine closer to him before looking back at all the others in the room. "This matter is settled. Now if you will excuse me, I would like to take my wife back to our quarters. George, whatever agreement you had with my father is non-existent now." Alexander took Jazmine's hand, leading her back to their quarters, not caring about the tantrum that his father and Meredith were throwing in the office. He had already asked the staff to move her belongings there. Brian was trailing behind them as they got to the room Alexander asked Jazmine to go in, he just wanted to speak with Brian real quick.

"I'll meet you inside. I will get the bath ready." She kisses him on his cheek before heading inside.

He waited until she closed the door before he turned towards Brian. "Brian, I want you to keep an eye on my father, Meredith, and her father. I also need you to bring Lucas to my office tomorrow morning. He needs to pay for what he did to Jazmine." Alexander rubbed his hands over his face, he was tired and still needed to deal with this. He just wanted to be with his wife, to show her how much he loved her.

"Don't worry sir, I will take care of all of it. Lucas will be waiting for you tomorrow. I have also arranged for you to see some guards for her majesty." Brian gave Alexander a slight bow. He liked Jazmine, she was not like these nobles and she always had Alexander's best interest at heart. He's everything to her, she would give him the world if she could, the same goes for Alexander, she's his everything, and would give her the world or die trying. "Sir if I may, Congratulations." Brian holds out his hand for Alexander to shake.

"Thank you, Brian. I should have known that you would know. We will meet the guards tomorrow. For now, I'm going to take care of my queen and my unborn child." Alexander smiled as Brian nodded. Alexander headed towards the bathroom. He wanted to spend this time with Jazmine, he wanted to spend the rest of his life with her.

The next morning Alexander left to meet Bastien at his office, Jazmine was still asleep when he left and he didn't want to wake her up. He felt at peace, knowing he could now tell the world how he feels about her. They decided to have a royal wedding for the country to be a part of. Alexander loved that she wanted to have their people share in their special times.

Alexander sat at his desk waiting for Brian to bring Lucas in. Alexander was furious at how he acted around Jazmine and what he did to her. He hated to think about what could have happened if they weren't there to save her. She could have gotten hurt, the baby could have been hurt. There was a knock at the door and Alexander called for them to enter.

"Your Majesty. Lucas is here as requested." Brian entered with Lucas. Both bowing to Alexander.

Alexander leaned back in his chair as he crossed his arms over his chest. "Lucas, what do you have to say about your behavior last night?" Alexander looked at him with so much anger in his eyes, Lucas felt like if looks could kill he would be dead in an instant.

"Your Majesty, I was just following your father's orders. He told me to get her out of there no matter who tried to stop me." Lucas stood there with a worried expression, he had to make them believe that he never wanted to hurt her. He could be in deep trouble if he doesn't.

"So, when Brian told you to let her go, you just assumed you didn't have to listen to my head guard?" Alexander stared at him.

"Sir, my orders were from the king." Lucas couldn't look at Alexander, he felt his gaze burning into him. He just wanted this to be over, to go back and find out what Charles wanted him to do next.

"Yes, you listened to my father even though he wasn't king anymore, you still didn't let up. You are hereby dismissed from being a king's guard. The reason being I can't trust you around my wife and I can't trust you to protect me or my family. You are also hereby banned from setting foot near the palace." Alexander turned from Lucas to Brian. "Make sure he leaves the palace and he is never to return." Brian nodded, taking Lucas by the arm. "And Lucas if you ever come near my wife again, I will kill you." Alexander smirked, motioning for Brian to take him away.

***

A few days later Jazmine and Alexander were on their way to the doctor. They needed to find out how far along she was and that everything was alright with Jazmine and the baby. Alexander didn't care as they were married for over eight months, but it made a difference as to when they would do the royal wedding.

Alexander and Jazmine walked into the doctor's office through the private entrance, the nurse motioning for her to lay back on the bed. Telling them that the doctor would be out soon. Alexander took her hand, giving her a gentle squeeze.

"Everything will be alright, love?" He leaned forward kissing her forehead.

"I'm just nervous." She smiled looking at him. She could see how excited he was about becoming a father. He had a sparkle in his eyes, the same sparkle he had the day they got married. She couldn't help but wonder if the baby would be alright. She was there the day Joseph and Amanda lost their baby and how hard it was for them. Joseph had the same look on his face as Alexander has right now when he found out he was going to be a father. It scared her to think that the baby could be taken away from them at any moment.

The doctor came in and greeted them, she moved over to the sonar machine asking Jazmine to lift her shirt. "Now let's see your baby. This will be a little cold, but it helps us see the baby better." She squirted the gel on Jazmine's tummy. Moving the wand over her stomach, Alexander's eyes grew wide when he saw it. Jazmine instantly locked eyes with him. He could see the tears in her eyes.

"There's your baby." She pointed to the screen showing them. "You are nine weeks pregnant and the baby is healthy." Alexander's smile grew wider, as he looked at Jazmine. The tears were running from both of them as they heard their baby's heartbeat; it was like music to their ears. Alexander squeezed her hand. He loved her more and more every day he got to spend with her.

The doctor printed out some photos for them, wiping the gel from Jazmine's stomach. "Now how are you feeling?" She turned to look at Jazmine.

"I'm feeling fine, just tired and I'm a bit nauseated but haven't thrown up. Other than that, I'm feeling great." Jazmine smiled. She didn't have many symptoms, if it wasn't for her being late, she wouldn't have known or taken a pregnancy test.

"If you do start to feel morning sickness just give me a call and I will prescribe you something for that." She got up. Alexander and Jazmine followed her. She told them what Jazmine should and shouldn't do and what she can and can't eat.

As they arrived at the palace and headed inside. Alexander told her that he needed to go over some things in his office, but he would meet her in their quarters. She nodded before she headed up the stairs. Alexander walked over to his office, he hadn't spoken to his father since the day of his coronation, but he was still angry with him for what he tried to do to Jazmine. Sitting at his desk he went over some papers from the council. All of them were happy that he was married, and they were thrilled about the fact that they would still give their people a royal wedding. They say that he got married before he knew that he was going to be the crown prince and knowing how King Charles was, they knew he had no choice but to hide his marriage from him until the time was right to disclose it.

Jazmine walked back to their quarters, she was smiling like a child on Christmas morning. Alexander and she had seen their baby and the baby were doing great. She was already so in love with that tiny human growing inside of her. She couldn't wait to tell Amanda. As she came to the top of the stairs, she saw Lady Jolene.

"Lady Jolene, it's good to see you. Are you heading back home?" Jazmine smiled as she reached the last step.

"Lady Jazmine, I'm glad I caught you. No, I'm not heading home." Jolene smirked looking Jazmine up and down shaking her head.

"Are you staying for the wedding then? It will have to be soon. Alexander and I haven't decided on the date yet but think it will be within the next month or so." Jazmine beamed at the thought of professing her love to Alexander again, this time in front of the whole country. Jazmine had hoped that now with everything over her and Jolene could become friends.

"No, I'm not staying for the wedding, because…" Jolene looked down at her hands, before looking back at Jazmine with a smirk. "I'm planning on making sure there isn't a wedding. Not yours anyway." Jazmine gasped, her eyes growing wide as she realized what was happening. Jolene never wanted to be her friend, she only wanted to get near Alexander, and seeing as he spends most of the season with her, she pretended to be her friend.

Joseph walked down the corridor seeing Jolene and Jazmine in a heated discussion. His eyes grew wide when he saw what she did. "Jolene no!" He shouted as he ran closer to them.

Alexander was just finishing his work when there was a knock at his door. He called for them to enter, and Brian came in with a worried look.

"Your Majesty, it's Queen Jazmine!" As Brian was saying the words Alexander's heart sank, jumping up he ran after him. Brian's face told him that something had happened.

CHAPTER 12

Don't Want To Write This Song

     Jolene stared at Jazmine, she wasn't about to give up on making her parents proud of her. She wanted to be their favorite daughter and to do that she needed to become the Queen of Castleberry.
     "Jolene, you never wanted to be friends with me. You just want Alexander. You are aware that we are already married and that the royal wedding is only for the country to share with us. So, there isn't a way he will marry anyone else." Jasmine rested her hand on the railing. She felt dizzy from standing too long and knew she needed to have something to eat. She should have had a little more breakfast than she did.
     Jolene lets out a dry laugh. "He will need a queen once you are gone." Jolene stepped closer to her, giving her a gentle push. Jazmine tried to tighten her grip on the railing, not wanting to fall, but her hand slipped, and she fell backward. She rolled down a few steps hitting her head with a cracking sound. The last thing she heard was Joseph shouting for Jolene to stop before everything went black.
     Joseph ran towards Jolene, he had just seen how she pushed Jazmine down the stairs. If he was a few feet further, he wouldn't have noticed it and it would have looked like an accident.
     "GUARDS!" Joseph yelled as he ran down the stairs to Jazmine. He got to her not wanting to move her as he wasn't sure if she broke anything. He could see blood coming from her ear and mouth. She was unresponsive but she did have a pulse and was breathing

normally. "You have to hang on. Don't you dare leave us?" Joseph tried to contain his anger and sadness. He wanted to push Jolene down the stairs but knew that he had to leave it up to Alexander.

Chase and Seth, Jazmine's new guards, came running up to Joseph. As soon as Chase saw Jazmine on the floor, he told Seth to get Brian and King Alexander. He shouted for another guard to come to help him while he pulled out his phone to call for an ambulance.

"Detain her, she pushed Jazmine down the stairs," Joseph demanded. He didn't know what was happening. Chase told the other guard to detain Jolene until the king arrived and told them what to do to her.

Alexander followed Bastien as they ran through the palace. It felt as if it was taking forever to get to Jazmine. Seth had already told Brian what he saw, so they decided not to tell Alexander until they got to her. Alexander's heart was racing, not sure what to expect. Brian only told him he had to come, something happened. As they arrived at the bottom of the stairs, Alexander saw Joseph on his knees on one of the steps with a tear-stained face. He couldn't remember the last time he saw Joseph cry. He froze as he saw Chase bending over Jazmine as she lay on the steps.

The paramedics came running past him but he stood there watching as he saw his whole world crashing down. Brian spoke to him but he didn't hear a word, he only saw Jazmine's body on the steps.

"ALEX GET YOUR ASS UP HERE!" Joseph shouted. Alexander snapped from his daze and ran up the steps taking two at a time.

"What happened?" Alexander leaned down on the other side where the paramedics weren't working. They were working fast to try and stabilize her, they needed to get her to the hospital as fast as they could.

"Jolene pushed her down the stairs." Joseph pointed towards the guard holding Jolene. Alexander watched her, he had so much hate in his eyes at that moment that his gaze alone could burn her to ashes. Alexander was holding her hand, praying that she and their baby would be alright.

"Sir we need to go." The paramedic touched his hand trying to bring his gaze back to her.

"I want to go with you." He got up, but she stopped him before he could walk away.

"I'm sorry sir, we need to get her to the hospital as soon as possible. Please just follow us." She could see the fear in Alexander's eyes. He just nodded as Joseph and he followed them down the stairs. They had Jazmine on a backboard, she had a neck brace on and her head was strapped to the board.

"Your Majesty, what should we do with Lady Jolene?" Chase asked, he didn't want to bother him with this, but Brian and Alexander were distracted, and he couldn't just do what he wanted to. If he could, she wouldn't see daylight ever again.

"Put her in a holding cell. I will deal with her once my wife has been taken care of," Alexander stated with disgust. He turned and walked after the paramedics. Joseph and Brian followed close behind him. Brian had already told Seth to get the car ready. As the paramedics were loading Jazmine, Alexander walked over to her. His heart was breaking seeing his wife as fragile as she was at this very moment. A few hours ago, they were so happy, seeing their little one.

"I will be right behind you baby. I won't leave you." He leaned down kissing her head. He turned to the paramedic. "She's pregnant. Please look after her and our baby." He pleaded with her and she nodded, making a note on the file. She then got in after Jazmine, the other one closing the door. Alexander stood there watching as they took his wife away. They took his whole world away in that ambulance.

As he got in the car, they followed the ambulance, all the thoughts going through his head of what could go wrong. She could be seriously hurt, she could lose their baby. Looking out the window, he knew once they get to the hospital, he will have to make decisions that he wasn't ready for.

"Joseph, you need to phone Amanda. I might need her to help me." Alexander gave Joseph a pointed look. He didn't want to think about it, but if there were decisions to be made he would want Amanda to know about it.

"Sure, once we get to the hospital, I will phone her. She's going to be alright, we have to believe that." Joseph clapped Alexander on the back. He hated seeing his brother like this. He hated that someone could do this to his brother in his own home.

Arriving at the hospital, Alexander bolted for the door of the emergency room. Jazmine was already inside. He needed to know how she was doing. As he entered a nurse found him taking him over to a private waiting area. Joseph and Brian once again followed them. She told them that the doctor will be out soon to talk to them.

Joseph went out to make the call. The call he dreaded making. He knew his wife would want to come, so he already arranged with Alexander to send the Jet to pick her up and bring her here.

Alexander was sitting in the chair, his leg bouncing as he waited for the doctor to come to see him. It wasn't long, but it felt like hours to him.

"Your Majesty, I'm Dr. Brooks." She held out her hand to Alexander as he greets her. "I'm working on your wife. Sir, I need you to sit." She motioned for Alexander to take a seat as she sat next to him. He could see that what she was about to say will not be easy to hear. "Her Majesty has taken a really bad knock to the head. We need to do a CT scan to determine if there is any swelling or bleeding in the brain. She has a dislocated shoulder which they have taken care of." She swallowed as she tried to give him the news as gently as she could. "The baby is doing well. Unfortunately, we can't promise the baby's safety if we take your wife for a CT scan." She gave him an apologetic look, he started to hate that look. She could see hearing this was hard on him.

Alexander sat there staring at the doctor. He wanted to scream to save her no matter what, but he lost his voice and wasn't able to say anything. He felt his breath becoming fast, he hated that he needed to make this decision, but he knew on his way here that he would have to make some choices that were hard to do. "Do what you have to. Please just try and save both, my wife and child." He watched as the doctor nodded, getting up to attend to her.

A few hours passed and Alexander told Joseph what the doctor had said. Joseph hung his head in his hands. He never wanted his brother to go through this. How will he tell his wife that her sister isn't doing too well?

Alexander sat looking out the window, he would give anything to hold her right now. To tell her that everything will be fine. He was furious with Jolene for doing this, he wanted to know why, but he first wanted to make sure that his wife was going to be alright. He wasn't going to leave her, not now, not ever.

"Sir, the press is outside. You will have to make a statement soon." Brian didn't want to give Alexander the news. He didn't want to bother the young king with unnecessary stress. The kind of stress that only the press can cause.

"I will give a statement in the morning. We need to find out how serious her condition is." Alexander rested his head against the window as he waited for any type of news on his wife. He snapped his head up as soon as the doctor opened the door.

"Your Majesty, we have the results from the scan." Dr. Brooks looked at Joseph and Brian, giving Alexander a questioning look as if to ask if she could speak in front of them. He nodded for her to continue. "Her Majesty has a small bleed on her brain, nothing to be concerned about for now. We will know more once she wakes up. Other than that, she was very lucky, this could have been so much worse."

"How long until she wakes up?" Joseph asked as he could see Alexander trying to fight back the tears.

"We won't know. It could be hours or even days. She will wake up once she is ready to." She could see the news was hard on them. She wasn't sure how this happened, but she could see that their king was devastated. "I can take you to see her, Sir. It would help her to hear your voice." Alexander nodded, getting up to follow the Doctor.

A few feet from her door they heard machines going off and people running into her room. The doctor turned, telling Brian to take Alexander back to the waiting room. As she turned and ran into Jazmine's Room.

CHAPTER 13

Heaven

Alexander stood there, he didn't want to move away from her room. Brian took his arm trying to get him to go with him. "Sir, I need you to come with me. Let the doctors work." Brian got Alexander to turn around and follow him. He hated what was happening, he should have had guards by Jazmine's side the minute she was announced as Alexander's wife.

Brian and Alexander arrived at the waiting room once again. Alexander felt defeated. Joseph got up as he saw the look on Alexander's face. He knew that something was wrong. Only a few minutes after they walked in there was a knock on the door. Brian opened it, to find Amanda and Christian on the other side.

"Baby, you made it." Joseph wrapped his arms around his wife as she buried her face into his chest. After greeting Joseph, she walked over to Alexander hugging him. Brian and Christian were standing off to the side waiting for them to have their moment.

"How's she doing?" Amanda asked, sitting down next to Alexander and Joseph. Joseph had his arm around Amanda's shoulders with her hand on his thigh.

"I'm not sure. She was doing alright and on my way to her room her machines went off. The doctor told Brian to bring me back, and she ran to her room. Now we are waiting to find out what is going on." Alexander hung his head in his hands. He was king and the one person he wanted to keep safe, but he was not able to keep safe.

"She's a strong-willed woman who loves you deeply. She will not give up. She will be fine." Amanda rubbed her hand on Alexander's back. She just wanted her sister to be safe, she still wasn't sure what happened, but she knew she needed to be strong for Alexander and Jazmine.

"You need to know something." He rubbed the back of his neck nervously, trying to find a way to tell Amanda. "She's pregnant." Alexander gave them half a smile, as Amanda's eyes filled with tears.

Amanda hugged Alexander. "She and the baby will be fine. You know she's a fighter, and having a baby is what you and Jazmine always wanted. She has to be alright." Amanda tried her best to keep her tears from running down her face, but as she turned to look at Joseph she broke down, he pulled her to him as she rested her head on his chest.

They were sitting in the waiting room for a while. Alexander told Amanda what happened the night of his coronation while Joseph told her what happened just before the accident. He wasn't sure what was said, but he saw Jolene push her down the stairs. He told them that if he had blinked, he might have missed it and it would have looked like an accident. That the way Jolene did it, was made to look like an accident.

As everything came to light Alexander realized the things Jolene did during the season, he should have seen the warning lights. He was so concerned about Meredith and Clara that he overlooked Jolene. But then again, she was always nice to them and looked like she was friends with Jazmine. He never thought that she would do something like this.

There was a knock on the door before the doctor came in. She looked around at all of them when Alexander jumped up walking over to her. "How is she?" He stopped in front of the doctor.

"She's resting right now. She had a setback due to her injuries. We were not able to detect any other injuries. We will know the extent of her injuries once she's awake." She turned to Alexander as he struggled to keep his emotions in. He heard what the doctor said, he just wanted to make sure she was alright. He wanted to be able to touch her and be with her, to tell her how much he loved her and needed her with him.

"Can I see her?" Alexander asked, turning to give Amanda an apologetic look as if telling her sorry but he needs to see her.

"Yes, please follow me. I have to ask that it is only the family that goes on for now." She gave them all a look. She knew they were all worried, but she also wanted Jazmine to rest as much as she could.

They all nod, following the doctor to Jazmine's room. Once outside Alexander lets out a sigh of relief that he would be able to see her this time. Joseph, Amanda, Christian, and Brian would wait outside to give Alexander time with Jazmine.

Alexander walked into the room, scanning the room to take it all in, his gaze landed on Jazmine in the bed. His heart raced as he saw his wife laying in the bed with machines attached to her. She had a bandage around her head, and her arm was in a sling. Other than that, no one would notice that she had been hurt.

He walked over to the bed taking her hand in his. He brushed his other hand over her cheek before he leaned down giving her a sweet kiss. "My love, I'm here. I'm never leaving you." He felt a tear run down his cheek as it landed on her cheek. "I love you so much."

Alexander sat there for a while not saying anything, just watching her breath. He laid his hand on her still flat stomach, he wanted them to know he was there for them no matter what.

Amanda and Joseph came into the room, seeing Alexander laying with his head next to Jazmine's side, they were happy that he finally fell asleep. Amanda walked over kissing Jazmine on her head. "Hey Sis, I need you to wake up. You have an adorable husband that needs you right now. And I need you." She brushed her hand up and down Jazmine's arm, watching her sister and Alexander sleeping. They didn't want to wake him, he needed his rest.

Joseph walked over to his wife putting his arm around her as they watched Jazmine. Joseph has seen Jazmine in many ways but never has he seen her so fragile, he hated what Jolene had done to her. He should have helped Alexander, he should have made sure that she was safe when Alexander wasn't able to be with him. Amanda squeezed his hand as if knowing what was going through his mind. That he was blaming himself.

A few days have gone by since the accident, and Jazmine has still not woken up. Alexander was concerned not only for her but for the baby as well. He had asked the doctor if there was something wrong, and she had assured him that she would be fine. She will wake up when her body has healed. The truth was that there was no reason for her not to have been awake yet. They have done all the tests, but for some reason, she hasn't woken up.

Amanda was there with Alexander every day, Joseph brought Alexander some clothes as he didn't want to leave the hospital. He wanted to be there when she woke up, he wanted her to know that he was next to her always.

Alexander was sitting reading over some documents that Joseph had brought him from his office. He needed to do some work while he sat next to Jazmine's bed. He would talk to her about what he wanted to do and how much he missed her, how much he wanted to see her beautiful eyes. How much he wanted to see her remarkable smile. How much he wanted to hear her laugh that made his heart flutter.

There was a knock on the door and Alexander called for them to enter. Brian entered and bowed to Alexander. "I'm sorry, Your Majesty. I have some news that you need to see." Brian handed Alexander the newspaper that came out that morning.

Alexander took the paper, his eyes grew wide as he took in the headline. "Brian, who gave this to them? How did this get out?" Alexander brushed his hand over his face, the headline running through his mind. **QUEEN JAZMINE ATTACKS LADY JOLENE! NEW QUEEN UNSTABLE!**

CHAPTER 14

She Got The Best Of Me

(8 Months Ago)

Alexander and Jasmine got off the plane, her eyes going wide realizing where they were.

"Alexander, how did you do this?" She smiled, throwing her arms around him. She doesn't know how she got this lucky, but she loved this man with all of her heart.

"I know how much you wanted to come here. I want our honeymoon to be perfect." He leaned in kissing her passionately.

Alexander and Jazmine spend the next two weeks enjoying Bora Bora during the day and enjoying each other at night. Alexander knew he had to tell her what was going to happen once they head back to Castleberry, he just wanted to enjoy these last few days together. He wanted to make sure she knew how much he loved her, and that she meant the world to him.

Jazmine watched as Alexander sat down on the plane. Their honeymoon is coming to an end. She sat next to him taking his hand in hers. "Are we going to talk about what made you so stressed?" She gave him a look, knowing he had something on his mind.

"Baby, you know I love you more than anything in the world...." He looked into her eyes trying to see how she felt, he knew she loved him. "You know that Joseph abdicated and that makes me the crown prince." Jazmine nodded knowing that this is going to complicate things. "I still need to join this year's season. Joseph tried

to get me out of it, but my father insisted." Alexander could see the worry in Jazmine's eyes. "You will be made Duchess as soon as we get to Castleberry, but we will have to keep it and us being married a secret until the end of the season. Brian will make sure none of our information will be accessible." Alexander brushed his hand over her cheek as she smiled at him.

"Then I will do it. If this is what we need to do to be together I will do it. I love you so much." She leaned forward kissing him. Both of them snuggled in for the rest of the flight. They would have to act as if they are not in love. But Alexander knew that his love would shine through no matter what.

(Now)

Alexander sat next to Jazmine's bed looking at the newspaper. How could they do this, he needed to give a statement. He stood motioning for Brian to exit the room.

"Brian, set up a press conference. I need to tell the people what happened." Alexander turned to Brian as soon as they got outside.

"I will phone Ana right away." He bowed, turning to walk away. Alexander saw Christian walking towards him giving him a questioning look. Alexander handed him the newspaper. Christian ran his hand over his face as he read the headlines and the article.

"This has your father written all over it. Has she woken up yet?" Christian could see Alexander was stressed and tired. He didn't want to leave Jazmine's side until she was awake. He wanted to be there when she woke up. He wanted to be the first person that she saw when she opened her eyes.

They went back into the room, Alexander and Christian talked when the doctor came into the room. "Your Majesty, we need to do a scan to make sure the baby is healthy." She moved the sonar machine to the other side of Jazmine. Christian clapped Alexander on the back before he exited the room.

The doctor lifted her hospital gown, putting some gel on her stomach. Alexander could swear she has started to get a tiny baby bump. "Uhm mm…." Alexander and Dr. Brooks snapped their heads up looking at Jazmine when they heard her moan at the coldness of the gel.

"Jaz…. Baby I'm here." Alexander cupped her cheek with his hand, a tear running down his face.

"Al…. Alexander, you're on my IV." She smiled as her eyes fluttered open. Alexander got up making sure to remove the IV line from under him. She took his hand before her eyes grew wide.

"The baby??" Her breathing became faster as her heart rate skyrocketed. Their baby could have been hurt. Alexander tried to calm her, but she was frightened of what the fall had done to their little one.

"Your Majesty, I'm Dr. Brooks and we were just about to check on your baby when you woke up. You have been out of it for almost two weeks." Dr. Brooks took a look at her vitals before turning back to the sonar machine.

She took the wand and rubbed it over Jazmine's stomach. Alexander and Jazmine waited for the image to appear on the screen. "Right there's your little one. And the baby looks good. You measure eleven weeks and three days." Dr. Brooks pointed to the screen before letting them hear the heartbeat. Jazmine's free hand flew to her mouth as she heard it, tears running down her cheeks. Their baby is safe and healthy.

"We made that" She grabbed Alexander's hand as he gave her a loving look.

"That we did love." He kissed her. He loved seeing her excited about seeing the baby.

Dr. Brooks left. She was happy with how things were. She had told them that if everything goes well Jazmine could go home in two days. Christian came back into the room seeing Jazmine awake, he smiled and walked over to her. Alexander told her that he needed to make a statement and he would be back shortly. He gave her a sweet kiss as he heads out.

He walked towards Brian, waiting for him to give him the clear that he could go out. Alexander followed Brian out, seeing all the people and press that showed up. They were shouting questions as soon as they saw him. He held up his hand to get them to be quiet.

"Good day, I will be giving a statement as to what happened at the palace. Yes, there was indeed an incident between Queen Jazmine and Lady Jolene." The crowd gasped at hearing his words. He held up his hand to get them to quiet down again. "Lady Jolene was at fault, she pushed the queen down the stairs. The queen is in the hospital and doing well. Lady Jolene will be dealt with once the queen can go back home. Thank you for coming out today." Alexander turned walking back into the hospital, not giving them a chance to ask any questions.

He walked down the hall back to Jazmine's room. He saw her, Christian, Joseph, and Amanda laughing through the window. That was the most amazing sound he has ever heard.

A few days after returning to the palace, Alexander was sitting in his study. Jazmine was in their quarter going over some wedding preparation with Amanda. They needed to do this before she started to show, and they wanted to involve the Castleberry people. They wanted to show them that the monarch has the people's interests at heart.

There was a knock on the door, Alexander called for them to enter. He saw his father walk in with Jolene and her father.

"What can I do for you?" He glared at his father. "And why is she out of her cell?" Alexander asked with anger lacing his voice. Brian was supposed to make sure that she doesn't come out of the cell.

"Your Majesty, if I may. I want to plead for my daughter." Her father gave Alexander a pleading look.

Alexander nodded as he watched Jolene's father closely. "I will hear you out. You should remember that your daughter committed treason. She attacked the queen and could have caused her to lose the heir to the throne." Charles snapped his head towards Alexander. Jolene's eyes grew wide, realizing she was in so much trouble right now.

"Sir, I want to take Jolene back home. I will make sure she never comes near the queen or you. I do understand why she thought she needed to do this. She wanted to make her mother and me proud. She thought that we didn't notice her. What she doesn't know is that we are already proud of her." He looked over to Jolene, smiling at her. Alexander watched him considering what he had just said.

"Would you mind if we spoke to the queen? I don't want her thinking that I'm making this decision without her." Alexander raised his eyebrow as he waited for Jolene's father to answer. He nodded telling him that would be fine.

Jazmine enters the room after Brian comes to get her. She looked from Alexander to Jolene and Charles. She smiled at the unknown man in the room. Alexander introduced her to Jolene's father. They told her what he wanted, and he explained everything to her. She sat there listening, looking over at Jolene a few times, she could see the hurt in her eyes.

"I'm not one to hold grudges, but Lady Jolene could have killed me and our baby. I need to hear from her why I should agree." Jazmine gave Alexander's hand a little squeeze as he smiled at her. She was handling this like a true queen.

"Your Majesty, I am sorry for what I have done. I never wanted to hurt you… I just wanted to prove to my parents I was able to do this. To win the prince, they had me do all the training and I am good at everything, but I'm not capable of having someone love me." Jolene hung her head as a tear ran over her cheek.

Jazmine watched her and could see that she genuinely felt remorse for what she had done. She looked over at Alexander and knew he also saw it. She nodded to him, silently telling him he knew what to do.

"We will agree to have Lady Jolene go home with you. She will not be welcome back in Castleberry again. Maybe after a few years, we can revisit this but for now, she's not welcome. Brian will escort you to the airport." Alexander stood up and shook Jolene's father's hand before he motioned for Brian to take them.

After they left Alexander stood there waiting for his father to leave. He saw Charles looking at Jazmine, he was unable to read his father at that moment.

"Father, is there something we can help you with?" Alexander stood half in front of Jazmine not sure what his father wanted to do.

"I'm sorry for ever doubting you son. Seeing Jazmine act like a true queen just now, made me see what you have always seen." Charles Stood up and walked over to his son. He hugged Alexander. Jazmine got up as well and squeezed Alexander's arm as she walked toward Charles.

"You tried to protect your country from an outsider. I'm not saying what you did was right. What I am saying is you need to trust your sons more. They are your family, and even a king needs his family." She smiled offering her hand to Charles. He looked at her taking in what she just told him.

"I'm sorry for everything I put you through. I am ashamed of what I did. Could you two forgive me?" Charles took her hand and pulled her into a hug as he looked toward Alexander. They both nodded, feeling so much more at ease knowing that now Charles could be a part of their lives. They sat in the study talking for a while. Alexander and Jazmine told Charles all their plans for the wedding. He asked them about the baby. They spend the afternoon talking and making plans. Finally, their family was together again. They could grow as a family now.

***

(A Few Months Later)

Alexander laid in bed as the sun rays lit up the room, he watched as Jazmine laid next to him with William on her chest. He had a rough night and she knew the only way to get her newborn to settle down was to put him on her chest. This was still Alexander's favorite way to wake up in the mornings, seeing his wife and baby boy.

Jazmine stirred next to him and he smiled as he leaned in to kiss her. "Morning love," He smiled down at her.

"Morning, did I fall asleep with him on me again?" Alexander chuckled as he nodded. He carefully moved William off of Jazmine. She smiled seeing Alexander being so gentle with him. Her heart swelled with pride as she watched him.

The last few months had gone by way too fast. They had their royal wedding and Honeymoon again. The people were excited when they found out that the royal heir was already on the way.

Alexander and Jazmine found out they were having a little boy shortly after the wedding and Alexander was so excited he had the nursery done within two weeks of finding out. He and Christian had done it. Christian doing most of the hard work just to avoid his duchy.

Alexander looked over, meeting Jazmine's eyes. She moved closer to him as he wrapped his arm around her. They sat there watching their baby sleep in Alexander's arms, feeling complete.

With everything they went through, they knew one thing was for sure.

Love always wins.

THE END

ABOUT ANNEKE BOSHOFF

A rugby and netball mom, who spends way too much time next to the fields cheering for her kids. Writing helps to relax me and puts my very wild imagination to good use. I love creating new stories and characters. I also get way too attached to my characters.

LOVE ME 'TIL THE END

by Ayana Lisbet

CHAPTER 1

Isabella

My mother Julia recently married a guy named Tommy, who's a drug addict. They have been dating for only six weeks. Like seriously, they don't even know each other. But it's whatever. This is my last couple of weeks of college, and then I can go wherever I want. My father is in the city of Springbrook, in Virginia, while my mother lives in the middle of nowhere where it takes fucking four hours to get to my father. My baby brother, Mateo, is six years old. My mother doesn't even take care of him. All she cares about is shopping for clothes, shoes, purses, and... oh, more clothes. But not for us. For her.

When my parents were going through divorce, the judge gave my mother custody over me and my brother. When I was a minor, my brother and I stayed with my mother during the week, and then on weekends we would go to my dad's. Now that I'm in college, my brother is with my mom during the week, and the weekend is with my dad unless I come home from college. She would hit us. And when the judge asked her, she lied, "Oh they fell down the stairs, they are clumsy, you know how kids are."

Every time I am home, I take care of my brother. I bathe him, I brush his hair, and I make sure he has everything and is taken care of. I have class three days a week so the other four days I go home and make sure he's cared for. As for my stepfather, Tommy, I can't stand him whatsoever. He literally gives my brother and I weird vibes.

***

I am sitting on my bed with my little brother, Mateo, on my lap. He is watching his favorite show PAW patrol and giggling at it. I am partly watching cartoons with my brother as I was talking to my best friend, Carly.

Carly has been my best friend since we were in first grade. We met in first grade and have been inseparable since. Carly is wearing her brown hair in two ponytails with her pink and blue strap dress and her black flats. I am sitting in the corner of the classroom with my notebook in front of me. "What are you making?" Carly asks me.

"I'm sketching clothes I want to make. I'm going to be a fashion designer when I grow up. I want to make clothes for everybody," I say, as I continue to sketch some designs.

***

"Isabella, what are you doing tonight?"

I look down at my brother, Mateo, as I am talking to Carly, "I am not doing anything, but I can't go anywhere I have my brother. You know how my mother and stepfather are."

"Your dad?"

"Dad is actually working late tonight. They have him doing extra shifts. We would've gone to his house today, but he couldn't."

"Alright, but I will be taking you out this weekend. You focus on getting what you are going to wear, and I'll figure out your little brother."

"Fine, but I like my house. I don't like going out," I say as I get up.

"Bella?" Mateo asks, as I am talking on the phone.

I look at Mateo and say, "Keep watching your cartoons. I'm going to make us something to eat for lunch. I'll bring your food upstairs when it's done."

"Okay," Mateo says, rolled up in his spiderman blanket and drinking his apple juice.

"Alright Carly, I got to go. Talk to you later."

"Alright, Isabella, take care. I'll talk to you later."

I hang up and put my phone in the back pocket of my dark blue jeans and go downstairs. I grab some chicken tenders and some French fries and preheat the oven. As the oven is preheating, I put the chicken and French fries on a baking sheet, and my mom interrupts me.

"What are you doing?" my mother asks.

"Making my brother and I some food since you seem to not care about him. I might be going to dad's later," I say, as I am seasoning the chicken and cooking it when Mateo comes running down towards me.

"What's wrong, Mateo?" I ask, looking down at him.

"I want daddy?" he says, looking sadly at me.

"Daddy's here," our mom says.

"No, that's not daddy."

"Yes, he is!" Julia says, with a frustrated tone in her voice.

"No, he's NOT!" Mateo screams at his mother.

Mateo is crying while my mom goes towards Mateo, trying to hit him. I go and grab Mateo from my mother, looking at her with hate. "Why would you do that? He is only six years old. He doesn't see Tommy as his dad, and I sure as hell don't either."

"Tommy is his father. Unlike your father. He barely helps take care of you guys."

"NO!! My father does everything for us. You barely feed my brother. The only reason we live with you and that I come home is because my brother is here. And my father does everything. When we go to his house on the weekend, he is always there. When dad was living with us, he was the only one that paid attention to us, unlike you. All you wanted was to sleep."

Julia looked at me and went to hit me. "I did everything for you. I sacrificed my modeling career to have you guys. Your father was just some guy. Now here I am trying to raise your children."

Storming off, Julia goes to her room and slams the door. Mateo is curled up in the crook of my neck. I look down at my brother's crying face. "Mateo, you okay?"

"No, Tommy hurt me." He points to his arm, and I see a big handprint, and a cut on his stomach.

I go up to my little brother and see the purple bruise starting to show up on Mateo's stomach with the cut that is on his stomach. I sit down with him and clean the cut.

Why the fuck would my mother let him do this to my baby brother? I mean he is little, and he doesn't do much. He was in my room watching tv. So, he would have to go to my room in order to do that. My brother needs to get out of here. He is not safe here. My mother doesn't care about him.

Putting my brother down, I say, "Mateo you are okay. I will always be there for you, okay? I will never let you get hurt like this again. Let me see your bruise again."

Lifting his shirt, I can see the hand print starting to turn a dark purple. "Mateo, does it hurt if you touch the bruise?"

"Yes."

"Okay, let me get some ice and we can go sit down in the living room watching a movie while you eat your lunch."

"Okay."

I would never have thought that my mother would do that or let that happen to him. I guess my mother doesn't care about my brother. I need to do something and make sure that my brother doesn't have this happen again.

As we are both eating our chicken tenders and French fries, my dad, Sebastian, calls.

What is my dad calling me for? He's supposed to be working. I hope he's okay, and nothing is wrong. I don't know what I would do if my dad weren't with us anymore.

"Hey, daddy," Mateo and I say together.

"Hey babies, how are you guys doing?"

"We're good, daddy. Mateo and I are eating some lunch right now. Then I'm going to see where or who can do my hair for me. I want to get some red in my black hair," I say while eating my food.

"You both pack a bag. You're coming to my house this weekend. We're going to hang out. My girlfriend is going to pick you guys up. She wants to hang out with you guys. I miss you both."

"Sounds good. I miss you, too. I'll pack our bags, and we will be ready when she comes after work. I love when I hang out with you. I always have fun."

"Me too. I just want you to have fun. And also, Isabella Luciana Cortez, you are going to go out with your friends. I hate that every time you go home you're taking care of your brother. So, you and your friend are going to the soccer game. I got both of you VIP tickets, and you guys will be going Friday night?"

"That's tomorrow?"

"Yep pumpkin, you're going," he says.

***

Mateo and I went to the park at the end of our court. When we got there, Mateo ran to the slides.

"Weeeee," Mateo squeals as he goes down the slide, making me laugh.

This right here is my little brother. The sweetest brother. The one enjoying his childhood. The one I never thought I needed in my life. I am grateful for my brother. If my brother is safe and happy, then I am happy. Without my brother in my life, I'm not sure where my life would be.

"Well, well, well." Two people come up to us.

CHAPTER 2

Isabella

"Irena? Santiago? What are you doing here?" I ask.

"Dad told us you came home. We have been trying to see you every week when you come home. But every time we do, you never answer our phone call, or you leave before we see you," Irena says.

"Baby sis, what's wrong?" Santiago asks with his hand on my cheeks.

"Mom is not taking care of Mateo. That's why I never stay on campus more than the three days I am in class," I say, as I look into Santiago's eyes.

"Well, your mom is horrible. I mean our mom is no better than yours and Mateo's, but I just can't believe that dad never gets happy ever after. Like our mom was dad's high school sweetheart, then she got pregnant with us about a month after graduating then he found out that she was cheating on dad while she was pregnant with us. I have no words," Santiago said.

"Dad is the sweetest person, and he gives everyone his attention," Irena expresses while she is looking at Mateo.

"Yeah, I feel bad. I want to talk to dad to get custody of Mateo. I don't want him with mom and her drug addict boyfriend."

In a stern and mad voice, Irena looks into my eyes, and says, "Isabella, why haven't you answered our phone calls, huh?"

"Umm.. I…I…"

"Hello, Isabella?" Irena says.

"Irena, stop! Go sit down, and I'll talk to Isabella," Santiago says, furious at Irena.

Irena walked to the chair and whispers, "Always have to be the big, bad supportive brother."

"Isabella, come here," he says, with his arms out. As I went into them, I wrapped my arms around him. "What's wrong, baby sis?" he says, looking down at me.

"I felt bad. Originally, I was busy with school and then making sure Mateo was okay. Then I got scared because I was afraid you would be mad at me?"

"Why would I be mad at you?"

"Because... bec..."

"Isabella, breathe for me... Take a deep breath for me. I need you to relax for me," he tells me as I am breathing.

"Now, tell your big brother why I would be mad at you." He walked to the table as Mateo came and sat on Santiago's lap.

"Because, I changed my major, and I didn't finish college like I was supposed to." I look down at my hands.

"Isa, I knew you weren't happy with your major. I knew you would change it, and I am happy you changed it. I support you to the end. Now, tell me what you changed your major to."

I smile at my big brother with a giggly face. "I changed it to two majors. Graphic Design and Marketing."

"I'm not surprised!" my brother says.

"You're not?" I say confused.

"Nope, I'm not. Every time I was doing my homework when I was in college, you would see what I was doing. Or when I got my first job and you saw some graphic things I was doing and you were excited. I always saw the happiness in your eyes."

Looking down at Mateo, Santiago was enjoying his baby brother. "Mateo, let's go play."

Mateo looked up at Santiago. "Swing?"

"Sure, come on." Santiago and Mateo walk to the swing set hand in hand.

I am down at the table watching my brothers playing. *I am so happy my brother is not mad at me. I was also with my big brother when he came over or when we used to hang out. People used to think that Santiago was my dad. My dad wasn't mad as he loved how much*

Santiago loved me and would do whatever for me. My brother used to cancel things especially when my mom didn't want to take me.

I am sitting as soon as I see my sister sitting in front of me. "Yes, Irena?"

"Are you going to go to dad's today?"

"Yes, Irena, I'm going to dad's," I say.

Mateo is asking, "Bella, come and play?"

"Alright, I'm coming."

Then, as we were playing, we were having a blast. It is like having family time. And we enjoy our time together. Mateo is running around giggling and screaming happily at his big brother and sisters. His brother and sisters are chasing him around the park, excited that he is happy. Ten minutes later, my phone rings.

Ring... Ring... Ring...

I pick up my phone and it is my father. "Hello?"

"Hey, pumpkin? Where are you?" Sebastian, my father asks.

"Oh, I was with Mateo at the park down the street, and then Irena and Santiago came to see us. Right now, Santiago is playing with Mateo."

"Oh, okay, well why don't you ask your brother to bring you as he is coming over today, anyway."

I walk to Santiago and Mateo, asking, "Santiago, can you take us to dad, since you're on the way there?"

"Yeah, no problem."

***

Santiago, myself, and Mateo were all sitting down on the couch talking with our dad happily. Irena is sitting on the couch, really mad. "So, kids, did you have a great time together?" Sebastian asked.

"Yes, we had fun." I smile up looking at my brothers.

"Not me. Isabella will not tell us a thing about what she is dealing with. Well, at least me." She looks angry with me.

"What are you talking about?" Sebastian asks Irena.

"Isabella has been not calling us and then when we do, she doesn't answer. So, I asked why? And she was sitting there," Irena says, angrily.

"Stop right there, Isabella was trying to tell us, but you wanted her to spill it right that instant." Santiago rolls his eyes.

"Whatever, Santiago. Every time you always support Isabella. You always baby her. I'm your full blood sister, and you never treat me like that."

Sebastian got up and screamed into Irena's face. "Stop that right now. You know your brothers love you both. How can you say that? You also know nothing that she is having to deal with."

"But daddy…," Irena said.

"NO!! Isabella has been struggling with her life," my dad said as he looked at me. "Isabella, do you want to tell your sister, or I can tell her?"

Wrapped up in Santiago's arm I look into my father's eyes. "Can you tell her, please?"

"No worries, pumpkin," he says, looking at me.

I hope my sister doesn't look at me differently. She is never supportive of me. She always said you are never good enough. You could lose ten pounds, or you can't do that. She was never supportive of anything I did.

"Your sister first changed her major, and she didn't believe that anyone would support her. I am sure your brother supports her major. On top of that, her boyfriend left her for another girl, and during the time they were together, and even now, he is still being abusive to her."

"She deserves it. She doesn't give him anything that he wants," Irena says, looking at me.

"Irena, out!! If you can't support your sister, then you can leave."

Irena leaves while Santiago rubs my back. I am holding tight to his waist. Mateo is playing with his toys on the floor happy and content.

CHAPTER 3

Isabella

Santiago stayed last night and made sure I was okay. After we eat dinner, Santiago, dad, and I have a great day. We all were playing card games and enjoying the time together. Santiago still is supportive of me changing my major, however he is a little disappointed that I didn't tell him about what my relationship with Andy was like, and how he is still mistreating me even after we broke up.

It's ten in the morning and Mateo comes and wakes me up. "Bella, get up. Daddy is making us breakfast, and it is ready."

"Okay, Mateo, let me get up, and I'll go downstairs. Is Santiago up?" I ask Mateo.

"Nope, I'm going to go wake him up." Mateo says, running out of the room to Santiago's room.

Everyone went downstairs and sat down in the chairs in the dining room. Sebastian gave everyone their plates and looked at Santiago. "Santiago, any plans for you, today?"

"Other than meeting a client around three? Nothing."

"Well, I hope everything goes well with your client and nothing goes bad," Sebastian tells Santiago.

"Isabella, are you ready to go to the soccer game with Carly tonight?" Santiago asks with curiosity.

Eating my bacon as I look up from my plate, I smile nervously. "Not really. I hate crowds. I hate leaving my house. I just want to be in my bed and re-read *Erin McLuckie Moya's Hell Hounds Series* or *AV Asher The Truth & Lies Duet*."

Like seriously, Erin McLuckie Hell Hounds Series is to die for. It's steamy romance and Bear, from Cautious and Conditional, is a badass that I wish I had someone like him. Plus, motorcycle club omg, that is my weakness. I love to get lost in Bear if I could.

Now, AV Asher duet. That series I probably have read too many times to count. I haven't put the book down. I literally have that book in paperback and eBook. If they were audible, I'm sure that I would get that copy too. I mean who doesn't have a book in more than one form.

"Isabella, the spot I chose for you guys will not be crowded because I got you guys the suite, so you will not be crowded there. And please have fun. Plus, I know you love soccer," my dad says, looking into my eyes.

"True, I do love my soccer. Okay, I'll go," I say, looking at my daddy.

I go to the couch to watch tv, when my two brothers jump on me making us giggle. "You two are too much. I love you guys to pieces."

"We love you to pieces, too, Bella," Santiago and Mateo say as they curl up together.

"Let's watch a movie together before you need to get ready, and I need to leave to meet my client." Santiago looks at Mateo and I. We are all cuddled up on the couch watching one of Mateo's favorite movies, Finding *Dory,* when my phone rings.

I pick up my phone. "Hello?" Silence. "Hello? Anyone there?" Breathing. "I can hear you huffing and puffing. Answer me, dammit."

"Bella, what's wrong?" Santiago asks me. I am shaking next to them. Santiago grabs me, putting me in between his legs. "Isabella Luciana Cortez, what is going on?"

Looking into his eyes, tears roll down my eyes while Santiago rubs my arms "I... I... got a phone call... b-but I don't know who it is."

"Look at me. Give me the number, and I'll have a buddy of mine check it for you. You go get ready for your soccer game tonight and have fun."

"Okay, here." I show Santiago my phone and what the number is as the doorbell rings.

"I'll get it, Bella," Sebastian says, walking towards the door.

Sebastian opens the door, seeing that it is Carly. "Hey Carly, ready for the soccer game?"

"You betcha. I can't wait for this game. Where is Isabella?"

"Living room with Mateo," he says walking into the living room.

Carly comes into the living room and sits on the couch. "Hey, Isabella, ready?"

"Yes, I'm going to get ready."

I walk to my room and grab my soccer jersey with my favorite number, five, and put on my light blue jeans with rips in the thigh and cuff up at the end along with my white air max to pull the outfit together.

Once done with my outfit, I decide to put on some make-up, but not too much. Just adding some foundation, a little eyeliner and mascara and call it a day. *Well, that is amazing and looks perfect.*

I am sitting on my bed, trying to calm down. Fifteen minutes later, Santiago comes into the room and sees me lying there staring into space.

Santiago walks up to me and says, "Are you okay?"

"Yes, I am okay. I'm just afraid that Carly is going to leave me alone in a compact area, and I won't find a way out," I say looking into his eyes, tearing up.

"First, you need to breathe for me. Second, if that happens like she has done many times, which I hate, call your best friend Jasmine. And if you need to, call me, and I will come pick you up. Now, get up and I will walk you out."

"Okay."

We went to the car and once we got in the car Santiago looked into Carly's eyes while she was biting her lips and curling her curly, wavy hair around her fingers. "You better watch my sister. You know she hates crowds and going anywhere besides her house or being with her family. So, I repeat, take care of my sister."

"Fine, whatever."

***

When we get to the arena, it is already packed. We walk into the arena and go to the suite. "So, Isabella, do you think we will get to find some hot guys that will take me home?"

Rolling my eyes at her, I didn't pay attention to her. "We didn't come here to check out the guys. We came here to watch the games."

"Yeah, Isabella, but they are hot and all."

"You know this is pointless; I think it's best that we go our separate ways. All you care about is to try to get my brother's attention, but my brother has a fiancée."

"WHAT??! Isabella, you're so stupid. I don't even know why we are even friends. All I wanted was your brother."

I run to the bathroom and run into a soccer player. "I-I s-sorry"

"It's okay, breathe with me. Breathe, calm down for me." I mock the soccer player and calm down.

"Now, sweetheart, what made you so scared you would cry your beautiful green eyes out?" he asks me.

"Me and my friend came to the game, and she was going on about her finding someone to go out with and stuff. I was telling her we are coming to see them play and stuff, but then she kept going on about the hot players. I told her our relationship is pointless, and she called me stupid, and she's only friends with me because she wanted my brother," I say looking up at him.

"Don't worry about her," he says as the whistle blows.

"That's me. Go sit at your seat and enjoy the game."

"Will do." As I walk away, he yells, "Sweetheart, that jersey you're wearing is the best player, but that may be biased, as that is me."

"What?" I say as I turn around quickly, but he was already gone.

CHAPTER 4

Greyson

I look back to the most beautiful girl I've ever seen. Even with a teary face with puffy red eyes, she is the most beautiful girl ever. And what kind of person would make anyone like her feel like shit? What kind of person would try to use her to get to her brother? That is so stupid. And to make her feel like that, that is not okay.

Once I made sure she was calm, the whistle went off, and I wanted to be there for a few minutes longer, but I needed to go and get ready for the game. And the one thing I don't get when I leave is her name. But the one thing I will do is make sure I find out who she is and what she is hiding. Who hurt her?

"Andrew, ready?" the coach asks me.

"Yes, coach, ready to beat these Knights," I say with excitement.

Every year for the past six years since I got recruited for the Bears, we won every single game, and we won the championship game. We have been undefeated, and we are going to be undefeated. Oh, and yes, I am also captain. I am the youngest captain ever, and couldn't believe it when they named me captain after a couple months being recruited.

"Bro, let's crush those Knights. Those Knights haven't been able to beat us for the last six years, and I am hoping it continues," Taylor says with power in his voice.

Taylor has been my best friend since middle school. We have been supportive of each other since. My family wasn't supportive of me playing soccer in the beginning. Now, some are and some are not. But it's whatever. However, Taylor's family isn't very supportive. Well, his sister is supportive. His parents threw him out when he was recruited. I still can't believe we've been friends for that long.

We are playing like we always have, the crowd cheering us on. This is the biggest game yet. However, the Knights, well they can go sit this out. Like seriously, they don't even play as a team. Every time the Knights don't do what the coach wants, he gets even more angry and furious if that is even possible.

"Guys, what's wrong with you? You're supposed to be playing like a team, not like you're walking at the store with your grandma on a Saturday night," the Knights coach screams at them.

"Let's go Bears! Let's go! Let's go Bears! Let's go!!" the fans cheer, making me smile. That even though we are not even trying that much we are crushing them in the first quarter.

Throughout the game, I am distracted trying to figure out who the mystery girl is. And when I will see her again. She is all I can think of. Making her smile and making her enjoy her time.

"Andrew focus," Coach yells, even though we were beating them in the first forty-five minutes twenty-five to five. Like seriously we don't need to do much.

As the whistle blows for the end of the first round, I sit in the bleachers and try to find those sweet green eyes and black wavy hair in the seats. But I can't find her. I can't explain it. She makes me feel things I never felt before.

"What are you thinking about, Greyson?" Taylor, my best friend asked.

"Trying to find this girl that I saw Well, bumped into when I went up to the stands. She was so beautiful. When she bumped into me, my heart stopped. She had the most beautiful eyes. She wore makeup but didn't wear that much like all the other girls do. She was the sweetest. She had my jersey number on, but it's funny. She didn't realize it was me she ran into," I say, looking into the stadium with starry eyes.

"Looks like the 'no, I'm not dating anyone' has a crush now. And a crush that sounds like the one for you," Taylor says.

"Shut up! No girl has made me get this feeling. Yes, all my exes left me or used me for my money. At the time I didn't care, but as I grew tired and after the last one, I was like nope, I'm done."

"Boys, game time. Let's crush those Knights." All of us are running to the field and getting our game faces on.

Taylor got the ball, and zoomed through their players passing the ball to me, which landed me with a score. That was in the first ten minutes, too.

"God dammit, what's wrong with you guys? Focus. Those Bears are going to crush you. And it's the beginning of the season. You don't want to start it like this," the coach kept screaming throughout the game.

Keep playing the best you can. Once the game is over, you can find your girl. Well, unless you don't want to find her.

Of course, I want to find her. She is my soulmate. I would die for her. She needs me just as much as I need her.

Goal after goal of the Bears scoring and tiring out the Knights, the Knights won the game with forty-five to eight. The Bears are still undefeated.

"WE CRUSHED THEM!" Taylor says with excitement, making the whole team laugh.

As I went up to the stadium, I was signing some autographs when I saw one girl crying with some girl.

Pushing through the crowd with my two best friends behind me, I ask, while looking into her eyes, "Are you okay, sweetheart?"

Looking up at him with tears in her eyes, she says, "Yes, Greyson Andrew, I'm okay."

The girl next to her was biting her lips and looking up at me. "Yes, we are fine. Just she said that she ran into you earlier. And like what kind of guy would run into her? I mean come on. She is not even all that."

CHAPTER 5

Isabella

    I can't believe how my friend Carly is. When I came back from running into Greyson, she didn't believe me. She kept going on and on that she was better and that he would never go for a girl like me. And now, right in front of me she repeats the same things.

    Greyson looks at her with anger. "First off, she is beautiful and one of a kind. I have never had anyone make me feel things like that. I never had anyone get me distracted from a game, and a good distraction. You are not my type. I would *never* go out with you. So, do yourself a favor and stop trying to hurt her, because you think she doesn't have anything. Well, news flash, she has everything and more than I want."

    "Fine! Isabella, find your own ride home?" Carly says, walking out of the stadium.

    "B-But..." I said looking at Carly.

    "Isabella sweetheart, look at me. We don't want you to get overworked. Let's go somewhere quiet." I look up into his eyes.

    "Okay."

    I follow Greyson and his friends, we go to one of the suites and Greyson has me sit in a chair. Greyson bends down and looks me in the eyes. "Breathe."

    I breathe and let it out. Once I calm myself down, I sit there looking at them all. "I need to call my brother. He is going to be mad."

    "Why?" the three soccer players say, together.

"Because Carly did this before. She would leave me because things didn't go her way. I never understand why she also puts me down and hurts me. I guess she wasn't my friend," I say looking at them all.

I dial my brother's phone, and it is ringing. "RING... RING... RING..."

"Hey baby sis, what's going on?"

"I-I-I'm..." I say.

Greyson interrupts me and says, "Breathe for me. You can't get upset. You need to calm down. I am right here. I am not going anywhere."

"Sis who's that...?" Santiago asks

"It's Greyson Andrew, Taylor Johnson, and Coby Adams," Looking at them all and they all are smiling at me.

"I call that bullshit."

"No bubba, it's really them. I can put you on speaker." I look around at them.

They all shake their heads yes, and my brother says, "Yes, do it." They all watched me put my phone on speaker and they all sat down with me.

"Hello?" Greyson says with his deep voice that makes me shiver.

Never thought a guy that plays professional soccer would make me feel like that. Every time he looks at me it makes me giggle, like he is the best person in the world.

"Hey man, I didn't think that you would be with my sister. It's not because she is not pretty or anything. My sister is gorgeous. I just thought about her and her fear of crowds and her being shy that it would stop her. Plus, she and I have always watched soccer games when we were younger."

"No worries. Your sister is gorgeous," Greyson says winking at me, which makes me blush fifty shades of red.

"What's going on, sis, I'm on the way to my office right now and I thought you and Carly were going to the mall. She just called me and told me." He sounds confused.

"What? No! She left me here at the stadium. She didn't believe me when I told her that I bumped into Greyson. Before the game, she said the usual."

"Sis, I'm on the other side today, but let me get in the car and I'll pick you up. And sis, I don't want you around Carly anymore. Why haven't you told dad about her?"

"I don't know," I say, looking down at my hands.

"Hey man, if you want, I can take her home for you. And you meet you at the house?" Greyson says to my brother.

"I will say yes, but only if my sister is okay with it."

I look around at the guys and am nervous. "What do you say, Isabella? Do you mind if we take you to your house? We will meet your brother."

"Okay."

"Alright, sis, talk to you when you get home. Relax for me. We will talk about the game later. I'm sure you had fun."

"I did, but I wish you would come." I look around the stadium, which is now empty.

"Dad never told me he got tickets, let alone tickets for you and Carly until I saw you guys. But next game we will go together."

"Okay."

We all are walking down to the garage where his car is. He was driving a red Ford F-150 truck. Once we got there, we all got in the truck.

"So, Isabella, behind me is Taylor, my best friend since middle school. And next to him is Coby. Coby, I met when we were recruited."

Smiling at Greyson, I say, "Greyson, you know I know you guys. I grew up watching soccer. My brother and I. My half-sister nope. All she cared about was boys and makeup and stuff. She even dated my brother's best friend. My sister broke my brother's friend's heart."

"Wow, that's crazy for her to do," Coby says.

"Yep, it was. My brother doesn't really care much about her after that."

"So, Isabella, what do you do?" Coby asks.

"Well, I am getting my degree in Graphic Design and Marketing, I will be done in a couple of weeks," I say, smiling and giggling.

Throughout the driving, they have me feeling calm and content with my life. They don't look at me weird. They ask me all kinds of questions.

We are pulling up when my brother walks out and says, "Hey sis."

"Hey bubba," Isabella says as Santiago pulls up a coke for her. And she starts drinking it after a night that she has had. "Thank you," Isabella says.

"You're welcome." Turning to the guys, Santiago says, "Hey, you guys want to come in. We have some beers. We can hang out or whatever."

"Sure, I'm down," Greyson says.

They all go in, and Santiago grabs the beers when someone comes down the stairs. "Sissy, bubba?"

"Hey buddy. Why are you up?" I say, looking at the clock as my dad comes down.

"He wanted you. I was going to put him in your bed. I guess he heard your voices and ran down here."

"No worries."

I sat down next to Greyson with Mateo on my lap. Someone opens the door while Santiago passes the beers out."

"Irena, what are you doing here? Daddy kicked you out. He doesn't want you here if you are going to be rude to Isabella, but also trying to use the way I treat her against her. Get out," Santiago says.

"I don't get it. Why does Isabella get your attention? I am your sister. She is our half-sister."

Irena comes to me and yells at me like I did something. Santiago grabs her. "Stop."

"Isabella, you want to know who your boyfriend left you for? Huh?" Irena yells while Santiago is in between us.

"I really don't care about it, Irena."

"It was me. He left your sorry butt for me. He said you were boring. You didn't give him anything. He felt like he was dating a child."

"Irena, I know he left me for you. He told me. And I don't care that he left me for you. I mean he didn't cheat on me. He told me he left me for you. But you don't understand what I went through. I was scared to leave that relationship. He was abusive to me. Not sexually abusive. Physically and mentally. I couldn't tell dad. It took me a while to tell dad."

***

It's Friday, Greyson and I have been talking since I saw him last week with my dad. He didn't let me go when we were at my father's house. He was so sweet. When my sister left, well, more like my brother dragged her out, he checked on me to make sure I was okay. We all decided to watch a movie. My brother picked a movie, and we all watched the movie. We all enjoyed the movie, and it was amazing.

Ring... Ring... Ring...

Looking at the phone, I saw it was Greyson calling. Smiling down, I answer it, "Hello?"

"Hey sweetheart. What are you doing tonight?" Greyson asks.

"Nothing really. Just going to see my little brother later and maybe sit at home and read another romance novel. Why?"

"Well, I was going to ask you to come out with me. We can go and have a picnic and do some painting together."

"I love that, Grey. What time?" I asked Greyson as I was looking outside on the balcony, drinking my coffee.

"If you want, we can do lunch time or we can do dinner time. What do you want, sweetheart? I don't care."

"Let's do lunch," I say as I look around feeling like someone is watching me. "I will pick you up at 11:30."

"Y-yeah, okay," I say, while still looking around.

"Sweetheart, what is the matter?" Greyson asks concerned.

"It's nothing. I am just overthinking. But seeing as it's almost ten o'clock I should probably get ready." I look at my watch.

"Yep, sounds good."

Walking to my room, I get dressed for my picnic with Greyson. Looking in my closet, I am looking for what I am going to wear.

Well, let's see what I should wear. Well, we are going to have a picnic and go painting. So, a nice shirt with jeans will be good.

Looking through the closet, I find my white blouse with blue flowers embroidered shirt with my dark fitted blue jeans. Walking to my door length mirror, I wet my curly hair and brush my curls out to make them look wavy with half it up in a clear clip with two curls dangling on the outside of my face.

Sitting down on the balcony on my chair, hearing the birds chirping through the calm afternoon, reading my book. As time passes, Greyson comes and walks up as soon as I see a shadow. "Hey, sweetheart, ready?"

"Yep, Grey? Is this okay or should I change," I say, twirling.

Walking up close to me to stop me from twirling, Greyson looks into my eyes. "Sweetheart, you are beautiful, but can you please go get a jacket? Just in case you get cold."

"Okay." I go inside and get my dark blue jean jacket with little bedazzled lavender on the jacket.

Walking back out, Grey looks at me with his sweet caring eyes. "You love lavender, don't you?"

"Yes."

Greyson helps me into the truck, I watch him as he walks around the truck.

Man, he is sexy. Never thought I would ever get a man like that. Fit in all the right places. Sweet, caring. Has eyes for me. Every time we talked on the phone or when we hung out, he gave me his undivided attention. Plus, he has been my support since we met. Never thought I would ever find someone, again. There will be so many things I would want to do with that man. Stop, Isabella, focus.

Getting in the car, Greyson pulls out and looks back. "Sweetheart, do you want anything else for the picnic? I got some chips, some fruits and some sandwiches made."

I look into his eyes. "No. That's good."

"So, how's college classes going?" Greyson asks, driving to the park.

"It's going well. I have one final left. It's Monday, but everything else looks good. My grades are good right now, so I can't complain."

"That's good, sweetheart. I'm so proud of you. Even though you changed your major, it's okay. I actually got a degree as well. I haven't used it, but I'm thinking of using it." Greyson watches the road, making sure he was not hitting anyone.

"Really?" Isabella asks, surprised.

"Yep, right when I got recruited to be on the team, my father said, 'You need to get a degree. What happens if you get hurt, or you can never play again.' I thought what he said made sense, so I got two degrees. I got a degree in accounting as well as a degree in business administration."

"Really?" I ask, looking at him. My eyes look like they are going to pop out.

"Yes, sweetheart. I am going to open a business soon. As I love helping others, I thought having a business that could help the community would be great."

"I think it will, and you are amazing. You show so much care. Especially the first time I met you. You saw how Carly treated me and you were there for me. You took me home when my brother was on the other side of town. You call and check on me just because."

Finally getting to the park, Greyson looked at me. "Isabella come out, let's go eat our food and hang out."

Getting out of the truck, I kept feeling something. I couldn't figure out what was going on. Walking quickly to Greyson, we sit at this nice picnic table. Wooden table that has the bench made of wood as well. Something that you would be sitting at, at a campground table.

Greyson noticed something was off. "Isabella? What's wrong?" He is looking at me as he takes the food out.

"Nothing is wrong."

Stopping what he is doing, Greyson looks up. "I don't believe a word you say. I have known you for such a short time and you are not telling me the truth."

Closing my eyes, I breathe. "Grey, please don't be mad at me."

"Alright, I will not, but honestly there is nothing to be mad at."

Looking down at my hands, I say, "A couple days ago I got a phone call. When I answered they didn't answer. I hung up. Then a couple times after I felt like someone was watching me, but when I looked nobody was around me. I'm scared." I wipe the tears from my face.

Across from the table, Greyson grabs my hands. "Look at me. I will do whatever to keep you safe. Did you tell your brother?"

I shake my head and look down. "No, I'm scared. He has always been protective of me. I love him, but sometimes it is too much."

"How about this? When we go over there, as I'm sure your brother is going to be over there, I'll help you tell your brother. Your brother needs to know."

"Okay."

"Greyson, how was it growing up? Like with your family?"

"Well Isabella, my mom didn't support me at all. My dad is supportive. In my opinion a little too much, but I don't mind at all. Especially since he told me I should get a degree and knocked some sense into my head."

"Your dad is so sweet. Maybe I can meet him?" I ask, drinking my coke.

"Yep."

After finishing the food, Greyson looks up. "Let's go walk to the painting and we can see what we are going to paint."

"Okay."

Greyson grabbed my hand, and I held his hand. Walking down the sidewalk, hand in hand while I swish our hands back and forth like we are sprinting on Sunday afternoon. Once we get there, we sit down at two easels and see that they are painting the sunset at the park.

While sitting down, Greyson's friend, Taylor, calls. "Hey man, the coach called. He wants us for an emergency practice tomorrow at 7am. Don't know why or what it's about?" I heard Taylor tell Greyson.

"Sounds good. I'll be there. I'll talk to you later; I'm going to hang out with Santiago."

"Santiago, Lily's brother Santiago," Greyson says, sounding confused.

I look at him, confused. "What is going on with my brother?"

"Well, apparently, my best friend, Taylor, is going to be seeing your brother. And who knows what? And I have an emergency practice tomorrow. We don't know what that is about or why."

"Let's get started on this painting. Let's do this together." Greyson says.

"Did you sign us up for a couple paintings?" I ask, squinting my eyes at Greyson.

"Maybe?" Greyson smiled at me.

I look at him. "You're something else."

Oh, he is something else. Finding things I love to do and doing them with me. Knowing something is bothering me and making me spill it. Being supportive of me almost finishing college. On top of that, he is going to help me tell my brother what is going on. Who is this man, and where has he been all this time?

Like with my ex-boyfriend. He didn't care about me. He only cared about himself. If he wasn't ready to do anything, he would push me away. He didn't like people insulting him. If someone hurt him, he would hurt me when we were alone. Not sexually hurt me, mentally hurt me. He got mad when I had no time for him. He got mad when I went to see my family. He wanted everything to be about him and nothing else but him.

But this is my life. When he finally left me, for my sister I was grateful. However, now I am wondering who is stalking me and where they are. Why? Why me? Of all things, what did I do to deserve this? I never did anything to anyone that would hurt them. I am always supportive of everyone. When someone asks me for their help, I stop what I am doing and do what I can to support them.

***

Once done, Greyson and I get ready to go to my father's house.

The painting is not the best painting, but the painting is the best because of the memories. Like enjoying our life together. Sharing memories about our past and future. And this has been the best day with Greyson. I mean, talking to him is great, and the time we hung out after the game was great, but today was special.

We are driving to my dad's house. When we get there, we walk into my brother and Greyson's best friend, looking at each other like they're in love, like they want to be together. Taylor is close to Santiago, while they are sitting on the couch. Well, that is until they heard the door slam.

"Hey guys, how is everything?" Taylor and Santiago look at Greyson and I.

"Everything is great. We had fun. We made this painting. I am going to put it on my wall of paintings. I love it," I say, looking at Greyson.

Once everyone is sitting on the couch, I ask, "Santi what's going on? You have a fiancée. Don't say it's nothing. I saw the way you looked at him. And it wasn't that look you give your fiancée."

"Sis, I lied to you. My fiancée... we broke up. She didn't feel a connection with me. She fell in love with someone else, so we decided to go our separate ways," Santiago says, looking into my eyes.

"So, what about you two?" I look at them both, moving my eyes from side to side.

"We are just hanging out as friends."

My brother is hiding something. That look they gave each other was a look of love. Could my brother like him? Could my brother be gay? Will I support him? Of course, I will. He would support me and has been with me since the beginning.

I am leaning on Greyson's chest. "Isabella, you need to tell your brother, please. He needs to know." Greyson looks down at me.

"What is it?" Santiago asks with concern.

"You know I got the phone call the night I went to the game."

"Yep, I remember." I keep looking into his eyes.

"Well, I got more of those messages. I didn't think anything of it. Then recently I felt like someone was watching me but when I looked around, nobody was around me. I-I don't k-know what to do?" I look down with my hands in my lap.

Getting up from the couch and bending down in front of me, Santiago, says, "Isabella, do you want to come live with me? Plus, maybe a change of environment will be better?"

"Okay, let's do that."

CHAPTER 6

Isabella

I finally graduated with a degree in graphic design and in marketing. Right now, I'm working in a firm doing what I love. Helping others. My brother and I have dinner together every night. He makes sure I am okay, and I don't need anything.

My brother wants to go to the next game, so later tonight we are going to check the schedule for the Bears and see which game we are going to go to next.

As for my mother. She has been calling me every day and telling me how much I am not perfect, and not worthy of being with someone as well as not worthy of being her child. My father was pissed off when he found out. He went to her and told her if she didn't stop, he would have the court give him rights for Mateo so she would have no contact with us. We will see if that lasts though.

Greyson called me last night and told me that he has a surprise for me. If many people know. I HATE surprises. I just want to know what it is. But nope, he wouldn't tell me either.

Here I am, sitting down on my bed, when my brother comes in. "Hey Santi, how are you?"

"Good. Want to see when we are going to the game next, and we can schedule everything?" he says as I look at him.

"Yep."

We sit at the table and look at the schedule and the next game is in two weeks. "Isabella, why don't you invite your best friend, Jasmine, and we can all three go to the game?"

"Yep, I'll ask her," I say as I pull my phone out and dial my best friend's phone number.

"Hello?" Jasmine answers sleepily.

"Did I wake you up Jasmine?" I ask looking down.

"Nope, I'm slowly trying to get up. What's up?" Jasmine asked.

Looking at my brother, I say, "My brother and I are going to the soccer game in two weeks, and we were wondering if you wanted to come with us. My brother is getting the suite?"

"Really? I want to go to a soccer game; I'd love to go. When is it?" Jasmine asks so excitedly that it sounds like she is high on sugar.

Looking down at my computer, I say, "It is on the 23rd at 4pm."

"Well, sign me up. And tell your brother that I'll pay him back."

"Okay, I will."

"She is coming. She said she is going to pay you back for the ticket."

"She doesn't need to, but knowing your friend she is going to want to pay me back for that ticket," he says, looking at me, happy.

My brother is buying the ticket when I fall asleep on the couch. As soon as I fall asleep, I feel a blanket go over me. A soft, fluffy, blanket.

***

Greyson

Isabella is my life. My everything. I have no words to describe her. She is so beautiful. She is so sweet. Like helping her father take care of her brother when they are with her mother. Putting others before her. That is someone special.

I called her brother earlier and asked him for permission to date his sister. Don't get me wrong, I know it's her choice, but having her brother's support will definitely mean so much to her. After he said yes and threatened me, I asked him what the perfect date for Isabella would be. I never thought this would be his answer. "Simple dinner, and going to a bookstore. More specifically, an indie author bookstore."

Driving to her brother's house, I get scared not knowing what she will think or what her brother will think. But first I need to relax.

Finally, arriving at the house, I get up and knock on the door. As the door swings open, the most beautiful girl opens it. "Hey, Isabella. How are you?"

"Good."

"Isabella, can we talk?" I ask.

"Sure, let's go to the balcony."

After walking to the balcony Isabella sits down next to me. I looked up and say, "Sweetheart, I talked to your brother, and he gave me his blessings, so Isabella will you be my girlfriend?" I ask, looking into her eyes.

Isabella stares at me, not saying anything. I grab her hands. "Isabella?"

"Yes, Greyson, I would love to. You have been amazing to me. And if my brother gave you his blessing, then I am happy. My brother is my support system, and he always will be."

Isabella leans on top of me, and I rub her head. As I am rubbing her head I ask, "Sweetheart, would you like to go out tonight? Like our first official date?"

"Sure, but what do I wear?" she asks, turning and twisting herself.

"Beautiful you could wear a trash bag and that would be fine. But just wear what makes you comfortable. I don't care what you wear."

"Okay."

Isabella runs into her brother and hugs him so hard. You can hear them both laughing. "What's that about?" Santiago asks his sister, Isabella.

"Thank you for giving Greyson approval to date me," she says, looking up at her big brother.

Who knew siblings would do whatever for their siblings? I mean all of my friends' siblings always fight and they are not like these two. I adore their relationship, and I hope their relationship continues to grow. They are not perfect, of course, but they are always there for one another.

"Go, have fun. I have to go hang out with the guys. I want you to be safe and remember if he ever hurts you, I will hurt him!" Santiago looks up at me.

"Hey man, I will never hurt this sweet girl," I say, holding my hands up.

***

We just got to the restaurant. Nothing fancy, Isabella is sitting across from me. Isabella is fidgeting and acting very nervous. Isabella is wearing her wavy jet-black hair out and decided to dye her hair with red highlights recently. It's not that bright tomato red, it's more the burgundy dark maroon red.

"Isabella, are you okay?" I ask, looking up at her.

"Yes, I am okay. I just like to stay home and stuff," she says, looking around herself.

"Do you want to go home? If you want, we can go home. I don't mind. I don't want you here if you are uncomfortable."

"It's okay, but can I call my brother really quickly? I feel like he is going to get hurt. And if they ask, I want a lemonade, please?"

"You got it, sweetheart."

A waitress comes by and in her thick southern belle accent, asks, "Hey love, what can I get you, today?" She gives the flirty smile she has.

"Can I get a lemonade, please as well as one beer? I also would like to order some garlic parmesan fries and onion rings as well," I say, looking at the menu as I order.

"Is that all, hot stuff?"

"Yep."

"I'll get your drinks and put your order in to give you a few minutes to decide."

What's wrong with women? They throw themselves at guys. And think that every guy wants them. Omg, well we don't. Well, at least not the man who wants a relationship, who wants a family, who wants an amazing woman who cares about them and not their money.

Isabella walks back looking better. "Everything okay?"

"Yep, it's good. They are going to the house, and he made me feel better. I don't know why, but my brother and I always get this feeling. I know he ignored his feelings with my ex, and regrets it to this day."

"Your brother and you must be really close then?" I ask as the waitress comes to put our fries and drinks on the table.

"Are you guys ready to order?" she asks, looking at Greyson.

"Sweetheart, you ready?" I ask, looking at Isabella.

"I..."

"Of course, I am sugar," the waitress answers.

"I was talking to my girlfriend, who is sitting right across from me." The waitress turns and looks furious.

"Yes, babe, I'm ready."

Isabella goes first and asks for her food, "I would like a bacon burger, cooked medium well with fries. Can I also have some ranch on the side?"

"Sure."

"And I'll have a cheeseburger, well done with regular fries."

Once she left, Isabella and I relax and joke about having a great time. This girl is amazing. I love her to pieces. "Isabella, what did you do today?"

"Well, nothing much. I did some graphics for my friends. I did this when I was in college and loved it. So, I am continuing to do it while I am working. So, after my brother got home, we went to get tickets for your next game."

"Baby girl, why didn't you ask me? I could've given you the tickets that I got." I look into her eyes.

"It's okay. My brother got the suite for us and my best friend, Jasmine," she says, looking into my eyes.

The waitress finally comes with our food and softly hands me my food, then once the waitress hands Isabella her food, she dropped her plate so close that the ranch got everywhere.

"Ooops," the waitress says.

I got pissed as hell. I get up from my seat and scream, "Are you serious right now? What the fuck would you do that to someone? I want a new waitress now!"

"You're a soccer player, and she is not all that. You could do better than that girl. She talks quietly. She doesn't raise her head much."

"So, like you?" I ask her.

"Well yeah, I mean come on. Like I have passion. I have a body and confidence in myself. And she is not even all that great."

Laughing at the waitress, in my deep voice, I say, "You don't know shit about me. You don't know what I need or what. But know this. I adore this girl and I love her to pieces. So, get your manager and a new waitress for me."

A manager comes out, asking, "What seems to be the problem?"

"Your waitress over here basically dropped my girlfriend's food, which had the ranch splattering everywhere. Not only that, she also flirted with me in front of my girlfriend and called my girlfriend names."

"Come here baby." I say, looking at Isabella, who comes into my arms. I whisper, "Want to come to my house?"

"Nope, not today."

We get our food and go to her brother's house. As soon as she walks into the house, Santiago is watching tv. She goes to him and hugs him. He doesn't care that she was dirty, the look she has shows all he needs to know.

Santiago saw me and asked me, "Can you go to her room and get her a clean shirt from her closet? Her room is two doors on the right."

"Yep, you got it bro." I walk down the hall grabbing a purple t-shirt that says, *'Live your life, not others'*.

I walk back to the living room, handing him the shirt as he is trying to pull his sister's shirt off. "Nooo," Isabella says.

"I'm just changing your shirt, if you don't want me to look fine, but I want you out of this shirt and into a clean one."

"It's okay, Santi," Isabella says, looking into his eyes. Isabella is sitting in Santiago's lap with a blanket around her, while he takes the old one off, and puts a new one on.

Isabella is laying on her brother as he calms her down.

"Isabella, can you please tell me what happened?" he asks, looking down, rubbing her hair in his lap.

"We went to dinner and then some girl kept flirting with Greyson in front of me. He told her to stop, but when she brought our food, she dropped mine so the side and the ranch splattered."

"I'm so sorry sis, but remember there is someone out there for you. And look, Greyson likes you. He has been at your side. He will always be there for you when you need him. He could have left you, but he stayed. If he truly cares for you, he will make sure you are doing okay."

"That's true. Santi, he told the waiter that he loves me." Isabella smiles trying to hide her smile from me.

"It's true, Babygirl. I love you so much. You have been my world since we met. I have no words to describe you. It's funny because whenever I go to the store, I buy things you may like. Food, drinks, and small items."

"That's cute." Isabella says.

"Isabella, dad is having a cookout this week. He invited both our moms." Santiago says looking down at her.

"Don't leave me alone." Isabella says.

"That's fine. I will not." Santiago says to Isabella.

"Wait, what do you mean both our moms?" I ask them. And they looked at each other.

"Greyson, my sister Irena, and I are twin siblings. My dad and my mom had us after high school. However, my mom didn't want to be in our life. Then my dad met Isabella's mom and my dad had her and Mateo. However, Isabella's mom didn't want to be with him, and he left," Santiago explains.

Isabella looks at her brother and they shake their heads. Isabella gets up and sits on my lap and looks in my eyes. "Will you want to come to the cookout this weekend? You can meet my parents, and then we go to the lake. Normally, Santiago, Mateo, and I go after we have a cookout."

"If you want me there, then yes," I say, looking into her eyes.

"Yes, please."

"Okay, then I will be there. What time is it?"

"My dad said, noon on Saturday, so we all probably can go to the lake between three to four o'clock," Santiago says.

"That's perfect, as I have a game Sunday. And looks like I'll have an audience."

"Glad that we can come. However, we want to see a win. We want to see you kick a goal. We know you can. But the question is... How well will you do it?"

"Oh, you got jokes."

The three of us are laughing. This is the relationship I missed. My girlfriend is here. Her brother is here and he jokes and is like a best friend to me. And we all have a great time. Not only that. They invited me to come hang out with them and their parents. One thing I need to watch is their sister. She wouldn't stop flirting with me. She needs to stop. I guarantee if her brother finds out, he will be pissed. I will handle this, because I want him to have one less thing to worry about.

CHAPTER 7

Isabella

I am sitting at my office trying to find the perfect size keychain for this company *Inking & Creative* that they like made. It's a business for small authors. They want their books on their keychains and still have the name bold. It's four o'clock and in about thirty minutes I will leave.

Alright, let's figure this out. So, tomorrow morning, I just need to send it out for proof and get the approval of everything going on.

After trial and error for the next twenty-five minutes, I get the designs down. The books are in their blue stack as on their logo and had their name in bold white outlined in black over the logo. I send the designs to the company to get it approved. So, tomorrow if they send it back then I can work on it.

I sign out for the day and go across the street to my brother's apartment. Which is so nice that he lives right across from my job.

Greyson was going to pick me up from work, but seeing as he wants to go to his house and hang out today, I need to get clothes, so I went to my brother's apartment to get it. Just as I was walking up to the house, Greyson says, "Hey, sweetheart, what are you doing?"

Looking at him sweaty after his practice, with the cheesy but cute smile he gives me. I love him to pieces. I mean he has told me already and multiple times. I haven't yet, but I think I will show him how much, tonight.

"I'm just going to get my bag for tonight and then I'll be right back down." I look at him.

"Alright, be quick, please."

After grabbing my overnight bag and getting in the truck, Greyson grabs my backpack and puts it in the back seat. "Hey, baby girl." He kisses me on the cheek.

"Hey Grey, how was practice today?"

"Brutal, I'm so tired after this practice I could go to sleep for days." He drives us to his house.

"Babe, we could have done a different day. I wouldn't mind at all."

"Babygirl, it's alright. I have time for you. It's just a pain in my muscles that I can manage."

"So, babygirl, what do you think of us making homemade Lasagna, and eating that for dinner? It would be amazing," Greyson says, as we are driving to his house.

"Lasagna, yep. So, let me guess. You have everything already, and you were hoping I would say yes to that?"

Smiling at me Greyson says, "Well, not necessarily. I did have everything and did ask your brother what he thought, and he was definitely happy with it."

"I'm sure he was, however he may not be happy with what may or may happen after dinner..."

"What?!" He turns his head so fast that he can't think anymore when he turns into the driveway.

"OMG this is where you live?"

"Yes, this is my house?"

"This is not a house, this is a mansion. My brother has a big house, but this is like three of his houses put together. And his house has five bedrooms, an office, and a fully finished basement," I say, with my crystal eyes popping out of my head.

"Well then, welcome to my mansion. Oh, I forgot to tell you, I sorta have a cute fuzzy roommate?"

"What?"

As he opens the door, two fuzzy little boxers come running to the door.

"Aww, they are so cute. What are their names?" I bend down and pet them.

"The one on the left is Daisy. She is a sweetheart. Then the other on the right is Jasper. Now, Jasper is something else."

They get in and they are on the couch cuddling. Daisy is laying right on top of Greyson, while Jasper is laying on his feet.

"Jasper, come here."

Jasper jumps on his lap, and looks at me. "Isabella, these are my babies. Ever since I moved out, when my mother didn't support my dreams.

"Why two dogs?" I look down at them both snuggled up on his lap.

"Well, when I went to go get a dog, I saw Daisy, however, then I saw Jasper over here. I couldn't help but take them both."

"Let's go make dinner," he adds, looking at me.

"Yep, umm, lasagna with cheese on top."

Greyson takes out the already cooked meat and warms it up. He takes the noodles out to cook in a pot of hot water and salt.

"Alright, Isabella, we will wait for the noodles to cook, while we are cooking we can relax."

"Or we can do something else?" I say.

Mischievous, Grey looks up, asking, "Do what exactly."

"Oh, I don't know? Maybe something that you would want to do. Something that you love to do and you can have."

He grabs me, setting me on the island. He stands in between my legs and starts to kiss me on the lips. I pull Grey by the waist and wrapped my legs around his hips. As he massages my lips with his lips, I moan in his mouth.

"You are perfect, baby!"

"Really?" I ask, looking under my eyelashes.

"Yes, babygirl. Why would you second guess yourself? You are perfect in my eyes, always."

"It's nothing." Just as the water of the noodles bubbles, Greyson goes to check on them. As he is checking the noodles, there is a girl coming into the house with two babies.

"Babe? Where are you?" some girl with pink hair says, with big lips that look like she has had plastic surgery just done.

Greyson turns off the stove and turns around furious. So furious that he could easily burn her with his eyes. "Firstly, don't call me that. I'm not your boyfriend. I broke up with you after you decided that I wasn't what you wanted."

"This is your daughter and son. My boyfriend doesn't want them," she tells Greyson as he crosses his arms over his chest.

Greyson looks at them, "those kids aren't mine. Look at them, they look nothing like me."

"Well, I had them only eleven months ago. And we broke up about a year and half ago."

"I don't believe you, so we are getting a parental test before I will claim anything."

She looks at her kids. "What am I supposed to do with these kids until we do the parental test?"

Greyson and I look at each other then, look at her. "They are your babies. You have them. You take care of them," Greyson says.

She leaves with the kids, stomping her feet like she was told she couldn't have any candy or she couldn't stay up.

Greyson and I both sit on the floor in the living room while the lasagna is cooking. I am staring in his eyes, facing him. "What baby girl?"

"Nothing. It's just you are the first person to make me feel comfortable and I love you for that. My boyfriend from college he took forever, and when I was finally comfortable it wasn't like you make me comfortable... I love you so much."

"I know we said it to each other really fast, but I do. I have no words. When we met I felt connected. I don't understand it. It's something I never felt before. Like the missing piece I never knew was out there."

Beep, beep, beep, the ringer to the lasagna goes off. Both of us get up and get our plates of lasagna. Sitting at the island, we are enjoying our dinner.

I looked into his eyes. "Greyson, who was that girl? Why did she come over today?"

"That girl was my ex. I dated her on and off for some time. After the last time, I was done. And for her to come over I don't know."

"And the children?" I ask, looking into his eyes.

Staring into my eyes, he says, "Isabella, I have no idea. I never knew she had kids. And I don't believe that she was pregnant with my kids. I left her the last time because of the drama her and her family caused. They kept saying things that were not true. There were times I had to travel for my soccer games. They didn't understand, and got mad. I couldn't stand that."

"I hope you are right, Grey. So, are you ready for your next soccer game?" I say, looking up at him as I eat my food.

"Honestly, yeah I am. I am prepared for this game. I have no words why I'm not nervous, but I can't wait to crush those Vipers."

"Babygirl, how was work, and how do you feel about the stalking? Still happening?"

"Yes, it's still happening. Work is amazing. I just do my thing. I love it, and can't wait for more projects to do."

"That's amazing. Well, I support you 100%."

"Thanks, babe."

Sitting at the quiet table, I am done eating my food, so is Greyson. We are looking out the window at the pouring rain. The slashes of rain hit the window. The gray cloudy sky. I curled up to Greyson.

"Babygirl, let's go upstairs and we can relax and watch tv." I am wrapped in his arms.

"Okay."

Hand in hand, we walk up the stairs and into a room. A king-size bed with gray fitted sheets and black walls. Then a dark cherry wood dresser. We both change into some comfortable clothes laying together in the bed, cuddling up together. I am looking up at Greyson, as he is getting the movie ready to watch together.

As we are cuddling, I look up. "Greyson, thank you so much for today. I had a great time."

"You're welcome, babygirl." Greyson says.

CHAPTER 8

Isabella

I just woke up cuddling into Greyson after the most amazing night. Greyson is my guy. Greyson never pressured me to do anything. He makes sure I'm cared for. But I hope he doesn't leave me. Now, we have to get ready to see my and Santiago's mom at my father's house. I am not looking forward to that. Especially since my mom hates me, my brother's mother hates me. And whenever my mom, my dad, stepdad, and my brother's mom are all together there is nothing but fighting.

Greyson is slowly kissing my neck as I stare into space. He doesn't realize that I am awake. Slowly Greyson rubs my back and keeps kissing me until I look up, smiling at Greyson. "Hey, babe."

"Hey babygirl. What was cooking in your mind?"

"My parents. And what trouble will happen tonight when we get together," I say, looking down.

"Babygirl, don't worry about that, right now. Let's go get ready and I can take you to breakfast, before we have to go over there for lunch. If you need me, let me know."

"Sure, Greyson, that sounds good."

I go to the bathroom, while Greyson goes to take the dogs outside. As I am getting ready, I am smiling at myself, as I am putting on my black jeans with my white blouse.

"Babe?"

I look down the stairs and see the front door open and nobody is there. The dogs are inside.

"Babe?!" I run everywhere upstairs looking for Greyson.

"GREYSON!! Where are you?!"

No, no, no. Where is Greyson? My baby. I want him. He is my world. I adore him. I run through the house opening all the closets and doors with tears running down my face.

"Jasper, Daisey, where is daddy?" Then as soon as I say that, Greyson comes up from the basement.

As soon as Greyson sees my tears, he drops the bag he has and goes to wrap me in his arms. "Babygirl, what's wrong?"

"I-I th-thought someone took you. I called for you and you didn't answer and the front door was open." I hold tight onto Greyson's t-shirt.

"I left the door open for the dogs. And I promise if I ever get taken, I will fight for my life. Let's go get breakfast and then we can walk around the park or something." He rubs my back.

"Jasper, Daisey, come on. We are going on a ride."

The two of us, with the dogs, get into the car and we drive to get breakfast at a town breakfast café, the "Empire Café". It's a small, quiet café that serves anything you may need.

I am jamming to Try, by Colbie Caillat, making Greyson smile throughout the drive as we are holding hands.

At the park, we grab the dogs and sit on the patio waiting for a server to come. I am leaning against Greyson, looking out at the sky and tracing little swirls on Greyson's arm that wrap around me.

A waitress comes and looks up. "Hey, Greyson."

"Hey, Mary. How's college going?"

"It's going well. Mom told me to thank you for helping us pay for my college and her medical bills. It means the world to us."

"No worries. You both are family to me. Whatever you need, let me know."

Shaking her head, she says, "So, what can I get you guys?"

"Um, can I have two orange juices please? I'll have two eggs scrambled with cheese and onions and sausage on it. With six slices of bacon. Can I also have three pancakes and…"

"Babe chill, we have lunch with my parents."

"Don't worry, girly, Greyson is just teasing me. He always does that to me. He is going to get orange juice, his scramble eggs with cheese, onions, sausage, bacon and three slices of bacon, and toast. So, what do you want?"

"Just scramble eggs, and some slices of bacon."

"You got it."

"Who is she?" I looked jealous at Greyson once the waitress walked away.

"Baby, relax. She is like my sister. She is a friend from high school. When we were in high school, she barely had anything. Her dad walked out on them when her mom got cancer and she was trying to take care of her mom as well as finish school. So, I gave her a helping hand and paid the whole medical bill as well as paying for most of her college tuition as she wouldn't let me pay for the whole thing."

"Sorry, babe. I just didn't want to lose you. I love you so much. When I was in high school, like 11th grade. My boyfriend at the time we promised each other that we would marry each other as we love each other and we didn't see each other with anyone else. Shortly after we graduated high school he passed away and his mother didn't tell me. I found out from his grandma as she asked me why I didn't come to the funeral."

"Oh, babe?? Listen, did you ever get to see your boyfriend's grave?"

I shake my head. "No??"

"Do you want to see it and get closure?"

"Yes, but I'll have to call his grandma. His mom and dad hated me. They felt I was changing their son. Like he was going to games, he was hanging out with my family. He was not skipping classes as much. He was more happy, and you know, being an actual kid."

"Well, take it one step at a time, I will always be with you." I look out to the sky.

I smile and finally ask. "Babe, is your friend Taylor gay?"

He looks at me, saying, "What do you mean, asking if Taylor is gay?"

"Do you remember when Taylor and my brother were really close when we came back from the picnic and went over to my dad's?"

Thinking, Greyson says, "Well, I have never seen Taylor dating a guy or hanging out with a guy like that. But, he could be scared to come out... so he could be gay. If he is, I honestly don't care?"

"Me either. If my brother is, I don't care. I love my brother so much. He is my protector. He loved my first boyfriend. Now, my second boyfriend nope. I wish he had told me that he didn't like him, but he never really met him like my first boyfriend."

"Why didn't he?"

"My boyfriend kept making excuses at the last minute so that he couldn't come to see my brother. I forgot I need to help so and so with moving their furniture, so and so need help with this. I am meeting my professor for this. I have a game I have to prepare for. I have to go study for an exam."

The waitress came with our food. "Here you go."

As we are eating, Greyson looks at me. "Isabella, your boyfriend sounded like a piece of shit. Like you don't say you wouldn't bail every single time. And Isabella, you don't need to worry. I love getting to know your brother."

"Babe, what do you think of me opening a business? I always wanted to. And I would love to, and I was wondering what you think?"

"Love, I know we haven't known each other that long, but if you want to open a business go for it. I will help you anyway I can."

"Okay, I am going to ask my brother, however, I'm pretty sure I have my answer. I may ask my dad, but I don't know."

"That sounds good."

Grey is done with the food, with the dogs at his legs as I was still eating. "So, do you guys think you'll make it to the final championship game?"

"Yes, definitely. I love doing what I'm doing. We go to practice and work really hard for the championship. I work on my business during my off-season. I have a clothing line.

"That's amazing." I am so proud of him.

"You want to see some of the designs me and my designers have created for this season's line."

"Of course, I want to see your designs." I eat my last bite.

Greyson puts $100 on the table and says, "I'll show you. They're in the car. Well, the bigger designs and some samples as well."

We walk to the car and Grey opens the door for the dogs to jump in. I get in the car and Greyson hands me the designs along with the samples.

"Babe, I love it. It's amazing. The sweats are designed unique. It's not like other sweats and the material I would die for."

"Thank you so much. So, park or home. As we still have time till we have to go to your father's."

"Park, please."

"Alright."

Driving to the park quietly, I sit there fidgeting with my hands as Greyson turns into the parking lot and says, "Stop."

"What?"

"Get out of your head. Don't worry about your parents. It's on them, not you. If they are going to fight over some stupid shit, then that's on them. Not you. Not your brother."

"Okay." I shake my head.

We walk to the grassy area and sit down with the dogs running back and forth playing with each other. I am leaning against Greyson. Greyson is rubbing my back up and down as I am rubbing his chest.

***

Greyson

I can't believe Isabella just fell asleep in my arms. She must have not gotten much sleep last night. Or she may have problems that she hasn't told me yet.

Isabella's phone rings, and since she is still sleeping, I answer it. "Hello?"

"Hey, Greyson, where is my sister?" Santiago asks.

"She is sleeping right now, in my arms while we are at the park."

"Oh, okay. My father is mad at my sister for something, not sure what, as it makes no sense. Please don't leave my sister when you come. I don't want my sister to get hurt."

"What is he saying?"

"That my sister doesn't love him. How she left him for me and then now she doesn't hang out with him as all her time is with me or her new boyfriend. And something about him going to make him pay for what she's been doing to him."

"That makes no sense. Like your sister hasn't been with me that much as she's been busy with stuff and I've been busy with my stuff."

Isabella starts to wake up and gets more comfortable in my lap as I am talking to her brother.

"Exactly, but I'll see you guys in an hour."

"Yep, we are getting ready to go back to the house. We were at the park just to enjoy the weekend weather."

"Good luck getting my sister to leave."

Hanging up the phone shaking my head, I look at Isabella. "Let's get going. We will stop at my house to drop the dogs off and then go to your dad's."

"Okay." She gets up and starts shaking."

"Here, put my jacket on. You're cold."

"Jasper, Daisey, let's go."

As we are running to the truck, we jump in and Isabella gets in. Jasper jumps in the front with Isabella and cuddles into her as she pets him. "Aww Jasper you wanted to be up here."

"Babe, can we bring the dogs to my dad's?"

"Sure, that's fine."

While driving to her dad's house, Isabella is playing with little Jasper who is licking her face and making her happy. And Daisy is in the back, sleeping. Once we get there, everyone is there. Her brother is outside.

"Hey Greyson."

"Hey Santiago. How is everything inside?"

"Don't ask, I couldn't stand being in there another minute. As soon as I got there and all the parents were there, they started arguing."

Isabella holds onto me. I look down. "What's wrong? Ever since you got up you've been clinging to me."

"I feel like something bad is going to happen soon. Don't know what, though?"

As soon as we walk in we see they are still fighting.

Some woman in her late forties is yelling, "Well, that's why I left you!"

"No, I didn't leave you for that. I left you because you said you didn't want to be a parent. You signed your rights away from Irena and Santiago. All you cared about was your image. So, when you were pregnant you hid in the house and asked people to get you things, or you went really late."

"So, are you okay with your daughter dating some soccer player? And a professional soccer player at that?"

"What?" Isabella's father yells.

"Isabella?" he yells.

"Yes dad."

"Please tell me that your boyfriend is not a soccer player. At least not a professional soccer player. They don't make much. They are only with you for one thing only. They'll use you. Get you pregnant and leave."

"How would you know that?" Isabella asks.

"They are all like that!"

"Well, first, yes my boyfriend is a soccer player. A PROFESSIONAL soccer player. He is not poor. He has enough money that he lives in a house that has six of our three bedroom houses in it. He has his own clothing line. He is supportive of me opening my own business for me."

"I don't understand why you're so mad for your daughter to date a soccer player?" Greyson asks.

"You'll leave her and she'll get pregnant and she will raise it herself."

"Okay, so, say we do get pregnant, and we do go our separate ways. I will have an account for our kids that she will also be able to get into, to help take care of our kids.

"Sure whatever."

Isabella's mother looks at Isabella. "Plus, he would leave Isabella. I mean look at her. She is not even that pretty. He will leave her for some supermodel and leave her to fend for herself. I honestly question myself, why I have the ugliest children ever. She has been a chubby child since she was a kid. She was always slightly overweight. I had a fluffy stomach. Not in the right shape."

Isabella leans on me. Holding on tight. I pick her up with her mom continuing to talk to her like she is not special.

"I agree. She is not that special. My daughter Irena is more beautiful than your daughter."

Santiago and I scream at them, "ENOUGH".

"My sister is beautiful. I love her to pieces. If my sister wasn't my sister, I would totally date her. And dad, why are you standing here letting her mom rip her apart? She has been daddy's little girl. Well, unless she was with me."

"I love my girlfriend. And until you guys can accept my girlfriend for who she is, we will not be coming back. My fluffy girlfriend with her creative side. She may not be a supermodel. But I love her for her. I don't need someone that only eats salad."

Santiago screams, "Mateo, come you're going to stay with me for a little bit."

"Is sissy going to be there?"

"Sometimes."

Walking outside, Santiago looks at Isabella who hides her head in my neck. "Sis, you still want to go to the cabin. We can still have fun. We can do whatever."

"Okay."

We all go to the cabin. Santiago invites his friends from high school and some of Isabella's friends from high school and we all chill out in the cabin playing poker. Isabella is sitting on my lap rubbing my stomach and slowly falling asleep.

"I swear this is the second time today she fell asleep on me. And every time she falls asleep, she is rubbing my chest."

"I think it's you, man. She probably feels safe with you." Santiago says.

"I am not sure. There are times where I have to reassure that she is beautiful because she never felt like she was beautiful."

"That is her mom, and her ex."

"Her ex?"

"Yep."

"When I was on the phone with her, there would be times when they would be fighting over her being mad that he is not hanging out with her, or that he is not meeting us or what not. But one time he said, 'Well maybe if you lost a hundred pounds, then maybe I would want to be seen with you.' Okay, my sister was, and still is a little on the heavy side. She is not the skinny supermodel stick, but I love her the way she is."

"That's messed up."

"But her ex isn't wrong," one of Santiago's friends said.

"Shut up. My sister is beautiful. She is amazing. Any guy who loves her will love her for her. You are like the people that hurt her. News flash, girls that don't have a skin to show. Like they don't have little something is people that pay to get it taken in most of the time. And frankly, I would rather have a fluffy girl, because all the imperfect things that she may think are imperfect are perfect to me."

"I disagree. Your sister needs to lose weight."

"Out."

"What?"

"You will not disrespect my sister and try to hurt her. She is finally with someone after her first love got killed. And I thought she would never find her second chance at love.

"I'm going to put her down in our room, and then I'll come back."

Walking to the bedroom, I put her under the blanket with one of my sweatshirts over so she can sleep.

I can't believe her brother's friend said that. I get that fluffy, chubby girls are not for everyone, but saying that to your friend about his sister crosses the line. Like you've known her probably most of her life. I am sure her brother's friends said things to her, but she didn't tell her brother.

Everyone went out to start cooking burgers and hot dogs. Somewhere sitting outside enjoying the weather, talking.

"Hey Santiago, question for you. I'm not out to have you second guessing your friends or anything, but I have this thought. Could it be possible for your friends, especially the one that you kicked out, that did something to your sister that hurt her so much that made her insecure?

"I guess maybe it could be. But I don't know as she hasn't told me anything. But if that was the case, I would be pissed at him. Like I was very open to him about how I felt when guys shamed girls. My sister isn't fat. She may not have a flat stomach but that's fine. But he did say it a couple times and I was mad."

"Understandable. And honestly, I like people who are a little imperfect. Well, in my eyes they are perfect. I'm not trying to say…"

"Dude, I understand you're not saying she is not perfect. Don't worry. I like you so much."

In comes Isabella, wrapped in my sweatshirt, and goes into Santiago's arms. "Santi, why are you friends with Morgan?"

"Remember when I came home with cuts, broken bones and stuff in middle school?" He looks at Isabella as she thinks.

"Yep."

"Well, the reason I didn't die was because he saved me. But I think now I should remove the toxic from my life and just focus on the positive. You. Mateo. My life. And sis, open that candle and bookmark business. I support you either financially, emotionally, or whatever."

Smiling down at her brother, she wraps her arms around him, and doesn't let go.

They all have fun together and are content with each other. Everyone is laughing and smiling, and enjoying the life they have.

Looking down at Isabella, Santiago asks, "Isabella, did Morgan do something to you?"

"Yes, he made me self-conscious about myself around the time I was in high school, I think. And I didn't want to tell you."

"You should have."

"Sorry."

"It's alright."

CHAPTER 9

Isabella

It's the day of the game. Greyson has already left. My brother and I are ready to go. We are going to go grab Jasmine on the way to the game and get to our seats. Greyson told us when we get there to let him know, as he wants to make sure everyone gets there safely.

My brother and I haven't talked to our parents since we left our dad's house. We are bringing our brother Mateo to the game as well. We got a last-minute seat that actually is right next to us. If it wasn't, who knows what we would do?

"Call Jasmine and tell her we are on our way to get her."

"Alright."

Ring... ring... a soft, calm voice answers, "Hello?"

"Hey Jas, my brother and I are on the way to come pick you up. We will be there in about thirty-five minutes."

"Thanks. I will be down at the door, so just call me when you're here and I'll come out. Do you want me to bring anything?"

"Nope, just bring your cute self."

"Alright, later."

"She said to call when we get there."

"Sounds good. Are you ready to see your boyfriend at the game and see our team do well, today?" Santiago looks at her.

"Yep, I am. Santi, thank you for standing up to your friends that always made fun of my weight, even though I still feel self-conscious of my weight."

"No worries, I love you, baby sis. You will always have me in your corner."

We finally reach her apartment. Once we get there she runs to the truck and gets into the car. "Hey Santi. How is everything?"

"Good. Enjoy life!"

"I'm sure. Your fiancée told me she just found out she is pregnant."

"Well, not by me. We separated and called off the wedding a couple of weeks ago, because we have different views and stuff."

"Oh, okay."

***

Getting to the arena, we all sit in our spots when Greyson comes up with his friend, Taylor. Taylor looks at Santiago and gives him that sweet smile. My brother tries to hide his smile from me, but he could never do it. Well, not when he is standing right next to me, anyway.

"Hey, baby girl. You guys got here safe."

"Yep, all good. Greyson, this is my best friend, Jasmine. Jasmine, this is Greyson. The one who took me home when Carly left me here on the first game," I say, looking at Jasmine.

"Well, nice to meet the wonderful person who met and helped my friend out."

Looking at me, Greyson says, "Isabella, I just came up here to check on you. We need to go back down as we are getting ready to play."

"I'm sure you will, babe. You guys have been practicing every day, and you guys are amazing. So, just focus on the game and make sure you're doing the best you can do. Win or lose, I love you so much."

"I love you, too."

They walked down for the game and as soon as the game starts you can hear my brothers, Jasmine, and I screaming for our Bears.

"Go, Bears, let's go! You can do it. Let's go!"

People are staring at us, but we don't care. Our team is amazing, and we will win. As we were chanting, you can see that the other team is looking at us crazy and side- eyeing us. We don't care. We are the Bears and we are going to root for them.

The Bears are not doing as great as the last game, but they are fighting for the game. Greyson is fighting for the ball when the player pushes him. And no, it wasn't some soccer push.

The whistle is blowing like crazy. A yellow flag has been raised with the Bears having the ball and it helps the Bears to lead. Not necessarily because they couldn't do it, but because the Vipers caused them to lose the ball and point.

As the game goes on, the Bears have kept kicking the soccer ball to their goal back-to-back. The Vipers were doing well in the first half with a tie ten to ten, but come the second half the Bears are winning, so far with a twenty to thirty lead. With five minutes left in the game.

Mateo is sitting in Santiago's lap. "They are winning, bubba?" he asks, pointing to the Bears.

"Yes, they are. Does Mami take you to any soccer games? Or daddy?"

"No, daddy works a lot and Mami is always with her boyfriend." Mateo looks up at his big brother, Santiago.

"Well, then I'll take you to some more later this year. Maybe it can be just the two of us," Santiago says as he holds our brother.

Mateo gets up and stands up on Santiago's lap and hugs his neck, just as the Bears kick a soccer ball from the midfield to the goal. Making the goal that ends the buzzer from no other than Greyson Andrew.

Greyson is pounded with the guys all on top of him having a blast before they all go back to the locker room. What a way to end this game.

"Well, Isabella, let's go. I don't want to lose you. Want to go to my house or are you going to your boyfriend's?"

"Yours?"

We get into the car, Jasmine looks at me. "Isabella, that was amazing and your boyfriend, omg, that was so great. Like they all got that ball to the goal and made sure they went home with a win. I mean I'm not a soccer player, but if soccer is like that I may have to be a soccer supporter."

Santiago and I shake our heads, leading to Santiago's house. Once there, Mateo goes in and into the living room, or what he calls the TV room. I mean there is a tv in there, but it is what he calls it.

"Mateo, you want to go outside and play?" Santiago says.

"Okay."

They walk out as the doorbell rings. At the door is a bouquet of flowers with a card on. Heading back to the kitchen with lavender flowers and some roses.

"Oooh, who are these lovely flowers from?"

"Open the card," Jasmine says as her phone rings.

Looking down, she sees it was Greyson. She smiles while reading the card:

To my love, the one I can never live without.

"Hey Grey, congratulations on the game. I was so proud of you, so was my brother and my little brother. He was pointing at you the whole game."

"Your little brother came?"

"Yes, my brother didn't want to take him home after what my parents said to us last night. My brother bought a last minute ticket and luckily it was right next to us."

"Makes sense. I am on my way, I called your brother and we thought of doing a cookout with all the guys and stuff with your brother."

I shake my head okay. "Sounds good, Grey. Thank you for the flowers."

"Flowers? What flowers?"

"Some flowers came to the house for me, and I assumed you sent them to me. It was my favorite flower with a card on it."

"I never sent any flowers to you."

"W-What? What do you mean that you never sent me any flowers? Nobody other than my brother and you know what my favorite flowers are." I look around like someone is watching me.

"I don't know what to tell you, babygirl, but I haven't sent you any flowers," Greyson says as Santiago and Mateo come in.

"Alright, I'll see you when you get here," I say while I go and jump on my brother.

"What's wrong?"

Shakily handing him the card, I look into his eyes. "Someone sent me these flowers and cards, but Greyson never sent me these flowers."

He wraps his arms around me and rubs my back as Greyson comes in. "Isabella, it's okay. I will figure everything out for you. I promise. Now, why don't you go with Greyson, while I make some phone calls and then start the food?"

I shake my head, I go and sit next to Greyson while he looks at me. I am rubbing on the inside of his leg over and over while Mateo comes over to me and curls himself next to me.

"Bella, you play with me," He asks, looking into my eyes.

"Sure, Mateo. What are we playing?"

"Mario karts," Mateo says as he grabs his controller and sets up the game.

I am sitting on the couch playing Mario kart with Mateo. Mateo is giggling up a storm, having a great time with me. After four times Mateo beat me in three of the games.

"Bella, you do good. We play later. The food is done," Mateo says, pointing to Santiago bringing the food.

"How much did you cook, Santiago? Looks like you were cooking for half the world." I look at the mountain of hamburgers, hot dogs, wings, fries, and seafood.

"What do you expect sis? We have the soccer team, and the soccer team is filled with hungry guys. Plus, we can have leftovers."

All the soccer players run into the kitchen, with their hungry stomachs, filling their plates with hamburgers, hot dogs, and wings as much as they could fit on the plate.

I still can't believe that all the soccer players are over here. But then again, I can. My brother is always welcoming of my boyfriend's friends. Well, at least the one that he met. He's met only three of them and liked them all, and we all went our separate ways because of our differences, but the one he didn't meet he didn't even want to meet my brother. This tells me he was hiding something.

"Sweetheart, go get your food. We are all going to watch a movie together. But a cartoon because your little brother is here."

I get up from the couch as Greyson sits on the couch, I go to the kitchen and grab a plate and fill my plate with wings and ranch, while I make my brother Mateo's food with hamburger and hot dog.

Everyone sits on the couch. The soccer players are all on the couch, I am on the floor between Greyson's legs, with Mateo sitting next to me all watching Cars.

Fifteen minutes after the movie starts, Mateo was asleep. My phone starts ringing. I pick it up and look at it, like it is a ghost. Finally, looking up I say, "Santiago, it's the same person that keeps calling me."

He runs to me and grabs the phone. "Hello, who the frick is this?"

No answer. Santiago hangs up the phone and calls his friend. They all sit there tracking the number. Once they track the number, it shows as registered to the one and only, Robby

"Isabella, it's okay, he will not do anything to you. Remember you have me, and I will do whatever it takes to take care of my baby sister."

I shake my head. I sit down on the floor, rubbing Mateo's head and trying to relax.

***

Greyson

Looking at Isabella, I can tell she looks sad and is trying to fight her demons. Santiago grabs Isabella, putting her on his lap and rubbing her back, while looking into her eyes. "Stop. You always knew why I didn't love Robby. Robby has always been someone I didn't understand. But we will get him. You have me, your little brother, and Greyson," Santiago says.

Getting to Isabella's eye level, I look Isabella in the eye. "I love you so much. I will be with you and your brother and we can always do whatever we need to make sure you're safe."

Shaking her head, Isabella goes into my arms, wrapping her arms around my torso.

"Is she sleeping, man?" Santiago asks as he is grabbing Mateo to put him in his bed.

"Yep, she is." I look down at her.

"Good, then we can figure out something to help Isabella with this. I hate that this is happening to my sister."

"Maybe we can get some people to follow her and see who is following her or something," I say looking at Santiago.

"Nope, that would never work. She wants her privacy."

"I'm sure that I can get her to say yes. If she says yes, I'll pay for your trip anywhere in the world for three weeks." I say looking into Santiago's eyes.

"And what do you want if you win?"

"I want you to help me plan the getaway of her dreams, and find her ex so I can talk to him about what he did to her."

"Ahhh... deal."

CHAPTER 10

Greyson

It's been almost two weeks now. Santiago has his friend looking for her ex, so we can talk to him. And why would he do that to her? Like for real. Of all the people, he just had to stalk her after he was the one that hurt her.

"Greyson, are you going to practice today?" She screams from the kitchen.

"Yes, baby girl, why?"

"Well, I want to go to my brothers. And I was wondering if I can bring the dogs to my brothers with me as well."

"Sure, that's fine. I will stop by your brother's tonight, as tomorrow we are going to an away game. I know you wanted to come but couldn't."

"Yep, that's good."

I grab the leashes and everything that Isabella would need for the dogs while I am away from Isabella. Their dog beds, the bowls, food, and their toys.

The dog jumps into the car while we all drive to her brother's house to drop them off while she heads into the office to get her new project for these two authors that she just took in.

One author is a fantasy author, while the other author is a romance author. They all are looking for keychains, bookmarks and small little stickers designed right now. Then in a couple months they want some help promoting their books to the world.

***

Isabella

"Hey girly, ready to see your new authors? One of them is getting here in five minutes, the other one called and said that they will be here around one o'clock," one of the girls in the office says.

"Yes, I am. Can you bring them to my office when they get here? I'm going to get everything set up on my computer."

"You got it."

Walking into my office and turning on my laptop as well as my desktop computer, I make sure I have everything I need.

Alright, I have all the forms I have for her to sign. I have the design I created that maybe she will want to use or we can make something from scratch. I have my tablet in case we need to do some other designs. And all my programs for my designs are open, as well.

"Isabella, Kylie James is here for you." I look up to see one of my amazing authors I get to work with.

"Thanks."

"So, Kylie, how are you? Are you excited about the cover reveal? Your books are getting published and released soon."

"More excited than you know."

"Alright, so Kylie, since you asked for some stickers for merch, I have these made for you. The first one is your logo." I point to a blue rose with little butterflies around the rose with her name in the center.

"Oooh, I like those, but can we have my name kind of stand out? Like maybe putting it in bold or my name in white font?" Kylie describes to me as I work on the design for her.

I sit at my desk with Kylie in front, watching me change some things as she describes what she is looking for, smiling as she gets what she wants.

After finally finishing the final product of her stickers, "So, well, what do you think of this design?"

"I love it, Isabella. So, I know I said I wanted this in stickers, but could you maybe also make this in a keychain as well?" she asks, looking at the design, eyeballing the image.

"Yep, definitely. I'll add that to the form."

"Alright, now we have these three designs for the three bookmarks design you want for your latest sweet romance book. What do you think of these?"

With a happy, excited face, Kylie looks at them. "I have no words for this. This is perfect, the perfect design. You got my version better than I thought. The font is perfect, the images you used are perfect. I love them."

"So many stickers, bookmarks, and now keychains."

"Well, I want 100 of each of the bookmarks, so 300 hundred bookmarks. Let's do 100 keychains and 100 stickers."

Writing the information on the form with everything we need I say, "So, Kylie here is what you're going to get. Can you sign this making sure everything is correct? I will get the design started today, and we will get them ready and hopefully we can get them finished and mailed out to your house in three to four business days. Just take these to the front and they will get all your billing information and everything will be ready for you."

"Sounds good. I can't wait to see the final product of everything."

As Kylie was walking to the front, a tall skinny tan man with tight, curly hair, said, "Isabella Cortez?"

"Yes?" I look up.

"Um, I have these flowers and a box of chocolates for you."

I grab them, the lavender flowers with some red roses in between them. And the box of chocolates. There is a card with a little red heart on it. I sit down at my desk as the guy leaves, while she is reading the card.

My love. I hope you love the flowers I sent you.
Can't wait to see you soon. I've been thinking of you.
Xoxo

Shaking my head, I look up. "Noooo, this can't be." I turn my head, looking around me to see who could be watching me.

If I tell my brother this, he is going to be pissed and be even more protective of me. I love my brother, but I don't need him to be all protective. Whenever my friends would hurt me, he would be protective. I'm sure if my brother ever met my ex he would, however my brother never met him as he always said he had plans. Which in my defense was probably a red flag that I should have seen, but I was being naive. What did I expect? I thought he was the first person that loved me after my boyfriend died.

I sit there, finalizing all the designs and eating my lunch before my next author comes. I go to warm up my oven roasted chicken with broccoli leftovers, when her boss comes to me. "Hey Isabella, this guy came for you and dropped some lunch for you and dessert."

Looking around confused, I ask, "Who sent this? Because my boyfriend is at practice right now, and won't be out of practice until two, today."

"Isabella, I don't know, but it was this guy with curly brownish hair, blue eyes, kind of thin, and good looking I guess," he says, shaking his shoulder.

"I don't know anyone like that."

I look out the window as my boss looks at me. "If you need to go home. Go home. Or we can call the detective to see who this could possibly be."

"Sure, let's call the detective. But I might have to call my brother. If I don't, my brother will be pissed at me and scream at me all night." I look down at my phone.

Shaking his head, Isabella's boss calls the detective walking out the room. While I call my brother. As I am calling my brother, looking out the window feeling nervous, fidgeting with my fingers and twirling my fingers, front and back of each of my fingers wondering what I will be telling my brother.

"Hello?? Isabella, what's the matter? I am about to go to a meeting, so can you make this fast?" he speaks as fast as he can.

"Sa-Santiago, I think he found me. Whoever was following me because two times today, I got mysterious packages and I'm scared. I have no idea what's going on." I could feel the tears running down my face.

"WHAT??"

"Someone brought me flowers and chocolate and then a couple hours ago, lunch and dessert. However, Greyson couldn't possibly send me anything, as he was still at practice and wasn't going to get out until two o'clock, possibly three o'clock today, as they are getting ready for their away game."

Santiago calms down. "Isabella, first I want you to go home. I am in a meeting to figure out who sent those flowers to you at the house. I guess it's more than one person. Once I figure it out, I will come home and tell you everything I found, okay?"

***

I sit at home, curled up on the couch, scared at every sound that I hear. I'm curled up with a red fuzzy blanket. Jasper and Daisy are curled up next to me. As soon as I jump from any sound, both of them would push their warm bodies to me, which causes me to calm down while I watch tv.

The door opens, and I wake up from my sleep. Santiago goes and sits next to me as I slowly get up, looking at Santiago as he is watching some of his Law and Order: SVU. Daisy and Jasper are shaking and walking in between Santiago.

"Santiago, did you find anything?"

He looks down at my eyes, breathing very slowly. "Well, sorta."

"What do you mean, 'sorta'? You either found something SANTIAGO, or you DIDN'T. I need to know. I am so fucking scared that I have no words. Like, I feel as scared as when my ex-boyfriend died. When he said he was always going to be there and then I got those letters from some guy. I miss him so much, Santi." Tears run down my face.

"Alright, well, we sorta found something. And don't interrupt me, yet. I am still confused about what we found. But first we found out it wasn't one person doing it. It was more than one person. We think two to three people. Maybe more. I don't know how to say this, but we know one of the guys is your ex from college. I'm sorry baby sis. But there is something I don't understand," Santiago says looking down.

"What?"

"Your ex from high school. They ran his information, and it made no sense."

CHAPTER 11

Isabella

It has been three weeks since my brother told me what they found. I still am speechless. My brother is here and my brother and boyfriend have me under house arrest. I can't go anywhere without one of them, but they prefer if I go with both of them. I work from house and my boyfriend has gone to another game

My brother and I are still confused about how my ex is still alive. Like it makes no sense. His family called me weeks after he died. Saying he is dead, and that we buried him. I got no 'I'm sorry to tell you he died, and you can come to the funeral at this place and this time.' Nope! It was weeks after he died. I was heartbroken. And if he died and my boyfriend knew and he hurt me, I'm going to be pissed at him.

I am sitting at my makeshift desk and making more designs for my future project when I get bored, so I go walking to the store to get something to make for dinner.

Alright, let me get some food. I walk into my favorite grocery store getting things to make my dinner. Chicken, potatoes, onions, parsley, tomatoes, and chicken broth. Then, walking around the store, I felt like someone was watching me, but turning around I saw that nobody was. Walking down to the chip aisle, I kept feeling it, so I turn around seeing the same guy who was near me while I was walking near the chicken.

"Can I help you?" I ask as I turn to the guy.

"Are you Isabella Cortez?"

"No, why?"

"No reason." I walk away from the guy, go to the register and pay for my stuff as soon as my brother calls.

Ring... Ring... Ring...

"Hello?"

"WHERE THE FRICKEN HELL ARE YOU ARE? We told you not to leave the house without us, because the guys are still out there and we are trying to find them." Santiago screams at me.

"Well, one I am at the store, I'm walking back to the house, and two I think they found me already."

"What do you mean?"

"Well, I felt like someone was watching me. The first time I turned around, and I didn't really see anyone. Then as I was walking to the chip aisle, I felt it and then went and turned and there was a guy staring at me. He asked if I was Isabella Cortez, of course I said, 'no', then he walked away.

"Come home. Your boyfriend is here. He called me when you weren't here, like you should have been. He called you and you didn't answer so that is why he called me."

"Sorry."

"It's fine. Just get here, please?"

"Okay."

Walking down the sidewalk to the house, I pinched myself to ask how I did that. *Like seriously. My brother and boyfriend are always supportive. I love them both. I don't even know what my life would be without them.*

Walking into the house, I go to the kitchen and put the groceries on the counter and see Greyson laying on the couch. Walking to the couch I lay on top of him.

"Hey Greyson," I say as he slowly opens his eyes.

Looking into my eyes, Greyson frowns, "You don't leave the house without either one of us or letting us know. You know the reason why. We do this because we care for you. We want you safe. What would've happened if he took you from the store. Your brother and I would have been hurt for you. We would have definitely done everything we could, but there is no reason for us to do that if we don't need to."

"I'm sorry, I didn't think about it. I'm just tired of being home alone. I miss going into my office. I want to be able to live my life," I mumble, looking down into my lap.

Around the corner, Santiago comes and bends down to me "Look, if you are tired here, we don't mean it, but you never tell us. If you told us, we could have done something. And you should have told us that you were going to the store today."

"I will. I'm sorry, I didn't think of your feelings. I don't want to be without either of you."

***

It's been two weeks. My brother, boyfriend, and I talked. We all decided that I can leave the house to work two of the five days. And when I do go, one of them will pick me up. It may not be much, but it is something. Plus, my brother has some leads on who it could be. So, fingers crossed that they find this guy or guys.

My boyfriend has been literally the sweetest. Whenever he comes over and I watch my girly shows, which is rare as I prefer my action movies, he just sits there and watches with me. Or when we go to the store and he's tired, he would still go with me.

My boyfriend hasn't come, and it's my time to go home. I pick my phone up and dial my brother. Ring… Ring… RING…

"Hello?" Santiago answers.

Looking around, I say, "Santiago, Greyson isn't here, and it's been an hour. I called him and he didn't answer."

"Isabella, let me call your boyfriend, and I will call you back…"

While waiting for my brother to call back, I am doodling on my sketch pad for inspiration for the home office that I took over from my brother.

My phone rings. I look, and seeing that it is my brother, I answer it. "Hello, Santi?"

"Yes, sis. So, he didn't answer. So, just go home. I have a friend that is near the house that is going to come to the house so he will be there or almost there when you get there."

"Sounds good," I say, as I pack my things. "I'll call you when I get home and let you know if your friend's there or not."

"Alright, love you, sis. I have to get back to work."

Hanging up the phone, I walk down the sidewalk, towards the house where a man is standing next to the door. As soon as I reach the door, I see Santiago's friend, Mike, there.

"Hey, Mike, how have you been doing?" I say, as I open the door.

"I'm good. I just heard what has been going on with you from your brother. What your dad and mom have been doing to you. What you have been dealing with the stalking, and all that."

Looking down at my hands as I sit down on the brown loveseat, Mike sits in front of me, I fiddle with my finger. "Yes, I can't believe they would do that to me. Like, why would my parents say that to me?"

Mike gets up, wrapping his arms around me with me resting my head on his shoulder. "I don't know why your parents did that to you. But look at this, you have your big brother with you. You have your boyfriend, and your little brother."

Shaking my head, I say, "That's true, but I miss my dad. What did I do to deserve what my dad did to me?"

"I don't know Bella, but why don't we watch a movie together? Later, I will get us some dinner. That way, it's here when your brother gets home."

I get the remote and start flipping the channels, until I find some action and adventure movies that we both would want to watch.

I am so grateful that Mike is here. Whenever my brother was in middle and high school, and even in middle school I would want to hang out with my brother and Mike. Mike has always been like a big brother to me. He would actually come up to see me in college when I was there. We would go to lunch or dinner together and would walk around, maybe go to the movies, the store or just the park.

***

Mike

Isabella slowly falls asleep in my lap as Santiago and Greyson came in. Santiago says, "Hey man, thank you for coming over a little early."

"No worries," I said looking down at Isabella as Greyson comes over and sits in front of me.

"So, how long has my sister been sleeping?" Santiago asks me.

Looking down at Isabella, "Your sister has been sleeping since within ten minutes of watching this movie. And I haven't moved since then. I didn't want to wake her."

Greyson gets up with a face and is about to pick Isabella up. "Noo, you don't pick her up!" Mike and Santiago say, in unison.

"Why can't I pick MY GIRLFRIEND up," Greyson asked with frustration

"Listen man, I get you want to pick up my sister, but once she is sleeping you don't want to wake her up. So, if she falls asleep on the floor, you leave her. If she falls asleep on your enemies' lap you leave her," Santiago expresses to Greyson.

Greyson stands up looking into Santiago's eyes, "So, you want me to let my girlfriend sleep on some fuckboy and expect him to take care of my girlfriend. Like I was supposed to pick up my girlfriend today, and I found out when I got there that my girlfriend left."

"Firstly, Mike is not a fuckboy. If anyone is a fuckboy it's me. And secondly, Mike has been my best friend since middle school. Mike has always been close to Isabella, when she needs him."

"My sister called me an hour after you were supposed to pick her up and you didn't. so, I called you and you didn't answer. So, since she wanted to go home, I called my friend and asked if he could come a little early and let my sister walk straight home. Maybe, if you answered your phone or came to pick up my sister when you said you would, we wouldn't have a problem."

"So, you're okay with your boy to fuck her?" Greyson looks into Santiago's eyes like he could kill him.

"No, I don't. But, my best friend would never do that to her. He has treated her like a princess ever since she was little. Isabella was always around me when we were younger. Whenever I had friends around, she would want to come. Not because of my friends, but because of me. She hated staying at home with her mother. She was always in my shadow. She was near me, like 24/7 or she asked for me. When I wasn't home, she would either sleep in my bed or wait up for me. So DON'T you ever say that about my sister."

"Mike, what do you want for dinner? I'm going to make something for dinner," Santiago says, getting up from the couch."

"Bro, here is $100, go buy some food for us. Your sister was sleeping, talking and wanting General Tso, in her sleep."

Smiling and shaking his head, Santiago says, "OMG! What is new? My sister has always loved her Chinese food. But sure, I'll order some. What else do you want?"

"Come on man, usual."

***

Isabella

I slowly wake up and look around. I am concerned by Greyson's face. His scrunched face with his eyebrow arched.

"Babe, what's wrong?" I ask, showing my concern.

Breathing heavily, Greyson looks into my eyes. "You, for one, left work before I could pick you up, and when I came here, you were sleeping on him."

Getting up from the couch, I slowly straddle Greyson's lap, wrapping my arms around his neck. "You, my baby, have nothing to worry about. I love you to pieces. You didn't come pick me up. So, I called my brother, seeing as you guys have me on house arrest."

Greyson grabs my face looking deep into my eyes. "But I called you to let you know I was running late, that my coach wanted to do some emergency testing on us."

I side eye Greyson. "No, you didn't call me. See?" I hand Greyson my phone.

He scrolls through my phone as I lay on his shoulder watching him looking at my phone. "Sorry, baby girl. I guess I didn't call you."

"Greyson, it's okay, it happens." I say, rubbing his cheek.

"Can we go to your room?" he asks, looking down at me.

I get off Greyson and take his hand. The two of us walked past my brother and into my room. Greyson sits on the bed with head in his hands.

"What's wrong?"

"I was mad at Mike for sleeping with you, and I sorta called him a playboy and all these bogus things." He looks down at his lap.

"Okay, listen babe, Mike isn't one. He is the sweetest. Whenever my brother was at work or something for school, he would come over and hang out with me as my father used to work really late and my mom, well, you know my mom all cares about is herself."

"I know now. I just feel bad."

"Just tell my brother and Mike that, and they will understand."

I look into Greyson's eyes. "Grey, did you ever get a paternity test done? And did you get the results?"

"Oh yes, I got the letter, today. Well, that is one reason I came over. I wanted to open the letter together."

We both open the letter. Once we open the letter it reads.

Greyson Andrew is 99.9% not the father of baby A and baby B.

I look into his eyes, Greyson says, "I knew they weren't mine. But the real question is why did she say that they were mine."

"Probably because she either wanted child support or she wanted to get rid of them. She probably thought you wouldn't do a paternity test."

Greyson sits, looking into the ceiling curled up into me. "I think so, too. But I'm just glad that it's over with. I want to live my life with you."

"Me too, babe, me too."

Watching tv, we slowly doze off and fall asleep content with each other and ready to live our life together. Living the life we deserve. A life where we are there for each other.

CHAPTER 12

Greyson

I am still the jealous boyfriend, and I haven't changed. I don't call people out or anything.

Today, we are surprising Isabella for her birthday. I can't believe that it's been almost six months since Isabella ran into me at the game. Isabella is the sweetest person. She still doesn't believe that she should be in love. Every time we are home alone and I say something sweet to her, Isabella always looks at me uncertainly, or like she doesn't believe me. I will keep telling her this, until she believes me. She deserves love. She deserves a future with someone that cares for her.

Isabella has left to go shopping with her friends today. They will be shopping with Mike while Santiago and I set up her party. The food, the decorations, her presents, and making sure everything is ready for her and she is treated as a queen.

"Hey man, so when do you know who could be the one that is hurting your sister? I don't think that your sister can handle this anymore," I ask Santiago as we get the food to cook.

He stands up tall. "Look Greyson, I get that you want to help. I get you're my sister's boyfriend, but we can't rush anything. Life is precious. If we make one mistake, we can make a mistake with everything."

***

Santiago

I get up and finish the decorations when my phone rings. Grabbing and looking at the flashing light on my phone, it says, "Isabella," picks up the phone and answers it.

"Hello, Isabella, what's wrong?" I said while putting the finishing touches on the decorations.

"Santiago, I miss Linkon. He was so sweet. I love him so much. It hurts."

"Linkon would have wanted you to live your life. He wouldn't want you to stay single. Enjoy your life, sis. If you want, we can do something in honor of your ex."

Isabella cries. "Y-yes please I will love that."

"Okay, love you, sis. Take care of yourself. And be safe."

"Yep, buba," Isabella says and hangs the phone up.

***

Greyson

Once Santiago and I finally finish with the decorations and food, Isabella walks in. Once she walks in, Isabella sees what they did. Above the tv in purple words is, **Happy Birthday, Isabella,** with turtles around the wall.

"Aww, bubba, you did this for me," she asks, looking into his eyes.

"Yes, I did. It's your special day, and I remember what happened on your birthday several years ago. I don't want you alone. I know when you were in college you were with Mike, as he went up there with you and celebrated. He wouldn't want you to be alone. He would want you to have the best birthday ever." He looks at her.

"Yes, you're right he would. But I still miss him."

"Who?"

"Linkon." Santiago says, looking into my eyes.

Isabella goes to sit next to me. I am rubbing her face and see the sadness in her eyes. "Isabella, who is Santiago talking about?"

"Linkon is someone special to me. Linkon was my ex-boyfriend who died after high school. Remember, I talked about him?"

"A little bit." I look into her eyes.

"Well, I didn't even know about his death until his grandmother asked me why I didn't go to the funeral. Then, I was like, what?! She knew I didn't know what was going on, nor knew that he died."

"Aww I'm sorry."

Everyone is sitting and enjoying the time. Isabella is sitting in my lap relaxing and enjoying her birthday. I can sense that she wants her brother, but doesn't want to let go. Every time I look over she is looking at her brother and then she looks at me biting her lip.

"Go baby, I know you want to be with your brother," I say, looking down into her eyes.

"You sure?"

Shaking my head yes. "Yes, baby girl, I'm sure."

As Santiago is talking with Mike with his elbow on his knee and hand on his face, Isabella moves his hand and sits on his lap and slowly calms down. I knew right then and there she needed her brother. I may be mad right now, but at the end of the day she needs him. Slowly, I go up to him and ask what is wrong with her.

"Greyson, she didn't tell you her history of her and her boyfriend, Linkon, did she?" he asks, looking down at her.

"Nope, all I knew was she was his girlfriend."

Looking up at me and breathing out while rubbing her back, Santiago says, "Greyson, Linkon was Isabella's first real love, her first everything. They had their life planned out. I saw their life, and I was happy for them. Isabella was at her grandparents' house for the weekend and Linkon had a dirt bike track competition, and a soccer game that weekend. He was sad she couldn't go see him compete in either one, but he understood as her grandma wasn't well. They found out her grandma had cancer. Well, she stayed two nights. The two nights that she was there they talked, and then she went home the next day. She called him that day, when she got home with no response. She called a couple more times that week as she thought he probably was mad that she didn't make it even though he understood. Well, fast forward three days, Isabella got a phone call from his grandma asking why she wasn't there for his death. But she had no idea, when the grandma realized that she told her that Linkon died five days ago. The day he died was the day after her birthday. On the day of her birthday, he got her lavender flowers with roses, and her favorite chocolate for her, since they couldn't be together. "

"I feel bad for her. I had no idea. I mean, I suspected that something was going on as today she hasn't been as happy as normal." I look at Isabella. "Isabella, let's go get some food. You need to eat."

Getting up from Santiago, Isabella and I go to the kitchen. Getting a plate each, we grab our food. Isabella and I sit on the couch as we eat our food.

Santiago gets up and bends down in front of Isabella. "Isabella, I have a surprise for you. You want to see it?"

Shaking her head quickly with a smiling face, she says, "Yes, I want to see, now. Please, can we see now?"

Giggling up a storm, Santiago stands up. "Yes, you can, but can you put this blind fold on? Then we will be able to see it."

Squinting her eyes, she looks at her brother suspiciously. "Are you trying to kill me or hurt me on my birthday, Santi?"

"I'm a man of many talents, but let's go, Isabella."

Isabella, Santiago, and I walk down the hallway, to the office room that once was Santiago's. Slowly, I remove Isabella's blindfold as Santiago says, "Okay, you can open your eyes, now."

Opening her eyes and walking into the office, she says, "Ooh this is nice. That's my computer, and my painting. And... Why is this room more for me than for you?"

"Isabella, because this is for you. I want you to have your own office for your business. And I already filled your business plan, however I may have changed it."

"To what?" She sits in her new blue chair.

"Linkon Enchanted Marketing Service." He points to her new website and new business.

"You did this for me?" She sits crying into my shoulder.

"Yes, Isabella. I knew you wanted to open this business. I know you have an author wanting to ask for your help. I'm sure you already have four authors that they adore."

Running to her brother, she squeezes him and says, "thank you so much. I love it and I can't wait to be sitting here doing what I love so much."

***

Isabella

Yesterday was the best day ever. My brother and boyfriend surprised me with a birthday party. I wasn't having a great party in the beginning, then it turned out amazing. My brother gave me his office and made it for me. It has all my organizers that I would want. Then surprised me with my very own and special business name. What more can I ask for?

As for my boyfriend, he gave me some of my favorite and unique kind of keychains that were made of my favorite animals. Well, one of them. Plus, he also told me he is surprising me tomorrow, with a present that hasn't been ready yet.

Sitting in my office working on my author's sign-ups form that we will be using for readers and making sure everyone will be able to get their copy. Never in a million years would I think I would be enjoying this. Yes, this is a part-time job, but this doesn't feel like a job. Every day, or every couple days, I make a bunch of graphics, videos, or whatever I need. I share with our groups and share the teaser, coming soon, sales, or whatever I may need to share about that week. I make sure all my authors are on track for their release and there are no speed bumps in their way.

The phone rings on my desk and I look down at my purple phone case with pink peony flowers and see Greyson's name flashing. "Hey, Greyson, what's up?"

"Ready for your surprise. I am on the way to your brothers. I shouldn't take that long, probably maybe thirty to thirty-five minutes away."

Looking around at my desk filled with papers and things to do I breathe. "Yes, that's fine. I need to be back at two to get ready for a meeting."

"No worries, we will be back then."

Sitting at my desk, I feel blessed.

I still can't believe my brother gave up his office room. When I was living with my parents, the one thing my brother said was he was either going to make his game room or an office room for him when he started his own business. Not only that, but to get my own business and have it set up for me has me speechless. I love him so much.

My brother has always been my support system. A system I never thought I would have. There were days that I hated my parents. They didn't understand that my dreams were never what they wanted. My parents wanted me to be an accountant or be a lawyer because I was good at writing and math. However, I never saw myself as being someone doing numbers 24/7 or defending others 24/7, either. Yes, I love the bits and pieces I know about those subjects, but not to live my life on. I wanted to own my own business. I have my own schedule. Help others by being as creative as possible.

Since I started my business while I was trying to figure out what my life is, it has been amazing. Not only was I able to be creative by making video, graphics, bookmarks, and anything possible it showed my inner child. But I found a person I never thought I would find. Someone that was hidden that I didn't know who I was. But with this, I was able to excel and do everything I possibly could.

Startled, I turn around and hear a bang on the door. Walking to the door, I look out the white wood front door, seeing Greyson.

"Hey Greyson, you came early." I look at the clock in the corner in the dining room."

"Yeah, well traffic wasn't bad today. Which led me to come here earlier than I thought I would. So, are you ready to go now?"

"Yep, let's go. I'm going to put my shoes on." I walk to the closet and grab my flat, cream colored shoes.

Once I have everything and head to Greyson's truck, we get in and drive for five minutes. "Alright, now Isabella, I know your brother gave you that office at his house and you adore it, but I got this for you." He opens a door to a building.

"What is this?" I look around at a plain empty building.

"Well, when you told me you wanted your own business, I thought it would be amazing to have an office that is not in your house. Somewhere where you can leave and don't have to worry about sleeping."

Half-smiling, I look around and turn to Greyson. "Grey, this is really sweet and all, however an office outside is not necessary for my business, as I make my own hours and I get to decide when I want to work. However, I love the comfort of my home. I do love the thought behind it, though."

We walk out of the office, where Greyson's walking to the park and we see a beautiful purple and rose table with some of my friends. Looking at them with my green hazel eyes and back at my boyfriend with tears dropping down at my eyes, I say, "Grey, did you do this for me?"

"Yes, babygirl, I did this for you. You guys have been together from the very beginning, and I know you all adore each other, and will be there together for much longer."

Looking down at them, I walk down to the three girls sitting at the park with their books in front of them. "Hey, Isabella, we are all so glad that we got to meet you. You have been our rock since the beginning. You helped us promote books, read our books, and are always there for us when life takes us on a storm," a dirty blond curvy and short tan woman in her early twenties says.

Looking at her, I say, "That is true, Aubrey. I have no words to say. Helping you, Aubrey, and you, Kendall, and Alexa have been a dream come true. I never thought this was something I would want to do, but after helping you guys then getting more authors it became my dream. A dream that seemed far-fetched to me for many years. That after many years of seeing people do something that I wanted to do, all I did was say, 'Fuck it.' and let me do me and do the best I can do."

The three girls look at each other and then at me. After staring at each other, Aubrey looks up. "Isabella, did you just say that? What happened to our sweet Isabella? Isabella, who is the sweet angel that is there for us."

Pointing to my heart, I say, "Sweet Isabella is here. The Angel is still there. But after many people, well, a couple people, saying I couldn't do that even though there were things I have been doing for years in the book world, I would shut down everything. Then I said nope, this is something I enjoy, and I will fight for what is mine. I have been doing this for longer. I have put my name out here. I have the support of many friends and will always help the amazing authors out here in the indie world."

"So, Aubrey has everything going with your life. Your future. And everything?"

"It's incredible! I still can't believe you got me a bestseller for my newest mafia series and that I've finally reached fifty Amazon reviewers in two weeks. I'm not sure what I did to deserve you. Just know that I will NEVER let you go. You are my protector."

"Aubrey, I am just the promoter, the cheerleader, the person that will continue to support you. You, on the other hand, are the writer. The writer of amazing stories that people will read and love."

I was looking at my friends, laughing and smiling at each other. I never thought I would have such amazing friends. But here I am with my best friends.

"Isabella, so are you ready to help me get the best release as you did with Aubrey?" Kendall, a tall, thin girl with jet black hair and dark brown eyes, asks.

"You know, I always make your release amazing," Isabella said. Turning towards everyone: "Why are you here, and why are you holding your books? Aubrey, you have two of your own, one of which has yet to be released. And Alexa and Kendall, why do you have your books."

Well, the first thing is that we are giving you this. We all signed this book to our favorite reader, our number one fan, and our amazing family."

"Wh-what?" I look at them like they are speaking a different language.

Alexa grabbed her hands and said, "Isabella, you are amazing. Before you, it was hard for me to sell books. And now look at me. I'm not selling two hundred books a month yet, but I'm making money and loving it."

"But... that is not all," Kendall said while looking me in the eye. "We have all decided to move here. Well, we did. We live near you. Your brother helped us find the perfect place, and when we told your boyfriend what we were doing, he got us first-class tickets. "

I lean into Greyson's chest with tears in my eyes. Alexa, Kendall, and Aubrey were all looking at me. "Well, girls, you guys are amazing, and I am grateful for you guys. What do you want to do, because we were all supposed to be having a meeting right now, and I guess the meeting was a decoy?" Isabella squinted at them.

"Yep, that is what it is," Kendall said with a smile.

Alexa looked up at me, "Isabella, what is new because we can see something in those hazel green eyes that shine in the sun when you are happy. But those eyes are filled with fear and sorrow.

"Well, um..." I look down at the table.

What do you think they'd think? Wouldn't they want me to help them? Would they want to return and not live here any longer? I enjoy doing it for my friends. Unless you have decided to cross me, big or small, everyone is my family to me.

"Well, girls, I have been stalked since I broke up with my boyfriend, and it has gotten to the point that I will get flowers or whatever I enjoy delivered to my brother's house. I thought it was from my brother or Greyson sending it to me. I also got a phone call from someone, and when I answered, nobody was there."

Looking up, my friends had tears dripping down their faces, "Aww, Isabella."

"I hope whoever is doing this gets caught," they say all at once.

"Yep, my brother is working on it."

"Amazing, now here are your books. And yes, I know you have our books already, but these are special. These are signed copies that may or may not have one extra book that will never be published just for you and a copy," Alexa said, handing me her books.

Who would have thought my three favorite friends and authors from high school would have sent their books to me? I love them to pieces. Once we all went to college, they moved west, while I stayed on the east coast. While we were in college, they were writing to their hearts' content and publishing stories back-to-back. Well, not back-to-back, more like every two to three months apart.

These are books that have helped me through my abusive boyfriend. I had always wanted a family but never had one. There were times I wanted a family and never came back. But at the end of the day, I would have left my friends to fend for themselves, and I would never want that. Life is short, so instead of waiting till after college, I decided to make the best of my life and follow a dream that I could while figuring out my life.

CHAPTER 13

Isabella

It has been an incredible month since my friends returned. Since then, my life has not been the same. Every day, I see my friends, in particular. We will continue to complete our tasks. They work on their stories, and I work to make sure they have everything they need to publish their book.

My life is now as best as it can be for what I have been going through. Yes, the stalking is still happening, but my brother got a ping last night, so he has been searching for it since yesterday after he got it.

Sitting at the table with Aubrey, we decided to get some food. So, we decided to go out and walk across the street to the sub sandwich.

"So, Isabella, will you ever have a book published? I am positive that you have several stories," Alexa glanced at me.

Looking out to the crispy blue sky with fluffy white clouds, I say, "I do not know. I do not know where to start. Okay, let me rephrase this. Yes, I know what I am doing. But it is different when you are doing it for your book than promoting someone else's books."

"Yes, definitely, but you are not alone. You have me, many readers and authors. You've made a name for yourself. "Isabella, you love books," Aubrey says.

"That is true."

As Aubrey and I were about to walk into the sub shop, two guys came up behind them and took them. I looked at Aubrey, and she looked terrified. Before I could even say anything, I passed out.

***

I was slowly waking up and looking around. Once finally adjusting to the bright light, I saw Aubrey next to me, tied up. "Aubrey, are you okay?"

"Yes, I am good. It's nothing that I can't handle. Now we need to get out of here."

Two guys walked in, "Well, look at what we have here, my lovely girlfriend and her so-called best friend, Aubrey."

"WHAT THE FUCK? ANDY? MORGAN?? WHY?" I say to my ex-boyfriend and my lovely brother's best friend.

"You see, babygirl, you left me, Isabella." My ex-boyfriend looked furious at me, "Isabella, it was always about you. If you wanted to do this or if you wanted to see this person, nothing was about me, Isabella."

"NO!! That is not true. What happened was that you did not want to see my brother multiple times. You always had an explanation for refusing to hang out with me. Additionally, you and my sister have consistently told me that I am not attractive enough and do not deserve anyone. Don't worry; my big brother will come and grab you when he gets here."

"Oh, you mean that sweet brother of yours? The one that is finally getting married to his fiancée after they found out they have a daughter together." Morgan looked at me with evil eyes.

"Nope, my brother is not."

"You girls are not even all that. I only dated you because your mother paid me to. She said that your so-called ex-boyfriend died and that she was the reason behind it. And she will do whatever to hurt you."

"W-What?"

"Aww, little chubby Isabella is hurt and scared," Morgan said as Isabella's older sister Irena and Carly showed up in short pink lace dresses.

"Hey, girls, What are you up to?"

"Nothing much, babe, just see what you're doing with our kidnappers," Carly says, looking at me.

"Nothing special. I'm going to see how much Santiago is willing to pay for his adorable baby sister."

Walking through the door are thirty guys, one being my big brother and my boyfriend. Morgan, Carly, and my ex-boyfriend were, "h-how?"

"I told you to leave my sister alone, Morgan. But no, you had to kidnap her. She is my younger sister. And to think I was your friend is insane."

"Why?" My brother asks. "You were her best friend, or at least you said she was. However, I never thought you were. I want you three to stay away from my sister. And if I find out that you ever do this again, you will be sorry."

The cops then read them their Miranda rights and took them to jail. My life may be fine for the time being, but the stalking has slowed. Who knows who it could be?

My boyfriend is my world. My brother is my world. These are the two people I never thought I would need. Now I am going to go home and do what I enjoy. But first, I cannot wait to see my boyfriend at his game, where I am sure he will dominate.

CHAPTER 14

Greyson

I am so grateful to be able to find my girlfriend. She is the sweetest person. I love her to pieces. Not only that, but I want her to come to my next game, which is one of our final games. She didn't come to the others as she was busy with things. But that is fine; it's life.

So, if it hadn't been for her turtle-themed necklace, which her brother had given her, we might not have found them. However, she was wearing it. It's no surprise that her brother's friend, her ex-boyfriend, and her best friend, who left her at the first game, were there. So, once we got there, not only did we save the girls, but they also got arrested.

"Babe, where are you taking us?" Isabella asked as I was driving.

"Nothing exceptional, your friends want to hang out. So, they organized a movie night. Who knows if your brother would go out after this? He was supposed to go out with buddies. We shall see."

Aubrey was using her phone to watch a movie as Isabella was curled up next to Aubrey in the back seat. She giggled the entire time as I was driving, wearing a fuzzy pink hoodie.

The idea of losing my girlfriend is so unsettling, and I never considered what I would do in such a situation. But the time has come to live the life that we have always dreamed of.

***

Isabella, Aubrey, Kendall, and Alexa all stay in the living room to watch movies together.

Her brother Santiago came out in a fitted blue shirt and some tan dress pants.

Where is he going? You don't dress like that when you go out with some friends. When you go out with guys, you go to the bar, get some beer, and get drunk. But he is dressing like he is going on a date. Based on what Isabella and I walked into a couple of times, he's likely going out with my best friend, Taylor.

Shaking my head, Santiago looked up at me and says, "What?"

"Santiago, you and I know you are not hanging out with the guys. You dress like that when you're going on a date with someone."

"Whatever, man. I got going. I will see you later. Take care of my sister?"

Sitting curled up with my girlfriend and enjoying life with her is an understatement. I know I have my game tomorrow and need to leave tomorrow morning early to get my stuff before going to the arena but curling up with Isabella is what I look forward to every day.

Ten minutes into the movie, the girls all passed out, so I covered them with blankets, and we all fell asleep.

***

I felt like I had only slept for three hours as I felt like someone had smacked me in the head. I slowly got up and saw Santiago in front of me. "What the fuck, what was that for?" I ask, still wrapped up with Isabella.

"You are late. You need to get to the arena, and it is one, and you need to get to your house for your stuff, and you have not left yet. And I am sure you wanted to grab something to eat before you have to meet with the team."

"Dammit," I said, running, getting my shoes on, and grabbing my keys.

I was driving as fast as I could to get to my house when I ran into my closet, got my uniform, and got back into the car. I am driving back to the arena and making sure I get there in time to be able to play. If I do not play, my surprise will not go as planned for Isabella.

Finally getting to the arena, Taylor came out of the locker room, "You are here in the nick of time. Coach is going crazy at people who are still not here. Greyson, get ready; we have a game to win. You have a surprise to give your girlfriend. "

"Certainly," I say as I dashed into the locker room.

I hope Isabella says yes. I know we are young. Well, Isabella is young anyway. I know she just finished college and is finally starting her business, besides all the other things she does, but I can't wait. I love Isabella so much. She is the first person I think of when I get up. She is the first person I want to talk to every day. I want to live my life and see where things go, but only time will tell.

I was sitting on the bench waiting for all of us to get on the field when the coach looked at us and gave us the same speech every game. 'Work hard, play like a team, and win like a team.'

We finally got to get on the field, me in front and center, having the best game ever. If we win this game, not only are we going to the semi-finals, but if Isabella says yes to my questions, it would be the best news ever.

***

Isabella

Since we arrived at the arena, I have sensed their conflicting emotions. It is a scary feeling, but it is also a happy feeling. What could happen to cause me to feel those emotions before the game starts?

We are running late today, so we did not have time to see Greyson before the game. I love him so much that the only thing I can do is be cautious of what is happening next.

I am watching the game, and it is the first half of the game, and the guys are crushing this. Greyson has scored four goals, and Taylor has scored four goals. The Tigers barely had the ball.

Every time the Tigers have the ball, the Bears swipe it from them.

I am not sure how the Tigers got this far. The Tigers have yet to score, and the Bear steals the ball almost every time they have it. The other team is either terrible or had a bad day.

Greyson noticed me and made me smile with his red cheeks as he looked out at the stands. "Come here," Greyson called out to me. I walked down the stand until the security guard stopped me, "Ma'am, you are not permitted to go over there."

"It is okay; she is with me," Greyson said, looking me in the eyes.

Looking into his crystal eyes, Greyson held onto me, trying to calm down and regroup before they played the 2nd half of the game. I rubbed my hands through his hair, trying to calm him down while Taylor came over.

"Hey, Isabella. How do you like the game so far?" Taylor asks, walking towards Greyson and me.

"Well, considering you guys are winning, then I say I love the game. However, these guys are having an off day or are very bad. And if they're that awful, I can't imagine how the other teams are. "

Shaking his head, Taylor sat on the bench as Greyson sat next to him, pulling me onto his lap. "Well, Isabella, I say they're terrible because I don't recall the Tigers ever winning many games. Grey, our coach, also wants us in the locker room in two minutes so we can plan our next move and kick their asses, even if we are winning."

"Okay, babygirl. We must leave. Remember to cheer for us."

"You got it."

I loved the game. Once I got back to my seat, I leaned onto my big brother. Santiago turned to face me while the boys were in the changing room. "What was the point of that?"

"I'm unsure. Greyson asked me to come down while nobody ever goes down there. Oh well, I managed to figure it out somehow."

I sit in my seat next to my brother, eating the salted popcorn while my brother was looking at me with a curious voice. "Isabella, what is wrong?"

Breathing out, I looked out to the field and say, "Santi, ever since I got ready today, I felt different. I am not exactly sure what it means."

Looking into my eyes, Santiago bent down between my legs as best as he could in the seats. "Listen, baby sis. It's okay to feel that. If something happens, it happens, and you know that everyone will do everything to stop it. You need to take it day by day and enjoy this game. Your boyfriend wants you to enjoy the game, not overthink something and not enjoy the one thing you love."

I hug my brother and look out at the green soccer field, shaking my head.

Alright, I need to breathe. My boyfriend and my family mean everything to me. My happy place is with my brothers. So, I'll do what I can and take things day by day.

Out comes the Bears, ready to beat the Tigers and win their next title. All in their tight red jerseys with their number and name on their jersey, getting ready for the whistle to blow for them to play. They are determined to get the ball to their goal with all their might.

I watched my boyfriend cheering them on. As time went on, Taylor and Greyson had the ball most of the time, leaving the other team tired of chasing them around and the team winning thirty-five to five.

Everyone was about to leave for the VIP area when Greyson came onto the center field and looked out at the fans. But his eyes finally landed on me right in the center.

Sweet mother of Jesus, what's he doing? Please, please don't you dare do it. No, no, no!!

"Thank you to each one of my fans for supporting us through this year. We have a semi-final game next, then if we go to the final. I hope to see everyone out there. My girlfriend, whom I met over a year ago, is my missing piece. With everything going on, I want to see my girlfriend, Isabella Cortez, in my life. She is worth everything. There is nothing that I will take for granted. She is my soulmate. My endgame."

With a twinkle in my eyes, I was crying, and Greyson passed the mic to Taylor while he picked me up and took me down with him.

"Isabella, Greyson is so much better with you. You both deserve each other. When Greyson told me at the first game about you, I could see he had found his one. He always told me he wanted the one, and I never understood. But when I saw the twinkle in his eyes, I knew you only mattered to him. You have my support and the team's support. Greyson is our baby brother. He may be the captain, but we are all older than him." Taylor says.

Looking down at me with Greyson's hand holding me up, I looked up at this all. "Greyson is amazing. I never thought I would find love. There are days I wonder if I am dreaming. I am grateful each day that I have Greyson by my side.

Isabella, baby, you are beautiful. I'm not sure if I would ever be this happy without you. I have you and my two babies."

"Yes, they do. But you are beautiful. Never say that about yourself."

"Since the season has one or two games left, I would love to offer you guys the trip of your dreams. Well, us guys. But first, you need to hear what Greyson's surprise is for you." Taylor pointed to Greyson.

Greyson put me down on the ground. "Listen, I know things have been moving fast, and I am grateful for that." But listen, I cannot live without you. So will you marry me and make me the happiest man in my life?"

I looked everywhere. I'm not sure what to think. *Oh my God, I can't believe my boyfriend is proposing to me. I mean, we have been dating for almost a year now. We have gone on many dates but never expected my boyfriend to ask me. What do I want?*

Closing my eyes and breathing, "Yes, baby, I love you." You are my light and my soul. I have no words for you."

Walking on the field are Greyson's ex-girlfriend, Jacie, and a tall guy walks down. Jacie said, "You left me for her. Some girl who got her ex-boyfriend killed. Well, almost, and now he does not know why."

"What?" Greyson asked.

"Yeah? Look at her," Jacie said, walking toward them.

With tears in my eyes, I saw my ex-boyfriend. The one boyfriend I never thought I would ever see.

"Linkon, how? Your grandma and your mom told me you died. When I was at my grandma's house, they never told me until after your supposed funeral, when your grandma asked why I did not go."

"What? Do you mean to tell me you never tried to kill me?" Linkon was looking at me.

"No, I love you so much. I never stopped loving you. You were my world."

Greyson and Taylor looked at each other, and Greyson looked into Isabella's eyes. "Isabella, let's all talk in private." Greyson said.

Shaking her head, they all went to the locker room. When we got to the locker room, I sat on one bench next to Linkon, while Greyson sat on one in front of us.

I had tears going down my face, "Linkon, when I called you that time, and we got into a fight, I was mad, but I called you the next day, and you did not answer, then the next day and did that for a couple of days. Then I got a call from your grandma asking why I did not go to the funeral. I did not know you supposedly died. It hurts me so much. I never thought I would find love. You were always there for me. You support me. You told me to follow my dreams. That whatever dreams I wanted, you would be there for me."

"Isabella, I do not understand. Your mom and my mom said you did not want me. That I never gave you attention or that I was never thinking of your needs. Then your mom said I should not be dating someone like you." Linkon says as he clasps my hands.

Looking into his eyes, "Linkon, I never said that about you. I was talking about my brother's girlfriend at the time. I told my brother his girlfriend never gave him her time or thought about his needs."

Looking down at me in my eyes, "Isabella, I am sorry about what my mom and your mother did to you. I regret it every day. So how are you and your boyfriend, or should I say, fiancé?"

"It is great," I say, holding onto him.

Greyson finally stood up and knelt between my legs. "I know you want your boyfriend back, Isabella. When you look at him, I see the same love in your eyes that you have for me. I'm not going to let you pick between the two of us."

"What am I supposed to do now?"

EPILOGUE

Isabella

It's been three years now. I have finally healed from my heartbreak. Well, it was not an ordinary heartbreak. It was a heartbreak that I never wanted to experience. I finally talked to my mom, and she hates me more. I have not talked to her since the day that Linkon told me what was happening. Linkon does not speak to his mother anymore after what she tried to do.

As for my sister and me, we have yet to talk. I went to my father's house with Linkon and Greyson. My sister thought she could get my boyfriends with her red crop top, shorts, and make-up. If you look at my sister, it looks like she has four inches of make-up on her. Well, that was a mistake. Greyson pushed her away, and Greyson and Linkon want nothing to do with her. She kept calling me names that neither Greyson nor Linkon would accept. However, my father adores me and hates what happens.

At least two times a week, I have lunch with my father somewhere, and once or twice a month, I go to dinner with my father and family.

You might be thinking about my love life. Greyson wanted me to go back with Linkon because we had history, and he knew how much I missed him. However, Linkon was okay with letting me go and be with Greyson even though he would get hurt. In the end, they decided that they would be together with me. I love them both to pieces, and I cannot express how much I love them.

I never thought I would be able to find my true love after what happened to Linkon, or so I thought. But, no, I discovered my two true loves. I am grateful for them every day.

Greyson is still captain of the soccer team; they have won the championship game for the past three years, and I am so proud of him. Linkon is running the business with me, as well; as soccer training for little kids

After two years of the three of us together, yesterday Linkon proposed to me at the lake house that his family has. The three of us went up there to celebrate the celebration of our lives. Well, that is what I thought, and it was not. When I walked into the wooden cabin, there were rose petals outside leading to the pool and candles around the pool. I saw Linkon on his knees, saying, "Isabella, I am so grateful every day when I get to wake up with you, and never in a million years did I think I would find my soulmate again, but I did." So, Isabella, will you marry me? "I looked with my teary eyes, I shook my head and whispered, "Yes." But Linkon, how is that going to work? Like, Greyson and I are going to get married. But on Jan. 15th, that is a little less than two months. '

Greyson says. "Baby, we talked, and we are going to get married to you. Legally you will be married to Linkon, but we will both be married to you. Linkon does not have any brothers to take his name, and I have a brother that can continue that on."

"I love you both." I hug them together.

Greyson looked at Isabella and said, "Now, let's celebrate you two getting engaged." I know your fiancé over there has a romantic date for you later tonight, which he said I could go to, but I told him.

"Babe, please go. If Linkon said yes, then yes."

If my fiancé says my other fiancé can come with us, he is coming. I do not care if I have to push him or what to make sure he is coming with us. He is my person. He is the one that led me to find my ex-boyfriend, but then again, my ex-boyfriend, and now fiancé, was the one that led me to Greyson. If Linkon's mom and my mom didn't do what they did, I would not have experienced heartbreak, would not have met my college boyfriend, and would not have met Greyson. Life happens, and each day I live, I accept all my heartbreak because, in the end, I found my way back.

"Fine, I will go, but we are all watching a movie first."

Walking up to the bedroom, is a big king-size bed in the center of the room and a flat-screen TV on the wall. When I walked into the room, I saw decorations in gray and silver, with some purple and blue in the room. I was getting myself comfortable in bed. "Linkon, did you paint this room because I do not remember it being this color when we came here during our summer and winter break."

"Yes, baby girl. My father gave me the house, and I knew you loved the colors gray and purple, and I knew Greyson loved blue, and you knew I loved gray. I also painted the other rooms and may change some things in the kitchen. Not sure yet. "

"Well, I love this room." I laid my head on his chest as Greyson came and cuddled Isabella, watching a movie together.

***

Isabella got up and finally decided to do something sweet for my fiancé's. Never, in a million years, will this happen. As for the surprise Linkon has, I hope he is doing what I think he is doing. He had this idea when we were in middle school. And he said, "One day when I find my soulmate, this is what we will do."

Isabella went to the kitchen and made her double chocolate mousse with extra whipped cream. Isabella walked in and whipped some cocoa powder and heavy cream when she felt arms around her. "Babygirl, why did you leave us? "Linkon asks.

Leaning back, "You guys are sleeping. Besides, I made us some chocolate mousse before we got ready for your surprise, Linkon."

"Fine, you win, but can I have some of that before you scoop them into little jars?" Looking into the bowl.

Shaking my head, I looked up at Linkon. "You, my sweet fiancé, are something else, but here you go."

"Hey Greyson, how are you?" I asked as I was putting the chocolate mousse in jars.

"Fine, just wish you'd stayed in bed with us," he said as he walked over to me and wrapped his arms around my waist.

Looking up, I say, "Next time. But here's some chocolate mousse."

I looked up from her island when I saw Linkon's mother at the door. I turn my head to Linkon and say, "Linkon, your mother is here."

"WHAT?!?" he screamed, leaping from his seat. "Mother, what are you doing here? I have not talked to you since Isabella told me that she never said all those things. What was your problem? I love Isabella. Isabella has always been my soulmate. What is so wrong with her?" staring his mother down.

"Look, Linkon. There is nothing special about Isabella. Why not date her sister? Her sister is perfect for you. "

"Yes, someone that spreads their legs at every human who looks her way. Yea, nope, I passed. Isabella is my soulmate like I said. Isabella and I will be getting married. You are not stopping us. Isabella and I will have a future with each other, whether it is just us or with kids. So, stop trying to hurt us; you have already done that the past five years. I thought my girlfriend did not want anything from me after I woke up from a coma."

"Not only that, you did not even tell me that my boyfriend was in a coma. If I had known, I would have been with him every step. I loved him, and when we were in high school, I could not imagine my life without him," I said as I walked over to Linkon.

"What about your pathetic little dreams?"

"Do you mean the marketing business she wanted to open up? Baby girl, how well is Enchanted Marketing Service doing?" Linkon looked down at me.

I am sitting on the bench on the island looking up at Linkon's mother. "Well, if you must know, we are fully booked till the end of the year. We make hundreds of dollars a month. We are an internet success. Linkon has now helped me run the business so that we can add some more clients to our list."

"You can see that the business that you said would not make anything has turned us into success. We have nothing to worry about. We love what we do. We may work more than we typically do, but we enjoy it."

With frustration, Linkon's mother left the house, stomping her feet like a three-year-old who doesn't like it when someone says no to ice cream.

"Ready, baby girl?" Linkon asked.

"Yes, Linkon." Turning around to Greyson, "Let's go. We are not leaving you. And you know that I will use Linkon on you and your soccer team."

Widening his eyes, "You would not?"

"Want to bet?"

"Fine, let me get a chance to wear some comfy clothes."

Once we got to the field, there was a soccer ball on the field. Isabella looked up at Linkon. "Did you do this?"

Shaking his head, "Yep, let's go play." I turned towards Greyson, "Let's go play soccer. I can show you what my fiancée showed me in high school. Let's see if this professional player can play better than me and Linkon."

"Well, you are on." The three of us enjoy playing soccer as the sunset behind us turns into an orange red. We were playing around, having fun, and enjoying our life together. I eventually got the ball from the boys and scored into their improvised soccer goal.

This is my life with my two fiancée's and the life I never understood I deserved. I will forever be grateful to them. My support of my family, especially my brother, is on another level. If only we could live here instead, that would be great.

"Hey babes, I have a question for you." Looking at them.

"Sure, what is up?" Greyson asked as Linkon turned around.

Turning herself as she was nervous, Isabella says, "Guys, I know we all have a life outside of this house, but do you think we can move here?" I mean, it is peaceful, and I have everything here."

Greyson was lying down and smiling while Linkon went up to me. You know, I knew you were going to ask me that.

"What?"

"Yep, so I asked Greyson if he was okay with that, and he was fine. Your brother is moving into the house across from us. Your dad and your little brother will be ten minutes away. Your friends will be a couple of houses down from us."

"You guys are amazing, but what about your business, Linkon? And your practice Greyson?"

Linkon looked at me and said, "Isabella, I can do whatever I want from anywhere. Plus, soccer season is in the spring."

Shaking my head as Greyson's was "one more thing for you, but we need to go to your dad's."

"Well then, alright then, let's go to my dad's house," the three of us ran back to the house and got into the car.

What could be at my dad's house that we do not have here? What surprise could be at my dad's that only my dad will be able to tell me? Well, at least I think they don't know. Well, only time will tell. I love the ride, especially since the sky is turning a beautiful orangey red color.

Once I reached my dad's house, my dad handed me the envelope. As I grabbed the pink envelope and opened it, there were three tickets to Greece. Looking up with tears, I was like, "What did you do this for?"

"Bella, this is for your guy's honeymoon. I knew you three would get together, and I am okay that you do," looking at Isabella with sweet, caring eyes.

My dad turned to the guys and said, "If you guys ever hurt my baby girl, you will be gone, and nobody will ever be able to find you guys."

"We love her, and there is nothing that would want us to hurt her."

I never thought that the day my dad forced me to go to the game with Carly, who decided to leave me, would lead me to find my Greyson. The one that was always there for me and supported me. The one that helped me find my first love. I never imagined having two loves in a million years. That is indescribable. Love is worth everything.

Now here we are, living our life and finally finding our one true love. The love that will be worth fighting for.

Greyson and Linkon are my world. They love me for me. Linkon and Greyson are my end goals. The person, no matter what, I'll fight for them. Without them, who knows where I would be?

My soulmates.

The light in the darkness.

My Kings.

THE END

ABOUT AYANA LISBET

Ayana is an author of poetry and sweet romance who has always had a pen and paper or a book in her hands. She always had stories in her head, and she decided to get her stories on paper. When she is not reading or writing, she is at home enjoying her life with friends and family, and helping authors achieve their author's goals.

Writing has always been something that Ayana enjoyed doing. She does not only read and write, but she also enjoys taking pictures or watching the sunsets, sunrises, or doing anything creative, whether it is sketching, graphics, or making videos.

Family is everything to Ayana. Blood or not. If you need Ayana, she will help you, big or small.

DRAGGED OUT KICKING AND SCREAMING

by D.L. Howe

PROLOGUE

Grayson

(12 years old)

Pins and needles have taken up residence in my lower half, but ask me if I care to move.

Over an hour ago I stuffed my lanky frame, that's tall for my age at five foot seven, into my mother's favorite curio cabinet.

Why, you might be asking?

Because the doors are mesh and easy to see out but not in.

For many years it's been my favorite hiding place because it means I can watch him. My mother's nearest and dearest friend.

My father likes to joke that my mother is Soren's beard because he's gay. Soren is his name, Dr. Soren Delgado, a reconstructive surgeon. And not the kind that does routine rhinoplasty but much like McSteamy in Grey's Anatomy who helps people who need it. People born with abnormalities or suffered from horrible burns. It's a distinction he prides himself on which makes him even more beautiful in my mind.

His beauty isn't only skin deep but down to his very soul.

He's the reason I knew I was gay for as long as I can remember. Not that it matters, I'll never tell. Not that I have too many people to tell. I hate leaving the house. Meeting new people makes me break out in hives.

Last year, I finally convinced my parents to let me do online school, which worked to everyone's benefit because I worked so far ahead that I skipped two grades. After years of meltdowns and full-on panic attacks, my parents took me to a psychologist. It was no surprise to anyone when I was diagnosed with several things that boiled down to agoraphobia.

It was such a relief when they stopped blaming me for overreacting and finally understood that this wasn't something I chose. Who in their right mind would choose to live in a self-imposed prison?

But Soren is the only exception. He's the only person I look forward to seeing. I keep wishing and hoping that today will be the day that I force myself out of my mother's curio cabinet so I can finally meet him face to face.

Unfortunately, today's not that day.

My heart drops as I watch him gracefully pull his tall, perfectly sculpted body from the deep seat of our plush leather couch. He hugs my mother goodbye and as he turns to leave, he pauses, staring at my chosen hiding spot.

I freeze as those crystalline blue eyes seem to bore into my mousy brown. Only when my mother utters his name does he turn and follow her out of the room.

After they've gone, I realize I'd been holding my breath and suck in deep gasps of air.

Before she returns, I clumsily open the doors and practically fall out of the cabinet. My legs are too numb, incapable of standing quick enough before she returns and gives me one of her knowing grins.

"Spying again, I see." She winks causing a heated blush to flush my neck and cheeks.

I scowl. "I wasn't spying."

"Mmm, so you've taken up contortionism then."

I push my chin out. "Perhaps I have."

She chuckles softly before trying to ruffle my shaggy mahogany hair, but I wave her away.

Instead of getting mad she only shakes her head in humorous exasperation.

"Dinner will be ready in twenty."

***

Soren's visits have always been like clockwork. Both he and my mother are doctors. While he's a plastic surgeon, my mother is an OBGYN. They're always off on Sundays, so they brunch and gossip to their heart's content while I hide and watch every nuance of every single thing he does.

Yet, when the next Sunday rolls around and there's neither hide nor hair of my favorite doctor, I begin to panic. I haven't felt this kind of nagging urgency in over a year. Not since I was allowed to stay home where it's safe and quiet.

But where the hell is he?

Is he sick?

Did he have an accident?

What if he needs help, and I'm the only one who realizes it?

I'm completely useless and I've never hated my agoraphobia more.

With a shot of adrenaline, I jump from the confines of my cabinet and proceed to rush around the house until I find my mother. Which isn't difficult. If she's home, and she isn't sleeping, she's in her office.

She doesn't notice me as I charge into the sanctuary of her private space as her eyes, exactly like mine, carefully scan a textbook on obstetrics, specializing in cesarean. She's so absorbed I have to practically sit in her lap, which is quite the feat considering I hate touch of any kind.

She shudders in surprise. "Good grief, Grayson, what in the world do you think you're doing?"

I skip the niceties; small talk has never been my forte. "Where is he?"

Her brows furrow in confusion. "Who? Your father?"

I want to shake her in exasperation, but I manage to rein it in. "No, where's your friend?"

As if she has dozens of friends, and what do I know, perhaps she does, she contemplates my question. When she finally manages to answer, it brings no relief.

Far from it.

"Oh, Soren? He moved to California."

Anguish, the likes of which I've never known, takes up every cell of my body.

I'm at a loss for words before I finally stutter. "B-Bu-But he di-did-n't even say g-goodbye."

Concern draws across her expressive face. My mother would never make a good poker player.

"I'm so sorry, love, but you've never even met him. I had no idea his leaving would impact you so strongly."

Of course, she doesn't know. Even if she does know that I spy on them. Perhaps she only believed I was bored and looking for entertainment. Which is good if she believes that. No one needs to know how the sad little hermit longed for the attention of the beautiful doctor.

CHAPTER ONE

Grayson

(23 years old)

Loud roars inundate my ears thanks to my headphones. My thumbs speed over my Xbox controller as I talk trash to my only friend, Bryce.

He says he's twenty-one and like me, he lives in his parent's basement in Chicago. As far as I know, he could be anywhere from the age of nine to ninety-nine, living in Timbuktu. I've never even seen his picture, only heard his dulcet tones when he smack talks over the airwaves as he tries to kick my ass in anything from Mario Kart to Call of Duty.

Today's game of choice is Mortal Kombat, one of my personal favorites. As long as I can be Scorpion, I can kick anyone's ass. It's always music to my ears when the familiar growl of "get over here," echoes around my skull.

I'm in the middle of a round when I notice movement from my peripheral, but I'm too busy to turn away. Even when I see my mother in my face, I wave her away but she's not having it. She pulls one headphone away and squawks far too loud directly in my ear.

"I have some news." She beams.

"Can't it wait? I'm a little busy here."

She huffs. "Fine, then I guess you won't care that my good friend Soren…"

As soon as his name leaves her lips everything else disappears. I don't bother saying goodbye before I pull the plug on our game and give my mother my full attention.

"As I was saying, my good friend Soren is moving back to Kansas City. He'll be staying with us until he finds a place of his own."

I gape, utterly flabbergasted.

He's coming back. After eleven years, the man of my dreams is coming home.

***

That night as I brush my teeth, I lean in and study myself in the mirror. Physically I know that I'm a handsome man. I'm certainly not conceited, it's just obvious. I have the angular face of a model, and my lanky body thanks to boredom and increasing weight training has filled out with lithe muscles.

While on the outside I may seem appealing, it doesn't mirror what's inside of me. Inside, I'm a muddled mess, still filled with the excruciating fear of leaving the house only to go for a swim in our secluded pool out back, let alone see other people.

Through years of therapy, I've managed to work my way up, one baby step at a time. Finally, in my first year of getting my doctorate in mythology, I'm able to go to one or two classes a day. I sit in the back corner, which is considered no man's land, but progress is progress.

I may be able to go to class, but the professors know not to try to include me in discussions or question answering. Not unless they want to watch a grown man fall to the floor in a full-on hissy fit. It's not a pretty picture, for anyone, so I'd rather avoid it.

At any cost.

But considering how stellar my work is, no questions are asked. It's well-known, at least to the teaching staff, that I'm a bit of a prodigy. Even if my big brain is wasted on Greek Gods and odysseys rather than medicine, like my mother, or math, like my father.

My love of Greek mythology started early when dad read bedtime stories of Prometheus and Theseus. When you don't have many friends, I had none, by the way, books became your bosom buddies. Men such as Euripides and Homer became my confidants. So, no one was surprised when I carried my passion on to college.

I think my mother was relieved because my only other passion was video games. Better to have her gifted son obtain a useless degree rather than go into game design.

A bit snobbish?

Well, yes. Both of my parents are rather pretentious, but they come by it honestly. My mother is from Connecticut and my father is from here, the very neighborhood we still live in, Mission Hills. One of the richest neighborhoods in the country and it's brimming with blue bloods, not that I've met one.

Much to my dismay... did I mention I'm extremely sarcastic?

Even if there's no one to appreciate my satire.

Anyways, my parents met in college, Yale, of course. My mother already knew Soren. They had been as thick as thieves since they were children. To this day my father is still jealous of their closeness. The only reason he puts up with it is because of Soren's proclivity for taking it up the ass.

Of course, I heard this from my father's mouth, and yes, I was spying on them at the time. You must understand that spying is one of my only sources of entertainment, even if it's rude. I couldn't stop if I wanted to, otherwise, I'd be climbing up the walls, and nobody wants that.

And as you can see, I've gone off on a bit of a tangent.

Now, where was I?

Ah yes, inside, I'm a mess. So, when the man of my dreams returns, I doubt I'll be able to build the confidence to meet him once and for all. And unfortunately, at six foot five I've grown too big to fit inside my mother's curio cabinet.

I think about it hourly until the day of his return arrives. I've yet to come up with a solution, so when he and my mother walk in the front door, I stand behind the corner of my father's library where my mother never goes, but it has the perfect view of the front door.

As soon as he walks inside, I can't tear my eyes away from him. It's been eleven years, but he's scarcely changed. Perhaps there is a bit of gray feathering his temples, maybe a tiny line around his mouth, but he's still as beautiful as ever. He's still my Soren, and when he smiles, I swear my heart stops.

And then his sky-like gaze traces over the rooms, they freeze when they land on me.

Dammit, I knew this wouldn't work. Blast my ridiculous height and the bulk I've added to my gangly frame. But it was that, or resemble Shaggy from Scooby Doo, and nobody wants to fuck Shaggy.

But I can't seem to move, I simply stand in some sort of suspension while he looks me over from head to toe. And if it wasn't too good to be true, I'd swear he appreciates what he's seeing if the small gape of his mouth and the drowsiness of his eyes is anything to go by.

But that's absurd.

Right?

CHAPTER TWO

Soren

Stepping foot outside of KCI was a breath of fresh air. Even though Kansas City wasn't my original home, it came to be the place I loved the most. It's underrated, but it's the best of both worlds. With a big enough metropolis to provide entertainment down to wide open spaces where you can lose yourself in the reserve of nature and all its splendor.

While I enjoyed my time in San Francisco I was ready to return to this, to my dearest friend. Even though we talk almost every day I missed her more than words could say. If it weren't for us batting for the wrong team, I'm sure I would've married her.

Much to Jacob, her husband's dismay, Caroline is my soulmate and I'm hers.

Being back in this city is nice but pulling my best friend into my arms is everything.

I breathe in her familiar scent of roses and disinfectant and let loose a hearty sigh of relief. Now, I'm home.

"You look beautiful." I nose into her silky chestnut hair.

She pulls back to glare at me. "I look a mess. I've been up half the night delivering twins."

I pull her back in. "You always look beautiful."

"And you're either crazy or blind," she mumbled into my chest.

"I'm always crazy about you."

She pulls away again and I reluctantly let her go but grasp one of her hands in mine. I'm relieved when she entwines our fingers.

She wrinkles her nose at me. "Don't let Jacob hear you say stuff like that."

"Or what? He'll follow through on his twenty-five-year promise to knock my lights out?"

She shrugs, smirking. "You never know."

***

Our mouths have run a mile a minute the entire ride to The Rhode's palatial mansion as if we'll run out of time before we tell each other every little thing we missed in the past decade.

The Escalade's interior goes silent as I take in the familiar home of white-painted brick and manicured tea gardens. It looks like something straight out of an old-fashioned fairy tale.

"Admit it, this house is why you said yes when Jacob asked to marry you," I snark.

Caro may have come from money but not this kind of money.

She smacks my chest hard enough that it smarts, and I wince before rubbing it absently.

"It also helped that I was four months pregnant at the time."

It's not a secret because how else can you explain why they got married in the middle of our sophomore year at Yale?

Plus, her swelling belly was a dead giveaway, and fortunately, Grayson was an August baby. Just in time for all of us to return to school while poor Grayson was reared by a parade of nannies and servants here in this very house.

He rarely saw his actual parents until he was almost eight years old. It's no wonder he's closed himself off. The people who brought him into this world wanted nothing to do with him while paid servants only paid him enough mind to make sure he was clean and fed. Otherwise, he was left to his own devices.

While Jacob has many faults, as soon as we all moved back, he tried to make up for the lost time. It helped that as a mathematician, he was able to work from home. His love of Greek mythology rubbed off on the boy, and it became his life's work. Much to the chagrin of his parents.

The likelihood of him following in either one of their footsteps was slim to none, not when he can barely step foot outside of this house. He can barely mumble one or two words to the servants, let alone have a full conversation with the people who brought him into this world. Even though I was a regular fixture in this house for five years, he never said a word to me.

Yet he did hide in a cabinet in full view of the room Caro and I always occupied. It became a bit of a game whether I could catch his eye through that mesh door. I think I finally did on the last day I was here.

Now, as I follow Caroline inside, as I look around the familiar entryway, I find him. Like a game of Where's Waldo, I spot his rather large frame badly concealed by the corner of his father's office.

Through the years, I've seen little more of him than the irregular photographs. He was always a lovely boy, but now he's grown into a considerably attractive young man. Far too young for me, but he's enticing enough that it's hard to look away.

Caro's words do the trick though. "Are you coming in? You're letting all the cool air out."

I snort because it's not like they need to worry about paying what I'm sure is a ridiculous electric bill, to begin with. But it's enough to wake me up and get me moving. As we move deeper into the house, closer to the boy who's as good at hiding as an ostrich with its head in the sand, it's difficult to look at anything else.

The house is elegant, and beautiful by anyone's standards, but Grayson Rhodes is a wet dream come to life. And even though I'm far too old for those kinds of dreams, I can't help but appreciate every inch of him.

What a shame to keep this treasure hidden, even if it's in a gilded cage. A cage is a cage, no matter that his mind put him in it.

I know for many years, his parents blamed him for doing this to himself. I'm the one that convinced Caro to take him to a psychologist because God forbid if their shitty peers were to discover that the Rhodes weren't perfect in every way.

By the time he was diagnosed, it almost seemed too little too late. If they had known when he was little, it would've been easier for him to learn to maneuver the world despite his many mental challenges. The older he gets, the harder it is to change. As the saying goes, you can't teach an old dog new tricks.

But he's taken several steps that have at least enabled him to go to the actual university for his doctorate.

His parents are no help. No doubt the guilt of their previous absence has led them to coddle him. To let him get away with hiding in his room, only to come out for food or the lure of books.

I have this urge to lure him out. What would his face look like the first time he could walk out in the world and instead of terror written across his face, relief?

I'm not sure why it matters to me. Perhaps I'm intrigued, perhaps it's my love for his mother, or more than likely, it's my need to fix things. There's a reason I became one of the top reconstructive surgeons in the country.

I'm the man you come to when everyone who came before me failed. I can fix the unfixable. And once I've put my mind to something, I'm like a dog with a bone. I don't let go until it's immaculately clean.

And now, I've decided I'm going to annihilate this boy's fears.

CHAPTER THREE

Grayson

He's sitting by the pool reading a book. It should be the most mundane thing I've ever seen but that's far from the truth.

I'm enthralled, as I am with everything he does. The way his pale blue eyes travel over the page. When he uncrosses his legs and recrosses them the other way, it's mouthwatering. Then my favorite part is when his tongue peeks out to lick his thumb to turn the page. I swear my dick hardens more each time.

It's a race to see who finishes first, him and his book, or me.

Now and then, he'll reach toward the nearby table to grasp his sweating glass of iced tea. Watching his throat work as he swallows gulps of the refreshing beverage reminds me of how hot it is. How much I'm sweating through my long-sleeved black button-down and black jeans.

My outfit isn't convenient for the sweltering July heat, but it's good for hiding in the shadows. I'm not sure what I want more, a sip of his cold drink or his tongue on me instead.

Which is crazy, I hate being touched, but I've dreamed of nothing more than feeling every inch of this man's skin against mine for as long as I can remember.

Suddenly, he sets his book down and rises from his seat. He looks around the manicured garden, around our ridiculously huge pool, perhaps looking for a stray maid, but it's Sunday, and the servants have the day off. Dad is golfing, and mom is out of town for a conference.

It's only us.

It eventually occurs that he could be searching for me, but I never come out here, not until he came back anyway.

I suppose he's decided the coast is clear because he reaches back for the neck of his t-shirt and pulls it over his head. My mouth immediately salivates as I take in all his tan muscled skin. From his broad shoulders to his firm pecs. I'm impressed his abs are well defined, and he even has that Adonis belt I've heard so much about in my MM romance stories.

Fuck!

I'm so hard right now the imprisonment of my jeans feels like steel bars.

I press down on my ever-growing bulge, only giving myself the tiniest relief. Then, he makes it so much worse when he toes off his sandals, unbuttons his cargo shorts, and lets them drop to his feet.

Holy shit!

He's not wearing any underwear, and my god, that ass. It's round and firm enough to bounce a quarter off of. I mean, I would guess so; I absently search my pocket for change, like I'll have the audacity to check my theory.

Those thoughts quickly disintegrate as he turns around giving me a full view of everything he's working with. It's not like I have a lot to compare it to, except myself, or the few times I've watched gay porn.

I was too afraid my parents would check my internet history, so I barely have the balls to watch. Yes, I know you're asking about the books, but there are far too many books in both my physical library and my electronic one. Plus, I've barely spent a minute with my nose outside of one, so they've become immune to what I read.

While I might be a bit bigger, it's not by much. He practically has a third leg hanging between his spread thighs. His balls are heavy, swaying back and forth behind his impressive member.

Why is he hard?

Before I can contemplate that question, he turns away and jumps into the pool.

He's graceful as he slices through the crystal-clear water, a similar shade to his eyes. I watch avidly as he goes from one end of the Olympic-sized pool to the other. Back and forth, back and forth, mesmerizing as a swinging pendulum.

Far too soon, or perhaps not soon enough, he's pulling himself up the side of the pool. When one elegant foot lands on the side, opening his legs to give not only a better view of his swaying genitals but his surprisingly smooth and shiny hole.

My dick is on the verge of bursting through my pants while I'm drooling as I imagine what he tastes like. How much I not only want to lick that rosebud, but to shove my tongue inside as deep as I can.

I only catch the deep moan escaping my mouth.

He stands up straight as rivulets of water slide down every hill and valley of his delectable body.

What I'd give to be just one of those drops of water.

CHAPTER FOUR

Soren

I'm trying to force myself to concentrate on this book. It should be easy, it's one of my favorites, but I've read the same damn sentence a million times when I finally give up and place it face down on the table next to me.

I grab my tea and take a leisurely sip, and I swear his stare intensifies. I swallow too quickly, just stopping myself sputtering the cool liquid all over. I pull at my collar; I know it's a hot day, but it feels like I'm standing in the sun.

I pull to my feet and look around for anyone but my constant observer. When I'm sure we're alone, I start to strip. I make sure I take my time, draw it out, and keep him on the edge. Whatever it takes to draw him out.

The lines are beginning to blur already. Whether I'm doing this for his well-being or for my selfish wants. But does it matter? Two birds with one stone and all that.

When I dive into the water, it's not enough to cool my body. My cock is still hard as stone and aching something fierce. The worst part is how empty I feel. It's been too long since I've been filled with a nice big cock. He's so tall, so broad, I can only imagine he's working with something along the lines of what I need.

I shouldn't be thinking about this, not with him. He's way too young. Let alone that this is Caro's kid. But it's not as though this is a one-way street. I saw the way he looked at me, the way he ate up every inch of my body. His stare alone is one of the most titillating things I've ever experienced.

What would his touch feel like?

I go back and forth in my mind as I swim across the length of the pool until my body is dragging with fatigue. I push myself further until I'm too exhausted to go another inch.

After I pull myself out, I don't bother with a towel. Not when I want him to take his fill, to not miss an inch of me. I may be twice his age at forty-five, but I've worked hard to maintain this body. So, there is no self-doubt, no uncertainty that he wants me. He only needs to know that I'm a sure thing.

I wander through the sliding glass door, sure to leave it open for my admirer. With every step, I leave behind watery footsteps, like breadcrumbs for him to follow. When I head for my destination, I graze my hand over the curio cabinet that I knew he hid in as a boy before falling gracelessly onto the overstuffed leather couch.

With my legs spread wide, I slowly run my palms up my thighs. Teasing both him and me before I cup my full, throbbing testicles and squeeze until it hurts. Until a gasp escapes my mouth quickly followed by a guttural moan as I massage away the ache.

I don't stop, not as precum bubbles from the tip of my crown and leaks down my length. When I'm edged about as far as I can stand it, I gather some of the natural lubricant pooling around my base and rub it over my tight hole. I throw my head back on a groan as I slit my eyes and search out his hiding spot.

I find him in the shadow of the grand staircase. He's watching intently like I knew he would. My eyes gravitate to the impressive bulge tenting his jeans. Satisfaction inundates my arousal because I knew he'd be big, that someday he would fill me just right.

Until then... I slide my sticky fingers up my body and detour around one pebbled nipple. I pinch, twist, and torture myself until I'm heaving with my neediness. I force my continued exploration until I suck a single digit deep. I thrust it in and out, making it nice and wet before I lower it to my ass.

I don't ease it in, no I want him to know how I like it hard and fast. I like the edge of pain, so I don't waste time before I shove another followed by a third until I'm fucking myself on my hand.

With my free hand I squeeze the head of my cock, more precum erupts, and I smooth it down, slicking my length to ease my hand as I jack myself harshly.

"Fuck!" I hiss.

I'm losing myself to the pleasure, but I never take my eyes off him. I watch as his hands creep towards his dick but every time he gets close, he snatches it away. His self-control is impressive yet aggravating.

What will it take to make him lose control?

I edge myself over and over again, hoping he'll finally give in, but he never does.

Unable to hold off any longer, I jerk forward and widen my eyes so there's no mistake that I'm looking right at him. I can tell by the widening of his eyes and the way he freezes like a deer caught in the headlights.

And then I say in my most seductive voice. "Come out, come out wherever you are."

CHAPTER FIVE

Grayson

No amount of porn, there are not enough smutty books on the planet to compare to the sight of this gorgeous man getting himself off on my parent's couch. It's obscene, of course it is, because that's where they watch movies and eat popcorn. I used to take naps on that couch. And now it's been tainted, soon to literally be painted by come. And it's the most erotic thing I've ever seen.

I'm so lost in the show he's putting on that at first, I miss his statement. Until it's on repeat inside my head.

"Come out, come out wherever you are."

That's when it all came crashing down, and I realize he's been watching me as hard as I'm watching him.

How long has he been watching me?

The whole time?

Was this show all for me?

And if it was, why?

What's the purpose?

Is he playing with me?

Once my body awakens from its daze, I flee. Rushing up the stairs on speedy feet, almost tripping before I reach the top. I don't stop until I reach the safety of my bedroom. I slam the door shut, it's loud, echoing throughout. I twist the lock and lean back against it as I try to catch my breath and calm my speeding heart rate.

My cock is pulsing, practically bursting out the top of my jeans. I don't dare touch it for fear of getting caught. Yet, as I wait on pins and needles, nothing comes. Not a sound can be heard except for my slowly calming breaths.

Yet, my mind is busy running the reel of what I just saw. From the beginning, when he first removed his shirt, until he was about to come all over my mother's favorite couch. It's on repeat so my dick never deflates.

Not even when I force myself to take a seat at my desk. To go over old schoolwork. When that doesn't keep my attention, I grab my favorite book, but I can't get past the first page. I start up my Xbox, and for twenty minutes, I allow Bryce to kick my ass one game after another until I finally give up.

I fall to my bed in defeat as I rip my jeans open and grasp my hard length. In less than five strokes I'm coming all over my hand. But even as the greatest orgasm I've ever felt continues to pulse through my body, I know it's not enough. It will never be enough.

Then a very important question occurs to me. Does my dream doctor want me as much as I've always wanted him?

***

I've avoided him for over a week. I've holed up in my room, only leaving for food. Even then, I wait until the middle of the night when I'm sure everyone has gone to bed before I sneak down to the kitchen.

On the eighth night, my luck runs out.

I've got my head in the fridge as I shove roasted chicken in my mouth when a throat clears. I freeze, which isn't anything new. With a chicken leg between my teeth, I slowly turn to find the very person I've been avoiding.

"Hungry?" he asks, as if that wasn't obvious. "You should've tried it when it was still hot, it was delicious."

Slowly I pull the leg from my mouth and finish chewing before I manage to speak to the man of my dreams for the very first time.

"I like it cold." Go me!

One corner of his mouth quirks up. "Is that so?"

I nod, jerking my head up once.

He steps forward, and I step back. We do this as if it's a choreographed dance until my back hits the counter, and I've nowhere else to go. My dark eyes frantically search for my escape, but there's none.

And then he's there, toe to toe, chest to chest, nose to nose.

His voice caresses my lips making me shiver.

"You've been avoiding me."

A hand reaches toward my cheek, and I flinch, he freezes.

"I'd never hurt you."

I realize too late that I've been holding my breath. Why does this man make breathing so difficult?

I suck in a deep, heaving breath before I finally utter. "I know."

The centimeters between his hand and my cheek disappear until I'm engulfed in warmth.

With little thought, as if my body has a mind of its own, I lean into his hand. His thumb brushes over my bottom lip, and my tongue slips out, tasting him. This time he's the one to shiver.

"Will you answer my question, Gray?"

Nobody calls me Gray, and in my mind, I'm doing the happiest of dances. The embarrassing white boy dance with little rhythm and jerky movements. Because this man gave me a nickname. For the rest of my life, only he's allowed to call me Gray.

"I've been busy."

It's the flimsiest excuse to my ears, so I'm sure he'll call my bluff.

But he doesn't. "I want you to join us for dinner tomorrow. Can you do that for me?"

I suddenly feel like I could do anything for this man. All he needs to do is ask.

My nod is subtle, but he sees it.

"Good boy."

Then he's walking away leaving me feeling... empty... bereft.

For the first time, I'm looking forward to a social engagement. It's only dinner with Soren and my folks, but it's progress, nonetheless.

***

The following evening, I dress in a pair of my nicer jeans and a white button-up that I doubt has ever seen the light of day.

When I join them at the vast dining room table, both my parent's eyes widen subtly. If it was anyone else, it would've been unnoticeable, but I know all their little ticks. They quickly hide it with a smile.

"What a pleasure to have you join us, Grayson," my mother simpers as my father nods in agreement.

This is the first time I've ever joined my family for dinner. Mostly, I eat in the kitchen with staff or take it up to my room. It's not lost on anyone that I'm closer to the cook and maid than my parents. Even though they've put in the effort to make up for the first eight years of my life, they still sort of feel like strangers sometimes.

It makes my life sound lonely, and as far back as I can remember, it was. But you can get used to anything, and I grew accustomed to only having my own company.

I'm a social pariah, so I have no idea about etiquette or how I'm supposed to react when Soren starts questioning me like The Spanish Inquisition.

"How are you liking KU? Did you ever consider our alma mater? What do you think you'll do with a doctorate in mythology? Who's your favorite Greek God and why?"

They feel never-ending as I'm inundated with one after another.

And my parents do nothing but watch us back and forth as if they're at Wimbledon. Even if it is one-sided because while he asks his questions, his answer is only stilted silence until he goes on to the next one.

Finally, he asks. "Are you ok?"

And the answer to that is quite simple.

An astounding no.

Unable to verbalize even that one syllable I rise too quickly, sending my chair to the floor. I pay it no mind as I rush from the room and back up to the sanctuary of my bedroom. Where it's safe and quiet.

Even if it is away from the only man I want to spend time with.

CHAPTER SIX

Soren

I should be ashamed of myself. I know I'm pushing him past his limits, but I can't seem to hold my tongue. I think if the shoe were on the other foot, I would feel as uncomfortable as he looks. But I can't stop. I need to push him, and I don't even understand why.

It was only a matter of time before he flees and when he does, I feel emotionally destitute.

I wipe my hand over my face in exasperation. Both at myself, at Gray but, most importantly, at his parents, who now eye me with aggravation. I may not be a parent, but even I can see that they've failed miserably at every turn.

"What was that?"

I'm surprised when I realize the aggrieved question came from my dearest friend. Which is good, at least she has some sort of mama bear instinct. Even if it is wrongly placed.

I'm explicitly honest, for all our sakes. "Someone needs to push him out of his comfort zone."

Jacob chortles mirthlessly. "Well, congratulations. I'd say you succeeded swimmingly."

I narrow my eyes at him, it's no secret that we've never liked one another. So, no punches need to be pulled. "At least *I'm trying*."

"And what the hell is that supposed to mean?"

I shake my head in exasperation. "First, you force him into every panic attack he's ever had because you refused to believe that there was something wrong. Until I, yes I, insisted that he be seen by a professional. Then, when he was diagnosed with a plethora of disorders that all equate to agoraphobia thanks to you two selfish assholes who left him alone for the most impressionable years of child development. Instead of taking the steps to help him manage his fears, you coddle him. You've allowed him to hole up in his room for over a decade."

By the end of my tirade, I'm practically yelling, but I don't care as long as they hear what I'm saying. It may be none of my business, but somebody needs to give a shit about this kid.

Jacob rises to his feet. "How dare you speak to me in my own house about how I should raise *my child*."

I snort. "You had twenty-three years and you've failed miserably."

"Get out!" he snaps.

Caro pops to her feet. "Now wait just a minute, Jacob..."

"Don't tell me you're on his side. I know you've always been his fag hag, but are you seriously going to allow him to speak to us like this?"

I lean back in my seat as I watch them go back and forth. Jacob is getting closer to losing his mind as my best friend remains the pillar of calm, cool, and collected. It would be impressive if she wasn't part of the problem.

Then, tears well in her pretty brown eyes, and I start to backtrack in my mind. Until I remember that beautiful boy who is right now hiding in his room. Where he'll continue to hide for the rest of his life unless somebody does something about it.

And who better than me?

I grasp her hand, and she looks at me, her features brimming with regret.

"You're right," she says, and her husband gasps, making her return her attention to him. "It's true, Jacob. We've been so busy with our careers, allowing our son to fall deeper into this abyss of nothing."

Jacob slumps into his chair, resentment, and failure written all over his face.

Finally, he asks. "What do we do?"

It's simple when you think about it. "We fight. We go to him on our terms until he comes back on his."

***

That night, I camp out in the kitchen to await his arrival, but it never comes. I return every night. On the fourth night, he appears on quiet feet. I wait until he's elbow deep in a bowl of mashed potatoes before I speak.

"I see you've finally chosen to sneak out of your hole."

The look on his face could be considered comical if this wasn't so depressing. The fact that he fears any kind of attention. That he's more comfortable slinking around this big empty house, sneaking into the kitchen in the dead of night to relieve his hunger, rather than interact, even with his parents. Even with me, the man he's had a crush on for most of his life.

I can pretend I'm doing this only for him, but that would be a lie. I was intrigued the minute I saw him upon my return. He's one of the most beautiful men I've ever seen. But more than anything, he touches my heart, makes me feel something more than lust for the first time in forty-five years.

The need to protect him is there, but more than anything, I want to help free him, I want to see him fly.

I clear my throat. "I owe you an apology." His eyes widen, making me smirk. "I pushed too hard; subtlety has never been my strong suit."

He wipes his hands on a paper towel and takes his time as he throws it away before he turns back to me.

"What exactly are you trying to do?"

It's a loaded question if I ever heard one. One that begs for honesty, so I give him just that.

"I want to help you get out of your shell."

He swallows several times; reaches for a glass of water that he drinks deeply from until the glass is empty.

His voice still comes out scratchy, breathy. "Why?"

I look down at my bare feet and rub my hand over the back of my neck sheepishly. I'm never bashful, but this kid makes you feel like you're in the center of the brightest spotlight.

"I like you."

He coughs until I think he's choking. I rush to his side to beat against his back.

He waves me away. "I'm fine."

I hold my hands up in surrender.

When he gets himself under control, he crosses his arms over his chest defensively, but I can't say that I blame him.

"You don't even know me."

And who's fault is that?

"I know you're super smart in different ways to your parents much to their chagrin. I know that you're lonely, that you wouldn't have chosen this for yourself. And most importantly, I know you've almost always had a crush on me."

I smirk devilishly at him as he goes from deathly pale to as red as a tomato.

Before he can freak out and run away again, I carry on. "I'd like for us to get to know each other. We'll go at your speed, but with little nudges from me, but I'd like to help you leave this house. Go someplace other than your university for an hour or two at a time."

He huffs. "And what if I don't want that?"

I shake my head. "We both know that's not true."

It grows so quiet only the whir of the refrigerator and muffled cicadas outside can be heard.

"Will you be a good boy and let me help you?" I finally ask.

So much time passes, I'm sure he'll turn his back on me and leave. But then he surprises us both by nodding.

CHAPTER SEVEN

Grayson

That night I lay down, but sleep is elusive. I'm far too restless. My body, my mind is inundated with both excitement and fear. It's something I've always dreamed of, having all of Soren's attention, but now that I have it, I feel overwhelmed.

Be careful what you wish for.

I toss and turn for hours before I finally fall into a fitful slumber.

It feels like no time has passed when there's a rather loud banging echoing around inside my head. Eventually, I realize it's coming from outside my door. When I push my hair out of my face, I see that it's a little after 6 in the morning.

"What?!" No answer, just another knock. "Who is it?" Another knock. Frustrated, I drag myself out of bed and throw the door open where I find Soren looking refreshed and perfectly dressed and quaffed. "Wha...?"

"Get dressed, we're going out."

I try to ask why, but he's not having it. He shoves me into my room and rifles around my closet until he finds an outfit similar to his own. Relaxed, yet trendy.

When I don't move to dress, he begins to do it himself until I freak out and shove him off.

"What the heck are you doing?"

With all seriousness he states. "If you refuse to do what you're told, I'll do it for you."

I gape at him. Who the hell does this guy think he is?

I start to ask him just that when he resumes stripping me.

"Ok, ok. I'll dress myself."

He smirks. God, why is that so sexy?

"Be ready in ten, or I'll be back to finish the job."

I doubt a threat has ever been more alluring.

With much trepidation, I slink downstairs after I've put on the clothes he laid out for me. Half the clothes in my closet were bought by my mother. Without much use for suits or designer wear, most of it was left untouched.

The new clothes feel scratchy against my skin. I pull at the neck of the light summer sweater as if it's strangling me. It feels like it anyway.

Downstairs the empty halls echo with my footsteps, making me feel self-conscious. The urge to flee is high, but I force one foot in front of the other until I find my tormentor sprawled across a chair at the dining room table.

The room is abandoned otherwise, even this early in the morning it's not uncommon for both my parents to be long gone at work. This reminds me why he's not at work, so I ask him as much.

"Your mother didn't tell you?"

As if my mother speaks to me regularly.

I simply shake my head no.

"I don't start at the hospital for another few weeks. Plenty of time to pull you out of your comfort zone."

Dread more than I've already felt since last night's proclamation inundates me from head to toe.

"You don't have to do this," I offer mildly while inside I'm begging anything, anyone to make him change his mind.

He winks, and I deflate. "Oh, but I want to."

"Am I some kind of social experiment?"

He scoffs, appearing far more taken aback than I would've expected.

He slides to his feet. I watch his muscles bunch and expand, which in turn makes my mouth go dry.

Why does he have to be so hot?

He steps too close, but I decide to buck up and hold my ground. Even if it makes me tremble.

This time when his hand reaches for me, I don't flinch, which is a feat all in itself.

When he takes my hand, the most unforeseen thing happens. I relax, and it couldn't confuse me more. But that doesn't take away from the fact that I liked it, and it only makes him more fascinating to me.

"This isn't a game to me, Gray. I want to help you."

His thumb rubs back and forth over my wrist making it hard to think but I push through.

"What's in it for you?"

He pulls me closer until I stumble into him. Until the only thing holding me up is his arms around me. I should be panicking, at the very least trying to push him away. But then I do the unthinkable, I lean into him, and wrap my arms around his waist. My ear is against his chest as if the rhythmic thumps of his heartbeats are the most therapeutic thing I've ever felt or heard.

How could I have ever known how starved for touch I was until this very moment?

His raspy voice breaks me out of my revelation.

"I have many selfish reasons for helping you."

"Give me one."

It sounds like I'm begging because I am. I need to know that he doesn't feel sorry for me. Or at least that it's not his only reason.

Warm, soft hands engulf my cheeks, raising my face to his. His lips are close enough that I feel his words.

"I want to feel close to you."

Kiss me, I silently beg.

I'm certain I've suddenly become telepathic because he does.

It's soft, so soft it feels like butterfly wings against my mouth sending tendrils of quivers radiating out of my body. I wait for him to deepen it, but he never does.

Instead, he looks so deeply into my eyes that I lose myself in the pools of clear blue until I'm sure I've found his very soul.

"Do you want that?" he asks raggedly.

Slowly, so he can see that I am sure of my answer, I say it firmly. "Yes."

CHAPTER EIGHT

Soren

I lead him outside to my brand-new Escalade. I open the passenger door for him. He looks at me in question, but I only wait. I watch indecision run over his features; he's fighting with himself. Whether he should do what I'm telling him to do or run away.

I don't want to push him on this, I desperately want him to choose this... to choose me.

Perhaps he sees that on my face as he grudgingly climbs into the vehicle. I reach around him to buckle him in,

One of his brows cocks. "You know I'm capable of buckling myself in."

I grin almost bashfully. "I wanted to do it."

I want any reason to touch him, and I think he's starting to want that, too. It not only makes me harden, but it also expands my heart. I like him, perhaps more than I've liked anyone in a long time.

I know they say that age is just a number, but what could we possibly have in common? His life experience is nonexistent. I doubt he's touched another soul, not since he was a child. Even then, I'm sure it was rare.

But none of that matters. My need to protect him, to show him anything and everything, to take care of him is enough. I don't need any other reason to want him as I do. We're both adults, as long as it's consensual, nothing else matters.

With a full head and heart, I jump behind the wheel and smile at him. In turn, he offers a grimace that makes me chuckle.

"Stop acting like you're on your way to your execution. I promise you're going to enjoy this."

He doesn't look convinced. "And what exactly is it that we're doing?"

I'd like to surprise him, but I know that won't help. He needs to know, to prepare himself.

So, I take a deep breath and lay all my cards on the table. "A friend of mine is an art curator at The Nelson. As a favor, he's opening the doors a few hours early to let us check out the new Greek Mythology display."

When I saw the event online it felt serendipitous, so I made the call. Keith was only too happy to help me out after I explained everything. I left out that Gray is Caro's kid, it didn't feel pertinent and honestly, I didn't need that kind of judgment. It's nobody's business but mine and Gray's.

I keep one eye on the road and the other on Gray. I watch as his eyes widen in shock which quickly morph into wonder. He certainly has a soft spot for this shit. It's almost like he has a one-track mind. Makes me wonder what it would be like when that mind is consumed with me, but I'm getting ahead of myself.

It's a dream, sure, but one that I'll do everything in my power to make a reality.

The roads are packed with traffic, even this early in the morning, and I can see the havoc playing over his face from my peripheral. I question whether it's a good idea, but decide to go ahead and take the chance.

My hand moves away from the steering wheel, slowly making its way over to Gray's thigh. Softly, I lay it against him, He tenses but he doesn't pull away. I take it as an invitation, so I squeeze him affectionately.

When I chance a glance his way, I'm pleased to find the tiniest smirk quirking his plush mouth. God, I want to kiss him again, a real kiss, but one step at a time.

By the time I'm pulling into the museum's empty lot, all the tension that had eased out of his body is back with a vengeance.

I squeeze again. "It'll just be me and you."

He swallows thickly. "And your friend," he says raggedly.

I put the car in park before I turn my body towards him. "Keith is only letting us in, and then we'll be alone. You want to see this, don't you?"

He'd been staring out the windshield, looking resolute. Pride swells, and I want to tell him, but I doubt he'll appreciate it. Perhaps afterward, he'll accept my praise.

After a long pause, he finally nods and turns to me. "Thank you for doing this."

I lean in and carve my hand around his throat. His pulse beats spasmodically against my palm, so I gently grasp him firmly.

"I'd do anything for you." Once it's out of my mouth, I know it's true.

His mouth gapes as if he'll speak, but nothing comes out.

So, I answer his unasked question. "I'm serious."

He nods firmly as if we've come to an understanding.

I smile. "You ready?"

He offers his awkward quarter smile. "As ready as I'll ever be."

I let him go as we both get out. I round the vehicle to join him but leave a foot of space between us. He's the one to kill the distance, and I couldn't be more pleased when he takes my hand in his and entwines our fingers.

I want to say something, anything, at least look at him. Instead, I keep my gaze ahead as we walk toward the entrance.

Keith is already waiting for us with the door open. He's much older than I am, no doubt far past retirement age. But the man loves his job, I'm sure he'll stay until they cart him away.

"Good morning, and welcome to The Nelson."

I explained to him in advance about Gray's agoraphobia, so he takes it in stride when the man beside me remains silent. When he doesn't acknowledge him.

"Feel free to explore to your heart's content. You have a good two hours before we open, so take your time."

Two hours isn't enough to see everything that this well-established art museum has to offer, but I doubt we'll leave their newest exhibit.

And Gray doesn't disappoint as he closely examines every piece made available. Some pieces he studies for ten, fifteen minutes. He appears to be especially enamored of a painting called The Lament for Icarus, depicting a man with an extensive wingspan as he lay dying surrounded by water nymphs.

He tears himself away to look at me. "Do you know the story of Icarus?"

I nod. "Vaguely, but why don't you tell me."

His gaze goes cloudy, as if he's remembering the first time he heard it. Did Jacob read it to him from one of his many tomes?

"His father, Daedalus, invented the wings made from feather and wax so that they could escape from Crete. He had warned Icarus not to fly too high or too low. Too low, and the sea would dampen the feathers, making them too heavy. Too high, and the sun would melt the wax. But Icarus was too prideful and ignored all his father's warnings. He flew higher and higher, exuberant with his sudden freedom. But his father was right, of course, and when Icarus realized it, it was too late. He plummeted to his death where he perished in the sea far below."

It's a tale as old as time, one that's been reincarnated several times throughout history. A warning to wayward children to listen and comply with their parents.

Yet, in Gray's case, the opposite is true. He listened to his parents and found himself the prisoner of his mind. The only way to free himself was to do exactly what Icarus had done, to fly higher and higher. But in Gray's case, I would be there to catch him when he falls.

We slowly move through the exhibit. I watch him study both ancient artifacts and art alike. For every piece, he has some history to share that I soak up like a sponge. Not because I have much interest in the subject matter, but because I'm enjoying watching him flourish like the most exotic flower.

His beauty is as unique as a rare orchid. It requires much care so as not to bruise or wilt.

Even as we leave the display behind, he carries on with one story after another, barely stopping to take a breath all the way out to my car. But once we're inside, he clams up, making me turn to him.

"Are you alright?"

For the first time, he offers me the most radiant grin. "I'm wonderful. I can't thank you enough."

I lean my forehead against his. When he doesn't pull away, I'm silently counting my blessings.

"You're wonderful," I rasp. "You have such a beautiful mind and heart to say nothing of your exterior. You know that, don't you?"

He lets loose a shaky breath. He opens his mouth several times, but no words escape.

"Watching you in there, it was breathtaking to see you thrive. I want to see it every day. I want to make you bloom in every way. Will you let me?"

His head snaps back, brown eyes widening in shock. "You couldn't possibly..."

I throw all caution to the wind and grasp his face as I pull him in for a kiss. Unlike last time, this one isn't gentle. I don't start slow, and hope he'll let me in. No, I take everything I want as I lash my tongue against his. As I bite his full lower lip and suck it into my mouth. It's desperate and needy and conveys everything I'm only now realizing that I feel for him.

I want him, everything that he's willing to give me, and some that he's not. But I'll do whatever it takes to get it.

When I eventually tear myself away, we're both breathing hard. His eyes are wild as they search my face.

"Look as hard as you want because all you'll see is how much I want you. The question, my dear Gray, is if you'll continue with your fantasies, or if you'll let me help you make them a reality."

CHAPTER NINE

Grayson

I'm in a sort of daze as I watch the man I've only dreamed of having as he expounds all the reasons he wants me. It's a dream come true. Yet, why is it overwhelming me to the point of near asphyxiation?

Why the hell can't I breathe?!

My face feels tight, like an overblown balloon that's on the cusp of exploding. I'm not sure if that would make it better or worse. But the pressure building inside me with no release is more than I can handle.

Then the warmth comes. So tiny at first, like the smallest pinprick, but it quickly expands as the feeling travels from the middle of my back outwards. By the time it reaches my extremities, my awareness returns.

I take inventory, first that I'm bent in half, my head between my legs as heaving breaths saw in and out of my lungs. The air slowly begins to flow easier as I realize the reason for the warmth.

It's his hand that is currently rubbing up and down my back in the most soothing manner.

His voice is soft as it coos, "Shhh baby, just keep breathing with me. In and out, nice and easy. There you go. You're such a brave boy."

Tears prick my eyes. It just hits me all at once that nobody, not once in twenty-three years has ever tried to comfort me. A gut-wrenching sob breaks free as I realize how much I like it, how much I need it. Especially how much I don't want to lose it.

For over ten years after my diagnosis, I never tried very hard to work my way out of this hole. I never found a reason to try. But now? Now, I have every reason to try, and he's cocooning me into his big, warm body. Even though I'm not small by any means, he makes me feel protected. As long as I have him, nothing will ever hurt me.

If he asked me to speak in front of millions of people, I would do it just to see him smile at me. If he asked me to visit the mall days before Christmas when it's wall to wall with insane shoppers, I would do it just to hold his hand.

When I eventually feel I have myself under control, I sit up. I find Soren watching me, his features full of concern. And I feel contrite.

"I'm sorry," I grumble.

"You have nothing to be sorry for. You took a big leap today, and I couldn't be prouder."

God, those words make me feel like I'm standing on top of the world. Does he have any idea what he does to me?

Then, he chuckles. "Took the breath right out of you with only a question. I can think of several ways I'd prefer to do it."

That makes me blush, and further heats my body for an entirely different reason. I'm not sure whether it's temporary insanity, or if my curiosity gets the best of me because I ask, "Like what?"

He jerks toward me, surprise written all over his face. But soon, devilry is eclipsing anything else.

"I suppose that's for me to know and you to find out. That is, if I can tempt you?"

Shit, I've been tempted by this man for half my life. But now what will I do when he's offering me everything I've always wanted?

I do the only thing I can do.

I say, "Yes."

He falls back, perhaps in shock, but he covers that quickly. A lazy smile spreads as the hand still soothing my back moves lower, centimeters at a time until I'm literally on the edge of my seat. How far will he take this? How far will I let him?

When he stops just short of my ass, I barely contain a pouty complaint. But he sees it, I'm sure he's always been able to read me like a book.

"Tsk, baby boy. Good things come to those who wait." He leans in for a quick peck before settling back behind the steering wheel. "Now, buckle up."

I automatically do as he says after I shove my hands under my thighs to keep from touching him.

He smirks at that. "You can touch me as much as you want."

Feeling bolder than I ever thought possible, I reach for the large bulge tenting his linen slacks. But his hand catches me around my wrist and places my hand on his thigh, mere inches from my previous destination.

"Don't be naughty, Gray. You don't want to give me a reason to punish you."

Goosebumps spread along my body like wildfire as my dick hardens painfully.

What kind of punishment?

I wonder to myself, for fear of what? I'm not sure. Whether of the punishment itself, or if I say something and he'll withhold it.

CHAPTER TEN

Soren

Gray's easy acquiescence both excited and unsettled me. Mostly because it upset my plans to woo him slowly. I wanted him to be sure before I took him to my bed, but I can't deny how much I want him.

Of course it's because it's him, but also because of how much I desire to teach him, to mold him. To see all the wondrous expressions that cross his face, the way his body will undoubtedly react to every ounce of pleasure I plan to squeeze out of him.

I want to make my mark. Even though I want him to be mine, I'm not naive to believe that I'll be enough for him. He's a May to my December. While he's on the cusp of a reawakening, I'm at the twilight of a life well lived. I have no regrets in my life, but I know deep down when this comes to its inevitable conclusion, that it'll hurt. The day will come when Gray leaves me for far better pastures.

And I know without a doubt that his leaving will leave the biggest stain on my soul.

I just manage it, but I do push those negative thoughts down into the abyss of my deepest, darkest secrets until it's all but forgotten.

Too soon, we're pulling into the long drive of a modern glass house. Ten-foot-tall windows make up almost every wall showcasing the interior consisting of teak wood floors, the sleek lines of white leather sofas, and tables made from driftwood and resin in every shade of greens and blues.

The house was built over a bubbling creek that you can hear throughout the first floor, creating this oasis in a tiny bit of woods in the middle of a busy Kansas City.

I avidly watch my beautiful boy take it all in with wide chocolate eyes before he turns to me. "What is this place?"

"My new house. It's quicker to buy a house outright when you don't have to go through escrow. I knew as soon as I stepped inside that it was exactly what I wanted."

What I don't say is that I pictured Gray here. Even if he never found his way out of his prison, I thought I could give him one with a better view. With all the views.

The most insidious part of me hopes that he won't escape, not if that freedom means flying away from me.

Fortunately, I've never been a selfish man. Not only my conscience, but my heart would never allow it.

"What do you think?" I asked with far more confidence than I feel. "Do you like it?"

When I look back at him, I shudder to find him studying me as hard as he was just appraising the house.

"It's gorgeous. I think it fits you to a T."

I'm dazed as I heat from a full body flush. I've never been known to blush not since I was a boy. But I believe Gray is going to make me feel several new things during our time together, and I can't wait.

I open my door, grateful when he follows suit. Even though I wouldn't mind throwing him over my shoulder and carrying him over the threshold. Believe me, the thought isn't lost on me.

I shake the ridiculous thought aside and settle for placing my palm against his warm back and leading him inside.

I show a great amount of restraint as I allow him to wander and explore to his heart's content. When all I want to do is push him against every vertical surface to ravage him in every sense of my wicked imagination.

Yet, when he finds the floating stairs and makes his way up, my giddiness expands because there are only two rooms upstairs. One is a luxurious bathroom with everything one could desire, from a waterfall shower to a jacuzzi tub big enough for four.

The second is a master bedroom that for the time being is bare except for the biggest California king-sized bed I could find. I covered it in black sheets, imagining Gray's pale soft skin framed by its vast comparison.

I wanted to take my time. I didn't mean to start today. I only wanted him to see it, to know it was here for him if he wanted it. But seeing him in my bedroom, all my good intentions go flying out the window as my lizard brain takes over, and there's nothing I can do to stop it.

"Take off your clothes," I rasp.

He startles, turning to me in stunned silence.

I can't help it. I prowl toward him on sure feet. Not surprised when he backs up, not realizing that I'm corralling him toward our destination, my bed. When the back of his knees hit the frame, he barely stays on his feet.

His hands go up, as if that will keep me away, making me grin. I don't stop, even as his hands press against my chest, until my body is as close to him as is humanly possible. Until not even a hint of air can move between us.

I keep my hands clenched by my sides, refusing to touch him until invited. No matter how scared he is, he'll ask me to touch him.

"Don't you want to be a good boy, Gray? Or do you want to be punished?"

Indecision wars over his face, his eyes rapidly moving back and forth. I can see the exact moment he chooses, and I couldn't be more surprised.

"Punish me," he breathes so quietly I almost wonder if I imagined it.

"Are you sure?"

He nods succinctly, up, and down three times convincing me of his choice.

"Very well."

I don't waste a moment as I reverse our positions. I sit on the edge of the bed as I pull him between my spread thighs. Keeping my gaze locked on his, I efficiently unbuckle his belt, his button, and zipper. I push both his shorts and underwear down his sinewy thighs down to his ankles.

In a quick movement, I kick his feet out from under him and maneuver his falling body over my lap. Of course, he struggles, but I'll have none of it. I push down on the back of his neck and lock his legs under one of mine.

"You've made your bed, Gray. Now lie in it."

I chuckle when he turns that hurt puppy dog look up at me because it's easy to decipher curious longing underneath that facade. In the back of my mind, I fear that this will make him backtrack, but he still looks at me with trust, so I carry on.

My gaze travels back and forth between his face and his ass as I bring my hand down in punishing strikes. Not hard enough to bruise, but hard enough to leave the most delicious red handprints.

His expression morphs from shock to pain and then his mouth gapes and his eyes grow drowsy with undeniable lust. His cock grows with every smack until it's driving into my thigh. For so long he stays silent forcing me to up my game. To spank him harder and harder until he finally gasps, lets loose a few shocked screams before moaning incessantly.

"You're such a dirty boy, enjoying your punishment. You like it, don't you? You relish the thought of me leaving my mark. Admit it, Gray."

"Yes," he chokes.

"Tell me," I command, my voice brimming with authority that won't be denied.

"I love every touch," He forces out. "I want your hands everywhere. I want you to bruise every inch."

Before I can second guess myself, I throw him on the bed and rip away every stitch of clothing. Then I take in his wondrous body sprawled out across my bed. I knew he would look amazing against the dark sheets.

CHAPTER ELEVEN

Grayson

I knew deep down what his punishment would entail. Even though I've never known myself to enjoy pain, I couldn't help craving it. Perhaps, it's because it's him. Because I could see how much he hungered for it, and I yearned to please him.

But once it started, I knew my reasoning was far greedier. As much as I loved being soothed by him, I freaking needed his punishment. That first spank was a shock to my system, but as the warmth spread from his harsh touch, I knew I thirsted for more, so much more.

As his touch grew harsher, faster my breathing grew heavier, not with exertion, but with neediness. I knew he was silently demanding my cries, no matter what kind. But this need to disobey, to make him chastise me further, kept me silent.

And it worked. Dear God it worked.

Tears sprang to my eyes as the pain became all-encompassing, as it radiated up my body, my clenched muscles increasing the intensity, until I had no choice but to cry out.

At some point, even though his force never lessened, the pain became a dull roar until everything but pleasure all but disappeared.

When I floated back down to earth I found myself cushioned on his fluffy bed, the man of my dreams standing over me bare. A wild look covered his face, making anticipation rather than fear radiate through me. All my fears disappeared as my desire for this man took over everything.

"I need you, Soren."

It's the first time I've said his name, and it comes out reverently.

"What do you need, baby?"

Fuck me, I love when he calls me that.

"I need you to touch me," I plead.

"Where?"

His voice wavering as his body tenses, I think with the need to do exactly as I ask, but he requires permission.

If that's what he wants, then permission is granted.

"Everywhere," I gasp.

As soon as it leaves my mouth, he's on top of me. The weight of him, the hair on his chest raking against my bare skin. The feel of his engorged length rubbing against mine. It's an amalgamation of everything I've ever wanted.

And when his mouth, teeth, and tongue dance with mine, I feel complete for the very first time. I feel wanted, needed, and accepted for everything I am. Both the good, and all the bad. I know without a doubt that my bad far outweighs the good, something he's aware of, and he still wants me.

I cry out when his glorious mouth leaves mine until it moves over my jaw, his teeth nibble the shell of my ear. As his tongue lathes down my neck until he's sucking this sensitive spot where my neck meets the shoulder. I never knew there could be so many erogenous zones on the body, but I swear he's hitting every single one.

"God, you make me feel so good," I grit out.

It turns to a gasp when his hot tongue moves over a nipple, running it back and forth until it's the hardest little point.

"Jesus fucking Christ!"

He sucks it into the heated cavern of his mouth, and I can't stop my body from arching into him, silently begging for more. In return, or perhaps in retribution, he rubs his hand down my neck, over my shoulder until it reaches my neglected nipple to pinch and twist until I'm crying out in both unbearable pain and the greatest pleasure.

"Yes! Fuck me, yes!"

I wonder if I could come from this alone.

I glance down my body at my cock standing straight up toward the ceiling as precum bubbles and slips down my length. The head is an angry red as I watch it pulse. I can't see them, but I can feel my balls drawing up so tight against my shaft that it's just a matter of time before I erupt.

But do I want to come from nipple play alone?

The hunger to feel more, to feel everything makes me cry out. "You're gonna make me come."

And like I hoped, he draws away; the relief and discontent inundate me until that magical mouth moves down to my happy trail. Sea blue depths gaze up at me, their intensity upping my appetite as I thrash my head back and forth against the pillow.

"Touch me, Soren. Please God, touch me."

His devil-may-care smirk undoes me, when his tongue meets my skin, I'm done. I know as soon as he touches my cock I'll erupt, and there's nothing I'll be able to do to stop it. But then he surprises me when he goes around the most prominent part of me. His soft touch and meandering kisses travel down one leg and up the other. He takes his sweet ass time until my entire body is shaking with my desperation to come.

A sheen of sweat covers every single inch, and I'm crying, fucking crying, as I beg him to finish it.

"Please Soren, let me come."

Instead of giving me what I need, he sucks first one ball, quickly followed by the other. The pleasure is like nothing I've ever felt before but it's not enough. I need something, anything. Whether he touches my cock, licks it, sucks it, hell, even just breathes on it, I know that will be enough to tip me over the edge.

But he does none of that. Just leisurely explores my testicles, my taint, even allowing his tongue to feather over my hole until I'm an even bigger, quivering mess.

My face is covered in tears, my mouth as dry as the Sahara from all my screaming, and my body aches in both pain and the most excruciating pleasure.

When he sits up, I want to scream and sob until there's nothing left.

While he appears serene. "Do you want to come baby?"

What kind of fucking question is that?

I've only been begging for it for who knows how long.

I somehow manage to speak; it comes out on the barest husk. "Yes, I need to come."

"What will you give me if I make you come?"

What?

Are we playing some sick game of Let's Make a Deal?

But then none of that matters. Nothing matters but this undying ache for relief.

"Anything," I rasp.

He gives me the biggest shit-eating grin. "I fully plan to hold you to that."

And then he takes me down to the back of his throat and swallows.

It's enough as I shoot my seed in what feels like an endless flow down his throat.

"Holy shit, you're amazing! You're everything," I rattle off as the greatest orgasm leaves me spent.

My body is a useless mass as he pulls off and climbs back over me. I'm at his mercy, as if I wasn't before, but now there's no other choice. His mouth covers mine, and when I open for him, I not only taste the salty earthiness of my spend, but I feel it dribbling into my mouth. I'm in shock as he feeds me my essence, and while a part of me feels sickened, the bigger part is heated once more.

I moan into his mouth as I accept every drop.

"Don't swallow," he murmurs.

Then his tongue plays over mine, as we exchange the fluid back and forth, until I can't tell his taste from my own, until we become one.

All good things come to an end, but I'm too exhausted to care. I can barely keep my eyes open as he wraps his body around mine.

The last thing I remember is him whispering directly into my ear, "This is just the beginning, baby."

CHAPTER TWELVE

Soren

I must have dozed off shortly after Gray did, because when my eyes blink open, the room is dark. My back is cool, but my front is so warm as Gray cuddles closer, his face pillowed against my chest, his legs entwined with mine. Our softened cocks are nestled together as if they can't bear to be apart.

I watch as first, my shaft hardens before my boy's continues suit. Even in sleep, we are in sync.

As much as I want to explore him more, make him beg and plead before I give him pleasure only I'm allowed to give him now, I need to soothe him. He doesn't know it yet, but he's mine, at least for the time being. And with my ownership, so are all his orgasms.

His hips begin to rock, but I stay them with my hands against his slim hips making him grumble sleepily.

"Stop," he whines.

"Shhh, we've plenty of time for that."

Before he can complain further, I climb out of bed and head for the bathroom. I run the bath, setting the temperature just this side of scalding.

When I return, he's sitting up in bed, rubbing his eyes, reminding me how much younger he is, but I shake it away.

Not now.

"What are you doing?" he mumbles adorably.

"Running us a bath."

His groggy features brighten. "Really?"

I nod happily as I pull him close before lifting him like a groom carrying his bride.

He yelps. "Put me down. I'm too heavy."

"Nonsense."

I kiss his temple, effectively soothing him.

The bath is almost filled so I place him inside making him hiss at the temperature. I make sure to place him over a jet so when I turn them on, he squeaks in shock, quickly followed by a groan of pleasure.

"Holy shit! Who knew?"

Me, of course.

I slowly climb in, over his body until I'm straddling him. I align our pulsing cocks as I begin to thrust against him. With the pressure of the pulsating jets of water against his virgin hole and our hard lengths chafing against each other, I know his relief will be quick.

This is good because I held myself back earlier, and my own need for release is excruciating. I've never been happier to be right when after a dozen thrusts, he throws his head back and cries out.

"I'm gonna come again. Holy shit I'm coming!"

I feel his seed hit my dick, and it spurs me on to quickly follow.

I crush my mouth against his as rope after rope pulses out of me.

Fuck me. If it's this good now, how much better could it possibly get?

***

The answer to my previous question is it could get so much better.

Gray blew my mind with his capacity not only to try new things, but how quickly he picked them up. The first time he gave me head was messy and clumsy but perfect because it was him.

No matter how many times he gagged, or I told him to use his hand, he was relentless in his mission to deep throat. Nothing was hotter than his face covered in saliva, tears, and my come. The instinct to mark every inch of his body was all-consuming. Even knowing this is temporary, I wanted to do everything to make him mine.

The burden of stopping myself from bruising and biting was driving me insane. So much so that I could no longer hide my frustration.

He lay spent against my chest, but as he came down, my heart rate ratcheted as fear overcame all my good intentions.

He sat up, his chin on my chest as he looked at me with those big, sad, puppy dog eyes that got me every single time. I could never lie to him, at least not outright if he asked.

"What's wrong?"

I sigh deeply, studying his lovely features as I contemplate the best way to answer.

In the end, I decide on raw honesty. "I don't want to lose you."

Confusion spreads. "You won't lose me. I'm yours."

Naive words that go straight to my heart like a stabbing knife.

I weave my fingers through his shaggy hair and pull tight, making him moan. "I'm only here to help you. When you're free, you'll discover you have so many options. So many better options than me."

He jerks and pulls away until he's sitting straight up. He looks as though I've killed his puppy.

"Are you insane?"

I try to keep it lighthearted as I shrug. "I've had my moments"

"This isn't fucking funny, Soren."

No, it's not, and saying what needs to be said is cracking my heart. When everything is said and done, I know it'll crumble until there's nothing left.

"I'm not trying to be funny, Gray."

He flinches when I say his name. He's never hidden how much he loves when I call him, baby. It's not lost on either of us that I don't call him that now. It pushes a wedge between us, one that's needed for us both to escape unscathed.

Well... as unscathed as we can be.

"Why are you doing this?"

His voice breaks on that last word, and it breaks off the biggest chunk of my heart. Fuck me, I hate this. But it's necessary.

"Because I'm not good enough for you. You deserve the world, and I can't even offer you half."

Now, he's on his feet, pacing across the expanse of my gigantic bedroom. Even though it hurts, I can't help but appreciate his body. Long, lightly muscled legs that I'll never forget wrapped around my body. The curve of his spine is beauty in motion. If I were an artist, I'd draw him over and over again to immortalize his beauty.

I sit up straight when he stops directly in front of me. Surprise encompasses all of me when his hands cradle my face, forcing me, as if I don't always want to look at him.

"I have wanted you my entire life. How can you possibly think that I wouldn't want to keep you?"

Unbidden tears flood my eyes, and I try to blink them away to no avail. When he kisses them away I break. I've always been strong, stoic to a fault, but this boy tears down all my walls, leaving me exposed to the pain I never knew existed.

Not until this moment.

He climbs into the bed until he's sitting with his back to the headboard before he pulls me onto his lap. I surprise myself when I go willingly. I can't remember the last time someone comforted me. No doubt I was a small child. But I go to it like a duck to water, like this boy was born to take care of me as surely as I was born to care for him.

With my head over his shoulder, he soothes me with his hands over my skin and his soft crooning in my ear.

"Shhh, my love. I believe you're overthinking all of this. But if you honestly think that you can get rid of me, let alone that I would ever leave you now that I finally have you, you have another thing coming. That will never happen."

Fingers grasping my hair he pulls me back enough to slant his mouth over mine. Our kiss ravages before it soothes, it kills demons before it brings life. Until nothing remains but us. Until two become one.

The most unexpected comes out of his mouth when we eventually pull away.

"If you ever try to leave me, I will hunt you down. Do you understand me, Dr. Delgado?"

I shout out a laugh. It's that or cry, and I think I'm fresh out of tears before I nod my acquiescence.

"I promise I'll never leave you, but I won't stop you if you want to move on."

I know I'm stubborn.

He shakes his head. "Do you have so little faith in me?"

My blues fuse with his brown. "I don't want to hold you back."

He snorts. "Soren, you're the only person that's ever pushed me. You didn't just crack my shell, you eviscerated it."

It's true. We didn't only fill our time with learning about each other's bodies. Even though that was a big part of it.

I took him everywhere from empty movie theaters to restaurants to the busiest festivals.

Only yesterday, we ventured to the big farmers market. On a Saturday. It was packed. Even though he had plenty of panicked moments, he never tried to flee. We worked through each moment as it came.

And as a reward, I blew him in the Escalade.

"But..."

He cuts me off with a kiss that effectively melts me. Makes me shut up.

"You're mine," he says against my lips. "And I'm keeping you."

CHAPTER THIRTEEN

Grayson

After I made my proclamation that Soren was mine, he didn't argue anymore.

Did I think that was it?

That he suddenly believed me?

No, I wasn't that naive. I would simply have to show him every day for the rest of my life that I meant every word. The exchange must have exhausted us both because when we woke, it was to his alarm.

I hated it when he went back to work because I no longer had his undivided attention. But I couldn't be selfish. People needed him far more than I did. I could live with it because his nights were always mine.

But I didn't think I could wait anymore. For six weeks we explored each other's bodies until we knew them better than our own. But he never let us go all in. He never even let me push a finger inside of him. After our conversation, I think I understood why. He thought our time was finite. Perhaps, he would've never crossed that line. But now we've reached a precarious understanding.

After he shut the alarm off, he pulled me back into his arms, but with a mission in mind, I push him down. I kiss down his body, making him squirm. Little noises of appreciation slip from his mouth. The lower I go, the louder he becomes until he is moaning endlessly as I tongue his hard length before swallowing him whole.

When I was eventually able to take him in my throat, I doubt I had ever felt prouder. I also discovered that I enjoyed it as much as he did, at times coming hands-free merely from sucking him down my throat until he filled me.

But this time, I have another destination in mind. When I pull off, he grabs for me, but I entwine our fingers, holding them captive as I fondle his balls in my mouth, loving the feel, the taste of him where his essence was the strongest. I mouth his taint, making him jerk before I lathe the flat of my tongue against his tight hole.

"Oh yes, that's it right there, baby."

I smile, loving his words as much as his taste. I doubt I'd ever get enough of him.

But when I pushed my tongue inside, he pulled away. I tried to chase after him, but he was quicker than I could've imagined. Suddenly, I am trapped beneath him.

"Wha?" I ask stupidly.

"You can't do that, Gray."

My name was a bucket of ice water to my heated system.

"You don't have my permission to penetrate me."

Now, I'm really confused.

"But I thought you liked that. I thought you were a bottom."

A power bottom, but a bottom, nonetheless.

"I am, but you still need to ask first."

I smirk. "Fine, can I have your ass?"

"No, you may not."

My smile drops. "But why?"

"I won't cross that final line until your parents know that we're together."

And I thought his earlier words were a shock to the system.

I struggle beneath him. He reluctantly moves to let me up. I once again find myself pacing his spacious room.

Who the hell needs this much space?

I do.

I'm not sure how many passes I make before I finally stop in front of him where he's sitting on the edge of the rumpled bed. With sheets that stink of us and our non-penetrative lovemaking.

Focus, Grayson!

"Are you forcing me out of the closet?"

He smirks, which aggravates me to no end, even if I find it endearing.

"You can say no. I'd never force you to do anything."

"Ha!" I shake my head in exasperation. "But you'll manipulate me, offer me an ultimatum. There's little difference."

He gracefully pulls to his feet, and for a moment I forget my anger as I take in his tan, leanly muscled frame. I shake myself out of my stupor when he tries to pull me into his arms.

"Nope. No touching."

We both know I'm a sucker for his skin against mine. I'd probably agree to anything in his arms.

He huffs. "Baby, it's not only for your benefit. Yes, it mostly is, I want you to be free in every sense. But your mom is my dearest friend, the only person I love more than her is you."

We both freeze… neither of us has said the L word before. And he just said it like it was the most obvious thing in the world.

"You love me?" I squeak.

This time I can't stop him when he pulls me close.

"Of course, I love you. Falling for you was both the easiest and the hardest thing I've ever done."

It feels a bit cheap now, but I can't not say it back. "I love you, too."

"I know."

I laugh. "Thank you, Han Solo."

He pulls away looking confused.

I wave it away. "Never mind. It's a nerd thing."

I lean in and rub my cheek against the soft hairs on his chest as I consider what he wants. Eventually, I come to the realization that he was right. I don't want to keep sneaking around. Even though they haven't been the best parents, they deserve to know.

Finally, I relent. "Fine, I'll come out to my parents."

He kisses my forehead, reverently.

"Thank you, baby."

***

The following night we have dinner with my parents. Deja vu hits me right in the chest as I enter the gigantic dining room. Rather than take the seat next to my mother, I sit beside Soren. If my parents find this odd, they don't show it, or say anything. But that does nothing to relieve my nerves.

I feel like a live wire. Shivers relentlessly shoot through my veins. My fingers drum over the table as my knee jumps up and down. Until a warm hand clasps my thigh, running a soothing thumb under my shorts until my body eases enough to be still.

I pick up my fork but promptly drop it. I try a few times before I just give up and bury my hands in my lap. With the table hiding his movements, Soren takes a hand and clasps them. When I look up, he's giving pointed glances at my parents, who are already looking at us.

I get the gist; he wants me to spit it out.

I open my mouth several times to do just that, but each time nothing comes out.

My mother is the one to break the silence. "Grayson, are you alright?"

Nope!

Not in the slightest.

But some things are like Band-Aids. It's better to rip it off all at once rather than one hair at a time.

So, with every bit of courage I have, I rush out. "I'm gay, and Soren is my boyfriend."

I wait with bated breath for the inevitable. The fear, the anger, the soul-crushing disappointment.

What I get instead is this: My parents look at each other and smile before they breathe out one word…

"Finally."

CHAPTER FOURTEEN

Soren

(Six Months Prior)

When I moved away eleven years ago, I fully expected my lifelong friendship with Caroline to wither and die. I had been incredibly ignorant to believe my tenacious bestie would ever let me go.

We'd been through everything together. From my coming out, to her budding relationship with that idiot Jacob, to her pregnancy. I may not have agreed with everything that came to pass after Grayson was born, but I still supported her. After all, that's what friends are for.

Through thick and thin we've stayed together. I even moved to Kansas City, which I thought was two steps up from hillbilly country. It didn't matter that I was wrong, I would've done anything for her.

But then when I was offered the head of reconstructive surgery at San Francisco General Hospital and Trauma Center, it was an offer I knew I couldn't refuse. Even if it took me halfway across the country, away from the only person who truly meant anything to me.

Of course, she was understanding, even pushing me to accept when I questioned the merit of leaving the home I had learned to love. But I did, and I never regretted it for a moment.

And not a day went by where I didn't talk to her by text, phone, or FaceTime. It still wasn't enough; I miss her like a severed limb. There are not enough visits to make up for the time away.

When her lovely face pops up on my phone screen, my smile is ear to ear.

She chuckles. "Why are you so smiley? Did you meet someone?"

This question is a constant in her arsenal. She's never hidden the fact that she worries about my relationship status. But nobody could ever compare to her. It's not that I wanted her physically, but that didn't stop me from comparing her to every man I met, and I found them all wanting. Only worth a night or two before it was time to move on.

"I have better news," I hedge.

She crosses her arms over her chest, giving me her patented, 'I'm waiting,' face. "So, spit it out."

I huff. "You take away all my fun." She only waits. "I got a new job."

Her eyes widen because I don't know how many times I've told her how much I love my job here in San Francisco. While that may be true, nothing can stop this gnawing ache from missing her.

"Where at? A different hospital in Northern California?"

"Nope," I shake my head. "At KU Med."

She jerks back. "Here?"

I laugh. "No, in Katmandu. Of course there."

Her eyes widen in wonder. "Are you serious? You're coming home?!"

My smile grows impossibly larger. "I'm coming home, sweetheart."

We go on to discuss house hunting, and if I should rent one of those temporary apartments before she blurts out. "You should stay here. It's not like we don't have plenty of room."

That would be perfect except for one thing. The elephant in the room that we've always tiptoed around, but there's no avoiding it if I'm to stay with them for any period of time.

"What about Grayson?" I ask meekly.

She rolls her eyes, but I don't miss the concern spreading across her features.

"I mean he usually sticks to his room," she admits sheepishly.

Then we get into the only argument we ever have. Dr. Caroline Rhodes is a wonderful human being in almost every way, but she's a miserable mother. Something she's admitted to several times.

As we go back and forth, she suddenly blurts. "If you know so much better than me, why don't you put your money where your mouth is?!"

I'm taken aback, both by her tone and her statement. "Are you serious?"

"As a heart attack, Soren. For years, you've given your unsolicited opinion. Well, here's your chance to prove it. And while you're at it, why don't you seduce him."

I tear back in utter shock. "What the fuck, Caro?!"

She shrugs unrepentant. "What? It's not like we didn't know he's had the biggest crush on you."

"Yeah, but he's your kid."

She looks at me with all seriousness. "He's not a child anymore, he's twenty-three. More than old enough to make his own choices, and my money says he'd pick you."

"And the fact that I'm old enough to be his father doesn't bother you?"

"Pfft!" She waves my concern away like it's a bothersome gnat. "You could never be confused with his father. Plus, don't think I haven't seen the lust in your eyes when I've shown you pictures in the last few years."

My face heats because she's right. Her son grew up to be an amazing-looking man. The perfect mix of both his parents, who are attractive in their own right.

I need to change the subject, so I backtrack. "So, you want me to break him out of his shell and the closet?"

She considers it shortly before nodding. "That's exactly what I want."

"And what's in it for me?"

She snorts, and I can't help but smirk because obviously.

"Well, when you put it that way... but none of this bothers you?"

She sobers. "I may have fucked up as a mother every step of the way, but it doesn't take away how much I love my son. I want him to be happy. I want you to be happy. And maybe, just maybe, you can find that together."

Fuck!

What can I say to that?

With little other choice, I reluctantly agree.

CHAPTER FIFTEEN

Grayson

I sit frozen in my seat after Soren and my mother finish explaining their plan to seduce me. I should feel sick. It makes the most sense, but all I feel is this strange overwhelming sense of wonder.

Not only did my parents know I was gay, but they knew how I felt about Soren. My parents set me up with a man twice my age.

What kind of Twilight Zone am I living in?

But then I remember the life I had before Soren, or the lack of one. At least not one worth living.

Of course, I'm confused. I should be angry. Not only at my mother for planning this behind my back, but at Soren for agreeing to it.

Then, it hits me. I turn to find him already staring at me, nerves radiating from his pores.

"Did you only do it as a favor to my mother?"

He reaches for me, but I shove my hands beneath my thighs, making it clear I don't want to be touched.

He sighs, making pointed glances at my parents, who from my peripheral, I see studying us like ants under a magnifying glass.

My father is the first to rouse from his stupor turning to my mother. "Caroline, why don't we go check on dessert?"

She turns a confused expression his way. "We didn't make dessert."

He rolls his eyes, a common occurrence. "Then perhaps we should find something."

It takes her a moment before understanding dawns. "Oh yes. I wouldn't mind a little something sweet."

They both stand and my father practically drags his wife from the room.

After a drawn-out moment, I turn back to the man by my side who appears contrite.

"I know it's all a little fucked up," he admits.

I snort. "Ya think?!"

"There's something I need you to understand about me and your mother. I know you're aware that we've been close for most of our lives, but it's a little more complicated than that. When I came out at fifteen, my parents disowned me, and Caroline's family took me in. I've always loved her like a sister. I owe her so much, there's nothing she couldn't ask of me."

"Including seducing her only son."

He nods stiltedly. "I know she hasn't been the best mom, that she's never worn her heart on her sleeve, but you must know how much she loves you. She was so worried about you, and she felt like she had reached a point of no return. All she wanted was for you to be happy."

That's when something occurs to me. "She wanted you to be happy, too."

He looks at me blankly.

"She did this for you as much as she did it for me."

He considers my words carefully. "Yeah, I think you're right about that. When she first asked, I was astounded, but the more I considered it, the more sense it made. I knew about your crush, probably before you did. I thought it was adorable, but I never considered it anything more than puppy love. I almost agreed to do this on a whim, not thinking I would follow through with it. But then the day I arrived, I caught you waiting to see me. The way you looked at me caught my interest... I knew you had grown into this gorgeous man, but seeing you in person I realized I had underestimated the attraction I'd feel. I wanted you from the first moment I stepped into this house two months ago. The more time we spent together I realized it was so much more. I've never found anyone I wanted to spend time with outside of a quick fuck. Not until you."

This time when he reaches for me, I give him my hand, his relief is potent. I know I shouldn't give in this easily. What they did was wrong in so many ways, but how can I look this gift horse in the mouth?

This, right here, is everything I've always wanted since I was eight years old.

So, what if my parents paved the way?

I tug on his hand, making him smirk as he leans in to press soft lips against mine in a chaste kiss.

"Take me home, Dr. Delgado, so I can make love to you."

We don't bother saying goodbye to my parents.

"They'll forgive our rudeness," Soren mutters against my mouth.

He pulls away reluctantly before dragging me out of the house as if the hounds of hell are on our heels. Or more likely, the needs that have been building since we first laid eyes on each other since his return.

He breaks every speeding law on the short drive that still feels like an eternity. As soon as we're out of the car, his mouth is on mine where it belongs. Where I hope it'll always belong.

We're barely through the door when we start ripping articles of clothing off. Fabric tears and buttons fly as our hunger for each other erases any kind of nuance or civility.

As we get each other naked, we rush toward the stairs, practically crawling up each step until we reach the top, and he's laid out on top of me.

"We can't do it here," he grumbles. "I want our first time in our bed."

Oh God, he said *our* bed, not his. It's the first time he's said something that equates to any kind of permanency.

With renewed vigor, I keep him in my arms and rise to my feet.

He gasps. I'm betting he didn't realize how strong I am. Hell, I'm not sure I did either. But for him, I think I could rise to any occasion... literally.

I chuckle to myself.

"I can't imagine what you find amusing right now," he mumbles unhappily.

My smile grows as I take in his annoyed expression. "Of course I'm amused. This is the happiest moment of my life."

Yes, I'm young. Yes, I've lived inside of a box for most of those years. Most of them haven't been that great, but I still managed to find my happiness. I'm a big believer in making yourself content. That you'll never find true joy with someone else unless you find it within yourself.

And believe it or not, I did find that. I never dreamed that I would ever find love in my life. I never knew to dream for more. I knew I wanted Soren, but I never thought I'd have him. And when it became a reality, I was suddenly filled with a new dream. The kind that filled me with hope and effervescence I never expected for myself. And now that I have it, I'm never letting it go.

So, yes. I have had many happy moments in my life. They may not compare to others, but they meant a lot to me. So, saying this is the happiest is pivotal, a time I will treasure until my dying breath.

When my mind wanders back to the present, I find Soren staring at me. There's wonder in his eyes and the biggest smile splitting his face.

"God, I love you!"

My eyes blur with tears as my heart expands, almost painfully by how much I love this man

"I love you, too."

Everything slows down as we cherish every second that follows.

Our kisses are long and drawn out, tasting each other, savoring every tiny aspect. Our hands are lazy as we map each other's bodies. His muscles are a little more defined, with more hills and valleys to explore.

His body is hairier, thicker across his pecs that I enjoy resting my cheek against before it thins down his abdomen. I enjoy licking his happy trail as it leads me to heaven. The hair is there, too, but maintained and manicured, so it perfectly frames his cock.

His dick is a little longer than mine but thinner, the crown more purple than red, resembling a mouthwatering plum. But he tastes better, reminding me of a combination of the sea and earth at the same time. It's a taste I've never experienced before, and I doubt I'll ever grow tired of it. If he doesn't come in my mouth, I lick it off wherever it lands, savoring every drop.

As I dip my tongue into his slit, he arches up off the bed, a guttural moan falling from his lips like rain, natural and fruitful. I tongue him thoughtfully, taking my time to taste and feel every texture of his shaft. At times, I nibble gently or lap at him like a kitten would with a saucer of milk until he's straining, fisting the sheets as he begs for more.

But I don't, not yet. I'm beginning to understand why he's enjoyed playing with me, drawing out my pleasure. Not because I enjoy his suffering, but because I'm loving my exploration, and I don't want it to end.

I don't know how much time passes. His body is covered with sweat, and he's quivering as he glares at me with desperation.

"I'm begging you Gray, please."

I smirk. Perhaps, I do like making him suffer. Turn around is fair play, after all.

But instead of quenching his thirst, I lick him from tip to stem before I begin offering his big, heavy testicles the same attention. His balls, unlike his bush, are bare. I'm assuming waxed. It's a lovely contrast to the rest of him, I love the feel of that slick, velvety skin on my tongue. Sucking one, then both, feels indulgent like I'm a kid in a candy store.

As I suck, I bury my nose in the hair here, the smell so strong and musky and just all him. I lose myself in the bliss of these activities, barely feeling the strain as he tugs at my hair.

Eventually, I rise from the heaven of his body to gaze over every hill and valley until our eyes clash.

He's looking worse for wear, his blue eyes crazed, his chest heaving as he fights for his next breath.

"Fuck me, Gray. You're killing me!"

He tries valiantly to pull me up his body, but we're both learning I'm stronger than I look. And right now, there's only one thing that I want.

"Do I have your permission now?"

Confusion crosses him.

"Permission to penetrate you," I explain.

Understanding dawns like a wrecking ball to the gut.

With wide eyes, he nods as he stops trying to pull me on top of him. He reaches for the drawer of his nightstand, clumsily pulling out the lube and a condom. I throw the lube to the bed as I hold the condom up.

"Do I have to use this?"

He considers it. "I had my last check-up a month ago, and I'm clean."

It's answer enough because we both know that I am. I toss the condom away.

"Good, because I want to fill this ass, and then watch it slowly leak down your crack. After I've filled you, I want to watch you walk around as my seed drips down your legs."

He shivers at my words, his eyes glaze over with lust.

"Do it," he whispers.

I keep our gazes trapped as I push his legs up where he holds them against his chest.

"Mmm, I love how bendy you are."

He doesn't have time to reply as I grasp his lower cheeks and pull him open. His hole is a shiny pink pucker, also free of hair like his balls. It's mouthwatering, and I can't stop myself from falling on it as a man starved.

His taste is like his seed but deeper, darker, and wholly addictive. With the tip of my tongue, I explore every wrinkle eliciting mews of pleasure. Only when I've had my fill do I flatten my tongue, lapping at him until his hole is soaked, creating an easy path for when I finally dip my tongue inside. I'm careful at first as I work it past his tight heat before I shove as deep as I can, making him jerk up and cry out.

"Oh, fuck yes!"

I smile into his ass as I take turns pushing my tongue in and out and sucking deeply. Good god, I'm pretty sure I could come just like this as my hard length digs into the mattress. But when that thought begins to become a reality I reluctantly pull away.

Kneeling between his wide-spread thighs I grab the lube and slowly dribble the viscous liquid over his tightening balls. Avidly watching it drip between each testicle as it leaks down his crack. I also watch his reaction, and I'm not sure who's enjoying this more. His face is so slack with desire, he's practically putty in my hands.

With little patience and this need to join him, I begin fingering his opening now slick with both lube and my spit. I press the pad of my thumb against his pucker, looking up at him for permission. He only nods before I slowly push inside.

Goddam, he's so hot and tight that my cock jerks in anticipation.

How the fuck will I ever last?

I'm sure I'll blow as soon as the tip's inside.

With that thought, I firmly grasp my base tight, perhaps in vain, trying to hold off my consuming need.

I slowly thrust my thumb, once, twice before he's begging for more. I pull out before pressing two fingers inside, my digits strangling. I'm barely able to pull them apart as I scissor them.

This may be my first time, but I've become a porn expert since we began. As soon as I knew Soren was a possibility, I consumed everything I could find about taking a man's ass. How to prepare him and please him. I may be a virgin, but I was certain I could do this, that I could give him pleasure.

And by the look on his slack, obscenely desirous face, that certainty is cemented.

I lean forward to glue my mouth to his. Hungry tongues and teeth both work together and against each other as we battle for domination. But when I push in a third finger, I know I've won the battle as he goes slack beneath me. As he accepts whatever I'm willing to dish out. Which is everything.

He's practically humping my fingers when the fight in him returns. "Fuck me, Gray. Please. For God's sake fuck me already."

I smile against his lips. "No need to bring God into this."

But I finally give him what he wants. I pull away, back onto my haunches as I grease my length with a good amount of lube. I watch his beautiful face as I lazily fist myself before notching my crown against his pulsing opening.

"I love you so much."

Then I'm sliding inside with ease, all the way to the hilt, and we both sigh in relief and pleasure. He's everything I've ever wanted and more. So tight, so hot and we fit together perfectly. Like puzzle pieces. Like we were made for each other.

I'm so lost in this perfection that I forget why we're here. My mind eventually clears of sparkles and fairy dust to find him smirking at me.

"I need you to move, baby."

We both laugh until I do move. Those chuckles quickly turn into moans and groans as we each find our pleasure. For me, it's immediate because I've been sucked into heaven. His is found when I switch angles and find that magical spot inside him.

I know the exact moment because he throws his head back with a long, drawn-out groan.

Also, because he begins repeating. "Right there! Don't stop!"

I don't. I keep hitting it with renewed vigor and purpose. The desire to come has become all-consuming with the need to bring the love of my life pleasure.

His straining cock is standing up at attention, precum soaking his length, pooling around his base as it leaks down to where we're joined, only adding to how good this feels.

I begin to reach for him, intent on making him come when he slaps me away.

"No, I'm gonna come. I want to come from your dick alone."

With renewed fervor, I fight to give him that. Moving my gaze between where I'm pushing into him, his straining cock, and his gorgeous face. My love for him grows until nothing else exists but him... us. The rest of the world simply fades away until we're the only thing that's real.

Animalistic grunts, the slapping of skin against skin, and the squeaking mattress encompass our bubble as we both speed toward completion. It's no doubt the most beautiful sight I've ever seen when ribbons of cum shoot from his tip, striping his heaving chest. His luscious lips open on a scream.

I fall on him, my mouth swallowing my name as my hips brutally slam into him. The pleasure begins slowly, gradually building until it completely encompasses every molecule of my body. Then it explodes, my orgasm raining down on me until there's nothing left but every good feeling I've ever felt combined.

Slowly but surely, my body comes back together, and I find myself cradled in the warmth and love of Soren's body. His arms and legs are wrapped around me as my still hard dick remains buried deep inside him.

I look up, his features no doubt mirroring mine with total gratification.

"Was it everything you hoped for?"

I scoff at him. "Did you not see me disappear in a blast of ecstatic dust?"

He laughs long and hard making him tighten around me. We both gasp as I begin to move again. He doesn't complain, not once, as I take him repeatedly through the night and into the wee hours of the morning.

We make love until we're both puddles of pleasure, until our hunger for food and the need to pee finally pull us from the haven of our bed.

With great pleasure, I watch as my fantasy comes to fruition as my cum slips from the deep recess of his ass as it drips down his long, muscular legs.

EPILOGUE

Soren

Even though it became my greatest dream, I never quite lost the dread that hung over my head that Grayson would eventually leave me. He's one of the most beautiful men I've ever seen, and as I helped crack his shell, as I watched him ease his way into society, the surety of that grew.

It was a double-edged sword to help free him from his prison. I wanted nothing but happiness for him, but I hated when everyone began to see what I always knew. Not only is he aesthetically pleasing, but he's brilliant. A beautiful mind, if you will. He's giving and sweet-natured and so charming he woos everyone he meets.

Once he broke out of his shell, once the shyness fell away like shedding his old skin, he became this man that drew everyone to him. Me more than anyone else. I thought I had loved him five years ago, not long before he first made love to me. But as time passed, I realized that had been the tip of the iceberg. Before I knew it, he had taken over all of me, until I didn't exist without him.

A single glance feels like the greatest spotlight. It heats my cold soul from the inside out until I'm radiating, shining like the sun. I feel like that all the time because he looks at me almost constantly.

The only time we're apart is the long dreary hours of our jobs. As the head of reconstructive surgery, that time is unfortunately plentiful, but he's also busy now. Two years ago, he was able to accept a professor gig at UMKC. So, sadly our jobs take up far too much time, but every other second is spent together.

Eventually, Gray proved to me that there was no place that he would rather be. That was cemented the day he dropped to one knee.

It was in the middle of Loose Park as we walked our matching corgis Eros and Psyche. I'm certain I looked as confused as the dogs as he dropped. Understanding only dawned as he pulled a small, red velvet box from his pocket.

I gasped, a girly giggle slipping from my lips in a most unusual fashion. But I can't deny how giddy I am as I bounce on my toes.

Our dogs join me as we look expectantly at the man we all adore.

"Soren this has been a long time coming. I've wanted you for more years than not, so for me, this is the most obvious culmination. You're my everything; my greatest cheerleader, my best friend, and the only lover I will ever want or need. But it's not enough. I want it all. I want to be your partner in life, I want to be your lawful husband. Would you give me that honor? Will you agree to marry me?"

My head is nodding so fervently, I know it'll hurt later, but I don't care. I fall to my knees as I pull him into my body where he comes easily, happily. I palm his cheeks, and his neck before carding my fingers through his soft dark hair.

My lips caress every inch of his face, kissing each eyelid, nose, cheeks, and jaw before settling against his mouth.

Without drawing away, I tell him all the ways I'm saying yes.

"I didn't know romantic love existed for me until I had you back in my life. I watched you grow up from afar. Found it adorable how often you hid from me, but all the while I saw you anyways. I always saw you. Back then I had no idea what you would come to mean to me, but I thank my lucky stars every minute of every day when I figured out that you were mine. I'm sorry I didn't realize that I was yours sooner, that I was stupid enough to believe that you could ever love anyone else. Never again, baby. Never again will I not believe in all of you, in all of us. The answer is yes, a thousand times yes."

We fell on each other, making out in the middle of a busy park as our dogs yipped and jumped all over us.

And today as I walk toward him on an aisle made on the beach, surrounded by everyone we love, and the most beautiful surroundings nature could offer by the Pacific Ocean, I know none of it matters.

It all simply fades away until there's nothing but Gray and Soren.

We repeat after the officiant as we promise to love and to hold until death do us part. But it's not enough. I lean into him, my mouth against the shell of his ear.

"I don't just want your life, my love, I want the after too. I never want to let you go. Even when time and the universe disappear, our love will endure."

Then we kiss long before the officiant announces us married.

But I suppose we were always meant to break a few rules.

Anything for each other.

THE END

ABOUT D.L. HOWE

Born and raised in Kansas City, Kansas. The proud mother of an amazing son and two crazy cats. When I'm not reading and writing, I'm working with kids with mental health.

THERE ALL ALONG

by Darley Collins

CHAPTER ONE

Josie

"Try not to be a Jealous Josie tonight."

Jealous Josie. The old nickname had Josie Heiner wrinkling her nose. "Do you have to call me that?"

"Oh, Josie, really." Her mother rolled her eyes before turning back to the bags of take out that lined the kitchen counter. "I don't know why you make such a fuss over something so trivial."

"Trivial. Right." Twenty years of having her family taunt her with that awful nickname was 'trivial.' She'd been five the first time someone called her Jealous Josie. It had been Christmas and Aunt Beckett had just given her twin brother Kyle a gift certificate for a year's worth of dance lessons. Josie had received a little cat shaped purse. According to family lore, Josie had burst into tears and started blubbering about how it wasn't fair since she was the one who wanted to be a ballerina. She may or may not have accused Aunt Beckett of loving Kyle more. The one absolute in the whole thing was Aunt Beckett saying "don't be Jealous Josie" before telling her to look inside the little purse; there had been tickets to see Cats on Broadway. It had been the perfect gift for a girl obsessed with dance and felines. Jealous Josie had stuck though.

"I'm just saying..." Ruth Heiner glanced over shoulder, her blue eyes boring into Josie's. "Kyle said he had something important to tell us. If it's what I think it is... well... we don't need Jealous Josie making an appearance."

"Oh. My. God." Shaking her head, Josie shot her mother a disgusted look before stomping towards the living room. Despite what her mother thought, she didn't sit around sulking every time something exciting happened in Kyle's life. She was happy for him, cheering him on the loudest.

In fact, while everyone else had been busy trying to talk Kyle out of opening his own dance studio, Josie had been at the bank co-signing on the business loan. She'd even helped him plan the perfect proposal. Would a jealous person do that? Most of her family seemed to think so. They didn't seem to understand that a person could be happy for someone else while bemoaning their own failures over a pint of mint chocolate chip; which is exactly what Josie was going to do after Kyle dropped his engagement bomb.

'You are so going to owe me,' Josie thought, picking up a silver framed photo of Kyle and her at their high school graduation.

A faint smile curved her mouth upward. They looked almost identical with their long blonde hair and winged eyeliner. Kyle had left three days later for a dance intensive in New York. When he returned, his hair was shorter and he'd grown at least five inches taller. He'd also returned with a determination to open his own dance studio. The peel of the doorbell startled her back to the present. She carefully set the picture back in its place and reluctantly walked over to the front door. It was too early for Kyle and Jonas, which left good ole Aunt Beckett. Rising on her tiptoes, Josie peered through the peephole and let out a groan. There was no mistaking the perfectly coiffed silver hair.

Aunt Beckett.

And, Josie gulped, the old woman had a death grip on a violently shaking pet carrier. "Please don't be another cat."

"I can hear you, Josie" Aunt Beckett wheezed, her heavily made up face moving closer to the peephole. Josie took a faltering step backwards. "Might as well open the door... got a little something for ya."

A groan vibrated in Josie's throat. It was definitely a cat, probably a special needs one knowing Aunt Beckett. The seventy-five year old woman had a soft spot for cats most people wouldn't attempt to take on, which wouldn't be a problem if she took care of them herself; instead, she liked to pawn them off on Josie. "I can't take another cat, Aunt Beckett," she said in place of a greeting as she swung the front door open.

"What's one more?" The old lady wedged past, leaving the scent of cigarettes and expensive perfume in her wake. "Found the little guy in the parking lot of that quack your mother makes me go to for the diabetes."

"Dr. Thomas isn't a quack," Ruth called from the kitchen. "He's one of the best doc-"

"He's a quack. A bossy one at that. Always trying to tell me what I can and can't eat. I'm old. Let me eat and die in peace." The wrinkles around Aunt Beckett's watery eyes deepened as her lips tipped into a smug grin. Without warning, she thrust the pet carrier into Josie's hands. "Named him Derek after the quack. He's only got one ear and can't eat anything with chicken or he gets the runs."

"Aunt Beckett, no. I told you the last time I can't-"

"One ear, Josie. He has one ear and gets the shits if he's not fed the right food. Ain't nobody going to adopt an ugly cat with stomach trouble."

Arguing was futile. Once Aunt Beckett decided something that was that, and she had decided years ago that cats were the perfect distraction for whenever something life altering went on in Josie's life. The first had been a Cornish Rex named Muffin. He had been bald with saucer-like eyes and giant ears. She hadn't wanted much to do with the poor thing at first, but after Dirk the Jerk Jennings dumped her for some cheerleader two towns over, Muffin became the main man in her life. Cats two and three had been a bonded pair of sisters named Pancake and Pickle, whose owner had passed away; keeping them from terrorizing Muffin had distracted her the summer Kyle was gone to New York. Number four, Cupcake, had been a straight up guilt trip. *'Poor Cupcake is old and fat. Ain't nobody going to adopt an old, fat cat.'* Even her mother had chimed in. *'Poor thing, at her age she deserves to live out the rest of her days in comfort, not locked in some plastic box.'* Now, she had a parking lot cat that was missing an ear and had food allergies. Great. "This is it. I meant it. No more."

"If you say so." Aunt Beckett trudged over to the sofa and flopped down. "When's your brother getting here? Soon, I hope. It's bingo night."

"Not soon enough." The sooner Kyle and Jonas arrived, the sooner Josie could leave. She'd stick around for the congratulations, endure a few more of her mother's Jealous Josie jabs, and then she would use the built-in escape Aunt Beckett had provided for her by claiming her new cat needed to go home. Kyle would understand, he knew what their mother was like. Knowing him, he had his own exit strategy in place and would show up at her apartment with hard pear cider and the wedding planning binder that Josie was certain he and Jonas had already started.

Eyes narrowed, Aunt Beckett leaned forward. "Your mama isn't cooking is she?" Josie shook her head. "Thank the lord for small favors."

Small favors were all well and good if they were talking about her mother's lack of cooking skills, but what Josie needed was a big favor. Scratch that, what Josie needed was a miracle. She needed her mother to stop comparing her life with Kyle's, or at least pretend to accept that Josie wasn't jealous every time her brother had something good happen in his life. "She had me pick up an order from Alfredo's."

"Pasta." The word spat out of Aunt Beckett's mouth, her lips curling into a sneer.

"Pasta." It was on the tip of Josie's tongue to remind her aunt that at least it wasn't her mother's leathery pot roast and slimy green beans, but she didn't. Aunt Beckett knew what the alternative was; the remark was still made.

"I suppose it beats that meatloaf surprise she tried to kill us with the last time." The elderly woman groaned as she slowly rose from the sofa. "Guess I better check on her, make sure she isn't adding anything to that overpriced pasta she bought."

"You do that," Josie muttered. Ignoring the bickering coming from the kitchen, she dropped to her knees next to the carrier. The cat really was homely. Scars crisscrossed the peach fur; the worst of them near where an ear should have been. "Poor baby," she whispered, her heart melting. Aunt Beckett had been right, his grotesque appearance combined with digestive issues weren't exactly selling points to prospective adopters. *Damn you Aunt Beckett.* "Mom," she called out, "I'll be right back."

Ruth popped her head out of the kitchen. "Don't you even think about leaving me alone with that woman." Josie gestured towards the kennel. "Dear God," her mother whispered, "another one?"

"Yup." Her mother let out a sigh before gesturing towards the door; the hurry back was unspoken but still loud and clear. There was an unspoken rule in the family about not leaving Ruth and Aunt Beckett alone together. None of them knew why the pair bickered so much, just that it dated back to when Ruth was a child.

Living in the apartment above her parents garage had a few perks, the most obvious one being she could make hasty escapes; quick returns as well if her mother sent her a passive aggressive text. The downside was she couldn't blame traffic for any delays, which meant she settled the newest member of her cat tribe in the bathroom, blew kisses to the other four kitties, and was back in her mother's living room in under ten minutes. Just in time for Kyle and Jonas to walk through the door.

"I smell happiness," she teased, hugging her older brother by fifteen minutes. Her body stiffened when he volleyed back he smelled jealousy. She tried to pull away, only to have him hold her closer.

"I'm only playing," Kyle whispered, squeezing her tight before stepping back. "You don't have a jealous bone in your body. If anything, you're too giving and supportive."

Jonas murmured his agreement before pressing a kiss against her cheek. "Which is why I want to thank you for helping plan the most perfect proposal ever."

"No thanks needed." Throughout the course of her brother's three year relationship with Jonas, Josie had learned that 'thank you' was code for gift. A gift was the last thing she wanted; it would tarnish something she had done out of love. There was also the fact that, aside from Kyle, Jonas had terrible taste; it was why Josie had been enlisted to help with the proposal in the first place. "Seriously, just seeing the two of you getting your happily ever after is enough for me."

"We insist." The 'we', paired with the excited smile that spread across Jonas' face and the way Kyle wouldn't look at her, raised the hair on the back of Josie's neck. Whatever form of gratitude Jonas had cooked up, Josie had a feeling she was going to hate it. She wouldn't be able to decline either, not with her mother present; she'd become ungrateful Josie if she did. "My sister Robin married this ridiculously hot guy who comes from a huge family of ridiculously hot siblings."

"And," Kyle interjected, "Jonas has managed to get you an introduction to the hottest one of all!"

No. No. No. A blind date with some semi-relative of her future in law was worse than the yoga goat session she'd been gifted for her birthday. Only desperate people let their relatives, or in her case almost relative, set them up on a date. "Um." Her gaze darted back and forth between Kyle and Jonas. Excitement and expectation shone on their faces. For a split second, Josie almost gave in. What harm could come from one teeny, tiny blind date? Worst case scenario, she got a free meal. Then rationale sank in. There was no way she could say yes. If the date went south, like most blind dates were prone to doing, then she and 'the hottest one of them all' would never hear the end of it. That only left her with one option. "I have a boyfriend."

Kyle blinked. "You have a boyfriend?"

'Tell him it's a joke. The three of you will laugh it off and then you can firmly tell them you're not interested in Jonas' sister's brother in law or whoever this guy is.' The truth was on the tip of her tongue, ready to come out, only to falter when her mother and Aunt Beckett stepped into the living room. It was one thing to admit to lying about a relationship to Kyle, admitting to such a lie in front of her mother who was fixated on accusing her of being jealous all the time was another. "I have a boyfriend," she repeated.

"Since when?" Kyle demanded.

"Uh." She licked her lips, her mind searching for a time when Kyle had been busy. A busy Kyle was a forgetful Kyle. "Last month." It was perfect. His studio had put on a huge recital and for weeks he'd had to be reminded of things that didn't pertain to ballet, tap, or jazz. "I told you about him right before your recital."

"Are you sure?"

Before Josie could respond, Ruth let out a gasp. "Didn't Dirk Jennings move back here last month?" Aunt Beckett, the traitor, affirmed that Dirk the jerk had indeed moved back and he was the deadbeat father of three children by three different women. "Oh my God! Please tell me you're not dating him again."

Burying her face in her hands, Josie groaned inwardly. Dirk the jerk was the last person she would date, kids or no kids. He'd dumped her two days before prom for some Wesville cheerleader; baby mama number one if Josie remembered correctly. *'It isn't too late to say gotcha. Sure, your mom will use this as another reason to call you Jealous Josie and Aunt Beckett will find a litter of deformed kittens to drop on your doorstep, but at least they'll stop assuming you're desperate enough to rekindle things with Dirk the jerk.'* That just left

Kyle. Would he be understanding of what was probably the first real lie she had ever told him? *'He will,'* her internal voice insisted. *'He may be mad at first but Jonas will think it's hilarious. If Jonas laughs it off... and he will... then Kyle won't be able to resist laughing it off. In fact...'* Her internal dialogue came to a screeching halt. "What did you just say?"

"I said, I'm relieved." Kyle shot her a pointed look. "I was starting to worry you had given up or something."

Disbelief coursed through Josie. "Given up on what?" She inhaled sharply when Kyle muttered something about life and love. "Why would you think something like that?"

"I don't know Josie, maybe because you still technically live at home, you never date, and you have four cats."

"Well," their mother started. *'Please don't say it mom. Just this once keep your mouth shut.'* "Aunt Beckett brought her number five this evening."

"Jesus," Kyle whispered. "Five cats."

Ruth cleared her throat. "How about we leave Josie's cats alone and eat dinner before it gets cold."

"How about these two," Aunt Beckett gestured towards Jonas and Kyle, "announce they're getting married already so I can make it to bingo on time."

An uncomfortable silence hung in the room; heavy to the point of being stifling. Josie could almost hear her mother accusing her of ruining the night. Just when it felt unbearable, Kyle wrapped his arm around Jonas' waist. He pressed a gentle kiss to the taller man's cheek before turning towards the rest of the room with a smile. "Yes, Jonas and I are getting married. Now," he looked directly at Aunt Beckett, "go. Have fun showing those other old biddies how bingo is really played."

"Oh no she doesn't." Ruth scurried towards the front door, blocking her aunt's exit. "I didn't order all that food for nothing. We are going to sit down, eat, and celebrate. Including Aunt Beckett. I insist."

"And I *insist* on making it to bingo on time. Move it or lose it Ruthie." Josie could see her mother's nostrils flare, her blue eyes darkening with an unreadable emotion before her mother repeated her demand that they all sit down, eat, and celebrate. "Oh, for the love of..." Aunt Beckett rolled her eyes upward. "We all know you're going to throw some party or what not. I'll celebrate then."

"Listen here-" Ruth started, then sighed. "Fine. Go." She stepped away from the door. "I'll let you know when the party is." If reverse psychology had been the goal, it failed miserably. Aunt Beckett didn't have to be told twice. She shuffled out the door without so much as a goodbye. It took every ounce of Josie's willpower not to chase after the old woman and beg her to *'take me with you.'*

CHAPTER TWO

Josie

Dinner went the way Josie suspected it would. Her mother spent the majority of the evening fussing over Kyle and Jonas, asking about wedding plans and when would be a good time for an engagement party. For once, she couldn't even be bothered by her mother focusing on Kyle, the engagement was exciting news. At least it would have been if she hadn't lied about having a boyfriend. *'It was a lie of necessity,'* she reasoned. Was it though? Was creating a fictional boyfriend just to get out of a blind date really a necessity? Necessity or not, the lie had been told and her little fib had revealed a side of her brother she hadn't seen before. *'Stop dwelling on it. So, Kyle thinks you have too many cats. Big deal.* You *think you have too many cats.'* It wasn't the dick comment about her cats that bothered her, it was the way her brother seemed to think she had no life. *'Well...'* She scowled, shutting down the thought before it could continue. She had a life. Maybe it wasn't full of romance the way Kyle's was, but she had life. A life that now included a fake boyfriend.

'One thing is for sure, I can't be dumped *any time soon.'* Josie fought back a grimace as Kyle pulled her close for a goodbye hug. If he thought she had no life before the boyfriend lie, she could imagine what his opinion of her would be if she was 'dumped.' Poor Josie, all alone again with her cats, like that was a fate worse than death. Josie had watched too many of her friends jump into relationships out of fear of being alone. It was like they'd rather pretend they were happy with their serial cheaters than wait to find the right person.

"So," Ruth drawled once Kyle and Jonas were out the door, "care to explain that little boyfriend stunt you just pulled."

Well, poop. She should have known her mother would catch on. Ruth had always had a radar when it came to lying. Josie had hoped between her mother's favoritism and Kyle's engagement any suspicions would be overlooked. "What makes you think it was a stunt," she asked carefully. The smart thing would be to fess up and beg her mother to let her be the one to tell Kyle. "It's because I have no life right?"

"What?" Frowning, Ruth gave her an odd look. "Why on earth would you... oh. Kyle. He shouldn't have said that." Her frown deepened. "You know that has more to do with him than with you right?" Josie shrugged. "Well, it does. Kyle isn't like you... he doesn't know how to be alone. He equates happiness with being in love. And you..." Josie felt her body tense up. Here it came. Jealous Josie. "You know better. You learned early on there is more to life than being in a relationship."

This was a side of her mother that she had never seen before. She didn't know if she should embrace it or take Ruth's temperature. Better to embrace it. Even if it was short lived, she would be able to look back and say there was at least one moment where her mother understood her. "And yet I'm always jealous." She cringed as the words slipped out of her mouth. She'd wanted to avoid that topic. Jealous Josie always had a way of ruining things.

"Oh Josie, I really don't understand why you take that so seriously." And there it was. The dismissive mother who didn't take her feelings into consideration.

"Maybe to you." Josie started only to press her lips into a thin line when her mother insisted it was just a silly nickname. "It's not just a silly nickname. It is how most of the family sees me."

"Well, that's just not true." Ruth crossed her arms.

"It is true." Her frustration mounted as her mother shook her head. "Anytime something good happens for Kyle, I'm called Jealous Josie."

"That doesn't mean any of us actually think you're jealous of your brother."

"Then why say it?"

Ruth opened her mouth only to snap it shut. "I don't know. I guess we... I... thought it was funny. I didn't realize it actually bothered you." From the way her mother shifted around, Josie knew that her mother knew that wasn't the entire truth. She'd never made her feelings about Jealous Josie a secret. She'd told her mother over and over again she didn't like it. Yet, Ruth had persisted. What good would come from continuing to rehash it though? Not a darn thing. "Look, for the sake of moving forward, I'll try to make the effort to not call you that anymore." Now... back to this fake boyfriend business."

'And that is that,' Josie thought with an internal sigh. "All I ask is that you let me be the one to tell Kyle."

"Were you not listening when I said Kyle equates happiness to being in a relationship?" She'd been listening but she didn't know what that had to do with coming clean about her boyfriend lie. "You can't tell him the truth. It'll just cement his idea you're a lonely, cat lady who has no life."

"Then what do you suggest I do?"

Ruth smiled. "We find you a boyfriend. Or," the smile widened, "we find someone willing to pretend to be your boyfriend."

If only it were that easy. "And where are we going to find one of those?" There was no stopping her groan when Ruth said the dread words: dating app. "Do you even know of any legit dating apps?" Josie's experience with dating apps was limited to the hook ups her best friend Cristina partook in.

"Well, my friend Lori has met plenty of wonderful young men using this app called Cub Connect." Josie cringed inwardly. Her mother's best friend Lori was known for two things: her delicious cupcakes and her love for dating guys young enough to be her son. Crossing her arms, Josie waited for her mother to make the connection. Cougar. Cub Connect. It didn't take long. "You know," Ruth continued, her cheeks flushed, "maybe Cub Connect wouldn't be the best choice."

"Probably not," Josie agreed.

"Oh!" A smug smile twisted Ruth's lips into a smirk. "What about Love Buzz? Kyle met Jonas through Love Buzz."

Technically, Kyle had met Jonas when Jonas dropped his niece off for dance class. The fact that the two wound up romantically connecting when Kyle signed up for some speed dating event sponsored by a dating app was of little consequence. Plus, if Josie remembered correctly, Love Buzz was kind of expensive. She needed a short term fake boyfriend, not an overpriced subscription that left her open to crude messages from guys looking for a good time. "Maybe I can borrow one of Lori's cubs."

Ruth snorted. "Oh honey, you're not their type."

"You don't know that."

"You're young and broke."

Her mother had her there. "Well, I can't afford Buzz Love." And that was when her mother said the magic words: free trial. According to their website she would have 30 days to find out what the buzz was all about. If she wasn't drunk in love by then, their expert matchmakers would continue searching for her happily ever after for the low cost of $59.99 per month. "I can't believe I'm actually doing this." She buried her face in her hands. Maybe Kyle was right. Maybe her life had reached a point where people should be concerned. Normal twenty-five year olds didn't spend Friday nights setting up dating profiles with their mothers. *'There's always telling Kyle the truth and letting him set you up with Jonas' sister's brother-in-law.'* The fact that she found joining a dating app with her mother's help more appealing was disturbing. She hesitated for a moment and then handed her phone to her mother. "Here, let's just do it before I change my mind."

Half an hour later, accepting a pity date with Jonas' ridiculously hot sort of relative sounded really good. It had to be better than arguing with her mother over what to put in the dating app profile. Ruth insisted on telling the truth: *'I am a happily single cat mom who just needs a temporary fake boyfriend to get my brother off my ass.'* The more Josie dug her heels in, the more determined Ruth became. "Look," her mother waved her phone in Josie's face. "Even Lori agrees that you should just be honest. You'll attract the right person that way."

"You told Lori?"

"Don't worry, I told her I was asking for Aunt Beckett."

It was the perfect lie. Worst case scenario, Lori asked Aunt Beckett how her hunt for love was going. Aunt Beckett would tell her to buzz off and then call Ruth to complain about her weirdo friend. "Lori give 'Aunt Beckett' any other pointers?"

"We need to include the cats." A groan escaped Josie's lips before she could stop it. Her cats were what got her into this predicament to begin with. If her own brother saw her little furry babies as a sign she had no life, she could only imagine what strangers would think. "You want someone who's going to appreciate your little clowder." Her profile was going to be a real winner. Single cat mom of five looking for a fake boyfriend. Just seeing the words made her cringe. "Oh, and you need to post at least one bikini pic."

Tucking her lower lip between her teeth, Josie silently sat by as her mother filled in the rest of the profile. It was just easier. Plus, it was nice having her mother fixated on something in *her* life for once. The benefit of letting her mother take control was Ruth thought to add things Josie wouldn't have. Like cooking. Josie had inherited her mother's inability to cook but she could order take out like a pro. Or that she didn't mind watching football, so long as the guy she watched it with understood that by "watching football" she actually meant scrolling through funny cat videos while everyone else screamed at the television. "You're not really going to upload a bikini pic are you," she demanded when she realized her mother had finished her profile and was uploading images.

"It probably couldn't hurt, but no. That is where I draw the line. We want a nice guy willing to do a nice girl a favor...not some pervert who thinks you look hot in a string bikini." Ruth ducked her head, tapped on the screen a few more times, and then handed Josie back her phone. "There. It's done. With any luck the right guy will find your profile and we can turn your lie into a reality."

CHAPTER THREE

Josie

Either Josie had the worst luck ever, or online dating was a bigger cesspool than her and her mother had suspected. Maybe it was both. Whatever the case, her inbox seemed to attract perverts who thought nothing of sending dick pics or, worse, inviting her to meet them at some sleazy pay by the hour hotel. It was comical how quickly they ghosted her when her mother responded to their requests for her to send nudes by sending them pics of her hairless cat Muffin. Somehow, among the hairy balls and oh so romantic 'are you dtf' five semi-normal guys read her bio and were open to the idea of being a fake boyfriend; benefits not included. Part of her was skeptical, like what sort of guy swipes on a girl looking for a pretend relationship. The other part, the part who was still pissed about being accused of being a lonely cat lady with no life, prayed that at least one of the guys turned out to be legit.

Like Your_Mr_Right.

It was one of the cheesiest screen names Josie had ever come across; the sort that belonged to some putz with an arsenal of bad pick up lines. Instead, the guy's blurry profile picture suggested that he had an infinity for beanies, flannel shirts, and granola. Their chats consisted mostly of their mutual love of cats, the Chai tea at Delia's Coffee House, and families that wouldn't stay out of their love lives. If ever there was a reason to connect, it was over cats, Chai, and brothers who meant well. On screen, he seemed like the perfect fake boyfriend candidate, the kind of guy her mother said she would totally order take out for and force Kyle to back off on trying to introduce her to the younger brother of Jonas' brother-in-law.

Tugging on the too short hem of the light blue sundress her mother had picked out, Josie took a deep breath before entering Delia's. Meeting at the quaint little coffee shop had been Ruth's idea. It had seemed like a safe, logical choice for two strangers who loved Chai. The fact that Jonas' family diner was across the street and she could run over there for help if the guy turned out to be a creeper had also played a factor. A single girl meeting with a stranger she found on a dating app couldn't be too careful. Or so her mother said.

She scanned the crowded interior, looking for a dark haired man wearing a red t-shirt. There were two. Either of them could have been Your_Mr_ Right. One gave off a boy next door vibe; nice enough looking; with short dark curls and a few scraggly hairs on his chin that she guessed were meant to be a goatee. The other was what her best friend Cristina would call a grade A hottie. Everything about him screamed hot, sweaty sex in the back of a cab because you just couldn't wait to get home. Josie let her gaze linger for a moment before turning back to the first guy. Men who looked like sex on a stick did not troll for fake girlfriends online.

"Your_Mr_Right?"

Both guys glanced up. The hottie let out a snicker, but the boy next door's face lit up. "CatMom828?"

Hearing someone say her screen name out loud made her grimace. It had sounded so cute when her mother suggested it. Now it just sounded as cheesy as Your_Mr_Right. "Yup. That's me," she finally said. "I'm CatMom828." The Hot Guy let out another snicker. No doubt he found it all amusing, and she couldn't blame him. Two strangers with ridiculous screen names awkwardly introducing themselves in the middle of a coffee shop. "It's nice to meet you."

Your_Mr_Right's smile widened and he motioned for her toward the table where he had been sitting. "I hope it's alright, but I went ahead and ordered us both some Chai."

"Oh. Um. Thanks?" It was difficult to spit the words out. She reminded herself several of their conversations centered around how fantastic Delia's Chai was and how it was their go to order. Poor, clueless soul probably thought he was earning brownie points. "Just... maybe next time wait to order?" Hot Guy chuckled again. And again, she shot him a hard look. So, Your_Mr_Right made a dating no no; it didn't give sex on a stick the right to laugh.

"Shoot. You're right. I'm sorry." His face crumpled. "You're not going to leave now are you?"

Another soft laugh erupted from the guy a table away. Josie shot him yet another dirty look. "No," she reassured the man in front of her. Chai faux-pas aside, he seemed like a nice enough guy. Their online conversations had been friendly. "I'm Josie, by the way."

"Will. Not William, Willard, or," his lips curled up, "Wilbur." There was a story there. Josie could feel it. And, from the look on his face, Will (not William, Willard, or Wilbur) planned on telling on it. "I dated this girl in high school who used to call me Wilbur… you know after the pig in *Charlotte's Web*. I was sort of chubby back then and I guess she thought it was funny. It wasn't."

"I'm sorry," she said lamely, not knowing what else to say when he shot her an expectant look. She offered him a sympathetic smile. He took it as an invitation to spill out his whole life story. His mother had set up an account and chosen his screen name; something Josie could relate to. He had considered speed dating but the idea of that many rapid dates freaked him out, so he bailed before the event even started. His ex-wife had left him for a woman, but they shared custody of their three cats. And, last of all, he missed the girl who had called him Wilbur.

"Have you thought about looking her up," Josie suggested. It was counterproductive. Will was a nice guy. The sort of guy who would readily agree to be a fake boyfriend.

Will shook his head. "Not really. She's probably married with a kid or two by now."

"Maybe. Or," Josie leaned forward, "maybe she misses you too."

"You think so?" He looked at her with so much expectation in his eyes she didn't have the heart to say no, or question why he would want to reconnect with someone who nicknamed him after a pig. "You don't mind…" he gestured towards the door.

"Best of luck." Arms crossed, she rested her forearms on the table, and watched the most promising of the five hurry out. Back to square one, she thought. She picked up her phone to shoot off a text to her mother, letting her know Your_Mr_Right was a no-go.

"That was interesting."

Josie looked up to find Hot Guy staring at her, a slow grin stretching across his lips once he realized he had her attention. Her heart did a little flip. Hot guys rarely noticed her, let alone engaged in conversation. "It was something."

Blinking, Josie looked up to find the hottie staring at her, a slow grin stretching across his lips. Her heart did a little flip. Hot guys rarely noticed, let alone spoke to her. "It was something." Before she could say anything else a petite young woman with dark hair bound over and pulled out the empty chair across from him. It was just as well, Josie thought standing up. Guys like that were never interested in girls like her. When she caught him staring again, she gave a little wave and made her way out of the coffee shop.

CHAPTER FOUR

Josie

Love Buzz was full of crap. There was no rhyme or reason to the matches they suggested. Nor did there seem to be a way to report the perverts who kept invading her inbox. And the decent ones were snatched up quickly. She'd left her date with Your_Mr_Right determined to make it work with one of her other four candidates. What a joke that turned out to be. Two randomly disappeared. No thanks but no thanks, just there one minute and gone the next. The third had been nice enough to message her and wish her luck but he'd made a connection with another girl. That left her mother's selection. NahTNurse. The name alone was enough to make Josie cringe. Paired with a profile full of muscle flex pics and an intro that included Venice Beach as his favorite vacation spot, it had taken a lot of convincing. Her mother could claim his messages were sweet all she wanted but sweet men didn't choose screen names like NahTNurse or post pictures where they were slathered in baby oil. Ruth was insistent though. *'He's a nurse, Josie. A nurse! And look, he had a cat!'* There had been a random cat pic among the 'look at my oils abs' but Josie was pretty sure it was a stock photo. When she brought that to her mother's attention, Ruth brushed it off. *'All striped cats look the same.'* They didn't but saying so wasn't worth the argument.

'Maybe he is a nice guy. You never know.' The guy had given solid advice on which dermatologist to take Aunt Beckett to for the rash she'd picked up at bingo. Josie was going to cling to that, not the photos of oily muscles and potentially fake cat. Who knew, maybe

NahTNurse would turn out to be the perfect fake boyfriend. Doubtful, but miracles were known to happen. He'd also been a good sport about letting her decide where they would meet. Like last time, she went with Delia's. She told herself it was because she enjoyed the Chai and chocolate croissants, not some misplaced idea that the Hot Guy would be there again.

This time, Josie made a point of arriving first. Instinct drove her to the same table she had shared with Will. As luck would have it, Hot Guy was sitting at the table he had occupied the week before. "Not meeting Wilbur again, I hope," he joked when she was closer.

"No." Josie laughed, shaking her head. She shrugged out of the light weight cardigan she'd thrown on over yet another sun dress her mother had chosen, and draped it over the back of her chair. "You will be pleased to hear he made contact with his ex and they are meeting up this weekend."

"No kidding." He started to say more but abruptly fell silent.

"Damn girl, you're way hotter than that picture."

Eyes widening, Josie jerked her gaze away from 'Hot Guy' and stared up at a tall, redheaded man standing next to her table. Even if he hadn't been wearing the designated pink polo, Josie would have recognized him from his pictures. "NahTNurse?" A cough, followed by a snort of laughter came from the next table. *'Yeah, I know buddy. I feel the same.'*

"Yeah, baby, that would be me but you can call me Tanner." He yanked out the chair across from her and flipped it around before straddling it. "You need to do something about that profile, baby, it's false advertising." He wiggled his brows.

"It is?" There was nothing wrong with her profile. Everything about it, including the photos, were an honest representation of who she was. Her mother had made sure of that.

"Yeah. You're much sexier. When I read about all those cats and how you're needing a fake boyfriend I thought for sure you were going to be a porker who stole some hotties pic to lure in unsuspecting guys like myself." She was going to murder her mother. Murder her. "So, Josie," the way he said her name made her skin crawl, "I have one question for you."

"And what's that?" She didn't bother to hide her disdain. If Tanner noticed how frosty she had become he hid it well.

"Are you a natural blonde?" He wiggled his brows again. "Does the carpet match the drapes?"

The question didn't deserve an answer. Without saying a word, Josie stood. She ignored his demands that she sit back down and made a beeline for the door. *'You are never choosing my dates again'* she texts her mother before logging onto the Love Buzz and blocking NahTNurse.

***

"I'm sorry."

It had been four days since the NahTNurse fiasco. Four days of her mother simultaneously apologizing and trying to get her to try again. Third times the charm and whatnot. Whatever. There was no way in hell Josie was going on another blind date with some sleazeball her mother had picked out on an overpriced app. Her disdain for being set up by relatives was one of the reasons she'd been on the hunt for a fake boyfriend. It was her own fault. She could acknowledge that. Having her mother's undivided attention had felt good, she'd let it blind her.

"He was so nice in his messages."

A plate with leftover pizza appeared in front of her; pepperoni with black olives and extra cheese. Nose wrinkled, Josie picked off the greasy discs of meat. "He was my bad karma for lying," she muttered before taking a small bite.

"Doubtful." Ruth plucked the discarded pepperoni from the side of Josie's plate and popped them into her mouth. "You're too nice for bad karma."

"I lied to my family about having a boyfriend."

Her mother rolled her eyes. "The only person who bought the lie was Kyle... and I'm not entirely certain he did."

Josie set her pizza down and pushed the plate away. For all her turmoil over telling Kyle the truth, she didn't like him assuming she had lied. *'You did lie.'* "Did he say something?"

"Just that it's weird he hasn't met him."

Fair. If the boyfriend was real, Kyle would have been the first to meet him. It was how they did things. "What did you tell him?"

"That you'd introduce us when an introduction was warranted." Ruth gestured towards the half-eaten piece of pizza. "Finished?" Without waiting for a response, she scooped the plate up and tossed it into the trash. "Now… don't be mad… but I've been messaging with someone on your behalf. He's been nothing but a gentleman. I told him I… *you*… would meet him for coffee later tonight."

CHAPTER FIVE

Josie

Heart2Heart. The screen name was cheesy but no more so than the last two and her mother was right, his chats were always polite. Not once did he ask her to send him 'kitty pictures' or what kind of underwear she was wearing; 'are they thong or cheeky' seemed to be the most popular. Heart2Heart just wanted to chat. His favorite subject was trying to help the colony of ferals that lived in the wooded area behind his house. The cats, and her mother's pleas, were the only reason Josie found herself walking into Delia's for another date.

"Back again?"

A surprised squeak slipped past Josie's lips. Heart pounding, she turned to find 'Hot Guy' standing behind her. Relief mixed with dread shot through her. Relief that he wasn't last week's pervert; dread because he had witnessed the debacle with the pervert. "I could ask you the same."

"You could," the hottie agreed. His lips twitched for a moment before stretching into a crooked smirk. Any hope she'd been holding onto that he didn't recall the 'does the carpet match the drapes' went out the window. He definitely remembered. And thought it was funny. "I come here for the coffee though, not to meet people I don't know." He had her there. She wasn't at Delia's for the coffee, and she definitely didn't know any of the guys she was meeting. "You know," he continued, "there are a lot of sickos on the net."

Josie narrowed her eyes. "There's also a lot of judgmental assholes who hang out in coffee shops." Who was he to judge how she met people? For all he knew she enjoyed the thrill of meeting men off the internet. Maybe she got off on hooking up with strangers. Okay, so she didn't but the guy behind her didn't know that.

Her comment didn't seem to offend him so much as amuse him. He laughed, holding open the coffee shop door for her. "So, who are you meeting this week? Another Mr_Right or Naughty Nurse?"

Naughty Nurse. NahTNurse. Oh my God. How had her mother missed that? How had *she* missed that? "Neither," Josie snipped before sighing. She couldn't blame him for laughing. Her first date had been obsessed with his ex and the second one...she shuddered. Hot Guy had been a table away both times. At this point, he was part of her journey. "Heart2heart," she muttered. He burst out laughing. "Go ahead. Laugh. His screen name is cheesy but so far he's been a perfect gentleman."

"I'm sure he has," Hot Guy chuckled. He shook his head and wished her luck before heading straight to the table he always occupied.

Josie turned her attention to scanning the cafe for her date. Her stomach knotted up when her gaze fell on a solitary man standing near the pastry case. The navy blue sports jacket with a red rose in the lapel was impossible to miss. So was his neatly trimmed gray beard, salt and pepper hair, and the little sign that said Heart2Heart. Crap. Heart2Heart was old enough to be her father. *'No wonder your mother got along with him so well.'* Turning abruptly when he glanced in her direction, she made a beeline for the Hot Guy's table. Without asking, she sank onto the chair across from him. "Not one word," she warned.

"Wasn't going to say anything," Hot Guy quipped. He leaned across the table, his brown eyes meeting her blue ones. "Old guy with the flower is Heart2Heart isn't he?" Her lips puckered. "Not into geriatrics?" She shook her head. "Then why did you agree to a date?"

"I didn't. My mom did." Damn it. She hadn't meant to say that. Hot Guy's curiosity was piqued, interest shown in his eyes. He was smart enough to remain silent. "His profile said he was in his forties." Even that had felt too old for her but Ruth had presented a solid case when she brought up using the guy's age as the reason why "the family" hadn't met him yet.

"Maybe he doesn't age well." He threw his hands up when Josie shot him a hard look. "Hey, you sat at my table, remember?"

"It made sense at the time." Chin tucked against her chest, Josie studied her cuticles in an attempt to keep her face hidden. The bell over the door jingled. "Was that him? Did he leave?"

"Yup."

"I feel horrible. I'm a horrible person." She could feel her nice guy image slipping. First the lie to Kyle, now this. She'd blown off an old man who was probably lonely and in need of a friend.

"You probably did the old guy a favor. Most likely his ticker would have given out in the throes of passion."

Her lips formed a silent oh. "You're an ass!"

For the second time in less than a week, she stormed out of Delia's with Hot Guy's laughter trailing after.

CHAPTER SIX

Josie

Agreeing to meet SouthernCharm247 happened in a moment of weakness. She'd been on the verge of sending Kyle a confession via text, convinced the reason none of her dates worked out was bad karma from lying. Aunt Beckett stopped her. "You're in too deep. If you don't see it through, you'll never hear the end of it." For a solid five minutes she was livid with her mother for spilling the beans. Love Buzz and the hunt for a fake boyfriend was supposed to be their secret. "Oh please," Aunt Beckett scoffed, "you're a terrible liar. The only reason Kyle bought it is he doesn't think you have the balls to lie to him. Now, are you going to spend the rest of your life being guilt tripped into every blind date Kyle wants to set you up on or are you going to meet SouthernCharm247?" With options like that, how could she refuse.

Josie toyed with asking him to meet her somewhere other than Delia's, mostly because she couldn't stop thinking about 'Hot Guy.' The more she went over their last encounter, the more she realized she overreacted. He had been trying to make an awkward situation less tense. If she went to Delia's and he was there, she knew she would spend the evening wishing he was her date, not SouthernCharm247. Her mother made the decision for her. 'Delia's is your go to place,' Ruth explained when Josie asked why her mother had taken it upon herself to tell SoutherCharm to meet her there.

"I'm sorry."

The words caressed her neck as she stood in line waiting for a frozen mocha. A faint smile turned the corners of her lips. She'd known he would be there. He was always there. "Apology accepted."

"So," Hot Guy stepped forward, his shoulder brushing against hers, "who's the lucky guy this time?"

'You,' her heart pleaded. It was a smoke dream. Guys like him were friends with girls like her. Nothing more, nothing less. "SouthernCharm73." Her eyes rolled before she could stop them. If this date went the way her last three did she was calling it quits. She'd delete her account and convince her mother to back up her *'I was dumped, boo hoo'* story. If Kyle pushed about Jonas' pseudo relative she would sniffle and say she was too heartbroken. Maybe he'd actually believe her. "He's going to be wearing a yellow sweater. Buttercup, not canary or mustard."

"Huh." An odd look crossed Hot Guy's face. "That's weird."

It was on the tip of her tongue to ask him what he meant when the barista called out her name. She side-stepped a mother with two small children.. "What's weird? That he was so specific about the color of his sweater?"

"No." Hot Guy shook his head. "I think I know the guy. I would have sworn he was engaged though."

And there it was. SouthernCharm247's flaw. She knew he had to have one. All of her dates had one. "Keep the change," she told the barista before turning around to face Hot Guy. His attention was focused on a man in yellow near the door. An all too familiar man. Her fingers started to shake, losing their grip on the clear plastic cup she'd just taken from the barista. It splattered across the tiled floor, leaving clumps of whipped cream and frozen coffee on her black booties, as well as Hot Guy's white running shoes. Her lips parted, an apology forming when a string of curse words and salty tears replaced it.

"Josie." Kyle said her name so softly she almost didn't hear it. He bodily blocked her exit, leaving her with no option other than to stand in front of him. "You might as well come clean."

The moment of truth had arrived. It was inevitable. From the moment they were born there was a connection Josie couldn't explain. Kyle called it twin-epathy. Whatever it was, they always knew. If the other was hurt, scared, or lying... they knew. She'd give him credit. He'd let her carry out her little fib longer than expected. *'He also said those hurtful things knowing how they would make you feel.'* "Why? So, you can tell me some more about how pathetic my life is?"

"I never said your life was pathetic. I said I was relieved that you found someone because I was worried that you had given up."

"What does that even mean?" She shoved her fingers into her long hair, pushing it off her face. "Given up on what Kyle? Life? Love? You're going to have to be a little more specific. And while you're at it, let's talk about why I don't move or get serious with anyone." She let out a choked sound when he stood there, staring at her. "When dad got sick, who gave up ballet to help mom take care of him? When mom lost her job, who moved out of their condo and into a tiny garage apartment to help with the bills?"

"Nobody asked you to do those things Josie."

He was right. Nobody had asked her to give up ballet or her condo, but someone had to do something. Since no one else had stepped forward, she did. It was her role in the family. Kyle was the golden child everyone loved and raved about; while Josie was the one holding it all together behind the scenes. "You're right. Nobody asks because you all know I'll already say yes." She shoved past him, pushing open the glass door. Her body collided with another man in a light yellow sweater. It took her a moment to realize it was Jonas. "Move," she choked.

"Omigod, Josie. Are you okay?" The genuine concern in his hazel eyes broke her. The tears she'd been holding back burst free. He was such a nice person, always worried about others. Why couldn't at least one of the guys she met be like that? "Kyle's just inside. We were going to surprise you. Stay here... let me go get him."

"No!" The last person she wanted to see was Kyle. She didn't know why her brother hid behind a Love Buzz account to get her to meet up, but the result was a disaster of epic proportions. "I just... I need to go."

The door to the coffee opened. Hot Guy stepped out, concern stamped across his features. The concern melted into confusion. "Jonas?"

"Hank?" Jonas blinked, then chuckled. "Wow. Talk about a small world. Josie," he wrapped arm around her trembling shoulders, "this is the guy Kyle and I were telling you about. My sister's brother in law."

A buzzing filled her ears. Hot Guy… Hank… was the blind date she had been avoiding. It was karma. Karma was screwing with her for lying. "I can't.. I just.. I have to go!"

CHAPTER SEVEN

Hank

Hank Mancini tore his gaze from the retreating form of the tiny blonde he'd come to think of as his coffee buddy and shot the man next to him an annoyed look. Thanks to their siblings dating since preschool, he had known Jonas Bruno most of their lives. The slightly younger man was a bit too dramatic for them to be the sort of friends that hung out on the regular, but they had a mutual understanding. Besides, Pete marrying Jonas' sister Robin made Jonas family. And since Jonas was family, quizzing him up about what the hell just happened in the coffee shop was fair game. "Want to tell me what that was all about?"

"My fiancé being a total dickhead." A v formed between Jonas' brows, his gaze flicking from the coffee shop door to the car peeling out of the parking lot. He shook his head, his lips pressing into a thin line. "I tried telling him to leave it alone. If she lied to him, it was his own fault for saying the things he said to her. I even told him setting her up with you was a bad idea. He wouldn't listen. He just kept on..."

Frowning, Hank barely heard the rest of the explanation. It was like his mind latched onto 'setting her up with you' and the rest was just background noise. The conversation took place at his niece's fifth birthday party. While the rest of the adults sipped on juice boxes laced with vodka and watched their kids combat it out in a bouncy house, Hank hid in the spare bedroom with the family cats. It didn't take long for Jonas and Kyle to join him. Over cake and kittens, Hank let it slip he missed being in a relationship. That was when Kyle brought up his sister. His sweet, beautiful sister who loved cats and thought about everyone but herself. When they offered to arrange a date, Hank shrugged. Why not, it wasn't like there were any better offers. And then he met Coffee Girl. He'd shot Jonas a text nixing the blind date, he'd met a girl at the coffee shop. "Wait. Did you just say the woman who just left is Kyle's sister?"

"Mmhmm." Jonas rolled his eyes and then let out a gasp. "Omigod is Josie Coffee Girl?"

Hank scraped a hand down his face as Jonas' words sunk in. Kyle's sister Josie was Coffee Girl. He had shut down being set up on a date with the woman he wanted to ask out. *'Don't forget the part where she invented a fake boyfriend to avoid going out with you.'* He dismissed the thought. Josie didn't invent a fake boyfriend to avoid going out with *him*, she invented a boyfriend because nobody would listen when she said no. Kyle said it himself: she thought of everyone but herself. The boyfriend lie had been her way of making her brother accept 'no.' Hank couldn't say that he agreed with lying, but he understood why she did it. "Josie is Coffee Girl."

"Ha! This is too perfect. Wait until I tell Kyle." Excitement lit up Jonas' face, only to fall away. "He didn't trick her to hurt her, you know? There were… words… said that Josie took the wrong way. Kyle wanted to confront her but their mother talked him out of it. Said maybe Josie needed to do this…maybe it would help her find a life of her own." Jonas shook his head, glancing toward the coffee door where Kyle stood wringing his hands. "You heard her in there. She doesn't think twice about giving up things she loves if it means helping the people she loves."

"And we all let her." Sadness hung from each of Kyle's words. "I know you probably think my family doesn't appreciate her, but we do. I could have opened my studio on my own, you know. I had the money for the down payment and everything. I only asked Josie for help because I thought if I made her a partner she would start to dance again. And mom, well, she let Josie move into the garage apartment because she wanted them to be closer. With dad… I can admit it was selfish. He was so sick and Aunt Beckett kept harping on about *'this is why you need to pre-plan your funeral.'* A dance intensive over a thousand miles away seemed like the perfect escape. I wasn't thinking about mom being a wreck or Josie holding it all together."

"I'm not the one you should be saying this to," Hank said.

"You're right. I need to tell her but so do you… Hot Guy." Kyle smiled ruefully before holding out his hand to Jonas. "I guess it's time to face the music. My mom's been blowing up my phone ever since Josie left."

Hank stared after them. He wanted to ask what Kyle meant by 'Hot Guy' but he had a feeling he already knew. Hot Guy was Josie's version of Coffee Girl.

CHAPTER EIGHT

Josie

Glutton for punishment. That was what Josie was. She was a glutton for punishment; otherwise, she wouldn't have gone back on that stupid dating site. It all started because her mother reminded her that she had to close out her account or she would still get emails from other members wanting to chat with or meet her. There had been over twenty such messages in her inbox when she went to close her account, and she had deleted them one by one, all but one from a new member named ItMustBeFate. Inside she found a rather sweet note asking her if she believed in Fate. It should have crept her out, the way this man seemed to know exactly what she wanted, it didn't though. If anything, it piqued her interest, and she found herself sending him a message back.

In need of more punishment, she started corresponding with him, volleying messages back and forth. The messages slowly became the highlight of her day. For once, it seemed like another human being actually got her. He seemed to understand all her fears, and offered encouragement when she spoke of how hard it was rebuilding her relationship with her brother was.

After a month the messages led into chatting via instant message. Unlike some of the others he didn't want her to talk dirty or participate in some cyber orgy; nor did he instantly start pushing for a meeting. No, he just wanted to talk to her. Occasionally they flirted with what might happen if they ever did meet, but Josie felt she knew him well enough to know it was just flirting. Which was why she took the next step and asked him to meet her at Delia's.

On the night they were to meet Josie couldn't help but wonder if she really wasn't asking for punishment. Sure, he seemed like a nice guy, but so had all the others. And there was the issue of why she had picked Delia's as their meeting place. Deep down she wanted to see *him* again. *He* was never far from her thoughts, but the few times she had dared to ask how he was, Jonas had been tight lipped. She couldn't help but worry that she was using this date with ItMustBeFate as an excuse to hang out there, maybe see him again.

"Stop it," she whispered, smoothing the front of her cream-colored turtleneck sweater. Paired with dark washed jeans and a pair of Uggs, the outfit was perfect for a coffee date. Nice, but not too dressy. "This guy is perfect for you. Don't mess it up because of some silly crush on a guy who could contact you but has chosen not to." Nodding her chin decisively, Josie gathered her chocolate colored peacoat into her arms and headed out the door.

Twenty minutes later she hurried from her car to the front door of the coffee shop. It felt a bit odd to be coming back, and she couldn't stop the racing of her heart. Inside could be the man of her dreams. On the drive over she had come to the decision that if things didn't work out with ItMustBeFate and *he* was there she was going to go for it. It was a win/win situation, and she couldn't help the bright smile that spread across her lips.

She glanced around the crowded shop. Her date would be wearing a red t-shirt which she found a bit humorous. Catching sight of a flash of red in the corner, Josie started in that direction. Halfway there she stopped. The red flash had come from a familiar table, *his* table, and *he* sat there, wearing the same red t-shirt he had worn the first night she had seen him. She told herself he wasn't the one, that it would be too much to ask. Then he rose, walked toward her, a soft smile on his face. She didn't resist when he leaned close to her, his mouth next to her ear.

"It must be fate," he whispered.

THE END

ABOUT DARLEY COLLINS

Darley Collins is an Oklahoma based author that loves bringing her small town to life for others to enjoy. A recent empty nester, she enjoys traveling with her husband and caring for their 5 geriatric rescue cats.

LIFE AFTER THE STORM

by Havana Wilder

CHAPTER ONE

Fortune

Keeping my breathing steady, I push harder and run faster as adrenaline courses through my veins. A thin layer of sweat covers the nape of my neck, and fear washes over me as I think about the possibility of our lives being cut short. The only things that can hinder us from surviving are our physical limits and self-doubt.

My shoes pound heavily across the ground, causing mud to slosh up my leg. My calves burn as my breath forms clouds in the air. I desperately attempt to create some form of traction while my slippery feet fly over stones, slick leaves, and jutted out tree roots. My right foot nearly slips out from beneath me when I lunge over a downed tree, and quickly right my stance, picking my pace back up.

At this speed, I can barely see a few feet ahead of me, let alone focus on my best friend who's leading us out of harm's way. Wind whips my hair back from my face as cold air bites into my lungs. Thuds of footfalls approaching closer cause each of our feet to bound forward, despite our sheer exhaustion. Coming to a clearing, I can't hear myself think over the sound of raging water.

"Well, this is a nice change of scenery." Leo stops abruptly, hands landing on his knees as he bends over, trying to catch his breath. A cynical smile spreads across his face, revealing two prominent dimples on each cheek.

My breathing quickens, trying to appease my need for oxygen. Once I'm able to speak, I point out the obvious. "It's a waterfall on a steep cliff, and they still are chasing us and trying to kill us." Closing my eyes tight, out of fear of falling, I yell loudly, waving my hands toward the thundering falls.

"It's just bread, and we're literally starving." He's not lying. It's been a long time since we've had a full meal.

"Clearly, they don't care if we live or die."

Shouts are getting louder as they near the edge of the woods, closing in on us.

"Here, eat." He rips the bread apart and we both shove it in our mouths.

When we're nearly done chewing, he opens his mouth, showing his half-eaten food. "Come on." He takes my hand, interlacing our fingers together.

"No, no, no. There's got to be a better way. A different way to escape them." I'm terrified of heights, and he knows this.

"There they are. Get them!" a man shouts from about fifty yards away from us—the one Leo swiped the bread from, no less.

"It's a nice cool spring day for a frigid swim. Do you trust me?" He grips my hand tighter.

Fear floods my veins, causing me to do things I'd never do if I were thinking straight. Closing my eyes, I nod yes.

"Hold your breath." And with that, he tugs my hand, taking me down the ravine, plunging into the depths below. Once we're under the force of the water, our hands are ripped apart. It's dark. I can't see anything. I'm struggling to reach the surface.

Attempting to calm my racing heart, I count to ten, kicking my feet as hard as I can. Counting up to twenty, I swipe my arms frantically as I fight to swim upward. I'm all the way up to one minute. My lungs burn from not being able to inhale, and I fear this may be the end. Unable to scratch the surface, my efforts are fought in vain, and my body begins to sink. Right before I lose consciousness, I feel a strong hand grasp around my wrist. As I'm yanked out of the water, I spurt liquid out of my mouth, coughing relentlessly.

"Don't ever do that to me again!" Leo shouts, fisting his hair as he tugs at the wet strands.

"Me? How about not ever taking me over the edge of a raging waterfall ever again?"

"It was the only way for us not to be arrested and have our hands chopped off, or worse, starved to death in a nasty, rat-infested prison cell." He's not wrong. I think I'd welcome drowning over either of those scenarios.

Crashing onto our backs, we lay there, trying to catch our breaths, while contemplating our near-death experience.

"How is it we keep ending up in these situations?"

"I've known you for ten years, and I still don't know." Rolling over, I playfully slap his chest. He places his hand over mine as his dark charcoal eyes, etched with concern, pierce mine.

"You really had me scared. I couldn't find you, and I thought for sure you were dead."

"But I'm not dead." I give him a reassuring smile.

"Fortune, don't you know I could never live this life without you?" His eyes go soft, and I suddenly can't breathe at the thick air between us.

"Leo, I didn't mean to scare you. Too bad my name doesn't make us fortun…"

He doesn't let me finish. Pressing his finger to my lips, he hushes me. "Shhhh, I can hear them coming." Quietly, we both rise, and within seconds, he's pulling me away from the rapid falls and off into the woods.

After we've run for who knows how long, the sun sinking at a rapid pace in the sky, he stops and twists his body around, searching for something.

"What are you looking for?" I whisper.

"There's a hidden cave here somewhere. It's stocked with blankets, pillows, canteens, extra clothes, and maybe even some food. I came out here with the guys and helped them supply it a while back." He furrows his brow, remembering our friends before they were captured and sent away to supposedly go rummage up food in other territories.

"Ahhh, there it is." He starts walking to an extremely large overgrown bush. "Everything is more overgrown than when I was here last.

"You think we're getting through that?"

"Not through, behind." He motions for me to follow. Once he has the thicket pulled back just enough for me to squeeze behind, he follows, letting the limbs drop back into place.

"It's pitch black in here. How do you know where to go?" I feel along the wall, following the sounds of his footsteps. "And how do you know something's not living in here?"

"I've been here a few times. And nothing lives in here because there's hardly any wildlife left. When I went hunting in a separate direction..." He takes a deep breath. "And they were captured. I got probably the last deer in the area."

"Listen, it's not your fault what happened to them. They just happened to be at the wrong place at the wrong time," I try to reassure him. "And you're not the only one who wasn't with them. I went to the creek to wash all our dirty clothes when all that went down. No, I didn't hear their screams or watch them being carted off like you did by the time you got close enough to the road, but I can't blame myself for those horrible Elite soldiers taking them, and neither should you."

"We're going to find them," he says matter-of-factly.

"Yes, we are, but first we have to get these other scoundrels off our tails."

Once we're deep inside, he manages to start a small fire. "We need to dry our clothes, so we don't catch a cold." He lays out a few sticks against the wall of the cavern for us to place our soaked garments on.

"I'm just supposed to strip and hide under a cover until they dry?"

"We've known each other since we were eleven. Come on. Do you really think you've got something I've never seen before?" He winks at me as he pulls his shirt over his shoulders, revealing his corded abs. His chiseled chest muscles bunch and flex as he gets trapped in his own top.

Hiding a smirk, I stride over and help him finish, wrenching it over his head. When he's free, he stumbles back a few steps. Glancing up, he notices my amusement.

"All right, magician. Let's see how easy you can get out of your clothes."

"Oh no. You turn around." A little laugh escapes him as he gradually turns away from me. After straining to get my top off, I end up slapping myself in the face once the sodden garment is off.

"You okay back there?" It's his turn to mock me.

"Shut it." I can't get out of my pants standing. It's like peeling paint off my legs. Resorting to laying on the ground, I shimmy and squirm to no avail. Taking a break from wrestling with my jeans, I lay there, resting my arms completely defeated while fully exposed in my underwear and halfway taken off pants.

"Need help?" He cranes his head over his shoulder. One look at me and he full on belly laughs. Covering his mouth, he attempts to muffle his hysterics, but there's no use. I know I'm reaping what I sowed by laughing at him.

"Nope! I'd rather lie here and catch pneumonia than you lift a finger to help me." I try to kick him, but he's just shy of my foot making contact with his shin.

"Look." He hiccups. "I'm sorry. Let me." Taking the hem of each pant leg, he yanks. In one fell swoop, they're off.

"What? How did you? You know what… never mind, I don't want to know." I know he's had many girlfriends and, to be honest, what he did with them is none of my business.

Sulking, I yank the blanket around my shoulders and face the fire.

"Just because I'm taking off clothes better than you, doesn't mean it's what you're thinking." I hear him rip off his wet jeans and watch him out of the corner of my eye as he places them on a rock.

"Oh really? And what am I thinking?" I snap my head in his direction.

"That I've had a lot of practice with this maneuver on other females."

"Leo, if you have, that's between you and them. Spare me the details."

"Sure, I've had the occasional rendezvous with a few, but they were never permanent."

"Clearly." Each time I watched him go out with one, it ripped my heart in two, but I never wanted him to know that it did, so I hid it from him very well. "And why, pray tell, are you not with one of them now? Is it because you felt sorry for me because the famine hit, and you didn't think I'd survive on my own? Is it because you thought I'd be captured for thieving a loaf on my own and the king would have me tortured and you couldn't have that on your conscious?" My words are laced with bitterness and hurt.

"Hey." He takes on a gentler tone. "Hey, look at me."

I don't. I continue to stare into the flames while my freezing body shivers slightly.

Taking his thumb and forefinger, he turns my chin until I'm looking right at him. "I'm not with any one of them because none of them are you."

Warm, glowing flames glint across his eyes as he gazes longingly at me while he cups my face and tilts it up. My belly flips as my entire body flushes with warmth. I steady my breath, peering into the glow behind his ebony eyes, and grin as the water drips from my hair down my face.

"I was young and dumb and never thought you'd see me as anything more than a friend. I'm not here with you now, risking our lives out of some moral obligation." He doesn't quite say he loves me, so I try to drag it out of him.

"What do you mean?" I'm shocked, but more interested in what he has to say.

"I've not been with anyone for over a year. I think you know what that means."

"No, I don't. I have no idea how or what you feel." My voice comes out weak and filled with desperation.

"What I feel for you is a cross between loyalty and genuine, everlasting love between lifelong friends, but then the dark side of me dwells on a ravishingly wicked, sinful desire of a passionate romance."

"Oh…" I can't even form words. Swallowing thickly, I finally manage to ask. "And you chose now to tell me how you feel. Why?"

"When I thought I lost you back there, I thought I'd lost my whole world. I'm tired of being afraid of how you'll respond. I won't lose you without you knowing exactly how I feel about you. I'm not only going to tell you, though… oh no. I'm going to show you."

"Good god, if you'd only known how long I've wished to hear those words. I wanted to show you… tell you how I felt." My body's trembling for an entirely different reason now.

"Come here, beautiful."

In one swift move, he has me sitting on his lap with nothing between us other than the thin fabric of our undergarments. He strokes my cheek with the pad of his thumb. My eyes close as he grazes my chin with his lips, and the entire world spins.

Slowly, he moves down to kiss my neck, and I suck in a sharp breath of air. I feel him trail his tongue over my shoulder. My skin is feverish as warmth consumes my body, and my temperature spikes. I make an eager, involuntary hum in the back of my throat. Then suddenly, his lips come crashing down on mine.

My insatiable hunger and need for Leo is quenched by a single taste, creating an inferno of happiness that burns through every cell of my body. Everything inside of me weakens as he lays me back on a blanket, covering us with the other one. Leo pauses our kissing briefly to look for assuredness in me. My gaze doesn't falter, and his pupils flare with desire. I wrap my legs around his waist and tug him closer. His arms begin to tremble as he hovers just above me. I trail my fingers up his spine, leaving chill bumps in their wake until I get to his neck. Locking my fingers together, I draw him closer until his lips are but a hair's breadth away.

"Don't be shy now because it's me," I whisper.

His lips crash down on mine, our mouths moving back and forth with fervency. Each of us demands that the other's lips part, and once open, our tongues swiftly drink in the flavor of the opposite person. He breaks away momentarily, fastening me with a firm stare.

"I have a confession to make." He's breathing hard and fast. "I'm not in this for a one-night stand. You're mine," he exclaims, pausing a second. "For life."

"Is that so? I'm yours? And what does that make you?"

"Yours." His breathing picks up, and he grips my hip hard. There's definitely going to be his handprint there tomorrow. I'm fully enamored with him as I lay there, and the urge grows even stronger in my stomach. It's like a thousand hummingbirds are dancing inside me. Except for the dying fire shining and reflecting a little in Leo's eyes, it's almost pitch black.

My tongue brushes across my upper lip. Taking the hint, he wastes no time devouring me in a passionate kiss. Then, as we're flesh to flesh, he consumes me totally, completely claiming me as his, while a red-hot fire spreads from my stomach to my heart before finally exploding in my mind.

"This moment right now…," I whisper as our foreheads press against each other after our moment of pure ecstasy. "This is a moment I will never forget."

"Me either." He rolls off me, drawing me close to him.

Laying my head on his chest, listening to the steady drum of his heartbeat, I'm lulled into a peaceful sleep in no time.

CHAPTER TWO

Leo

As the flickering embers gleam on her fair skin, I admire her. She is unquestionably a warrior most days, but also a broken mess on others. And, on occasion, a combination of the two. But there's no denying it. She's here each and every day: withstanding, unwavering, fighting, striving, surviving and living. And now she's mine.

Her eyes roam behind her closed eyelids as she sleeps peacefully. This is likely the best sleep she's had in a while. I smooth her wavy blonde hair away from her face, revealing her high cheekbones, full lips, and perfectly arched eyebrows. My eyes linger over her lean form, and it hits me… she has no idea how long I've been in love with her, or how long I've wanted to admit my feelings to her. God, what's wrong with me? She felt the same way too, and I had no clue. Damn. I could have lost her by pursuing easy girls just to get my mind off her. As I mentally scold myself, a noise sounds outside of the cave, and I realize we need to get up and get going.

"Pssst. Wake up, For." She doesn't budge a muscle at me cooing her nickname that I've called her since we met when we were children, so I wave some jerky under Fortune's nose to tickle her senses. I kinda hate to wake her, but I kinda love teasing her, too.

"Wha… wait! Is that…" Barely squinting her eyes open, she snatches the dried meat from my hand and devours it. "Mmmmm. Tis us oh good." She moans and laments, rolling her eyes in the back of her head.

I muffle out a laugh. "Do you mean *this is so good*?"

"Mmhmm."

"Well, once you're done eating, we need to head out. Since I saw the direction they carted our friends off to, we'll head that way, and never look back at this territory. Who knows, maybe the grass is literally greener on the other side?"

For the past two years, this area has been hit hard with a lack of crops, wildlife to eat, fowl in the sky, and fish in the waters. I'm not certain if it's only in this territory, or if it's the entire continent, that's been affected. One thing's for sure, if we stay here, we'll likely die from starvation or from being executed by the Prime Minister's Elite army. He feels that if there are fewer mouths he has to feed, it's less likely the famine will affect him or his hierarchy at the palace.

"Our clothes aren't quite dry yet. I'll wrap them and put them in this knapsack and hopefully we can either hang them out to dry or lay them by another fire tonight." I fold them and shove them in the bag.

"What are we going to wear?" She pulls the covers close to her chest.

"Are you being shy after what took place last night?" I tease.

A flush creeps up her neck and onto her face. "No." She avoids my gaze. "I'm chilly, and I refuse to walk out of this cave in nothing but my underwear with only a cover draped over me."

"I'm calling your bluff. If you're not being bashful, come here and let me show you what I have for you to wear."

"Is that some kind of sexual innuendo I don't get? I know I'm new to all this intimacy stuff, but that sure sounds vulgar."

"Bwahahahaha." I accidentally laugh hard and loud. "You've got to stop making me laugh. I don't want to be a dead giveaway of our whereabouts."

"I'm glad you find my lack of knowledge in flirting amusing." Huffing, she tosses the blanket to the side and seductively lurks toward me.

"You vixen! Don't tell me you don't know how to flirt. Look at the way you're peering at me through your lashes, sauntering slowly while stalking me like a feral animal who's about to have their last meal." My god. She's in see-through underwear revealing all her delicious breasts, and the way she's prowling has me so turned on now, I can hardly think straight.

"Well then, are you still calling my bluff about being shy?"

"I most definitely am not. Not anymore." Shaking my head, I attempt to get these lustful thoughts out of my skull.

"Good. Now what am I supposed to wear?" She's standing directly in front of me, practically nude, and my brain fails to function. I can't form words, can't speak, can't even mutter.

"Ut-um." Clearing my throat, I point to the corner of supplies. When she gets to the clothes, she rummages through them until she finds something she thinks will fit.

"How do I look?" She twirls around in baggy khaki pants that she's bunched around the waist to one side, holding them up by the belt loops, and a shirt two sizes too big for her.

"Like a potato swallowed you." Pushing myself up from the ground, I make my way to her. Sifting through the bag, I search and come up short of anything that'll fit her petite form. "Let's see." I take a rope and feed it through the belt loops and tie it snugly around her. Taking her shirt, I pull the hem to the side and coil it in a knot.

"Better?" I ask.

"Much." Lifting up onto her tiptoes, her lips land firmly on mine, and in one smack, they're gone all too soon. "Thank you, oh inventive one."

"Improvisation is my middle name." I smirk.

"No, it's not. It's Edgar." She winks at me.

"We could have gone the rest of our entire lives without mentioning that."

"Why? I don't know why you're embarrassed by it. I love your name, Leo Edgar Woodruff."

"Good, because one day you're going to be Mrs. Leo Edgar Woodruff." Not the ideal way to propose, but in this day and time, nothing's traditional anymore.

"Promise?" She glances up at me, tugging on her shoes.

Marking an X over my chest, I say, "Cross my heart and hope to d..."

"No. Just promise me," she interrupts me. "That was a rather morbid way we used to swear to each other as kids. I can't believe we used to say that." She smiles, crinkling her nose.

"Yes, For, I promise." Holding out my hand, she takes it as I lean over, placing a light feathered kiss to the top. She folds her arms around my neck, pulling me into a tight hug. When my arms embrace her back, I can feel her ribs.

"We've got to get out of here, find our friends, a new place to live, and get some meat back on your bones. You're getting skinnier every day."

"Am not."

"Are too. Two years ago, I could feel your ribs, not see them. If you get sick, catch a cold, or worse, pneumonia… you have no reserve."

"Okay fine. I am a bit thinner than I'd like to be, but I'm far from emaciated."

"Oh, don't I know it." I slap her tight bum and make my way to the heap of necessities. Thumbing through the mound, I find we have enough jerky between the two of us to last at least two weeks if we eat it sparingly.

After we get the rest of the stuff packed up and on our backs, I douse the smoldering embers and we cautiously venture out into the forest once more. Taking a deep breath, I thread my fingers with hers.

"You good to walk?" I know she's gotta be sore from last night, even though I went easy. It was hard to keep from being rough, but I managed.

"I'm a little tender, but fine. Let's go." She smiles playfully up at me as we head in the direction of where I think we can find our comrades. Once we find them, my plan is to free them, and get us all to a better place where we can all live without being on the brink of starvation or the heels of death, while avoiding the Royals blood thirst for population control and their Elite army bending to their every command—or whatever it is they want to call it.

Trudging through the woods, the sun escapes through the canopy of trees, dusting the ground with speckles of light. We can see our breath as we exhale, so the sun can't fully rise soon enough. The dew dappling the ferns and grass wet our clothes, doing nothing to ward off any coldness we're trying to combat. The more Fortune shivers, the more calories she burns. I've got to get her some place warm, and food in her system.

Stopping for a brief moment, I tug out one of the blankets and drape it over her shoulders. "Here, this should help keep you a little warmer." I gently kiss her forehead, then lock our hands together, getting us back on our way.

"Thank you, but I'll warm up the more we walk."

"This will merely help that process along." I glance over at her to wink. Her cheeks turn rosy. "Have you always blushed at our closeness and I somehow missed it?"

"I don't know. I do know that since we were young, I liked you more than a lot. As for blushing at your show of affection, I probably always have. You know I'm shy, and any sort of attention, whether positive or negative, shows on my glowing face, neck, and arms. I even get splotchy on my chest when I think I'll have to speak in front of a group. So, you probably never knew if I was responding to you in desire or embarrassment. I'm complicated. I know."

"Now that you mention it, you do pink up when all eyes are on you, regardless of the situation."

"True. Don't feel bad for not being able to read me. I'm not an open book, and for that, I'm sorry. Who knows? If I'd told you sooner how I felt, we could've prevented all that promiscuity on your part." She elbows me on the side.

"Hey, there weren't *that many*." My eyes pleat on either side.

"Melony. Leah. Justina. Tiffany. Lorelei. Wendy. Cara…"

"Okay. Okay. I get it, there may have been a few, but why the hell do you know all their names? And for the record, I didn't sleep with them all."

"I know because I know. And okay then, how many?"

"You seriously want to know?"

"I wouldn't have asked if I didn't."

"Ugh. Three." I'm too ashamed to look at the disappointment on her face.

"Huh." It's not a question.

"What does that mean?"

"I just thought there'd be more." This time I do look at her.

She shrugs, kicking away a random stick out of her path.

"Are you disappointed?" I have no idea what she's feeling.

"Oh heavens no. I'm glad. I'm also glad you've not fathered three children from any of them."

"I'm not that much of an idiot. I took precautions, even if they told me they'd like to have my children." I puff out my chest proudly.

"Hahaha." Her genuine laugh is loud, sending a couple of birds in flight. I cup my hand over her mouth.

"Shhhhh. I don't want to give away our location. They're no doubt still searching for us."

"Oh goodness. I'm sorry." She tucks herself closer to me as we hike further into the woods. "Can I ask you a question?"

"Anything."

"How did things go when you ended it with Cara? I know she's part of the Elite, and they don't take kindly to being dismissed."

"Let's just say I have had an even larger target on my back since then. She wanted me to commit to her, get married, to have children, and for us to build a life among the Elite. The worst mistake of my life was dating her." The feeling of remorse floods my soul.

"Was she one of the three?" For can't hide the hurt skirting behind her eyes.

"No, I made sure that I never took it that far with her. Thank God." I shove my hand in my pocket to keep from forming a fist, wanting to punch a tree for the pain I've caused For.

"When you ended it, that's when you came straight into hiding with us, isn't it?

"It is. I know you and Owen, Vivere, Eli, Graham, Aliss, Feather, and Malic were in hiding to keep from being deported or taken inside the castle walls to be servants or slaves, or to keep from ultimately being killed off for being seen as an extra mouth to feed that brings no benefit to the Royals or the Elite's army. So, when I told her we were through, she went running to her clan, told them about me calling it off, and then they all started charging after me, to do who knows what? I scaled the walls and sought you all out. I'm sorry I was M.I.A. for those two months."

"No apologies necessary. I'm just glad you came to your senses sooner rather than later."

"Yeah, well, it took me long enough to realize I was being an idiot, and in the process, I got a nice price placed on my head."

"You know what I don't understand? We were all in the same school learning how to fight in combat, and herbology, so if we got in a predicament, we wouldn't necessarily starve. Were we all not just children among each other? We were all friends at one time."

"Yeah, but the moment we didn't test to be in the Elite group, we immediately set ourselves apart as defiant. Not pledging our loyalty to the Royals made us rogues who were forced out of the province. They wanted us to die off without them outright killing us. They're bitter."

"Yet you saw Cara and thought to pursue her?"

"I was lulled into that group by her promiscuous ways. Yes, I thought about trying out for the Elite for a brief moment. We all have our lapse in judgment now and then. Only, I was smart enough to not tap that easy piece of ass, no matter how much she flaunted it in my face. Every time she'd try to seduce me, I'd have a vision of you, and would think to myself, *what the hell am I doing*? You've always been the one."

"Aww, and you've always been the one for me. Do you think that since you've been out of there for a year, they'll stop searching for you?"

"Unfortunately, they have nothing else better to do than to look for me and stir up trouble."

"Don't worry. We'll get as far away from here as possible." The hope in her eyes gives me hope, too.

"Come hell or high water, we'll get out of here and build our life together… with our friends." I give her hand a good squeeze.

We continue on until it's high noon and her stomach starts growling. She wraps her arms around her middle, trying to muffle the sound, but it's obvious she's hungry. As I contemplate what we'll eat, I hear rushing water nearby. When we get to the river, I fish out the net from my bag.

"Hopefully, we won't come up empty." I cast it into the water and drag it back in. Nothing. I do it again and again and again until my arm feels like it's going to fall off from pitching it so many times. I will not give up until I have a fish, crawdad, or something edible.

Snap! I twist to the sound of what I think is a snare.

"I set a few traps that were in my bag while you were fishing." She removes the carcass of a squirrel and sets it beside a small mound of firewood.

"Well, thank god for that." I hang the net over a tree limb, letting it dry before I put it back up.

"I'll get the fire started if you want to skin it and get it ready." She takes the fire starter. Sparks fly at the base of the kindling. Leaning over, she blows on it, getting dry leaves burning.

Unsheathing my knife, I glimpse in her direction. She cleans off the bloody trap, and places it in her sack with the other two she sat out. It's no surprise to me that I caught nothing, but I'm rather astonished she was able to capture a squirrel. I've not seen one in over six months. Maybe because it's been winter and they're just now coming out of hibernation. But then again, before the coldness set in, I still didn't see any. Perhaps, her name does bring fortune with her, she just doesn't know it.

After we get our fill, we put the tiny fire out and hide any remnants of us being here. We follow along the river for a good way. It's a fantastic way to hide the sound of our footsteps, but if they've set the bloodhounds to find us, that's a different story. There aren't many left, and I'm not entirely convinced they'd waste precious time sending them after us, but then again, we'd be dumb to ever let our guard down.

It's nearly nightfall and we come to a clearing and what appears to be a dirt road, most likely the road they took our companions down. They were traveling north.

Squatting down next to an oak tree, I look for moss. Moss typically grows on the north side of trees. When I find a few trees with moss all growing on the same side, I point in the direction we're to travel in, in conjunction with the road. We can't speak while we're this close to where civilization might be, so I press my finger to my lips, indicating to stay quiet. We can't walk directly beside the road. We've got to stay hidden. Not only that, but we've also got to find shelter for the night. The weather never got warm enough for Fortune to shed her blanket, despite the extensive traveling we've done.

While we're hiking, I look for any place we can either pitch a tent or stay inside another cave. We continue on until the moon is shining high above us. We've got to rest. If my legs are aching, I know hers are as well, but she'll never complain. Even if her insides were turned out, she wouldn't whine. As I come to a halt, she does, too. I stand there circling around, looking for anything that will keep us from the harsh wind and freezing nights. Even in the summer, the nights drop to a cool temperature.

"There," she whispers, pointing to some vines swinging from the top of a rock.

Pulling a few strands aside, I reveal a hollow tunnel. I peek inside the best I can to see if any danger lurks. Nothing obvious jumps out. Taking my blade out, I crouch down, slinking inside and moving in front of her to block her if anything attacks. If something does, I'll take it head on first. When we're several paces inside, Fortune lights the end of a stick.

"Where did you find that?" My voice is barely audible.

"I made it. I just wrapped some fabric on the end of this." She waves the branch slightly. "And then used the fire starter on it to see if it would light. It did." She's grinning from ear to ear. "Now we have a torch of sorts."

"What would I do without you?" Shock and amazement are clearly plastered all over my face as she smiles with pride. "And you said I was inventive."

"I learned from the best." She winks. "But I don't know how long the fabric will burn, so I suggest we find a place to crash soon."

"You got it. I want to get as deep inside as we can if that's all right? I know your legs have got to be aching like mine."

"I'm fine. Don't worry about me."

"I know you're fine." I give her a sultry once over, taking in her flawless body. "But you can't stop me from worrying."

"Ugh, fine, you big brute. Let's get moving."

"Would you look at that?" I twist around, noticing a lantern. "Let's see if it'll light?" She hands me the torch. Wiping off the cobwebs and dust, I open the glass to the lantern and place the flame to the wick. It lights immediately. "Yes! Good fortune is finding us." She mentions from time to time her name isn't living up to its definition.

"Ha. Ha," she retorts sarcastically.

"Let's see if we can get just a bit deeper, and then we'll call it a night."

"Sounds good." She sticks by my side now that we can see better. We walk a good distance further. It appears this is a tunnel that goes on for miles.

"There's no end in sight." For's eyes droop with sleepiness, her shoulders sagging, while her feet drag across the ground.

"All right, let's cop-a-squat here, then." We take out our bedding and set it up against the wall so I can constantly be on the lookout if something or someone finds us. "I'll sleep behind you."

When she lays down, she kisses my lips as if she's done it a hundred times. "I love you. Please sleep tonight. I'm not convinced you slept last night."

I smile, staring into her crystal blue eyes. "I love you more than you'll ever know." She doesn't need to know I've been awake the entire time, and I have no intentions of sleeping tonight. Grinning back, she flips over, and I tug her close to my chest. After a few minutes, her back relaxes against me and her breathing evens out, indicating she's fast asleep.

My arm lays directly behind her head. I bend it upward, resting my head on the palm of my hand, giving me a beautiful view of her. Knowing we've got an unknown future ahead; I lay here holding her a little tighter, appreciating every moment we have together. We never know what tomorrow's going to bring.

CHAPTER THREE

Fortune

Waking to a rustling sound, I'm immediately aware of the loss of warmth behind me. I squint my eyes open to see Leo packing up our things. He must sense me looking at him because he stops what he's doing to glance over at me. A faint smile appears on his face as his ebony eyes pierce mine. Lately, I've noticed his eyes are often purple underneath. Whether that's from the constant worrying he does or the countless sleepless nights watching for hunters while attempting to keep us from being found, I don't know.

"Morning, beautiful." His husky voice causes my heart rate to pick up. "I've searched a little further into the depths. It seems this follows the road traveling north. I think we can stay underground and get as far as it'll take us. We've got enough food for at least two weeks. There are a few natural springs along the way that'll allow us to fill our canteens in. What do you say?"

"I'm with you. Whatever you think is best and safest, let's do it."

"I love how much you trust me." His grin widens.

"Leo, you should know by now that I trust you with my life."

"I do. You ready to get a move on?"

"Mmhmm."

We trudge on in the endless tunnel, heading hopefully closer to our friends and away from the Elite, soldiers, and this territory all together. Even though we're underground, it's not as chilly as it is outside, which seems odd, but I'm grateful for it.

"I wonder if this is how vampires like it?" I scan the tunnel with my eyes, exploring it in front of me.

"What?" Leo asks, confused.

"You know, being where it's always dark and away from prying eyes?" I shrug.

"If they were real, I'm sure this would be right up their alley. Only, they'd probably starve to death with food supplies being limited."

"They wouldn't be eating animals, I'm sure. There are still enough people to satisfy their cravings. I think I'd lead them right to the Elite and their soldiers who kill for fun." He cracks up.

"True, and I'd help you." We walk on in silence for a few more minutes.

"How long do you think it'd take us to get to the other territory?" I change the subject.

"I think at least a week on foot, but I don't think the soldiers, or anyone, are aware of this access tunnel we've stumbled upon. I'm hoping it'll land us in the other territory."

"You and me both. I can't wait to have a fresh start."

"Me too."

***

We stay in this passageway for another week, and I think I can see the end because there's a faint light. Maybe it's the sun setting, and it's shining in through some brush up ahead, a good ways away. We decide to stay a bit further inside to ward off any cold before going back into the woods in the morning.

As we get to a spot to call it a night, the dirt above the tunnel starts sprinkling down on us. Terrified, we halt, taking out our sleeping bags and listen for any odd sounds. The steady drip of water is the only sound we hear except our breathing. Then a sound comes overhead. "Five." We stop in our tracks.

"What the...?" Leo asks, but it's cut short by another shout. "Four."

"What are they counting down for?" I grip his hand tightly.

"Three."

He begins dragging me in the reverse direction of the exit.

"Two."

I drop his hand and we take off in a full-on sprint.

"One."

As electricity rips across my skin, dirt pours down all around us. Leo is thrust forward by the explosion and me up against the side of the tunnel. Unfortunately, there's a perfect hole above me that's shining the sun right on me. Two soldiers see me, and they reach in to heave me out.

"Ah, you're the rogue on the run with Leo." He backhands me, splitting my lip open. The bitter, coppery taste of blood fills my mouth. The other one feels the need to get in on the abuse as he punches me right in the eye. Other soldiers stalk up to see what these two have found. As I watch them approach ravenously, I see there are several dead bodies lying around me. My heart immediately drops, thinking it could be our friends, but I don't have time to investigate because one soldier stops directly in front of me.

"Hold her up." The two who have already hit me forcefully hold me up under my arms to face this menace. Wham! He sends his fist into my stomach, knocking all the air out of my lungs. Spitting blood and air all over his face, the other two throw me to the ground as I try desperately to fill my lungs with air. They yank my arms behind me, tying me up, rendering me useless. As I'm shoved even closer to the ground, I see one of the people I thought was dead wobble and stand up, trying to make a run for it.

A soldier sees him and presses a button in his hand. Another explosion goes off, sending that man's limbs in all sorts of directions, killing him instantly.

An involuntary screech escapes my lips. My ears are ringing, and my vision is blurred, but when I'm finally able to focus, I realize that one of the man's arms is literally right beside me. Attempting to keep from vomiting, I bury my face in the dirt and pray they don't find Leo.

"If she's here, he's bound to be somewhere." Take her and make sure she doesn't know where she's going. Suddenly, my whole body is violently thrust even more into the ground as someone hits me on the back of the head. Dark spots cloud my vision until I see nothing but black.

CHAPTER FOUR

Leo

As I gradually climb out of unconsciousness, I reign in my senses slowly. First, I notice the thick smell of damp, earthy rock. Secondly, I zone my attention on the steady drip echoing. Then a terrible sinking feeling hits my stomach as the dirt and stone at my back begins to crumble.

I move out of the way just before I'm buried alive. Frantically, I search for Fortune and can't find her. My heart rate and breathing pick up as chaos reigns all around. Explosions echo too close for comfort and the scent of blood adds an unnerving weight to the air.

No, she can't be buried underneath all this. I start sifting through rubble, throwing rocks out of the way to find her. As I'm about halfway through the pile at my feet, I hear a shriek and know it's her. How she's out of this tunnel and in the arms of the enemy is beyond me. I start running to where light is shining above. Jumping up, I climb out only to find guns pointing at me in all directions by the dreaded territory's Elite soldiers who kill for fun.

"On your knees," one of them barks. Glancing over at who they're holding, I see one of our friends, Vivere. She's already been shoved all the way to the ground, in bindings, with a dickhead's foot planted firmly on her back and a gun pointed right at her head. She turns her head to look at me. Her lip is busted, her eyebrow is bleeding, and there are several cuts and scrapes on her arms. She has tears welling up in her eyes.

As the feeling of impending doom hits me, an indescribable desperate feeling also consumes my soul. I twist, side sweeping the guy immediately to my left. Taking his gun, I butt him in the head, knocking him out cold. One of the soldiers shoots at me, but I duck behind a tree before it can hit me. Peeking around the other side, bark flies up as another one shoots.

"He doesn't have any armor. Let's get him," someone says.

"What about her?"

"Take her away with the other ones. We'll take care of this one. We can't let them cross the border, or they'll be off our turf, and we have no rights over there."

I hear her scream as the man obviously hurts her while making her stand. I don't wait for the others to come at me around the tree. I step out, setting my sights on each one, landing a bullet in each of their heads before they even know what hit them.

The man holding Vivere, or Vi as I call her, has her by the hair of the head with the gun pointed at her temple, staring straight at me. We've practiced simulations like this several times. I nod and when I do, she drops down to the ground with all her body weight, even with the tight grip on her head. When she falls, it yanks him forward, giving me a clear shot. With one blow, his brains are splattered all over Vivere and the surrounding foliage.

I rush to her side, freeing her from the ropes. "Where's For?" I demand.

"They took her, Malic, Aliss, and Eli." She drops her head, then continues. "Graham, Feather, and Owen didn't make it."

"Damn it." I shove my hand into my tousled hair, but I can't dwell on the dead. I must focus my energy on the ones still alive, more importantly, Fortune. "Where did they take them?"

"I'm not sure, but they went in that direction." She points over the road and down the hill. Helping her up, she dusts all the dirt and grime off her, while I pull out random strands of straw and leaves sticking out of her hair. When she's somewhat steadier on her feet, we strap all the guns to our body in various different areas.

"How did you all end up here?" I question, as we hurry in the direction of where they took off to.

"Malic picked the lock to the cart, and when the truck slowed down to take us out and execute us, we flung the doors open and took off. We ran into a few more rogues here. We've been here for three weeks, trying to find a way over the electric fence to the other territory or wait for the gates to open and sneak inside, which obviously hasn't happened. The soldiers, not being able to find us, set bombs and traps. All the other rogues we were camping and hiding out with all were killed by the explosions, too. It's only you, Fortune, Eli, Aliss, Malic, and me now against all of them." Tears are now streaming down her face. I hate that some of our friends didn't make it, but I'm glad that not all of them are dead.

"Well, we just took out over half of their group. So, with any luck, the odds will be in our favor now. We just need to find them before they get too far." At this, we take off sprinting, following boot prints and straining to look for the bloody trail the soldiers left in their wake because the sun is setting.

When we get to the end of the tracks, she and I crouch down. We're at a chain-link fence locked with a deadbolt, surrounding what appears to be an army camp.

"We'll have to wait until it's dark before we can sneak inside."

"Looks like there's way more of them than there are of us. Those odds aren't looking so good now."

"Don't worry, I'll help you get inside," an unfamiliar male voice sounds behind us.

Whipping around, my eyes widen as I see a man in the same uniform as the ones we just got away from, completely unarmed.

"What?" I'm a little dumbfounded.

"Why didn't you kill me? You only knocked me out." He crosses his arms over his chest.

"Ohhhhhh. You're the first guy I took out." I size him up and down. "I'm not in the habit of killing for fun like your kind."

"I don't kill for fun. I was raised as a soldier, like you all were. When I pledged my allegiance to the province, I didn't think they'd put me in a group who were simply put on missions to eliminate unwanted civilians for no reason at all. I thought I was agreeing to protect our territory from invading countries trying to steal our rations of food, causing us all to starve. Rest assured, we're not all blood-thirsty killers."

"Yeah, I don't believe you. The only reason you've not killed us is because we have your gun," Vivere snaps.

"I swear on my life, I'm not a murderer. I have shot a few men, but never killed anyone. Even though the generals drill into us that rogues are the ones who are vicious killers, and have been exiled because they've gone rogue, not because they simply didn't want to test to get into a group of Elites or become soldiers. I've come across a few different rogues who were merely doing their best to survive out here. They shot at me but didn't hit me. That's when I knew they weren't killers. I knew they could have made their mark if they wanted to. I mean, everyone will go back to their primal instincts in situations like these. I don't blame them for protecting themselves. I have no desire to be back in that group. But for now, you're going to have to trust me. I will pretend like I'm still in the group to get you all the clothing you need to get inside. So, don't shoot me when you see me go into soldier mode."

"You're serious." It's not a question.

"I am. And I hope when you're able to escape, you'll let me go with you."

I glance at Vivere and she gives me an uncertain look. "Prove you're true to your word, and you can go with us. Do you know how to get over the electric fence, so we're free from this territory?"

"Considering I didn't even know there was a tunnel you were hiding in, I'm definitely not privy to how to escape our territory. We're taught this is our home until we die. Even with planning my own escape, I've never even had the smallest hope I'd have the chance to leave here." He stands there scratching the scruff on his chin. "I may have the opportunity to sneak into the general's tent and steal a map, or at least look at one to figure out if there's an entrance we're not aware of, while you all get your friends."

"Speaking of. Where did they take them?"

"They're in a holding area. Tomorrow, they'll be taken back to the castle guillotine and be made an example of in front of the entire province. It's imperative we get them out tonight."

"All right. We need to move fast." I glance at the lock on the gate again. "What's your name, soldier?" He doesn't have a patch with his name on his left pocket of his shirt.

"My name is Gage, sir. At your service."

"I don't take slaves and don't give orders. I got as far away from that lifestyle as possible." I make sure he understands me loud and clear.

"Well, sir, I owe you my life. I'm forever indebted to you. I'm confident you will learn to give orders."

Shaking my head, I dismiss his comment. Now's not the time for arguing. "Okay, Private Gage. How are you getting us inside?"

He smiles a grand, toothy grin. Reaching his hand in his pocket, he pulls out a plethora of keys on a round key chain. I smack my palm to my forehead. "Oh, of course. What was I thinking?"

"There's no way you could have known." He finds the one he needs, then leads us closer to the gate, but we stay hidden behind the trees, even if it's dark. "There's a hill over there. Stay put until I get you two uniforms. When you've changed, you'll have no problem getting into the holding area. If they are chained up, you'll need these. I don't know which one will unlock them, but it'll be one of them. After you have them freed, meet me at the other end of the compound. I'll get us out and on our way, and closer to the next province. Hopefully, I'll have a way to get us inside, or at least more knowledge of where and how to get us over to their territory. If we make it, they'll grant us amenity as refugees."

"That's what we've heard," Vivere acknowledges.

He's careful not to jingle the keys. Placing them in the lock, Vivere and I hold our breath until the lock is off, and the gate is open enough to let us inside. Both she and I dart to the mound to hide behind until we've been given a fresh set of clothes.

As we're hiding, Vi finds a puddle, and begins rinsing all the dried blood from her face, arms, and hair.

"I cannot wait to get out of these clothes." She tugs the top away from her chest, glancing at the chunks of flesh caked on it.

"I second that. We'll need to hide them." I begin digging a hole with a sharp, flat rock. While I'm shoveling away dirt, I hear constant sniffles. When I turn my head, I watch tears drip off her chin at a steady pace. I stab the stone into the ground and make my way over to her.

"Hey, it's going to be okay," I try to reassure her.

"It—It might not be. This blood, it's a mixture of Feather's and Graham's." She points to her sleeves. "And these brains are

Owen's." She gestures to the side of her pants. "They had me tied up. I couldn't try to save them." She whimpers, wiping her nose with the back of her hand. "All I could do was watch."

Not knowing what else to do, I gently lay my arm around her shoulder. Her sobs turn into hot torrents of grief, pouring down her face as she buries her head into my neck. There's no undoing what's been done. She can't blame herself, like I've blamed myself for the past few weeks of their capture. This place is an abomination, and the sooner these devotees realize that, the better off they'll be.

While I'm doing my best to comfort Vi, clothes start raining down on us from above. Tilting my head up, I see Gage is above us. He puts his finger over his lips, indicating for us to keep quiet. Vi rips off her shirt, not caring that she's only in her bra. She vigorously dries her tears. When she's done, she has wiped her eyes so much they're red and puffy. Yanking on her clean uniform, she avoids looking at both of us guys. I turn my back to her and shed my stiff, dried, bloody linens and don the godforsaken uniform I swore I'd never wear. After she and I are dressed, we turn our attention back to Gage. He hops down, handing me a piece of paper.

"Here's a map… Well, a quick sketch I did of the compound. It has the most important things on here for you to lookout for, where to find your friends, and where to meet me. Be at this tree no later than two a.m." He points to a drawing of a tree all the way on the other side of this area. "You have a few hours. I'll meet you there." He hands me his keys.

"There are probably twenty to thirty keys on here. How the hell am I supposed to figure out which one will work? This is going to be extremely fun. And by fun, I mean not fun at all." I shove the ring into my pocket.

He clamps me on the shoulder and squeezes once. "I've got faith in you."

"Well, that makes one of us." Pinching the bridge of my nose, I close my eyes tight, and tell myself that I can do this. As I'm reciting this silently, Vi stands right beside me.

"No. That makes two of us. I've seen you get us out of some very sticky situations before. Don't doubt yourself now. If Gage, who's only just met you, knows you can do this, I certainly do, too."

"We've got this." Wiping my sweaty palms onto my shirt, I look at Gage and say. "If we're more than ten minutes late, leave. We'll find our way out." I nod once, as does he. Then I slink into the shadows with Vi. Gage takes off in an entirely different direction.

Each tent we make it to, we're sure to stay completely out of sight. Moonlight filters through tree canopies dappling the ground with various shades of blue, somewhat illuminating our trail on the outskirts of the barracks. When we finally make it to the prisoner hut, we see two soldiers manning the entrance. Now, we just have to figure out how to take them down without causing a scene.

"Choke hold?" Vi whispers to me.

"Sounds good to me. You take the left; I'll take the right."

Both of us grab each guard without us making a sound. While they're drifting off to sleep, we drag their bodies and hide them behind the tent.

"I'll pretend to be keeping watch while you free them. Try not to take long."

"No pressure." I smirk. "I'll do my best."

When we make it back to the front of the tent, there's still no one else around. Vi begins pacing back and forth as a true soldier, and I sneak inside. Visibility is slim to none here. There's a place where the moon has an unobscured direct path of light shining on the back of the tent. Slinking to where that spot is, I unsheathe my knife and try my best not to trip over sleeping bodies lining each side. When I get to the illuminating cloth, I stab and rip it slowly, letting the beams shine inside. Holding the cloth open partially, moonlight shines on my friends, my love, and a couple of people I don't know. All of them are shackled and bound on their hands and feet.

Fortune sluggishly begins to stir when the light lands on her face. Squatting down beside her, I cup my hand over her mouth to keep her from screaming or saying anything. Her wide frantic eyes finally land on me, and her breathing begins to slow. I fish out the keys and begin trying to jam one after the other in the locks until one finally clicks it open. When I free her, I instruct her to exit out of the slit and to hide. Getting them unchained one by one, I end up with the last two people I don't recognize.

"They're fine to free. They've been camping out with us and trying to find a way to the other territory. They lost all their friends.

They only have each other and us," Aliss says, pleading their case very well. Vi thought all of them died, but I guess not. She'll be happy about that. After everyone is freed and out of the back of the tent, I wait until Vi's shadow is directly in front of the tent opening before I poke my head out to let Vi know.

"Pssst." I get her attention.

"About time," she whisper yells. A drop of sweat streams from her forehead down her cheek.

"How are you sweating when we can see our breath in the air?" I tease.

She huffs. "Are they unbound or not?"

"Yes. They are waiting for us on the other side of the tent." Opting not to walk around, we duck back inside, then go through the tent until we exit. When we're out, everyone is pretty much flush against the linen wall. "Our destination is on the other side of that hill." I point to our rendezvous area. We only have a half hour until Gage will go on without us, but I doubt it'll take that long before someone notices the prisoner tent is vacant. I grab For's hand and lead her in the direction we are to head to. I hold on, perhaps a little too tight, but I'll be damned if I lose her again.

We make it around the mound just in time for alarms to start blaring. Gage is standing there waiting for us with another person. Great! More people I'm not sure if we can trust.

"This is Corporal Lindy Mendez. She and I grew up together and have the same opinion of the Elite and Royals."

"That's fine." My eyes snap to her. "Nice to meet you. Not to be rude, but we need to get out of here, like now."

"I was able to sketch a map of a way out of here and two possible entry points for the province of Drodal. They don't starve their citizens and have a safe haven for evacuees." He points to what appears to be a mountainous range. "We go through here, then up and over here. It'll take a couple of weeks at best. It'll be freezing on the top of the mountains, even if spring is almost here. We need to travel the most during the nights and rest as much as we can during the day."

"Lead the way." I all but shove him to the fence line.

When he gets to the fence, he bends down, rolling away a small stone which has a key hidden under it. Unlocking a hidden trapdoor, we all slip down into another tunnel, one by one. When everyone is in, he locks it back but from the other side. "We planted this getaway route last year." He gestures to Lindy.

I clasp his shoulder. "We're glad you did."

"We were able to snag food and water as well." Lindy holds up a bag of sustenance.

"Fantastic. Let's get as far away from here as we can for now. We can revisit the need for nourishment later."

"Yes, sir." Gage takes the lead with Lindy by his side. I can't believe we have two more weeks before we'll actually be able to rest our heads without targets on our backs. Nevertheless, we must trudge on.

CHAPTER FIVE

Fortune

The soldier who appears in front of me is large and broad-shouldered. His brawny arms and tan skin stand in direct contrast to the warm and friendly smile on his face. *I can't believe he found me.* Blinking several times through swollen eyes, I make sure I'm not seeing things. I just knew my life was over or about to be over in the next few hours. I'm not entirely sure how Leo found me. I'm just glad he did. I was glad to see my old friend, my new lover, my now forever. When we make it below ground again, we all take off running in silence, listening the best we can for anyone who may have found us or might be following us. The further we get away from the compound, the less we can hear of the alarms.

I'm not sure for how long or how far we've run, but there are no sounds of anything other than all of our huffing. We've stopped as prompted by a soldier that Leo seems to trust.

"We're far enough away. We should be able to eat, then continue on." The soldier hands each of us a ration of bread and dried beef. I don't even contemplate if it's poisoned or not. I'm starving, so I nearly inhale the food. Leo twists the cap off his canteen of water, and I guzzle it, too. Now that we're all taking a short break, I realize that I don't see all of my friends who were captured here with us.

"Where's Feather, Owen, and Graham?" I scan the group to make sure I didn't overlook them.

"They didn't make it." Leo looks down at the ground and kicks a pebble away.

I glance over at Vivere and see that her eyes have obviously been bleeding with pain. Tears escape my lids, followed by my fist meeting the tunnel wall. I can't scream, can't breathe, and can't believe they're no longer with us.

"Hey, hey. Don't hurt yourself. There's nothing we can do now except move forward and strive to obtain our freedom with the friends here with us now." He takes my hand and kisses my bloody knuckles, but I can't seem to turn off the waterworks. Sliding my back down the wall, I crumble into a disheveled heap as my grief pours out. Vi makes her way over to me, encasing her arms around me in a tight hug. After a few minutes, I'm able to stop sobbing. Wiping my cheeks every few seconds while everyone else finishes their food, I eventually pull it together.

"Enough resting, we must move," the soldier barks.

Leo holds his hand out to me, lifting me to stand. "When we get to the end of this tunnel, there are bags of supplies, backpacks, warm clothing, and blankets. Everyone will need to grab as much as you can. You'll be responsible for your own well-being with the provisions stashed away. Should you lose any of your supplies, it might be a death sentence for yourself. Be sure to keep it safely secured to your body." He pins us with a knowing look. None of us say anything, knowing he's correct. I'm simply grateful for our escape. And now, as my grieving heart wants to rip apart at the thought of losing my friends, I know their deaths will be in vain if I don't continue with a new hope that the group here before me, stands a chance at a better future outside the walls of this territory.

Picking up our pace once more, we propel forward blindly, following this soldier to wherever he's leading us. My thighs ache, lungs burn, and cold sweat pours into my eyes as we finally begin to slow down. At the thought of taking a rest, I lean my body against the cool stone. It bites through my drenched shirt, sending cold chills through my overheated body.

Untwisting his canteen, Leo holds it out for me to drink. "Here, you needn't get dehydrated on top of exhaustion, lest you collapse."

Giving him a fake smile, I take the water and guzzle it down. I don't want to drink it all because I know he needs it, too. Gulping my last swig, I hand it back to him. "Here, you need it, too." He takes it from me, giving me a sidelong glance. "Don't look at me like you don't require hydration as well." Leo goes to put the lid on it instead of drinking, and I'm about to protest, but soldier boy starts talking again.

"Once we get packed up, there's a stream nearby. We'll refill our canteens and head for the hills. There's a cave we can all crash inside to stay warm. Even though it'll be cold, we'd be better off traveling at night instead of during the day. That's when the soldiers will be out looking for us." The soldier and his comrade start handing out satchels, totes, galoshes, and other things for us to survive with.

Quirking an eyebrow at Leo, he takes the hint and finishes off the water.

"So, you trust them?" I quietly ask, nodding to the two soldiers.

"I do." He gives a curt bob of his head.

"And why?" I don't remember much of the ambush, but I do remember that they were hell bent on killing us.

"Gage and Lindy have been looking for the opportunity to get out of this hell hole, and we just so happen to be a group of rogues refusing to bow to the Royals, swearing to kill anyone who doesn't benefit the kingdom. He's tired of seeing innocent people suffer and wants no part in the killing spree. He and a few of his buddies are the ones who've been making this tunnel and stocking supplies, so that, given the right opportunity, they could make a break for it."

"I'm still skeptical, but I trust you and your judgment." Wrapping my arms around my knees, I wait for my cue to strap all the resources onto my body. Once everyone is packed up and ready, Gage instructs us to follow him. When we resurface, it's still dark. He leads us to the stream, and we stay on our guard as we fill our canteens to the brim with water.

"We need to walk in the water to keep from making tracks, so use your rubber boots and try to keep water from going inside your shoes. You don't want to catch your death out here." We all do as we're told and stay close to the water's edge, so we don't splash water over the top of our boots, and to keep our clothes as dry as possible. It's pitch black out here, save for the full moon overhead, shining brightly as it lights our way. Silver moonlight shines through the tree canopies, dusting them with sparkles. A heavy breeze stirs the leaves, speckling the light along the waterway. My heart grips with emotion as we race to get to the cave. We try to tread as quietly as we can, but moving against the current is difficult and with us needing to get to our destination as soon as possible, has us struggling even more to all but run in this frigid mess.

When the sun finally decides to make an appearance, a worried look crosses Leo's face. "What's wrong?" I say, only loud enough for him to hear.

"We shouldn't be out in the daylight."

"It's dusk. The sun isn't fully up yet."

"Doesn't matter. Those killers are on the prowl, and I can't lose you again. No, I won't lose you again," Leo corrects himself as he moves to get closer to me. A warmth fills my insides at his confession, and I loop my arm through his. The sounds of everyone stopping in front of us catches my attention. When I look ahead, I see Gage has stopped. He's searching the riverbank in front of us. When he spots what he's looking for, he points in the direction we need to go.

Only once we finally get inside does Leo let go of me. Assisting me in taking off my wet shoes and jacket, he drapes them over a rock near the fire that Gage has going. Me and the other girls make a partition, hiding ourselves from the guys, so we can take off the rest of our wet clothing. After we're in dry clothes, we join the guys around the fire. We all eat a little something, but we're all beyond tired. It's nice and dark in this large cavern, so we all get our sleeping bags, ready to crawl inside. Leo takes his spot next to me. He unzips his blanket entirely and lays it on the ground. I eye him suspiciously. He doesn't say anything, simply takes mine and unzips it, too. Laying it on top of his, he slinks underneath the top cover. Throwing the edge of the cover aside, he pats for me to join him.

A sly smile curves on my face as I slowly inch under the covers, too.

Wrapping his arms around my torso, he snuggles me against his strong chest. "I was terrified I'd never see you again." His warm breath grazes my neck, making my heart race in my chest.

"Me too," I whisper.

"I'm never letting you out of my sight again." His grip tightens on me as he declares his promise, and in this moment, he has my heart bursting at the seams.

"You know, some people would say that's a bit stalkerish," I tease.

"You know, I don't give a second thought about what other people say." His lips skim the bottom of my ear, causing my stomach to flip-flop and other areas on my body to heat up. Feeling his lower half pressed hard against me, it's obvious I'm not the only one aroused by our close proximity. There are too many people in here for me to make a move. So, I lay here, willing my heart to stop thrashing against my ribs.

"We're all the way into the back of the cave. No one's around us, nor can they see us." His hand trails to my lower abdomen and my breath hitches in the back of my throat. As he makes circles around the hem of my shirt, my hand finds its way to his pleasure spot, and I gently caress the outside of his pants. If he can tease me, I can return the favor.

He lets a low grumble out, vibrating his chest against me. While his fingers work their way lower and lower, my willpower lessens. Giving into my desire, I flip over onto my back, and let him work his magic while I fumble to undo his britches. As he hovers over the top of me, my eyes dart to the fire that's now been extinguished. I can't see anyone. And the snores of a couple of guys are the only sounds above our heated breathing.

Tugging him closer to me, he searches my eyes. Seeing the glint in them, he takes the hint, crashing his lips onto mine and consumes me right here and now. It doesn't take long to send me over the top. Arching my back in sheer bliss, Leo covers my mouth with his shoulder to keep any moans or sounds I might make from being heard. Being with him this way is surreal. I don't know if I'll ever get used to this feeling. I've longed to have this type of relationship with him for forever, and I'll relish and revel in each moment we have together. To know he's mine and loves me the same is enough to make me hit a high point twice as he reaches his peak.

Collapsing on top of me, his heavy breaths match mine. "You like the idea of almost getting caught, huh?" he jokes as he rolls off me.

"You're not wrong." Heat flushes up my chest all the way up to my face. "It is kind of a turn on, but that's not why I caved." I pull the covers over our heads. "I'll jump on any opportunity to be with you." He chuckles and heaves me closer to him. I flip over until we're back in our spooning position.

"I'll let you jump me anytime, anywhere." He nuzzles his nose into the base of my neck. Silently laughing, I close my eyes and let peace and exhaustion lull me to sleep.

***

We awaken to soft shakes to our shoulders and whispers to get up. Rubbing my bleary eyes, I attempt to glance around us, but it's pitch black in here. I can't tell if it's night or day but clearly, it's time to move. I've slept so well I haven't even moved positions from where I fell asleep. It's nice to be able to have some sense of tranquility in this world of chaos.

As we wrap up our sleeping bags and gather our things, we meander out of the mouth of the cave, only to find the moon is hidden by thick cloud coverage. If it storms, it'll be a blessing and a curse. The sounds of our footsteps will be muffled, but we'll get so cold, hypothermia could set in. Leo's holding my hand so tight, I think it might start cramping, but I won't complain. The security of him being near is worth any discomfort my hand might temporarily feel.

He tugs me close and whispers. "Sorry for being so intense. I just want to have you securely by my side. It gives me peace of mind knowing our fingers are locked together. They'll have to pry you from my cold, dead hands before I'll let you go."

"Neither of us are dying. Please don't talk like that."

"We're not promised tomorrow. I'm just saying…"

"Well, stop saying it. We're together now, and come hell or high water, we're getting to the other territory safely."

"That's right," he affirms at the same time the sky flashes bright as lightning jets across the sky. One, one thousand, two, two thousand, three, three thousand. Rumbling thunder sounds only three seconds from the light, indicating the storm is directly overhead. Not long after the first few streaks brighten the sky, do enormous rain drops begin to fall. We're climbing up a mountain that's already slick from melting snow, now we're adding to it saturated stones, slippery mud, and slick leaves, so someone's bound to twist an ankle or get hurt much worse.

"Stick close to me, and I'll make sure you don't fall." Leo lets go of my hand to firmly grab my upper arm. Even though we have rubber boots on, there's still no grip on this drenched ground. Our pace is slowed by heavy rain blinding us, causing it to be difficult to see which way to go, as well as the terrain being more dangerous to hike. A few have already slipped, and either cut themselves on the jagged rocks or ripped their clothes while obtaining some nasty scrapes and bruises. Nonetheless, we trudge on. Our sheer determination to not get captured by the Elite is enough ammunition to continue without looking back.

Torrents of rain sweep sideways, stinging my exposed skin. Even though my eyes are less swollen, it's still nearly impossible to see with the onslaught of rain. Strong wailing winds send me flying backward as we near the peak of the mountain, nearly causing me to topple over the edge. Leo's death grip is the only thing that's keeping me from plummeting to my death. He wraps me close to his chest. Fear mixed with relief overwhelms me, and tears mix with the deluge. I wrap my arms snuggly around his chest and don't let go until my thrashing heart settles down. Our allies have stopped to give me time to regroup. Once I've recovered enough to continue, I nod, giving the confirmation I'm good to go.

I wish things were different. I wish we could just be on the other side already. I wish we didn't have days on end before we're even close to crossing the border, but that's not reality. Reality stinks, and I know that in the end, it'll all be worth it for a better life. Inhaling a deep breath, I begin to put one foot in front of the other. Looking down, I watch my every step. The trek down the mountain will probably be even more dangerous.

I've resorted to sliding on my bottom in some spots because the path is too steep, and I'd rather not crack my skull in attempting to walk down the slippery slope. Leo, love his soul, refuses to let me go at it alone, so he slides with me. It's a much faster way to travel down, and the rest of the crew quickly follows suit. It only takes a few more hours before we're at the bottom, and it's just in time because the sun is cresting the horizon. My shivering body longs to stand directly in the warmth, but I know that's an impossibility. Instead, we hike through the freezing stream to wash most of the mud off our clothes before we find another place to rest. I can only tolerate a handful of minutes in this water before my bottom lip trembles, and my body begins to quiver uncontrollably. I'm not the only one. Vi's teeth chatter so loudly I can hear it above the rushing waves, and Aliss's lips are bluer than the water.

"We've got to get shelter and heat now," Leo's voice carries above the rushing river.

"There should be another cavern nearby. It's deeper, and we can have a larger fire inside. Keep your eyes peeled for a lion head rock poking out of the side of the mountain. That's where we'll enter, but for now, let's get out of the water." Gage points in the direction we're to go, only I can't feel my feet. Stumbling to climb out, I slip and hit my chin so hard it knocks me out for a few seconds. When I come to, I'm being cradled as my head bumps against a firm chest. Looking up, I see that Leo is carrying me while running.

"There!" I hear Malic shout. Turning my head to see where he is, I watch him slap his hand over his mouth.

"It's fine. No one should be this far yet looking for us," Gage assures. "But let's make haste, everyone's freezing."

I attempt to wiggle out of Leo's arms. That cave is just a few feet away. I'm sure I'll be fine to make it.

"Not a chance. I'm not putting you down. Stop squirming. I don't want to drop you," Leo growls, while giving me a firm look. Heeding his warning, I cease moving.

When we're inside, all the females head to the back and strip down. Our other belongings are in waterproof totes, so we're fortunate to have dry clothes to change into as well as dry blankets. Struggling to get off my pants, I sit down and tug them from the ankle to wriggle them loose. I slap myself in the face from pulling them so hard and hit my lower lips that I now realize is busted most likely from my face plant on the bank only moments ago. Geesh, just one more thing to add to the not so wonderful things over the course of this escape plan. Swallowing my pride, I ask Aliss and Vi to assist me in my failed attempt to undress. They do so without question or laughing. I truly have the best friends anyone could ask for.

Once we're changed, we make our way to the guys, who are already in clean clothes and sitting around the fire talking. We drape our wet things on random sticks and stones to dry. Hopefully, they'll be dried out before we have to set out tonight. If they're still damp, it'll only add to the weight we have to carry.

Huffing, I place myself directly beside Leo and lean over onto his shoulder, careful not to rub blood on his clean shirt. Staring into the flames, I'm deep in thought when someone waves their hand in front of my face.

"I said, isn't that right, Fortune?" Malic says a bit loudly, from my other side.

"Hmmm? What? I'm sorry." My puffy lip causes my words to come out funny.

"I was just saying at this pace, we'll be there a lot sooner than we expected."

Rubbing the side of my swollen face, I say. "I sure hope so."

Lindy squats down beside Gage. "We're definitely moving a lot quicker than we'd anticipated. If we keep up this pace, given no one gets ill or severely injured, I'd say we'll shave off a few days for sure."

My heart leaps in my chest. I'll be damned if I let my track record of obtaining injuries get in my way. Sitting bolt upright, I attempt my best smile.

"Someone's excited." Leo's arm around my waist squeezes a little.

"Knowing we'll be there sooner ignites a new hope. Today was… trying at best. I'll do whatever it takes to get there sooner," I exclaim. Everyone else around the flame murmurs their agreements as well.

"The sooner we get some shuteye, the sooner we can wake up and continue on." Eli takes Aliss's hand and escorts her to their sleeping bags. They've always made a cute couple. I'm glad they finally see it. Next, Malic lends his hand to Vivere, assisting her as she stands, and both of them make their way to their covers. After everyone is situated, Leo leads me to our stash of blankets around the wall far away from everyone, so that they're out of sight, but not so far away we can't feel the warmth of the fire.

I snuggle up close to my handsome hunk of a man, burying my cold nose into his chiseled chest. His pectoral muscle jumps in reflex, and I let out a slight giggle.

"You think that's funny, huh?" Leo drags the cover over our heads.

"Just a little." I gaze up to see the tiniest light glimmer in his eyes along with the most devious smirk. "Oh no," I refute. I know what he's thinking. "You can't. You'll wake everyone up." My protest does nothing to deter his mischievous finger from digging into my sides, tickling me.

I buck forward, pressing my mouth entirely to his chest to muffle out my laughs. Doing my best to not laugh out loud, I try my hardest to pry his hands away from my waist. He doesn't give. The only thing I can think of to get him to stop is to grab his manhood. I don't know what I was expecting when I grabbed it, but being firmly erect was not one of them. He immediately stops goosing me and inhales sharply. My eyes have adjusted to the dark, and I can see a flash of desire burn in his eyes. He flexes in my grip, and I refuse to let go. Rubbing lightly up and down, his breath gets more haggard. His hand trails up my side and under my shirt until it's firmly cupping and caressing my bare chest.

Not fair!

My fingers fumble, but eventually get his button undone, and I mimic his flesh-on-flesh encounter, never tearing my eyes from his. My heart rate picks up and I can feel his beating through his chest. As he massages deeper, I do as well. It only takes a few more strokes until his lips come crashing down onto mine. I let out a little yelp involuntarily.

"Oh. I'm so sorry. I forgot about your lip." He backs away instantly.

"It's a pain I'll greatly enjoy." I press my lips gently to his. He moves his hot, soft lips against mine in a rhythm only our mouths know the dance to. When he deepens the kiss, it sends red-hot fire zipping up my veins.

I don't know how long our mouths are tangled up in each other or how long it took to rip our clothes off each other. Leo does things to my body and makes me forget who I am and where I'm at. Every inch of me is blazing with need. He hovers over me, and I stare deeply into his dark eyes that have become so infinitely cherished to me. His eyes burn with a desire, identical to my own, and I pull him down into a ravenous kiss.

Suddenly, we're flesh touching flesh, and when the space between us is concealed, the world stops and starts all at the same time, while the cosmos stand still in the galaxy, and I willingly give him every part of me, our souls join as one again. Regardless of what our future holds, this man will know I love him with every part of my being.

CHAPTER SIX

Leo

Waking up with Fortune nestled comfortably against me is the best feeling in the world. I can't wait until we get out of this hellhole and solidify our freedom. When we get outside, our breath billows up in circles while we discuss the safest route to take. At least the moon is out tonight, even if it's only half a sliver. Silver glistens against the remaining snow and rain puddles. Deciding to take the path with the thickest foliage to cover our tracks, we take off at a rapid pace.

We've been going nonstop for hours, only breaking for us to relieve our bladders and to snack. It's nearly dawn, and we need to find a place to bed down. Once we find a suitable area, we're forced to sleep high up in the trees in makeshift hammocks above the ground. We lay in them two by two so our body heat helps keep both people warm. Even though it's broad daylight, our sheer exhaustion from our fast pace of traveling with little to no breaks means we'll have no difficulties slumbering. As Fortune gets situated in front of me, my arousal becomes very evident. She doesn't let it hinder her, though. These arrangements don't make for the ideal place to fulfill my desires with her, but I'll just dream of a day when we can do as we please at liberty, without the chance of being caught. I hold her snugly to my chest and as her breathing evens out. Only then do I allow myself to drift off to sleep.

***

We continue at a rapid pace day in and day out, always on high alert, for the next week and a half, knowing the enemy is hot on our trail, even though we've been vigilant to cover our tracks. We see their campfires at night, way off in the vastness between us. They have no need to hide their whereabouts. They couldn't care less if we know where they are. Their primary goal is to kill and eliminate those who oppose the ways of the kingdom. I feel like I'm about to explode with excitement when we can see our escape route in the far distance, but because the sun is rising, we're forced to take shelter one more time before victory awaits us on the other side.

"Your heart is racing incredibly fast and pounding extremely hard," Fortune mentions after we crawl into our sleeping bags and she's flush against my bare chest. "Are you okay?"

"I will be after we step foot onto friendly territory. I can't believe we were born and raised here and are now identified as an enemy, causing us to literally run for our lives every day. It's so messed up."

"You're right it is. Fleeing mass poverty, cruelty and fear, and shacks for homes is necessary. Life has always been hard unless you're an Elite or royalty. Facing the harsh reality of our outcome if we stay isn't an option. Knowing they most likely killed our parents when we were in school being trained to be Elite makes me want to vomit. There's no way they just disappeared. To make matters worse, the leaders who have control are warped in their way of thinking. Instead of coming up with a solution to the drought; like importing water from neighboring countries, they make them enemies by threatening them if they even attempt to come here for any reason whatsoever. This control is too significant. Harsh rules are made only to benefit the rulers. To hell with the little peons like us. I keep holding on to the hope that after tomorrow, we'll be away from their twisted, demented ways and will have a bright future awaiting us." She curls her fingers with mine, tugging my arm over her side.

It takes more than a few minutes to calm my racing heart in anticipation of the better life that awaits us, but I eventually do.

No sooner do I doze off, do I hear the emergency bird call from Gage, warning us to get up and either prepare to fight or run. We're swinging in our hammocks high above the ground. I poke my head over the edge of the sack, searching for him. When I make eye contact with him, he points to brush moving not too far away, indicating that our enemies are closer than we anticipated. We forgo wrapping up our swaying beds and leave them suspended in the air to climb down to the ground.

He ushers us close, giving us instructions to stick closer together, be armed and ready, and to follow him, doing our best to leave no trace of our steps. I'm not sure if it's pure adrenaline from running for our lives, or the rush of knowing that we're this close to freedom, but we get to the electric fence in a matter of a couple of hours.

Buzzing and humming indicate the thing is on and ready to do damage if anyone or anything touches it.

"How do we get past the fence?" Malic asks the question we're all thinking.

"There's a refugee tunnel. We just have to find it," Gage states.

"Do you know where the tunnel is?" Vi's hand lands firmly on her hip.

"If I did, I can assure you it'd be blown to bits by now because that would mean the Elite would know and would destroy it. So, be glad I don't." Gage isn't trying to be a smartass, but he's not wrong. If they knew where it was located, it'd be long gone by now.

"Let's get to looking then." Fortune takes my hand and leads me to a thicket in front of a hill only a few paces away. Everyone else searches frantically with weapons in hand. I keep watch while she tears through the shrubs and feels around for anything that would indicate there's a secret pathway there. She pops her head out every once in a while, pulling leaves out of her hair and vines off her arms to give me an update. This time when she steps out, she swipes a stray hair from her face as her dirty fingernails rake across her cheek, leaving a trail of mud.

"Any luck?"

"Actually, yes. The ground is about to give way in a certain spot that's entirely covered with ivy. I need help to remove all the vines, but I'm afraid we'll fall through, and no one will be able to find us."

"Let me get their attention." I take a tiny mirror and reflect the sun off it to shine into our friends' eyes. After I get everyone to notice us, they quickly head over. I fill them in on what Fortune's found, and we rapidly get to work. Sure as the world, when the ivy is removed, there's an enormous gaping fissure in the ground. We braid several vines together and keep the majority of them as close as possible to disclose this area.

"It's now or never. Let's go down one by one. Once we're inside, we'll follow the path. It's vital we cover it back up. Therefore, the last one down needs to drag the vines back over this opening as they descend," Gage advises.

"I'll go last," Eli offers. Aliss crosses her arms over her chest and gives him the stank eye. "Look, I know you're not keen on this idea, but someone has to do it."

"Then I'm going second to last. You know, just to make sure you make it down." Her arms unfold, and her fists land firmly on her hips. He throws up his hands in surrender.

"Okay. Now that we got that settled, let's get down quickly. They're moving fast." Gage hops down and holds a hand up, helping everyone else down.

I think to myself. *Finally, there's a light at the end of the tunnel.*

CHAPTER SEVEN

Fortune

Right before Eli descends as the last one in our group into the crevice, the ground violently shakes. Gravel and dirt tumble down all around us as the Elite detonate explosives. My entire body is shot to the other side of the rocky terrain, and I'm almost knocked unconscious. Willing my body to stay alert, I search the area to see who else has been injured. My swollen right eye is swelling even faster, causing it to close entirely, and the coppery taste of blood, once again, fills my mouth. Not that I could control my body being flung into the rocks. I'm still ashamed to look at Leo with a black eye and puffy face, but I do it anyway.

"We need to get everyone to the other side now," he yells, crawling toward me. I can't tell if he has any injuries because we're all covered in dirt and dust from the boulder being blown to smithereens. We scramble to find everyone, get a head count, and verify everyone is accounted for. Most of us lost our weapons when the eruptions started. When we get to Eli, he confirms he was able to cover the escape route right before the blasts began.

After we get everyone safely out of the tunnel, avoiding raining rock and rubble along the way. There are friendly, yet scary, armed forces awaiting our arrival. They quickly assist us above ground.

No sooner do we stand, do we hear shouts from the other side of the fence, followed by arrows and any other sharp object they can project over or through the fence line. This militia immediately begins firing back at them with fire blazing arrows, while instructing us to get to a safe area. One soldier gives us different arms to retaliate with if we're able.

Even with my eye swollen shut, I can send a few arrows their way. I accept the bow and a quiver full of sharp arrows. When I knock one into place, I get ready to fire it when suddenly Leo collapses at my side. There's a lot of smoke and debris causing thick clouds of dust, but when I make it to his side, my eyes land on an arrow that pierced him through and through. It's under his clavicle, but protruding through his back. He's about to try to remove it, but I grab his hand immediately.

"Don't. We don't know if it's severed any arteries. Just stay here and let us take care of things. It shouldn't take long." I grab his hand and squeeze.

His jaw clenches and unclenches as he traces my face with the bloody fingertips of his free hand. He begins coughing. At first, it's just a mild cough, but then quickly turns into a coughing fit. When he pulls his hand away, there's fresh blood on his palms. My eyes widen when I realize that his injury is really bad. I don't want to leave his side, but I know if I engage in battle, it'll help this get over sooner.

My voice is thick with emotion when I ask Leo what he wants me to do. He says. "I want you to kill them and not feel any regret for it." Then he looks away, spitting out blood.

I grip my bow tightly, but before I can stand up, Vi yanks me to my feet, nearly ripping my shirt collar. Shredding seams of the material, she fights to get my attention. Glancing down, I notice there's small, frayed strands sticking out from her fist. *A torn shirt is the least of my worries.* Her wild eyes dart from me to the group on the other side of the electric fence.

"We have to end them before they do us," she shouts.

"I know, but first, you need to let me go and get your weapon." I grip her hand and gently pry it away from my clothing. Nodding, she scurries to grab her bow.

Standing side by side, we launch our arrows over the fence and nail several targets. As they drop, we keep reloading and send arrows flying. We've got to get Leo and the other injured people help.

It seems as if it's over as fast as it starts. The Elite have either retreated or perished, so we gather our things. I run over to where I left

Leo and panic when he's not there. All I see is an enormous puddle of blood where his body was laying. The air is thick with smoke, but I can see forms off in the distance. They're shouting, but I can't make out what they're saying. I take off in their direction. As I get closer, it's very obvious they're giving commands and orders to give medications and do things that are life-saving measures as they carry a few bodies in cots to a building nearby. I glance down at each person I get to, searching for Leo. So far, none are him. My heartbeat accelerates at an alarming rate.

I race past the soldiers and make a beeline for the all-brick structure. There's a red cross painted on the side of it, indicating it's a medical clinic. I bust through the doors, and it's even more chaotic in here than it is outside. People in uniform are yelling directives. Suffering patients are screaming out. However, nothing can shift my focus or determination to find Leo.

Slowly assessing each of the wounded, I eventually make it to the back of the structure and see a few mounds that have got to be bodies covered in sheets. These once white sheets are now littered with blood soaking through them pretty heavily in certain areas. My heart stops. All sounds of chaos become silence around me as my ears go deaf and my entire body numbs. I drop to my knees and uncover one of the forms. My lungs refuse to function until I make sure it's not him. Only when I realize that it's a soldier from this territory, do I allow myself to inhale oxygen.

I force my legs to walk over to the next form. Slowly, I uncover the next body. Biting my swollen lip so hard I draw blood, I hold my breath, praying it's not Leo. The head is twisted away from me, but the body is so bloody I can't tell if it's him or not. My shaking hands grab the face, and I nearly drop it from how cold and firm it is. Rigor mortis is already setting in. I have to know, though. I tell myself this person is dead; he won't feel anything. I twist until the neck cracks so I can tell if it's him. I exhale a sigh of relief when I realize it's not.

Out of the corner of my eye, I see the third sheet. I swear I see it move slightly up and down. Racing to this person's side, even if it's not Leo, this person isn't dead unless my eyes are deceiving me. I don't take my time removing the sheet. I rip it off and find Malic. A blood-curdling scream involuntarily escapes me. The entire room falls silent.

"He's not dead," I scream, and it all but echoes. Two soldiers run to my side. One presses his fingers to Malic's neck, while the other one listens for breathing sounds.

"He's alive. Quick, get him to a bed!" Both guys immediately take Malic and begin working on him. Vi is at the other end of the room and takes off in a sprint toward me. When she gets to me, I can tell she's been crying her eyes out.

"Will he make it?" she chokes out in sobs.

One of the men gives her a sorrowful look. "It's too soon to tell, but we'll do everything we can to save him."

I clamp her on the shoulder. "Stay here. I've got to find Leo."

"Who?" one of the men working on Malic asks.

"A guy who was shot with an arrow. I asked him to stay put, so I could help fight off the Elite, but when I got to where I left him, he was gone." I'm hardly able to maintain my composure as tears threaten to spill.

"He's in the other wing. Our healers are performing surgery on him. They won't let you in to see him until they're done." He pauses briefly to glance at me. "I know you're torn about what to do. Your friend here looks like she's in shock. I think it'd be best if you stay here with her. The healers will come here to look for someone to update as soon as they're done." Turning his gaze away from me, he continues to get back to working on Malic.

I wrap Vi in my arms and direct her attention to me. "Hey, have you seen Aliss and Eli?"

"Yes, they're okay. Minor injuries being tended to." She points at the door where both are sitting next to each other while being bandaged up. Relief and joy flood my veins but dissipates just as quickly when one of the medics starts doing chest compressions on Malic. I twist Vi's body away from him in an attempt to keep her from witnessing this. My heart is tearing open as I pray that he makes it through this.

"Clear the way. We need to get to the healers fast," one of the medics hollers.

Vi crumples to the ground as we watch them take off with Malic's body to the surgical wing. Her entire body racks with shudders. "Please, Fortune. Please." She grabs the inside of my knees and buries her head into my legs. Her hot tears are soaking my pants as she begs me to tell her he's going to be fine.

I open my mouth to speak, but nothing comes out. My voice is mute. I don't contradict her pleas or want to give her false hope, so I just sit beside her, holding her while I simply stroke her hair and cry along with her. Even in all our preparation for battles, nothing could have prepared us for this. The very real reality of potentially losing someone else so close to us is too much to bear.

We stay like that for a few moments before someone lightly touches my shoulder and says in a soft voice. "Someone's here to speak with you." Twisting, I look up and see Aliss. She points for me to peek over at whoever it is. Slowly, Vi unburies her face and lets go of me.

"Go see what they need." She wipes her dripping nose with the hem of her shirt.

Aliss scoots beside Vi. "I'll stay with her."

Vi lays her head on Aliss's shoulder and waves me on.

Through my blurry eyes, I try my best to focus on the man waiting for me to give me whatever news he has. Bile creeps up in the back of my throat, and it takes all I have not to vomit right here and now.

Swallowing thickly, I stammer out. "Y—You asked for me?"

"Hello, I'm General Luther. I was told to update you on your friend's condition." He pauses as he takes in a deep breath. One I'm sure is to prepare himself before he drops a bomb on me. Tears prick the back of my eyes, but I refuse to blink. "He's unconscious, but alive and breathing." His grim features tell me he doesn't want me to have high expectations of his outcome, but it's too late for that.

Hope washes over me like a flood. "He's—he's not dead?" My voice grates against the back of my throat.

"Yes, as of now. I don't want to give you false optimism. He lost a lot of blood. We were able to stop the bleeding and fix the arteries, but… but I can't be certain he'll pull through. Now it's just a waiting game." He rakes his hand down his face.

I clasp my hands together. "When can I see him?"

"Now, but he needs rest. Follow me. I'll take you to him."

I stick close to General Luther as we weave through more people. I had no idea they had this many soldiers here. I didn't have the chance to really see how many in their militia were here waiting on refugees. I make sure that as I pass; I give each of them a slight smile of gratitude. They didn't have to put their life on the line to help complete strangers, but they chose to anyway. It takes a few minutes that feels more like years to get to the surgery wing.

When we finally arrive inside the area where they're recovering, the general leads me to a cot near the middle. After I get to Leo's side, I pause and watch the slow rise and fall of his bare chest that's now got bandages around the worst wound he sustained. I don't make it to the chair against the wall beside his bed. My strength gives out, and I collapse to the ground, grabbing Leo's hand that's dangling beside the bed. I kiss the top of it, leaving behind a trail of tears and saliva. I hug and kiss his hand, clinging to life, while begging the heavens above to please let him pull through this. Several minutes pass, and the general let me fawn over Leo, even though he told me to let him rest.

Once I'm able to stand on my weak legs. I lean over Leo, stroking his gaunt cheek. "Leo… Leo, if you can hear me. I'm here." My tears spill onto his eyelids and face. He attempts to blink. Finally able to peel his brittle eyes open. He lets a tiny grin curl the corners of his lips. I gasp as a joyous smile forms on my face, a complete inconsistency to my swollen puffy eyes, runny nose, and busted lip.

"Fortune…" his voice rattles as he begins to cough. After his hacking fit settles down, he continues. "I—I didn't know if I'd ever see you again." He forces back his own tears, stating the theme sentence of our relationship that at any given moment of these days, we're not promised tomorrow.

"Don't ever scare me like this again," I repeat the words he once said to me as I gently lay my head on his chest where he's not injured and hug him as easily as I can.

He takes the palm of his hand and tenderly places it on my cheek. "For, I love you so much."

"I love you too, Leo." I raise up off his chest enough to peer into his eyes with my one good eye, so he can see how much I mean my words.

"Sorry to break up the reunion, but we need to move him to a safer, more relaxed area. It's not too far from here, and you're welcome to go with him, but I've got to get back to the injured," General Luther states.

"Ohhhh, the gentleman they brought in here not too long ago. Can you tell me about him?" I ask before I leave this compound. "I also need to let the others know where we're going."

"No worries. You can tell them. They'll meet you there at some point or another. The area you're going to is for new refugees." He rubs the back of his neck and doesn't make eye contact with me. "Now your friend... he's got a heartbeat, but he's not breathing on his own. We're going to work on that. We do have devices that can do it for him, but if that ends up being the case, he'll be in a different area until his situation changes either way."

Leo grabs my hand and squeezes. "Who are you talking about?"

Now it's my turn to avert his gaze. "Malic. I'm not sure what injuries he incurred, but he's fighting for his life like you were... are... I don't even know what I'm saying anymore."

"You all need rest. Go update your friends, and I'll have transportation ready for you when you're done." General Luther starts walking over to some guys with paper and pens. One takes a ring of keys from his belt loop and hurries away. That's my cue to get to moving.

I glance at the door, then back to Leo, torn between wanting to stay by his side or going to tell my friends what's going on.

"Stop fretting. Go. I'm not going anywhere." He lets go of my hand and nods to the exit.

"Okay, but for the love of God, if you're not here when I get back, I may lose my ever-loving mind." I give him a stern look.

"Now, they may have me loaded up. So, keep that pretty little head of yours intact, because I'm going to be looking at it and cherishing it for the rest of my life." He winks, sending butterflies to my stomach at the most inappropriate time.

"Fine. I love you." I kiss his lips gingerly, then all but run to Vi and Aliss.

When I make it to them, Eli has joined them. *Yes!* He looks as good as someone can that's just come away from a serious battle.

"I'm glad you're all here." I tell them about Leo and his recovery, and about Malic. Lastly, I tell them I'll eventually see them wherever they're taking Leo and me.

After we say our goodbyes, I head back to the other wing. I get there just in time to see them toting Leo off on a gurney. I run up to get beside him as they load him in. We ride in the back of a truck machine thing they call a medical transport. It's a bumpy ride, but Leo and I never unlock our hands.

When we get to the area for the new refugees, we're greeted by two lovely ladies named Tory and Claire. These ladies have clean clothes and warm food awaiting us. After Leo and I are situated comfortably in a very spacious room, they briefly go over some rules and regulations they have here, then leave us alone.

"If you need anything, don't hesitate to come get me. My door is always open. It has my name carved into the wood. It's hard to miss," Tory mentions as she quietly closes the door behind her.

"Alone at last." Leo lets a growly grumble from his throat.

"Ha! Sir, you are in no condition to do anything other than rest." I playfully push his good shoulder.

"Ow." He winces, and I immediately feel like I'm going to puke.

"I'm so, so, so sorry. I didn't mean to hurt you."

He grabs my wrist with his good arm and tugs me close to him. "The only way you'll hurt me is if you don't get in this bed right now, so I can at least hold you."

Mortified that he'd joke with me like this, I cross my arms over my chest. "You really made me think I caused you pain. You can lay there alone now."

He attempts to raise up onto his elbow and face me. This time, he winces for real. "If you don't get in this bed now, I'll personally get up and carry you to bed." He can't, and I know he can't, but I don't put it past him to try.

"No. Fine. I'm coming." After I turn the lamp off in the room, I crawl over the top of him and nestle myself against his uninjured side, laying my head on his chest.

"Now... I can finally rest." He kisses the top of my head, and it's not long before both of us are snoozing soundly.

CHAPTER EIGHT

Leo

It's been a couple of months, and both Fortune and I are fully recovered from our wounds. The officials here can finally perform our nuptials. How I went so long without admitting she's the one for me is a damn shame, but at least now she'll be mine forever.

All of our friends are here to witness this glorious day, even Malic, who's still not fully recovered, but is doing ninety percent better than he was two months ago. Skimming the crowd, my heart is full as I take in all those who care about us and want to see us happy. I feel the same way about them.

As music begins to play on the piano, the double doors to the cathedral open.

Fortune sets her sights on me. Her blue eyes flicker with strength, despite all the hell she's been through. A mischievous grin appears on her gorgeous face, leaving me completely breathless. I remind myself to inhale, so I don't pass out.

I expand my chest, taking in a deep breath while thinking to myself, she's the most beautiful person I've ever laid eyes on.

Finally, she stops in front of me. Our eyes meet, and I give her a lopsided smile.

She grins back as the official takes his place.

Taking Fortune's hands, I guide her to face me as she whispers. "You're very handsome."

"Not as gorgeous as you are." I wink.

The clergyman clears his throat, then begins. "Today we are gathered here to celebrate one of life's greatest moments. To cherish the union of Leo Woodruff and Fortune Samiski. This is a commitment made between two people who love each other, respect each other, and desire to spend the rest of their lives together. The purpose of this ceremony is to unite two souls into becoming one." He hands me the silver band for Fortune, who's still smiling at me. "Leo, you may say your vows."

I hold For's left hand. "Fortune, I'm sorry for not acknowledging sooner that you are the love of my life. If I could, I'd go back a few years before life began to get more complicated than it is today. I'd tell you all the ways I planned to make you happy. How I wanted to build a life with you and live forever with you as my forever partner. But I can't change time. So instead, I'm going to live the rest of my life promising to make it up to you, giving you my eternal devotion, loyalty, honor, and unconditional love. I vow that I will always be here for you, never letting go of your hand. I'll always try in every way to make you happy. I look forward to building a life and family with you. I can assure you that from this day on, and until I breathe my last breath, I'll be by your side as your protector, friend, and eternal soulmate."

The clergyman continues. "Leo, do you take Fortune to be your wife?"

Sliding the ring onto Fortune's finger, I promise. "I do."

He turns his attention to For, handing her my silver ring. "Fortune, you may say your vows."

The crisp air whips her hair around her face and she shudders. Shivering, she clasps my warm hand and promises. "Leo, there's not been a day in my life where I didn't know that you were the one for me. I wish I would've told you sooner, but it's okay because we're here now, recognizing, declaring, and acting out our love for one another. I vow to always be here for you. To love you in your weakness and in your strength. To be your biggest ally, and to protect your heart at all costs, facing whatever challenges come our way together. In everything, I promise to be your wife, friend, and soulmate forever. I swear to love you unconditionally and eternally, even after I breathe my last breath." She winks at me.

The clergy coughs to clear his throat, fighting back tears that fill his eyes over this beautiful moment. "Fortune, do you take Leo to be your husband?"

Sliding the ring onto my finger, she promises. "I do."

The official glances between the two of us. "The love you two share will forever join you as one. Leo, you may kiss your bride."

I step forward, closing the space between us, and place my hands over her cheeks, drawing her closer to me. Our friends begin to celebrate with whistles and applause as I capture her delicious smooth lips with mine in a long, fervent kiss.

For touches her lips when she finally comes up to take a breath, caressing them gently. "Wow. That was amazing, and a little dizzying. My knees are so weak. I'm not sure I'll be able to walk a straight line."

Letting my forehead rest against hers, I murmur. "Yeah, kissing you is always amazing. I love you, Fortune."

She takes my hand in hers and twists our fingers together, whispering. "I love you, too."

THE END

ABOUT HAVANA WILDER

Havana has always had a vivid imagination and is an avid dreamer. After discovering her love of fantasy romances, she decided to put her dreams into reality by becoming an author herself.

JIMENA: PART 1

by Kindra White

DISCLAIMER

This book ends on a slight cliffhanger and will continue in the second part of Jimena's story, which will be released soon.

PROLOGUE

Holding her white cotton nightgown, she stopped it from swooshing as she walked swiftly but silently through the vast white halls of La Finca. Her eight-year-old little feet barely touched the Spanish style tiled floors, just like her papi taught her.

She was hunting for leftovers of her favourite dessert in the kitchen, Brevas Caladas. Plump figs cooked in sugarcane syrup with creamy white cheese, just thinking about how it would melt in her mouth with the tasty flavours of sweet and salty together. Her mouth was watering as she sped up her steps.

However, before she could round the corner of the last hall to the kitchen, she saw through the glass walls of the dining room that the lights in the pool house were on and there were movements inside.

Throwing a quick look at the kitchen knowing that the sweets would be in there waiting for her, she debated if she was going for the sweets or not and looking back to the movements outside in the pool house, her curiosity won from her need to eat sweets late at night. Deciding that after satisfying her curiosity, she would satisfy her sweet tooth, she changed course.

As she opened the door to step outside, she paused for a moment, remembering about the cameras. The little girl looked up for them. First the ones hanging from the rooftop's corner, both corners. Then for the one her papi thought she didn't know about, the one hidden in one of the guava trees. If Rodrigo, the head of security, saw her outside at this hour, he would tell her dad. And she wasn't keen on having her dad upset with her at this late hour for being out of bed.

Curioso, she thought as she frowned and squinted at the cameras. The little red lights that always blinked below the cameras weren't blinking as they were supposed to. Her beast, her Pantera negra, became wary, and she was close to the surface. *Just under her skin, scratching her from the inside, ready to shift and protect her from harm, just like her bruja powers swirling around her, protecting her without casting a protection spell. Her mami was teaching her the way of the long line of Vasquez Brujos.*

Sniffing the air, using her beast's nose, she made sure that there wasn't anything to harm her in the backyard. There was the scent of old leather mixed with smoke and sandalwood, the scent of her papi and a similar scent as her dad but not quite, instead of the smoke there was a scent of rain in the morning, her tío Hernan and another male scent that was kind of familiar but she couldn't make out what it was with all the iron scent; blood. Lots of blood if she had to go by the pungent scent of iron, mixed with the rancid smell of vomit and faeces that were covering the third scent.

The foul scent made her wrinkle her little button nose and caused her beast to snarl and the swirling of protective magic shields to slow her down, but neither the scent nor the snarl nor the magic shield stopped her from wanting to know what was happening in the pool house. It made her more curious as an urgent feeling crept within her. A chilly breeze blew past her, making her shiver in the dead of night.

Even though every fibre in her body told her to turn and run back to her room, to hide and forget that she ever saw the lights on in the pool house and ese holor rancio.

She couldn't. Her dad taught her to be strong and to make tough decisions, no matter how dangerous the situation might be. If she ever was going to be taking over the family business from him.

The need to know what was happening and that her papi and her tío were okay took over as the little girl took those steps that got her closer to the pool house, which after this fateful night she wouldn't go anywhere near that cursed building again.

As she got closer, she heard her dad's voice. He was using his calm voice, the voice he uses when he was not happy with someone. The same voice he had used with her once when she didn't obey him and almost got trampled by the wild horses he got. She could only hear snippets of the conversation, if you could call it a conversation.

"... dónde las escondiste?... burlarte de mi?" Her dad's voice got that edge to it now, the don't-fuck-with-me voice. The little girl

wanted nothing more than to go inside and see what was going on, who was her dad talking to like that. But her beast wanted to get her as far away from that place as possible. The beast was now growling in her head to make her do as she wished.

Ignoring the beast's warnings and pleas to get her to safety and summoning the protective shield back, she walked up the stairs and toward one of the enormous glass windows in the back corner, where it was dark with shadows and she knew no one would find her. But before she could get to the corner, she heard punches hitting something soft and wet repeatedly and muffled moans of pain.

She got to the window and peered carefully inside. What she saw almost made her throw up. All the blood on the floor, the blood that was still dripping from what was over from the person strapped to the chair. There were pieces of what looked like small cut up meat, but then realisation hit her. Her eyes grew wide as she clasped a hand over her little mouth. Those weren't small pieces of meat, those were cut up fingers.

Her curious and wide eyes went of their own accord to what was left of the person's hands, two bloodied stumps still tied together on his lap. She could make out that the bound person was a man, with blood dripping from all his cuts and his mangled hands, adding to the growing pool of blood he was sitting in.

Another wave of vomit rolled upward, filling her little mouth and burning her throat while her eyes filled with tears when she saw it was her papi and her tío who were torturing the bound man.

She almost lost her balance while she took a step back as her gut tightened when she recognised the person they were torturing. Under the black, almost swollen shut eyes, split lips and what appears to be a crushed nose was Miguel dos Santos, well what they left of Miguel.

He was her dad's right-hand man from forever. She couldn't remember a time when Miguel wasn't with her dad following him like a shadow. Doing his bidding, helping with the family business of exporting coffee and spice. Miguel, who was always nice to her and gave her caramelos when papi wasn't looking. Miguel, who wouldn't kill a fly.

Grabbing hold of the first thing in front of her to keep herself from tumbling through the window glass in front of her, the little girl accidentally opened the door she hadn't noticed next to the enormous glass window and stumbled into the room where the three men were.

Falling flat on her face, she heard a surprised intake of breaths and one muffled groan. The little girl slowly lifted her head, with trembling lips and a racing heartbeat, not knowing what would happen to her.

She was met with two sets of glowing yellow eyes looking at her. Her dad and uncle half transformed into their jaguars, ready to attack. She covered her little head quickly with her arms, but not quickly enough.

The little girl didn't want to see her dad's face like that, ugly, twisted with rage, while long white whiskers were slowly growing from his upper lip while he hissed at her through his huge, sharp feline fangs. But she saw his face, and that visual would stay with her, engraved in her memory till the day she dies.

"Esteban! espera! Es Nena, tu hija, hermano." She heard tío Hernan's warm voice turned gruff by the shift, warning her dad. The little girl ventured a peek between her folded arms around her head and saw her dad had stopped some steps away from where she was lying on the floor, with the pool of Miguel's blood covering the beautiful light blue with red designer tiles.

When put in groups of four, they form a beautiful flower in the centre. She was worried that all that blood would stain the tiles and make the flower ugly. The little girl squeezed her eyes shut as she thought that would be the last thing she should be worried about.

"Hernan, get rid of that." There was the sound of a gun going off, making the little girl wince and look at the lifeless body of Miguel on the chair as it hit the floor with a thump sound. "And clean up all this mess." The little girl's dad commanded, his voice toneless, cold even. It didn't sound like her papi. Her dad's voice was always warm and proud when he talked to her and the rest of her family and friends.

As the little girl was about to speak and make excuses why she was lying on the pool house floor, instead of being asleep in her warm bed in her room on the top floor of the finca. She was hauled from the cold tiled floor and dragged by her upper arm behind her dad toward the main house, back inside the finca. He didn't stop till they reached his office.

He opened the door and let the little girl go in first, closing the door behind them as he followed her in. However, before she could take a seat in one of the two leather chairs in front of the big, dark wooden desk. Her dad grabbed her by her shoulders and turned her around to face him.

His face was grave, but she could see he was tired. She always could see through his facade, *su mascara*. She knew her dad well, and she knew what happened back in the pool house pained him. But Esteban "El Jefe" La Fuentes, her papi does not show emotion of any kind.

"*Los sentimientos son para los débiles, Nena. Grabá eso en tu cabezita. One day it will be the one thing to keep you alive.*" He would always tell her that whenever he got the chance.

He squatted in front of her, so he could be on the little girl's eye level. He titled his head to the side, frowning while he pressed his lips together into a grimace. Letting out a heavy sigh, he shook his head slowly in frustration.

"*Nena, no sé por qué estabas andando por la finca a estas horas de la noche. But it's not safe for you to be roaming around alone. Tío y papá tenemos asuntos que atender y tú, mi niña, no puedes estar...*" Before her dad could finish talking, she heard a click, followed by a loud gunshot.

"*Papi! No!*" the little girl screamed as warm blood spattered all over her white cotton sleeping gown, giving it a gruesome ombre colour effect, from innocent white to angry dark red. As she kept screaming, she had her hand outstretched, as if wanting to save someone.

***

Blinking rapidly and shaking my head, I tried to make that *maldita noche* disappear, stopping it from hunting my every waking hour and sleepless nights. The loud screams always brought me back to the here and now, and as always, my throat was throbbing with pain and I had my hands outstretched. Trying to prevent what happened years ago from happening all over again. Trying to save the little girl.

But in vain, because that little girl died a long time ago on that cursed night. Jimena "Nena" La Fuentes died that awful night and ceased to exist. Now, years later, only I, Jerry LeFontaine, was over and far away from that world I was born into.

Welcome to my story.

CHAPTER 1

Jerry

Checking my reflection in my compact powder mirror, I ran my index finger and thumb along the corners of my lips, touching up the imaginary smudge of my perfectly outlined plump nude lips, as I waited for the town car to slow down and stop in front of the hotel entrance, one of my boutique hotels, The LeFontaine boutique hotel.

Before I could put my compact powder back in my toiletry bag, Henry, my old landlord, from when I first got to Crescent Point, a long time ago, turned into a father figure, and now helped me run my little hotels, opened my door. "Good day and welcome back, Jerry. Any suitcases or just the carryon this time?" He greeted me as he stepped aside so I could step out of the car and walk past him.

"Good day Henry, no suitcases this time, only the carryon. No need to take it up. I'll do that myself, thank you." I stopped next to him to give him a quick peck on the cheek before I continued up the stairs to the entrance with my carryon in hand.

Henry has been helping me since I started my little B&B next to the Marina. Only four rooms, but all with a killer view and with a customer service, not even the Queen of Sheeba had.

Henry is loyal to me, he is loyal to a fault, has been always there for me and very protective of me. He gave up running his renting apartments business to help me run my B&B. He made me feel safe when I had no one and loved when I felt unworthy of love. As a father would with his daughter, he took it upon himself to guide me into the hotel business.

The fleeting thought of my father passed through my mind. It made my heart ache just for a moment. How I wished I had my *papá* next to me guiding me. But that would never be possible. He was dead to me as I was to him.

Taking some deep breaths, I looked up at the entrance of my boutique hotel. My lips curled into a proud smile at seeing the logo I had made with the letters of my new last name. The letters L and F intertwine beautifully together in stylish calligraphy with the name directly underneath the logo; *LeFontaine, A Boutique Hotel.*

Pride grew inside my chest, seeing how far I came with no help from *them*. How well, correctly and above all, legally, I built *my* legacy. With blood, sweat, and tears. I shuddered at the thought of blood, making my beast growl in my head. I have had such a big aversion toward blood ever since... *No, deja de vivir en el pasado. You have made it Jerry; you created this imperium. Leave the past in the past and keep moving forward.*

Taking the last steps up, with my head held high, proud of what I have achieved, I walked through the open doors, held by Wren. As soon as I stepped into the lobby, a dreadful feeling instantly washed over me, making me slow down my steps toward my office as I looked over my shoulders. A habit I developed ever since I got out of *la familia*.

"Jerry, stop being paranoid. They are far away and don't know where you are. Take deep breaths." I told myself this was just me being on edge around this time of year. This month was my *papá* and *mamá* wedding anniversary. This year, they would celebrate their forty years of marriage.

This year would have been the last year of my dad running *the business* and passing it on to me, the heiress of his legacy. What wouldn't I give to see his face on the day of *el festejo* and his *princesa* wasn't there and nowhere to be found.

The thought of Esteban La Fuentes' plans going to hell, where he also belongs, made the dreadful feeling disappear like snow on a sunny day. The thought of that made me smirk, just thinking how angry he must be that his legacy would be worth *mierda* without me and going down the drain.

Taking a good look at my surroundings, in search of those familiar faces I haven't seen in over eighteen years. But luckily I only saw new and unfamiliar faces. However, there seemed to be more men than I'm used to in my hotel. That means that my little boutique hotel started to be popular among the business men too, and not just rich men's wives looking for a weekend getaway.

Shrugging off all doubts, I continued toward my office, stopping only by the reception to give them my carryon to send up my suite and to make sure they followed my instruction of not booking the other suite on the floor where mine was. I longed for some alone time, no noise, no people, total peace. After the weekend, I had with Liz, Remy and *el pendejo de* Devin Olivier.

I should have ended him with what he did and wanted to do to me a long time ago. My beast snarled low at me for stopping her that night from shifting and tearing Devin apart, piece by piece, to feast on his corpse and bathe in his blood.

But I couldn't. I swore I wouldn't be a savage and let my beast loose to do what she wanted. I wasn't an animal like *them*. Going around killing people so savagely, even if they had wronged me. And Devin had wronged me. Ugh! Just letting that night play back in my mind makes me sick to my stomach. I can still smell his alcohol scented breath and feel how his hands grabbed me roughly and pressed me against his body.

My hand was trembling as I got hold of the door handle of my office and opened it. Switching the lights on in my minimalistic decorated office, the thought of that night kept playing like a distasteful film. How he ran his purplish tongue over his thin lips before he tried to kiss me. And when I didn't let him, he grabbed one of my boobs and squeezed it hard till I screamed in pain.

How he got a sickening triumphant look all over his face before it transformed into an ugly mask. No trace of humanity was left in his gleaming eyes. That was the moment I knew I had to do something that I didn't want, but was necessary, necessary for my self-preservation.

I called to my *bruja* powers in the hopes that a show of my abilities would scare him away. But that wasn't enough. He didn't even flinch when my entire body glowed with my witchy powers. That made me relent some power to my beast, just enough to make Devin think twice about touching me again.

My beast reacted just as I hoped. She made me let out a loud growl, increasing in volume from deep within my body. I knew my eyes changed to hers, as I could see ten times better than with my own eyes, even the little blond hairs on Devin's face. As at last, my teeth elongated into her sharp feline fangs. His eyes grew enormous in his head as he saw my little transformation and let go of my boob while he stepped away from me.

My beast made me growl at him one more time as I showed my feline fangs. He stumbled over his own feet before he ran away. I never had to deal with him directly after that night. But seeing him again last weekend at the Marina and seeing how he was preying on Liz made my blood boil again and my beast wanted to rip him apart.

Sighing, and taking another cleansing breath, I pushed the Devin incident back to where it belonged, in the past. Together with all the shits I have gone through.

I looked over some papers that Norah, my assistant, had left behind for me. Some deals I had pending with Greyson. A new venture I was about to start, real estate development. But that had to wait till after I had my break from everything, recharge and then deal with all that.

Putting the contracts aside, I checked if I had any messages or anything that needed my attention urgently. But seeing that there weren't any matters that needed my attention right away, I put everything on my to-do pile for next week when I'm done having my mini vacation.

The thought of being away from everyone and everything put a smile on my face as my mood improved. However, there was this whisper in my mind that kept reminding me of the constant looming feeling I have been having for a few months now. Since then, it was constantly present and in my mind that something bad was going to happen or something bad was coming my way.

I stretched my arms above my head, calling upon my powers, and asked them to take away any thought that wouldn't help me right now and fill me with positive energy. Just like how my mother taught me when I was only a child and had night terrors after the incident at the pool house.

Closing my eyes, I could feel the electricity of my magic surging through me, cleansing me of any doubt, bad thoughts, and replacing it with only good thoughts and positive emotions.

Putting my hands on my desk, I pushed myself up from my chair. Straightening the skirt of my navy pencil dress, I stepped away from the desk and walked around it, my heels clicking on the marble floor, walking up to my office door, opening it and making my way to reception to get my key and to finally get the peace and quiet I so craved.

As I got back to the lobby, I felt a black aura settling around me. Like an impending doom. My beast was on high alert, growling and hissing. The hairs on the back of my neck stood on end, the feeling that I was being watched weighed heavy on me. Yet, I couldn't see anything that could indicate that someone was watching me.

Whoever it was and was watching me, I refused to give them the satisfaction of seeing me nervous because of it. I pushed my shoulders back, arranging my resting bitch face. I strutted with my Louboutin heels, clicking all the way to the reception desk.

"Hi Michelle, can I have my key, please?" I asked the receptionist who was at the desk. Weird, Michelle wasn't supposed to be working the morning shift. Nancy was when I came in. "Michelle, where is Nancy and why are you managing the reception desk if this is not your shift?" I cocked my head to the side and waited for her response.

"I... I... I came in to take Nancy's shift over as she..." She cleared her throat as she continued. "uhm, Nancy called me because she, she, wasn't feeling well." She smiled, but her smile didn't reach her pretty green eyes. As she gave me the card key of my room, her little well-manicured hand was trembling.

"Oh, okay." I frowned as I tried to figure out how fast Michelle got here as I saw Nancy when I got here. But I dismissed the situation as I wanted nothing more than to relax and if they could fix it like this without bothering me, I was glad.

"I hope she feels better and thank you for coming in on such short notice, Michelle." I took the card key from her hand. As I was about to turn, I saw a drop of sweat rolling down on her face, from her temple toward her chin. And it wasn't even a proper summer yet.

Jerry, there is nothing wrong. You are on edge, tired and in need of a good relaxing few days. I reprimanded myself as I gave Michelle a smile and sashayed to the elevator next to the lounge.

Finally, my week of letting my hair down and leaving civilization behind for a few days would start. Pressing the button to call the elevator down, I took a last look behind me and let my eyes scan the entire lobby. My eyes landed on a gentleman sitting across from where I stood. Dressed in a black suit, his blond hair styled sleek back. He looked handsome.

His lips slowly transformed into a wolfish grin as he caught me checking him out. He dipped his head in greeting as the sharp ding of the elevator made me jump. I smiled back at him before walking into the elevator.

As I turned back to wait for the elevator to take me up to my room, the mysterious handsome man winked at me just as the doors of the elevator slowly slid close. However, his flirty behaviour didn't sit well with me. I couldn't put my finger on why, but the feeling I had before of being watched seemed to settle when we locked eyes outside the elevator.

"Jerry, *chica,* you are seeing things that aren't there. The gentleman just wanted to be friendly. Stop thinking about things that won't happen. You are here to enjoy and enjoy you shall." I told myself on the way to my room.

Happy to start this vacation, finally.

CHAPTER 2

Jerry

"*Esteban! espera! Es Nena, tu hija, hermano.*" A man yelled, but weirdly everything was black, pitch black. I was in a black abyss, falling. I couldn't see anything in front of me. Oddly, at the same time I thought I was falling, I found myself walking and not descending anymore. I kept walking, silently, keeping my steps light on the cold tiled floors. I didn't know why I was moving lightly, but I kept walking, not looking back.

The echoes of footsteps were bouncing all around me in this black abyss, following me, making me speed up my pace. I needed to keep one step ahead of them, always. Otherwise, they would catch me and make me go back. Back to that world I didn't belong to.

"*Hernan, get rid of that.*" An angry male voice yelled behind me and before I knew it, a gun went off, making me wince as I let out a yelp. I couldn't move, the sound paralysed me. No matter how hard I tried, I couldn't move. The darkness was heavy, pressing on me, holding me in its clutches. But I had to keep moving, always keep moving. I had to stay one step ahead of them.

Wheezing, gasping for air I turned around to see who was behind me but instead of seeing who was following me, was a light shining on the floor, lights you might find on a stage when the presenter walked on the platform but instead of a show I looked directly in the cold, dull, wide-open eyes of a man lying on the tiled floor in the middle of a pool of dark red blood. I think it was a man.

The face of the person kept changing from a jaguar head to a human face.

  I was nailed to the floor. As much as I tried to move, I couldn't. I knew I had to try harder. I had to keep moving, always moving, always one step ahead of them. Even through the darkness, I had to keep moving. My heart felt as if it was going to explode, that hard it was thumping in my chest. Blood rushed through my ears, making it sound like I was standing in the middle of a storm, the wind whipping around me.

  "Los sentimientos son para los débiles, Nena." The voice behind me whispered, making the hairs on the back of my neck stand up as a cold tingle ran from the top of my head all the way down to my bare feet, making me shiver in fear. I couldn't move my fingers as the footsteps were slowly getting closer. The pain in my chest was growing with every passing sound of footsteps that were getting nearer.

  Another loud gunshot next to where I stood.

"Papi! No!"

  "Noooo…" I screamed as I opened my eyes and sat up straight. I was in a bed that wasn't mine. It was too soft. Then I remembered I was at the hotel, and not at my house. I was all drenched in sweat, with tears streaming down my face. My throat throbbing with pain while my heart was racing like a wild animal caged up, trying to escape its enclosure. Gasping for breath with one hand over my heart in an attempt to keep the damn thing inside my chest and the other at my throat, I tried to calm myself.

  Fucking nightmares! I cursed, and my animal growled low while she was clawing her way to the surface.

  "¿Cuándo me dejarían en paz estas pesadillas pendejas?" I asked no one in my room as I threw the comforter off of my legs as I got up from my bed. I walked to the ensuite bathroom, turning on all the lights in my bedroom on my way. The suffocating darkness from my nightmare had done a number on me. I was still shaking and feeling the pressure on my cold sweaty body as I entered the bathroom, limbs trembling and knees feeling weak.

  Turning the lights on, I went directly to the washbasin to splash some cold water on my face and on the back of my neck. Hoping the cold water would drive away this looming feeling that *they* were close. *They* will find me soon. I think that was what my nightmares were trying to tell me these last few nights. That it wouldn't be long now before they would catch up with me and drag me back to *La Familia*.

I turned the faucet open, letting the water run till it became cold enough that I knew it would chase the residue of the lingering darkness from my mind. Cupping my hands under the running water, I let it fill up and splash my face. Once, twice before I looked up to gaze at my reflection in the mirror.

"You look like *mierda, cariño*." I told myself as I let out a humourless laugh, which came out all shaky and strangled. The woman looking back at me from the mirror had dark circles under her normally warm, sparkly brown eyes. But at that moment, the brown colour was dull, just as dull as the dead man's eyes from my nightmare, devoid of all warmth and sparkle, surrounded by thin red veins that clouded the white of her eyes.

I screamed as I shook my head and slammed my hands on the edge of the basin. As if that would make the haunted look on my face go away. Or the sense of impending doom disappear.

"*Coño* Jerry, you are a fucking strong woman. Pull your shit together." I told my reflection in the mirror. Breathing in through my nose, exhaling out of my mouth a few times and concentrating on slowing down my heart beat, as I pushed the dread feeling out of my system.

Who will El Jefe send after me? I didn't know why I was wondering who would come after me. I already knew who *he* would send to hunt me. As I also knew that the one he was going to send wouldn't pass the chance to hunt me down like a wild animal.

A hot shiver rolled down my spine, making my lower belly tightened as my core clenched in anticipation. My nipples puckered into two aching peaks, while my vagina walls contracted a few times in emptiness as arousal coated my pussy.

"*Hijueputa!*" I cursed at the reaction of my body as it remembers the sensual touches of *him,* Ángel Sánchez.

He better not accept the assignment to come looking for me if he knew what was good for him. I was prepared for the growl I was certain my beast would let out at the thought of him, but to my surprise, my beast just purred like a domesticated house cat in heat.

She was excited about the knowledge that Ángel would be the one hunting us.

Between getting my beast calmed down, my body to behave normally at the thought of Ángel hunting us, and getting the looming feeling of impending doom that they would find me to go away, I totally forgot that I had booked a full body Swedish massage with Josefin for today.

Josefin, who ironically was a Swedish woman, and was hired to give Swedish massages. She was a miracle worker, her hands were angels' hands. They could get the toughest knots out of any tensed up muscle in a body.

Looking forward to my massage, I decided that worrying about something I didn't have control over was futile. With my mood slowly changing to one I could relax and enjoy the rest of my time away, I got out of my still damp sweaty silk nighty and threw it into the hamper as I got into the shower.

I turned the shower on, adjusting the water just right to let the scalding hot water pour down from the oversized shower head. I stepped right under it and let the hot water ease my taut muscles in my body as it beat down on me, revelling in the warmth that was seeping into my cold bones after the nightmare.

By the time I finally turned off the shower and got out to dry myself off, steam swirls surrounded me. I tossed the wet towel in the other hamper next to the one with my sweaty nighty, as I grabbed the white robe hanging from the back of the door, put it on, tied the belt into an easy knot and went to blow dry my hair.

After what felt like hours in the shower, I emerged from my bathroom, energised, full of positive thoughts, and ready to tackle anything coming my way. Even a horde of *El Jefe's soldados*. I wouldn't go down without a fight. I'd kill them all before going back to a life and world that I didn't belong to, and I surely didn't want.

I walked toward my closet and got my caramel leather Hermès carryon out and carried it over to my bed and laid it on top of the bunched up comforter. Opening the small compartment it had on the inside, I grabbed my Glock43. I may have left the *Cartel world* behind, but I'm not stupid to think I would ever be safe. Closing the top lid of the carryon, I went to the dresser next to the closet and got my black leather thigh holster from one of the drawers.

Setting the Glock on the dresser, I opened one side of my robe and put my right leg on the vanity chair and slipped the little leather holster on. Picking up the Glock from the top of the dresser, I looked at it before sliding it into place in the thigh holster. My full lips curled at the corner. *Let them come. I'm ready for all of you malparidos!*

Happy with myself, I took my leg off the chair, straightened the robe, and made my way out of my room in search of food. I gave my team of customer service explicit instructions to stock up this suit with food for me. I even told them to tell the chef to make me *Brevas Caladas,* my favourite *dulce*. A reminder of home at happier times. My plan for this week was to stay in this suite until I can handle being surrounded by people again.

I got into the kitchen. It was just like the rest of the suite; walls painted cream, the cabinets were of a light brown colour that my interior designer called golden pecan. *Don't know why they couldn't just say it's light brown?*

Shaking my head, I turned on the coffee machine and pressed the upper right button for the kind of coffee I wanted. Then I walked over to the chromed fridge. Opening the fridge door, my lips stretched into a wide grin. Upon seeing the two medium size plastic containers fully filled with *Brevas Caladas.* I couldn't contain myself. I quickly opened one container and popped one of the brevas into my mouth, indulging in the sweet and salty taste of the fig with white cheese while getting the fruits out of the fridge and onto the counter of the breakfast bar.

As I made myself a fruit salad with papaya, mango, cantaloupe, banana and pineapple. I drizzled some passion fruit sauce I found in the fridge over the mixed fruits in the bowl and sprinkled some roughly chopped mint leaves over the fruits. Happy with my breakfast of fruit salad, I sat down at the kitchen table with my steamy mug of mocha latte.

My beast wasn't happy. If I left my diet up to her, I would only eat meat the whole day. She was still grumbling while I ate my breakfast.

"Calm down, girl. I'll eat a juicy steak for dinner. I'll even ask the chef to cook it *blue* for you. But stop with the soft growling at me this early in the morning." I said to my beast, hoping she would calm down and leave me to eat in peace. She was not amused with me, to say the least. It has been almost a year that I haven't let her out to run and hunt.

I couldn't risk it. I couldn't risk *them* feeling me shift and come for me. Eventually I would have to let her out to go hunt in the forest like the big cat that she is. But I'd rather risk her going feral on me for not shifting enough than *them* catching up with me.

There was a knock on the door just as I popped the last small cubed piece of papaya in my mouth. I rolled my eyes as I sighed heavily. I had told Josefin when I booked with her she could just come in and set up in the smaller room. *Why the hell was she knocking?*

"Josefin, come in. The door is open." I called to her from the kitchen as I pushed my chair back, stood up, and took my bowl and coffee mug to the sink. Before I could turn around, came another knock, harder than before.

It drove me nuts as Josefin kept knocking when I told her she could come in. Taking a deep breath to not snap at her when I let her in, I walked over to the suite door. I couldn't help but growl as my irritation at Josefin grew as she knocked for the third time.

I opened the door, my month half open, ready to scold Josefin, but instead, a sense of vertigo took over as my thoughts were swirling so quickly in my mind that it was hard to form any type of coherent words.

"You!" was the only thing that I could get out of my mouth as it went dry while an electric current coursed through my veins and ended in my core and made it clenched. *Damn you thirsty body of mine!*

"Hola, Nena." *He* said with his raspy and deep voice as he smiled at me. His too hot and sexy smile that should be punished for being so sinful, showing pearly white sharp teeth. His full lips curled even more as he took me in with hungry eyes. I could feel his grey eyes all over my body undressing me and if it was possible fucking me right there on the spot, I could see his desire burning hot in his slade grey eyes. But there was a sliver of apprehension there, too, as he cocked his head and ran his tongue over his bottom lip before sucking it in and biting down on it.

My treacherous body was reacting like we have never parted ways a long time ago, all tingling and the dormant fire in my centre sparked to life.

Fuck! They finally caught up and came for me. Keep your head in the game, Querida. You need it more than to let your body take over.

Before me stood Ángel Sánchez, in all his glory in a tailor made all black suit and black button-down shirt, with the first two buttons unbuttoned, some black tattoo lines peeking from under the opening of his shirt. Radiating power and raw sex appeal.

My body didn't want to catch up with my mind, it kept reacting to the desire in his eyes, as my mind switched to whether we were fighting or fleeing.

Before I could react and do something about Ángel standing in front of me, something flashed as there was a swift movement of his hands and I felt a sting in my neck. I instinctively brought my hand to the spot where something was burning and spreading through my system as I looked up at Ángel, eyes wide open. *What did he do to me?* My heart was beating like a bat out of hell, my eyelids were getting heavier and heavier with each passing second. My limbs turned to jelly on me and they couldn't hold me up anymore as I swayed on my feet.

The last thing I remembered was his face, his devilish sultry smile, and his powerful arms catching me as I fell forward and the darkness pulled me under.

CHAPTER 3

Ángel

I covered the champagne glass in front of me with my hand as the cute flight attendant of the private jet was about to pour some more. I shook my head and gave her a polite smile. She smiled back as a blush coloured her cheeks and spread to her ears. Her eyes went to my tattooed hand, at the jaguar skull with the two crossed pistols under it, as rune lettering adorned my fingers. If I had to believe Doña Graciella, they were runes of protection.

I cleared my throat and dismissed the flight attendant with a wave of my hand. I needed my mind clear for the next step. My mind was working overtime, calculating, recalculating, planning, and coming up with an escape plan for if what was coming up would go sour.

The easiest part was done; getting *her*. The trickiest part was next. If I succeed, to get into the country with *her* unnoticed by *El Jefe*, it would mean I get to live another day to ask forgiveness.

It was always better to ask forgiveness than to ask permission.

Esteban wouldn't be too happy with me as I'm disobeying his direct command of bringing *her* immediately to him, and we all in *la familia* knew very well what would happen if we pissed him off. It wasn't pretty. However, I had to risk it. For *her,* I would risk it all. I would even shoot the moon down for her, burn the world to the ground if she asked me to. Jimena was mine, and I had to stake my claim before her father did.

My beast growled in possessive agreement. It has been a long time coming. He was scratching me from the inside, getting very close to the surface. My teeth elongated and changed into feline fangs. My beast wanted to force the shift, but I had an iron hold on him, no shifting until I willed it. He wanted to mark her and mate her beast.

It was easier said than done. And if I knew my kitten well, she would rather die than to belong to me. Letting out a chuckle, I looked out of the small round plane window while that thought passed through my mind.

No correction, she would rather kill me than bear my mark and belong to me. I almost made her mine years ago, but I fucked it up and she slipped through my fingers and got away. But this time, this time, she will be mine. No matter how long it would take, even if I have to do it by force.

I was looking forward to her fighting me on this. Deep down, I knew she would. She was always temperamental. She did everything with such passion. I used to love to see that fire of defiance burning hot in the dark depth of her eyes, when I told her that one day we both would rule the Cartel side by side.

It would be my pleasure to break her to my will and see her begging me for more with the same fire in her eyes burning hotter, not in defiance, but with desire for me.

My slacks were getting tight around my crotch as my cock was half erected. Just by thinking about how she would squirm in my arms while I was breaking her and making her mine.

¡Ella será mía para siempre, incluso en el más allá!

There was never a doubt in my mind that there would be another woman than *Jimena La Fuentes* for me and my beast. I can't lie. I had my share of women, but no one could tip to my Nena. From the moment I saw her for the first time. We were mere *dos peladitos*, barely out of diapers. I think we couldn't have been older than five.

It wasn't love; it was more than that. When our eyes met, she became my world, my sun and stars. At that age, I didn't understand what mates meant, but I knew early on that she was made for me, just like I was made for her.

While growing up together, she became my haven, my sane sanctuary from the savage world we were born into. She was everything nice and warm that the world we both came from didn't have. She always made me laugh with her goofiness and her *locuras*.

My father was her father's best friend and his best *teniente* and because of that, her family and mine were almost living in one house. We spend more time at their *finca, Quinta Graciela* than at our own.

However, one fateful day, around her eighth or ninth birthday, all changed. She changed. My Nena was no longer my happy and free spirited girl anymore. She became sad and closed off from everyone, even from me. Where once was warmth and laughter was only coldness and sadness.

I never found out what happened to her. She refused to let me in, to tell me what changed her drastically. She rebelled against everyone and everything when she was in her teens, around her *quince*. The loving and sweet girl was no more. It seemed as if she died and a new cold and numb girl took her place. She was ill tempered and hated everything, including me.

Even more so when I started my initiation with *the family business* when I turned eighteen. The business she loathed took me from her. She never made it a secret of her feelings toward her inheritance.

"Now they have their claws in you too. *Me cambiaste por el cartel.*" As she said that, fat tears rolled down her angry face while she forcefully whipped them away as she turned away from me. One night, we ditched her bodyguard and went straight to our secret hideout just outside of the city. A colourful *casita* close to the jungle, with a small garden in the backyard, it once belonged to her great grandmother, *Doña Gloria*, the greatest bruja that ever existed.

"*Nunca*, never Nena! I'm yours, as you are mine. You and me against them." I followed her to the window where she stood looking at the moon and stars. I took her in my arms and kissed the top of her head, and then I kissed her tears away. On that night, I promised her I wouldn't become like her father, that I would not succumb to the savagery of the Cartel.

But sadly, I couldn't keep my promise for long. Once you belong to the Cartel, it's kill or be killed.

I was making a name for myself by climbing the ranks within *la familia* swiftly. Which gained me the trust of Esteban. It didn't matter that my dad was his best friend. *En el cartel* trust and respect were the currency and if you betray that, the payment was your life.

By the time I was twenty, I already killed more treats for the family and closed more deals for the business than any of the other *Tenientes*. I also got a larger territory to manage and my own group of *halcones y soldados*. Which put a bigger strain on my already rocky relationship with my Nena because of my actions.

But my ultimate betrayal that made her hate me had yet to come.

A movement next to me and a muffled soft moan caught my attention and brought me back onto the plane. I turned to look at the woman next to me, deep asleep by the sedation.

I put a silky lock of her jet black hair behind her ear as I leaned her head on my chest and draped a possessive arm around her while I kissed her hair softly. With my other hand, I trailed my fingers lightly from her collar bone toward her hands in her lap.

I could still see her face when she opened the door and was face to face with me. How her emotions flashed in her eyes, one after the other, from surprised and stunned to anger and hatred in just a few seconds. She never was one that could keep her powerful emotions to herself.

The one thing you sure had to keep in check if you wanted to keep breathing in this world of ours that I'm dragging her sweet ass back to was emotions. Showing emotion, just for a tiny fraction, could mean your death in the cartel.

I marvelled at the softness of her body. Taking advantage that she was out of it to enjoy her body close to mine, I could feel her warmth seeping through my clothes, soaking up this bliss moment with my Nena. Because once this feral kitten wakes up, she will be all sharp edges with even sharper claws, ready to tear everyone piece by piece. Starting with me once she figures out what I have planned for us.

Inhaling her sweet scent, made me lick my lips as I wondered how sweet she must taste. Her scent was a mix of sweet strawberry soap and her natural scent; so delicate and subtle as the Night Lily, with just a hint of the lingering fragrance of her arousal. I knew better not to let my guard down around her exquisite scent. She was poisonous when handled with violence.

¡Coño hombre! That succulent heady scent of her arousal that hit me hard when she saw me this morning. It took all my self-control to not grab her by her hair and drag her over to the couch and eat her out and feel her warm honey gushing all over my tongue and lips and then fuck her hard. Make her scream my name while she comes undone till she begged me to stop.

"Carajo! She is going to be the death of me." I murmured to myself as I adjusted my full-blown erection, making the suit pants very uncomfortable. I can't wait to be buried balls deep in her juicy and warm pussy while she clenched hard around me. Enjoying every moan and gasp, I draw out of her sweet, plump lips with each deep stroke of my hard cock.

Looking up from her body over mine, I lock eyes with Gabriel, my most trusted *soldado* and my beast, and I let out a low warning growl which made him show his throat to me submissively in the hopes he hasn't offended me.

I would kill anyone that looks at Jimena without my permission, or breathe the same air as her. She was mine alone and I alone would be the one that could feast my eyes on her beauty. As soon as we got to my estate, that would be my first command to all of my men, if they knew what was good for them and if they valued their lives.

But before I could do all of that, we needed to get into the country unnoticed by anyone. Not even by my own men on the streets. I couldn't risk them going blabbing to *El Jefe* that I was back. That wouldn't be best for my plans or my longevity.

As I kissed her temple, Jimena let out a sigh and her eyelids fluttered as she tried to open them. Her eyebrows knitted together as she scrunched her freckled nose, fighting the sedition to wake up.

I immediately motioned to Gabriel to get me another syringe with the next dose for her. It seemed that my feral kitten was fighting her way through the sedation too soon, but I couldn't let her do that, not yet anyway. Gabriel passed me the syringe and a small, wet disinfectant square.

"I hope you are having sweet dreams, Nena *mía*. You'll be home soon with me, where you belong." I whispered while I got the syringe out of the vein in her arm and swiped my thumb over the small drop of blood that appeared on the spot where the syringe punctured her flawless skin. I brought my thumb with the one blood drop to my lips and had a taste of her. Closing my eyes, I let out a moan of delight as my beast fought me for control to shift.

    Opening my eyes, I caressed her exposed arm as I kissed the tip of her nose while I felt her become heavier against my body as the sedation did its work once more.

CHAPTER 4

Jerry

Ugh, my head! The thing was pounding like a motherfucker and to make matters worse; it was pounding on the rhythm of every beat of my heart. It felt like someone was punching me in my head with every pump of blood it did. And there was this pressure on my brain while something held me down, surrounded by darkness.

I tried with all my might to get my brain to work again. To remember what happened to me. Why I was shrouded in darkness. And the most important thing; who did this to me? Try as I might, I couldn't get my mush of a brain to work. The thing kept pounding, making it difficult to sift through the muddled thoughts.

It was impossible to search for answers in my mind the way it was. Like wading through mud or getting out of quicksand. Slow, tedious and exhausting. It was driving me crazy. I could sense the answers so close, but yet so far. The answers I wanted kept going in and out of focus. Making it as if I was searching and looking through an unfocused camera lens.

I almost got what I was searching for a few times, but every time I got close and grazed the edge of the thought or image I was after, it would slip through me like sand would through my fingers. Irritating the shit out of me.

I needed to keep fighting the heaviness and darkness that surrounded my mind, as I had to figure this thing out. I knew it was going to be a Herculean task to do, but I wasn't one to give up. My thoughts were cloudy and murky. The figures that kept moving just outside of the perimeter of my perception were shrouded under layers of a dense, dark grey mist.

While I kept wading through my muddled and foggy brain, a terrifying thought crept into my mind. Adding to the panic that was bubbling up. *Was I dead?!*

Was that the reason I couldn't remember anything and my mind was as if they put it into a blender? But just as I was contemplating the possibility of being dead, my head throbbed painfully. Putting me in a state of agony as the pain split my head in two, feeling like someone opened the top of my head and squeezed my brain.

If I was dead, I couldn't feel that much pain, right?

Okay Jerry, take a deep breath and... woah, Jerry?... Who was Jerry? Was my name Jerry? But something deep inside me growled. It seemed to come from my soul. The sound was faint, yet I clearly heard it in my mind. The growl was one of disagreement with the thought that my name was Jerry.

I let the name roll a couple of times in my head to figure out how I felt about it and to find out if I agree or not with the faint growl in my head. I must be crazy, debating if the growl was right about the possibility that my name wasn't Jerry. However, there was this lingering feeling that I somehow trusted the growl. The growl was familiar, and I was sure that deep down, it would protect me. Don't know how, but that protective feeling was very strong.

The growl sounded louder and stronger in my mind, letting me know that what I just thought was true, that it would protect me. It was like the growl wanted me to know it would help me figure out this foggy mind of mine.

Was I losing my mind? Believing in a growl and that it would protect and help me? Come on girl, you got this. If my brain needs this to recover what it has lost, then I'll accept this growl phantom thing.

As I gave into the growl's feeling of protectiveness, memories flashed rapidly across my mind's eye. Thoughts, images pinging back and forth, which made me more dizzy. Which gave me the sensation of sinking further into the dark pit that was my mind.

Just as I thought my mind would trap me forever in this limbo of darkness, a vivid image flashed distinctly in my mind. It was the image of a handsome, dark-haired man with a sharp nose, high cheekbones, square jawline and full lips that were curled into a roguish smile.

His magnetic, silver grey eyes flashed and changed for a moment to the green of his beast in triumph. The handsome face that appeared clearly in my mind was no other than Ángel Sánchez.

Racing thoughts crashed down on me, forcing me to remember what happened; me opening the door, expecting Josefin to only find Ángel at my door instead. The sting in my neck and the darkness that followed shortly after the burning sensation.

Ese hijueputa, malparido! He fucking drugged me.

I wanted to scream, tear him apart, limb by limb. Slowly. However, nothing happened. I couldn't move anything, not even my little pinky. I tried my eyes again, still heavy, and felt glued shut. Next, I tried my lips. I wanted to scream at him for kidnapping me.

How dare he?! I will have his head for this transgression against me.

Maldita sea. I hated to be at his mercy. Hated to be at anyone's mercy but my own.

I had to give it to him. He found me. They finally caught up to me.

The rage that was brewing inside me because Ángel had me turned to rage against myself. I got sloppy; I got too comfortable in my little bubble of lies I created years ago.

I believed in my own bullshit of lies. That I was far enough from all of them, from my father and La Fuentes Cartel. That he and his *socios* wouldn't dare touch me while I was building my imperium in Crescent Point.

I truly was living in the fairytale of my own creation, thinking I was safe. Protected by Greyson and his powerful pack. Since we were business partners. How could I have been so naïve?

Esteban La Fuentes always gets his targets. Tarde o temprano, he takes what he wants.

How foolish I have been in thinking that my father, the head of all heads of the La Fuentes Cartel, wouldn't come for me after all these years. I had disrespected him once and, knowing my *papá*, he would rather kill me than let me disrespect him a second time, his daughter, the heiresses to his legacy, or not.

I scrunched my nose at the thought of me becoming the new capo of the cartel as my eyebrows knitted together while a soft sigh escaped my lips.

Yes!!

I was getting control over my body again. I tried one more time to open my eyes or move a limb. But to my dismay, nothing would react as I wanted them to, just my eyebrows and nose.

Fuck me. I need to fight this drug, whatever the hell Ángel injected me with.

A light touch of fingers brushing over my immobile arm toward my belly and waist had me recoiling from the soft caress. I was one hundred percent certain that it was Ángel who was caressing me. The possessive, jealous bastard wouldn't allow no one else to touch me. I kept trying to move away from the touch, but I couldn't get my body to do what I wanted. The son of a bitch drugged me.

As the images of this morning were flashing in the right order, making my blood boil because I got caught and the growling from earlier sounded angry and louder, something stung me in my arm. It burned just like it did this morning.

"I hope you are having sweet dreams, Nena *mía*. You'll be home soon with me, where you belong." His raspy, dark voice whispered next to my ear, then he kissed me on the tip of my nose. I knew if my body wasn't sedated, it would have erupted into goosebumps while heat would set me aflame and make my freaking pussy all wet with my arousal, waiting to be filled by Ángel's cock.

Stupid body. I would have rolled my eyes if I could.

I was being dragged by the man I swore I would never love again, back to the world I wished I didn't belong to, the world I ended ties with a long time ago. I didn't want to have anything to do with all of them in *la familia*. And here was my unfaithful body, reacting to his touch and voice, craving his dick while the drug kicked in and darkness pulled me under again.

TO BE CONTINUED IN PART II

Jimena's story continues in Jimena Part II: Women of La Fuentes Cartel.
Coming in the beginning of 2023!

ABOUT KINDRA WHITE

Fantasy and Paranormal romance author Kindra White is a mother of three and a wife. Born on the island of Aruba, she is an avid reader who took the plunge and started creating her own books to help break the stigma that women face. She currently lives in Enschede, The Netherlands, where when she's not bringing readers more books, she enjoys baking a killer cheesecake and taking care of her family.

When You Forget Me

by Lorelei Johnson

CHAPTER 1

Elspeth

The night was warm, the moon full, an auspicious sign according to my mother as she fussed with my hair for the thousandth time. Auspicious for who, I wasn't sure, but I doubted it was for me. If I had to say I had any kind of luck, I would have said it was bad, or at least wonky. Perhaps I was paying off karma from a past life, which seemed monstrously unfair but I sure as hell hadn't done anything in this lifetime to warrant it. The tiny town I lived in didn't exactly present a lot of opportunities for such things.

It was the night of my twenty-first birthday, so I was now officially allowed to join the coven, something all young witches dream about. Most counted down the days until the ceremony, wishing away the time as they anticipated the moment their life would truly begin. Not me. Every day I gave that calendar the side-eye, hoping I could ignore the impending initiation, all while praying to the goddess that my powers would finally manifest as my mother insisted they would.

I wasn't the only one who had doubts. There was some dispute amongst the council over whether I should be initiated or whether we should wait. Because like my luck, my magic was a little wonky.

Growing up, the other kids would tease that I was a bad omen, and who could blame them, really? Whenever I tried a spell, disaster usually followed, or sometimes nothing at all. When I was eighteen, I tried a spell to turn my hair red, but what resulted was a cotton candy pink tipped with platinum blonde, making me look like a tub of ice-cream. I never bothered to change it back, though, since I kind of liked it. My best friend, Bianca, told everyone she'd done it for me because no one would believe I'd done it on purpose. If they'd known it was the result of another botched spell, they would have snickered about it incessantly.

I secretly hoped the council would vote against me joining until my magic stabilised. But my father wouldn't hear of his only daughter being refused her right to join the coven. The Evans witches had a strong, proud history, and there was no way he could admit his daughter was a total failure as a witch. My parents were convinced that my powers simply hadn't awakened yet. After all, great power takes time to manifest, and the prediction ceremony to assess a witch's magical potential was never wrong. Or so they said.

So, there I was, in my white lace dress and my hair looking like melted ice-cream – much to my mother's dismay because I refused to let her change it – being led to a ceremony I had spent the last twelve months dreading.

As my mother led me through the mansion, the entire coven was present, dressed as formally as I was, the whole place lit with candles as the coven drank champagne. They all looked at me, most with scepticism or judgement, but I was used to those looks. They all doubted the power that was predicted to reside in me. Hell, I doubted it, too. But there were a few who believed it because of who my father was. I preferred the scepticism to the expectation; at least I couldn't disappoint those who weren't expecting anything.

As I walked, I felt a heated gaze on me that sent a shiver down my spine, like I was being watched by a predator. I forced myself to keep my eyes forward until Bianca bounded up to us. 'Mrs Evans, I'll take her,' she said with a wide smile.

'Alright, but make sure she isn't late,' my mother said. She kissed me on the cheek and offered me a smile that didn't quite reach her eyes. My father was a stubborn proud man, and while my mother didn't want me to be held back any more than he did, she didn't quite share his *it'll be fine* attitude. I knew she worried about me.

Bianca linked her arm with mine and steered me to a small room with hurried steps that could only mean one thing: there was gossip on the tip of her tongue. She shoved me inside and shut the door. 'Did you see the way Chase was looking at you?' she said, fanning her face dramatically.

'No,' I answered somewhat truthfully. I may not have seen it but I had felt it. And not for the first time.

For the past six months I'd felt his gaze on me whenever we were in the same room. I wasn't going to tell Bianca that, though. She'd run away with it and I'd never get her back to reality.

There were only three reasons Chase Danvers would look at a woman with any seriousness: power, money, or he hadn't already fucked her. I satisfied two of those criteria, three if the prediction my father clung to so desperately turned out to be true. There was something about him that I didn't trust, a darkness that made me wary.

'I wish he'd look at me the way he looked at you,' Bianca sighed dreamily.

'You should stay away from him.'

'You're not still on about that feeling he gives you? No offense, but your magic isn't the most reliable.'

'Well gee, tell me what you really think.'

'Give him a chance,' Bianca said. 'Who knows? Maybe you'll be the reason he settles down.'

'Taming the player is your dream, not mine,' I said flatly. I was only glad that no one else had noticed his attention to me. Having Bianca berate me was one thing, but to have the pressure of the entire coven telling me to give their golden boy a chance? No thank you.

'Well, when you reject him, steer him my way,' she said, hiking her shoulders in a shrug that told me she was finally dropping this line of conversation.

I smiled but I had no intention of steering him towards her. I didn't want him anywhere near her. My magic might be wonky, but that didn't mean I should ignore my instincts entirely. Chase Danvers was bad news.

'Alright, I'd better go join the circle. Stay here, and don't be late or your mother will have a fit,' Bianca said.

'Yeah, yeah, I know.'

Bianca grinned and ducked out of the room with a bounce in her step, leaving me completely alone with my anxiety. As part of the ceremony, I was supposed to do a spell to see what my affinity was. There was a fifty percent chance nothing would happen, and a fifty percent chance something would explode. Either way, it was sure to be a total embarrassment.

'I thought she'd never leave,' a dark voice said.

My body tensed but I forced myself to turn around. 'Chase, what are you doing in here?' I asked, keeping my voice calm despite the fact that my heart was hammering against my chest.

'So, you do know who I am. You've been ignoring me,' he said, a flirtatious lilt to his voice and he flashed that charming smile of his, a well-practiced move in his playbook.

'Goddess forbid a woman should ignore you,' I said, rolling my eyes. 'You didn't answer my question.'

'I've come to see you, of course.'

'And why would you want to see me? We've hardly even spoken before.'

'You're not going to make this easy for me, are you?' he asked, raking a hand through his hair. 'That's one of the things I like about you.'

I found myself analysing his every movement, wondering if it was staged or real. The smile that didn't reach his eyes, the confidence in his shoulders that conflicted with the expression on his face. The words were perfect, too perfect, as if he was trying to herd me somewhere.

But this cat was not about to be herded anywhere. Not by him.

'Stop trying to charm me and tell me what you want,' I snapped. I was in no mood for games, I already wanted to run and Chase wasn't making it any easier.

'I knew there was something different about you. Most girls would be flattered that I'd even notice them,' he said, and the playfulness fell from his face. He seemed almost...proud. I suddenly didn't want to know what he wanted anymore. I just wanted him to leave.

'Look, Chase, this isn't a good time -'

'Elspeth, when you go out there tonight, I want you to go out there as mine.'

I blinked. Then again. My brain scrambled to register what he'd just said. 'You barely know me, what makes you think I'd agree to that?' I couldn't remember a single time we'd actually had a conversation. No doubt we'd heard plenty about each other, as one would expect in a small town and a small coven, but when we were young, he'd snickered along with the rest of them.

So, what was different now? That uneasy feeling began to stir in my stomach. Whatever his reason, I doubted I was going to like it.

'That's my fault,' he said, giving a small shrug as if that was a minor detail. He took a step towards me and I took one back, but he seemed unperturbed. There was a darkness slithering around him, as if the shadows around him were living beings. 'I'm not good at...feelings, Elspeth.'

'Feelings?' I squeaked. Why was he talking about feelings? As far as I was aware, Chase Danvers did not have feelings, certainly not for her.

'I'm in love with you,' he said, something like authenticity in his voice. I blinked hard, shock rendering me speechless. What the hell was he talking about? He couldn't love me. It was absurd and the very thought filled me with dread. What was it about him that had the hairs on my neck standing on end? I couldn't pinpoint it but I knew that professions of love shouldn't feel like that.

'Chase, I don't...' Something flashed in his eyes that silenced me. Chase was the most powerful warlock in our coven, he was destined for a council position, no one doubted that. How could I fight against him with my abilities? I needed to get him to leave without pissing him off.

But Chase Danvers didn't take rejection well. I wasn't sure that he'd ever *been* rejected before.

He stalked towards me, his movements slow, calculated, like he was stalking prey. My heart hammered in my chest as I stepped back again but the wall met my back, giving me nowhere else to run.

'Why would you – are you under a spell?' I asked. None of this made any sense. He'd never shown any real interest in me before. It was some kind of prank, right? Or a potion gone awry. There had to be a logical explanation to...whatever this was.

'Have you really not noticed?'

'How could I notice anything when you're with another woman every other week? This' – I waved a hand at him – 'is just a little out of character.'

He reached me then, standing close. Too close. I could feel the darkness slithering across my skin. 'Don't you see how great we could be together? When your power manifests, there will be no stopping us.'

'I don't have any power.'

'You do,' he said, gliding his fingers along my jaw and I swallowed hard. 'I can sense it in you, lying dormant, waiting.' I could feel his breath on my skin and my stomach knotted, but he didn't seem to notice my anxiety. 'I covet you above all else,' he murmured, his voice seductive but his words unsettling.

'Chase that...isn't love,' I managed to say, my words slow and calm as I tried not to anger him.

'Isn't it?'

I slipped away from him, putting some much-needed distance between us, distance which seemed to set my confidence free. 'Wanting to possess a person for their power isn't love, and I won't be your trophy. There are plenty of witches here who would die for that honour, and they are far more powerful than I am.'

'Are you rejecting me?' Something dark twisted his expression, tightening that knot in my stomach.

'I won't go out there tonight as yours,' I said carefully. 'I won't be anyone's if I don't believe his feelings for me are real,' I added, hoping that he would see this as more of a no-for-now and buy me some time.

'If I can't have you, Elspeth Evans, no one can,' he snarled. He raised his hand and started chanting as a shimmering shadow began to dance in his palm. 'Memory unbound, time unwound. A curse to bind, my life to thine. Let none remember you but me.'

'Wait!'

The shadows lurched from his palm, sailing through the air, wrapping around me, sliding over my body, burning at my skin. I cried out as fear gripped me, but I couldn't get free of them. All I could do was endure it until the shadows began to dissipate, melting into the room as if they never were.

'What did you do to me?' I demanded, voice firm as my body trembled, the sticky feeling of dark magic lingering on my skin.

'I've erased you, my dear Elspeth. No one can love you if they can't remember you. When you've come to your senses, I'll lift the curse.'

'Come to my senses?' I screeched. 'You're insane!'

'No. I just know how to take what I want. Most females like an ambitious male.'

'I will never accept you.'

'Then you will live as a ghost for the rest of your long life,' he said. His gaze softened as he looked at me. 'Why did you make me do it? I don't want to hurt you, Elspeth,' he said, reaching out his hand as if to caress me.

I slapped it away and glared at him. 'Fuck off, Chase. Don't you *dare* blame me for this!'

I pushed out of the room, breaking into a run as I headed towards the circle that had gathered. I looked around at the confused faces, no one said anything as I passed, only shooting quizzical glances as if wondering who I was. I found my parents standing together, my father muttering something about magic.

'Mum, dad,' I said through panting breaths. 'Please tell me you remember me.'

They turned to me with confusion and my heart sank. 'We don't have a child. Who are you?' my father demanded, anger flaring his nostrils. 'Are you the cause of this?'

'Please, let me explain -'

My mother gripped my father's arm and he looked down at her, patting her hand comfortingly. When he looked back at me, his gaze was blank. 'Sorry, who are you?' he said, the anger gone from his voice, as if the conversation we'd been having had completely vanished from his mind.

Tears pricked at my eyes. I scanned the room but all around me people murmured in confusion. No one seemed to know I was there. As soon as they looked away from me, I was forgotten.

Standing in the shadows, leaning against the wall with a smirk on his face, was Chase Danvers, admiring his handiwork. There was no sympathy in his eyes, no regret or remorse. I knew there was no way he was going to remove this curse until I agreed to his terms, until I agreed to be his.

Over my dead body.

He wasn't the only powerful witch in the world. There had to be someone who could break this damn curse. I took a deep breath and ran.

CHAPTER 2

Elspeth

(Chicago: 2 Years Later)

It had been a long time since I'd been in a big city like Chicago. Mostly, I steered clear of them because it was a lot harder to find the paranormal community when they were surrounded by so many humans. For one, there was a lot more ground to cover, and two, they had to cover their tracks better. But I was running out of leads.

For the last two years I'd been tracking down every witch even rumoured to have the power to break my curse, but so far they'd all been a bust. Either they weren't powerful enough, or I couldn't track them down before I was forced to move on to the next town.

Chicago had the best lead I'd ever managed to dig up. The voodoo priestess, Angèlie Laveau, was rumoured to be in these parts. Of course, getting information on her whereabouts wasn't exactly easy when people forgot you as soon as they looked away.

It made everything just that little bit more difficult.

I walked up the rusted stairs to my room at Earl's Motel, a rundown place not fit for a crack den. I didn't have a lot of options. Earl was high most of the time, he couldn't remember anyone, so it hardly mattered that he didn't remember me. He knew all he needed to, that the room was booked and the tenant paid on time. Paid in cash, too, which he preferred. No paper trail, perfect for tax evasion.

I'd been in the city for a week now and I hadn't found anything on Angèlie Laveau. The paranormal population in big cities seemed to be much more careful about talking to strangers, and they were even less inclined to speak to someone they couldn't remember. Hold their gaze too long, they suspected magic. Let them look away and I had to start the conversation all over again. It was getting ridiculous, and I couldn't stick around much longer.

Chase would catch up with me soon.

I opened the door, looking around my *home*. It stirred that ever-present anger in me. I was forced to live in filth, stealing money and anything else I needed to survive, all because some warlock couldn't handle rejection. And still my magic was practically non-existent. Whatever power he'd sensed in me clearly wasn't there.

I popped the top off a beer and eyed the contents of my wardrobe sceptically. It was a jumbled mess of styles. Most of it wasn't what I would call *me*, since it was a closet full of disguises designed to help me fit into any situation. Tonight, I was headed into a paranormal bar. I wasn't sure what to expect, since I hadn't come into contact with many other species in my home town or in my travels. Or maybe I had but I hadn't noticed. I'd been focused on finding witches with the power to break my curse, not playing spot-the-paranormal. The elders of the coven had warned us of the dangers of other paranormals. Witches had many enemies simply because of what we were. But I was getting desperate, so I was willing to try anything. I could be walking into a vipers den, I could be walking to my death, but I was beginning to understand that there were worse things than death, especially for an immortal.

I drained the last of the beer and pulled out a black dress. It was mid-length and tapered, accentuating my curves and making my boobs look great, but I hated wearing it. I wasn't used to drawing attention, in fact, I'd spent most of my youth trying to do the exact opposite. But I needed to draw attention tonight. This was my last chance to get to Angèlie Laveau. If I couldn't find her in the next couple of days, I was shit out of luck and it would be time to move on.

I took extra care with my make-up and my hair, though there wasn't much that could be done about the colour. I promised myself when I broke the curse I would change it, but it stood now as a reminder of my failure. I tied it up, letting a few strands fall loose, kissing my neck. Satisfied, I pulled my pumps on – easily my least favourite shoes because they hurt like a bitch – and headed back out into the strange city.

The bar was easy enough to find because I'd scoped it out earlier, tucked down an unassuming flight of stairs with a star carved into the cement. If I hadn't watched paranormals going down there, I would have missed it entirely. Nerves fluttered in my stomach. I took a deep breath and rolled my shoulders back before striding towards the door as if I belonged there.

A large male stood in the door dressed in a tuxedo and wearing an earpiece. His hands were clasped in front of him as he eyed me up and down. 'Haven't seen you around here before,' he said in a gruff voice. 'This is a private establishment.'

'And yet I wouldn't have found it if I hadn't been told of it,' I said. In truth, I hadn't been told about it so much as I had eavesdropped on some paranormals talking about it. That was how I knew the place was called *Myth*. There were no signs to label the place, but I supposed that was the best way to keep away curious humans who strayed too far.

'You smell human,' he said, but he wouldn't have if he suspected that I actually was human. Unless he had some way of erasing my memories. That would be a change.

I could sense *he* wasn't human. Unlike many paranormal beings, witches didn't have heightened senses like smell or sight – at least, not in the traditional sense. We did have a kind of third sight. Some, like seers, had a stronger third sight than others. I was actually grateful to belong to the less talented side of that category. For those of us with a muted third sight, we could sense other beings and see strong auras.

I begged my power to work as I held my hand out, palm up. A small flame flickered to life, dancing on my skin for a moment before snuffing out again.

'Ah, a witch. You new to town?' he asked, suddenly warming to me.

'Yes, I've only been here a week,' I told him, keeping my voice calm as my impatience began to squirm.

'Well, enjoy your night,' he said with a smile and pushed open the door for me.

My shoulders almost sagged in relief. I smiled up at him and entered the bar. It was like nothing I'd ever seen before. Blue lights kept the room dim but elegant. Black leather stools lined the bar, white leather chairs surrounded small tables. Candles flickered on the bar and each of the tables, even the booths in the back corner. It was pumping; people everywhere and all of them paranormal. Some had glowing eyes, glowing skin, pointed ears, fangs, claws. I ran a hand over my dress and swallowed hard. I was a step away from being underdressed in this sea of glittering jewels and designer fabrics.

Where would I even start?

I headed to the bar, sitting on one of the empty stools at the end where I could see the room around me. I'd start as I always did, by observing.

'Can I get you something, love?' the bartender asked, flashing me a smile. He was beautiful to look at, his green eyes shimmered like jewels, his hair like fine silk, tucked behind pointed ears. I found myself wondering what those ears would feel like. I shook myself before I actually reached out for them.

What a strange reaction. Was it magic or something to do with what he was? I felt completely out of my element.

'Cosmopolitan, thanks,' I said, realising I still hadn't answered his question for all my staring. He smiled and gave me a nod, then walked to the back to collect the ingredients. I'd never actually drank a cosmo before but it was the only cocktail I knew the name of and I wasn't sure beer was going to give the right impression in this place.

I watched as he prepared the cocktail, wondering what manner of being he was. I wasn't very good at telling who was what yet, but there was something elegant about his movements and his lean figure. He pulled out a glass and a lost look settled on his face. When he'd been making the drink, he'd been on autopilot. He'd probably made the same cocktail thousands of times. But now that he had stopped to think about what he was doing, he had no idea.

'That's for me,' I said and he looked over at me. His brow furrowed for a moment before he strode towards me.

'Sorry, not sure where my head is tonight.'

'No problem,' I said with a warm smile.

He poured the liquid into a glass and placed a very pink cocktail in front of me. 'Cash or card?'

'Can you tell me who that is?' I asked, pointing behind him.

He looked over his shoulder and froze for a moment, as if his brain was rebooting, then looked back at me. 'Sorry, did you ask me something?'

'No,' I said with a smile. His brow furrowed in confusion and he shook his head, mumbling to himself as he walked away. I took a sip of the drink and scanned the room again. Was I kidding myself? How would I get anyone to talk to me in this place?

My gaze snagged on a man staring at me with curiosity dancing in his dark eyes. He was incredibly easy to look at with his blonde hair pushed back from his face, falling almost to his shoulders. His lips were curled with amusement. Had he seen my trick with the bartender? It wouldn't matter. Once he looked away, he'd forget everything. I pulled my gaze away, taking another sip of my cocktail as I tried to ignore the strange fluttering in my stomach.

CHAPTER 3

Roman

I approached the table Marcus always sat at. Same table, same bar. He was nothing if not a creature of habit, something that would likely get him killed one day if someone powerful enough had the inclination. As the head of the Enforcers in Chicago – a vampire run organisation that was responsible for keeping order amongst the vampires – Marcus thought he was untouchable. But if I had learnt anything in this business, it was that everyone was touchable.

'Roman!' Marcus said, moving a nymph from his lamp and slapping her on the arse to send her on her way. She squealed in delight, shooting a sultry look over her shoulder as she sashayed away.

'You never change,' I said as I took a seat.

'You're one to talk.' Marcus hailed a waiter, holding two fingers up. 'Good job in Memphis.'

'You have something else for me, don't you? What happened to my hiatus?' I wouldn't exactly but cut up if it was ending, since the hiatus was Marcus' idea, not mine. I lived for the job. As an enforcer, I was responsible for hunting down rogue magics and paranormals, and I was fucking good at it.

'Oh please, don't act like it was your idea. And I am putting you on leave after this one. You're going to spend a week in a den of nymphs if I have to throw you in there myself.'

Marcus was my polar opposite. He was always seeking out pleasure like a junkie seeking his next hit. I, on the other hand, was a workaholic. Not that pleasure was something I abstained from, I just didn't seek it between the thighs of every nymph that shook her tits in my face.

'Who knows? Maybe you'll find your bride there,' Marcus said with a wink.

'That's about as likely as you admitting you're a sex addict.' The waiter returned, placing the drinks on the table in front of us; blood served in fine crystal. I took a sip, letting the delectable flavour coat my tongue before swallowing it. The bar was run by a half fae, and whatever he did with the beverages here made them taste a thousand times better than anything else in existence. Was it legal? No one cared. No one seemed to care what the other half of his lineage was, either, though he guarded the secret closely.

'What's the job?'

'There's a malevolent magic heading this way. The oracle has seen a darkness descending on Chicago.'

'That's nice and vague. This darkness have a name?'

'You know it doesn't work like that. I've had witches scrying for days, but so far nothing.'

'You've been paying witches for days? I'm surprised you have any money left,' I scoffed. Witches weren't exactly fond of vampires, and vice versa. We had a long and bloody history. As such, they tended to charge us more than any other species for magic. And they charged a lot for magic to begin with.

'It has not been cheap,' Marcus said irritably.

'Is it really such a big threat?'

'You didn't hear Lorena's screeching. That woman has never seen anything that made her react like that.'

Lorena was an oracle that had been with the Enforcers for longer than I had. A vampire oracle was especially rare, she was probably more protected than the vampire king himself. Rumour had it she was a witch who had been turned, but no one really knew the truth of that.

'Okay, where do I start?'

A tantalising scent suddenly hit me, sending a tension through my entire body, my ears twitching, my fangs aching. It was intoxicating, consuming every part of me. I scanned the room, my eyes locking onto a gorgeous creature in a tight black dress, pink hair tied up except for a few strands kissing her neck where my lips long to be.

She took a seat at the bar, crossing one leg over the other, flashing her creamy thigh before tugging the fabric down. She wasn't comfortable in that dress but it was comfortable with her.

'Roman?' Marcus' voice barely registered as I strained to hear her voice over the noise.

'Cash or card?' the bartender asked as he placed a drink in front of her.

'Can you tell me who that is?' she asked, pointing behind the bartender.

He looked over his shoulder and froze for a moment, his brow furrowing in confusion. 'Sorry, did you ask me something?'

'No,' she said, flashing a beautiful smile that made my fists clench. An ugly feeling stirred in my chest, a possessive feeling. As if she felt my gaze, she looked over at me, her eyes stopping on mine. They were grey like the sky in a storm, her eyeliner making them more alluring than anything I'd seen before. All too soon, she looked away, leaving me with a pang of emptiness.

'Roman!' Marcus snapped.

I tore my gaze from the woman at the bar and my head spun. Her scent never left me but her face faded from my mind, as if being swallowed by a fog, until I couldn't remember what had captured my attention at all. 'What did you say?'

'It's unlike you to be so taken by a woman,' Marcus said, looking over at the bar.

'What woman?'

Marcus looked back at me then, his brow furrowed. 'What?'

I breathed in that intoxicating scent and my gaze was drawn to the bar, to a woman sitting in a black dress, sipping a cosmopolitan. Something about her was familiar and yet I was sure I hadn't seen her before. It was as if something was hovering at the edge of my mind but I was unable to reach it.

How peculiar.

But there was one thing I knew for certain. She was my bride, the one woman destined for me, fated. I could tell from her scent, from the way my instincts screamed at me, from the unquenching desire to be near her. I never imagined I'd find her here. How many times had I come to this bar? She'd never been there before, I was sure of it.

'Can we get started tomorrow?' I asked, not taking my gaze from her.

'Sure,' Marcus said, a smile in his voice.

'Great.' I barely had the word out before I was walking towards her as if there was no one else in the room. Her scent was maddening, the closer I got, the less control I felt. She continued to look around the room, and continued to sip her drink, as if she was determined to ignore me. It was infuriating and tantalising at the same time. I leaned against the bar and she finally looked up at me.

'You're new around here,' I said.

'That obvious, huh?' she asked, her glib tone making me smile.

'I'm here a lot, and I'd remember seeing you.'

'You'd be surprised.' There was something self-deprecating in her voice, a deep-rooted sadness in her eyes that clawed at me. Who was this woman? She took a sip of her drink, drawing my attention to her lips. Her tongue darted across them before she put her glass back on the counter. 'Wait, was that a line?'

A chuckle left my throat, which seemed to surprise her. 'Do you want it to be?' I leaned in slightly, unable to help myself, breathing her in. God. I wanted to take her out of here, back to my place. I wanted to touch her, to kiss her, to *taste* her.

'You're looking at me like you want to eat me,' she said cautiously.

I shook myself mentally and offered her a smile. 'There are a lot of things I'd like to do to you.'

'I might be meeting someone,' she said, turning her gaze from me.

Jealousy stabbed at me. The idea that she might be waiting for another male the idea that another male might take her home tonight, might touch what was mine – I took a breath to calm myself. She was running her finger along the base of her glass, her eyes following the movement, and realisation hit. 'Am I making you uncomfortable?'

Her eyes snapped back to mine. For a long moment she said nothing, as if she was contemplating her next move. 'Are you going to tell me your name?'

'Roman. And you are?'

'Elspeth.'

Elspeth. My bride's name was as beautiful as she was. If only she was a vampire, or even a shifter, that would make things so much easier. Then she would recognise me as her mate, too. As it was, it was clear she was a species that didn't have a mate. A siren or a witch perhaps. It was hard to tell, she smelled human, which meant she was not long into her immortality. Not having a mate would make it that much harder to win her over. Especially when she looked like she was on the verge of running.

'What brings you to Chicago, Elspeth?'

'I'm looking for someone, but I'm starting to get the feeling she doesn't want to be found,' she admitted, a flash of irritation in her eyes. Interesting.

'And are you searching now, or are you here for pleasure?' I could feel her walls coming down. She might not see me as her mate but there was an attraction there that even she couldn't deny. It was in the way she twirled her hair around her finger, the way she nibbled at her bottom lip, that uncertainty in her eyes. Anticipation unfurled in me like a cat waking from a nap.

She was almost within my reach.

'Neither,' she said.

Within reach but still fighting it. She didn't know that now that I'd found her, there was no way I could let her go. 'So, then what brought the most beautiful creature in Chicago to this bar tonight if not for work or for pleasure?' I asked, taking a strand of her hair and curling it around my finger.

Her heart beat quickly in her chest, her cheeks began to flush pink. The signs of lust were making themselves known, her body telling me what her mind was too afraid to admit. It stirred something primal in me. 'I bet you say that to all the girls,' she said.

'I would never lie about something like that,' I said, holding her gaze so she could see my sincerity. Her lips parted as she inhaled sharply. I could scent her arousal now and I knew that if I couldn't taste her I would go mad. 'Do you want to get out of here?'

'Why would I do that?'

The urge to touch her was unbearable. I traced my fingers along her jaw, slowly gliding them down her neck. Her skin was soft and warm, and that slight touch made me want more of her. A shiver ran through her and a heat danced in her eyes, making my cock ache. If she had any idea what she was doing to me...

'Because you want to.'

CHAPTER 4

Elspeth

Roman's lips were on mine as soon as he closed the door, as if he couldn't bear to wait another second. His intensity was intoxicating, erasing all my doubts, quieting that responsible voice in the back of my mind. His touch was cold but skilled, everywhere his hands went tingled. I felt more connected to him than I had with anyone before. Maybe it was the loneliness of the last two years catching up with me, but in that moment I didn't care.

'Where did you go just now?' he asked, his breath caressing my skin as he gripped my hips, pulling me against him. His firm erection ignited a heat in my core.

My heart was pounding in my chest and I let out a shaky breath. 'Nowhere,' I said and pressed my lips to his in an attempt to distract him. I needed him not to ask questions. He wouldn't remember this in the morning, and I didn't want to think about that.

He brushed his lips along my jaw, trailing them towards my ear. 'Liar,' he breathed before taking the lobe between his teeth. I moaned as I melted into him, a throbbing sensation beginning to build between my thighs. 'So responsive.'

It was hard to believe anyone could *not* respond to him. Each touch felt tailored for my pleasure, each kiss took my breath away. I slid my hands under his shirt, and his skin on mine felt electric as I traced his sculpted muscles. He cupped the back of my neck, capturing my lips once more. I gasped and he slid his tongue into my mouth, twinging it with my own, making my knees buckle.

Roman ran a finger down my arm. 'How attached are you to this dress?'

'As my only clothing option right now, I'd rather you didn't destroy it,' I said, my voice sounding breathy to my own ears.

'Maybe I won't let you leave,' he murmured, running his finger back up my arm. He was driving me to distraction. My heart thumped in my chest, a yearning began to build, a yearning to be seen, to be loved, to be remembered. Something about Roman made that desire stronger than ever.

As if he expected he wouldn't like my answer, he silenced me with a kiss, melting my thoughts, my doubts. He slid his hand up my back then slowly unzipped my dress, gliding his fingertips along my spine. He slid the fabric down, pushing it over my curves. I felt a twinge of self-consciousness as it hit the floor and the cool air brushed my skin.

'Gods, you're beautiful,' he said as his eyes raked over me.

My cheeks warmed. 'I haven't had enough to drink for that kind of talk.'

'You'll have to get used to it.'

I didn't have time to process those words because his lips began to trail down my neck, chasing away any coherent thought. I wrapped my arm around his neck, twining my fingers in his hair as he kissed his way slowly down, over my collar bone, down my chest, the soft skin of my breast. His hand slid up my back, unclasping my bra with one swift motion that must have been well practiced. I'd never known a man to do that with such ease before.

Doubt began to coil at the edge of my mind. What was I doing? I knew better than to let people in. It only hurt more later and this might be more than I could bear. 'Roman –' I began to protest but his thumb flicked across my aching nipple, sending a wetness to my panties and a moan to my lips.

'Don't tell me you want to stop,' he breathed, his eyes on my breasts. 'Not when you respond so well to me.' His lips wrapped around my nipple and he gave it a sharp suck that made my knees buckle. I gripped his hair tighter as all doubt fled me. I couldn't stop now, not when I wanted him so badly.

He gripped my hips, pulling me against him, his hard cock pressing against me, my muscles clenching in anticipation. 'Ah,

Roman,' I moaned, helpless against his touch, his tongue, pleasure shuddering through me, igniting a heat in my core. I began to fumble with the buttons on his shirt as his tongue circled my nipple, teeth grazing flesh, another sharp suck, another shudder of pleasure. Goddess, had anything ever felt so good?

His shirt finally fell open as the last button gave way and my hands found his skin as if drawn by a magnet. His body was cold and firm under my touch, like marble. Muscles rippled beneath his skin with each movement and I wondered what he would feel like between my thighs.

He shrugged off his shirt to reveal sculpted arms and shoulders, everything about him was breathtaking and I wanted to explore every inch of him. 'If you keep looking at me like that, you're going to make me blush,' he murmured. He grazed the back of his fingers down my neck, between my breasts, slowly over my stomach, all the way to my panties. 'These need to come off.'

My breath hitched as he slid his fingers inside the fabric, sliding it down my legs, his cool touch sending a shiver through me, heightening my pleasure. He reached my feet and I stepped out of them, completely exposed to him as his eyes raked over me and he licked his lips. That hunger in his eyes made my breaths shallow, my need uncontrollable.

'Beautiful,' he breathed.

'This feels a little one-sided,' I said, my teeth sinking into my lip as my eyes dropped to his pants. His erection strained against the fabric, sending a heat through me.

He groaned. 'What are you waiting for?' The wicked glint in his eyes had me licking my lips as I reached for his pants. I popped open the button, gripped the zip and slowly slid it down, each movement carefully planned out, designed to increase his anticipation. By the sound of his ragged breaths, it was working.

I slid his pants down his legs and inhaled sharply at the sight of his erection, at the promise of pleasure. Before I could stop myself, I wrapped a hand around it and his hips bucked. When I looked up at him, there was a hunger burning in his eyes. He gripped my hand, pulling it from him. He lifted me into his arms and carried me to the bed, laying me on the mattress with a care that was a stark contrast to that look in his eyes. His gaze lingered on my naked body as if he was trying to decide what to do to me first. My nipples tightened under his gaze and he bent down, sucking one between his lips. My back arched as pleasure rippled through me.

His tongue flicked over the tight bud as his hands explored my body, gliding over my curves, his fingers teasing at my sensitive inner thighs until my hips rolled up to him as my body begged for more. His lips curled and he released my nipple, his lips trailing down my stomach, my mind already anticipating his destination. He pushed my legs apart, hooking his arms under my thighs. I exhaled a shaky breath as he bent down to kiss my core. His tongue slid between my folds, flicking over my swollen clitoris, each stroke slow and deliberate, as if he was gaging my reactions. He was chasing all rational thought from my mind. My hips rolled up to meet his tongue and a moan escaped my lips.

'You like that?' he purred.

'Uh-huh,' I managed to say, my eyes fluttering closed as my fingers gripped the sheets.

He pulled my hips against his mouth and I gasped as his tongue expertly lapped at me, steering me relentlessly towards ecstasy, the tension coiling tighter and tighter until it became unbearable. My body shuddered as the orgasm ripped through me with a force I had never felt before, but his tongue didn't still, instead he continued to stroke me as if he couldn't get enough of my taste.

Finally, when I couldn't take anymore, he pulled back and moved up my body, dropping a kiss to bare flesh here and there, a kiss to my collar bone, to my neck, until he was hovering over me. 'I think you're ready for me now,' he grated. The hunger in his eyes sent a flutter to my stomach and I licked my lips in anticipation.

Who was this male? The way he treated me felt as if he was worshiping me, as if his pleasure was derived from mine. He looked at me as if I was the only female in the world worth looking at. I was in very real danger of becoming addicted to this, and I didn't care.

Just for one night. Just let go for one night, I told myself as I reached for him, pressing my lips against his. He groaned against me and thrust into me. My back arched and I cried out as pleasure sparked, my body greedily accepting his firm length. The feeling of him moving inside me as he bucked his hips against me made my mind go blank.

There was nothing but our bodies colliding in a furious passion, nothing but the pleasure exploding between us.

'Ah, Roman!' I screamed as another orgasm ripped through me. My body quivered around him as he thrust until a guttural growl tore its way from his throat. I could feel him pulsing inside me as he nuzzled my neck, his breath caressing the skin there, sending a shiver through me.

After a long moment, he pulled out of me. I'd never had a one night stand before. Was I supposed to leave now? I found myself wanting to stay, even though I knew it was wrong to let myself get attached. Without a word, he pulled the covers over me and tucked me into his side as if that was where I belonged. I drifted into sleep as he stroked my hair, wondering what it would be like if I could spend eternity like this.

CHAPTER 5

Elspeth

I woke the next morning feeling heaven beneath me in the form of a soft, lump-free mattress and silk sheets. My eyes snapped open, and I froze, last night coming back to me in hot flashes of memory, aching muscles and residual pleasure. I hadn't slept with a man in a while, definitely not since I'd been cursed, but nothing in my memory compared to last night.

He'd also not lost his memory of me when he closed his eyes, which left me with questions. How did this curse work exactly? Did he remember because we were intimate? Because we never lost contact? Or was it something else? It left an uncomfortable flair of hope in my chest.

But all fairytales come to an end. Especially this one. I'd thought I could have one night of pleasure and leave it at that, but the things I'd felt last night scared the hell out of me. The thought of never feeling his touch again made my body ache with loneliness.

It was definitely time to go.

I looked over at Roman as he lay beside me, sleeping deeply, a strangely contented look on his face that tugged at my heart. I had to snap out of this. I couldn't get attached, for two reasons. One, it would be too painful for him to forget me every time we were apart. Two, Chase would probably kill him.

It was safest if I left and let Roman forget me.

I slipped out of the bed, picking up my clothes from the floor and pulling them on as quietly as possible. I didn't want to be there when he woke up with no memory of me. I should never have gone with him. I picked up my bag and slung it over my shoulder.

'That's rude,' Roman said slowly.

I froze then looked over my shoulder at him, trying my best not to look guilty. 'Do you even remember my name?' I asked. It was an unfair barb but it hurt me more than it would hurt him.

He pushed himself up on his elbows and tilted his head, his brow furrowing in confusion. 'You're a witch. You made me forget?' He seemed almost hurt by that, and I suppose if the roles were reversed, I'd be upset too if I thought the guy I'd slept with had whammied my brain to make me forget him.

Unfortunately, this was something I had no control over.

I smiled sadly. 'I am a witch, but I'm not a very good one. I didn't make you forget.' I wanted to ask him what he was, since he now knew what I was, but the more I knew, the harder it would be to leave.

'Then why is my memory hazy? Why can't I remember your name?'

'Hazy?' I barely kept my mouth from falling open. 'You remember something from last night?' With inhuman speed, Roman was suddenly in front of me. I gasped in surprise, taking a step back. There weren't a lot of creatures who could move like that. He was cold to the touch. Had I just slept with a *vampire*? Vampires and witches were as close to mortal enemies as most people came. I'd been warned countless times against the dangers vampires posed to witches. To all paranormal beings.

'I don't appreciate people messing with my mind. Now tell me what the hell is going on,' he snapped, and that's when I saw them.

Fangs.

I ran across the room, throwing open the curtain. 'Fucking hell!' Roman snarled as he fled to the shadows. I stood in the middle of the window, letting the sunlight surround me, my only measure of safety now. How could I not know what he was?

Wait. He didn't bite me. Everything I'd been told about vampires said they were cruel, dangerous, and couldn't resist biting their prey. They didn't care to. So why hadn't Roman fed on me? Was he saving that for later? Had I really spent the last two years fighting to lift this damn curse only to get myself killed by a vampire?

Roman paced at the edge of the light, frustration set in his expression. 'Why didn't you tell me what you were?' I asked, pressing my back against the window as if I could melt through it.

'I don't remember, but if I had to guess I'd say it was because I didn't want you to react like this.' He stopped pacing and crossed his arms over his chest.

'If you knew I'd react like this, why wouldn't you just choose someone else?' I demanded. If only I'd managed to sneak out. Why had I told him I was a bad witch? I could have bluffed my way out. Now I was a sitting duck and when the sun went down, I was royally fucked.

He seemed to be chewing on his answer but finally he said, 'Don't tell me you regret last night, witchling. I know you enjoyed every second.'

I flushed but I refused to take my eyes off him, like a spider I was too scared to kill, I didn't want him out of my sight.

Wait.

'How could you possibly know that?' I asked, searching his face as if I could find the truth there. But he was a vampire, he'd likely had centuries to perfect his poker face. He didn't remember my name but he remembered something. How much did he remember? Or was it all a ruse? Perhaps he remembered nothing and it was simply his ego talking.

'I guess you really aren't a very good witch. Your memory spell doesn't seem to be very thorough,' he sneered.

'It's not my spell. It's a curse.' The words rolled off my tongue as I stared at him. Words I'd only ever told other witches in the hopes that they could help me. Why did I tell this vampire? Was I really so desperate? I clamped my mouth shut and dragged my eyes away from him. I needed to get a hold of myself.

'A curse?'

He seemed surprised, but I kept my eyes on the floor as I tried to compose myself, slowly building my walls back up, the ones he'd so easily torn down last night. *Get a hold of yourself.* First, I needed to get out of here, then I needed to find that priestess. Roman might remember some things, but it was likely that with extended absence, he would forget entirely. Safer for him if he did. Was it safer for me, too?

'Answer me, witchling.'

'You haven't answered any of my questions. Why should I answer yours?' I snapped. When my eyes met his again I saw pity there, and it rankled. I didn't want his pity. But there was also something darker there, something intense and dangerous.

'Will you close the curtains so we can talk?'

'How do I know you won't kill me as soon as the light's gone?'

He raised an eyebrow at me, a look of amusement settling on his features. 'Do you really think a little sunlight would stop me? If I meant you harm, my fangs would already be in your neck.'

'Is that supposed to be reassuring?' I asked, though truthfully it *was* somewhat reassuring, in a twisted kind of way. So maybe he didn't want to kill me now, but what was to stop him from doing it once his curiosity was sated? What other option did I have? The sun would eventually set and I would be vulnerable again.

'I give you my word that you have nothing to fear from me.'

I wanted to tell him that was hardly binding, but this was getting me nowhere. It was only wasting time I needed to find Angèlie Laveau. How much longer did I have before Chase showed up?

'Fine.' I pulled the curtains closed, fussing with them until all the light was gone. My eyes took a few moments to adjust to the sudden darkness, but when I turned again, Roman hadn't moved. He was watching me as if I was a skittish animal, which was probably fair. If he was suddenly inches from me I likely would have yanked those curtains open again.

'Why didn't you bite me last night?' I asked.

He shrugged. 'We're not the mindless monsters you think we are. Well, some of us. Do all witches practice dark magic?'

Fair point. Not all witches were evil, but I could think of at least one in my acquaintance who fit that category.

'My turn,' he said, but then he paused for a moment as if he wasn't sure what question to ask first. 'What curse is tampering with my memory?'

A part of me was disappointed. I wanted him to ask my name again, for him to be more interested in me than anything else. Which was entirely narcissistic of me. We'd only spent one night together, a night he didn't remember with much clarity. In his place, I'd also want to know what was happening to me. I let out a long breath. 'It's a long story. In a nutshell, someone cursed me so that no one would ever remember me. Once they look away from me, they forget everything.'

His brow furrowed, and that darkness returned to his eyes. It should have scared me but instead it was strangely...comforting. As if he was angry for me. 'Why?'

'It's my turn to ask a question.'

'Witchling,' he said, a warning in his voice.

I rolled my eyes. 'He didn't handle rejection very well. Now I get two questions.' He looked as if he was going to complain, but he waved me on. 'Do you know a witch named Angèlie Laveau?'

It wasn't the question I wanted to ask. For some reason questions about him bubbled to the surface, but I pushed them down. I didn't have time to waste and getting closer to him was dangerous, for him and for me. Best case scenario, Chase would make him forget me. Worst case, he'd kill Roman and make me watch.

'The voodoo priestess? Sure. What's your interest in her?'

He knew her? I almost sagged with relief. Finally, I had a concrete lead on her. If I could just convince Roman to take me to her, this could all be over soon. 'I came to Chicago to find her. I'm hoping she can help me break the curse.'

'What will you do once you find her?' he asked.

'Why do you want to know?' It was troubling how tempting it was to tell him everything. But I also needed his help. I wasn't likely to find Angèlie Laveau without him, not when my time was almost up. I couldn't remember the last time I'd cut it so close. Chase could show up any day now, but Angèlie was my best hope. If she couldn't do it then it was all over.

'Will you leave?'

With the curse gone, Chase would have a harder time tracking me down, but he likely already knew I was here. I would have to. But there was something about that look in Roman's eyes that made the words die in my throat. 'I don't know if I'll have a choice.'

He took a step towards me, and when I didn't react, he took another. When he was inches from me, I realised I'd made a mistake. My heart hammered in my chest. He could probably hear my body reacting to him. 'If I protected you, would you stay?' he asked, gliding his fingers along my jaw.

Memories of last night flashed in my mind, and my breath hitched in my throat. 'Why would you risk your life for me?' I asked, searching his eyes. But I couldn't decipher what I saw there as emotions seemed to war in those dark depths. I shook my head, pulling my gaze away. What was I saying? How could I live with myself if I let someone die for me?

He put his finger under my chin, forcing me to look at him, and my eyes grew wide in realisation. 'You're going to do that mind control thing on me, aren't you?'

He chuckled. 'You don't know very much about vampires, do you? Compulsion doesn't work on witches.' His brow furrowed then. 'How old are you?'

'That's kind of a rude question,' I muttered, my cheeks growing warm. I didn't want to tell him my age because in the immortal community, I was very young. What would he think when I told him?

'Answer the question, witchling.'

'It's Elspeth, not witchling,' I snapped.

'I won't take you to the priestess if you don't answer the question.'

'That's low.' He had me and he knew it. I sighed. 'Twenty-three.'

He was silent for a long moment, and I felt my cheeks growing hotter. I tried to look away, but he kept my head in place. I wanted to know what was going on in his head, what that look on his face meant but I was too afraid to ask. Finally, he released me. 'Shower's in there. I'll get you some clothes, and then we can go see Angèlie.'

Before I could argue, Roman disappeared. I gaped at the empty space where he'd been just seconds ago. What the hell had I gotten myself into now? And how much would he remember when he returned?

CHAPTER 6

Roman

My mind was hazy, something I hadn't experienced in my immortal life. When I was human, I'm sure I had times like that, times when I'd had too much to drink and lost the night before, but this was different. It was like seeing things through murky water; it was there but somehow out of reach.

I remembered that there was a female in my apartment, my bride, and that she didn't recognise me as hers. I also remembered that I needed to bring her clothes, but I didn't know why. Her face was impossible to picture. Did she have pink hair? What colour were her eyes? I knew I'd touched every inch of her body, I knew that I'd liked what I saw, but I couldn't remember what that was exactly.

When I returned to the apartment, she was wrapped in a towel, her pink hair was wet, dripping water over her shoulders. My eyes followed the droplets of water as they slid down her creamy skin. Memories of last night flashed through my mind, snippets, incomplete, but hot as hell. Her lips on mine, her nails digging into my flesh, the feel of her around my cock. It was impossibly frustrating not being able to remember.

She looked up at me with sad eyes, searching for something. My chest tightened. What must it be like for her to be cursed to be forgotten by everyone? She wanted to know why I hadn't forgotten her the way everyone else had, and I had no doubt it was because she was my bride. Somehow, that fateful tie was tethering us. If I marked her, would I retain my memories of her? If I tried anything of the kind, she'd run, and as a witch, she could hide herself from me indefinitely.

I couldn't risk it.

I held out the clothes to her, and she took them, hovering for a moment before disappearing back into the bathroom to dress. I could feel my memory of her slipping away when she closed the door, sinking back into the murky depths. I recited her name over and over in my mind, determined to keep hold of it this time.

When she re-emerged, her hair was pulled back and she brushed her hands over her shirt. 'So, how much do you remember?' she asked.

'Enough,' I answered, folding my arms across my chest to keep from reaching out for her. Every instinct was screaming for me to mark her, to claim her, but after the way she reacted to finding out I was a vampire, I was sure she wouldn't take being my bride well. Not yet, anyway. I took her hand and she tensed for a moment, but she relaxed slowly and she didn't pull away. Holding her hand wasn't nearly enough. I pulled her into my arms. Holding her close seemed to bring clarity with it. Was that the key to remembering? It was nice to have an excuse to touch her, but it might not be necessary if the priestess could actually break the curse.

'What are you doing?'

'Taking you to your priestess. It's easier if you're close,' I lied. 'Close your eyes and take a deep breath. This is sometimes unpleasant if you're not used to it.'

'Oh, okay,' she mumbled, her cheeks turning that adorable shade of pink. She fumbled with her hands, as if she didn't know where to put them, finally settling on my chest. Her intoxicating scent enveloped me, making my fangs ache. I'd much rather throw her back into bed than take her to a priestess.

She closed her eyes, and I traced us to the voodoo store. It was tucked away, hard to find if you weren't looking for it. The front of the store was a human friendly "wiccan" store, holding the usual crystals and dream catchers and all the harmless things that humans couldn't get into trouble with. The back of the store was where the real magic was. And luckily, it was UV proof. The windows were spelled to keep out UV and prying human eyes.

'What the hell?' Elspeth said, her eyes wide in surprise. 'You can teleport?'

'It's called tracing. All vampires can do it. Did you really not know that?' I asked. How could she be so naïve to their world? How old was she? Had she told me that already? This curse was doing my head in.

'I've been expecting you, Roman,' Angèlie said with her thick New Orleans accent as she stepped through the beaded curtain. Her smooth dark skin almost glowed, her emerald green dress flowed down to her ankles, revealing bare feet, and gold adorned her wrists, fingers, ankles and neck.

Elspeth wriggled in my arms and I grudgingly released her. She brushed her hands over her shirt and offered the priestess a smile. 'Are you Angèlie Laveau?'

'Oui mon cher,' she said, her eyes appraising Elspeth. 'You're carrying a heavy burden, child.' Angèlie reached out and stroked Elspeth's hair, sympathy in her eyes. 'I cannot do what you seek.'

Elspeth's shoulders trembled, but she held herself tall. 'Oh, I see.'

My chest tightened at the sight of her trying to be brave, even as I could see the hope draining from her. I'd seen Angèlie many times over the centuries, I knew what she was capable of, and I knew she would help Elspeth if she could, but frustration gnawed at me. There had to be something we could do. 'Are you saying there's nothing you can do for her?' I demanded. Was I supposed to sit back and do nothing while my bride suffered? Was I supposed to relive the torment of forgetting her over and over again? If she snuck away in the day, would I remember her at all or would those hazy memories fade until I only felt the loss of something I couldn't even remember?

'The power to break the curse lies right here,' Angèlie said, touching an elegant finger to Elspeth's chest.

'I hope you're about to tell me true love will break the curse, because my power is a little...wonky,' Elspeth said, a quiver in her voice.

Angèlie laughed then, a musical sound that was almost soothing. 'There is great power in you, child. You only need to awaken it.'

Elspeth didn't look surprised at this news, instead she frowned. 'I don't suppose you're going to tell me how to do that?' From her tone, she clearly expected the answer to be no.

This female filled me with such curiosity. The more time I spent with her the more questions I had, and it was infuriating that I had no way of knowing if she'd answered any of those questions before or not. My memories of her still shimmered beneath murky water, sometimes they would near the surface enough that I thought they might break through, but then they would retreat again.

'Can you tell a bird how to fly or a fish how to swim? It isn't something you can be instructed in. It will come naturally,' Angèlie said with a bright smile that was a stark contrast to the look of dismay on Elspeth's face.

'There has to be something she can do to help it along, Angèlie,' I interrupted, unable to help myself. She quirked an eyebrow at me then, and I realised she already knew too much.

'My, how protective he is.' She smiled knowingly, and I forced myself to stay silent in case I revealed something I shouldn't. 'Perhaps there is something *you* can do,' she said, a suggestive lilt to her voice.

I shot a look at Elspeth, but she seemed lost in her own thoughts, which was a relief. The last thing I needed was for her to find out she was my bride and take off. I'd find her again eventually, but I had no idea how long that would take, especially if I couldn't remember her. That was enough to send any vampire spiraling into madness.

'Wait,' Elspeth said suddenly, dragging Angèlie's attention back to her. 'You didn't forget when you looked away.'

Angèlie's lips curled into a conspiratorial smile. 'The magic is strong, mon cher, but not for one like me. And once you awaken your power, it won't be for one like you, either.' She picked up a bag from the counter, already filled with items, and handed it to Elspeth.

'What's this?'

'It should help you on your path,' Angèlie said with a warm smile.

'I don't have any money,' Elspeth said bashfully, holding the bag out for Angèlie to take.

'Do not worry, mon cher. I'll put it on your handsome protector's tab,' she said, winking at me. Cheeky witch. But I waved a hand nonchalantly. At least she hadn't let my secret out of the bag.

Elspeth hugged the bag to her chest. 'Thank you.'

I took her hand, and she moved in close. Angèlie raised an eyebrow but said nothing. How would Elspeth react when she found out I'd lied to her? I wrapped my arm around her waist, but instead of relaxing into me as she had before, she stiffened and her heart began to race, like a deer who sensed a predator's gaze.

'Elspeth?' I asked, concern in my voice.

She shook herself. 'No, it's nothing. Sorry,' she muttered.

She was keeping something from me, whatever she'd sensed had put her on edge. That was enough to let me drop the subject, at least until I got her someplace safe. 'Hold on, then,' I said and when she'd braced herself, I traced us back to the apartment.

It put my mind at ease to have her in my home, where she belonged. Here, at least, she would be safe from all things. Now if only she'd tell me what those things were.

Elspeth pulled away from me, and I could tell from the look in her eyes that a thousand thoughts were running through her mind. What I wouldn't give to know what was going on in the pretty head of hers.

'Thank you for your help, but I should get going,' she said.

'Why do I get the feeling you mean to leave the city?' I asked, my voice sounding much calmer than the turmoil raging inside me. How long would it take me to forget her when she left me behind? How long until the only thing I remembered was my loss?

'I've stayed here too long already. I only came here to find Angèlie, but she can't help me.'

'That doesn't mean you need to do this alone. Stay here. My home is warded with powerful magic, you'll be safe here.' It was one of the perks of the job provided to all enforcers to keep our homes and our families safe. This was the first time I'd ever had a real use for it.

'Why would you do that for me?' she asked, and the scepticism in her eyes spoke to something primal in me. I wanted to tear out the hearts of all those who'd dared to hurt her.

But I couldn't tell her any of that.

Instead, I shrugged. 'Dealing with malevolent magic is my job, remember?'

'I don't know.'

I couldn't let her go now. She was so close to caving, and once she agreed to stay, I'd be able to convince her to stay with me forever. I wasn't an idiot. I knew the prejudice most witches held against vampires, and who could blame them? Our history wasn't exactly pleasant. Then again, witches had always been complicated beings. If I could convince her to ignore that history and accept me, then she would be mine.

But first I needed to help her break this curse and deal with the dead warlock who'd cursed her.

'If it makes you feel better, you can think of yourself as bait. A curse like that requires significant power to cast. I can't let a warlock that dangerous roam about freely.'

'You'd hunt down a warlock just because he's powerful?'

'I'd say casting a curse like this classifies him as malevolent, so yes.'

She looked like she was going to argue but she conceded. 'Okay, good point. But it's too dangerous.'

'You'd be making my life easier, and you'd be safe, it's a win-win.'

'How do I know you're telling the truth? Maybe you have another reason for keeping me here,' she said, that suspicion in her eyes again.

Clever witchling. 'Oh, there is definitely another reason,' I said, running my fingers along her jaw. That delectable blush rose to her cheeks, making my fangs ache.

'W-well, have you got somewhere for me to sleep?' she asked, backing away from me.

'You'll sleep in the bed.'

'But where will you sleep?'

'In the bed.' Her eyes went wide, that blush deepening in her cheeks. 'You didn't have a problem with it last night.'

'Last night I didn't think I'd see you again. Or that you'd remember me,' she said. Her heart raced in her chest, her breaths becoming shallower. My cock began to stiffen in response. She was going to be the death of me.

'I promise to keep my hands to myself,' I said, raising my hands to show my innocence. Although keeping my hands to myself was going to be an almost impossible feat.

'Really?'

I shrugged. 'Mostly.' There was no way I could go the entire night with my bride lying next to me and *not* touch her. But I could keep it PG for a night or two, I supposed.

She chewed on her lip, her eyes darting from the bedroom to the couch as she deliberated. If she thought I was going to let her sleep on the couch, she had another thing coming.

I let out a sigh. 'Fine, I'll take the couch.'

'No, I can't kick you out of your bed.'

'Well, those are your only options, witchling. What will it be?'

She nibbled her bottom lip before finally muttering, 'Fine. We'll share the bed.' She sat on the couch and began rifling through the bag of tricks Angèlie had provided with a keen interest, that blush still burning her cheeks.

I smiled to myself as I watched her. Oh yes, I was definitely going to win her over.

CHAPTER 7

Elspeth

I let out a breath and eyed the bag Angèlie gave me. I'd looked through it before but I couldn't remember what was in it. I'd been too aware of Roman's gaze on me and all my mind could focus on were the images of the last time we'd shared a bed and all the things that could happen when we did again.

After insisting that I stay at his apartment, Roman told me he'd be back soon, and I'd better still be here when he returned. A devious little part of me wondered what would happen if I took off, but it hardly seemed like a fitting way to repay him. Besides, I wasn't sure it was wise to piss off a vampire.

I pulled out the contents of the bag; a couple of books, some candles, sage, chalk, crystals – it was practically a starter kit. Angèlie Laveau had given me a witch starter kit. I half expected one of the books to be titled *Witchcraft for Dummies*. To be fair, it had been a long time since I'd really practiced. What was the point in practicing something that wasn't going to get any better?

But I didn't have much choice now. If Angèlie was right, then the only person getting me out of this mess was going to be me and if I had a shot in hell of making that work, I was going to have to figure out how to be a witch.

'Sorry, Roman,' I muttered as I grabbed the chalk and dragged it along his expensive floorboards. I'd drawn circles thousands of times, simple ones, complex ones, committing the shapes to memory as if by doing so I would suddenly catch up to the other kids in the coven. The placement of each line and symbol within the circle had to be exact or it could change the entire spell. As far as magical theory went, I had been the best in my class, at least until I'd given up on the whole idea of ever catching up.

Next, I picked up the sage and lit the end until smoke began curling through the air. There was something soothing about the process, as if I was going back in time, before any of this had happened, back when things were easy and my biggest problem was my stunted magic. I wafted the smoke around, cleansing the room before placing it in the centre of the circle.

Magic is a gift, it's a companion. You can't hear the magic if your thoughts are clouded, my mother always said. I didn't know how right she was but I also didn't know where else to start. So, I crossed my legs and breathed in the sage scented air, closing my eyes as I tried to focus. The last few times I'd tried this, my fear had taken hold of me, but this time was different. This time I was distracted by something else.

This time I was distracted by Roman.

When I closed my eyes, his face came readily to mind, the sense of safety I felt with him, the feel of his lips on my skin. Everything my family had told me about vampires didn't quite mesh with Roman. He wasn't savage or cold, he didn't seem to have any problems keeping his fangs to himself, either. What would it feel like to have them puncture my neck? Would it hurt or would it bring pleasure? A warmth began to build in my core and I shook myself.

Focus.

'What are you thinking about that's made you blush so deliciously?'

My eyes snapped open and Roman was leaning against the wall, a smirk on his face that didn't match the smouldering intensity in his eyes. 'I'm not blushing,' I said, trying to ignore him. I closed my eyes again.

Focus. Clear mind.

'Were you thinking about me?' he asked, his words murmured against my ear, sending a shiver of anticipation through me.

I opened my eyes again, sending a glare in his direction as he stepped along the outer edge of the circle. 'And if I was?' I asked, wanting to get a rise out of him as he had tried to do with me.

He stopped then, looking back at me with desire dancing in his eyes. 'Don't tease me, witchling, or you'll find yourself chained to my bed.'

My breath hitched in my throat, and I looked away, my cheeks flushing again. I could hear his steady footsteps as he made his way towards me, but I didn't dare look back at him until he took my hand and pulled me to my feet. 'What are you doing?' I gasped.

He pulled me against him, his arm snaking around my waist. He brushed my hair over my shoulder, exposing my neck to him and leaned in, sending a shiver racing through me as his breath caressed my bared skin. He leaned in slowly and my heart began to quicken. Was he going to bite me? Why didn't that scare me more? His lips touched my skin, sending a burst of heat and pleasure blossoming from the kiss. He trailed slowly down, over my pulse, his tongue darting over the vein as if he longed to taste it and I clenched my thighs against the throbbing need that he ignited there.

'Gods, I can scent your arousal,' he groaned.

Just then, his phone began to ring, buzzing from his pocket, snapping me out of my stupor. I took a step back and Roman growled in frustration, yanking his phone from his pocket. 'What?' he snapped.

I turned from him, taking a moment to compose myself. It had been a long time since I'd had any kind of relationship, was this how they began? Did he want something more with me or was it only physical?

I needed to focus. None of it would matter if I couldn't awaken my power before Chase found me, and he would find me. I'd stayed too long already. It would be better for everyone if I just disappeared into the night – or day, as it were – and let Roman forget me.

So why did the idea sting so badly?

Roman clicked his tongue. 'I'll figure something out.' He hung up the call, cursing under his breath.

'Is something wrong?'

'I have to go out again. Work,' he said. But instead of leaving, he took a lock of my hair between his fingers, letting it slide over them like silk.

'Are you hunting witches?' I asked, trying to ignore the intimate gesture and keep my breathing steady.

'It's not all about witches,' he said absently, his fingers brushing along my shoulder.

'Then what?'

He searched my face, tilting her head slightly as if it would help him answer whatever question was in his mind. 'You don't know a lot about our world, do you?'

I shrugged. 'There aren't a lot of other beings where I come from and the coven...well, they didn't tell us much.'

'So, you do have a coven then?' It was hard to tell with his schooled expressions, but it sounded like he was disappointed by that. Or maybe that was my wishful thinking.

I shook my head sadly. 'I never got the chance to officially join. Besides, even if I had, they all forgot me.'

'Are you going to give me the details of that curse of yours?'

'Maybe, if you start answering my questions.' He was too good at spinning things around and making me answer his questions while giving me nothing in return. Or maybe I was too easy to get information from, too desperate to tell someone my story. But whatever I told him, I couldn't be sure he'd remember.

'I work for the vampire council to enforce the laws and hunt down criminals, malevolent magics, that sort of thing. It's not always witches.'

There was a vampire council? 'Is the council in charge of all vampires, or just the ones in Chicago?'

He paused for a moment, as if deciding how much he should tell me. 'All vampires are ruled by the king. The council is a sort of government, I suppose. They work under the king, helping him to keep on top of running a global empire, as it were. But Enforcers have branches all over the world.'

It was entirely different to how witches ran themselves. Each coven was responsible for their own members, for staying hidden. Every now and then, a few of the covens would unite against a threat; usually one that would expose us to the humans or potentially end the world, but there was no king or queen or council to govern all witches.

'What are you hunting now?'

'Curious little witchling, aren't you?' he said, but he didn't sound irritated, more...amused. I wished I could get inside his head, to know what he was thinking. It was so frustrating how little he gave away, and how badly I wanted to know.

But I wasn't about to let myself go there. That was a slippery slope I could not afford to slide down.

'I'm looking for a weasel to ask him some questions,' Roman said. I could tell there was a lot he wasn't telling me. Was it like being a human cop? Was he supposed to keep everything classified? Maybe he just didn't trust me. I couldn't blame him for that. I hadn't trusted him with my truth, either.

'A weasel?'

'A shapeshifter. There are those, like werewolves, who can shift only into one creature, and shapeshifters who can change into any number of creatures. This particular shifter isn't very fond of vampires, and he'll be hiding in his home now that it's dark.'

'Why do I get the feeling that's a bad thing?'

He chuckled then. 'Your coven really should have taught you more. They left you completely vulnerable. Vampires can't enter someone's home without an invitation. Well, except for other vampires.'

'Is that why you didn't want me to go back to my motel room?' I asked, teasing. But his silence wiped the smile from my face. I swallowed hard. Had I put myself in greater danger than I'd realised?

'I would never hurt you, Elspeth,' he said, placing his hands on my arms. 'But it's true, I didn't want you somewhere I couldn't reach you.'

'Why?'

His phone buzzed again, and he released me. 'We'll talk about it later, I really have to go.'

'Maybe I can help!' I said quickly as he stepped away from me, preparing to trace.

'How are you going to do that?' Roman asked.

I scowled at him. 'I'm not totally useless, you know. You can't enter his house without an invitation, right? But I can. And he won't even remember I was there.'

'It's too dangerous,' he said.

'Too dangerous with a big bad vampire there to protect me?'

He paused for a moment, but I could see him coming around to the idea. 'Fine,' he said, tugging me into his arms. 'But when we get back, I'm going to fuck the sass out of you.' He claimed my lips in a searing kiss that took my breath away and set my heart racing.

I was in way over my head.

***

Roman traced us to a dark street lit only by the dim light of the streetlamps that seemed to struggle against the thick shadows. I was getting far too used to being in Roman's arms. As I distanced myself from him, his hand wrapped around mine.

'This is a bad idea,' he said. 'I should take you back.'

'This isn't my first B and E, you know,' I said, placing my other hand atop his, trying to pry him off, but he acted as if he hadn't even noticed.

'What if I forget you're in there and leave without you?'

A valid question that I did not have a good answer for. 'Maybe that would be for the best,' I said, the words escaping before I could stop them. But they were true. If he forgot me, then he would be safe from Chase. He wouldn't even miss me.

But I would miss him. I never realised how selfish I was before.

'What is that supposed to mean?' he demanded, gripping me tighter. 'Are you so eager to be rid of me?'

The hurt in his voice surprised me, and it stung my heart like a thousand tiny cuts. Why did I feel *so* connected to him? Witches didn't have mates as Lycans or vampires did, we were free to love whoever we chose. Could I be his? No. No, it was too ridiculous. I wasn't a vampire, hell, I wasn't even immortal yet. Besides, if I was his mate, he would have claimed me by now. That was something the coven *had* taught me. A vampire was compelled to claim his mate, and nothing could stand in his way.

All the more reason to let him go. It would only hurt more if I got attached, and then his mate came along.

'No, I'm not. But it would be safer for you,' I said. Before he could ask more questions, I shook him off. 'I'll go round the back, just keep him busy.' I walked away from him, not daring to look over my shoulder in case he changed his mind and asked more questions I wasn't ready to answer.

The shifter lived in a dodgy looking building with holes in the walls, rotting wood, and weeds as tall as my chest. The idea of walking through that probably snake-infested junk yard made me hesitate, but I had a job to do. For the first time in a long time, I could be useful instead of drifting through life like a ghost, making no difference to anyone. I took a deep breath and waded into the weeds, hoping that the things brushing against my legs were plants, and not of the poisonous variety.

The patio was so rotted I wasn't sure how I was going to sneak anywhere. I had a better chance of getting tetanus. There was a loud banging on the door and footsteps came from inside, stomping across the floor. I used the noise to cover my own steps as I crept along the patio towards a conveniently open window.

The shifter opened the door, and I could see Roman on the other side of it. 'Fenton, you've been dodging our calls,' Roman said, a menacingly cold edge to his voice.

'You can't come in here, Roman,' the shifter squeaked. 'And you can't compel me.'

'Oh? Friends in magical places, hey, Fenton? And did we go to the dark or the light for that little trick?' Roman sneered and the shifter began to sputter, but no actual words came out.

I was going to have to be quick. Fenton clearly didn't want to talk to Roman, and I wasn't keen on getting caught in his house. I slipped through the window and wrinkled my nose against the musty smell that assaulted me. The inside of the house was as grotesque as the outside. How could anyone live like that?

'Relax, Fenton. I'm just here to talk.'

I crept up the stairs, their voices becoming muffled by the distance. I opened one door after another, cringing as hinges creaked and floorboards groaned, but all I turned up was mould, broken furniture and squalor. How much longer could Roman distract Fenton? How much longer would he remember I was here, helping him?

In the last room on the top floor was a desk. Finally, I was getting somewhere. I sifted through old papers and sun-faded catalogues. Nothing. I pulled open the top drawer. Bills, random bits of junk. There was a card with an address scrawled across it, which I pocketed. It might be useful, and it might be a load of junk. I was hoping for the former.

As I shifted another chocolate wrapper aside, something caught my eye. A crystal? Larmia crystals were often used for communication spells. I picked it up, energy tingled in my hand. It had been used recently.

'Why are you bothering me?' a familiar voice snapped, and I dropped the crystal.

Chase.

Fenton was working with Chase? To what end? Whatever it was, it wasn't good. I should have known better than to stay. Chase was coming for me. How long did I have? Days? Hours? And how was I possibly going to say goodbye to Roman?

'Fenton, you little weasel!' Roman snapped.

I shook myself. That was my queue to get the hell out. I fled the way I came, bailing out the window before anyone could see me. As I made my way around the yard and back towards the street, the hair on the back of my neck stood on end, and I froze. I turned to search the darkness. There was nothing there, and yet I could feel someone watching me.

'Elspeth, what's wrong?' Roman asked, suddenly appearing at my side.

'No, it's nothing.' I looked up at him, a warm feeling nestling in my chest. 'You didn't forget.'

'Not everything, but enough,' he said, pulling me in close. 'What did you sense just now?'

'It's nothing.'

'How long are you going to keep lying to me?' Roman snapped.

'Why do you want to know so badly?' I countered, my temper flaring. I had my secrets, but there were things he wasn't telling me either.

With a growl of frustration, he pulled me tightly against him and traced us.

CHAPTER 8

Roman

I traced us back to the apartment, frustration grinding my teeth. How could one witchling drive me so crazy? I should be focusing on the malevolent magic coming our way, but instead my thoughts were consumed with her. What was she thinking? What was coming for her? Why wouldn't she let me in?

'What did you sense?' I asked again.

'Wouldn't you rather know what I found?' she countered, struggling against my grip. As if a witchling was any match for a vampire's strength.

I could feel her pulling away from me, closing off to me. It was bad enough that I couldn't claim my mate, that I was forced to forget precious memories of her each time I left her side, but the thought of losing her awakened something primal in me that would not be sated with logic and reason. Would she disappear, letting my memories of her dissipate until I couldn't remember her at all?

'Why won't you let me in, Elspeth?'

'I've only known you a couple of days. Don't you think you're asking a lot?'

Damn witches. It would be so much easier if she only recognised me as hers. But she did feel something for me, I could feel it. How could I keep her from running from it? I tightened my hold on her, leaning down. Her heart raced, her breath shallowing. She reacted so well to my touch, and it chipped away at my control.

'Here,' she said, handing me a business card for some pizza shop, clearly scrap paper because the address scribbled on the back was nowhere near that place. I tossed it aside, not willing to let her distract me from this.

'Do you know what I did forget?' I asked and dropped my lips to her neck. She moaned softly, her body melting into me, her hand gripping my shoulder.

'What?' she breathed, her voice filled with lust and my cock began to stiffen in response. I'd gone one night without touching her, but there was no way I could go another. Every instinct was screaming at me to take her, to claim her. I knew I couldn't claim her yet, but how could I resist her when she responded like this?

'I've forgotten what you taste like,' I murmured against her lips before taking them in a searing kiss. The warmth of her body against my cold skin was heavenly, feeding my need, making it unbearable. I needed her more than I had ever needed anything. If only I could make her understand without scaring her away. 'I've forgotten what it feels like to be inside you.'

She looked up at me, desire burning in her eyes, cheeks flushed. 'I haven't.'

'Don't tell me you want me to keep my hands to myself tonight, witchling,' I said, the words almost a plea.

She swallowed hard. 'I have...a condition,' she said between panting breaths as my hands began to roam her curves, sliding beneath the fabric of her shirt.

'Which is?' I asked before dropping a kiss to her neck. She stiffened as if she was expecting something else, and I realised what her condition would be.

'Don't bite me,' she said.

Which meant I couldn't claim her. Not that I should without telling her what she was to me. 'I won't do anything you're not ready for,' I promised as my hand reached her plump breast. But there would come a day when she would want it. She had no idea the pleasure she was denying herself.

She relaxed at my words and tugged my shirt from my pants. She began unclasping the buttons, her fingers making quick work of them as if she couldn't wait to see what lay beneath. When my shirt fell open, I shrugged out of it as her hands reached for me, tracing along muscles that rippled under her touch. She moved them slowly down again, her teeth sinking into her bottom lip as if she was doing something she shouldn't but had no intention of stopping. She unzipped my pants and slipped her hand inside, curling her fingers around my hard cock. I groaned as she slid her fist slowly up and down the shaft. Her cheeks were growing flushed with lust, blood rushing to the surface of her skin, making my fangs ache for what they couldn't have.

She ran her thumb over the tip of my erection, moving it along the slit until a pearl of moisture beaded there. Her tongue darted across her lips, her eyes focused on my cock. 'I want to taste you,' she breathed.

I nearly came in her hand. 'Gods, yes,' I said, keeping my hands still, afraid I'd wake her from her trance, and she'd change her mind.

She lowered herself to her knees and pushed my pants down slowly, as if she was enjoying the reveal. Her breath hitched as she gazed at my erection, a hunger dancing in her beautiful eyes. I balled my hands into fists to keep from gripping her head and shoving my cock between those plump lips, the effort causing a sheen of perspiration to form on my forehead.

She darted her tongue along the slit, a teasing little touch that sent a shudder through my entire body. Gods, this woman was going to be the death of me. She repeated the action, causing another shudder and when I looked down at her I realised she was watching me closely.

'Are you going to tease me all night?'

'Maybe,' she purred. I opened my mouth to retort, but she slid her lips around my cock, and the breath rushed out of me in a hiss. She slid down my shaft with her hot little mouth, her hand following. I pulsed in her mouth, my nails dug into my palms with the effort not to grab hold of her hair and thrust into her. She moved slowly back towards the head and gave it a little suck when she reached it, sending a rush of pleasure through me.

'That's it, baby,' I murmured, my eyes falling closed as she slid down me again, her hand pumping my shaft as her mouth enveloped me, her tongue licking up the beads of semen that she elicited from me. She moaned, the vibrations sending sparks of pure ecstasy through my body, decimating the last of my self-control. My hand within her hair with lightning speed, my hips rocking against her mouth, her hand around my shaft the only thing keeping me where she wanted me.

'Ah, fuck. I'm going to -'

She silenced me with a suck that hollowed her cheeks, sending me over the edge. I spilled into her mouth as she swallowed me greedily until I was spent, but in no way satiated. It seemed that where this witchling was concerned, I was insatiable. When she released me with an audible pop, I lifted her to her feet, capturing her lips in a fierce kiss. She gasped, and I slid my tongue into her mouth, caressing hers until she moaned against me. I could feel her tight nipples through her shirt, as if they were taunting me. I needed them in my mouth. I needed to feel them on my skin. I pulled her shirt over her head and undid her bra in one swift movement, tossing it across the room. Before she could say anything, I had one of those rosy buds in my mouth, and I sucked until she cried out with pleasure. I unzipped her pants as her fingers curled in my hair, her knees going weak as I tongued her nipple, and the urge to sink my fangs into her plump breasts was almost impossible to ignore.

She shimmied out of her pants, that sensual movement of her hips shooting my cock rock hard again. She kicked them away as they pooled around her feet, and the scent of her arousal filled my senses, sending all rational thought fleeing from my mind. I needed to be between those thighs. A growl rumbled in my chest as I tore the skimpy lace from her hips and flung it across the floor, enjoying the way her breaths shallowed and her heart raced in response to me. She was watching me, waiting for me to make my move. So many things I wanted to do to her, I hardly knew where to start, but I knew that I couldn't wait any longer.

I lifted her, and her legs wrapped around me. The head of my erection teasing at her entrance had her hips subtly rocking against me. I pressed her back against the wall, leaning into her, the feel of her skin on mine set my body on fire.

'Ah, Roman!' she moaned, and I was lost. With a single thrust, I was inside her. She cried out, arching her back, her nails digging into my shoulders as if to hold me in pace. Those cheeks were flushed with lust, her eyes shimmered as her teeth sank into her lip. I bucked my hips, building my rhythm until her voice filled the apartment, until her eyes fluttered closed, her nails digging harder into me. My fangs ached, and it took every ounce of strength I had not to sink them into her neck.

She screamed with her orgasm, her body shuddering against the waves of pleasure as her lithe little body gripped my shaft, milking another orgasm from me with a roar of satisfaction. Her head dropped to my shoulder, her nipples grazed my skin with her every breath. We stayed like that until I began to stiffen inside her once more. Though I wanted to take her all night, her mortal body was exhausted.

I pulled myself from her, and she whimpered as if mourning the loss of me. My male satisfaction shot right up, and the corners of my lips curled despite myself. I lowered her to the floor, holding her up until her legs grudgingly took her weight.

'The first shower is yours,' I forced myself to say. When she didn't move, I couldn't keep the smile from my lips. 'If you don't go now, then I'll be joining you.'

She hesitated for a moment, desire burning in those beautiful grey eyes. She opened her mouth but then seemed to think better of it. 'Thank you,' she said instead, her cheeks flushing again as she traipsed towards the bathroom, still blessedly naked.

Oh yes, this female was going to be the death of me.

***

My phone buzzed on the bedside table, and I swiped it up to keep from waking Elspeth. The name flashing on the screen made me groan. I had hoped to shut the damn thing off, but this call couldn't be ignored. 'Marcus, I mean this with the utmost respect, but this had better be good,' I said irritably.

'Funny, that doesn't sound very respectful,' Marcus said, a hint of a warning in his voice. If I was anyone else, I'd be in for some serious consequences. 'You're needed. I'll text you the location.'

I let out a sigh. 'Yeah, okay.' I hung up the phone and looked over at the gloriously naked creature sleeping next to me, wrapped in my silk sheets. The idea of leaving her left a bad taste in my mouth, especially knowing that it would mean forgetting. How much would I forget this time?

A message came through, letting me know it was time to go. I pulled on my clothes and opened it. I froze when I saw the address there, the same as the one on the card Elspeth had given me. The one I'd ignored. Whatever was going on, I was clearly going to have to pay Fenton another visit. With a final look at my bride, I traced.

The moon was high when I arrived at the scene. The docks. Not exactly an original place for a murder, but the smell of death hung in the air. Murders in the paranormal community happened from time to time, but one so close to an enforcer base was ballsy. And this place was crawling with Enforcers; not a good sign.

'Good, you're here,' Marcus said, nodding for me to join him.

'So, what's the emergency?' I asked when I reached his side. As he led me down the docks, the smell of blood grew stronger with every step.

'You were with a female.' It wasn't a question. And of course, he would have forgotten all about my meeting Elspeth at *Myth*. Was this what it was like for her? Having to have the same conversations over and over because people simply couldn't remember?

'Yeah, I do that from time to time,' I said, wondering where this was going.

'Sure, but you're never reluctant to leave their bed when I call. Is it her?'

The *her* he was referring to wasn't anything to do with memory. He meant was she my bride. 'You catch on quick.' Of course he did. I didn't think it would be so fast, but I knew I wasn't going to be able to keep it a secret for long.

'But your heart isn't beating. You haven't claimed her?'

In order to claim Elspeth, I would need to bite her, and she'd already told me that wasn't something she was interested in. Hell, she didn't even know she was my bride, and I wasn't sure how she'd react to that news. Probably not well. A witch and a vampire was an unusual pairing. I supposed I was lucky she wasn't in control of her magic, or I might have lost her before I'd even had a chance to win her.

'No. She's a witch,' I said. It was all the explanation I was willing to offer him right now, and I knew it would be enough to sate his curiosity. For now.

Marcus stopped. 'We're hunting a malevolent witch, and you didn't tell me you had one in your bed?'

'She's not the one we're looking for, her power hasn't been awakened yet.' As I answered the question, I was surprised to realise I was beginning to remember more of her, as if prolonged exposure made it harder for the curse to affect me. But I still didn't know how long I had before those memories began to fade, and I was eager to get back to her.

'Not awakened? How old is she?'

'Young.'

'I see why you haven't claimed her then. But you shouldn't delay too long,' he said. And he was right. The longer a vampire waited to claim his bride, the more savage the bite tended to be, as if some primal beast had been caged too long and now was uncontrollable. But that would take months or a weak mind, and I was not weak. She was not yet immortal. I couldn't afford any mistakes.

As we neared a warehouse, Marcus put his game face back on. The stench that assaulted my nose was almost unbearable. Decomposing flesh, congealing blood, and dark magic. 'It's one of ours,' Marcus said as he led me inside.

It was like something from a human horror movie. A corpse was positioned on a post towards the back of the room, hung like a warning, the head dropped carelessly on the floor. But the scene had been staged to keep the body away from sunlight, in case it took us a while to find it. Even a dead vampire would burn up in the sun, and all evidence would be gone.

Our killer wanted us to find the body.

A ring of salt surrounded the post, wide enough for someone to comfortably move around inside the circle. Char marks darkened the floor. It was a common enough spell, setting fire to the salt, but ultimately useless here. It wasn't used to burn the vampire – another way to kill one of us – it was all for show. Whoever our killer was, he was one for theatrics.

On the wall behind the body was writing in blood that made me freeze. *Elspeth is mine,* it read, and I could feel the malice in those words. Was this killer the one who had cursed her?

Was that what she had sensed?

The idea that some sick fuck thought to lay claim to my bride sent a possessive rage roaring through me, instincts screaming to protect what was mine, protect my bride. I imagined what it would be like to sink my fangs into his jugular and drain him, for the last words he would ever hear to be the growl of my voice saying *Elspeth is mine!*

'That mean something to you?' Marcus asked, his gaze fixed squarely on me. I'd given myself away, unprepared for the raw and vicious reaction that had hit me like a train. To lie to Marcus now when one of our own had been butchered wouldn't help anyone, least of all Elspeth. The best thing for her sake was to tell him what he needed to know so that I could return to her.

'Yes. Elspeth is my bride.'

It was clear to me now that Elspeth knew a hell of a lot more than she was letting on. I knew she had secrets, but something this dark, this powerful, I had never imagined. The idea that she thought she had to face that alone made my heart ache for her. How could I convince her that she didn't have to be alone anymore?

'Then you'd better get her to talk or I will,' Marcus said. There was no room for argument in his voice.

And he was right. We needed the information she had. But I'd be damned if I let Marcus or anyone else extract it from her. That would involve far more pain. In any other circumstance, Marcus wouldn't have given me this chance, but because she was my bride, he was ignoring protocol. I couldn't waste this opportunity.

'There's something else,' I said. 'Fenton had this address.' I handed over the business card Elspeth had found.

Marcus frowned at it. 'It looks like I'm going to be paying that weasel a visit then, doesn't it?' He pocketed the card and looked at me, a hard gleam in his eyes. He was speaking to me as my commanding officer now, not my friend. 'Get the answers from your witch, Roman. I'm giving you twenty-four hours, and then we're bringing her in.'

I nodded at Marcus. I wouldn't let it come to that. One way or another, I would get her to talk to me, because there was no way I could let the Enforcers take her. If she refused to talk to them, I dreaded what they would do. I knew the dread was warranted, having done it countless times myself.

I schooled my expression, bracing myself for the task to come, and traced back to the apartment.

It was time to find out what the fuck was going on.

CHAPTER 9

Elspeth

When I woke, the moon was beginning to rise. Without realising it, I was adjusting myself to vampire time, sleeping during the day when Roman slept, waking during the night when he did. I smiled to myself before rolling over, but that smile faded when I realised the bed beside me was empty. I felt a twinge of disappointment mingled with something stronger; warm and hopeful. Was I developing feelings for Roman? Shit. I knew I shouldn't have stuck around, but damn him, he got under my skin. I wasn't sure I'd be able to let him go now, even if I tried.

All the more reason to unlock my power and rid myself of this curse and Chase Bloody Danvers. Breaking his curse was never going to be enough. It would only make him pursue me that much harder and his rage would probably lead to my death. It was foolish to think otherwise. Chase was unstable. The dark magic he'd obtained was eroding his humanity, and I wasn't sure how much longer I had before there was nothing left of him but the magic he'd given his soul to. There was a time when that would have scared me into running three continents away. But now Roman's life was at stake, too.

For the first time in my life, I had someone to protect.

I threw the sheets off and pulled on a night dress Roman had bought me; it was cream silk and more revealing than I would have liked, but I wanted to do this quickly, before he returned. Partly because I was excited and partly because I wanted to hide the evidence if I failed.

I drew a small circle on the freshly cleaned floorboards – *Sorry, Roman!* – and rummaged through the bag Angèlie had given me. Inside I found everything I needed. It seemed Angèlie knew more than she had let on. I knew she was powerful, but I hadn't realised she was a seer. Most witches had the ability to some extent but a true seer was rare, and it was not a magic that most would wish for.

There was an old necklace inside the bag with an unassuming bronze pendant that could be easily hidden beneath a shirt. It wasn't the most modern piece of jewellery, but it wasn't meant to be seen, what was more important was what it would do if the spell worked. I placed the necklace in the centre of the circle and poured salt around the circumference, then placed a stem of forget-me-nots over the pendant. I sprinkled a small pouch of dirt at the southern edge, placed an empty jar at the west, a candle at the east, and a small bowl of water at the north. Then I lit the sage stick to purify the negative energies. Nerves fluttered in my stomach as I knelt on the cool floorboards. I placed the sage to the side and lit the candle, then took a deep breath and closed my eyes.

'By earth and water, by fire and air, by the arc of the moon and the sun, may this amulet hold his memory clear, and so that my will be done.'

I peeked one eye open. Nothing happened. I closed my eyes again and repeated the chant. And again. Frustration began to edge in, and I forced myself to push it away with deep breaths and determination. I wanted Roman to remember me, to remember the time we spent together. I didn't want to be the sole keeper of those memories anymore.

'By earth and water, by fire and air, by the arc of the moon and the sun, may this amulet hold his memory clear, and so that my will be done,' I said, louder, my voice more forceful.

A breeze brushed against my face, and I opened my eyes, excitement welling in my stomach once more. A blue flame burst to life, dancing around the amulet and consuming the flower as if it were an offering. When the flame slowly died, the amulet remained, perfectly unharmed, but I sensed magic in it now. A grin spread across my face. It actually *worked*! I did a spell, and it worked! I snatched up the necklace and clutched it to my chest.

'We need to talk,' Roman said, his voice firm, and I spun around in surprise.

I swallowed at the serious look on his face. I'd seen enough movies to know nothing good ever came after those words.

'Don't look at me like that,' he said, his eyes softening for a moment as he took a step forward but seemed to stop himself. 'I need to ask you some questions, and I need the truth from you.'

'What's going on?' I asked, a quiver in my voice.

'There was an attack by a warlock tonight. Your name was written in blood.'

'An attack?' My face paled as fear crept in. 'I stayed too long. I have to go,' I mumbled as my heart began to race, my breaths becoming shallow. I'd been so careful for so long. Chase hadn't gotten this close in a year and a half, I'd learnt my lesson over and over and yet I'd ignored the signs.

'Don't run from this, Elspeth, just tell me what happened to you. I can protect you,' Roman said, gently. I wanted to believe him, but he had no idea what Chase was capable of. No idea what he was getting himself into.

'No one can protect me from him.'

He crossed the room then and gripped my arms tightly. 'You're not going anywhere, Elspeth. Understand me when I say I will not let you go.'

I blinked up at him then, my heart racing for an entirely different reason. I knew I shouldn't let his words affect me, that one day he would find his bride and this would come to an end. He didn't realise how cruel he was being, how he was etching himself into my heart. But even if I might lose him to another one day, I wanted to pretend, just for a little while, that he was mine. Was that so wrong?

Besides, if Chase had attacked someone, didn't I owe it to his victim to tell Roman what I knew? Or was I just making excuses now?

'Elspeth, please. Tell me.'

I let out a long breath. 'His name is Chase Danvers, he's a member of my coven - or it would have been my coven.'

'He an ex-boyfriend of yours?' Roman asked, his voice low. Was he jealous? The idea that he might be jealous sent a thrill through me, even if it was totally unfounded.

'No. He approached me on the night of my initiation. My parents had been told that my magic potential was great, that I could be the most powerful witch our coven had seen in centuries. But I never could master even the simplest spells, that's why my hair looks like melted ice-cream.'

He ran a pink lock through his fingers then, all the way down to the blonde tip. 'I think it's beautiful,' he murmured.

'You're being awfully distracting for someone who wanted answers.'

'So, he approached you?' he said, though he made no visible effort to be less distracting. His proximity sent a tingle through me, and his scent made me remember the feel of his lips on mine. I did my best to stamp down the lust that had started to burn in me again.

'Yes. My family is wealthy, has a long and proud history, and I was supposed to be this insanely powerful witch, so he set his sights on me, I guess. There was something about him, though, a darkness that scared me. Not that I'd ever had any interest in him. His own interest had been very recent. I rejected him, and he cursed me.'

'But he didn't just let you go, did he?'

I shook my head. 'He's hunted me down for the last two years. I can't stay in any place too long, or he finds me. He got close a couple of times, and he's finding me faster each time. He's getting stronger, I can feel it anytime he's near. My coven doesn't use dark magic, but Chase does.'

Surely, the coven knew what he was now. It would be hard to hide that kind of darkness from so many seasoned witches. Was he still a member? Had he done something to them? I had no way of knowing because if I went back, he'd find me that much faster. He had likely even set up traps for me there.

All I could do was pray to the Goddess that they were safe.

'You've spent all this time alone?' The sadness in his voice was unmistakable, bordering on pity, so I shrugged.

'What other choice did I have? No one remembered me. As soon as they looked away, it was like I didn't exist. Until you. I don't know why, but...you're different.'

He ran his fingers along my jaw, his touch sending a shiver through me. Never before had a male affected me the way this vampire did. 'But it still affects me. I wish I could remember everything.'

'That's why I...I made you something,' I said, feeling suddenly bashful about presenting the amulet to him. I held it out to him in the palm of my hand.

'I didn't realise we were exchanging jewellery already,' he said, a smirk on his face.

'Well, it was going to help you keep your memories of me, but if you don't want it,' I said, closing my fingers around it.

He clapped a hand around my wrist. 'I didn't say that.' He gently pried my fingers open and plucked the pendant from my hand. 'Does this mean you awakened your magic?'

'It means I succeeded in a single spell,' I said, my frustration showing in my voice. I shook my head, trying to rid myself of the negative thoughts haunting my victory. 'It means you won't have to forget anymore. If it's strong enough to fight the curse, anyway.'

His lips stretched into a crooked smile.

'What?'

'This means you want me to remember you,' he said, and he leaned in, capturing my lips in a searing kiss. Cocky vampire. He put the pendant around his neck and was silent for a moment, but his face gave nothing away.

Finally, curiosity got the better of me. 'So?'

'I remember everything,' he said, surprise in his voice. 'You have a birthmark on the inside of your thigh.'

I blushed furiously and smacked him on the arm. 'I've changed my mind. Give it back.'

He clasped the pendant as I reached for it. 'Too late, witchling. I'm going to remember everything about you from this moment on.' He kissed me again, this time tenderly, full of feelings I hoped I wasn't imagining.

'Okay, I have to report in before the calvary storms in. I won't be long,' he said. He squeezed my hand before stepping into his study. I put a hand to my burning cheek and smiled to myself.

CHAPTER 10

Roman

After relaying Elspeth's story to Marcus, there was silence on the other end of the line. Finally, a gust of breath. 'Well shit, that puts a whole new twist on stalker ex-boyfriends,' he said grimly.

'He's not her ex,' I corrected, unable to stop myself. That piece of shit had no claim to my bride whatsoever, and the very thought left a sour taste in my mouth.

Marcus chuckled. Fucker set me up for that. 'But you know, we could use this to our advantage.' His words were slow, careful, an order in the guise of a suggestion.

'Don't make me do that.' The idea of putting Elspeth in harm's way sent a tension through my body. It went against every instinct in my nature. I was supposed to protect her, I promised her I would. She'd finally started to open up to me, I didn't want to jeopardise that now. 'There has to be another way.'

'There's always another way,' Marcus said. 'The question is, how many more need to die along the way?'

Chase Danvers was clearly powerful and he didn't seem to have a lot going on in the morals department. I doubted ethics would ever stay his hand. The way he'd staged the scene, the confident way he'd written Elspeth's name, he enjoyed his work, was proud of it. He would kill again, without mercy, without remorse, if he felt his message was not being heard. He'd issued a threat, now he wanted to see how I responded to it. I had become the focus now, secondary to

Elspeth. I was a clear rival that he needed to defeat in order to prove himself the more powerful male.

But for me to be known to him, he had to be watching her. Which meant that night at the shop when she'd stiffened in my arms, that night at Fenton's, she'd sensed him watching her. The fact that he'd been so close, and yet I hadn't picked up on him, was concerning. If he could mask his presence, then we were at a decided disadvantage.

And Marcus was right, though there were other options, the easiest, by far, was sitting in my living room, dressed in cream silk. She'd placed her trust in me, in my word that I would protect her. The pendant she'd gifted me burned against my chest as if sensing my guilt.

'Look, I know this doesn't sit well –' Marcus said, his voice sympathetic.

My hand balled into a fist, the other gripping the phone too tightly. 'You don't fucking know. You can't until you find your bride. Then you'll realise what you're asking of me.'

'This is the best way to keep her safe, too. The sooner we get this animal off the street, the sooner she will be free of him.'

Low blow. *If* we succeeded, it would mean Elspeth would finally be safe. But what if we didn't? There was a chance Chase would overpower us and take her from me. There was a chance she'd hate me for this.

'How many times have I let you down?'

I exhaled a pent-up breath. 'Never.'

'Then trust me now,' Marcus said. 'I'll make a blood vow, if that would ease your mind. I won't let any harm come to her tonight.'

A blood vow was unbreakable. If harm befell Elspeth, Marcus would die. And if he phrased his vow carelessly, she could get a papercut and he would die. It was too risky, but he would do it if I asked it of him. He knew I never would, and he knew he'd win the argument with that promise. Not that I'd had any hope of winning it unless I wanted to desert. That wouldn't exactly help Elspeth, either.

'You shouldn't make promises you can't keep, Marcus,'

'We'll keep her safe. But you can't tell her, we need her reactions to be real. We have to believe that he knows her too well. If he senses anything, it could blow the whole plan.'

I hated the idea of lying to her, but Marcus was right. If Chase suspected she was acting, he'd know it was a trap. He wouldn't get close enough, and it would make it that much harder to catch him. Who knew how he would retaliate?

'What's the plan?'

***

Elspeth smiled at me as I walked through the door, her cheeks tinged pink. It was like a knife twisting in my gut as I wrestled with my guilt. But I had to put on a show now. I told myself this would be the last time I lied to her, and I hoped it was true. It would start with telling her the truth, telling her she was my bride. I'd do it as soon as this night was done.

'Is everything alright?' she asked.

Observant witchling. I was going to have to be more careful. I pulled her into my arms and dropped a kiss to her lips. Her body melted against mine, another sign of the trust I was about to betray. 'I think we should take a night off.'

She raised an eyebrow at me as she waited for me to elaborate, but I left her hanging for a moment longer than necessary, a sadistic part of me getting a thrill out of the look on her face as she jumped to the wrong conclusion. As if I would ever let her go.

'Let's have a night where we can just be normal. I'm guessing you haven't seen much of the city since you arrived.'

She smacked my arm. 'You did that on purpose.'

'Yes,' I said without a hint of remorse, and she smacked me again for good measure. 'So, what do you say?'

'Are you sure it's a good idea?' she asked and chewed her bottom lip uncertainly. I hated that Chase had that effect on her, that he could take her bright, playful nature and smother it so easily.

All the more reason to kill him.

'He won't be expecting you to leave tonight, he's probably gone to ground. Every enforcer in the city is looking for him.' I could see her teetering on the edge, she wanted to say yes, but fear was holding her back. I tucked her hair behind her ear. 'I promise I'll keep you safe.'

'Okay.'

'Okay?'

'Yes. Let's do it,' she said, a look of determination settling on her face. It was so beautiful. I leaned in, kissing her lips once more. I was tempted to call the whole thing off and keep her in my bed for the rest of the night, but instead I forced myself to release her.

'What was that for?' she asked, her voice breathy, making my cock pulse with need.

I shrugged. 'Because I wanted to.' She flushed, the blood rushing to her cheeks making my fangs ache. 'Go and change before I take you out in that,' I teased.

I expected her to scurry away but instead she stepped slowly out of my arms, her hand keeping hold of mine until she was too far away and her fingers slipped off the ends of my own. That seductive look in her eyes almost sent me over the edge. After tonight, I was definitely going to cuff her to my bed until her legs were weak and her voice hoarse from screaming my name.

She didn't have many clothes to choose from. I hadn't picked up many for her. Not because I didn't want to, but I didn't want to freak her out. She was like a frightened animal that way, any sudden movement might send her fleeing, and I'd never find her again.

Well, now I could. With the pendant she'd given me, I would retain all my memories of her. I'd be able to find her again. But I didn't want to chase after her. I wanted her to stay. Would she stay when she found out what I was about to do? If we caught Chase, she would forgive me. I just had to hope Marcus and the team could manage that much.

She exited the bedroom in smoky jeans and a black blouse with sheer sleeves. She'd pulled her hair back, letting a few loose strands fall around her face. She didn't look like a girl on the run, she looked like someone who wanted to enjoy life. And I was going to give it all to her once this night was done.

'So, where are you taking me?'

'Well, I don't know. We could go on the famous ghost and vampire tour.'

She frowned at me. 'That's not even remotely funny.'

'It's a little funny.' She shook her head. 'Fine. We'll start with dinner, and the rest you'll just have to wait and see.'

'But you don't eat.'

'But you do.' I pulled her into my arms. She closed her eyes, wrapping her arms around me as she rested her head on my chest. Again, she was telling me she trusted me, and again, that guilt twisted like a knife in my gut. How the hell was I supposed to pull this off when all I wanted to do was keep her here where she was safe? I'd lived for three centuries and this might just be the hardest of my life.

CHAPTER 11

Elspeth

Eating with a vampire was perhaps the most unnerving thing I'd ever done. He took me to a beautiful little restaurant by the river and told me to order whatever I wanted. On a normal date, a girl might wonder what she could order so as not to seem unladylike, but I couldn't exactly order less than Roman in this situation. He was drinking red wine – another thing I couldn't do because I couldn't stand the stuff – and would not be ordering anything else. I decided on the pasta, because you could never go wrong with pasta, and I was actually hungry. Though Roman had tried to provide for me, his hunter/gatherer skills left something to be desired.

    A beautiful waitress walked towards us with an extra roll in her hips for Roman's benefit. She should have swayed his attention, in all honesty. She had beautiful olive skin and perfect features, the kind you'd expect to see on a magazine. I wasn't exactly a slouch, but I was definitely on the more average side of the spectrum. My boobs were fine, but I had been told more than once that my butt was too narrow, and Bianca had always tried to coax me into the sun to *get a tan on that pasty complexion.*

    And the waitress had a much more acceptable hair colour. Why hadn't I changed mine already? She flirted with Roman right in front of me, twirling a strand of luscious blonde hair around her finger as she batted those *come-fuck-me* eyes.

Damn it. I was getting jealous. But I had to forgive the poor girl because to her I didn't exist. It was an unwelcome reminder of my current predicament. So much for normal. But logic didn't keep the sour taste of jealousy from coating my tongue.

Roman clearly noticed because there was a smug curl to his lips as the waitress left us. 'Are you going to set her on fire?' he asked casually.

Little did he know, that was not entirely unfeasible. I tore my eyes from the woman and pushed the jealousy from my mind. How embarrassing would it be to not only get caught feeling jealous, but to have my magic act on it? No thank you.

Thank the Goddess he didn't say anything more on the subject – though that look in his eyes said he wanted to – or I would have had to leave before trying the food.

And the food smelled incredible as it was placed in front of Roman by a waiter with a disgruntled look on his face. I looked over to find the waitress pouting. Clearly he hadn't liked her flirting with Roman, probably because he wanted her for himself. Ah, young love.

When the waiter left, Roman placed the bowl and the cutlery in front of me. I felt like a ghost that only he could see. I sighed inwardly.

'Don't look like that,' Roman said, taking my hand and pressing a light kiss to my fingers. 'I see you, and I'm much more important than anyone else here.'

A laugh escaped my lips. He had a way of making everything seem...brighter. Funny, I never would have expected that from a vampire. I picked up my fork and speared a piece of penne, then popped it into my mouth, waiting for the explosion of flavour.

But having Roman watching me so closely as I ate the steaming bowl of pasta made me so self-conscious I could barely taste it. 'Are you just going to watch me?' I asked.

He sipped his wine. 'What else should I do?'

I tried to ignore that seductive lilt to his voice. 'Don't you eat at all?'

'Are you offering?' he purred, desire flashing in his eyes, and I felt my cheeks flush at the idea of his fangs piercing my skin. It was a thought that should have terrified me, so why did I find it so tantalising? 'What a tease you are, witchling. I might have to punish you for that later.'

'What if I wasn't teasing?' I asked, my words slow as my embarrassment grew. I wasn't used to any of this. I hadn't flirted with anyone in years, I hadn't ever felt such intense feelings for someone before. When I looked up at him, his body was tense, his eyes were trained on me, a hunger burning there that ignited a throbbing need between my thighs.

'You're making this incredibly difficult, Elspeth,' he grated, his voice husky.

My heart thudded in my chest and I swallowed hard. I couldn't believe my own desires. Did I truly crave a vampire's bite?

'How is everything tonight? Can I get you anything else? Another glass of wine, sir?' the waitress asked, smiling beautifully at Roman, breaking the spell.

I cleared my throat and stared back down at my plate as that slimy jealous feeling slithered in my chest again. Would I have stretched out my wrist to him right here if she hadn't interrupted? Would he have whisked me back to the apartment and taken my neck? Or perhaps my thigh.

Stop thinking about it.

'We're fine, thank you,' Roman almost growled, sending the waitress scurrying away. I could feel his eyes on me but I refused to look up. This was getting out of hand, and I needed a moment to think. Finally, I heard him lean back in his chair and my body relaxed a little. I didn't know if I was disappointed or relieved that he didn't push the subject.

When I finished my food, and had a better hold of my emotions, I looked back at him and forced a smile, trying to get back to where we were before. This was supposed to be a date, after all, and I found that I was excited for it. 'Okay, where to next?'

He paused for a moment as if he was deciding what to say. Hadn't he planned this out? It was short notice, I supposed. 'Let's go for a walk.' He threw some bills on the table as he stood and held his hand out to me. I accepted it and as he laced his fingers through mine, my heart skipped a beat.

Oh boy, I was in serious trouble.

The moon was high in the sky when we stepped outside. It was almost full, and it shimmered on the river. A gentle breeze danced through my hair, caressing my face. There wasn't a soul in sight. It was as if the night was ours alone.

'I never realised how beautiful the night could be,' I said, feeling my worries drifting away from me. The night had been a time of fear for me since my curse began, always jumping at shadows, worried that Chase might appear at any moment. I had no doubt that it was the vampire beside me who was making me feel safe now in the cover of darkness. He made me feel like anything was possible, but admitting that would probably give him a big head. Besides, I wasn't ready to admit it. Saying the words out loud would only make it harder to leave.

As if I could leave. I was beginning to realise that ship had long since sailed.

'Were you born a vampire or were you turned?' I asked as he led me along the edge of the river.

'I was turned.'

'How old were you?'

He raised an eyebrow but answered, 'Thirty-two.'

Most immortals settled into their immortality when they were at their strongest. For most witches, that was around twenty-five. But I was beginning to realise that I knew very little of the immortal community I was a part of. The coven had kept us ignorant, kept us isolated. It was true that there weren't many other species in our little town, and covens tended not to move around. I was beginning to sense there was a disadvantage in that, not just to the coven as a whole, but to the members. There was so much of the world we never got to experience. I used to dream of going home, of joining the coven, but now I wasn't so sure. Could I really go back to quiet country life?

'Do you ever miss the sun?' I asked.

'You're full of questions tonight.'

'This is a date, isn't it? The point is to get to know each other better.'

A smile stretched his lips though he didn't look down at me. 'I don't really remember what it felt like. It would be nice to walk in the sun and not burn to death, I suppose. But the only way that would be possible is through magic, and most witches aren't too keen on the idea of granting us immunity to our biggest weakness. Besides, to change a creature's very nature would take incredibly powerful magic.'

'Sure, if you were changing a creature's nature. But it might be possible to enchant an item, like I did with that pendant, to work as a kind of...ward rather than altering a being's genetic makeup.'

He looked down at me then, his steps halting. 'Are you saying such a thing is possible?'

'In theory, yes. If you're asking if *I* could do it...well, probably not with my current abilities. But maybe, if I figure out how to awaken my power.' There was a look of bewilderment on his face. 'Well don't look so surprised. You've helped me since I met you, I'd only be...returning the favour,' I said, dropping my gaze as my cheeks flushed again. I needed a better poker face.

'Elspeth, I have to tell you something,' he said, his voice taking on an edge of seriousness, of regret.

I blinked up at him, brow furrowed in confusion, a sinking feeling in my stomach. But before I could ask, I felt something else, a prickling feeling at the back of my neck, goosebumps on my skin, that slimy feeling of dark magic.

I spun around to see Chase standing only a hundred metres from me. Too close. Far too close. When was the last time I'd let him get this close to me? Fear gripped my heart, squeezing it so tightly I felt like it would burst. Roman clutched my hand, moving his body in front of mine. Tension rippled off him as he stared Chase down.

'I see you decided to ignore my message,' Chase said, a smirk curling his lips.

'I don't respond to threats,' Roman said calmly. If he felt anything at all, he didn't show it. Not anger, not fear, not hatred. He spoke as if Chase was beneath him. A dangerous game to play.

'Elspeth, I'm disappointed to see you slumming it with this filth, though he does seem very well trained as a guard dog. Tell me, would he die for you?' Chase asked, a hint of amusement in his voice.

As if of its own accord, my body moved, attempting to shield Roman from him, but Roman held his arm out to block my path. The smirk dropped from Chase's face, replaced by a malicious glare. 'Don't tell me you have feelings for this creature,' he spat, his hands balling into fists. He began pulling magic around himself, I could feel it growing thicker in the air, making it harder to breathe.

'Stay behind me, Elspeth,' Roman said, never taking his eyes off Chase.

'He'll kill you!' I couldn't let that happen, I wouldn't let that happen. I struggled against Roman, but he was too strong.

Shouts sounded and people began to materialise in the area, surrounding us. Vampires.

'Well, what do you know? I appear to have sprung a trap. The funny thing about traps is, they usually require bait. Lucky your vampire had such tempting bait at hand, all wrapped up in skinny jeans,' Chase said, amusement twisting his features.

Bait? This whole night was a lie. Roman *used* me to get to Chase.

'Elspeth, I can explain everything,' Roman said as the vampires began moving in on Chase.

But Chase didn't seem to care at all, and that sent fear slithering down my spine. 'Until next time, dear Elspeth,' he said. The vampires moved in with inhuman speed but before they could reach him, Chase disappeared, swallowed up by the darkness.

'Spread out! Find him!' someone shouted, and the vampires began dispersing.

I stood frozen, my brain stuck on a loop. *He used me. He used me. He fucking used me!* How long had he been playing me? How could I be such a fool? An invitation to a normal night together, I should have known it was too good to be true. He'd never wanted me, he'd only wanted to use me. My body began to thrum, like ants marching beneath my skin. Emotions roiled inside her. Anger, hurt, betrayal.

Bastard!

'Elspeth,' Roman said, turning to me, apology in his eyes.

Fuck his apology. I trusted him, and he used me. I let myself fall for him like a fool, and he was only thinking about his fucking job.

He reached out for me, but I pulled away. 'Don't fucking touch me!' I snapped. The air crackled around me, lightning forked across the sky. Static in my fingertips, body shaking. Anger or magic or something more? I didn't know. I couldn't think. Something in me was breaking. 'You'd think that I would have learnt my lesson by now.'

'Elspeth, calm down,' Roman said carefully, taking a tentative step towards me.

'Calm down?' I demanded. Another fork of lightning snapped across the sky.

'Roman?' a male voice said. Concerned. I didn't have time for him. My body hummed with strange energy.

'Don't, Marcus. Stay there,' Roman said, holding his hand out to the male, his eyes never leaving me.

'You used me.'

'I'm sorry. I didn't have a choice.'

'There's always a choice!' He took another step towards me. 'Don't!' Wind whipped through my hair, that energy in me growing stronger.

'I know you're angry, witchling, but you have to calm down. Can't you see what you're doing?' Soothing. I didn't want that tone from him.

But he was right. Somehow the wind and the lightning were responding to my emotions. I had to stop myself before something bad happened, and I knew it was only a matter of time now. I closed my eyes and took a ragged breath, then another, until my breathing became steady. *First rule of magic, Ellie, clear your mind,* my mother's voice whispered in my mind. In. Out. In, out. In… I let out a long exhale, feeling the energy inside me dissipate as the wind began to still, the night growing silent once more.

When I opened my eyes, there was relief on Roman's face, and it made that anger boil in me once more. 'I'm leaving,' I said, my voice calm.

'What? You can't!' Roman said, his relief replaced with panic.

'I'll not be your puppet, Roman.'

'Let me explain, I –'

'I don't want to hear it. I should never have stayed this long,' I said, hardly recognising my own voice. Hard, cold, emotionless.

'Elspeth, Roman's right. You can't leave,' the vampire, Marcus, said, slowly approaching us. 'If you leave, Chase will disappear again.'

'I would have thought you'd want that,' I said.

'No, we need to stop him. Whether he's in Chicago or somewhere else makes no difference. He'll go wherever you are, so we need you to stay.'

Stupid, stupid girl. Why did I stay? Why did I trust a vampire? I had magic in me, I'd proved that just now. But controlling it was another matter entirely. If I tried to run, these enforcers would only hunt me down. I had two choices before me, I could go willingly, or I could go as a prisoner. But there was one thing I would not do.

'Fine. But I won't stay with Roman,' I said, refusing to look at him.

'Elspeth –' Roman began, but Marcus cut him off.

'If that is your wish, but our accommodations aren't as nice as Roman's apartment.'

'I don't care. Let's just get this over with,' I said, suddenly feeling tired. Perhaps it was the magic, perhaps it was emotional. I walked towards Marcus ready to accept my fate.

'Elspeth, please,' Roman said. I looked back at him, and his eyes searched mine.

'Roman,' Marcus said and shook his head. He took my hand. 'Hold on,' he said. He was going to trace, but he made no move to pull me close. I should have known Roman was lying about that, too. Everything was a fucking lie.

I closed my eyes and let Marcus take me away.

'Welcome to the Chicago Enforcer base,' Marcus said a moment later.

I opened my eyes to find myself in a room that was nothing like I'd imagined. I'd expected a sort of police station or a military base, mostly concrete and cold. Instead, it looked like I was inside a mansion with the best of everything money could buy. Crystal chandeliers hung from the ceiling, expensive art lined the walls, the floors were polished marble. 'Wow. This place is impressive,' I said despite myself.

Marcus smiled. 'I'm glad you approve. You know, we always have room in our ranks for a talented witch.'

'You don't know me very well, I'm not that talented.'

'Yet. But there's definitely raw potential there.'

'I still plan to leave when this is all over,' I said. Joining a group like the Enforcers did sound appealing. The idea that I could use my magic for the good of others instead of just hiding out in a little country town was something I never would have thought about two years ago. But I didn't want to put myself so close to Roman. When this was done, I needed to put some distance between us. 'How are you going to keep me here when you forget me?'

'Were you banking on that to escape?' he asked, an approving smile on his lips. 'I remember everything Roman has told me about you, though it is fascinating to forget one's memories so completely.'

'Not the word I'd use,' I said bitterly. But if this little plan of theirs worked, I would soon be rid of that problem once and for all. What would I do then? I might go home to see my parents, and they would finally remember me. But after that? Maybe I'd just start fresh somewhere else. Perhaps I'd finally get lucky in love, not that my track record was so good on that front.

'Elspeth, I know you're angry that Roman used you, but he was under orders. He couldn't tell you because your reactions needed to be genuine,' Marcus said. 'Chase would have known if they weren't.'

'Why are you telling me this?' I asked bluntly. I didn't want to hear it, I didn't want logic and reason. For the first time in two years, I'd let myself trust someone. For the first time in two years, I'd had hope. And he had broken that trust. He'd chosen his orders over me. And why wouldn't he? I wasn't his mate, there was no reason for him to protect me. It was better this way. A little hurt now to save a lot of hurt later. 'It doesn't matter. Where am I staying?'

Marcus let out a sigh, guilt furrowing his brow for the briefest of moments before he schooled his expression again. 'This way,' he said and led me through the mansion.

It took only a few minutes before he stopped, seemingly confused as if he didn't know why he was going this way. He turned around, his eye widening when he saw me. 'Elspeth?' he said after a moment.

'Yep.' It seemed I was back to being forgotten. Though it took him a little longer than most people. Was that a vampire thing or something to do with what Roman had told him? Roman had managed longer than Marcus, but perhaps that was for a different reason.

Or perhaps I was looking for excuses.

My heart ached at the thought of being back at square one with no one to remember me. 'You should probably set a reminder or something, so you don't forget to feed me. I'm still mortal, you know.'

Marcus frowned. 'Yes, you're right. Are you sure you don't want to go back to Roman? He seems to be able to remember you better.'

'Especially now,' I muttered and rolled my eyes. I should have taken that damn necklace when I left. Perhaps there would be another opportunity to remove it, but I didn't know if that was a good idea either. Would I be able to do it if I saw him again?

'What does that mean?'

'Nothing, it doesn't matter. This me?' I asked, pointing to an open door leading to a room with a single bed, a desk and little else.

'Yes, this is where you'll be staying. If you need anything, you can ask any of the men here. I'll arrange for someone to collect some things for you. At dawn, the mansion goes into lockdown, you won't be able to leave. Helps to keep the sun out.'

I nodded my understanding, a wave of exhaustion hitting me hard. I didn't have the energy to escape, and I didn't care. I would stay in my little cage until they caught Chase, or until he came for me. Then this thing would finally end.

'I'll leave you to it then,' Marcus said with a tight smile that told me he wanted to say more. I was grateful that he didn't. When he closed the door, I kicked off my shoes and crawled into bed, letting go of everything as unconsciousness took hold of me.

CHAPTER 12

Roman

I was pacing the apartment when my phone finally rang. I'd called Marcus four times already with no response. What the hell had taken so long? It took all my strength not to follow them to the base and demand to see Elspeth, and the only thing holding me back was the thought that I might push her further away.

But I didn't know that I could hold off much longer.

'If this is what it's like to have your bride, then I don't think I want mine,' Marcus said.

'How is she?' I asked, ignoring his jab. He'd understand when he found his bride. Until then, there was no point trying to explain it to him. She'd been in my life a matter of days, but her absence was everywhere. The apartment was too quiet, her scent lingered on my sheets, her clothes and supplies were still here, but I wasn't sure she would ever come back.

'Sleeping. I think.' Marcus said, uncertainty in his voice. 'Wow, this curse of hers is a real mind fuck.'

'Yeah, it is.' Or it was before she'd given me that pendant. Now, I couldn't forget her unless I took it off. Damn it. I needed her back.

'Look, I'm sorry things turned out this way. Give her time. Tonight was a shock, but I'm sure she'll come around.'

'I want to see her.'

Marcus sighed. 'I won't stop you, but at least wait until tomorrow. Let her rest.'

'What are we going to do about the warlock?' I asked. If I couldn't see her then I would have to focus on hunting him down.

'We won't be able to lure him out again. He might seek her out, but if he's smart, he's gone to ground for a bit to figure out his next move. I've got witches scrying for him. Maybe now that we have a name, they'll have more luck.'

'So, we just sit and wait?'

'Get some sleep. With any luck, the witches will have something for us soon.'

Before I could argue, Marcus hung up on me. Fucker. How was I supposed to sleep? I knew Elspeth was well protected at the base, but that didn't calm the agitation crawling through me. I needed her here. But Marcus was also right, I should let her rest. She's had a long night, and the kind of magic she'd been using would have taken a toll on her. Maybe she would be more forgiving when she had some time to think it over. But I didn't want to give her too much time in case she settled on the wrong conclusion and solidified that opinion.

This was going to be the longest day of my life.

***

The sun was finally beginning to set. I hadn't slept at all, but I'd attempted to make myself look presentable. Emotions knotted in my stomach, emotions that were strange to me. I was nervous, I was worried she wouldn't forgive me, and I was fighting the feral instincts that snarled at me to claim her and sort the rest out later.

Finally, the light disappeared, and I traced to the base. Marcus was waiting for me with a shake of his head. 'You sure the sun was down before you left?'

'Where is she?'

'You should have claimed her. It's making you crazy,' Marcus said with disapproval.

'I couldn't exactly force it on her, could I?' I snapped.

Marcus let out an exasperated sigh. He scanned a few post-it notes stuck on his desk. I raised an eyebrow but said nothing. Marcus *hated* post-it notes. But on them I realise he'd scribbled reminders, each one about Elspeth. When she last ate, a reminder to check on her, which room she was in. He snatched up that fluorescent yellow note with a frown. 'This way,' he said, then led me through the base.

Her scent grew stronger as we neared, and agitation exploded in me, scuttling under my skin. It was unbearable. If she did forgive me, I was never letting her leave again. Finally, Marcus stopped and waved his hand at a door. He walked away without saying a word, and I was glad of it. I didn't want to waste any more time. I knocked on the door.

'Yes?' She sounded tired, and there was a hint of melancholy in her voice that squeezed my heart because I knew I was the one who put it there. I pushed on the door, and when she saw me, a scowl settled on her face. 'What are you doing here?' she asked flatly.

'I need to talk to you,' I said, stepping into the room and closing the door behind me.

She let out an exhausted breath. 'There's nothing to talk about, Roman. You were just doing your job. I knew this was never going to last. It's better that it happened now.'

'What are you talking about?'

'You're a vampire. Even if you felt something for me, one day you'd find your mate, and that would be the end of it. You did me a favour, really.' Her words were resigned, almost apathetic. Almost. But there was a sadness in her eyes, as if she was doing something that was inevitable, but she didn't want to. Was that my own arrogance, or had she truly come to have feelings for me?

'*You're* my bride, Elspeth.'

She blinked at me. 'What?'

I closed the distance between us, and she didn't pull away. 'I knew it the moment I saw you at *Myth*.'

'But I – why didn't you tell me? Why didn't you claim me?' she asked, the words falling quickly from her tongue as she tried to make sense of what I was telling her. Did she want me to claim her? I stifled a groan, my fangs aching at the very thought.

'I was afraid you would run,' I said, tracing my fingers along her jaw, my self-control teetering on the edge of a blade. Being this close to her when she was on the verge of running from me sent my instincts into a frenzy. 'Was I wrong?'

She opened her mouth to argue but clamped it shut again, and the petulant expression on her face was answer enough. She would have run.

But she wasn't running now.

I leaned in, my lips hovering above her ear. Her intoxicating scent enveloped me. 'I could claim you right here if you want me to,' I murmured. Her breath hitched in her throat, sending a shock of need to my cock. She had no idea how hard it was to resist her all this time, to keep from sinking my fangs deep into her neck and taking her into me, to keep from claiming her as so that all the world would know she was mine.

She shook herself as if from a stupor, that frown creasing her brow once more as she pulled away from me. 'Then why did you lie to me?' she demanded, and I could see the anger building in her eyes. 'How could you use me as *bait* for the male I fear more than anyone in this world?'

'I didn't like the plan any more than you, but to draw Chase out, your reactions needed to be real. If he suspected, he never would have set foot in that trap.'

'But your trap failed! You did all this for nothing.'

'I had to try. It was the best chance I had at taking him down and keeping you safe.'

'I have spent two years running from that bastard, and you almost delivered me to him with a pretty bow tied around my neck!'

I closed the distance between us again, her hands beating against my chest as I backed her against the wall. 'Understand this, Elspeth,' I said, my voice dark, 'I would die before I let him touch you.' I held her gaze so she could see how serious my words were. I *needed* her to know that.

But instead of the forgiveness I'd expected to see there, her stubborn eyes began to well with tears. 'I don't want you to die!' she said, emotion robbing her voice of anger and robbing me of the last thread of my control.

I captured her lips in a searing kiss. Her hands pushed against my chest for only a second before her fingers gripped the fabric of my shirt, pulling me closer. As I deepened the kiss, sliding my tongue between her plump lips, she arched her back, pressing her breasts against me. Gods, I wanted her naked and in my bed, I wanted my cock and my fangs buried inside her. Her tongue brushed against one of my fangs, then the other, and I groaned as I realised she was exploring me. She grazed her tongue on the tip, and my body stiffened as the first taste of her coated our kiss. Never had I tasted anything so good, not in my three hundred years as an immortal. My fangs ached as something primal within me began to awaken.

'Roman?'

The uncertainty in her voice brought me back, and I took a breath to steady myself. *Reign it in, keep control*, I told myself. I caressed her cheek with a shaking hand but that uncertainty didn't fade from her eyes. Her teeth nibbled her bottom lip. *Gods, tell me she wasn't about to send me away*. I didn't think I could handle that.

'If you claim me, would you have to bite me?' she asked.

'Yes,' I said, my voice rough. Her hand went to her neck, a subconscious action, and I knew she wasn't ready. 'I can wait, Elspeth. Until you're ready.' It would damn near kill me, but I could do it, for her. I'd heard of vampires being driven mad from waiting, claiming in a frenzy, but I could hold the insanity at bay. I had to. If I lost control for even a moment, my mortal witchling could die.

She nodded once before stepping into me, wrapping her arms around my waist, nestling her head against my chest. I blinked in surprise. 'Take me home,' she said.

Take me home. She was going to stay. She was going to stay with me. I wrapped my arms around her and kissed the top of her head as relief washed through me. She might not be ready to be claimed, but I was sure that day would come. As I traced us back to the apartment, to *our home,* my heart felt more full than it had in centuries.

CHAPTER 13

Elspeth

We'd hardly materialised before Roman's lips were on mine, a searing, sexual heat radiating from him that was a stark contrast to the cool touch of his skin. Or maybe the heat was mine, it was hard to tell where he ended, and I began when we were like this.

Because I'm his bride.

The thought came unbidden to my mind, stiffening my body. Was it a good thing or a bad thing to be a vampire's bride? Roman was certainly not what I'd expected from a vampire, and the idea of being the only one for him sent a thrill through me, but it was hard to wrap my head around. Witches didn't have mates, and with all of eternity stretched out before them, they rarely married young. And I was still young. I hadn't even settled into my immortality yet. Could I commit to a vampire I'd known for a mere fraction of my life? The blink of an eye in the grand scheme of things.

He hadn't even said he loved me. Did I want him to? Did I love him? Goddess, the way my heart responded to that thought scared the hell out of me. But I knew I couldn't commit to him without love. A fated mate was one thing, but love was entirely another. Wasn't it?

He stopped kissing me and let out a sigh as he rested his forehead against mine. 'Where did you go?'

I didn't know how to answer that question. I didn't want him to know what was going on in my head. I wanted him to come to those feelings and answers on his own, not because I told him what I wanted.

I needed to know they were real when he finally said the words I needed to hear. If he finally said the words.

'Elspeth, I told you I'll wait until you're ready.' He kissed my jaw, then trailed his lips slowly down my neck until my mind began to blank with pleasure, and I let out a shaky breath. Heat began to build in my core. This male was impossible to deny, impossible to ignore.

'That's it. Come back to me,' he murmured, sending a wetness seeping into my panties. A moan dropped from my tongue and my eyes fluttered closed.

Goddess forgive me, I was falling hard for this vampire.

The sound of tearing fabric made my eyes snap open. Roman's lips were curled in a mischievous smirk, my ruined shirt in his hand. 'I'm not going to have any clothes left if you keep doing that,' I said, though I couldn't deny that it was hot as hell.

'No complaints here,' he said as he eyed me hungrily. He licked his lips and ran a single finger down my chest, between my breasts, slowly down to my jeans. Goosebumps raced across my skin and my muscles clenched in anticipation.

He unzipped my jeans and slowly slid them down my legs as he dropped to his knees. He tossed them away, never taking his eyes off me. With another tear of fabric, my panties were discarded, leaving me bare before him. He pulled his shirt over his head, throwing it aside with the same care he had my clothes - none at all.

He ran his hand up the inside of my leg, all the way to the apex of my thighs, though not touching me where I needed him before he trailed it back down again. He lifted my leg then, draping it over his shoulder. 'Lean back,' he said, and I did as I was told, a fluttering nervousness in my stomach as I leaned against the wall behind me. His lips brushed against my inner thigh and I gasped, muscles clenching again, need building, my body begging for more.

His tongue darted out, flicking over my sensitive clitoris. I moaned as my knees grew weak, and he growled with approval. My toes curled as his tongue explored, sliding between my folds, circling my clitoris, a tightness coiling inside me quickly becoming unbearable. His hand gripped my arse, fingers digging into flesh, pulling me to his mouth. His stayed other hand on my thigh, keeping me open to him as he lapped at me with his wicked tongue.

'Ah, Roman, yes!' I cried in abandon as I approached my climax, and his firm tongue dipped inside me, sending me over the edge. My body trembled as I cried out, waves of pleasure crashing through me, making my limbs weak, my mind blank. When he pulled back and gently removed my leg from his shoulder, the only thing supporting me was the wall.

He carried me to the bed, my body exhausted and throbbing, satisfied, but hungry for more. He pulled the blanket over me and removed his pants before climbing in with me, tucking me into his side.

'What about you?' I asked, my cheeks flushing with embarrassment.

'Tonight was about you,' he said, kissing the top of my head. 'And if you think I'm not satisfied as hell making you scream my name, you're wrong.'

'What if I'm not?' I asked before I could lose my nerve.

He raised an eyebrow and looked down at me as if I'd surprised him. I pulled the blanket back, my eyes trailing down his delicious body; wide shoulders, sculpted muscles, his firm erection. The idea of having him inside me made me lick my lips, and he growled in response. I straddled his hips, and his hands flew to mine as if magnetised, his fingers digging into my flesh, but just to hold. He was letting me take control now.

I watched him as I slid down on his erection, slowly pushing him inside me. The pleasure I saw in his face was intoxicating, the groan that escaped his lips empowering. The knowledge that I affected him as much as he affected me made me feel connected to him in a way I never had before. I sank my teeth into my lip as I rode him slowly, teasing him with my body, the power as intoxicating as the sex.

'Ah, gods, Elspeth,' he murmured, his hands tightening on me. He wanted more, but I wasn't ready to give it to him, I was going to make him wait. I let out a moan as I slowly sank down on him, letting him know exactly what I was doing.

A growl of frustration rumbled in his chest, sending a shiver of pleasure through me. Before I could blink, he had me on my back, my hair splayed out on the mattress as he loomed over me, his cock buried deep inside me, and my muscles clenched around his length.

'Don't you know it's dangerous to toy with a vampire, love?' he asked, that last word making my heart stutter in my chest. I didn't have time to analyse it. He thrusted into me hard enough to make my breasts bounce, and I gasped as pleasure shot through me.

'You like that?' he asked and thrusted again.

I nodded. 'Yes,' I said, when I could trust my voice to work. 'Yes.'

His lips claimed mine, and he kissed me deep as he slammed into me over and over again with his hard cock. I could feel the tension building in me as he took over, my aching nipples grazing his chest, the feel of his fangs.

A wicked thought came to mind, and I ran my tongue along a sharp tip. My blood stained our kiss, and he growled against me, his hips slamming into me with a final thrust that sent me over the edge. He consumed my scream as I came around him, as he came inside me hard enough for me to feel the pulsing of his cock as his seed spilled into me.

He kissed me tenderly for a long moment before finally untangling himself from me. He pulled the blanket over me and tucked me into his side, kissing my hair. His thumb drew small, soothing circles on my arm. He may not have said the words out loud, but in that moment, I *felt* loved by this vampire and I realised then that I wasn't just falling for him, I had fallen for him. The idea of saying the words made my cheeks flush with embarrassment. But I resolved to tell him. Tomorrow I would tell him how I felt, and I would become his. I would let him claim me.

CHAPTER 14

Elspeth

Roman left me alone in the apartment for the first time in two days. Marcus had called him in, and he wouldn't be ignored any longer. I couldn't blame him. While we were swept up in the glow of this new honeymoon period, Chase was still out there, and while he was quiet now, I knew he wouldn't stay that way for long. The look in his eyes at the river had been almost deranged. It sent a fresh shiver down my spine. Maybe there was a time when he might have treated me reasonably well if I'd married him, but now? I dread to think what that life might look like.

The enforcers were searching for Chase, using witchcraft to scry for him and their own trackers. But the darkness I'd felt that night made me doubt they'd find him. So much dark energy in one warlock...he'd always been powerful, but this was something else. Did the coven know about this? Did they still accept him as one of their own? Perhaps they didn't have a choice. The idea of my parents, my friends, the people I'd grown up with my entire life living under his control made me long for home. I wanted to know they were alright. But going home now would only put them in more danger, and they wouldn't even know who I was.

I let out a weary sigh.

I didn't like the idea of Roman looking for Chase. Now that he was on Chase's radar, he would be in more danger than me. At least Chase wouldn't kill me. Not yet, anyway. He'd want to have his fun first, after spending two years of his life chasing me down. But telling a three-hundred-year-old vampire what to do wouldn't go down well.

My only hope now was to awaken my power. I still didn't know how the hell I was supposed to do that. I'd felt it, though, at the river. I'd felt a power stronger than anything I ever had before, breaking through me like a storm. It was there, if only I could figure out how to control it. Maybe Angèlie could help me, but I couldn't get to her without Roman. He'd traced us there the last time, and I didn't know where 'there' was. Besides, if I started walking around the city on my own, I might as well text Chase to come and get me.

Suddenly the air shimmered, and a portal opened up next to me. A squeak of surprise leapt from my throat. 'Come on, child, I can't hold this open forever,' Angèlie's voice drifted through the shimmering space. 'You wanted to see me, didn't you?'

I stepped through the portal, eager not to waste this opportunity. If Roman was going to be risking his life for me, I wasn't going to just sit at home and wait for him.

Angèlie was waiting for me in the back room of her shop, ingredients and talismans lining the shelves and a big open space in the centre of the room for practicing spells. As soon as I was clear, the portal snapped shut behind me.

'How did you know I wanted to see you?' I asked.

'Mon cher, I know many things,' she said with a coy smile.

'Did you know I was looking for you for a week before Roman brought me?'

'Of course, but if you had found me, then you wouldn't have met Roman,' she said, that smile stretching into something mischievous. 'You haven't let him claim you.'

'How do you know that?' I asked before I could stop myself. Was it stamped on my forehead?

'Any supernatural being can see when another has been claimed. To make him wait so long, though?'

'What? Is that bad?'

'But you didn't come here to talk romance,' she said, completely ignoring my question. 'That would require much more wine, maybe a fire, and a lot more time than we have right now.'

It occurred to me then that Angèlie might actually be crazy. Was I making him suffer? Roman didn't say anything about it. I didn't want him to suffer, but it was a big thing to consider. By letting him claim me, I was essentially committing to this male, this vampire, for the rest of my life. For him, there was no one else, I was his fated mate, but for me...could there be someone else? Would I want there to be?

'You have begun to awaken your power, yes? I felt it the other night.'

'But I wasn't in control.'

'And yet, you controlled it.' She raised her eyebrows at me as if expecting me to see something obvious.

'Hardly. I could have hurt someone.'

'But you didn't.' Angèlie strode towards me, her white dress flowing around her bare ankles. 'You are too much in here,' she said, poking one perfectly manicured finger against my forehead. 'Magic comes from the heart not from the head. You *feel* it, you guide it, but doubt leads to chaos.'

'Are you giving me the Disney 'believe in yourself' speech right now?'

'If you want to call it that. Your fear holds you back, you must overcome it. You will face it when it is worth it to you. Then you will see.'

'Is that really all the help you can give me?' I asked, despair beginning to settle in. I wasn't any better off than when I'd been waiting in Roman's apartment. Angèlie held out a dark metallic crystal to me. 'Hermatite?'

She nodded. 'To balance your mind and your body.'

I took it from her and stuffed it into my pocket, feeling less than grateful for the confusing sort-of-assistance. I wasn't sure how it was supposed to help, but I could use all the help I could get.

Angèlie's face grew serious. 'Our time is up,' she said. 'You must go now.' She waved her hand in a circular motion and opened another portal. Portal magic was notoriously difficult, but she made it look like the easiest thing in the world. Before I could protest, she shoved me into the portal and snapped it shut as I hit the floor in Roman's apartment.

Angèlie Laveau might be one of the most powerful voodoo priestesses in the country, but she was also mad as a fucking hatter. Or was that just an act?

I let out a sigh and picked myself up off the floor. Roman still wasn't back from his meeting with Marcus, and the sun would be up soon. I set about closing all the blinds in case he got home late. I'd just closed the last of them when my phone buzzed.

Meet me outside. I have something to show you.

Roman wanted me to meet him outside? Now? It was only minutes until sunrise! I hurried out the door, racing down the steps. What was he thinking?

'Everything alright, miss?' the doorman asked as I burst into the lobby.

'Yes,' I answered automatically. I realised I'd never been to the lobby of this building before, I hadn't even known there was a doorman. No matter, he'd forget me in a moment.

Outside the sky was beginning to lighten, the dark of night becoming grey. I looked around but Roman was nowhere to be seen.

'That was far too easy, love.'

A chill shot down my spine and I spun around. Chase was leaning against the building, one leg casually crossed over the other, but his eyes were trained on me like a predator eyeing his prey.

'Chase.'

'It was pretty clever of you to find a place to hide that I couldn't get into,' he said, pushing off the building. It seemed the wards on the building were as good as Roman claimed. That would have made me feel better if I was still inside. 'Did you sleep with him?'

'Who I sleep with is none of your business.' I took a step towards the building, and he followed suit, mirroring my actions. He was enjoying himself. If I made a break for the door, would I make it inside before he caught me? He looked as if he wanted to find out.

'It *is* my business. You are mine, Elspeth.'

'I will *never* be yours,' I spat.

'Well, you're not his,' he said, his eyes dropping to my neck.

'And if I was?'

Chase shrugged but there was a darkness in his eyes. 'Better for you if you don't make that decision. He's going to die either way for touching what's mine.'

I took another step towards the building, and so did he. He was toying with me, amusement curling his lips, but one wrong move could spell disaster for me. 'What do you want, Chase?'

He cocked his head. 'Come now, love, you know the answer to that.'

'Well, you know I'm not giving you that, so why are you really here?'

'I came to make you a deal. You see, I could just take you, but you'd fight me every day of our lives together. You're selfish like that. You'd rob us of the happiness we could have out of spite.'

You're completely insane! I wanted to shout, but I clamped my mouth shut. Insane people did insane things, and that made them unpredictable. I stamped down the fear clawing at my chest and forced myself to appear calm. 'So, what do you propose?'

He smiled then, his eyes glinting with approval, and I felt like I needed a shower to scrub the disgusting feeling from me. 'Meet me on the night of the new moon. Come willingly, and I will...*spare*' – he spat the word as if it was a razor blade slicing his tongue – 'your vampire.'

With a flick of his fingers, a scrap of paper floated through the air towards me. Reluctantly I took it. An address was scribbled there, the place he wanted to meet. Was it supposed to be a sign of good faith? I doubted Chase was capable of doing anything on good faith.

'And if I don't?'

'You're a smart girl, Elspeth. I'm sure you can figure that out. I'll send a driver for you, that way you won't be late.' He waved his hand towards the door. He was letting me go, but he would only do that if he was sure of his victory later. I didn't wait for him to change his mind. I raced inside, slamming the door shut behind me. As I turned back to him, watching from behind the safety of the wards, he smiled at me, sending another chill down my spine.

How the hell was I going to get out of this now?

CHAPTER 15

Roman

'Where the fuck have you been?' I demanded, unable to reign in my rage. I'd gone back to the apartment to find Elspeth was gone. Panic had set in. I'd sent people to look for her, I'd scoured the city, and yet, here she was as if nothing had happened, dressed in a silk robe, staring into the empty fireplace. I didn't know if I wanted to kiss her or chain her to the bed so she could never leave again.

'What?' she asked as if coming out of a daze.

Reign it in, Roman. Reign it fucking in. 'Where did you go?' I asked slowly, aiming for calm and missing by a mile.

'I went to see Angèlie,' she said after a moment's hesitation. 'I didn't realise you'd come back.'

'You could have called me!'

Her brows furrowed as her temper rose to meet my own. 'That works both ways, arsehole!'

I let out an exasperated sigh and massaged my temples. 'You're right,' I grudgingly admitted. 'But you shouldn't have gone out alone.' I collapsed into one of the chairs, feeling drained. I reached for her, and she came to me, letting me pull her onto my lap. Having her in my arms eased the panic I'd felt over losing her. Maybe not claiming her *was* making me crazy.

'She opened a portal for me,' she said, nestling her head against my neck. She let out a contented sigh, but there was something sad about it, too. I had that feeling again, like she wasn't telling me something. I stroked her hair as tension began to coil in my body again. Would she tell me or would she continue to keep things from me?

'Elspeth –'

'I have to tell you something,' she said, cutting me off.

'Okay,' I said, the calm in my voice hiding the turmoil those words had riled within me.

'Chase was here today. He lured me outside,' she said. She held up her phone before I could say anything, and I read the message I never sent to her. He'd used me to lure her out. I was going to kill that fucker.

'How did you escape? Is your power finally awakened?'

She shook her head. 'He let me go. He said he wants to make a deal. He wants me to meet him –'

'No.'

'Roman –'

'No. You're not meeting him anywhere,' I said firmly. There was no way in hell I was letting her go to meet Chase.

'He said he'd kill you if I don't go,' she said.

'He'll try to do that anyway.'

'No, he said he'd spare you if I went with him.' She handed me a piece of paper with an address scribbled on it. I clenched my fist around it, crushing it.

'You're not seriously considering this?' My temper was slipping again, my instincts screaming at me. *Protect. Claim.* The thought of losing her was enough to drive me mad. 'No, we should use this. We know where he'll be and when.'

'On a new moon when those who practice dark magic are at their strongest?' she said. 'Roman, please. I don't want you to die.'

'Then stay.'

She looked up at me, a tangle of emotions in her eyes; fear, sadness, love. 'Okay. We'll do it your way.'

'That was easy. What's the catch?'

'There is a condition,' she said, her cheeks beginning to flush. 'I want you to claim me.'

My cock shot hard at her words, my fangs aching. 'What?' Had I heard her right? Her condition was to be mine?

'Roman, I love you. And the thought that I might lose you for good, I – I don't want to be in a world without you. I'm already yours so...I want to make it official. I want you to claim me.'

There wasn't a hint of doubt in her beautiful eyes as she looked up at me, offering me everything I had ever wanted. 'Are you sure?'

'Yes.' She pulled the sash on her robe, letting the silk fall across her bare skin. I sucked in a breath at the sight of her. She really was sure. And who was I to deny her? I couldn't if I tried. I felt as if something had snapped in me, and there was no turning back now.

I pressed my lips to hers, my hands gripping her waist, and I positioned her so she was straddling me. As my hands explored her skin, she rocked her hips against my straining cock, sending a shock of pleasure through me. I groaned as she slid her tongue between my lips, deepening the kiss. My hands tightened on her hips as she explored my fangs again, carefully, purposefully. She grazed it along one sharp point, and her blood ran across my tongue, stirring something primal in me. My cock was so hard, and she continued to rock her hips, her taste on my tongue, I felt like I was going to spend in my pants.

'I need you inside me,' she breathed, almost sending me over the edge.

'Gods, witchling. You're going to be the death of me.' I was far too close, and I'd be damned if I let her have all the fun. I moved by hand along her thigh, enjoying the way she squirmed as my hand drew closer to her core. I slid a finger between her slick folds, grazing her clitoris, and she cried out, her hips tilting to grant me better access, her head falling back as I explored her. I slipped a finger inside her, and she gasped with pleasure. I leaned forward, taking a tight nipple into my mouth with a hard suck, causing her muscles to clamp around my finger. I slipped a second finger into her as her hand gripped my hair, and she rolled her hips, fucking my fingers towards her climax. Wanton little witchling, I was going to come just watching her.

'Bite me,' she begged.

I couldn't even begin to tell her how I longed to hear her say those words, and with her plump breast in my mouth it was impossibly tempting. I released her nipple, and she whimpered. 'The first time I bite you, love, my cock will be buried in you so deep you'll wonder how you lived without it.'

Her muscles clamped around my finger in response, and my resolve shattered. I needed her. Now.

I traced her to the bed, laying her on the mattress before ripping off my clothes, the sound of tearing fabric barely registered. She looked up at me, desire burning in her eyes, lust flushing her cheeks, her pink hair fanned out beneath her. This was a sight I never wanted another male to see. She was mine. I pushed her legs open as I lowered myself between her thighs.

'Will it hurt?' she asked, uncertainty tinting her words.

'No, love. You've never felt pleasure like this before.' I brushed my lips over the artery in her neck, and she shivered. Anticipation? Fear? Maybe both, but after this night, she would never fear me again. I licked my lips at the thought of what I was about to taste, and my cock teased at her wet centre. She rocked her hips against me, a silent plea for more, for the orgasm she'd been so close to reaching before I'd stopped. Her breaths left her lips in wanton pants that made her breasts bounce temptingly.

With a single thrust, I filled her slick core. 'Yes!' she screamed, her muscles clenching around my cock, begging for more. God it felt so good to be inside her. I could feel my control slipping. I needed to be gentle with her, but I wasn't sure I had it in me anymore.

'Are you ready, love?' I asked, my fangs aching in anticipation.

'Yes. Claim me. I want to be yours.'

I slowly moved my hips, sliding back out, then thrusting back in, enjoying the way her fingers curled, the way her legs tightened around me as if she could prevent me from leaving. As if I would ever leave her willingly. 'Say it again.'

'I want to be yours.'

I thrust into her again and brought my lips to her neck. A shiver ran through her as my breath caressed her skin, and her back arched, her head falling to the side, a clear invitation that decimated the last of my control. My fangs sank into her neck and blood pooled in my mouth, coating my tongue as I drank deep. Pleasure shot through me, the likes of which I had never felt before. Her voice filled the room, her body trembling. Her orgasm hit hard, her muscles clenched around my cock, her nails dug into my skin, and my own orgasm followed with a murmured *fuck*. The word sounded so sexy from her lips. With a final thrust, I let out a guttural growl.

I pulled my fangs from her neck, and piercing the tip of my finger, I sealed the wound with my blood. It stopped the flow, and I licked the remnants from her skin, her legs still gripping me tightly, keeping me locked in her. A strange sensation began in my chest, the familiar but long forgotten beat of my heart. Slow, at first, stuttering, as if my heart was remembering how it was supposed to function. When I looked down at her, her eyes were glazed with ecstasy, her cheeks flushed, perspiration dampened her skin.

She was perfect.

She was mine.

CHAPTER 16

Elspeth

As I stared out the window into the dark, I felt different. The bite on my neck was still healing, but it was healing quickly. By the time I met Chase, all physical traces of it would be gone. But a mark would be left behind, his mark, telling all immortals that I was taken. To mess with me was to bring the wrath of my mate.

The pleasure from his bite had been incredible, unlike anything I'd ever felt before. No one had told me to expect *that*. It was almost laughable to think how afraid I was at the idea of it. Now, I couldn't wait to do it again.

My mark would also remain on him. After he'd claimed me, Roman's heart had started beating, as if I had breathed new life into him. No one had told me to expect that, either. I hadn't even noticed until he'd tucked me into his side and my head rested on his chest. But I was glad that in some way, I had marked him, too. Now, all would know that he was blooded, a mated vampire. And he was mated to me. A satisfied smile stretched my lips.

Roman wrapped his arms around my waist, pulling me back against him, his head coming to rest on my shoulder. He still didn't like this plan, but he knew it was the best way to get this done. He'd had the very same idea that night at the riverside. The tactic was slightly different, but in essence it was the same. I was bait. The question was, who was I bait for? Each side was making their own play, and I couldn't help feeling that my role in each was the same. There was a sinking feeling in the pit of my stomach, but I needed to do this.

'I still don't like it,' Roman said. He breathed in deeply, as if my scent could calm him, and I hoped it did. It was my fault he was suffering right now. I only hoped that after tonight I could make him happy.

'I know.'

'There are too many things that can go wrong. It's not too late to change your mind.' Even though he'd agreed to the plan, it seemed he was going to attempt to talk me out of it until the last possible moment.

'I'm tired of running, Roman. I'm tired of living in fear. I want to have a life with you, and that means Chase needs to go.' That didn't mean I wasn't terrified, of course, but I knew if Roman caught wind of that, he would probably chain me to the bed, and that would be the end of this plan.

He kissed my neck tenderly, right where his bite mark was fading, and squeezed me a little tighter. 'We could wait for your power to awaken properly.'

'No. No more waiting.' I had no idea how long it would take for my power to fully come online. I would have to trust in Roman and his team, and hope to the goddess that my powers weren't so wonky tonight. 'We'll never get an opportunity like this again. And the longer we wait, the more powerful he'll get.' I turned in his arms and looked up at him. 'I need you to promise me something.'

'What?' he asked, suspicion in his voice.

'If something happens tonight, don't throw your life away.' He scowled at me, so I pressed on, 'He won't kill me right away, but he would kill you. Please? If things go south, promise me you'll live to fight another day.'

The scowl deepened, the silence growing thick.

'Please, Roman. I need to know you'll be okay.'

He clicked his tongue in irritation. 'Low blow, witchling. Fine, I promise.' His eyes flicked to the window, and I knew it was time. My stomach flipped with nerves, and I pressed my lips to his, just in case it was the last time I ever got to do it.

'Don't do that, Elspeth. This isn't goodbye,' he said, caressing my face with his fingers. 'And if you keep acting like it is, I'm going to chain you to that bed and call the whole thing off.'

'Won't Marcus be pissed?'

'Fuck Marcus.'

'Don't let him hear you say that.' I kissed him again then pulled out of his arms. 'Don't be late,' I said, flashing him my best attempt at a smile.

As I turned away, he grabbed my hand. 'Wait.' He pulled me back into his arms, kissing me long and deep, leaving me breathless and ready to agree to anything he said.

'Now who's being unfair?' I asked as he pulled away.

'Be careful,' he said. He dropped another kiss to my lips before finally releasing me with a pained expression.

It took every ounce of strength not to run back into the safety of his arms, but it was time to face my fears and take back my life. I forced myself to leave his apartment without looking back, because if I let myself look back, I wasn't sure I could leave. When the door closed behind me, I felt my determination return. The elevator travelled slowly down to the lobby, and I expected to see the doorman behind his desk, but all was quiet and empty. I swallowed hard and exhaled a breath as I pushed open the door.

The chill of evening wrapped around me, the taillights of the taxi glowed red in the darkness, and I pulled my coat around me as if it could protect me from the uneasy feeling sinking in my gut. The driver got out, a blank expression on his face and opened the door for me. His zombie-like movements are a clear indication that he'd been spelled. My stomach knotted, but I had to do this. I climbed in, and he closed the door, then got back into the driver's seat. He said nothing at all to me, simply pulled away from the curb, leaving me to play out all the possible scenarios in my head.

The drive felt longer with the empty silence, but finally the driver stopped. He didn't turn to me, he didn't say anything, simply sat staring forward, both hands on the wheel at exactly ten and two. I shuddered and scampered out of the taxi, eager to be away from the shell of a man. Hopefully, Chase would simply have the poor man wake tomorrow with no memory of his evening trip.

The taxi pulled away as soon as the door was closed, and I realised too late that something was wrong. I wasn't overly familiar with Chicago, which Roman had been quick to point out, so he'd pulled up pictures of the location Chase had chosen. This wasn't it.

Shit.

The place Chase had brought me to was an abandoned building in a street that looked similarly abandoned. I doubted that was the natural state of this place, the slimy feel of dark magic clung to the air. The only light came from the flickering streetlights. Roman would want me to run, it was clearly a trap. But there were two problems with that; one, I had no idea where I was, so running would probably end up being a fruitless venture. And two, if I ran now, I'd be putting a target on Roman's back again.

One way or another, this was going to end tonight.

I took a deep breath to steel my courage and headed towards the building I'd been dropped in front of. The door opened with a loud creak that sent goosebumps scuttling across my skin. Inside the building had been lit with candles, the flickering flames looking out of place in the dilapidated building that seemed like a strong wind would blow the whole thing down.

'I wasn't sure you'd come, Elspeth.' Chase's voice echoed through the darkness, though he made no moves to show himself.

'I told you I would,' I said, looking around for any sign of him.

'Yes, but you, my dear, have a habit of running,' he said, his words almost a purr.

'Well, I had a very compelling reason not to, didn't I?'

He strode out of the shadows, stopping only inches from me. 'Yes, you came to protect *him*.' In this light, Chase's eyes looked almost black and insanity danced in their depths. His gaze dropped to my neck, carefully concealed with the collar of my jacket to hide the mark I now bore. His eyes narrowed and flicked back to me, his face twisting in rage. 'You let him *mark* you?' he snarled.

'I told you before, I will *never* be yours,' I said, holding my head higher, meeting his gaze head on. He was right, I did have a habit of running, but no more.

He leaned back then, an ugly smirk curling his lips. 'Oh, my sweet, naïve Elspeth. You have made this far too easy.'

'What are you talking about?'

'Now that you are mated, your precious vampire can find you anywhere. The question is, what shall I do to him when he arrives?' Chase said as he began circling me, malice gleaming in his eyes. He stopped behind me and leaned in, breathing deeply against my hair. 'What shall I do to you until he arrives?' he purred.

I spun around but he had already straightened up as if it had all been my imagination. 'What do you want, Chase? Why are you doing this?'

'Love, Elspeth!' he spat, his voice echoing in the empty space. 'After all this time, how can you ask that?' The shadows began to vibrate around him as his emotions heightened, the smell of dark magic beginning to build.

'Okay, I'm sorry,' I said, trying to keep my voice calm and steady, trying to soothe him. My magic was still unreliable at best, and I had no back up. If Roman could find me, then I needed to stay alive until he and Marcus arrived.

Please hurry, I begged. I wasn't sure how much time I had left, but Chase was deteriorating fast, as if he had leapt off the ledge and willingly taken the plunge into madness. I only hoped Roman's plan would still work.

CHAPTER 17

Roman

I paced, my agitation only growing. How long should it have taken the cab to get here? How long had it been? There was no sign of Chase, there wasn't even the slightest trace of his scent, as if he had never been in this place.

Something was very wrong.

'Roman, what's wrong?' Marcus asked, a hint of caution in his voice.

I was clearly not managing my emotions as well as I'd thought. 'She should have been here by now.' Saying the words out loud snapped something in me. Anxiety and rage began to tangle in my chest, making it hard to hear, hard to think. My instincts screamed at me.

Protect!

Marcus grabbed my chin forcefully and looked at me hard. I tried to rip myself away from him but the man had easily a millennium on me, and the older the vampire, the greater the strength. 'You claimed her.'

'Yes.'

'Then you can find her. But you need to calm the fuck down,' Marcus said.

I should have paid more attention when others told me about the bond with your bride, maybe then I'd have been better prepared. I took deep breaths, forcing myself to calm down. Her life depended on it, so I had no fucking choice. I focused on her, picturing the way she smiled as she looked up at me, that proud expression on her face as she'd presented the pendant to me, the warmth of her in my arms.

'Good,' Marcus said, relief clear in his voice. 'Now you need to reach out for her, *feel,* don't think. What do you feel?'

I kept her image in my mind and let everything else fall away. I wanted to demand how the fuck I was supposed to know how to do this, but then I felt something pulling at me, as if there was a string attached to my soul. I let it pull until I saw her in my mind as if I was standing right next to her.

'Where is she?' Marcus asked.

Elspeth was in an abandoned building lit with candles. There was nothing in it that could identify her location, no signs, no distinct markings. I couldn't scent anything, the only sense I had here was sight. I knew I could trace to her, all I needed was to see the location, and I could be there. But that would leave us without back up until Marcus could track me down.

'You're going to have to work fast, Marcus,' I said, not willing to open my eyes, to lose sight of Elspeth. 'I don't know where she is. Track my phone, do it fast. If you're late, we'll both be dead before you reach us.'

'Roman, wait!' Marcus said.

But he was too late. I wasn't going to leave Elspeth alone with that monster a second longer. I traced to her.

'Ah, good, the leech has arrived,' Chase said flatly, his eyes sparking with animosity. 'So good of you to walk right into my trap.' With a flick of his hand, I was flung across the room, shadows parting around me like a crowd. I groaned as my spine slammed into something hard.

'No!' Elspeth screamed. Her eyes were welling with tears, her body began to tremble, and I could smell a storm on the air.

My arms were pulled out to the sides, as if someone had physically grabbed them. Silver cuffs snapped shut of their own accord. Fucking witches. I just had to keep this one busy long enough for Marcus to find us.

'Must be hard for you, if the only way to get a female is to stalk her across the continent and erase her from memory,' I taunted, letting my lips curl into a smirk. 'Bit desperate, don't you think?'

Chase flicked his hand again, and a silver cuff snapped around my throat. My skin sizzled from the contact, and I gritted my teeth against the pain.

'Stop it, Chase!' Elspeth cried out, but the warlock ignored her, his eyes trained on me, right where I wanted them to be. While he was focused on me, Elspeth was safe.

'I gave her the chance to save you. I guess you weren't all that important to her,' Chase said casually, though the sharpness in his eyes didn't soften.

'Is that why she asked me to claim her?' I chuckled, ignoring the searing pain, trying not to think about the scene I was currently starring in. It was almost identical to the crime scene we'd uncovered.

'For all the good it will do you when your head rolls across the floor,' Chase said, then he looked over his shoulder at Elspeth. 'Say goodbye to your lover, darling.'

Chase's lips twisted into an ugly sneer, a smug expression as if he had already won. Elspeth ran for me, but Chase held out a hand, trapping her with an invisible barrier. She could not get near me, and I was relieved. If she couldn't get in the way, she would be safe. I only wished I'd gotten more time with her.

I could see the shadows moving as he chanted words I didn't recognise, sharpening into a sort of blade. I knew Marcus wasn't going to make it then. I looked at Elspeth, offering her a smile as tears dripped onto her cheeks. 'Look away, love,' I said softly. She didn't need to see what happened next.

She shook her head, her body trembling harder, her eyes flashing. The scent of a storm grew stronger. Wind began to whip through her hair. Chase clicked his tongue in irritation, casting a glance at her before returning to the task at hand. He threw his hands out, and the shadow blade hurtled towards me.

'No!' Elspeth shrieked. Glass shattered, time seemed to slow as the shards drifted through the air. The blade dissipated, as if it had been struck. Lightning struck sporadically outside as her feet slowly lifted from the ground until her toes were hovering just above the splintering floor. Her eyes blazed, the wind blew harder.

'Ellie, calm down,' Chase said, raising his hands as if in surrender.

'Don't call me that,' she snarled in a voice that wasn't hers. She flicked her hand at him, sending him flying across the room. He hit the wall with a loud crash. Another flick of her hand released me from my bindings, and I fell to the ground. Bloody rings marred my wrists and neck. I pushed myself to my feet, but she already had her back to me, her eyes trained on Chase as if she was a predator eying her prey.

Chase swallowed hard, and that scared the crap out of me. I'd never seen a witch lose control like that before, though I had heard stories of it happening, and none of them ended well.

'You wanted my power, Chase. So have it,' she said with a cruelty that sent a shiver down my spine. She slowly raised her hands at her sides. Shards of glass obeyed her command and slowly rose, their sharpest points turning towards the warlock. Without warning, she shot her hands forward, sending the shards hurtling towards him. He cried out as hundreds pierced his body. Blood soaked his clothes, dripping slowly to the floor from his fingertips. He dropped to his knees, and her lips curled. She was enjoying this, like a cat toying with a mouse.

Marcus and his team burst into the building, their eyes widening in shock. Marcus looked from Elspeth to me, and I shook my head, but I wasn't convincing him to stay his hand. Chase wasn't going anywhere. She may not have killed him yet, but he was bleeding at an alarming rate, and from the way his arms dangled uselessly at his sides, he wasn't going to be casting any time soon.

I slowly walked towards Elspeth, having no idea what the fuck I was going to say. All I knew was I needed to talk her down before Marcus took her out. 'Elspeth, you need to calm down,' I said.

The exact wrong thing to say.

The wind blew more violently, picking up dust and debris and flinging it around the room. 'He has to die,' she said in that strange voice, her eyes never leaving Chase.

'He'll get what's coming to him, love. But right now, you need to come back to me before you lose yourself,' I said soothingly as I reached for her hand. When my fingers were entwined with hers, she finally looked at me, but she felt so far away. 'Come back to me, witchling.'

A conflicted look twisted her face as she fought to control the power raging inside her. The wind began to ease, and little by little, her feet began to lower until they were on the ground once more. I pulled her into my arms. 'That's it, love. That's it. Come back to me.'

The wind died down suddenly, as if a door had been closed on it, the lightning outside ceased, and her body slumped against mine as if all the energy had been drained from her. I lifted her into my arms and she looked up at me as if she could barely keep her eyes open.

'I'm sorry,' she said.

'Don't be sorry, love. You saved me,' I said, trying not to show her the relief that washed through me. For one terrible moment, I thought I was going to lose her. 'What do you say we go home now?'

'What about –'

'Marcus will take it from here,' I said, cutting her off. If she never said that monster's name again it would be too soon.

'That's right,' Marcus said, his voice completely calm, as if he hadn't just seen her lose control of her magic. 'Get some rest, Elspeth, we'll take care of it.'

'Okay,' she said, resting her head against my shoulder. Her eyes fluttered closed, and she slipped into unconsciousness.

'If she ever scares me like that again, I might kill her,' I muttered, feeling completely exhausted as all the tension drained from me.

Marcus laughed heartily. 'Oh please, as if you have it in you.'

I let out a sigh. He was right, of course, but I was in no hurry to repeat the experience. With Chase in the care of the Enforcers, she was safe now.

'Take her home, we've got it from here.'

'Thanks, Marcus,' I said, but he waved me off as if he didn't want to hear it. He began barking orders as I traced us back home.

CHAPTER 18

Elspeth

I cracked open my eyes. They felt heavy, as if someone was holding them down. My body ached all over. When I looked around the room, it was dark and still, but the warmth in the air told me it was still daylight outside.

Beside me, Roman was sitting in a chair, his head resting on the mattress, blonde hair falling over his face. He looked exhausted. How long had I been out? How long had he been watching over me before he finally succumbed to sleep?

As if he sensed me watching him, he sat up. His eyes met mine, and relief washed over him. 'You're finally awake.'

'How long was I out?'

'Three days. Angèlie said you would wake, but I was starting to have my doubts,' he said, gripping my hand a little tighter.

'Three days?' Goddess, I must have used an enormous amount of power. I hardly remembered any of it, almost as if someone else had taken over my body and left when the work was done. A classic sign that a witch did not have control of her magic. 'What happened to Chase?'

'He's being taken care of. You don't have to think about him anymore. In fact, I forbid it.'

'You forbid it, do you?' I asked, raising my eyebrow. There were some females who liked being ordered about by males, but I was not one of them.

'Don't look at me like that.' He stood up and kissed my forehead, then fixed me with his gaze again. 'Can you blame me for not wanting my bride to think about another male?'

I couldn't keep the smile from my face. As I looked into those dark eyes, I felt like everything I'd suffered for the past two years had all been worth it. It had brought me to Roman, and he was pretty great. Though it would be a cold day in hell before I told him that. His ego was big enough already.

'Don't ever scare me like that again,' he said, gazing into my eyes, his fingers caressing my jaw. 'I thought I was going to lose you.'

'I hate to break it to you, but you're stuck with me now.'

He kissed me softly, as if he was afraid of hurting me. He looked as if he wanted to say something but he remained silent.

'What is it?'

'I suppose now would be a good time to tell you that your curse is broken,' he said.

My eyes shot open wide. 'What? How?'

'The way Angèlie explained it was that all that power you used fried the system. You overloaded it, or something.'

'My own magic was more powerful than his curse. That's what she meant when she told me I had the power to break it.'

'Why didn't she explain it like that? That makes much more sense.'

'Because she's a tricky voodoo priestess, and I suspect she likes messing with you,' I said, surprised at how easy it was to laugh with him now. I felt so carefree. Finally, I didn't have to look over my shoulder, I didn't have to run. I could settle down. I could have a life.

And my family would remember me. My friends, my coven. Hopefully not that cop I'd used my curse on so he'd let me go after he caught me shoplifting...

'What are you thinking?' Roman asked, almost as if he dreaded the answer.

'I think I need to go home,' I said. He nodded solemnly as if he'd been expecting this. 'Will you come with me?'

'You want to introduce me to your family? They're not going to stake me, are they?'

I laughed at the idea of my erratic mother staking a vampire. That was a scene that belonged in a comedy special. 'I want them to meet the male I love.'

'Alright. When do you want to go?'

'As soon as it's dark.'

I almost couldn't believe that after two years, I was finally going home.

***

I'd had to wait for nightfall to come home. Now that the curse was gone, my old life was waiting for me. My family, my friends, my coven all remembered me now. But for the first time since this all began, I didn't want my old life back, I had something else I wanted, something that was mine.

'So, this is where you grew up. It's...quaint,' Roman said.

I smacked him playfully. 'Don't be an arse. What do you think my parents will say when they find out you're three centuries older than me?'

'You're not going to tell them that, are you?' he asked, a look of horror on his face that made me laugh.

'Depends how good you are.'

I'd wanted to go home first, to see my parents, but I knew they weren't there, I could feel it, somehow. Since my magic had properly awakened, I was feeling a lot of new things. They were with the coven, they were searching for me. I could feel their magic prickling on my skin, soft and gentle like sunlight.

'Are you ready?' Roman asked, taking my hand in his and squeezing it reassuringly.

Two years I'd spent wishing they'd remember me, two years running and hiding and being totally alone. The last time I was here, I'd been preparing for my initiation, the day that was supposed to be the proudest of my life, and instead, I'd been cursed. Now that I was back, I was nervous. But I was as ready as I was ever going to be. I nodded and led him into the building.

The coven was seated in a circle, hands joined. A map dotted with blood lay in the centre, no doubt a mixture of my mother and father's. They were looking for me. It was why I could feel their magic.

'It's not working, Martha,' one of the council members said. She was an older woman with sympathy in her eyes. Her name was Agatha, the oldest member of the coven. When I was small, she would find me sulking after failing another spell at school. She'd give me a cookie and tell me *all things are better with sugar*.

'No, we have to keep trying!' my mother said, her voice cracking with desperation. 'We have to find her.'

'It's not working because I'm here,' I said, my voice more timid than I would have liked. After spending so long being forgotten, it was strange to suddenly call attention to myself.

All heads turned to me, but my eyes were on my parents. My mother gasped, tears springing to her eyes. She always was quick with her emotions; quick to cry, quick to anger. My father always joked that she was part furie. My mother tried to run to me, but my father stopped her, eyeing Roman suspiciously.

'Who have you brought with you?' he asked firmly.

'This is Roman,' I said. 'He's –'

'A vampire,' my father finished.

'Yes, he is,' I said, taking his hand and holding my head high to show I was not ashamed of that. 'He's the one who helped me break the curse.'

My mother let out a frustrated noise as she shook my father off. 'Honestly, Thomas,' she chided before running to me, flinging her arms around my neck and damn near squeezing the life out of me. But I didn't care. Tears spilled down my cheeks as I embraced her, letting her familiar scent envelop me.

'I'm so sorry, baby,' she sobbed as she stroked my hair the way she used to do when I was young. 'I'm so sorry.'

'It wasn't your fault,' I said.

My mother pulled back and sniffed loudly. She wiped her eyes and smiled up at Roman. 'Now, I know that vampires think a bite is all that need be done, but you'd best prepare yourself for a witch wedding,' she said brightly, only a hint of warning in her voice, though I knew she was far more serious than she was letting on.

I groaned with embarrassment, my hand shooting to cover the mark on my neck. I should have covered the mystical brand. At least until I was ready for my mother to go wedding crazy.

But Roman smiled wide. 'I'll participate in whatever ceremonies you like.'

My mother beamed, and I groaned again. 'You're making this worse,' I hissed at him, but that only seemed to increase his amusement. Bastard.

'There's so much to prepare. I've been waiting for this since the day she was born!' my mother declared happily.

'Daddy, are you going to frown at me the whole night?' I asked, finally turning my attention to my father. I wasn't in the habit of using that endearment, he'd been *Dad* since I was ten and too cool for such a childish name.

His frown deepened. 'You learnt that from your mother.' But then his frown fell away as he shook his head. 'I would have preferred a warlock, but no one has ever been able to tell our Ellie what to do,' he said. That was about as close to approval as we were going to get, and although I hated that nickname, I let it slide because it meant I was getting what I wanted.

'Have you eaten?' my mother asked. 'You look thin.'

'Dinner would be nice,' I said with a warm smile. It felt like forever since I'd had my mother's cooking.

'We'd better say our goodbyes then,' my father said. That was just like him. No matter the situation, he was sure to be proper at all times.

I smiled at the commotion around me. Each member of the coven came to me with a hug and tears or kind words. Agatha babbled about arranging my initiation right away and started muttering about finding a suitable house for me and my new family.

When they'd all said their piece, I was exhausted, but in a good way. I told my parents we'd meet them back at the house, I wanted to walk around the town. It felt so strange to be back. My mother was reluctant to let me out of her sight but relented. It wasn't like I was going far.

'Do you want to stay here?' Roman asked when we were alone. I looked up at him but his face was unreadable.

'There was a time when I wanted nothing more than to come back home. I dreamt of my initiation and being surrounded by my family, my coven.'

'But not anymore?' he asked cautiously, almost as if he was afraid to hope.

'See, I met this vampire while I was in Chicago, and he showed me a whole new world. I kind of like it there,' I teased.

He pulled me into his arms and captured my lips in a searing kiss. 'Good. I don't think I'd adjust well to country living.'

I laughed and shook my head. 'But I won't be sitting in your apartment all day waiting for you to come home, either.'

'No? Then what are your plans?'

'I want to be an enforcer,' I said.

Roman's eyes widened in surprise. 'You want to join a vampire law enforcement agency?'

'Why not? You protect others from malevolent magics and beings. Who better to join your team than a powerful witch?'

'That awakening thing gave you a big head, didn't it?'

I smacked him on the arm. 'Brute.'

He grinned at me. 'Well, Marcus will be happy.'

'But not you?'

'You can't expect me to be happy that you want to put yourself in harm's way on a daily basis,' he said.

'Well, you'll just have to make sure you're there to protect me,' I said. I stretched up on my toes and pressed my lips to his.

'Right now, I have other things in mind,' he said, looking down at me with a burning heat in his eyes. 'When can we get out of here?'

I smiled as a warmth began to ignite in my body. 'You have to survive dinner with my parents first.'

'Yes. I don't think your father likes me very much,' Roman said.

'He'll come around. He never could deny my mother anything, and she likes you just fine.'

'Well, I suppose we have something in common then,' he said and dropped a kiss to my lips. As we walked towards my childhood home, his fingers laced with mine, I felt lighter than I ever had before. For the first time in my life, I felt excited for what the future might bring.

THE END

ABOUT LORELEI JOHNSON

Lorelei Johnson is an Australian romance author, primarily writing Paranormal Romance and Fantasy Romance. She graduated from Flinders University, where she studied English Literature and Creative Writing before she discovered her degree was useless and she hated studying in an institution. She went into administrative work where she learnt just enough business sense to start publishing her own books.

Lorelei is fuelled by caffeine and sarcasm, priding herself as a true 90's kid. She labels her self-publishing as anti-establishment, but really she's just a chicken who decided to avoid the gatekeepers all together and enjoy the freedom to write whatever the heck she likes. Through her writing, she likes to explore the many facets of love and revel in a little magic and a little smut, of course.

THE STORYTELLER

by Louise Murchie

CHAPTER 1

Tabitha

The stabbing pain increases in intensity to almost unbearable levels by the time the hospital looms into view. I'm determined to get to where I'm going by myself, though it's excruciating to do so. The rattling of the bus and its ability to hit almost every pot hole and drain Birmingham City Council hadn't yet filled is astounding. It finally grinds to a halt and I fight my way out, trying to focus on the doors of the huge, curved white building before me. The Queen Elizabeth Hospital has undergone some major changes since I was here last. Now it was bigger, cleaner and also far more confusing.

I manage to stagger to a front desk, clutching the letter I'd scribbled down a few days before. I have no idea if I am at the right desk, and I no longer care. I just know that I require medical help. Now.

"Help, please!" I manage to utter at the smiling nurse behind a screen before the latest bout of side-splitting pain brings me to my knees and with it, blissful darkness.

***

Beep.

Beep.

The sound is regular, steady, and constant. I am warm and comfortable, something I haven't felt for years—not since I'd run away to protect myself. I have no idea how long I've been here. The bus ride is the last thing I remember. I adjust my position, making someone near me react. Someone I hadn't realised was there.

"Tabs?" The voice I'd dreamed about hearing so many times, whispers my nickname softly in disbelief and shock. I'd been gone for three years. I'd knowingly put him and his family into the spotlight of social services and probably the police. I just hope my departing note has helped them in some small way.

I try to open my eyes, but they seem glued shut. I try again, but still, they wouldn't open. I move my left hand, but it is sore, and something prevents me from moving it.

"Take it easy, lovely. That's got a cannula in it. Try the other one?" His voice suggests, somewhat stronger now, but still hesitant. I rub my nearest eye, then open them, only to shut them again as I groan against the light.

"What's wrong? Is it too bright?" His voice rises, a chair scrapes against the obvious hard floor, and then there's a swooshing sound, and it's a little darker. "Try that," he proposes. I try opening my eyes again, and I manage it this time, the bright sunlight no longer blinding me.

"Hey you," he whispers at me. I can only smile as his image goes blurry and for the first time in three years, I cry.

***

A nurse bustles around us. My crying sets off the machine that is constantly beeping, not liking that I am suddenly taking deep breaths, my heart rate increasing.

"Do you want him to go?" she asks quietly, into my ear. I shake my head slowly. Her hair is pulled back, but it's starting to get that salt-and-pepper look of an older woman. The nurse has kind soft brown eyes, a gentle smile and a slightly weathered, rounded face. He's the only person I want anywhere near me right now. He or his parents are the only ones I know I can rely on.

"Okay. Did he upset you?" She asks. I gently nod no.

She sighs, and I whisper, "happy." She smiles at me and then looks across at Frank.

"Try and make her stay calm," she tells him. "She needs her rest. That was a huge operation." He nods, and then she departs out of the door which closes quietly behind her.

"I didn't mean to upset you," he sighs to me when we're alone again. He's sitting across to my right, holding the hand that doesn't have drugs and everything else coming into me.

"You didn't," I whisper. It's been so long since I talked to anyone, I've nearly forgotten how to.

He moves the chair closer to my head. "I'm told you're allowed a drink," he tells me, holding up a small cup and a straw. I nod, and he helps me before I lean back with a happy sigh and close my eyes.

"You came," I state, still disbelieving my own ears and other senses. I knew he would; even if I don't get to stay in his life now, I knew he'd come.

"Always would for you. I've got so many questions, but they can wait for when you're stronger. Do you know what was wrong with you?" he asks. His voice is surer, gentle. He's changed a lot in the last three years. Gone is the chubby, older boy from a few streets away. Now, he's a strapping, fit, well-dressed god of a man that's sitting by me. If I hadn't heard his voice, I would not have recognised him. I shake my head slowly, unable to move it much faster than I am right now.

"Your appendix was rupturing," he tells me. I nod, understanding that the pain in my side, the flu-like feeling I'd had for days was down to something fixable. I'm glad I came home.

"I did hurt," I rasp, finding it strange looking at him. "I don't anymore," I say, trying to smile. I have no idea what I look like now, I haven't seen a mirror or my reflection for months. "Where's my bag?" I ask him. I wrote him a letter, explaining in writing what I thought I might never get to tell him. Since I can just about speak, it can do the job for me.

He moves, and I watch as he goes to the side cabinet by the machine and pulls my bag up, then brings it around to where he was sitting. I watch him as his t-shirt ripples with his movements, lost in the fact that the boy I crushed on in my younger teenage days is now an Adonis.

He looks at me, and I smile. "Front pocket," I tell him. He opens it and pulls out some envelopes. There should only be two. The third I was holding when I stumbled into the hospital. That much I do now remember.

"You wrote me a letter?" He asks. I smile and nod as best I can.

He gives me a look that sends a shiver of fear through me. "Nothing bad," I croak, and he moves the bag to sit back down. "Read it," I tell him. Honestly, talking is a lot of effort right now, and as he tears open the letter, I close my eyes to rest them.

CHAPTER 2

Frank

    I watch as the girl I adored from afar rests up in a hospital bed. After the nurse has been, I'm left holding an envelope as Tabitha goes back to sleep.

    Before I read what she's written, I pay attention again to the hollowness of her cheeks, the dark circles under her eyes, and her bony frame. Tabitha was always slim, but this version of her I know is sick. I have to keep that in mind as I read her letter.

Hey Frank,

If you're reading this, I'm in a bad way, more than I was when I ran away. I'm going to try and go back to Birmingham and aim for the QE. I know it's a trek to get there from Tipton, but that might be as far as I can get, and it's the best in the area by far.

Anyway, the pain in my side is bad, and I feel I'm getting a fever or the flu, I can't decide which. Knowing my luck, it'll be both.

I know you'll want to know what happened, and I hope I get to explain it to you, but in short, my step-dad was a piece of work. I know from national newspapers that he's killed mum. He's doing time for it, and I wish I could send him to hell myself. But I am not strong enough, I never was. He was and probably still is, a drunken letch and a brute. I also now know about my little brother, Shane; though I don't know where he is or how he's doing. Can you find out? Would you, please? I really want to know where he is when I get to see you.

I didn't feel safe. I needed to not be in his line of fire. Mum wouldn't leave him, though I tried to get her to. I couldn't let him force himself on me or carry out his threat. My first always had to be you. That's why I ran. I only intended to stay away until I was an adult, but I didn't want to go back, knowing he'd find out where I was as soon as I got in touch with you or mum.

Reading about mum's death in the newspapers was hard. I'll find her grave when I'm better, or maybe I'll meet her as a ghost, I'm not sure which, yet. I know he's locked away, which is why I know I can finally come home.

I'm sorry for all the hurt I've ever put you and your wonderful parents through. I hope my letter to you all was evidence enough for the authorities. And proof I was alive. If my leaving didn't make mum leave that drunken brute, nothing would.

My train to Birmingham is tomorrow, and I hope I get to see you soon.

Again, I'm so sorry. There's a letter for your parents.

I don't deserve to ask, but please, please be here when I wake up, if I wake up. Please?

Tabs.

    I swipe at my eyes, unaware that I am crying at her words. Now I know why she left, and it explains the two years before that too. I'd love to smash her step-dad's face in for her, but there's no way he's getting out of Long Lartin, unless it's in a body bag. Murder and child endangerment secured his place in that maximum security jail.
    As for her little half-brother, I know exactly where he is and how he's doing. I smile, knowing that I'll at least be able to help her out on that front. I fold the letter up, tuck it away and send my parents a message in our family group.

Frank: She woke up for a little bit. Gave me a letter she'd written. She's written one for you both. Best you read it when you're here.
Mum: I'll be there as soon as your dad is home to take over.
Dad: I'll be there in half an hour. How's the little man doing?
Mum: He's fine, as always! He knows something is different, though. Did Tabs say why she left?
Frank: Yes. It's in the letter. I'll let you and dad read it. Dad, come with mum. I'll take over from you both. Bring the tornado.
Dad: You're sure?
Frank: Absolutely. He can ride home in my car.
Mum: She doesn't know, does she?
Frank: She knows more than we thought she did. Best you read her letter.
Mum: Okay! Be there soon.

I sit back in the hard chair, watching Tabitha sleep. The doctor said she wouldn't be awake much when she started waking up. Her appendix was very close to rupturing, and from her note, she had been suffering for a little while. She'll need plenty of rest, clean drinks, and to do nothing heavy for a few weeks. If I know mum, she'll have finished sorting out the spare bedroom for Tabitha.

CHAPTER 3

Tabitha

When I next open my eyes, Frank's parents are at my bedside, the letter I wrote to them open and on their lap. I smile at them, and they beam back at me. Katie, Frank's mum, is stroking my face, but her eyes are swollen and red.

"You're too thin," she tells me. I chuckle. It's hard to eat properly when you're living rough.

"Let her be, Kate," Phil scolds her, though gently.

"My letter," I try to begin. Suddenly, Katie's crying. I was brutally honest with them, telling them why I ran.

"We know, and we know where Shane is." Phil's voice is strained and Katie turns to him.

"Where?" I ask. I want to sit up, but I'm not sure that's best right now. I still haven't had a chance to speak with the doctor, and I haven't the strength to move. "I didn't know I had a brother until the newspapers mentioned him."

"At home, with Frank. We've been fostering him since the incident with your mum. Thanks to your note to the police when you vanished."

Katie is still holding my hand, and I squeeze it. "Water?" I ask through parched lips. She nods, lets go of my hand and pours me a drink, then helps me drink it through a straw, just like Frank did earlier.

"What time is it? When did Frank leave?" I ask.

"It's about eight o'clock. Frank will have Shane in bed by now, after his bath." Katie looks so proud, and I can't help but smile. Her family has always looked out for me, but I couldn't make them face my stepdad. I had wanted to be back a year ago, but I was still too afraid of him.

Then, I read in a national newspaper that my mum had been murdered by him when he was high on drugs. From what I read from autopsy evidence from the trial, my step-dad had physically forced her to take them, and she'd had a bad reaction to them. He had been in an almost-drunken state when the police broke in, thanks to the neighbours hearing Shane constantly crying. The brother I didn't know I had.

"You took him in?" I ask gently, shocked that they would do that for him.

Katie looks at Phil who looks at me. "Should we not have?"

I can't tell them how grateful I am, and I burst into tears again. They saved my little brother. Okay, he has half of that dip shit for brains' DNA in him, but he's a part of mum. He's linked to me.

Katie looks at Phil in alarm. "Thank you!" I blurt out between sobs, which brings in the formidable nurse from yesterday as the machine, once again, goes nuts. She looks at me and decides it's not because they've upset me or that I want them to leave. It's almost as though she knows my history, which I'm guessing she probably does by now.

"More news?" She asks as she checks my vitals again. She looks at Katie and Phil. They nod.

"I need to know. I don't care how upset I get." I look over to Phil and Katie. "You saved him. You have no idea how grateful I am to you both. The debt...," I stop. The debt of raising a child that isn't theirs with no income for him.

"He's fostered to us, which means the state pays for his basic care. But Tabs, he's your little brother. There was no way he was going into a home when we could step in." Katie holds my hand, reassuring me with soft squeezes and thumb strokes.

"I'm so glad!" I blurt out, sobbing again. Phil leans across and hands me a tissue.

"The lawyer will visit when you're better able to handle the will your mother left. Until then, he's looked after, cared for and safe."

I nod slightly, letting the tears fall. I wonder why I stayed away a year too long.

CHAPTER 4

Frank

Mum and dad come home around ten, looking exhausted. I'm guessing they talked with Tabs and I'm keen to hear what they discussed. It can't have been much.

"She knew about Shane, but not where he was," Mum explains as she nurses a Disaronno with ice. I've never seen mum hold a drink like she is right now, I'm afraid she'll crush the glass. "I thought she was angry at us to start with when we told her he was here."

Dad grabs her hand. "She's weak from the operation and living rough, love. She didn't mean it as it sounded, and she did say she was glad we'd taken him in. I think it was a bit of a shock to her."

I blink at them. "She must've thought he'd be in a children's home or something, expecting the worst situation for him to be in." I look at dad as I try to think like Tabs for a moment. "If I'd been hiding for three years, because of my stepdad, I'd be expecting the worst too. Him in a home, not loved, not cared for, alone...," I stop. "It was probably sheer relief when you told her mum, nothing more."

Dad stands and sighs, pouring himself a generous single malt and downs it in one. I blink at him, eyes wide.

"What else did she say? You two never drink, not like this." Tabitha could hardly string a sentence together earlier, she can't have said much to mum. Then I remember the pain relief the doctors said they were putting through her. In her weakened, postoperative body, I'll wager they'd be knocking her sideways, and not just physically.

"She asked us about Shane. We showed her pictures, but she just wept. Oh, Phil, we did the right thing, didn't we?"

Dad goes to mum and hugs her, nodding.

"She's not herself, Mum. Did you see how haunted she looked? And the surgeon did say he was putting her on some quite heavy drugs, as she'd been living rough, maybe picking up goodness knows what. With what they had to do to her to save her...," I let the statement hang. This isn't the Tabitha we know, but there's a reason for that. There has to be.

"You're probably right, it's just been exhausting," mum tells me and I can only nod.

"For us all. Let's give it a few days, let's not talk about the important things with her until she's off the drugs and able to think straight. She's got a lot to catch up on and she did ask in her note when she was admitted that they contact us. She trusts us. She never trusted lightly before." My reasons and excuses for her are now exhausted. But I *know* Tabitha.

"I've already called Laurence James," I explain. "I have a shoot to do tomorrow, but as it's only over in Lichfield, I can head across, do the shoot then go to Tabitha. She'll have had a night's rest on the drugs and her brain will have processed some of her worries."

Dad looks at me. "You think she's been worried?" He asks.

I nod. "I can't show you the note she left for me, it contains a few personal statements," I let it hang, knowing that dad will pick up on that. He just nods, but his smile is one of his knowing ones. "But she told me she knew of Shane because of the newspapers. She's been imagining the worst for a year or so, I guess."

I can only imagine what's maybe been going through her mind. She was quiet and unassuming when she was younger and three years of avoidance will have fueled that. However, she's home now.

"I'm going to bed. I need to be up in the morning to drive over to Lichfield. They know I want an efficient turnaround for personal reasons."

I kiss my mother goodnight and hug my father, checking on Shane as I go to bed. He's fast asleep in his toddler bed and little sleep sack, content and unaware that the only family member that we're aware he has, has come home.

His hair is a darker shade than Tabitha's, but as I look at him, I see her. Their nose and eye shape they must get from their mum. I smile and head to bed, hoping my mind can shut down.

***

The following morning as I drink my protein shake, the phone pings. The shoot is on, as arranged, and the promise of efficient use of time is made. They'll have someone from the fashion house I'm modelling for to check things out as the shots come in, which is ideal.

I quietly head out to my car and head to Lichfield, grateful that the motorways are behaving.

***

By mid-morning, the fashion house photographer of Laurence James have agreed on the shots for the clothes the other guys and I had been modelling. The bonus is that I get to keep them this time. The three-piece suit looks particularly interesting with its square patterns that remind me of tartan. I nod to Omar as we change into our regular clothes, packing the suits away into their bags to take home.

"You okay? You seem... focused on something else," he asks me as we wipe the makeup off. Before Tabs left, I would never have thought I needed to wear makeup, but being a fashion and sports influencer means I need to have a certain look. Thankfully, I don't need a lot and neither does Omar.

"Remember I told you ages ago about that girl that ran away?" I ask, wiping the last of the makeup off and throwing the wipe into the bin. I'd told him about her when we both started with this fashion company.

Omar nods. "The one you fancied when you were growing up?" He grins at me, then he goes wide-eyed. "She's come back?" he asks, his voice quieter.

"Yeah, that one. Only, she's quite sick."

He stops and gapes at me. "What the heck are you doing here?"

"She's in the hospital and getting better, I've been with her most days. She woke up yesterday, and it's been hard explaining to her what's happening and trying to get answers."

He slaps me on the back and chuckles slightly. "Mate, give yourself and her the time. If she's that sick, she's not going to be thinking straight. And her coming home like that, that will have been a shock to you and your folks. Take it easy on yourselves."

I grin at him, taking his extended hand but grabbing his arm and pulling him in for a hug. "Cheers, mate. I needed to hear that."

He nods at me after giving me a resounding thump on the back. "Let me know if you need some help," he tells me. "Now, go, Romeo!" His teasing tone is welcomed, but Omar is about the only person apart from mum and dad, who knows a thing about how I once felt for Tabitha.

***

Tabs is sitting up in bed when I walk in, though her head is against the pillows and her eyes are closed. About ten minutes later, she wakes and smiles at me.

"Hey, you," she greets me in the age-old way we used to, and slowly she blinks herself awake. I smile back at her and sigh.

"What's wrong?" she asks me. "Please tell me I didn't upset your mum and dad." Her eyes go wide and tears begin to form.

"I had a busy morning, and you can talk with mum and dad later," I tell her, taking her hand. I notice the cannula is gone and across her left hand is a huge plaster.

"Busy doing what?" I can see her swallowing. "You don't look anything like how I remember," she whispers.

I chuckle and let it show. "Yeah, I changed that year. I decided I wasn't going to wait around for what I wanted anymore, and I started achieving my dreams." Her smile goes wide and her eyes shine, but not with tears this time.

"You went and changed your body. You never said you wanted to look like Hugh Jackman," she cocks her head slightly. "Or a Hollywood star." I beam at her, proud that she noticed. Is that what she was doing yesterday, checking me out? Perhaps she was; I pull my shoulders back a little.

"I was a lot of things when you left Tabs." I take her right hand and stroke it gently, lowering my voice. I never explained why to mum and dad, not really. Tabs leaving messed my head up. "I channelled all my thoughts and emotions into something constructive. Walking past a gym one day, I walked in. I got shown the ropes and did my first set of weights. Loved it."

I look at her in the hospital bed; she looks a little better today. I notice her eyes dart over me, focusing on my visible tattoos. "I used my brain too, I tried to study for my accountant's qualifications like dad wanted, but it's not me, not what I wanted. I took sports studies at college. While I can, I'll earn as much as I can from modelling and enjoy the clothes I get and the sports training that I do through the gym. I've met some great guys."

"So... you're a model?" She shifts in bed to turn to me as best she can, her eyes wide. "What's that like?" she asks me, her voice excited. I tell her about the fun parts of it, leaving the tedious, annoying parts and the sometimes crazy fans out of my description.

"As for the gym, it helped having something to do that was physical. I could take the pain out on the bench presses and let my mind wander, which was then free to absorb the information for my sports exams."

"I knew you hated the idea of being an accountant," she says. Her voice is quiet today, but steadier. She's asked questions today, and engaged with me, which is good. I sit back and watch as a nurse comes in with the doctor. Tabitha sits up straight and grips my hand.

"Ms Reid, good afternoon, how are you?"

Tabitha smiles at him. "I'm better, thank you. Sorry, you are?"

"Doctor Ramesh, I operated on you. Now, can I have a look at your surgery site to see how it's healing? I'll also explain what had to happen. Is this your boyfriend?"

Tabitha looks across at me. "Yes," she answers without a second of hesitation. I gape and close my mouth.

"Okay, if you're happy for him to stay whilst I check you over?" he asks, and Tabitha nods. "Let's get you laying back down shall we?" He nods to the nurse and the bed is lowered, then flattened. The blankets are pulled back and Tabitha's lower stomach is revealed. I watch as the doctor gently peels back the dressing. There's an angry-looking wound, but the doctor seems quite pleased.

"We would have preferred we go in via laparoscopic, but given that you were unconscious almost upon your arrival and with your note, we didn't want to take a chance it had ruptured."

He pokes around a little but Tabitha doesn't make a sound.

"This doesn't hurt now?" He prods deeply around where her scar now is, making me flinch.

Tabitha shakes her head. "No. A week ago, I'd have been in tears, curled up. It doesn't hurt today."

The doctor smiles and then asks the nurse to replace the dressing with a fresh one.

"As I was just explaining," he says, looking between me and Tabs. "We had to open you up, and I've used dissolving stitches. I do need you to keep it dry for five more days. You can wash but in the sink, not a bath or a shower. Given that you were on the streets for a while, I've also pumped you full of antibiotics to help clear out any underlying infections that may have been the cause of your appendix to do what it did. The surgery itself was straightforward." He moves out of the way as the nurse tucks Tabitha's gown around her and the blankets back down. "You were lucky that you understood something was very wrong. Another few hours, and that appendix would have caused lots more problems."

I understand what he's saying could have happened; she was close to her appendix exploding. I've been reading up on this since we were told why she was admitted. Developing peritonitis can be fatal, and given that she was seriously malnourished, they fed her via a nasogastric tube for a few days while the antibiotics kicked in.

"Thank you," Tabitha quietly tells him. He smiles at her and folds his hands over his lap.

"Now, I expect you to be in for about five more days. I'd like to see you eating. You scared us with the way you came in, but I'm hoping the worst is over."

"You're hoping?" she asks. I can hear the fear in her voice. The doctor sits on the edge of the bed and looks at both of us.

"Surgery of this type carries a risk that I hope I've alleviated. One in five people develops an abscess if the appendix ruptures. Yours was *dangerously* close to doing that, but I won't know if you have any abscesses until I check you over in five days. Until then, you're here in our care, and we will get you better."

He casts Tabitha a reassuring smile, and she smiles gently back at him.

"Have you eaten today?" he asks.

"I had some toast for breakfast, and I ordered lunch and dinner this morning," she tells him. He looks across at me.

"I suggest some extra protein bars, or the like, for Ms Reid." I nod, and he looks back at her. "You'll heal better if your body has some energy inside it. You're running on fumes." He stands up slowly, I guess so he doesn't knock or nudge the bed.

"I'll come by and see you tomorrow. Rest and eat until then." He smiles and walks out of the room, followed by the nurse.

Tabitha sighs and leans back against the pillows. She's trying to fish around for something underneath, but she gives up.

"What's up, Tabs?"

She sighs. "There's a remote that controls the bed," she tells me. I look around and I find it quickly. It was out of reach of Tabs' right hand. I give it to her, and she slowly raises the head part of her bed. She sighs contentedly.

I'm about to ask her what she ordered for lunch when an older lady comes in, carrying a food tray, wearing a polo shirt with the words 'Hospital Helper' on it and a logo of the Care Trust.

Tabitha smiles, and the food tray is placed on the bed table, which is wheeled into position. I watch as Tabitha raises herself to be more upright.

"We have tea and coffee there," the staff member points out as she leaves. "I'll be back to collect the tray in about an hour." I thank her, but tea and coffee just don't fit with my diet. I pull out a protein shake bottle, add in the protein mix and shake it up. Tabitha watches me intently.

"That's your lunch?" She asks me, her voice rising in surprise.

I nod. "I'll eat at dinner, but this is enough for what I need to maintain this," I motion up and down my body, and Tabitha licks her lips. My mind goes back to her note: *'I always intended on you being my first.'* I swig a mouthful of shake to avoid asking her about that part of her note.

Tabitha gets started on her lunch; a sandwich, some jelly, fruit and water. She chews the sandwich, and I'm tempted to offer her my protein shake. I look around for a cup and spy a plastic one, then I pour some out and hand it to her.

"It's gotta be better than that," I tell her, motioning to the food on the plate. That has to be the blandest, driest thing on the menu.

She drinks it and nods. "It certainly tastes a heck of a lot better!" she tells me with a grin on her face. She tries to open the bottle of water that's a part of her meal, but she can't, and I open it for her. For the next hour, I assist her in doing little basic things, such as helping her make her way to the attached bathroom and refill her water jug as I answer questions about her little brother.

"We tell him mummy is in heaven," I explain when she asks what we've told her brother about their mum. I know Tabitha was never a great believer in a God.

"I hope she is," she whispers as she slowly drinks some water. That was an unexpected response.

"Your parents showed me pictures, but I don't remember what he looks like?" She asks. I pull my phone out and show her the album I've been building for the last year. I take her to the start and for ages, she scrolls through images of Shane. From when we took him under our wing at six months old until last night when he was asleep... he's just over two. I have over four hundred. A few times I can see her almost reach out and trace his face on the screen, then she remembers it's a screen and stops herself.

"He can be here with mum in a little while if you'd like?" I offer. She's taking the fact she has a little brother quite well.

She looks at me and smiles. "Maybe, after a nap? I'm quite tired again."

I nod and reach out to stroke her hand, then I pull the table away and let her recline the bed.

"Are you going to go home, or stay here?" she asks me. The WiFi here is not bad, I'm able to work.

"I'd like to be here when you wake up," I tell her. The smile she gives me makes my chest contract, and I flex to ease the tightness.

"I'd really like you to be here," she confirms to me with a weak smile. Then she snuggles down, yawns, pulls the blanket up over her shoulder and closes her eyes. In moments, she's asleep, and I pull my tablet out so I can connect and catch up with my clients.

CHAPTER 5

Frank

Nearly two hours later, Tabitha stirs. I've responded to my clients, confirmed I'll be at two training sessions tonight and agreed with mum that they can bring Shane to meet Tabitha whilst I work.

"Hey, you," I smile at her. She looks a little better, and her stomach growls. She maneuvers the bed so she's sitting up and I pour her a drink, bringing the console table to her. The hospital staff took the dirty plates away not long after Tabitha had gone back to sleep. The nurse has been in too, checking all of Tabitha's vitals. Nothing disturbed Tabs.

"Mum says she'll bring Shane this evening for a quick visit."

Tabitha nods as she drinks a small cup of water. "I wish there was a way to get snacks here." She leans back into the pillows and closes her eyes. I grin and dig around in my backpack for a protein bar. I was going to have it later, but she can have it now. She needs it far more than I do.

I hand her the bar and she looks at me. "You're sure?" she asks. I nod.

"I've boxes of them back home. I've asked mum to bring you a selection of them." She smiles a huge smile at me, and I grin back. "Mum also said she'd bring you some grapes. You still like grapes, don't you?"

Tabitha giggles and nods, going red in the cheeks. I recall one of the first times she and I had met. She'd hidden in our garden shed. We didn't understand why at the time. She could have only been around thirteen. Dad found her, huddled into the back in a big coat, hiding from the wind and the rain.

He'd enticed her in and offered her a warm drink. While his back was turned, she had started eating the grapes in the bowl. The entire bunch was nearly gone whilst dad's back was turned. Once we knew who she was and where she was supposed to be living, we told her she was welcome all the time. I eventually took a liking to the quiet girl being around. She'd do her homework at the kitchen table with me. She wasn't shy, exactly. She was just quiet. But she'd eat anything and everything mum placed down in front of her as if she was never fed. Recalling her note, she probably wasn't.

She wasn't around every day and on the days she was, she left promptly at five o'clock, though. I'm keen to understand why.

"Do you want to talk?" I ask her, sitting back in the chair. We've spoken about Shane, and I know she'll get to meet him soon. There are plenty of things we need to discuss, especially without my parents listening in.

She shakes her head but smiles at me, her brown eyes shining. It's been a long time since I've seen her so animated.

"I don't, but I think you do. So," she smooths down the covers on her bed, "ask."

"Your note...," I begin, and her cheeks colour.

Then she answers me without looking at me. "I've left what few things I had behind to avoid some rough types a few times. The streets...," she shivers. "They're not kind. It's nothing like Conan Doyle writes them. They've got predators, gangs, rules and codes I never knew. I avoided most of them, I didn't want...," She reaches across and takes my hand in hers. "It was always you," she says, her eyes shining.

I lean in, keeping my voice low to not be overheard.

"You thought of me—in that way?" I ask her in a low, raspy voice. I wonder how long I've been on her mind.

She nods. "Regularly. It kept me warm, thinking you'd...," She turns her head away and closes her eyes. I reach a hand around to her jaw and cup her face, which makes her look at me in surprise.

"That I'd want you?" I ask. She nods. She's hardly breathing, or moving. I guess she learnt some skills on the street, she was always so expressive and nervous before, easy to read and understand. I lean in, close enough to maybe kiss her. However, she's too ill at the moment. So, I kiss her on her cheek, softly. "Oh, Tabs...," I lean my head against hers. "I have. I still do, but you need to get a lot better first," I whisper.

"*You* thought of me?" she sighs, her voice just audible. "Romantically?"

I chuckle. She doesn't see it. Maybe if she had she would have run to us, not away. I smile and nod. "I was going to kiss you properly on your sixteenth," I confess. I close my eyes, remembering how I planned it. That night never happened. But I've imagined it so many times in the years she's been away. It's progressed, matured, grown-up.

"Oh!" she replies, and I hear the surprise catching in her voice. "I messed up, didn't I?" she asks, her voice heavy and sullen.

I pull back to see she has closed her eyes and the tears fall softly. "No!" I whisper back, my voice hoarse as I wipe the tears away. "You did what you had to do, Tabs. We'd have faced him off and gone through the courts if we had to. Anything... that I wanted to do was just delayed for a few years. There's been no one but you." I sigh, recalling the few disastrous dates I've been on. "I tried, I've not been a saint, but no one was you."

That makes her cry more, but she's trying to smile, and her hand comes up to cup my face. "I'm so sorry, Frank!" she cries out and suddenly, her lips are on mine. They're soft, salty, and gentle.

"There's no need to be, Tabs. You're alive because of what you did. We get a chance, now." I dry more of her tears with my thumb. "Come on, let's get you cleaned up before that nurse decides I upset you too much," I tease. It gets a laugh from her, at least for now.

***

A different member of the volunteer staff comes in with food a little while later and I look at the time. Mum will be feeding Shane. I'll ask her to bring me something. At least this time Tabitha's meal looks like it's actual food. It's a small roast dinner and she manages to eat most of it.

Frank: Mum, can you make one of my chicken wraps, please? Tabs and I have had a good talk, but I haven't eaten anything, and I don't want to leave her alone.
Mum: Okay. We're nearly finished eating, so I'll make it up to put in the food bag I've prepared for her.
Frank: Don't bring all of Tesco. She can't eat that much!

I know I'm teasing, but my mother is used to the amount of food I can put away. Tabs can barely eat a small meal.

Mum: Do you have any sessions tonight?
Frank: Yes. But not until seven. I'll go straight from here, change there and meet you back at home.

Hospital visiting hours will be over by the time I'm done with my personal training sessions and nearly twelve hours with no contact is going to be hard. I look up at Tabs, an idea forming in my head. I wait until she's finished eating her meal, which she does. Slowly.

"Hey, I have a question. I get given stuff as part of my social profile." I watch as she looks at me with a small, quizzical look.

"Go on," she says as she eats some jelly. The roast potatoes don't look great, and I can't blame her for leaving them. However, the rest of the food on the plate is gone.

"I've got a spare mobile phone. It's new, never been used. I prefer slightly bigger phones, but if I were to get you a contract, would you use it?"

"Why would I use it?" she asks. "Who would want to talk to me?"

I chuckle at her question, she doesn't get it, despite what we said a little while ago. "So, I can call you," I say, putting my head against hers again, trying hard not to laugh too much and hurt her feelings.

"Oh!" I can see her pupils have contracted. She didn't expect me to want to call her, even after what we said? "I won't be away from you forever," she whispers to me.

"I know. But it'll mean I can call you first thing, or send you a message to check up on you when I can't be here...," Being able to text her or send her a secure message would be brilliant. "Or say good night in private," I whisper. My phone pings, and it's a text from mum. Tabs will have to ponder that one on her own.

"Mum and dad are here. Ready to meet Shane?" I ask her, tidying away the plate and everything to do with dinner. She nods and heads to the bathroom to do what she needs to do before the tornado that is her little brother arrives.

CHAPTER 6

Tabitha

Frank telling me he wants to buy me a mobile phone, or give me one, confuses me for a moment. Why would I want to talk to someone else, someone that wasn't him? But then, he's not always here with me. It would make sense, and I can also get the pictures off him of Shane. Perhaps a few of him, too.

His phone pings, and he tells me that my brother is here with his parents. I nod and go to make my way to the bathroom. Frank's there, hovering, helping, ready to catch me if I fall as I'm still a little unsteady on my feet. I need to get used to walking again now my side doesn't hurt anywhere near as much.

Frank helps me climb back into the bed. I almost hate him seeing me like this but I came back because my step-dad is in prison and I trust Frank. No, it's more than trust, though I'm scared to put these feelings into words. Frank has cleared away my dinner plate and I feel sorry that he didn't get to eat a decent meal.

Moments later, his parents are here with a little boy. He is tiny compared to Phil and Frank, but I know it's Shane. Phil picks him up and comes to sit in the chair Frank has just vacated. Katie is whispering to Frank in the corner, handing him boxes of food, and I sigh. She's catered for him, thank goodness. Though being honest, this is his mum, she's brilliant like that.

I focus on Shane and Phil, trying to make eyes at Frank.

"Hey, so you're Shane. Do you know who I am?" I ask him. Looking at him in his little jeans and hoodie, he looks like a miniature version of Frank. He snuggles into Phil, and I just smile.

Phil speaks up. "Hey, Shane, this is your big sister, Tabitha. We've told you lots about her haven't we?" I look at Phil as he looks up at me.

"Have you? What do you know about me? Because I don't know a lot about you," I wink at Frank who looked like he was about to protest, but he just nods and starts eating something Katie brought for him. It looks like a chicken salad wrap.

"Siser," he tells me. He's not pronouncing his T's yet, but the word is unmistakable.

"Yep, that's right, I'm your sister," I say. Frank pulls the lid off a box and comes over to me, placing it on my lap. It's full of grapes. I think Katie's put two bunches in here. Shane watches Frank put the grapes in my reach and he motions a grab with his hand.

"Would you like some grapes?" Phil asks. "What do we say when we want something?"

Shane looks at Phil, then me, then the grapes. "Come on, you can show your sister how good you are with your words," I can see him trying to work out if he can get away with just grabbing the grapes or not. I take one and hold it out.

"What do you say?" I ask him, echoing Phil's teaching.

"Pwese," he says. It's so cute I give him two. Then he holds his hand out for a third after shoving one in his mouth.

"Oh! He needs them cut in half first!" Katie tells me, and I blink.

Phil goes red. "Sorry love, I forgot!"

"Chew properly, Shane," Katie coaxes as she brings over a plastic knife to cut the grapes with. Then I see his little jaw move, and I grin.

"Good boy," Phil praises and Shane lights up, he smiles, showing off half-eaten grapes in his little mouth, and his eyes are bright.

"You're a clever boy," I tell him. He nods a few times, and he seems quite happy sitting on Phil's lap, so I don't try to get him to hug me. Frank comes over and hugs me.

"I need to go to work." He tells me. He doesn't look happy about it. "I'll bring the phone tomorrow. Sleep well!"

"Do an extra set for me," I tease. He turns and grins at me, waves at Shane and his dad and then he's gone out of the hospital room door.

"So, you two...," Katie asks. I blush. She probably always suspected I was keen on her son.

"We're... interested in each other," I quietly admit to her.

"I'm so glad! When you left...," she begins.

"I hurt him—and you both—I know. I'm so sorry," I state, my heart is heavy, just like my voice. "I couldn't ask you to get in the line of fire, not with him. He was violent with mum at times, I just tried to stay out of his way. I couldn't tell if he'd hurt you, too, and I couldn't stand the thought." I can just about see Katie, Phil and my little brother. I blink the tears away, and Shane pulls away from Phil, climbs up onto the bed and comes to cuddle me. He somehow manages to avoid shoving a little knee into my bad side, but when he throws his little arms around my neck, I melt. I squeeze him back as hard as I think he'll take. "My little brother," I remind myself again. Phil hands me a tissue and I dry my eyes. "You're fabulous, kiddo," I tell him. It didn't take me long to fall in love with him.

"You stepped up to take care of him, and I can't thank you enough. I kept thinking of all the places he could be." I pull my brother close to me again. Suddenly, he plants a small, wet, sloppy, grape flavoured kiss on my cheek. Beyond Frank's kiss earlier, this is the best.

I reach out and find Katie's hand ready to grab mine. "His social worker wants to meet you, but she's happy to do that next week."

I nod. "I need to speak with the Council, get put on an emergency waiting list for a house." Katie looks at me with shock in her eyes and her mouth open.

"You're not staying with us?" she asks.

I go to speak, to tell her no. "I didn't want to presume," is the reply that escapes my mouth, tears in my eyes again.

"It's settled then," she tells me. I look at Phil but he just smiles and winks at me. I know better than to refuse. This is why I wanted them contacted. Right now, I need someone to be my mum.

CHAPTER 7

Frank

I get in around a quarter past ten, noticing that mum and dad's car is in their usual spot. I touch the hood as I walk past; it's cold so they've been back a good hour, if not more. I head in quietly, on a high from my two clients and my own session.

I shut and lock the front door, and I can hear dad getting up from the lounge to check that it's me coming in. He nods to me, and I drop my kit bag at the bottom of the stairs. I showered at the gym, but I do need to wash my stuff.

"I persuaded Tabitha to stay with us," mum says as she sips a soft drink, her infectious smile makes me do the same.

"You mean you told her she was, and good." I grin at mum. "How did Shane react to her? He seemed stand-offish when I had to leave," I mention as I move to sit on the sofa.

"He was great!" Dad says. "First, she got Shane to mind his manners, then she talked about why she ran, rather than asking us for help. I had no idea her step-dad was previously violent to her mum." I managed to not gape at his comment, didn't Tabitha explain that?

"I thought he might have been," I reply. I shiver in both anger and hatred at her step-dad. At least he's where he can't touch her or Shane.

"She didn't want to presume that she'd be allowed to stay here, so started talking about a Council house. Then the tears started," I lift my head at dad's words but he's glancing at mum. "So, Shane climbs off my lap, climbs up onto the bed and kisses Tabs, then hugs her. He didn't want to leave but Tabitha said he had to come home to bed, so she could get better and come home with him when she was allowed."

I grin. Typical Tabitha, persuasive until the last.

"Then he comes home and does his bedtime routine like an angel," mum says. She certainly looks more relaxed this evening.

"I'm going to get Tabitha a SIM deal early tomorrow and give her one of those phones I was gifted," I tell them. Dad nods.

"That'll be good. She says you and her are *keen* on each other?" Mum coaxes. I grin and my cheeks suddenly feel hot. Mum's eyes flash and a knowing smile appears on her face. She always suspected, so I might as well come clean about how I feel regarding Tabs.

"I was always keen on her, no one else compared to her," I tell them.

"We know," dad says as he pats me on the shoulder.

"I'm glad you'll finally get a chance to explore this. I'll speak with the social worker and the lawyer tomorrow," mum decides, finishing her drink.

"Good night love," she tells me, kissing me on the cheek as she heads up to bed, dad following shortly after. I bid them goodnight and turn the lamps off, fix a quick hydration drink whilst I get my kit into the wash. Then I head to my room, finding two of the mobiles I was gifted. I'm not sure what style Tabitha would like, so I pack both, noticing I have a few spare SIMs too. I grab them, pleased that I don't have to head to a mobile shop tomorrow.

I get ready for bed and as I turn out the light, I whisper a good night to Tabitha in the darkness.

Shane's crying wakes me up early in the morning, and I'm in with him just as mum enters. He seems hotter than usual and I tell mum, who quickly strips him out of his sleep sack and down to his vest and nappy. She takes him to the bathroom just in time for him to vomit over the sink, himself and mum. Before long he's crying again, but I can hear mum soothing him.

"I'll grab the cleaning gear," I say. We're used to this and I hope that whatever bug Shane's got, doesn't affect Tabitha or us. Half an hour later, Shane's on the sofa, cleaned up, towels around him in case of round two. Mum's just finished cleaning herself up, but I did clean the bathroom. Now, I smell of various cleaning fluids, and I need a shower before I go to visit Tabitha.

"Siser," he tells me.

"I'll go and see her, but you've just been sick so you can't go to see Tabitha today." His little face falls as if he understands what I've gently told him. "If you're not sick again today, you can visit her tomorrow, okay? We need Tabs to get better so she can come home." Home. That word never had Tabitha in it before. Now it will.

Mum nods to me, then I head off and have a good shower, dressing in a blue ribbed crew top and casual trousers; smart but casual. I grab my rucksack, Chromebook and things I'd need to work remotely, then I head down and grab a shake for breakfast.

I ruffle Shane's hair as I go past to grab an apple and some fruit to eat on the way to the hospital. Mum meets me in the hallway and hands me two Tupperware boxes of stuff.

"One is for you," she tells me. I kiss her for keeping me on my protein plan. "The other is for Tabs," she tells me, smiling.

I look into it, and I can see it's the dividing one: she's stacked one side of it with packs of soft dried fruit, apricots, figs and mango. Then there are even more protein bars on the other side, stacked up so that there's a good dozen in there. I grin.

"Thanks, mum!" I kiss her on the cheek, load the boxes and head out. I'll be glad when Tabs is home, and I doubt I'm the only one.

***

When I get to the hospital, the doctor is with Tabs, doing another check on her surgery wound. She seems cheerful enough and the doctor sits next to her after covering her back up, the nurse hovering by.

"I'm happy to let you go home in a few more days. Your food intake is good, and given how your wound is healing, I see no reason to keep you in much longer. I'd like you to get weighed and have a full physical done by your GP. Do you have their details?" Tabs looks across at me, her face is a little shocked.

"I haven't had a chance to register with any yet," she mumbles.

"She'll be with the same one as me." I butt in, dropping my bag gently by her side. "I can get that sorted today, but I can tell you what their details are now." The doctor nods at me and Tabitha smiles, relief evident on her face. He hands me the paperwork and I sit at Tabitha's side, filling it in as best I can. My handwriting is not the neatest, I just hope it's clear. I remember Tabitha's writing, it was always so neat and, for the want of a better word, pretty.

A few minutes later, I hand the clipboard and paperwork back to the doctor.

"Now, remember. When you *do* go home, no climbing stairs, and no baths. Cloth and wash for a week until your GP says you can shower, but that should be in about ten more days from now."

He smiles as he leaves, and I grin at Tabs.

"We'd best get you registered with the surgery, then," I tell her, tucking the chair to be closer to her bed. "I'll go through the mobile setup with you afterwards." I melt at her smile.

"Thanks, Frank," she whispers and she leans back, closing her eyes.

"Are you tired?" I ask her.

"A little. I always seem to be after the doc's visit." I smile, and I pull out the box of food for her that mum packed.

"This isn't for all in one go," I tell her. She grins and then chuckles as she sees the dried fruit and the protein bars. "Oh wow...," I look across and the fruit is half-eaten.

"Something wrong with the grapes?" I ask her. I expected them all to be devoured by now. Tabitha shakes her head.

"The nurse said not to eat too many at once. Partly because my stomach is still small but two, it could clog me up, since I've not been eating properly for a few years."

"That is good advice." I lean in and kiss her on the lips softly.

"That makes things a whole lot better," she tells me. I lean my forehead against hers, and sigh happily. I notice she looks the same as she did yesterday.

"Right, let's get you registered," I pull my phone out of my pocket and dial the surgery, getting the ball rolling.

***

Half an hour later, Tabitha is semi-registered, the surgery taking details from us both, as she's still in the hospital. I get out the mobile next and set it up, calling the provider and getting it onto a contract for her. When it's all done, she looks at me shyly.

"Frank, how am I going to pay you back for all this?" she asks. Her voice is weak and quiet, and she doesn't want to look at me.

"Who says you have to?" I ask her. She snaps her head up, opens her mouth and then closes it. "You need to get back up on your feet and make plans for what you want to do now you're home. I can easily afford to cover a mobile bill like that. It's not a huge amount," I explain, hoping to pacify her anxiety. I understand now why she was always like a cat on a hot tin roof. It isn't an issue though, I spend far more on self-care products in a week than that bill will cost me for the month. Perhaps, I could cut back a little.

She shakes her head. "It's the cost of two nights in a homeless shelter in London, three if you're in towns and not a city."

"So? I want you to be able to ask mum, dad or me for anything you need right now. Or have the ability to use the internet and look things up. You can't, as you're in here with no way to communicate with us, but now, you do. Shall I show you how it works? We'll get you a Gmail account now, too," I tell her.

Another hour later, and she's got an email address, knows how to call me, mum or dad, and how to message us.

"Did you never have a phone?" I ask, and she shakes her head.

"No way was Lee ever going to pay for one; mum worked, bringing in what she could. He spent it on drink, then drugs, so I never had one."

I gape, then close my mouth. "Wish I'd known," I say.

"You couldn't have afforded one, and when I ran, I couldn't get one. They wanted a permanent address, bank accounts... it was impossible," she says, turning the handset over in her hand. "You're sure I can have this?" she asks me again, still unsure of everything that I take for granted.

I grin and nod, then take her hand in mine. "I'm very sure," I say, reaching across and kissing her. "Stop worrying about it, okay?"

She nods and smiles. Then she leans back against the pillows and sighs. "Always so tired," she whispers. I grab her hand and rub my thumb across her knuckles. Even her hands look underweight.

"Then sleep. The doctor did warn us that the recovery will make you tired," I remind her as I settle back into the huge chair. It's not as comfortable as the sofa at home or the desk in my room, but that's okay. I smile as I watch Tabitha slowly drift off to sleep again. When her breathing levels out, I contact my clients, go through their workout plans and arrange to meet one this evening.

***

Tabitha sleeps for a few hours, which isn't surprising. I've taken my usual protein bars and prepared my shake for when her lunch comes around. The hospital staff are quiet when they see she's asleep, but I gently wake her up as they set her lunch down.

"Hey, Tabs, it's lunchtime," I call out. She stirs and moves, wincing as she does so. "Careful," I tell her. I pour her some water, and I help her drink the cup before she unwraps her lunch, though she still looks pale. It's almost a child's meal of chicken nuggets, mashed potatoes and vegetables.

"Shane eats that," I tell her, teasingly. She turns to me and pokes her tongue out. I grin, and chuckle softly.

"I'm trying to eat," she admonishes. It's great to see the fire back in her again. "Besides, this doesn't require a lot of chewing." She puts another forkful into her mouth, and I watch. She chews but it's simple food, so it doesn't take a lot of effort. I suddenly understand what she means. It's less effort to eat this, but it's still calories. I sip my protein shake and watch her as she very slowly eats everything on the plate. If it had a pattern, I'd wager she'd have eaten that, too.

The dessert is a chocolate muffin. "Frank, I think I'd like a cup of tea, please?" she asks as she swaps the plates around.

"Of course," I reply, but not until I reach across and kiss her on the cheek again.

"Thank you," she tells me, hoarsely. She waits until I'm back with the tea, and I touch her hand, rubbing my knuckles along the back of her hand. Her skin seems too dry.

"Do they give you any moisturiser?" I ask. Her hands seem dry, and it's cold. She wasn't this cold before her nap. "Tabs, are you feeling worse?" I ask. She tries to look up at me and there's a sheen of sweat on her forehead. I press the buzzer to get a nurse in, and it's the formidable one from the other day. A fact I'm glad about.

"She seems to be burning a fever," I tell her, and she takes over, checking Tabs out, then her wound.

"Be right back," she tells me,, and she is back in a few moments with some basic paracetamol. "I've called Dr Ramesh to come up and the sister is getting you some blood work organised."

Tabs just nods and takes the pills as instructed. Suddenly, she doesn't want the muffin or the tea, and I can't blame her. I think back to Shane this morning and fire a text off to mum.

Frank: How is Shane doing? Tabs seems to be down with something here, too.

Mum: He seems fine. He's eaten a little, but not a lot. I'll try him with a banana in a little while. What's wrong with Tabs?

Frank: Not sure... the surgeon is being called up to see her and blood work is being called for.

Mum: She's in the best place to be ill

Frank: I know.

I look up and Tabs is shivering. I throw away the tea I've made her and pour out some of the pre-boiled water into the mug.

"Tabs, try drinking just some hot water, babe," she smiles at me weakly as I help her take a sip from the mug. "Slowly, it's hot," I tell her. She gives me a faint nod and leans back against the pillows. Half an hour later, another Doctor comes in, but it's not Ramesh.

"Ms Reid, I'm Doctor Jones." I almost scoff but Tabs isn't doing well. I just want her better. He's as tall as me and his light blond hair is short; he clearly likes the gym in his downtime. "I was part of the team that operated on you. Let's have a look and see what's happening, shall we?" A nurse brings in a machine with another following behind with other things. I push my chair back and watch as they work.

They give Tabs' wound an ultrasound, and I hear the doctor tell the nurse that the site is clear. Whatever that means, I hope it's good. Another nurse has extracted three vials of blood from Tabitha and the doctor signs off the paperwork she presents.

"As soon as," he nods at her. Then, she's off with her trolly and the paperwork.

"Ms. Reid, can you hear me?" He asks and Tabs manages a nod. He turns to the nurse. "Saline IV," he tells her, and she nods, vanishing off. Shit, they're putting another IV drip into her hand.

"She's left-handed," I tell him. He turns and looks at me as if he hadn't seen me before.

"Good to know, thank you," and he brings the drip machine around to her right side. I know that Tabs will use her left hand first and last time it caused issues. The nurse comes back with a saline drip, tape and needles, and I try not to cringe as they wire Tabs back up to a drip.

At last, the machine beeps steadily and Tabs seems to be resting but is looking worse than she did an hour ago.

"To bring you up to speed," Doctor Jones turns to speak to me. "Her wound site is clear, there's no pus or abscess there that I can see, and I've looked extensively. Is anyone else at home sick, or ill that's been to visit her?"

I nod. "She met her little brother yesterday, he's nearly two. He was sick this morning," I tell him. He nods, and he gives me a rueful smile.

"No need to look so worried, Mr Allen," he smiles at me. I hadn't realised I looked worried, though now he mentions it, I can feel the knot in my stomach; my short but quick breath. "It sounds like the little fella may have given her a bug, but one we can fight off. I'm going to have to ask that he's not brought here for forty-eight hours." I nod.

"Not a problem," I say.

He spies the grapes. "When did these appear?" He asks, pointing at the almost eaten tub.

"My mother brought them in yesterday," I tell him, and he nods in reply.

"I assume it was all washed," he asks. I nod.

"Yeah, mum would have done that... but she shared those with her brother. She handed them to him, though," I recall.

I can see the doctor's mind whirling, thinking. His lips have gone thin and he looks at me. "I think it best if they're binned, and the tub washed out thoroughly," he says.

"Could they have done that to her? To them?" I ask.

"If he's put his hands in the grapes, possibly. I'd rather not risk it." I look at him and I nod.

"We can buy fresh grapes," I tell him. I take the tub, empty it into the waste bin that the doctor tells me and I rinse the pot in hot water. Then he's back with some surface spray and paper towel.

"Got it," I tell him, spraying the tub, lid and every part of it I can, then wiping it down with the blue paper towel. I pack it into my backpack and then I wash my hands. I watch as he washes his hands and checks her vitals again.

The nurse comes in, and he relays to her about the extra hygiene needed for Tabs right now, and the hand sanitiser. The nurse nods and the doctor heads to his next patient as his pager goes off.

"I assume she won't be wanting dinner?" she asks me.

"I doubt it. But, she was looking forward to that muffin and a cup of tea," I quip. The nurse winks and motions to the bedside cabinet where we have stacked the other Tupperware tubs. I nod, but take them out and give them a quick wipe before stacking them back in Tabitha's cupboard.

CHAPTER 8

Tabitha

Beep.
Beep.
Beep.

The monitoring machine is back. Why? I move and groan, aware that there's something in my right hand this time.

"Easy," says a masculine voice. It's not Frank but his dad, Phil. "We think you caught a bug of some type from Shane," He's sitting off to my left side.

"Feel awful," I mutter, rather matter-of-factly.

"We know. We didn't realise," he tells me. He's here alone. I guess that Frank must be doing his personal sessions, and Katie is at home with Shane.

"Wasn't intentional," I quip. I manage to open my eyes, and he's smiling at me.

"Hey kiddo, how ya doing?" He asks, jovially but quietly. How can such a huge mountain of a man be so quiet?

"Not sure...," is my only honest reply. "No energy," I explain.

Phil just nods. "Need a drink?" He asks me and I manage a smile. He reaches across and pours me some water, then grabs a metal straw and helps me drink.

"Better," I breathe out, feeling the tightness in my throat ease. "Is Shane okay?" I ask.

"He's mending. He was sick this morning, but we're keeping him at home until you're home too. He's not coming in here again!"

Phil's laughter ripples through his statement, but it's also set in steel and determination. I won't get to hug him until I get to theirs.

"Poor us," I whisper, but I smile gently at Phil. "But he's okay? Frank told the doctor my brother had been ill," I recall that part of the conversation, but beyond being stabbed again, I don't recall too much after struggling to eat my lunch.

Phil nods. "Right as rain since. Katie's been telling him about bugs that live on your hands and that we need to wash the bad bugs off and why. He's really getting into it, especially since we told him you can't come home because a nasty bug made you sick again," he smiles at me.

"It might not have been him," I tell him. "I could have given him something just as easily." Phil nods.

"Or this place, we had to walk through a lot of corridors to get here," he tells me, "And Shane loves running his hands over things."

"Right hand this time?" I ask. Phil nods.

"Frank told them you were left-handed," he explains. I sigh contentedly.

"He's a star, your boy," I tell him. Phil leans in and smiles.

"We know," he winks.

***

Phil leaves when visiting hours are over, though I got introduced to video calls with Shane and Katie. My head hurts and I take the pills the nurse gives me as I settle into bed, still unable to sleep. I pick up my phone and message Frank, wondering how he is.

Tabs: Thanks for earlier, I went from feeling okay to not quite quickly!

Frank: There you are! Dad didn't wear you out?

I chuckle, then remember, Frank can't tell.

Tabs: LOL! No. I'll be glad when things settle down, and I can get out of here.

Frank: I can only imagine! I won't call you, just learned you video chatted with Mum and Shane, so you've gotta be tired.

Tabs: I want to sleep. I'm yawning, but I can't... no idea why.

Then the phone rings and his voice is low, quiet. "Will this help, do you think?"

"Hey, you!" I greet him, his voice instantly settling me. "And yes," I breathe back. Oh lord, yes!

"You sound a lot better," he tells me, and I chuckle softly in response.

"Wait until I am, I'll be home then," I tell him. His voice drops in volume and it goes soft.

"I know. It'll be great," he breathes in. "So, you go to sleep, I'll be there in the morning."

I smile. "Good night, Frank," I whisper but loud enough he can hear me.

"Night, babe," he huskily whispers back, then the static in my ear is gone, and I can close my eyes in peace.

CHAPTER 9

Frank

It took another week before Tabitha was allowed home. Whatever bug Shane had given her took three days to shake off.

Tabs is arguing with a nurse when I arrive to bring her home. I'd been at a personal session first thing, but she knew where I would be, and when I'd be there to pick her up.

"I just want a shower," Tab's voice wails from the bathroom.

"You're only supposed to have sink washes," the nurse tells her sternly from the bedside of the door. It's the same nurse that was there from day one, Clare. I smile and motion for her to back away from the door.

"I can come and help you if you want," I call through the bathroom door. Suddenly, it unlocks and Tabitha is standing there in a towel. Nothing else on her.

"I can't reach places by myself," she tells me. I glance back at Clare.

"I'll help her. It's fine," I tell her.

Clare looks at me. "No funny business," she warns and marches off, but she's smirking at me. I grin in reply, feigning ignorance with my hands, and Tabitha giggles. I wait until the room door is closed, and I let out the chuckle I'd been keeping in.

"Now, where can't you reach?" I ask. Tabitha moves back and heads to the sink which is made up of warm water with some shower gel and a scrunchie ball.

"My back," she says, looking in the mirror at me. My eyes catch the fire in hers, and I beam at our reflection, then shake my head.

"No funny business," I repeat, but I take the puffball and massage the shower gel into it. When I'm ready, Tabitha moves the towel so she is still covered at the front. She doesn't even try to keep the towel covering her arse, and I keep my focus on her back. In moments, I'm done, and I wrap the towel around her, patting it dry.

"Anywhere else?" I ask.

"I'm not allowed to bend down," she tells me. There's a bathroom chair in here, designed so you can sit in the shower if you wanted to. I pull it over and make her sit on it, then I help her wash her legs and feet.

"Sorry for being a bit of a yeti," she mumbles, just loud enough that I can make out.

"Tabs, do you want me to shave your legs?" I ask.

I watch as she purses her lips together and nods. "Yes, please... if you're okay doing that?" She stutters.

I look into her soft brown eyes. Right now, there's not a thing I won't do.

Mum went to town and brought Tabitha a lot of personal hygiene items. I think she would have liked another child, and preferably a girl the second time around. Alas, it wasn't meant to be.

I carefully wash Tabitha's legs, shave them for her, then I rinse, dry and moisturise them for her, hoping that she doesn't see how I'm reacting. I can't look at her face, she'd simply know. I expected little moans or giggles, but Tabitha is silently watching my every move. The nurse comes in to ensure Tabitha and I aren't up to any funny business, but I draw the line at helping Tabitha get dressed. Clare helps and Tabitha sits back on the bed, able to move around on her own as we wait for the dismissal paperwork Clare has gone to finalise.

Clare comes back half an hour later, flustered and deeply apologetic.

"Sorry! Got waylaid," she grins at us.

"That's okay," Tabitha replies happily. Being told that she can come home today was great news. Shane is at nursery, dad has said he'll be working from home and that's where mum will be.

"Now, remember a few more days with no showers. Sink washing, like earlier, is the most we need you to do. The stitches are all dissolving nicely but there are a few that haven't vanished yet. Wait until they are and your GP is happy that they've all gone."

She hands the paperwork to Tabitha to sign. When Tabs has done that and handed the clipboard back to Clare, she beams at us.

"Go on, get outta here you two! And good luck!" There are tears in her eyes and suddenly, Tabitha is hugging her, thanking her. Clare gets busy stripping the bed Tabitha's been in for the best part of three weeks and I see her wipe her eyes a time or two as I gather Tabs' things together.

***

I've grabbed Tabitha's bag, intentionally travelling with just my phone, keys and wallet today. I've training sessions booked for tonight, but not until I have Tabs home and settled

"Come on, you," I say, reaching for her hand. I let her set the pace and I led us to my car. She stops and gawps at the A class I drive. "I do well, babe," I tell her, helping her get in before I load her bag into the boot. Then I jump in, keen to get her home and hope I never set eyes on this place again.

CHAPTER 10

Tabitha

I tried so very hard not to react to Frank shaving my legs or washing my back. The towel could have slipped so very easily, and in part, I had wanted to, to see what he did, but I suspected the nurse would come in to check us after her warning. She did.

Frank, though, drew the line at helping me dress. Katie had told me she needed my size so she could buy me some clothes. To be honest, the rags I'd been living in weren't much, but I did insist on her only buying the basics of things; nothing fancy or frilly. She asked why, and I told her I didn't want her to buy that kind of thing for me. I'd buy the more expensive stuff myself when I had the funds.

She must have understood, though, and stuck to the soft fabrics basics as I asked. I can smell that she's washed it all for me.

Shane making me sick meant that I stayed longer in hospital, but I was now cleared to manoeuvre around stairs. I'm watching myself in the elevator, trusting Frank's physique to keep me upright, but he doesn't need to lend me that. Just holding my hand is enough and when he guides me to a small, silver Mercedes I balk.

"I do well, babe," he tells me. Then he drops my bag to the side and helps me into the car. The boot opens, closes and he climbs in, taking me home.

***

I alternate between looking out of the window, watching the roads change from the whacky Birmingham ones to the quieter Black Country ones, and watching Frank. Around Dudley, the drivers seem to be just as mad as they are in Birmingham. Frank drives with care and one guy gets annoyed at Frank's careful driving, giving Frank the two-fingered salute. I return it, which I think shocks Frank more than the other driver.

"He's a twat," I proclaim, aware that the guy could get out and cause a scene. Once we're through the Dudley area, things are calmer, and Frank drives me along streets I used to know.

A pub I had to walk past to get to school has been demolished and flats are being built in its place. The park is still there, though the railings have been painted and the equipment has changed a little since I saw them last. Then the car slows and he turns at a junction. His road. The access to where mum and I were, is a few streets away and I'm glad he's not taken that route home.

He takes something out of the console in the middle and points it at a set of gates, which pull back slowly.

"You've done it up," I whisper. The front door is now one of those ultra-modern ones with a half-moon curve in it that is a shiny grey, the windows have been updated and the house seems larger. The other car is off to one side and I notice the Audi badge on it, so I assume it is Phil's. The driveway is now tarmacked with a paving edge, a change from the slabs and grass I recall from years ago. There was some wasteland off to the left that was just left after they got rid of their caravan. It was just an underdeveloped area where grass grew tall until Phil would take the grass strimmer to it. Or pay Frank to. Now it's a part of the drive, extending it.

I can't form any words to describe how nervous, happy and overwhelmed I am right now. I don't even notice Frank turning the engine off, getting out or coming around to help me out until my door opens.

"Hey, are you ready?" he asks as he holds his hand out for me. I look at the house, and I swallow my nerves down, though it doesn't seem to help my dry mouth. "It's okay!" he croons out to me in a reassuring tone. "It's home. You've been here before, remember?" He reminds me, and I nod, smiling weakly.

"Yeah, but I was never going to stay or sleep in a bed in your house. Not back then." Frank tugs my hand and I slowly get out of the car.

"Times change Tabs. We have changed. Come on," he coaxes and he takes me to the front door. He doesn't get to open it, his mother does that for us.

"Oh good! Come on in, it's too cold out there for you in your condition," she tells me. It's late August, but the weather today is cooler than it has been lately. It's not the coldest I've endured.

CHAPTER 11

Frank

Helping Tabitha out of the car feels strange. She's acting shy, just like she was the first time when dad encouraged her to come inside for a drink and she ate the bowl of grapes.

Mum takes her and guides her into the living room while I head back outside and grab her bag. I drop it at the foot of the stairs and move around my parents' spacious home to follow them. They've moved and mum has her sat at the kitchen table already. Tabs looks at me with a plea in her eye.

"Mum, we had a drink before we left the hospital. Are you okay, Tabs? You look tired," I suggest, offering her a get out already.

"Tired? She just got here!" Mum starts, then she looks at Tabs and she smiles. "I'm sure that car ride was tiring for you," mum says, seeing what I'm seeing.

"I've been awake longer today than before. I'd just like to sit somewhere soft, please?" Tabs asks.

"Of course!" And mum gets on with bossing us both about. I grin and take Tab's hand, guiding her to the hall.

"A nap or the living room with the television?" I ask, giving her a choice.

"I think I'll try the TV first, please? I've been without one for so long, I've forgotten what they look like." She grins, but when she sees the size of the TV we now have, she goes speechless and quiet again. After half an hour, she's heading out of the living room, and I find her in the conservatory, taking deep breaths and holding her head.

"Too loud?" I offer, coming to sit next to her.

She nods. "Yeah, sorry, I've mostly had silence for the last three years... all the shouting and threats went when I left. I couldn't hear the arguments, and I was glad." She's fighting back the tears, and I go to her, hugging her.

"It's okay, let it out," I tell her and she does. That's how mum finds us ten minutes later, and she just nods, then closes the door quietly behind her.

"I'll bet you never talked with anyone about it, did you?" I offer. Counselling isn't something I thought Tabitha would ever need, but we all have our ghosts and demons. Some just hide it better than others.

Tabitha shakes her head and dries her eyes again on some fresh tissues. "Who would I talk with? There was an offer, with one Council at a hostel on the south coast. But the guy creeped me out, so I moved on." She shrugs, trying to act like it's normal. How could a counsellor creep you out? They were meant to help you. "Can I... stay in this room for a while?" She asks in a pleading voice. "I don't want to lie down, but I'd like to sit and just be. I had forgotten houses were noisy." She smiles as I nod in agreement, making herself comfortable, and I do the same. Minutes later, her eyes have closed, and she's asleep. I grin, as that's what I thought she would do, so I grab a blanket, put it over her legs, kiss her softly on the cheek and then go and join my parents.

***

An hour later as mum goes to fetch Shane from the nursery, I check on Tabitha. She's still fast asleep, but she's moved positions so she's more comfortable. I smile, feeling glad she's home as I look at her face, pain-free, content. Looking up counselling on the phone, or how to go about organising it, distracts me from Shane barrelling into the house, all keen and excited to see Tabitha. I stop what I'm doing, and I crouch down to his level.

"Hey, little man," I call to him, and he comes over to me. He can't quite reach the door handles yet but it won't be long until he does. "Tabitha is asleep, resting. You can go and sit with her if you want, but you have to be super quiet. Her body still needs to get better and sleep helps, okay?" He nods and holds a finger to his mouth, making me beam. "Exactly. Now, go take your shoes off like nana said," we've been calling my mum his nana, so he didn't get confused.

He runs off, takes off his shoes and does what mum instructs him to do. Then he comes to me and once again, he puts his finger over his mouth. I grin and do the same, then I let him into the conservatory. The huge corner sofa folds out into a bed, but Tabitha is occupying just one part of it. Shane jumps up and crawls gently over to his sister. He seems to understand more than we've ever told him for a two-year-old. He snuggles into Tabitha's sleeping form, and I grin; his gentleness endearing him to me more than ever before.

"Blanky," he tells me quietly, and I nod, moving the blanket so he can get under it, too. I cover it over him, and he smiles. With sighs and yawns, he closes his eyes. Minutes later, he's asleep, too.

"Where's," mum begins to ask in a loud voice, but I shush her and point. Her face changes from one of frustration to one of love as she sees Shane snuggled up with his big sister, asleep.

Mum nods. He usually goes for a nap after nursery. Snuggling into his sister is just as good a place to take that nap as any.

***

While Tabitha and Shane nap, I continue on my quest to find out how to get counselling for Tabitha, and I'm surprised it seems to mostly be a process started by a GP. It's a good job we're meeting them early next week. We can ask at that point. Satisfied that there's no other way to do this, I check in with my clients, confirm the times of the gym sessions that I'm needed at and then eat. Drinking a protein and hydrating solution afterwards will be all I need, except for a shower.

I glance across from the kitchen to the conservatory, seeing that Tabitha is awake. Noting the time, I go and wake Shane up, too. I know if I don't, he'll be a nightmare at bedtime.

Tabitha grins as he slowly wakes up, and when he realises that Tabitha is awake, too, he's super alert, jumping up to hug her.

"Hey, little brother," she softly says to him as she squeezes him as tightly as he'll take.

"Siser," he says, and she chuckles, a sound so warm and fun, it melts my heart all over again.

"Yeah, sister," she confirms. "Where have you been?" Shane babbles on, and she picks up most of what he's saying. They talk about his day, and I hear mum starting to prepare dinner, the sound of the pans being pulled out from the drawers is distinctive.

"Shed," he tells her and points to the huge storage shed we have in the garden. I hold my breath, Shane knows what's in it, we've not had a chance to tell or show Tabitha yet.

"That's new," she comments as she turns to me. I nod, holding my breath. "What's wrong?" She asks, coming to me and she reaches out to touch my arm.

"Our fings," Shane tells her. So much for easing her into telling her we also emptied her mother's house.

"What is?" she asks him, confused for a moment. He points to the shed as the door to the kitchen opens.

"Our fings," he says and smiles at my mother. "Show siser," he demands, and my heart sinks.

"Show me what?" she asks with a lift in her voice.

"We... When what happened, happened and we took Shane in, the Council asked if we needed anything from there for him. We said yes, and... It's all in there," I nod towards the shed.

"You... saved some of my stuff?" she asks us quietly. Mum nods and Tabitha begins crying, then hugs my mother tight. "You didn't have to! Oh, I'd love to see what you managed to salvage," she wipes her eyes but there's a huge smile trying to fight through.

"I may have gone through what was left of your stuff," I tell her, wanting to get it out of the way. I did, and I saved as much of the things I thought important or necessary to her as I could.

"Thank you," she tells me gently as she touches my arm. There's a set of keys being jangled and dad appears, which makes Shane cheer.

"Let's start showing you, you might want some of it up in your room," he tells her. She nods.

"I have half an hour spare before I need to leave for the gym," I tell them. Tabitha smiles at me, warmth and appreciation shining from her eyes.

***

"Oh my!" she exclaims as she sees piles of large wooden and plastic boxes. Her dressing table was moved up a few days ago by dad and me. He wanted to restore it and loved doing it about a year ago. I wonder what she'll make of that.

"All my supplies," she breathes as she comes across two boxes with her art stuff. Her easel didn't make it, smashed to bits by her stepdad, not that I need to tell her that. She gently eases out watercolour paper, drawing pads, charcoal pencils and more drawing implements than I can begin to name.

"Drawing!" Shane squeals as he comes across another box of stuff that contains fat crayons and a colouring book.

Tabitha smiles at him. "Do you like to draw and colour, too?" she asks, and he shows her. For a two-year-old, he gets that he needs to draw in the lines, but hasn't worked out how.

"Aww, that's great! Shall we take some of this inside? That's okay, isn't it?" she asks as she looks at my dad. He nods with a huge smile on his face.

"Shall we take this whole box up for you, Shane?" Dad asks and Shane jumps about, happy as anything. They vanish, Shane leading the way, and it gives me a few moments with Tabitha.

"I hope you don't mind that I went through your things," I tell her, feeling my cheeks going a little red.

She chuckles and reaches across, touching my hand slightly. "I don't mind, I wasn't here. I'm surprised anything survived his drunken rampages." She smiles and secures a drawing pad and a box of drawing pencils off to the side. "Did any of my old clothes survive?" She asks, and I direct her through to a few boxes at the back.

"Mum can wash anything that you need washing," I tell her, and dad appears again.

"Dinner won't be long, and you need to get going, son," he tells me. I nod and I turn to Tabitha. She's already smiling at me.

"Have a good session," she tells me as her eyes soften. I grin at her and then nod to dad, heading out to my gym sessions.

CHAPTER 12

Tabitha

Watching Frank go out to his gym sessions is hard, but trying on all these clothes can maybe wait until they're washed and dried. They do smell funny, and they feel cold. Phil kindly grabs the two boxes and lifts them, taking them into the house effortlessly. I smile and shut the shed behind me. My art supplies were saved. I'll need to go through every tube and brush to see if I can still use them, but that's for another day when it's just as warm and dry as today. I'm hoping Frank will help me.

For now, I've grabbed a pad and my drawing pencils. I can at least keep my mind occupied and get back into my art while my body continues to heal. As I enter the kitchen, the scent of dinner assaults me.

"Katie, that smells amazing!" I declare as my mouth begins to water and my stomach grumbles. Loudly. I can feel the heat rise in my cheeks.

She turns to me and grins. "Pasta. something simple for you and Shane," she tells me. I can smell something else, too, and as I watch, she pulls out two chicken thighs that are roasting in the oven, bastes them and returns them into their warm hell. I must groan in anticipation because Katie laughs at me.

"I'll cook you a roast dinner and such when you're better, but Frank said pasta and salad would be good for you and Shane. You might even get Shane to eat his salad." She grins at me as she bustles about.

"I'm sure he'll eat whatever you put down in front of him," I tell her. "Can I help?" I offer and Katie shakes her head.

"When you're able to stand up a little longer. No heavy lifting, remember?" She grins at me. "I've got this," she says.

I leave her to it as she pulls out the potatoes and bastes them. I find the corner seat in the conservatory, and as I get comfortable, Shane comes in with Phil.

"Do you not like television?" He asks, and I shake my head.

"It's a tad too noisy for me right now, Phil. I'm sorry." I decide to be honest with them.

"Katie says she'll get that lot washed and dried in the next few days. Do you want to see your room?" He asks me, and I nod. I would. Shane jumps up and down, cheering.

"Siser next to me," he announces.

"Sister," I tell him, making the T sound harsher. "Sis-ter," I coax and he tries to copy. By the time we reach the stairs, he's got it.

"Sister next to me," he declares proudly once more, not missing the sound. I nod and grin as I grip the bannister tightly. My extended stay in the QE means I can handle stairs now. Well, I can at least attempt them! Phil comes up behind me, in case I fall, and I'm grateful. Shane leads the way and stops outside a closed bedroom door. All the other doors are slightly ajar, but this one is closed tightly.

I turn as the sound of another person is on the stairs, and it's Katie. I smile at her, and she nods to Phil, who motions for me to open the door. I do, tentatively, trying to keep a hold of my nerves. What I see is a beautiful room with fitted wardrobes on one wall, a white iron double bed with soft pink bed covers on them and some curtains that match. I can only gape in wonder as I spy my mum's old dressing table.

I finally gasp in shock and head towards it. It's been restored, repaired and it's not as shabby as it once was. The veneer has been removed and the whole thing is sturdy once again. The small stool has been reupholstered, too.

"Do you like it?" Phil asks gently.

I turn to him, but he's a blur, and I have to blink to see anything of him or his awesome wife.

"It's gorgeous! How did... wow!" The heart in my chest is working hard, beating double time. My lungs are just about functioning and my throat can't form any words that my brain is now formulating at the lightning speed it's thinking.

I grip the bed, taking in the simplistic design they've thought of, just for me. Phil's hand touches me on the shoulder lightly and Shane comes around to hug my leg.

"Sister like?" he asks. I can only nod in reply, my voice has stopped working.

"I love it!" I breathe out eventually as I wipe my eyes. Shane pats me on the leg and holds up some scrunched up tissue. I laugh and smile, thanking him.

"Sister not happy," he states, and I quickly get to his level.

"Sister loves it too much," I wipe away the tears with the knot of toilet roll he's given me. "These are tears of love and joy, little brother!" I hug him tight, breathing in his scent, using it to calm myself.

"Dinner's ready, come on," Katie says, and she leads the way back downstairs, a smile on her face and a light in her eyes. At the door to the room they've just gifted me, I stop and look around, taking in the nightstands, the lamps, the cleanliness of it, the sheer... femaleness of it! I was neat at home, my step-dad didn't give me a choice, and the room there wasn't even neutral. It was raw with bare walls, certainly not as furnished as this is. Here, it's softer, there's carpet, lights, curtains, wallpaper; it's homely. The tidy discipline that drunken brute served out might well come in handy as I now aim to keep this space spotless.

***

After a very simple but filling dinner that I, unfortunately, couldn't finish, Katie walks me through the rest of Shane's bedtime routine. We chill for an hour in the conservatory, which gives me many inanimate objects to sketch, so I can get my hand back into the art of drawing. I hug Shane as Katie takes him up for a quick bath before bed, but then I hear him shouting and Phil rolls his eyes.

"Let me," I tell him as he reacts, making him sit down. Carefully, I make my way up to the bathroom to hear Shane shout and scream.

"Is this how you behave?" I ask him as he splashes Katie. He stops mid-tantrum and closes his mouth. He shakes his head, and I try to help Katie up, but she manages it without any assistance from me.

"I'm going to get changed," she states, glaring at my little brother. She's been splashed good and proper. Her top is half-soaked.

"Shane, that wasn't very nice. Why are you playing up?" I scold him, placing the toilet lid down so I can sit on it as Katie heads out in a huff.

"Want you," he tells me, and I shake my head.

"No, that's not how it works. If you're not going to be nice to nana, I am not going to read you a story, or let you colour in with me." His face falls, and I press on. "Or come to bathe you. You have to be nice to the people that have loved you when your mummy and I couldn't be here." I look at him as he understands my words. "You do *not* get to be a brat, kiddo." He splashes his arms into the water, but it doesn't come out over the sides. "When Katie comes back, you need to say sorry to her. She's given you and me a home, a bed, food every day, love…"

Shane begins to cry, and I go across, but not before I put a towel down to soak up the water he's thrown out of the tub.

"You can cry if you want," I tell him. "But, you will have to say sorry to Katie, and mean it. Or I won't read you a bedtime story," I tell him.

His head jerks up quickly. "Story of mommy?" he asks, and I freeze in response. I wonder just how many questions the poor boy has of a woman who was taken from us both far too soon.

"I can tell you stories of our mummy, yes," I say, recovering some of my composure, "But, you have to be a good boy, okay?" I hear footsteps behind me, and I use the towel on the floor to finish mopping up the mess my brother has made. As I stand, using the bath as an aid, I look at him crossly. "Be good for Nana," I remind him as I begin to take the sopping wet towel and bath mat down to the washing machine, throwing a smile and a wink to Katie, leaving a very sheepish Shane to finish his bath. I'm at the top of the stairs when I hear my little brother apologise.

***

Shane cuddles up to me on my bed as I tell him a few short stories about our mother before she met his father. Stories of happier times, when we'd bake, or go to the park.

"You bake wif me?" he asks, and I nod. For a two-year-old, his speech isn't terrible, he can be understood.

"You've got to be well-behaved though. Kitchens can be dangerous." I repeat the words my mother used on me when I wanted to bake, but I was five then and dad had died a year or so before.

"I be good," he tells me and then a huge yawn erupts from his tiny mouth. For such a little boy, his yawn is almost adult-like.

"I'm glad! Let's get you to your bed," I state, but he begins to sulk. "Hey, no sulking. You have your bed in your room. I'm here now. I'm not going anywhere, but I need to rest in my bed, too. I'll see you in the morning, okay?" He nods, and I take him through to his room, being watched by Phil. He helps him to go to the bathroom one more time before he wears a pullup. Then he's back into his pyjamas, a sleep sack and he's in bed.

"Night, little brother," I tell him, kissing him before he gets to lie down on his little toddler bed.

"I wants blankie, like sister," he states, and I look at Phil, then Shane, not quite understanding what he means.

"You want a quilt?" Phil asks, working out what it is he means, and Shane nods.

"Quill," he says, and I smirk.

"We thought this might happen. Okay, take the sack off kiddo," Phil says, but Shane is like lightning, it's off just as Phil finishes speaking. Quick as a flash, there's a toddler quilt with cartoon superheroes on it for Shane being pulled out of the cupboard. I grin at Phil, and he winks at me. They were expecting this, maybe not tonight, but they were expecting it. I smile at Phil, then turn to my brother.

"Okay, get ready!" I call out as Phil fans the quilt over him a few times, then tucks him in as it surrounds him. Phil kisses him goodnight and leaves us for a moment. "Does this make you happy?" I ask him, and he nods, then he yawns again.

"Shane happy," he states and I kiss him on the forehead.

"Tabitha's happy, too. Now, you need to go to sleep so I can go to bed soon, too, okay?" He nods and closes his eyes, and I slowly get up. "Goodnight, little brother!" I say, turning to see Katie in the doorway, grinning at us both.

I smile at her, touching her on the shoulder as I slowly pass, then carefully make my way downstairs. The sound of the television draws me in, and I smile at Phil as I gently sit on the sofa. He turns the TV down a notch, and I smile.

"Thank you, but it's okay, I'm getting used to it," he nods and turns the volume back to where it was. Minutes later, Katie comes in, and together, I spend the first evening in a house that's a home, with no shouting, threats of violence or beatings. It's a beautiful evening.

***

An hour after Shane has gone to bed, I begin to lag. I'm trying to stay awake for Frank coming home, but I drag myself off to bed anyway. I get a little more emotional when I realise that Katie has been clothes shopping for me again and has brought me more casual clothes, jeans and tops, and a few pyjama sets that are funny, cute and girly.

I turn as I hear a noise, and I see her standing in the doorway. I go and hug her tightly, letting my love and appreciation show, even though I can't see her again.

"How can I ever thank you for all you've done?" I whisper at her through catching breaths.

"You don't need to. I wish you'd told us sooner about your step-dad," she laments. I shake my head.

"I love you endlessly, but there was no way I was putting you in the line of fire with him," I snip out in a determined voice. "I couldn't do that to you, any of you," I state. I hear a key in the front door, and Katie turns and moves to peer over the bannister. I follow, and over her shoulder I see Frank coming in, sweaty and half-dressed in his gym gear. He clearly wanted to be home as quickly as he could tonight. I can't help but grin at the sight of him, muscles peering out over his vest-like top, the shorts clinging to his fit, strong, sculpted legs. The tattoos on his right forearm are visible, as is one on his leg and the top left part of his arm that I can't make out.

I quickly swipe at my eyes and pull myself together. Then, he's there, saying hi to his mum and pulling me into a sweaty hug.

"Eugh!" I call out, making Katie shush me because of Shane. "Sorry," I whisper and push against Frank, who chuckles.

"I'll grab a shower," he nods to me, and he smiles at his mum, who grins at us, her eyes dancing in knowledge.

"I'm heading to bed," I tell him. I hadn't changed yet, which is a good thing, and as Frank heads up to the loft bedroom, I turn to watch him go. Only, I catch him looking at me with fire in his eyes. As he vanishes out of sight, I make my way to my room, change out of my clothes, put on one of the cute sets of pyjamas and sit on my bed, leaving the door ajar. I'm not sure what I'm expecting here, but I know this - I want to say goodnight to Frank.

Properly.

CHAPTER 13

Frank

I shower and dress in some loungewear I was modelling the other day, which is part of an upcoming Christmas collection, though this one is very understated in the Christmassy department. It's August, but this company does things months in advance so that the collection is ready on time. I head back down to the first floor, and I see Tabitha's door is open, the light is on, and she's sitting on her bed.

"Hey, you," I call out at the door. She motions for me to come in.

"Hey to you, too," she quietly replies when I go to sit on her bed. "Thank you for today," she tells me. There's a soft smile on her face; her hair is shiny, soft and untangled.

"Do you like what we've done?" I ask. It was a pure white bedroom before, there was no bed in here until the day after we'd been told she was back and in the QE. Dad managed to secure the bed frame from a colleague who had it in storage and he ordered the mattress online. It had arrived the day Tabitha woke up. When we've not been at the hospital or work, we've all been busy here. Mum especially loved decorating and making it girly.

"I love it, thank you," she tells me, reaching out for my hand. "I never expected this," she swallows, taking her time to form what she wants to say. "I never showed you..." She stops talking and takes a huge breath. "But if you cleared out my old room, you saw what state that house was in," she tells me. I do. Dogs in kennels and soldiers in the field have better decor and facilities than she did. I nod in reply, not trusting my voice. "That's why I wanted to be here most of the time after school. Your house, your life... It was a dream I wanted. Simple, I know, but you and your family showed me it was possible." She lifts her head from the spot she was looking at where our hands were nearly touching. "You gave me something to believe in." She's fighting back the tears.

"You deserve that," I whisper to her. She takes a huge sigh, and I lean in, my forehead pressing against hers. "You can start to live again."

I hear her sniff, and I pull back, then I pull her to me, holding her whilst her emotions overwhelm her. I need to put a box of tissues in here. She's going to need them.

"How?" she whispers to me after the crying has stopped.

"You take one step at a time, one day at a time."

She makes some kind of agreeing noise at my words and forces herself to smile. "You sound like you're more of an adult than I am!" She teases, and I grin.

"It's what I told myself when you left. One problem at a time, one day at a time. Baby steps or crawl. You have got the chance now to set goals, so decide what it is you want to do."

She nods. "I'm sorry I messed things up," she tells me. I lay down on the bed and pull her with me, cuddling her so we can talk quietly. She keeps saying this, and it's starting to grind on me.

"You didn't. You leaving as you did, I get it. But it gave me a kick up the arse, too. I'd still be doing what dad wanted, and as much as I love him, I don't want to do what he does. If you hadn't left, I might not have walked past that gym that day, gone inside, done a session on the weights, or spoken to a trainer. You gave me a reason to find my backbone. It set me up to do what I'm doing now, and I love that." I look down at her, and she's curled up. Her bad side can't be that bad anymore, she's laying on it. I smile at her. "So, stop blaming yourself. I don't want to hear you blame yourself for what I did, or how I reacted to you going. That's on me. Got it?" I said.

She snaps her head up at my gruffness but there's something there, an acceptance. "You don't blame me?" she asks.

Oh, hell. *Is that where her head is?*

"Not in the slightest. What you did was bloody brave. You got out. You highlighted a problem, social services had your mother and him on their radar as soon as your note was received. It was only because of that, that they reacted when the neighbours and the police broke in to find what they did. They...," I swallowed. "They moved away, Mr and Mrs Marsh." I finish telling her. "I hope they're okay. They were distraught when they found your mum dead, Shane covered in faeces and your step-dad out of his mind on drugs."

"Oh god!" She sobs for a few moments, then she composes herself. "They were always nice to me, but polite," she swallows.

"Talk to me. What are you thinking?" I encourage her, but she shakes her head. She doesn't want to share what she's thinking, and I can guess what it is, I thought the same. "I wish the police had gone in, not r. Marsh." I sigh and reveal more of what happened in those weeks. "The haunted look on his face for weeks afterwards was telling. They moved away a month after, renting a place somewhere down in Cornwall, only letting a few people know where they were, mum and dad among them."

Their house sold in months and beyond Christmas cards and the odd email now and again, we hardly hear from them.

Tabitha is crying again. "You can't feel guilty. You weren't here." She nods, but she's beating herself up over something that can never be changed. "Mr Marsh told us he was glad he went in, he photographed Shane and the conditions he was in, then brought him here. He was instrumental in adding child cruelty to your step-father's case," I add.

Tabitha is in full-on crying mode now, but I can't keep this from her. "Social services were here and mum offered to take care of him. She was always hoping that you'd seek us out first when you came back. They agreed, and he's been with us since that day. Dad and I went around days later when the police had finished, so we could grab some of his stuff, and yours."

I pull her to me, the anger surfacing at the state of the house when we went around. "How the hell did you live there like that, Tabs?"

She sniffles and wipes her eyes. "Be right back," I tell her and I dash to the bathroom, returning with a fresh toilet roll so she can blow her nose.

"I had no choice," she explains as I pull her to me again. "I was fifteen when I ran away, right after my exam results. He'd promised to make a woman out of me when I was sixteen because then it wasn't rape. He said he'd claim I consented." She blows her nose, and I bring the bin over to sit between us. We shift so we're sitting, and I open my arms out to hug her again. She nods and scoots up to cuddle in. "I had two days to plan, to get things packed and hidden. I'd wait until two or three in the morning, then I hid some clothes outside when he was too drunk or high to care. The day I went for my results was the last time I saw him. Or you and mum...," A fresh wave of tears hit and it doesn't stop for ages.

"I'm sorry," she tells me, but I tsk and keep her pinned to me. I kiss the top of her head and rub her arms.

"Stop apologising. You've had a lot to deal with. There's more to come, and as you told the nurse, it doesn't matter how upset you get. You'll have to deal with it. But," I pause, letting her look up at me and I smile at her. "I want to be there with you while you do."

Her arm flings across my torso, pulling me into her and she nuzzles into my chest. I can do nothing more than hold her and let her just be. Is it wrong that she feels so right in my arms, that she wants to cuddle into me for support? I sigh and close my eyes, committing to memory how she feels.

"I was hoping you'd say that," she tells me several minutes later.

"I know," I tell her, holding her to me for a few more moments. "I know."

***

Half an hour later, she's finally gone to clean herself up. I grin, then look at my top in the sliding mirror to see it's covered in her tears and snot. I don't mind, but I quickly dash to my room and put on a replacement.

I'm back at her bedroom door just as she returns.

"Oh! You... what did you do?" she quietly asks.

I motion for her to go into her room, and as she does, I make my way over to her window, closing the blinds and the curtains. She's sitting on the edge of the bed, watching me.

"I had to change my top." I grin, and she goes red in the cheeks.

"Sorry," she whispers, standing to meet me.

"No...," I command her, lifting her eyes to mine. "You don't get to apologise for being you, for letting go of the hurt or messing my clothes up. Not like that."

I look into her soft brown eyes, watching her irises dilate and contract as she processes what I've told her. Without thinking about it, I close the door and lean down, letting my mouth gently press against hers.

She sighs and opens her mouth. I gently explore her warmth, her scent. Her tongue comes to dance with mine, and I wrap my hands into her hair, turning her head to deepen the kiss. She tastes of salty pasta and squash, which until now, was just food, but it makes me so hungry for her. She moans quietly as she pushes herself into me, her softness, along with the lack of underwear, makes me react. She pulls back and purses her lips together.

"Oh, wow...," she breathes.

"I should let you rest," I begin, and she sighs. I lift her chin so that she's looking at me. Then I push into her, and she backs up to the door. "If I don't go," I grind into her slowly, and her eyes go wide. "And you're not well enough to do that, not yet," I tell her. She might be nineteen now, but she's dealing with a lot of emotional stuff. She's not where she needs to be for this between us to get physical, not yet. I kiss her again, gently this time.

"Good night, Frank," she whispers to me as I pull away. She moves and bites her bottom lip, then she looks at me through hooded eyes. I place a hand along her jawline, feeling her softness.

"Good night, Tabs," I grin, and then I head up to my room as I hear her door close quietly. I gently shut my door and head to my bathroom so I can take care of the problem I've let her create.

***

I head down after my second shower and check on Tabs, her door is ajar, but she's asleep, softly breathing. The clock says that it's just about nine pm now. I smile and head down to chat with my parents, spending a quiet evening in front of the TV with some of the people I love.

The following morning, I'm up and out of the door and heading to a personal training session before Tabitha or the rest of the house have stirred. I checked in on her as I went to bed, she'd moved the lamp to the floor, but she seemed to be peacefully asleep. When I looked this morning, the lamp was still on and I don't think she'd moved.

I grin as I walk past her room, the curtains make it very pink and girly, which I think was mum's intention. I make up a breakfast fruit and protein shake, then I head to the gym and my first client.

***

By the time I'm home again, everyone is out. Mum sent me a message, saying that she's taken Tabitha to the hair-dressers, Shane to nursery and she'll be back late morning. I grin and go grab a shower, focusing on what is going to happen today. I haven't told Tabs. Mum said she would, and I hope she has. I'm eating lunch when mum and Tabitha return. There's some colour on Tabitha's cheeks, her lips are glossy, and I realise she's wearing some light makeup.

"You're looking great," I tell her, admiring her form, and the confidence that she's gained. She twirls around and her long, straight hair has been altered so it's now wavy, the dullness that it had has been sorted out. There's a smile on her soft, light pink lips that I echo.

"Thank you!" she whispers to me, and I make her sit down.

"What did you do, besides the hairdressers?" I ask. They walk me through their morning from taking Shane to nursery school to the hairdressers, buying some fresh makeup. Tabitha yawns as mum busies herself at the cooker.

"You overdid it," I scold her a little and she smiles at me, her eyes soft.

"Maybe, but it was nice getting out and doing girly things," she grins. "What time is… I forgot his name again!" she chastises herself.

"Mr Carter," mum replies. Ah, the lawyer in charge of Tabitha's mother's will. Mum has told her. "And two o'clock," says mum as she hands Tabitha a plate of scrambled eggs with toast.

"I think I need a little nap before I meet with him. Is that okay?" Tabitha looks between mum and I, but we're both nodding.

"I think you need it," I tell her, winking at her. She eats the small pile of eggs and the slice of toast mum has made, and then she's off to bed for a nap.

"You seem distracted," mum tells me, and I shrug, nonchalantly. I don't want to admit to my mother that I didn't sleep well because the girl I'd been crushing on was home, and that I had to take care of business before I joined them in front of the TV last night.

"I'm okay...," I begin, but my mother chortles.

"You've got it bad," she tells me, and I can't help but grin.

"I do... but she's not there yet." Mum just smiles at me softly, pats me on the arm and busies herself around the kitchen, preparing dinner.

"She'll get there," she tells me, and I nod.

We will. I check in with my clients, seeing an update from one on their health journey and they've met one of their targets. I mail them back with praise and suggest they switch their attention to another part of their body, but pointing out we will be keeping an eye on the leg area, too. I take their latest images and post them to social media, singing their praises and dedication on each of the platforms I have. Instagram is the biggest one I use, with over four hundred thousand followers.

I get replies in an instant, praising him and me, but I know I'm not doing all the work. The hard part the client is doing. I'm just focusing their minds, telling them what to do, holding them to account and being there on their journey. I get on with engaging with my other clients before I take a break, making up a drink. I check the time and I realise I've not chatted with Omar for days. Grinning, I check he's free and moments later, he's calling me.

"'Ey up!" He greets me as I answer the phone. I head out to sit in the sunshine, getting out from under my mother's feet. "How ya doing?" he asks as I take a seat on the swing chair.

"Doing okay! You? Just wanted a chat," I share with him.

"Yeah, my cousin is getting married in late September, so we're preparing for that."

I grin. He has a huge family and the ceremony will be epic. It is always that way for Hindu weddings. "I'll bet it's all hands on deck," I chuckle at him.

"You've got no idea," he says, and I chuckle. Just last year I helped him out with one aspect of another wedding, and we were run ragged all week trying to get it all sorted in time. We managed it, though, because we said we would..

"Yeah, I do!" I chortle at him.

"How're things at your end? Is she home yet?" he asks, and I bring him up to date with Tabitha being home. I don't need to share that I've kissed her, that I want to do more with her.

"Keep it light mate," he reminds me. "Date her. Did you ever do any of that before?" he asks, and I stop my thoughts right in their tracks.

"No," I admit, and he laughs.

"Okay, I'll meet you for a coffee or something after the gym tomorrow. What time do you want to be there?" he asks, and we confirm a time. "'ll give you some hints my friend."

"Do I need them?" I ask, though I'm sure I do. My brain forgets to work when I'm in proximity to her ,,and one day I'm going to pull back and make her feel awkward, which will undo all I've done so far and all I want to do.

"Having a firm game plan helps, not just in the gym," he tells me. That galvanises me.

"We tell that to our clients all the damn time," I remind him. "Just never thought about it for dating a woman," I quip.

"Man, everything in life needs a game plan," he retorts. "I gotta go, later!" He bids me goodbye and hangs up as I quickly do the same. From here, I can see Tabitha's bedroom. I can't tell if the curtains are closed, but the blinds are turned against the sun and the window is open slightly. I smile, hoping that she didn't hear me. But if she did, she did.

***

Mum is busy with some laundry when Tabitha comes downstairs, still slightly sleepy, but she perks up when she sees me.

"Ready for a snack?" I ask her, and she nods. I don't know how much she weighs, we'll find out tomorrow at the doctor's appointment, but I can tell she's underweight. A diet isn't just about losing it. It's about being a healthy weight, though most of the people I train with are trying to lose the weight, tone up and shed the pounds. Tabitha might need a little toning, but losing the weight isn't on her agenda.

I prepare a small bowl of apricots, nuts and soft figs with a tall glass of squash.

"Thanks, Frank," she tells me and we sit in a comfortable silence as she eats.

CHAPTER 14

Tabitha

I set my alarm so I was up half an hour before the lawyer was due. Frank greets me, and he makes sure I eat something healthy as a snack, which I do slowly, grateful that I don't have to have this conversation alone or worry about what to eat. Just before two, Katie lets the lawyer in.

"I need to distract Shane, so we'll head to the park after nursery," she tells me. I nod.

"Won't he be too tired later?" I ask, and she shakes her head.

"Not today. He can go to bed earlier. Frank will be here for you." She kisses me softly on the cheek, then she heads out of the door. Frank makes Mr Carter a coffee as we get to know each other with some small chat.

"So, you're Emily's daughter? It's nice to meet you," he tells me and extends a hand to greet me. His hand is firm but soft, and he has more salt in the hair department than Phil, making him look older.

"Where shall we sit?" he asks and Frank takes us into the conservatory, to the comfy sofa. I find what I consider to be my spot and I sit, waiting, swallowing a few times more than normal. My throat is tight, and my stomach has a cacophony of butterflies in it.

"Perfect. Now, Tabitha, this is quite simple. Your mother left mostly everything in her will to you," he tells me as he pulls out papers from his briefcase. "There are some things that she wanted Shane to have when he turns eighteen." He pulls out a pair of reading glasses.

For the next half an hour, he talks Frank and I through mum's will. Since the house was rented from the Council, her estate was small. However, some of her jewellery which was saved thanks to Frank and his family, is mine to keep. Some of the items didn't make it because of that arse-hole of a step-dad, but I can only shrug. I cannot pass to my brother what I do not have. But what I do with mum's belongings is down to me. He won't miss out just because the items, her engagement and wedding band from *my* father, are missing.

"She had a small bank account, which has been held in trust for you and Shane. It's to help with your education, for college, so you get two thousand if you enrol. The rest is to be held in trust until Shane is eighteen, and he can decide what to use it for. Do you have a bank account?" I shake my head, indicating that I do not. "We'll get that sorted for you. I'll confirm some things in writing to you this week, which you can take to a bank and get an account open and anything else you need to do, like register with the doctors." He tells me which accounts might be good for a nineteen-year-old to open up. He's done his homework.

"Thank you," I reply to him. He picks up his coffee and leans back in the chair. "I'm seeing the doctor tomorrow," I inform him, and he takes down their details to email paperwork directly to them.

"Not a problem. Emily was quite insistent about her will being as it is. Her husband," he pauses, "was never to receive anything. Her first thought was of you, then Shane." He reaches into his briefcase and removes an envelope. "She asked that I give you this if anything were to happen," he tells me, his voice choking, and he's holding back tears.

"Were you a friend?" I ask, suspecting he was more. Or that he wanted to be.

He nods. "We were at school together," he tells me, and my heart sinks. Why couldn't mum have sought comfort in his arms when dad died? "But I was married when your dad passed," he tells me, and I get it. He wasn't available.

"Do I have to read it now?" I ask, looking between Frank and Mr Carter, wanting some privacy to read my mother's carefully crafted words. I know I'm going to be crying more when I do, and I don't want an audience.

"No, when you're ready. She did tell me you were good at art," he mentions, and I nod towards my sketchbook.

"I'm out of practice, but I'm getting back into it," I tell him. He smiles a warm, genuine smile. He picks up my A5 sketchbook and gives me a look that asks for permission. I smile and motion with my hand to carry on, not trusting that my voice will work right now. He flicks through the few drawings I've sketched of the garden swing, a chair, the lamp when it's on, the shadows of the vase, all inanimate. The older ones from when I was fifteen don't count in my view.

"She said you'd make a great artist." He hands me a college prospectus from his briefcase. "I don't know if you've thought of your next step," he tells me as he nods to the A4 brochure, "but I took the liberty of seeing what the colleges around here have available and what they need from you. A small portfolio, A4 size is ideal, for their A level art class. I understand you did well in art in GCSE."

I gape at Frank and gingerly pick up the brochure, then flick through it.

"When does college start?" I ask. We're in mid-August now. "And yes, I got a 7 in that subject." Mr Carter looks confused. "7 is quite high, a 10 is the old A**." He nods, understanding.

"Mid-September," Mr Carter tells me as he leans forward a little more. "Submissions are closed, in general, but I've taken the liberty and spoken with college admissions and the Dean. Given your circumstances, they'll take a look at your portfolio, and they have space on the A level art course. They just need to see your portfolio, if you want to go that way. Maybe add in some real-life drawings," he smiles at me as he hands me back my sketchbook.

"College," I whisper. I'd never thought of that as my next step, but it would have been, years ago. "That means I'll need support for the next few years, or more," I tell them. Frank grabs my hand and smiles at me, his touch instantly calms and grounds me, his smile focuses me.

"The support is there if that is what you want to do, Tabs." His sincere look hits me to the core; there's nothing his family won't do right now. Supporting my brother and me for the next three years. *Can I ask that of them?*

"You'd-do that?" I ask. I have no worries that the lawyer will be embarrassed to sit here and witness my meekness, I just don't care if he is bothered.

Frank nods. "We spoke about it, before you came back when we took Shane in. Mum and dad are up for the haul. They were with you before you came back. That's not changed." He shifts so he's facing me. "If we weren't, you wouldn't have a room upstairs," he tells me. I sigh, knowing that he's right. When I knew I'd need their help, it wasn't to this extent. At least, I didn't think it would be.

"There is one thing I need to clarify," the lawyer states and I turn to him, not letting go of Frank's hand. "Mr and Mrs Allen have made it known that they'd like to formally adopt Shane. His care was to come to you when you returned, but to do so comes with some stipulations."

I look between the lawyer and Frank. It's almost like being at a tennis match.

"Go on," I tell him, quietly, trying to keep the knot in my stomach at bay so I don't throw up.

"To look after him, you're to have a stable home and job. Unless you go to college and live your life as she wanted you to. Basically, you can take Shane on as a responsibility and jump through so many hoops that it'll make your head spin, or live your life and have him taken care of, but still be in his life."

I sit back and think about it, for all of two minutes. "I'm not ready to be his mum." I look at Frank, then at Mr Carter. "I've only just gotten used to being his big sister," I grip Franks' hand and he winces, so I lessen my grasp. This decides my future, and Shane's. *Do I have that right?* "I can't be his mum," I say, and the tears start. "I want to, but I am not ready," I tell them and Frank is beside me, hugging me from the side.

"We didn't think you were. But breaking you two up isn't an option we'd want to go for either," he confirms quietly, but loud enough so Mr Carter can hear.

Some tissue appears in my hand, and the box is placed between Frank and me. I dry my tears, but more are threatening to escape. I suck in a breath and pray; pray that I'm making the best decision for us both.

"I will do it if I absolutely have to," I tell Mr Carter, who nods. "But, I haven't lived, not really. I want to go to college, at least I think I do. I want to explore life, kiss boys," I don't glance at Frank, I don't need Mr Carter working out I'm keen on him, and it's part of why I named them as emergency contacts for the hospital records. "Go to parties,"

"Festivals," Frank adds. "Theme parks."

I nod. "I want to enjoy those things with my brother, make friends and find new things to do. I can't if I have to wipe our circumstances clean and begin again. I'm barely an adult as it is. But, I want to check with Katie and Phil first." I hold up my mother's letter. "And read this before I give you a definitive answer," I clarify.

Mr Carter nods and smiles. "You're as prudent and as wise as your mother," he smiles. "I'll give you a week to consider your final answer," he taps my sketchbook. "Though, I would encourage you to pursue *your* dreams." He stares at me intently, as if conveying something to me that he already knows.

"I need some time to think about my options please, Mr Carter," I repeat. He smiles.

"And just as polite and firm in your stance. Your mother was the same," he comments again. I pull my shoulders back and sit up a little straighter. That's the best compliment I think I've ever been paid.

Mr Carter finishes up his coffee. "You don't need to come into the office, but I'd like a number to call you on, so we can discuss things," he tells me. Frank reads him out my number. I haven't memorised it yet, but I intend to.

Frank sees Mr Carter out and whilst they're gone, I finger the letter my mother wrote to me. It's not a very fat envelope, it's less than a postcard in size and about that thick. I spy a letter opener on one of the shelves, and I use it, then settle down to read my mother's letter.

Her swirls are just as neat as they ever were, and I grab the box of tissues, suspecting I'm going to be needing them.

My darling Tabitha,

If you're reading this, I hope this short letter finds you well, safe and loved. Or on the verge of finding all that is good in this world, just as you are.

I'm sorry I didn't run away with you. I should have. I realise that now. I was angry and sad that you left. I didn't know he'd threatened you until much later, but by then, I was unable to get out.

When I found out I was pregnant, I wanted to hate the child that he'd given me, but I couldn't. I can't just leave him or take him with me. I didn't know where to go, and I didn't want to ask in case he found out.

Don't worry about taking care of your brother. I suspect when you come back, you'll visit Frank and his parents. Your note to them was quite clever, and so are you my brave, gorgeous girl!

Please, live your life! If you can help Shane, then please help. If you need to step in, then please do, but otherwise, remember <u>your</u> life is for you to live.

Please don't spend it fixing my mistakes. I wish I'd been brave enough to do it for myself.

I love you!

Mum

    I'm doing exactly what I knew I would after seeing my mother's writing. I push it away, not wishing for her last note to get damaged by the waterfall cascading down my face. My head hurts now, I find it hard to breathe. I think I'm alone, but strong arms are bound around me, turning me, the soft strokes to the back of my head and down my back tell me he's there, that he understands. I'm not alone. This is my life to live. But I still can't breathe, think or tell mum that I loved her, that I still do.
    The other person in this world that I have feelings for is holding me, and when I sort myself out, I know I'll need to be brave enough to tell him.

***

    I'm not sure what time it is when Katie and Shane come back, but when my brother sees I've been crying, he's by my side, hugging me.

I can see Katie is by the kitchen door and Phil is behind her. I motion for them to join Frank, Shane and me. This is their house, and they're acting like I own the place. I know I don't.

"I've got some decisions to make," I say, and I look at my brother. "*We* have decisions to make." I pause as his little face looks up at me. "Shane, would you like nana to be your new mummy?" I ask him, gently. He looks at me confused.

"Why not sister?" he asks.

I swallow. "Because then sister needs a job, a different house," I begin, but that's enough for his little brain to grasp.

"Don't want to leave," he states, his little face scrunching up and getting cross at me.

"That's good because I feel the same. So, how about Katie gets to be your new mummy, a second mummy, and I still be your big sister?"

He looks across at Katie. "Nana gets to be my mummy?" He turns to me. "And your mummy?" He asks, but I can only sigh.

"I am too old to get a second mummy," I begin, but Katie shuts me down.

"You are not too old," she tells me. "I'm happy to be mummy to you both," she says, and she looks between Frank and me. There's a knowing look sent to her son, and he leans in to whisper into my ear. I go wide-eyed as he whispers a short sentence: "I want you to stay." This is all too much though.

I nod. "Yes, mummy to us both," I tell my brother as I hug him tight. Katie just nods and leans into her husband. Frank pulls me to him and Shane follows me; but we spend half an hour just being, together, the five of us.

***

After Shane is in bed, we get to talk, as adults.

"Why didn't you say you wanted to adopt Shane?" I ask them because that was a curveball I hadn't expected.

Katie sighs. "We knew you'd want to take him on, but that lawyer always told us your mother's wish was to have you live your life, not fix her mistakes." Katie sips some of her drink, and I notice her hand shakes slightly. "Shane's not a mistake, but if you're going to be here, Shane is too. Mr Carter made it clear that he believed your mother's last wish was for you both to go do what you wanted in life." Phil's hand reaches across his wife's lap and grabs the hand not holding the drink.

"We always wanted that for Frank, even if we were slightly blinkered as to how," Katie continues. Yeah, he was on their track, until I ran, and as he said, it made him realise he had to go and get what he wanted, not to answer others' expectations.

I can't run away, not now. While I might not be responsible for Shane, I still want to be in my little brother's life. I need to be. And Frank's. This is *our* chance. I'm not throwing it away because I get scared. Not again.

"I'm not sure what I want to do. I didn't consider college until today and mum left me a nest egg, but I need to build on that," I tell them. "I can't work yet, and college starts in a few weeks. I would need to focus on my portfolio if I wanted to go that route." I looked through the requirements earlier. I will need to showcase my style, not just the still life, but real life, and in various formats, from drawings to watercolour, acrylic, crayon and collage. I chuckled at that, but I know artists' crayons are more expensive and blend better than the crayons my brother is just getting used to.

"We can get you what you need," Phil tells me, but I shake my head.

"There are plenty of supplies in that shed, I'm sure. I will take a look tomorrow," I promise, more to myself than anyone else. "If I need anything else, the funds will be there soon to take care of it," I tell them.

"How so?" Katie asks with a strange look on her face. She turns to Phil, not sure what's going on, then she turns to me.

"The nest egg Mum left I get, but only if I went the college route," I explain. I'm glad I have them to talk with, facing this on my own would be hell. "If I do, I get that money to pay for the course, the supplies. If I don't, it's kept where it is in trust for Shane; I guess it was to prevent Lee from getting his hands on it. I won't get access to it otherwise, but I get it if I further my education." I don't need them to know just how much I'm being given. "But, I will want to add to that, so I was thinking of taking a part-time job, funding my way through with the job and touching that initial fund to get what I need."

Katie and Phil nod with me, understanding.

"That sounds like a good idea," Phil tells me, giving me his approval for my plan.

"Telling Shane what happened with your mum was hard. I wish there was a way we could make it easier for him," Katie tells me. I shrug and snuggle into Frank, but somewhere out in the back of my mind, I feel an idea sparking up.

***

Later that night, we're all watching TV. I'm getting used to the noise. Katie has turned it down a few notches, though she complains she can't hear it as well. Phil tells her to go get her hearing checked, but she refuses, for now. I love how they banter, hold each other to account, all without a raised voice or screaming at each other.

Frank's mobile rings, and he heads out to take the call, coming back in near the end of the programme. Not that he'll care that he's missed most of it. I'm still not quite sure what's going on with the show we're watching.

When he comes back in, Katie drops the volume so we can talk.

"What was the call?" his father asks as Frank eases himself to sit next to me. He reaches out for my hand.

"Fashion shoot over in Northampton that they want me to do at the weekend. I've accepted. Just need to juggle clients around to free up the time." He turns to me and smiles. "Got you a pass to come with me," he tells me.

I gape at him. "Really?" I ask. I'm not sure I want to.

He nods. "There are plenty of people there, other models, who will happily pose for a photograph from an aspiring art student," he smiles at me, and my brain catches up where he's gone with this.

"Oh my god!" I squeal as I leap forward and hug him. "I'd love that! Yes, please!" I cry out. I glance across at Katie and Phil, who are grinning from ear to ear. "You're okay with that?" I ask them, and they nod.

"We'll tell Shane the truth in a way he can understand. You've gone to work with Frank for a few days so you can do some drawings for college. We just need to make sure you've got all you need." Katie grins at me. They've moved heaven and earth for me, made space and offered me shelter. I'm so glad I came home!

***

The following day, I'm up early, the same time as Frank. It's about six am, maybe just after. The sun is up, the coffee is on, and I grin as he joins me in the kitchen. Frank hands me a plate of scrambled eggs as it's just us up. Shane is still in bed, where most little boys ought to be. His parents are, too, not that I blame them.

"You couldn't sleep?" Frank asks me, and I shake my head.

"I'm excited! I need time to go through those supplies though, and I thought I could do it outside...," The day isn't warm yet, but give it another hour. "I wanted to take a short walk first, though." Frank nods in agreement.

"You want to walk past the old place," he says, reading me, and I nod, inhaling deeply. *How did he guess?*

"I need to," I whisper back. "Lay some ghosts to rest," I reply, quietly. Frank just nods and finishes his shake. I finish my breakfast, but not quite as quickly, and then we're quietly leaving the house.

***

It takes all of four minutes to walk the length of the three streets back to the place I grew up, where for a time, I was happy. Until mum found him. Lee Hill. It was okay, for the first year or so. Once they were married, though, the changes started. As I look up at the house, I recall the bad times that have played in my mind so often, the good times are hard to find. Frank's arms are hugging me tight as the sight of the house blurs, then he drags me away to a path and towards the park; away from there.

"Maybe that was too soon," he tells me as we sit on some swings, and he hands me a tissue. I haven't sat on swings since I was at school. It was on these swings I decided I liked Frank Allen, when I realised he was more than just an annoying boy of the family that offered me shelter. I really liked him.

"It needs doing. Just not sure it's going to get done in one visit," I shiver as I tell him.

"You've got the doctors today, I...," Frank stops talking and swinging. "I want you to consider something, please?" he asks me as he gazes at me with the same look in his eyes as he did when I told him about my letter.

"Something else?" I reply, wondering what he's going to spring on me now.

He nods. "Maybe consider some counselling, so you can start to put all this crap behind you," he moves off the swing as he talks, then comes to me and holds my hands, almost begging me. I can only nod in agreement. I need to talk to someone and asking Frank and his family to burden themselves with what is in my head doesn't agree with me. "You will? Seriously?" he asks me, his voice lifting and getting stronger.

I nod and smile. "You... You don't want to hear what's in my head," I take a huge breath, "but I know I need to get it out," I reveal. He pulls me up and hugs me tightly.

"Oh babe, you're just... utterly amazing!" He tells me and we begin to walk back to his house, holding hands. We take a different route back through the estate and my soul seems to be ascending as we walk, as I begin to start living again. My heart is lifted and I want the possibility of the life that's now before me. Mum told me to live, so that's what I'm going to do.

The doctor's appointment is at half-past ten, so I have a little time to start sorting through some of my art supplies. Frank helps me pull the two boxes out of the shed, and I sit down at the garden table, slowly going through everything, trying this tube or checking that stack of pencils. I'm surprised that most of it is intact! The acrylics aren't, but I didn't expect anything to have survived, or for me to be on the cusp of going to college. I have a stack of methods and mediums I can use right now. Frank grins at me just before ten am and removes his top.

"I'd love for you to draw me," he tells me, and I get to see just how sculpted he is now. On his left peck, an amazing array of tattoos are on display, the base of which is a Celtic dragon. It's not just his pec; it goes across to his bicep and down the top half of his arm to his elbow. He chuckles, and I remember to close my mouth. Then I blink several times. As I do, I can feel my cheeks go warm. I can't take my eyes off the ridges and contours of his chest and stomach, which he makes dance by flexing.

"Oh my!" is all I can say as I look at him.

"Where's your phone, babe?" he asks, and I blink.

"In my room," I quietly respond. "I'll go get it," I leave him standing in the garden looking like Adonis himself landed at my feet and quickly grab my phone, before returning to the garden. I can hear Shane stirring so I know we have to be quick.

"I don't know...," I begin and Frank just grins as he holds his hands out. Then he shows me how to use the camera, and I quickly take some shots of his upper body, standing in the sunlight as if he's taking a quiet moment to contemplate.

"You know," he tells me as he puts his top back on. "There are going to be guys there tomorrow who are more sculpted than this," he points to himself, and I do go wide-eyed again.

"Really?" I ask and he nods. "I best not act like I just did."

He laughs, coming over to where I've perched on a garden chair. "Babe, you'll get used to it by the end of the day. But," he says, standing between my legs to kiss me, "I am the one who gets to take you home." An alarm rings out on his phone, and he silences it quickly. "It's nearly time to leave for the doctors," he tells me, and I nod.

"Right... the doctors," I repeat, dragging my mind and body from where it's gone to the gutter, to the moment at hand. I gulp a few times, then nod as he backs away, his eyes dancing at my uneasiness. *Why does he seem to be enjoying seeing me squirm?*

CHAPTER 15

Tabitha

I tap my foot as I notice that the doctor is now running twenty-five minutes late. Whilst Frank and I put the art supplies back in the boxes and sat them in the shade, the sun will have moved, and I'm worried my few supplies might be damaged.

"Frank?" I whisper to him as we wait. The survival of the art supplies is worrying me. He grins and holds his phone up. His father has moved the boxes back into the shed, out of the sunlight. I grin. "Thank you!" I breathe out, then I notice that Frank asked him to as we are delayed going in.

"You'll come in with me? I... new people make me nervous," I explain, and he smiles, squeezing my hand.

"I'll just be there, but this is down to you, okay?"

I nod and sigh, then I stare at a spot in the pattern on the floor; anything to stop the mind-monkeys from running riot in my head. Finally, I'm called through, and I focus on what I have to do.

"So, Ms Reid, how can we help you today?" The doctor begins and she doesn't look at me. I wait until she does, and then I smile at her.

"I was homeless until a few weeks ago, then I had to have my appendix removed. Frank's family have taken me in as they're looking after my little brother."

The doctor turns to him and suddenly she's all smiles, her eyes light up. "Ah yes! I know of you... Mr and Mrs Allen have spoken of you a few times when I've had to tend to Shane. How is he?" She turns back to me, but the smile and acknowledgement she had for Frank, is not there for me. One thing the streets taught you is how to read people.

I explain that my brother is fine, but that the doctor at the hospital wanted a full work up. She nods and calls in the nurse, telling the nurse what she wants to have done to me, which doesn't seem too exhausting for a change.

"When you're done, I'll check your operation wound, and we'll come up with a plan for what needs to happen next, okay?" She smiles at me and she's friendly enough, but I can see her eyes following Frank as we leave one room and head to another.

***

"The doctors give you the time you need, which means they run a little late...," he tells me. My thoughts must show though because he gives me a funny look. "We'll talk about what's bugging you later on, babe," he tells me, touching the small of my back gently. I'm so glad he's here. I'd be walking away if he hadn't been waiting patiently with me. And I'd not be wanting to see the doctor and be frustrated because I left. Or I'd have run away. Again.

The nurse doesn't seem phased by Frank being there, she focuses on me. She makes me strip to my underwear, then weighs me, takes in my height and measures me all around. I can spot Frank making the same notes. Minutes later, I'm allowed to put my clothes back on, and then she stops me and gets me to lay down.

"Might as well get the doc in to take a look at that whilst you're already mostly undressed," she smiles at me. I rather like this nurse. She heads out and Frank smiles at me.

"You okay, babe?" he asks, and I nod.

I reach out for his hand and squeeze it as the doctor comes in. She stops for a moment, then smiles at us both and preps herself up by washing her hands and putting on some surgical gloves. Then, she's checking over what I'm calling my war wound. Whilst she's prodding quite hard, it's not painful.

"That's healing nicely, and I can't see or feel any stitches protruding." She says as she removes the gloves. "I had a good poke, and I am not concerned about anything residual being in there. So, from my point of view...," she reads the details the nurse has inserted into my medical file, "you're quite underweight, but nothing that can't be sorted. You're forty-six point two kilogrammes, and your ideal weight of about fifty-seven. It's a case of just eating healthily, regularly and getting enough exercise and sleep."

"What kind of exercise can I do? I wasn't sporty at school, and I'm not up for doing what Frank does." I notice the doc glance at him, and he shrugs.

"I don't want you to do any swimming in a pool, or have baths for a few more weeks yet, but you can certainly have showers now. As for exercise..." Frank hands me items of clothing, namely my socks and shoes, as the doctor talks to me. "Walks are great, do some light housework—get moving, get active."

I nod and finish getting dressed. "I'll do that," I tell her, and the determined look on Frank's face tells me he'll make sure I do it, too. "There is something I wanted to ask," I tell her, and she perches against the nurse's chair. "The reason I was homeless is that I ran away. I may...," I balk, trying to find the words I need. I look at Frank who nods. "No, I need to talk about it with someone." I look at the doctor, hoping I'm not asking for the moon here. "A professional someone," I confirm.

The doctor nods. "Okay, are you thinking anything in particular when you think about why you ran? You're Emily Reid's daughter, aren't you?" she confirms again.

I nod. "Yes, I am," I tell her, and she smiles.

"Emily was lovely. I keep forgetting Shane's her son, your brother." The doctor stands up straight and I realise she's nearly the same height as Frank. "Have you any suicidal thoughts, given what happened?" she asks gently, and I shake my head. It seems I might be rather known around the area.

"No, but the thoughts I have are all jumbled, and I can't ask mum," I share. The doctor's face softens, and compassion shows.

"Okay, there's a few places and people I can refer you to for trauma counselling, none of which happen here, though, I'm afraid," she says to me. I nod, I didn't expect it to, and I hope I don't have to travel too far.

"I'll send the referrals off this week. If you're struggling in the meantime, I suggest a diary of sorts, so you can write down things that you want to think about, or explore."

I nod, grateful for the advice. "Thank you," I say. Now, I feel bad that I thought she seemed to be paying attention to Frank at the start more than me, or making eyes at him.

"I'll see you when you need us, Tabitha," she says and nods to the nurse as she heads out.

"I'll check early next week and make sure the referrals have gone through," the nurse tells me. "Let's get your blood work done, then you can head off home." She tells me. Five minutes later, I'm sporting a large plaster on my inner arm, and there are a few vials of blood on the nurse's desk.

***

As we walk home, Frank pulls me up against the perimeter wall of a house and pulls me into his open legs, wrapping me into his space; into him. I breathe him in, glad to be out of the doctors and have that part over with. I'm going to enjoy a good shower when I get back before I carry on with checking my art supplies. His hug is all-encompassing, surrounding me and making me feel safe.

"What was going on back there?" he asks as he holds me tight to his firm chest.

I sigh. "The doctor was focusing on you, to begin with, not me."

He grins. "The doctor is a client," he tells me, but I shrug.

"Her face fell when she saw you holding my hand in the nurse's room, but only for a brief second."

He blinks. "Really?" he asks and I nod. "I don't take her home, Tabs. Never will. You're all that I want," he tells me as he kisses my temple.

I snuggle into him for a moment, then I start to pull away. "We need to go back. I probably still need to hit the art shops to get what I need," I remind him. Frank's smile is soft, genuine and he holds my hand firmly as we walk back home.

***

A few hours later, I had enjoyed my first full shower. Shane is now at nursery, and I've gone through both boxes of supplies. My art folders didn't get saved, and I make a list of what items I need to replace. I don't have the cash from mum yet, and I know what little I had on me won't cover the cost of a carry-case, let alone this small shopping list.

I'm sitting with the notepad and pen at the garden table. The sun parasol is up and Frank is sitting next to me, checking in with his clients to do what he does on his laptop. He looks up at me as I glance at him nervously.

"What's up, babe?" He asks me, and I share with him what I'm thinking.

"Would you lend me the cash until my account is set up?" I ask, showing him the list and the total I'm expecting it to come to. It's the best part of three hundred pounds. He just nods.

"Sure." He taps his phone. "I'm going to ask Mr Carter where he is on that legal stuff you need," he tells me, and I chuckle.

"I'm not expecting it until next week, and if I weren't going with you tomorrow, I'd not think about any of this." I look at the list again. Tomorrow. That's what I need to focus on. "Actually, I only need the A4 carry-case and the A4 sketchpad. The rest I can get when I've got the money," I tell him.

"Okay! Well, I've asked. Where would we get this?" He asks me, and I grin.

"There are a couple of places in Dudley, or there are arty supply shops in Merry Hill," I say, making him nod and smile.

"Can you be ready in about ten minutes? I'm just finishing up here," he says to me, and I grin.

"Yep!" I say, putting away the small case of things that I'm preparing which contains the pencils and pastels I want to take with me. I take my supplies inside, hugging Katie on the way.

"Are you two heading out?" she asks, and I nod.

"I need some storage folders and more drawing pads, so we're heading to Dudley to the supply shops."

Frank comes in at my back and grins at his mum. "We need to head out," he says to her, and she nods.

"Tabitha was just telling me." She smiles at me, and he chuckles.

"Shall we get going?" he asks me, and I hold back, I can smell fresh eggs that have been beaten.

"Not staying for lunch?" Katie asks, and my stomach rumbles at the mention of food.

"Eggy bread?" he asks as he looks around at what Katie is doing.

"Of course!" she tells him, and that decides it. We'll go after we've eaten.

***

An hour later, after a few slices of French toast, we're walking around Dudley to find the two art supply shops that I know are in the town. We locate the first one and venture inside the cool interior to be greeted by the smell of oils, pastels, crayons, paper and wood. I inhale and sigh contentedly. This could very well be my new favourite space.

"Can I help you?" an older gentleman asks us as we enter. I smile at him.

"I am in need of some supplies. An art folder, a drawing pad for pastel, crayons and charcoal." I go on with the small list that I require. The older man smiles at me as he helps me find the equipment I've listed.

Twenty minutes and a small bill later, Frank and I leave the shop, but we have a few items to carry. I can feel my cheeks going red at how much all this cost. It was more than just the A4 pad, my enthusiasm making it easy for Frank to purchase these for me.

"Don't worry about it," he tells me as we get to the car.

"I will pay you back," I promise, and he smiles at me.

"I know you will, babe," he says as we carefully put the folders and new supplies into the boot. "And I know it's a loan," he tells me as we climb in.

"I'm glad you know that," I smile at him. "It's important to me," I begin, but he reaches across and holds my hand.

"I know. Mr Carter replied. He's having the paperwork dropped off tomorrow, which means we can get you an account sorted as early as next week," he advises.

"That's great news," I reply as we head back.

***

I'm tired when we get back, but I take some time to pack my art supplies first, making sure I have all those stored safely as some are fiddly and breakable. Then, Katie comes in with a small suitcase for me.

"You can borrow this," she tells me as she places a small silver, hard case on the bed. "Until you can get your own," she smiles at me.

"Thank you!" I enthuse as I zip the art case shut and place it near the folder.

"Dinner will be at around six, when Phil is due home," Katie tells me, and then I hear Shane coming in, calling for me. Frank went to fetch him whilst I sorted through my art things.

"Sister going away?" Shane asks as he bounces onto my bed.

"For work, yes. I'm going with Frank to his photoshoot tomorrow so I can get some photographs of people I want to draw," I tell him. "It'll help me get into college," I explain a little more as he nods.

"Shane not come," he tells me, sadly.

"No, this is work. There won't be anything fun for you to do. Katie and Phil will be here to look after you and give you snacks. Do what you usually do on a Friday and Saturday. We'll be back on Sunday," I tell him.

He sulks for a moment, then I have an idea. "I am tired. Shane, wanna tuck your big sister in for a nap?" I ask as I yawn. I had wanted to do a pretend one, but that was genuine.

He nods and Frank smiles at me from the doorway. "I'll see to him," I tell him and Katie, who head off. Minutes later, my little brother and I lay on my bed. A blanket is over us, and I watch as sleep claims him, then me.

***

"Hey, you two," Frank's voice quietly interrupts my dreams, and I blink myself awake. Shane seems to do the same and then he's awake, sitting up and hugging Frank. He's like a switch; sleepy one moment, vibrant the next. I grin as he follows Frank to the bathroom, and I stretch. The smell of wonderful food reaches me and makes me get up. It can't be nearly six already, surely? But, it is.

After dinner, Shane and I sit in the conservatory, reading a book. I take my phone out and take some pictures of my little brother reading.

"Shane, can I draw you for my school work?" I ask, and he looks up at me, a smile broad upon his little face as his eyes dance.

"Yes!" he cries out and sits very still as I take a picture of his little face. Human faces are the hardest to draw, and getting their features right is going to take some practice. At least now, I know I can.

When Shane is in bed, I begin packing and Frank comes to "help" me. He checks the weather report, and I pack light. Later, when I'm alone, I add in a few of the nicer pyjamas Katie purchased for me. My bank account cannot come quickly enough.

CHAPTER 16

Tabitha

Early the next morning, we're on the road to Northampton, songs playing on the radio and we're both singing along to the ones we know. Then, he pulls up his Spotify and asks me to pick a band. There's a huge collection, and I'm not sure what I want to listen to. I've enjoyed the radio, but then I see *Pulp* and I grin. I pick them, and the car fills with the voice of Jarvis Cocker as Frank guides the car to our destination.

He thoughtfully made protein shakes for us both, and as we get stuck in traffic, we slowly drink them. I've started drawing my brother's face, getting the shape and the rough contours of his face down with the lightest pencil I own. By the time we've reached our destination, I'm a third of the way through, and I change my focus on what we need to do at the shoot site.

***

Frank guides me around to the area he was told we needed to be at and suddenly, there's a huge mountain of a man coming towards us, calling Frank's name. I move to stand behind Frank since I don't know who this man is.

"Omar!" he calls out, and then the two men are hugging, slapping each other on the back like they've not seen each other for months.

"How are you doing? You're looking a lot...," The big man looks across at me. "Oh, I can see why you're smiling more!" He grins at me, making Frank pull me in a little closer to his side.

"Omar, let me introduce you to Tabitha, my girlfriend," he tells his friend. I blush at the label, but as I try to shake Omar's hand, I'm encased in a hug. His arms wrap around me, squeezing me tightly.

"So, you're why he's been in knots for weeks! I can see why, too, pretty lady," he compliments as he grins at Frank, who goes red. I've never seen him embarrassed before, not like this.

"In knots?" I ask, though I think I understand what Omar is trying to tell me.

"Yeah, Mr Sourpuss here was worried about you and missing you like mad," he grins and Frank rolls his eyes, muttering a few swearwords under his breath as Omar teases him.

Someone calls to Omar and Frank, beckoning them over. Frank holds his hand out for me, and I grin as I'm escorted to a meeting area.

***

The shoot director walks everyone through what they're meant to be doing and what styles they're going to be wearing. I find a seat at the back near the make-up artists' booth, which is an event tent with two sides missing, but it stops the sun from melting the make-up and scalding those sitting in the makeup chairs.

I'm watching every muscled man listen to a woman about my height and stature give out orders and tell every model who is where with which photographer, wearing what line.

They break up into their groups of four and Frank rushes across to me, Omar hot on his heels.

"Liss has said you can sit here," he tells me and a taller woman is coming across, makeup brushes in her hand and she's glowering, but not at us.

"Hey, Frank, is this Tabitha?" she asks in a brash American drawl as she firmly places the brushes on the table.

Frank nods and hands me the car keys. "My girl. Look after her for me, yeah?" he asks as he plonks himself down in a chair. Omar eases himself into the one next to Frank, and they let Liss apply their make-up. I really ought to get tips from the lady. She had them done in five minutes!

"I sure can!" she exclaims as she brushes powder onto Frank's brow and around his face. "So, how'd you meet?" she asks and quickly, Frank gives her the abridged version; that I've returned and now live with him and his family. There's no explanation as to why I've returned, or from what.

"Tabs had a serious operation recently too," he shares with her. Liss nods.

"I got your girl, English. Now, off you go! Omar!" She turns to him and grins as if she's just seen him here for the first time. There's a queue starting to form and another makeup artist appears, then another. I realise I'm sitting in their work chairs, and I vacate it, heading back to the car to get my art supplies as Liss and her team work. Then, I'm back, and I wait on the fountain stairs as Liss and her team finish up.

"What ya doing?" Liss asks me as I settle back into a chair twenty minutes later.

"Building up my art portfolio," I tell her, showing her the drawing I've started of my brother.

"Man, that's good! You going to college for that?" she asks as she tidies up her makeup brushes and the various pots she and the team have had out.

"That's the plan, but I need to get a portfolio together," I tell her. "I don't have many examples of human still life and there's plenty here to draw."

I watch her work and I take out my phone. "Can I grab an image of you? Your style is very different, and I want to showcase females as well as males," I say to her, hoping she'll consent. She lets me snap a picture of her as she's bending over to put things away. The light, the way her colourful braided hair falls over one shoulder, the shape of her jaw and nose, and the shirt she's wearing that's now covered in makeup and not sitting on her shoulder properly make for a striking picture. I have the phone set to take multiple images, and I pick the best three, then delete the others.

"Hell girl, you've got a good eye for detail," she grins at me. I smile and I can feel the heat rising in my neck and cheeks.

"Thanks!" I gush, not quite sure how to handle the praise coming from her. "Err, I could do with some make-up tips," I whisper to her. "My mum isn't around to help and…" I shrug but smile. Liss grins at me, her white teeth showing through her dark skin.

"Sure thing, girl. I'll help. The last shoot takes place around four today, so we can do it then, okay?" She nods at me, and I nod back.

"Thanks, Liss. You're a gem," I tell her.

"Aww shucks. You English are so polite!" she coos at me, but I can only grin.

***

Throughout the day, I switch seats from the makeup booth to the fountain and back. Omar lets me take a photo of him for my portfolio, and so does another model who is as sculpted as Frank and Omar.

"Why don't you take a photo of me?" asks one guy when Frank and Omar aren't around. I shrug and do as he asks, but then he's hovering around me, not giving me space.

"Ty, whatcha doing with my girl here?" Liss challenges him when she comes back to the booth. The man, Ty, backs off a little as she stalks towards him like a panther, eyes slitted from the sun but the glare from them towards him is unmistakable.

"Just wanna see the girl draw," he tells her in a voice that cuts through me. I don't want to draw him. He sets me on edge.

"Ty, you better get back over to three before Lois busts your ass," she directs him. "Go on, shoo! And you leave my girl alone, ya hear?" she calls at him as he leaves. He answers with a wave but thankfully, he doesn't look back.

She sighs and looks at me when we're sure he's out of range.

"Listen, girl, you do yourself a favour," she says to me. I've come to like her American drawl. "He's trouble, arrogant, spiteful and an ass. You're better off deleting that photo," she instructs me, and I smile.

"Already have," I say, but knowing that his name is Ty is helpful.

"Good! Avoid that piece of euro trash, okay, sugar?" she tells me, and I nod, understanding that he's a whole load of trouble. Avoiding him is exactly what I intend to do.

A catering van pulls up and everyone suddenly takes a break. Frank and Omar find me, and I get dragged off by them both to sit in the shade of the huge house where one photoshoot is taking place. There's a perfect bench and both of them sit on either side of me.

"Liss says you had a chat with Ty?" Frank asks as he hands me an egg salad roll.

"You remember?" I ask, and he nods with a smile on his face.

"Every little thing," he tells me quietly. I blush, and Omar chuckles.

"You two are cute," he teases, and I shrug at him. "Avoid Ty," Omar says, his voice tight and growly, making this more than a suggested course of action.

"I'll try. He creeped me out a little," I tell them, and both men nod.

"Yeah, he's a creep in general, but don't be afraid to push back, and tell him to bugger off," Frank says. "I'll remind him later," he tells me, and I gape at him.

"You, will?" I ask, nervously. "I don't want to cause trouble," I begin, but Frank waves his hand at me as we eat.

"He's on thin ice with the bosses, Lois and Xander. He's been in trouble before when he's tried to get too friendly with the girls. The last one was a colleague of Liss'. She nearly broke his nose." Frank looks cross as he tells me. "There's also a female model that's quite keen on him and just as nasty. She's late in arriving," Frank sighs.

"Liss' friend didn't quit, but she won't come on-site to help Liss if Ty is here," Omar adds. I look between both men, and I have to ask.

"Why is he still working with you?" I ask.

Frank and Omar don't get a chance to offer me answers as an Italian man calls out for them. I get back to drawing my brother and take more photos of some of the other models, this time picking a few of the girls. I also take a weird picture of Liss' makeup table, the lines of all the pallets contrast with the roundness of the brushes. In colour, it will look amazing.

I'm concentrating hard when a voice speaks out, making me jump. Ty.

"Sheesh!" I begin, then I bend over to pick up the pencil I dropped. "I hope the lead didn't break," I whine. The last thing I need is broken pencils when I'm in the zone.

"You worry too much," he tells me, and I shrug, not looking at him or paying him attention. "You know, you can do much better than Frank," he whispers to me loudly, and I whip around.

"I could, huh? What if I don't want 'better'? What if he's exactly who I want; who I need?" I put my pencil and pad down, rising to the bait he's set. I know I shouldn't, but I hate bullies, and I was too timid and young the last time with my step-dad. Something inside me clicks. The fire is ignited, and I gun for Ty, my voice rising as I push back at him. "What if I don't want *someone like you* anywhere near me? What if your opinion isn't something I want? Or something I care about?"

"Oh, darlin'," he drawls, imitating Liss, and that's it. The small amount of control over my temper ignites.

"I am not your *darling*. I never will be. I didn't ask you for your opinion, or for you to bother me. You're a creep!" I can hear my voice rising. "Go away, leave me alone!"

"I'm a creep?" He begins and stalks towards me, his nostrils flaring as his hands go into fists. I hold my ground, even though he's scaring the living daylights out of me. Suddenly, he's not there. He's on the floor, and Omar is between Ty and me, angled so that he's protecting me. There's another man with him, telling him to get up.

"You're done, Ty. That's it. I've had enough of you harassing every female member of this crew or people who are invited here. Now, get your stuff and get the hell off my shoot!"

There's a crowd gathering around us now and suddenly, warm arms are wrapping around me, but they're not Frank's. They're Liss'. Then the other woman who was giving the assignments out today, is there, a tablet in her hand.

"You can't fire me. I'll sue you!" Ty proclaims as he gets to his feet.

"We can, and I just did," Lois fires back. "Gross misconduct and harassment. Ms Reid is a guest here. You harassed her, and you were on a final formal warning. Get out," she states in a tone that makes me shiver down to my toes.

Ty looks around at all of us and throws me such a look before Omar gets between me and his view.

"Later, princess," he spits, and I see a few of the larger guys like Omar escort him to get his stuff, then follow him to his car and watch as he drives away.

I sigh and hug Liss, enjoying the closeness of another human being around me right now.

"What did he say to you?" she asks, and I get embarrassed by everyone watching. Xander and Lois look around, and then shoo everyone back to their shoots, then they huddle around me. Liss backs away, and then Frank's there, holding me.

"What happened?" he asks, and I tell him how Ty made me jump, sharing what he told me about doing better. Frank goes very quiet, and I can see his jaw tick. Omar is behind me, and I can feel his growl as much as everyone around me can hear it.

"Little fucker," I hear Omar curse.

"He's a prized tool, for sure," Liss agrees and everyone nods.

"Well, he's gone now," Lois states. "Liss, your friend is more than welcome back. I'm sorry it took so long to clean house," Lois says to her.

"You had to follow your employment laws, I get that," she smiles. "It's over with now," she declares, and there are nods all around.

"Come to the pod I'm at," Frank tells me, and I nod with a smile. I've had enough attention on me today.

CHAPTER 17

Frank

I guide Tabitha away from the makeup booth, the scene where she stood up to Ty. One of the runners came to get me, telling me Ty was having a go at her, and I've never been so glad for all the cardio work in my life. Omar was with Xander, hashing out a plan for tomorrow due to missing suits when the ruckus hit, and I'm glad Omar was the first of us to reach her.

Between shots, I glance at Tabitha, keeping an eye on her, concerned that Ty will suddenly show up again. We all know he's a vindictive son-of-a-bitch. Then a gopher goes over to her and points her to certain spots. I watch, and I forget for a moment what I'm doing and where I am.

"Frank, that was fabulous!" The photographer announces in a rather jubilant tone. What?! Oh, hell.

"Sorry, zoned out," I tell him sheepishly, and the skinny Italian laughs.

"Look at these," he tells me, and I go over for a look as Tabitha is being ushered across. The angles are great and I realise, they got Tabs to move so she'd get me to look where they wanted me to.

"They do look great," I tell him.

"There's a hunger there that's not been present before," he tells me, focusing on my face for one image. Tabitha gasps as she joins us.

"That's an amazing shot!" she breathes.

"Yeah, it is. Pity I can't use it, though," he says, his fingers moving over the controls.

"Don't delete it," Tabs cries out, reaching out one of her tiny hands to pause him. "I can use it for my art course, if you'll let me?" she asks, and he nods. She gives him her email address and moments later, she has the unedited proof on her drive.

"Thank you so much!" she gushes at him, hugging him in thanks.

"You are very welcome, *mio caro*," he tells her. She wanders off a few feet to look at the image he's sent her, absorbed in the image of me. I can feel myself getting warmer and the jeans get tighter in the crotch.

"Frank, my boy, you look after that one, *capisci*?" Angelo tells me.

"I intend to," I tell him, and he nods, slaps my arm and starts pulling his kit together. Until the missing suits arrive, we can't do the final phase of the shoot.

Lois gathers us around, and I ensure I've got my arms around Tabitha as the new plans for tomorrow are announced, which is the suits. Omar is standing close by, too, watching and listening.

"And one more thing. With Ty being dismissed, his usual photo partner has resigned." No one laments Suzie not being on-site anymore either, and I'm glad we warned Tabitha about her. "So, we need another couple," Lois uses her fingers to air emphasise 'couple', "to do their suit shoot tomorrow."

Lois looks straight at me. I pull a face, but she grins and winks.

"Frank, a word, please. The rest of you can head off to your hotels. We're done for the day! See you all at seven at The Big Guys," she reminds us and everyone leaves. Omar and Xander come up to us, and I hug my friend.

"Thanks for earlier," I thank him. At least if I am not around, I know my girl is safe.

"Angelo showed us the shots he took, even the ones he couldn't use. You two would be great in the couples shoot tomorrow." Xander looks at Tabitha, who is squirming.

"Sorry, you want to, what?" she gasps, catching up to what Xander and Lois are asking. "I've never... I'm not..." She looks at me, eyes wide and floundering, but I also see some excitement in there. I smile, grabbing her hand as Lois grabs her focus.

"Look, you wear the clothes, cuddle up to Frank here. Angelo will be doing the shoot for you both. You just look and stand where Angelo tells you like you did today. You'll be with Frank, and it's an easy two grand," Lois tells her. It's just the five of us.

"Two thousand?" Tabitha confirms slowly, rolling the figure off her tongue, and Lois nods. It takes a few moments for Tabitha to respond, but no one pressures her into saying yes. It's much less than I'm getting paid, but I'm not just starting out.

"I'd need a contract, and I won't have a bank account until next week," Tabitha quietly informs them. That money will be a huge help to her right now, along with what her mother left her.

"That's okay. We can get that info from you when you've got it set up. But, if we can get a contract signed tonight, you'll get paid when everyone else does, which is always a week later anyway," Lois informs us, and Tabitha nods.

I can see Tabitha thinking, and she bites her lower lip. My chest contracts as she looks at Lois. "What would you like me to model? Is it my size?" she asks, and I grin as Lois guides Tabitha off to talk about the clothes for tomorrow, sharing the tablet between them. She's about the same size as Suzie, so there shouldn't be any need for adjustments before the shoot starts.

Five minutes later, we're back in our huddle, and Tabitha has agreed to join me and help Lois. I grin, It'll be good to model with her tomorrow, though it's not like we're on a catwalk.

"So, meet us at Big Guys at seven. Our treat," Xander says, and we nod.

"See you later!" I confirm, and we head off with Omar to the hotel we're all booked into.

***

Our B&B is in an old section of town, in an old Edwardian looking building, with a king-sized bed, an old armoire and an en-suite. The room is cosy and comfortable. Omar is across the hall from us, and we quickly freshen up and change. Though, it takes us nearly half an hour because Tabitha isn't fast at moving around right now. I shower while she applies a little makeup, and then we're walking to the burger bar Xander has picked, Tabitha walking between Omar and I.

We're talking about what to do on a shoot, how it usually goes, and the short videos they'll do at the same time.

At the burger place, we've commandeered one side of the restaurant and everyone puts their order in. Tabitha is in a small group of women near the window booths, and the chatter is at a decent volume. Liss is here, and so is her friend, the one who detests Ty. They seem to be having fun, and I join the guys as the beers get poured and the burgers start getting made.

We're all laughing and joking when it suddenly goes quiet, and I turn to see Ty walking in, with Suzie on his arm.

It takes all of three seconds for Omar, myself, and a few others to block the entrance to the section we're in, and he tries to push past.

"It's a free country, I'm allowed in here," he states.

"That section is for a private function, pal," the owner states, coming around from Ty's side of the restaurant. "And I can tell you now, you're not welcome."

He starts to argue but we're on a high street and two police officers come in, nodding to the owner as they wander up to our group.

"There's the door," the owner states, pointing. Ty takes a look at me, narrows his eyes at someone behind me, then he grabs Susie and turns to leave. The police, though, want a word, and he's guided outside. The wimp drops Suzie's hand and runs, but does not get far. Susie screams at him that he's a coward and talks with one policeman as we return to the party. Xander shakes his head as Lois heads out to talk with them, and we're surprised when he's handcuffed and put into a police car.

Tabitha has moved to be far away from the windows, and thankfully, she's not on her own. She's sitting with Liss and Rachel, but she looks pale. Ty showing up is typical behaviour. Him being arrested was the icing on the cake. I head over to their corner and Liss stands, making room for me to take her seat.

"Does he ever stop?" Tabitha asks me, and I smile.

"He will. They arrested him, though I didn't hear why."

There's a lot of noise now as Lois glides across the restaurant with a huge grin on her face.

"That'll take care of him." She grins and leans against the booth seats after she pinches a few fries from Tabitha's pile. "He got gobby with the police and Suzie dropped him in it by revealing his intentions for tonight. I gave them the background story, and my details so that they can come and talk with me, should they need more evidence."

"And what were his intentions?" Tabitha asks.

"To bully his way back onto the contract," she says, looking at me, but I have a feeling it wasn't quite just that. I see Lois glance quickly at Tabitha, then at me, and she nods. Yeah, he came here to intimidate Tabitha. Git.

***

Tabitha pulls herself together a while later when the joviality hits and we decide we're going to a club.

"I've never been to a club before," she tells me, and I grin, holding onto her hand tightly as we head down the high street. "Well, not properly," she says, but I don't press her as to what she means.

"You'll be fine, I'll be there, and you don't have to drink," I tell her. I know she doesn't like drinking, given what her step-dad would do when he was drunk.

We smile and hold hands as we're ushered into the nightclub. We're all taking turns to dance and watch the drinks, and a few hours later, we decide to head back. Tabitha looked like she was having fun when she danced with the girls, and she was close to me when we danced, her soft curves swaying close to my hips.

"Tonight has been a lot of firsts," she tells me as we head back, holding hands. Omar is walking with us.

"Such as?" he asks. We chatted in the club, and Tabitha told him why she ran away. He was as unimpressed as my family and I was when we learned the truth. Was that only weeks ago? It feels like a lifetime.

"Going to an actual club to enjoy it," she tells us. "Usually their air vents are the warmest place to huddle into at one am." She grins, but I can tell from the look on her face that she's not joking.

We're back at the B&B, and we head in, being quiet. Omar bids us goodnight as I open the door for Tabitha and let her go in first.

Omar grins at me, then hugs me, shoving a line of silver packets into my hand. I throw him the middle finger, but he just gives me a thumbs up with a huge grin.

***

Inside, Tabitha is in the bathroom. I quickly remove my jacket, then I undo the shirt by a few buttons before I walk in to find her. She's carefully removing her makeup, not that she's wearing a lot. When she does, she turns to me with a smile and I can't hold back any longer. I step towards her, wrapping a hand around her head and pull her body into me. My lips gently tease hers, and I slide my tongue along her lips. She opens them for me and I dive in, angling her so that I can taste all of her. Tonight, she tastes like cola, but that's not something I care about. Her arms wrap around me, inviting me to her, and I turn her slightly, aiming to get more.

I push up against her, wanting to feel her close, smell and touch her. We couldn't be any closer with our clothes on. I feel her hands against my chest, digging her nails into me, exploring me. I pull back and open my eyes to see her.

"Frank," she whispers as one hand roams downwards and she's cupping me through my jeans. She doesn't say a word as her other hand comes around my neck and pulls me in. I didn't think I could get any harder than I was, but I was wrong.

I wrap my arms around her and turn us, lifting her by the arse and walk her to the bedroom. She slides down my legs when I stop walking, and I quickly turn off the bathroom light, pushing the door closed behind me.

Her eyes are wide but she's trusting. I know I have a high bar to set here.

"Tabs," I whisper, and she smiles.

"Don't stop," she breathes at me as she pulls me to her to kiss her again. My mouth wanders from her to her jaw, and I can feel her breath, hear her soft pants as I nibble her earlobe and kiss her neck. Her fingers dig into my back when I hit particular sweet spots.

She arches back, making soft moaning sounds as my tongue and lips dance on her skin. I pull back and try to work out how to remove her dress, but she senses my unease. Tabs reaches around under an arm, unzipping it. She goes to push the dress from her shoulders, but I stop her, slowly teasing one arm down, kissing the skin as it's revealed. I do the other, and her perky pink lacy bra is revealed. Admiration and desire elicit a groan of pleasure from me and I massage one breast whilst my mouth finds the nipple of the other through the fabric.

I shiver, partly in anticipation, partly because of the low moans Tabitha is giving out right now. Moments later, I've unhooked it, and it drops to the floor, revealing her pert nipples. I switch my mouth's attention to the other breast and roll the other with my fingers, which makes her whimper a little more.

"You like that?" I ask her, and she nods.

"Oh yes," she breathes at me as I stop to wait for an answer. She tries tugging at my top, and I pause briefly to pull it over my head. It joins the clothes on the floor. Before I can do anything, she's kissing my pecs, licking her tongue over a nipple, and she's going lower, kissing my torso, my abs, then my V.

I get with the programme. I'm supposed to be the one making her feel good, and I encourage her to rise so I can kiss her mouth. Working my way down her body, I trail my tongue over a breast, under it, her ribs. I find a ticklish spot, and she erupts in giggles, collapsing onto the bed behind her. I follow her down, carrying on where I left off.

Her stomach is soft, and I kiss it as my fingers slowly trace their way down her core.

"Frank!" she whispers as my fingers begin to massage her through the pretty fabric.

"Yeah?" I answer, not bothering to hide the fact I'm erect, turned on and deeply aroused by this woman's touch.

"Oh god!" she breathes out as I slide my fingers into her hot, slick wetness. I climb back up to her mouth and kiss her senseless as my hand makes her body writhe, and her breaths short.

"It's okay, look at me," I coax her. She does, and she seems ashamed. "It's okay, I know." I lean in and kiss her. This is her first time if we go that distance. I won't until I know she's ready, though. I pull back. "I can stop, sweetheart, if that's what you want," I say, but she shakes her head.

"No, don't... oh!" She arches up, contorting as I flick my fingers inside of her, feeling her walls clamp around my fingers, and the juices flow down my fingers.

"So beautiful," I tell her. Before she can say another word, I push down to her knickers and remove them down her long legs. I could rip them, but these are new, so I'll save that trick for another day.

I pry her legs open and kiss up the inside of her thigh.

"Frank, what... oh!" She breathes out as I quickly find the centre of her. I suck a little on her clit, then nibble and bring my hand back to the party. I watch her face as I continue to bring her pleasure, I don't just need to make this good for her. I want to. Her whimpers get more frequent, and in the tightness of my jeans, my cock jumps, eager to be out.

Inserting a third finger makes her curl towards me, clamping my hand as another orgasm washes over her. God, she's so beautiful! I've never had anyone react like this for me before.

As she comes back to me, I stand and strip, so I'm as naked as she is, placing one of the silver packages near my knee.

"Tabs," I breathe, and she looks up, then down and gapes. "I need you," I begin, but she's there, reaching out, wrapping her hand around me, and she slowly begins fisting me. I can see her biting her lip.

"Oh God, sweetheart," I hiss at the pleasure she's giving me, the fireworks exploding inside of me, which makes her stop.

"Did I...?" she begins.

"Too good, Tabs. Don't stop," I command her, and she lets out a huge sigh.

"I'm glad I didn't hurt you," she tells me and carries on. I can see her biting her lip again, focusing on the task at hand.

"You're so dry," she admits minutes later as the friction does the job.

"Won't be when I'm all wrapped up and inside you," I promise with a growl.

Tabitha looks at me directly and nods. "Show me how, Frank," she asks, and I grin. "Teach me?" she begs softly.

"Keep doing that," I tell her, trying not to cum on her right here and now. Then she does the most incredible thing; she swallows me, sucking on me, the hollowness of her cheeks showing. Her hot, sweet little mouth is wrapping itself around me. No other blow job on the planet has ever made me moan and beg. "Oh fuck, yes," I tell her, thrusting my hand into her hair to hold her still. She manages a few more swallows before I pull out, and I grin.

I grab the condom and put it on, before leaning over her and settling between her thighs, angled so that I can still play with her. I run a finger into her, and she's still wet, wetter than before.

"You enjoyed doing that to me?" I ask between kisses.

"Yes," she breathes as she arches her neck back and I reach in to nip. I work her wetness with my hand, making her writhe and buck.

I stop and lean over her properly, kissing her. The head of me is just at her entrance. I kiss her deeply, angling her head as I slowly push into her.

She gasps and clings to me, making me stop.

"Don't stop," she tells me, and I push all the way into her.

I wait a moment, and she breathes out, giving me a sheepish grin before she reaches up to pull me to her. Such innocence from her. I feel my chest expanding in something I'm not quite sure. I shake my head and lean down to kiss her again as I withdraw and slowly slide back into her.

"Oh!" she gasps as I do it again and again, over and over, slowly, thoroughly, kissing her all the time. Her arms wrap around me, her fingers run through my hair and her kisses get more intense the longer I love her.

"You can let go, Tabs. Just feel," I tell her as my climax threatens to explode, but I need her to come first. Kissing her again, she listens. She explodes on me; around me. Her head is tucked into my shoulder, muffling her cries as she comes, making me come within her, shuddering my release deep into the condom as I kiss her deeply.

I come back to earth quicker than she does and I'm there, pulling kisses from her as she comes back to her senses.

"Wait here," I tell her, slowly and gently pulling out of her. Then I head to the bathroom and get a warm cloth, discarding the condom as the water slowly takes its time to warm up. When it does, I'm back at Tabs, patting the warm cloth between her, helping her to clean up.

"Does it sting? Did I...?" I can't bring myself to ask if I hurt her.

She reaches up and kisses me. "It was perfect." And she's wrapping an arm around me. From the bathroom light, I can't see any blood.

I rinse the cloth out and then turn the light off, heading back to bed. I close the curtains a little more, darkening the room, and I fish out another condom, placing it on the bedside table.

Then I'm crawling in beside her, pulling her to me, not wanting to let go. I stroke the side of her face as she starts to drop off, a smile on her lips.

"What's so funny, Tabs?" I ask, and she sighs, then looks at me.

"Do that with me again later?" she asks, and I lift her chin and kiss her deeply.

"Oh, babe, we've only just gotten started," I tell her.

"Good," she replies, a lift in her voice. Then she's snuggling into me, and damn it if I don't sleep through the night.

***

It's early when I hear Tabs get up the following morning. I check the sheets and then follow her, ensuring she's okay. She nods when I ask and wraps her arms around me.

"So often I've dreamed what it would be like," she tells me. "My dreams... they weren't anything like what you made me feel last night," she tells me.

"You didn't bleed?" I ask her. Not that I doubt she was a virgin, her reaction to my intrusion as I entered into her was testament enough of that.

"No... They're not always intact. I've...," She grins at me sheepishly. "I looked up how it might hurt the first time," she tells me, her cheeks go quite pink, nearly red. I blink. "And it didn't, not like the websites hinted it would." She reaches up to kiss me. I grab her and kiss her back, letting her feel the full weight of me on her.

Her hand grabs me, slowly jerking me like she did last night.

"I want to do it again," she tells me, and I grin.

"Give me five babe," I kiss her, then take care of basic business as she bounds to the bed, giggling and dives back into the covers.

CHAPTER 18

Tabitha

I dart back to bed to get under the covers, waiting for Frank to come back from the bathroom. I don't want to tell him there was a little blood. I want him to love me again like he did last night.

I grin as he shuts the bathroom light off, and I watch as he walks around to the other side of the bed. He climbs in, under the covers and grabs something from the side table, hiding it away.

"Come here," he says and opens his arms for me to snuggle back into. Once we're comfy, he lifts my chin and kisses me deeply. I shift so that I'm on top, pressing myself against him, needing him again. After a moment, he pulls back and looks at me intently. "You're sure? You're not sore?" He asks. My heart blooms at his care, his thoughtfulness.

"I'm good," I tell him, and I run my hands through his hair, pulling him to me. Then he turns us so I'm underneath him, and he's poking me.

"Condom!" I breathe, reminding him that he's not wrapped up yet.

His wolfish grin is my only answer, and as his hot mouth moves down my body, kissing and sucking as he goes. His attentions send shivers of desire through me that are new and captivating, making me breathless. He pays particular attention to my breasts, nipping and biting the nipple.

"So good," I manage to whisper as his fingers nip and pull at the same time. I wince at the pleasure and pain he's creating in me, the desire I have for him. I want him. Now.

"Frank," I plead, but he shakes his head.

"Soon, sweetheart. Just enjoy," he tells me, and I can do only that. His kisses feel like nothing else, little spots of heat that set the fire within me alight. Then his mouth is on me, and he tells me, no, he orders me to watch him as he sucks and licks at me.

"Oh my...!" I arch back as another wave of electricity shoots through me, making my legs jelly. Frank doesn't stop, and now his fingers are joining in. I grab a pillow and scream into it as he makes me come again, then I hear something tear, and I move the pillow to see him putting a condom on.

He's leaning over me, kissing me, and I can taste myself on him. How can he like that taste? Mixed with him, it's... beautiful somehow. His wolfish grin gets broader as he leans in to kiss me more thoroughly, biting my lower lip.

Then he's in me again, and I'm full. It's delicious and intense. He holds himself still for a moment.

"I can't go as slow as I did last night, Tabs," he kisses me. "Ride with me, sweetheart. Wrap yourself around me," he tells me, and I wrap my legs around him, somehow making him go deeper. My hips lift, and he pulls back. Then he's sliding home again, and again and again. His movements pick up speed, his kisses get more intense and the fire within me threatens to roar into an inferno.

I arch backwards, seeing stars, calling out his name as he comes within me. I can feel all of him shudder and I find his mouth, kissing him intently.

"Don't leave me," I beg him. I never want anyone else to love me like he just has.

"Not a chance," he tells me right before he kisses me back to oblivion.

An hour later, we're still cuddled up. We've not stopped kissing each other, and I can't help running my fingers over his form or breathing him in.

"You okay, sweetheart?" he asks, and I nod.

"I am," I reply, being honest. I sigh contentedly, just enjoying being held by Frank. I look up at him. "I didn't realise it would be...," I can't find just one word.

"Intense?" he ventures, and I can tell he's holding his breath.

"Yes... and so much more!"

"No regrets?" he asks me, his voice is raspy, nervous.

"None at all," I reach up and kiss him deeply, happy now I can touch him as I've always dreamed of being able to. "The idea of this... it kept me warm at night when I ran away. At first, it was just imagining the kisses, but..."

He places a thumb under my chin and pulls my head up, shifting so we can look at each other. "But?" he asks.

"Sometimes people would find a companion on the streets... it was hard to block out the sound of others having sex to stay warm."

He chuckles. "I don't fancy being watched," he tells me.

I purse my lips together and grin. "I was never made to, but the sounds... You can't block those out in a tent or bushes. I get now why they were made." I grin. "It only happened three times, usually in the summer in or around the hostels when we needed showers."

Frank checks his watch. "Speaking of showers, we'd better get one and get down to breakfast." He kisses me, but then he drags his fine, pert arse out of bed, and I let him pull me into the bathroom and the shower.

***

We are getting settled in the breakfast room when Omar joins us. I smile sweetly at him, and as I go to get some more juice, Frank gets up to do it for me.

"You okay?" Omar asks me, and I nod, smiling.

"Yes, thank you! Perfect." I grin back.

Omar gives me a wink as Frank comes back with two breakfast juices, and there's a look between them.

"What?" Asks Frank as he sits back down.

"Just asking your girl how she is," Omar replies as he places his cooked breakfast order. We talk about today's shoot a little more, what might be expected and my phone pings. It's Lois, asking for my shoe size, and I send it back to her, enjoying the company and the small touches of reassurance Frank is giving me under the table.

***

We pack our stuff into the car boot as we're heading home once this shoot is complete. I leave my pencils and artwork in the car; I know I won't have time to work on them until we're on the way home. Walking between Omar and Frank, I feel safe and there is a feeling of warmth from Frank's arm being casually slung over my shoulder.

Soon, we're back at the shoot site, and there's a rack of clothes in a tent and Liss to one side.

"There they are!" she exclaims and comes up to us, hugging us. "Boys, Rachel is going to get your makeup done." Liss looks at me. "You get me, sugar," Liss drawls in a stronger southern accent than yesterday, and it makes me chuckle.

I squeal as Liss pulls me towards the makeup booth. Omar hangs back for a moment and they have a quiet conversation. I can't hear what they're talking about.

Omar nods and pats Frank on the back, then they're being guided to the makeup chair. Lois comes up, greeting us cheerily. Then, she gets on with telling Liss the kind of look they want me to wear today. These suits are not quite wedding, not quite corporate, which needs to match my makeup. Lois explains the brief, the look they're trying to achieve; corporate by day, out to a club at night. I listen to Lois intently, taking the instructions, and I ask lots of questions as Liss works her brushes on my face. By the time we're done, Omar and Frank are ready and we head off to get changed while Liss and Rachel work on the other models.

***

Standing by the changing tent, Frank turns as the tent flap cracks in the breeze. Dressed in a dress and jacket, I'm a far cry from the scared, returning runaway. I feel amazing, more of an adult. Frank's eyes light up, his jaw drops and there's a fire in his eyes that I love seeing there when he looks at me.

"The shoot for you two is over that way." Liss turns to call on someone to bring over some water and other things. Angelo greets us with air kisses, telling me he can't mess up Liss' work. She'd kill him if he does. His humour makes me laugh, and I love how easy it is to follow his instructions.

"Ready?" Angelo asks as he walks before us and we nod.

***

After an hour, several changes and a few 'go's at it, we're done. Angelo declares he's happy and Lois is ecstatic about the look we've created.

"Angelo did the hard work, this light is changing fast!" I praise. He mutters something in Italian and shrugs his shoulders, I guess no one has said that about him before, or often.

"She's right, you did great! You all did!" Lois looks around briefly. "Let's get these packed up and you can take them home," Lois smiles. I nod and smile, helping her pack the clothes I was modelling into their clothes bags. Half an hour later, we're heading home.

***

I jerk awake as we're pulling onto the M5. I yawn and stretch, then I turn to smile at Frank.

"How long have I been asleep?!" I exclaim, we're not far from home.

"Most of the journey. I think before we got onto the motorway," he tells me with a laugh in his voice.

"Sorry!" I mutter, embarrassed. I had wanted to work on my art as he drove.

"Don't be, you clearly needed the sleep," he tells me. "And you didn't miss much." I chuckle and sigh, then I wiggle back into the seat. "I wanted to ask you something," he says as he changes lanes.

"Go on," I ask, turning to him slightly.

"I don't want to just sleep with you at home for the sex," he tells me, glancing at me swiftly.

"Go on," I encourage, wondering how long he's been thinking about what he's trying to ask me.

"And mum will be annoyed if you don't use your room," he tells me.

"Yeah, she would be," I smile. "So what are you thinking?" I ask, keeping my tone light, though there's a knot forming in my stomach.

"We mix it around and maybe not every night?"

I let my emotions show. "Why?" I whisper, fearing I've done something bad. Does he not want me?

"You still need your rest, and some mornings I'm up early to be at the gym for six. I don't want to wake you," he tells me. I let out the breath I was just holding, the knot in my stomach easing off.

"Oh! I don't mind being woken up, I'm sure I can go back to sleep quite easily," I tell him. He laughs. "And a few nights together in a row would be nice, rather than bed jumping all the time."

"Bed jumping?" he asks and throws me a strange look.

"Between yours and mine," I tell him. He nods and laughs.

"Okay, so we mix and match. I have the en-suite," he reminds me with a smile.

"Yeah, I know," I grin, wondering what his parents will think of this.

***

Frank pulls up outside the house and gets out to help me out. I smile at him and he pulls me to him, giving me a huge kiss. When we break apart, his parents can be seen through the blinds, and there's a huge smile on Katie's face. I can see her make her way to the front door, and she smiles.

"So you two had a good weekend?" She asks jovially and we nod.

"We had some fun, but we had a small incident with Ty," Frank tells her, and Katie hisses.

"Have they not gotten rid of him yet?" she asks and Frank laughs.

"They did this weekend. Tell you about it inside over a cuppa." His dad comes out to help with the bags and suits. I grab my artwork, and take it up to my room as we quickly unpack, then chill out.

***

Over a pot of tea and a toasted teacake, we tell Frank and Katie all about our weekend. We can hear Shane's voice from the top of the stairs about half an hour into our chat and Phil goes out to bring him down.

"We had to get a stairgate for the top of the landing now he's in a big boy bed," Katie says as Shane appears in the hallway.

"Tabifa!" he cries out and runs to hug me. I get off the bar stool and kneel so his arms can go around my neck. There's a huge wet kiss on my cheek and he squeezes me tightly. "You home!" he squeals, and I grin.

"Yes, we're home! Were you good for Katie?" I ask, and he nods.

"Yes." He looks at Katie, then goes to her and hugs her. Then he's trying to climb up onto one of the bar stools, so Frank helps him up. We sit and chat like this for another hour, feeding Shane snacks and getting drinks for us all as we bond as an extended family.

***

We get another chance to talk after Shane's had his bath, and I've put him to bed. He asked nicely tonight for me to do it, and I think Katie was relieved.

Frank must have been telling them more about Ty's antics as both Katie and Phil hug me tightly as I enter after tucking my brother in. I smile at Frank as I enter the living room.

"Tornado wants you," I grin, and he smiles, touching my shoulder lightly as he leaves.

"Frank says you'll be sharing your rooms?" Katie asks, and I nod.

"I hope that's okay?" I ask. She stands up and holds out her arms in a hug, which I jump up to embrace and take in. Being hugged, this intimacy, is something I missed out on, until Phil found me in the shed one wet, cold day. It was the only place I could find shelter, because being at home wasn't an option.

"It's more than okay sweetie," she whispers to me. "It's always been the pair of you," she tells me just as Frank comes back into the living room. He grins at us, and then comes to hug me for a moment. Then we settle down to watch a movie before bed.

CHAPTER 19

Frank

Tornado wanted me to help tuck him in. I think he's missed Tabitha and me. When I get back to the living room, mum is hugging Tabitha, telling her that it was always her and I. We sit on the sofa and I'm holding Tabitha's hand as we watch a movie.

Somehow, we make it to the end of the movie, and we head upstairs as mum and dad secure the house for the night. I go to head to my room but Tabitha pauses outside hers.

"Which one first?" she asks, and I grin.

"Either," I tell her. It doesn't matter, and she nods towards her room. I grin, nod and kiss her. "Back in a few," I share, and I dart up the stairs to grab some basics and my phone charger. As I'm coming back down, Tabitha is leaving the bathroom, dancing around mum and dad.

"Night," I whisper to them and head into her room, closing the door behind us.

I wait until I hear that the bathroom is empty before I go to use that one, leaving Tabitha to get ready for bed. When I get back, she's in bed, her side light is on, and she's smiling while biting her bottom lip.

I climb in, and she turns the light off, then I pull her to me and spoon her. I can tell she's wearing some shorts and a cami top, whereas I'm just in some underpants. Tornado being able to come into the rooms means I'd like to be clothed if he does.

"Do you know how many nights I've wanted to do this?" I tell her, pulling her close and breathing her in. "Just to hold you?"

I can tell she's shaking her head slightly.

"I'll bet they're as many as I've thought about it, too," she tells me, which makes my heart soar.

"Plenty more days to do just this, Tabs," I whisper to her.

"Yeah," she replies in a sleepy tone. "There are." Moments later, her even breathing is the last thing I remember.

***

My watch vibrates at six am, but Tabitha doesn't move. Her arm is around me from behind, and I gently slip out of her warm embrace. I kiss her on the forehead before I go to my room, get into my gym kit and head out. I peek into her room as I go past to see she's not moved. Grinning, I head out to the gym. My first client is at half seven, so I have time to spend on myself before the client's session. Then I'll be back here for a shower and breakfast.

***

Two hours later, I am home. The Tornado meets me at the door and hugs me. I try not to get any sweat on him, but that's a hard task. Tabitha sees me next and scrunches her nose up at me as I try to reach out to kiss her.

"Go shower first," she tells me as she laughs, dancing away from me and taking Shane with her. His giggles vibrate through the house, and I can still hear them at the entrance to my room.

***

Half an hour later, I'm downstairs so I can put my kit into the wash. "I'll take him to nursery. I need a walk," Tabitha says, and mum nods as I enter.

"I can come with you," I offer, but Tabitha shakes her head.

"You need breakfast, and I could do with some fresh air before I settle down to do some art work," she tells me. "Oh! Did that paperwork from the lawyer arrive, Katie?" She asks.

Mum nods. "Yeah, it did. It's in the conservatory, on the TV stand," mum tells her, and Tabitha goes to retrieve it. She reads through it quickly and nods.

"Okay, that's where I'll go when I've taken Shane in," she says.

"I need to go into town, so I'll come with you," mum says. Tabitha smiles at mum.

"Girls morning in town. Sounds ideal," she says and I have to laugh. There's hardly a choice of banks or shops.

"Why don't you go to Merry Hill instead? They've got more bank branches there," I suggest. Tabitha blinks, then nods.

"I hadn't thought of going there," she admits.

"Great idea," Mum enthuses and before long, they're all out the door, leaving me at home. I grin, make breakfast and get on with my work in peace.

***

Hours later, mum, Tabitha and the Tornado are home. There's some colour to their faces as if they've been sitting in the sun. Shane asks for some juice, and after mum gets it for him, Tabitha takes him up for a nap. Half an hour later, I'm getting ready to head back out for client sessions.

"Did you get the account sorted?" I ask Tabitha as I prepare some restorative drinks for afterwards. She nods.

"Yeah, Katie was great at keeping me on track with what I needed, rather than being 'upsold' to a different account. I'm glad she came with me," she smiles. I turn and I can see mum there, a knowing look on her face. I don't think mum would have let Tabitha go alone anyway.

CHAPTER 20

Tabitha

I have a few short weeks to get something together for college. I call and speak with Admissions, and from that conversation, I'm invited in for an interview. I've two sketches of humans, as well as everything I did before, which I didn't want to include, but I know I have to. I've not been back and active enough in my art to leave that work out.

I have a sketch of Frank on the go as a "work in progress", which is going to be charcoal when it's done, but for now, I'm drawing his form lightly, just to get it down on paper.

Frank and I have been sleeping together, much to my brother's confusion. But I've told him Frank and I love each other the same way Katie and Phil do. To take a break from college work, I've been working on a very special idea for Shane.

Explaining to him what happened to mum in words he can understand, hasn't been easy. Whenever we go to the shop, he eyes the comic books, and I got the idea to draw what happened in that style. A children's comic-style storybook.

The money from mum and the fashion shoot has cleared into my account, and I paid Frank back. I'm grateful he let me get things organised, allowing me to put myself in charge.

I also got Katie to take me to Merry Hill again, and I picked up some stationery items from there, including this specially sized sketchbook. I've other art supplies on order.

***

The day of my college interview arrives, and we're in Frank's room. He persuaded me I could get ready up here in more peace than in the main bathroom, and when I come down to breakfast, I appreciate the gesture. Everyone is around the table, helping themselves to breakfast. Shane's mouth is covered in fruit and yoghurt, which I wipe off before I let him kiss me on the cheek.

"How are you feeling?" Katie asks as she pours me some juice. Frank puts a bowl of fruit and yoghurt in front of me, and I smile a thank you to him.

"Nervous," I admit and Shane reaches up to hug me. "Aww, thanks, little brother! But, that's a good thing, right?" I ask as Phil hands me a clean spoon.

Everyone nods, which makes Shane do the same, and it's cute that my little brother nods so vigorously. I tease that his head might fall off if he nods any harder.

***

An hour later, I take in a huge breath and walk up the steps to the college entrance. Katie said she'd wait in the car park for me, so I know she's close. Signing in, I enter the dean's office, and I meet the head of the art department, another art teacher, the dean, and then the questions start.

Nearly two hours later, they've gone through every image I've created, taken, painted, drawn, sketched or thought about, including the storybook I'm making for Shane. I explain why and my background, which seems to intrigue them.

"Miss Reid, we'd like to formally offer you the place on the A level art course," the Dean tells me, and the others nod.

I grin, smile and cry tears of happiness. I got on the course! They explain again what the requirements will be, and I nod, listening intently to what I'm being told. Then I'm being escorted out, with the promise that the formal letter will be emailed to me in the next forty-eight hours. I do have to pay for the course, but that's okay. I know I have the funds to cater for it and a way to make more money if I need it. Lois promised me more work if and when I wanted it.

***

The champagne cork flies off to another part of the garden as the smell of sausages, burgers and steaks wafts over from where they are cooking on a huge barbeque. Phil and Katie decided that they'd have a little party, and I got home from the interview to find Liss, Rachel, Omar and Frank waiting for me. The cheers are loud, and I look around for Shane.

"Asleep," Katie says to me, but his voice comes through the monitor, and she laughs. "Well, he was!" she quips, and she heads off to bring him down.

Sitting in the garden with friends and family, celebrating my simple achievement, isn't something I thought I'd get to do.

"To Tabitha's success!" the others cheer, and we ensure Shane has a little bit of lemonade. Hours later, stuffed and in the dark, Omar, Liss and Rachel head home, leaving us to finish clearing up.

"Thank you, for tonight," I say to Katie as I help her clear up. My head is spinning, and I'm not sure if that's from the champagne, the company, or the euphoria of the day.

"You deserve it!" Katie tells me and I hug her. I burst into tears; I wish mum were here!

I sigh as I trudge up to bed. Today has been long and significant, but so necessary. My life is back on track, and it keeps getting better and better. Wrapped in Frank's arms, sleep finds me quickly.

***

For the next few days, I spend time drawing some of the story for Shane, starting with just mum and I. I'm curled up on the sofa in the conservatory, sketching out the last part of page three, a holiday we once took: the only one I ever remember she and I took. Shane is sat with me as I define some of the lines for the little girl and the mum. Frank is out with his clients and Phil and Katie are in the lounge watching their shows.

"Sista draw?" he asks, and I look across and smile.

"Yes. I'm making a story."

"Who for?" he asks, and I smile at him.

"For you. But it's not finished yet, okay?"

My little brother nods and snuggles into me as I focus on drawing. I take a break to put him to bed when he starts dozing off on me.

"Want to see story," he tells me as I work his pyjamas onto his little body and go through his bedtime routine. I grin at his determination.

"It's going to take me some time to draw it all out. Don't worry. As soon as it's finished, it's all for you."

"My story," he tells me, and I kiss him as I tuck him in.

"Yes, darling little brother. All for you."

***

Frank and I settle into a routine. At the start of the week, when we're busiest, we're in my room. The tail end of the week in his. My artwork gets underway, and the time to start college draws ever closer. I'm about halfway through the "comic of explanation" as I'm calling it for now, for Shane.

He asks about it, and I tell him when I've added in another square. It's still all in black and white, I've not coloured it at all, yet. I think I want to copy it before I do that. So, I have a blank master file. Frank suggested that I take photographs and save them to a cloud drive, so that I don't lose the work, which I admit is a pretty neat idea.

***

When college starts, it takes my focus almost completely until I find a way to balance everything out. If it wasn't for Katie, Phil and Frank, I'd be drowning with pressure, expectations, deadlines, social interactions and care for Shane.

"Thank you," I tell them one evening when Shane is finally in bed. "I would be struggling to do all you do, as well as any school work and care for Shane at the same time!"

Katie hugs me and tells me I'm welcome. I also notice she is wearing some discreet hearing aids.

"When did you get them?" I ask, and she blushes. I hadn't noticed the TV was lower in volume, until now.

"I decided to get them when I couldn't hear Shane was in the conservatory with you one evening. Phil and Frank could hear you both talking, but I couldn't." She waves her hand, dismissing the incident, but I can tell it affected her. She's gone red. "Oh, there's a letter that's come for you," she tells me and points to where we now have to keep the post. Shane has taken to using it all for drawing on if we're not watching him.

I smile, get up and take the letter with my name on it. It's pretty bland, a long white envelope with my name, the address and no return on the back.

I sit down with it and open it as the attention from everyone else goes to the action on the screen; only mine is on what I'm holding.

"You cheeky...," I declare, loudly. I read the letter again and hand it to Frank. I watch my boyfriend as he goes wide-eyed and sits forward. My ankles were on his lap as he massaged them while we were watching the TV.

"What is it? What's the letter?" Katie asks, and Frank hands the letter to his father.

"The cheeky son-of-a-bitch," he declares, and finally, Katie gets a hold of it.

"He can't contact us," she states.

I shrug. "He didn't contact you. He contacted me. The order states that he can't contact you about Shane. There's nothing about contacting me in it."

"We'll see about that!" Katie declares emphatically.

I swallow and look at Frank, who nods. I don't think he has any idea of what I want to say. I am not sure I do either.

"I want to face him," I declare, and that stops Katie from huffing. Frank's eyes go wide but then he nods, looking at his dad. Phil rubs his short beard, and he looks at his wife.

Katie glances around all of us, then back to me. No one is asking the question that everyone is thinking; even me.

"You're sure about that, lovely?" she asks. "You don't have to," she tells me, her voice dropping low as her lips become thin-set.

"I kind of do... I lived in fear of him for too long. I want to face him. I want to tell him to go to hell, and to never darken my door again. I want to ask him why..." I look at everyone in turn, but it's Frank who is with me, holding my hand.

"We get it. You won't be going alone though," he tells me.

I nod, slowly. "Thank you," I breathe out, letting my nerves dissipate at the same time.

CHAPTER 21

Frank

A few days later, Tabitha's appointment to go and see her stepdad arrives. She moaned about booking it online. Everything you'd think the Prison Service wouldn't want to know about you, they do.

I drive, watching her from glances at junctions. She was quiet when she came home from college yesterday, almost back to the girl I first encountered when she was just thirteen. She's quieter now, lost in that pretty, artistic little head of hers, and she's wringing her hands. I can only guess she's thinking about what she wants to say to her stepdad.

The sick feeling I have in the pit of my stomach won't shift, and it's been there since the visitation was confirmed. I noticed Tabitha didn't eat this morning, though I have packed a few snacks for us to have on the way home if she doesn't want what I have planned. Her weight is slowly increasing. The chart I created for her is helping her see she's physically getting better.

Everything for Tabs seems to be moving at break-neck speed. The counsellor's appointment has come through, and she's been writing in her diary almost daily, as well as adding a square or two at least weekly to the comic book she's developing for her brother. She seemed lighter, focused. Until that letter.

As I pull up into the car park for the prison, I cut off the engine and go around to Tabitha's side to help her out. I love how she's dressed today; tight jeans, a fitted top, jacket and boots. It's a warm day and she looks fresh, fit and vibrant.

"Let's do this," she tells me with a tight smile upon those lovely coral coloured lips. I heard her speaking with Liss about make-up and tones last night, something understated is what Tabs wanted. Looking at her this morning, I'd say she's achieved it.

She walks with determination and strength up to the entrance, and we book in, showing the ID's we were told to bring. She smiles at me the entire time we're being escorted through to the visitors' hall. Across a table… is him. Lee Hill. There are numerous guards around, and he's handcuffed to the table, given the severity of why he's in here.

I wish I could be kind, but seeing him gaunt with little hair and in a prison uniform of green trousers and grey shirt doesn't add to the appeal. Tabitha sits down, not once greeting him. He lifts his eyebrows, and when she doesn't say anything, he sighs.

"I can see you're not going to say anything," he begins. Tabitha shrugs, she's neither scowling nor smiling. "I wanted to say I was sorry. I've cleaned up." He shuffles backwards and sits up in his seat. He continues to look between us, but neither of us are offering anything to him. Tabitha usually fidgets, but today she's still as a statue.

"You could have put that in a letter," Tabitha says after long minutes of silence. "You could have done so many things, but you didn't." She stands up, indicating that our time here is over. "So, here's my parting words for you." Her voice lowers. "There's a court order being processed. A restraining order. You are never," she leans across slightly, which makes a guard loom closer. "I repeat, never, to darken my door, or my brother's, ever again. We do not want to see you, hear from you or be anywhere near you." I stand and motion to the exit. Then, she delivers the last blow. "You are as dead to us as our mother, you vile excuse for a man." I push the chairs in as I leave, proud as heck for her backbone.

Lee drops his head, and his shoulders sag. Normally, I'd offer encouraging words when I see someone as defeated and broken as him. Today, I don't want to. Tabitha waits at the security door for me to catch up, and she smiles at me, holding out her hand.

"I don't know about you," she says as we head outside into the fresh air, "but now, I am hungry."

I grin, knowing full well she'll be up for the diner breakfast I know that's in the next town up, Bromsgrove.

"I've got a treat for you," I tell her as I help her into the car.

"Oh?" she asks, and I nod. "What is it?"

"Tell you over breakfast," I wink as I start the car up.

"Then let's leave. I'm never coming back."

***

As we head up the motorway to Bromsgrove, I glance across at her. She smiles back and then giggles.

"What is it, Frank?" she asks, and I grin.

"You were very brave," I say to her as I set the car into cruising gear for a junction. "I didn't expect you to say anything much to him," I admit. "I should have asked you what you wanted to say," I reveal, something dad asked her about this morning.

"Until I saw that worthless pig, I had no idea what I was going to say," she sighs, and I pull off at the junction we need. There's an American diner, or there was, just south of Bromsgrove. I love coming here, even though it's a little far out sometimes.

"But I did it. Told him to never darken our door again. That's all I wanted to ever tell him." She sighs and looks at me as I pull into the diner car park. "He didn't look well, did he?" she asks, and I shake my head before I get out to go and help her.

"No, babe, he didn't." I hold my hand out as I reply.

"Do you think I should have been kinder?" she asks as we head inside. Across from each other in a booth, I take her hand and run my thumb over her knuckle.

"That's down to you, but after scaring you as he did, that promise... making you run away to protect yourself, does he deserve any kindness from you?" I say, hoping to stop the guilt trip I'm sure she's putting herself through.

She chews on her bottom lip, and then shakes her head.

"No... you're right." She smiles at me. "He scared me, he's left Shane and me motherless. If it weren't for you and your parents, our lives would be a whole lot worse than they are right now." She pushes up and leans across to me, then kisses me. "Thank you," she says as she sits back down. Then a waitress comes over and we ask her to give us a few minutes. I already know what I'll be ordering, so I don't need to look.

"Hmm...," Tabitha muses as she reads through what they have for breakfast. "Ah!" she declares and grins at me. When the waitress comes back a few minutes later, I can't help but grin as Tabitha orders the scrambled egg pancakes.

"Do you want the maple syrup on the side?" the waitress asks in a fake drawl. Tabitha smiles sweetly.

"Yes, please!" she nods and the waitress winks at her. "Also, can we have a jug of iced tap water, please?"

The waitress nods. "Sure, sugar!" Then, she turns to me and takes my order.

"Back in a mo!" She vanishes for a few moments but comes back with our orange juices, clean glasses and a jug of water for us both.

"Thank you," Tabitha says as the tray of drinks is put down.

"I'll bring it to ya when it's ready," she tells us and wanders off.

"I wonder how long it took her to get the accent?" Tabitha grins at me as she sips her orange juice. I pour us both a large glass of water and shrug.

"No idea... Probably a requirement of the job," I think out loud. Now that the hard part of today is over, it's time to tell Tabitha what I've gone and done. I just hope she's not too mad at me.

CHAPTER 22

Tabitha

Frank looks nervous after we've ordered food and he almost gulps the glass of water in one go.

"Frank, what's wrong?" I ask, and I put my glass down to the side. "Whatever it is, we'll work it out." I fear the absolute worst... that he doesn't want me anymore. I clench my jaw, trying to keep the tears at bay.

"I... did something," he tells me and takes his phone out of his pocket. Then, he touches the screen a few times and suddenly, my phone pings.

"What's that? What did you do?" I ask and he motions to my jacket pocket.

"Read what I just sent you," he tells me.

"You're dumping me over a message at the table?" I whisper, letting the tears fall.

"What? Hell! No!" He vanishes from my sight and then he's next to me. "Fuck, Tabs, no! Never that! You might want to finish with me when you've read that email! I'd never finish with you–you've just come back into my life. No way am I letting you go!"

He hands me a napkin, and I dry my eyes. I intentionally wore water-proof makeup this morning, and I'm glad I did. I take a gulp of air, then another.

"I'm sorry I made you think that! Shit, that's not what you were meant to think... I didn't even consider you'd go there!" He rubs his hands over his face and sighs. "Please, Tabs, read the email."

When I'm able to see, I open my phone, and I bring up my email. There is one from Frank, alongside the College notification emails.

"A publisher?" I whisper, then I look up at him. My breathing is fast, and I know my mouth is open. He nods.

"Read on," he tells me and I do.

Dear Mr Allen,

Thank you so much for the few pictures of the storybook your girlfriend is drawing. Yes, it's exactly the kind of work we're looking at. Addressing grief in children is a genre that's difficult to pitch right, but Ms Reid seems to have found a way to communicate the emotions.

We'd love to talk more. Perhaps with you both? Please have Ms Reid contact us on the details below.

Yours faithfully…

I look up at Frank.

"What did you do?" I ask, fearfully, my voice just barely working. "That book was never meant to get published. It's for Shane." I no longer feel hungry. All I feel is empty, ashamed, hollow.

He sighs. "Tabs, that work is too good to just keep for Shane. Sure, make it a personal one for him, but the story can be adjusted for the mainstream. Think of little kids reading your books, enjoying your artwork, and understanding the way they're feeling."

I gape at him, shocked he'd betray me.

"That wasn't your call," I say, gathering my things together. "Please let me out," I demand. He sighs and moves out of my way, offering to help me out of the booth. I refuse his help and somehow, get outside before I find the corner of the building, lean against it and let the tears fall as I try to stop my heart from breaking right here and now.

***

Frank comes to get me a few minutes later, trying to guide me back in, but I refuse to go with him. He sighs and goes inside, I think to eat our breakfast, or his at least. I don't care for what I've ordered now. A few moments later, he comes back outside with boxes and heads to the car. I stay where I am, unsure if I even have a ride home, but when he comes over and offers his hand, I walk to the car with legs that just about remember how to work. I don't want to sit next to him, so I get into the back, and I stare out of the window the rest of the way home.

His jaw ticks, but I don't care. My nostrils flare, my limbs are stiff and there's a pain in my chest and throat. That he'd even send off what I've drawn so far to someone, a publishing house, without asking me if that's what I wanted to have happen, is the ultimate betrayal. Dishonesty is one thing I didn't want to deal with, but it looks like I will have to.

I'm contemplating if I even want to finish the book for Shane.

***

As we pull up, Katie comes out to greet us, and her worried face intensifies as I go to her. She holds her arms out for me, but I don't step into the embrace.

"Did you know?" I ask, and she looks between Frank and me.

"Know what? What's going on?" Phil appears behind her, and he too looks concerned.

I turn to Frank and shake my head, then I look back at Katie. "Ask your son," I whisper as she moves to let me pass. I head upstairs, closing myself in my bedroom. I flop down onto the bed, and I let my emotions go like a dam, knowing I'll have to deal with this later on. Somehow.

CHAPTER 23

Frank

Tabitha's sad, tear ridden glare as she entered the house and then her slow climb to her bedroom, closing the door, made me feel like a total idiot. *How could I have not seen this happening?*

"What's happened?" Mum asks, confusion etched on her face as much as it is on dad's.

"I'll tell you," I say, motioning to the kitchen and bringing the breakfast boxes in, placing them on the counter. "I did something that I thought would be great. Turns out, Tabitha doesn't think so."

Mum sits on the chair and gives me the look that she gives Shane now; the one I grew up with when I was being unruly.

"What did you do?" Dad slowly asks, and I pull my shoulders back.

"I sent photographs of the first three pages of Tabitha's comic for Shane to a publishing company that specialises in kids' books. They're keen to meet her."

"Oh, Frank, you didn't," Mum sighs.

I look at dad, who is shaking his head. "Son, we love you, but that wasn't your call to make. I take it you didn't ask her about her intentions for that book."

I shake my head. "It's brilliant work, Dad. It deserves to be published," I begin but mum slaps the counter, hard.

"Francis Philip Allen, that was not your decision!" Mum glares at me, then she begins crying. I've just been full named and now I *know* I'm in deep trouble; not just with Tabs. "I thought we had taught you to have better respect for others than what you're displaying right now." She stands up and makes a step to the hallway. "I'm deeply disappointed in you, Francis. To do that to Tabs, after all the lack of control she's had...," Mum's voice cracks as she walks through the door; the feeling I had at the dinner intensifies as I realise, far too late, I've really screwed up.

I look at dad, and he's turned away to put the kettle on. He turns his head half to me and talks to me over his shoulder. Dad has never done that, even when I told him I didn't want to do the accounting exams he'd set his heart on me doing.

"You need to give her some time, son. What you did...," He sighs, deeply. "I get why you did it, but it wasn't the right thing to do."

"I thought it would be great for her to get her artwork out there," I tell him. He turns to me and the look of disappointment on his face is the final nail in the coffin.

"You didn't discuss it with her, Frank. Or even seek counsel from your mum or me. We knew she was never intending on publishing that book. It was always for Shane, exclusively." The kettle clicks off, and dad makes up a cup of tea, but not how he drinks it. How Tabs drinks it. "We've told her it's great work, but that decision was hers, son. You didn't have the right to do that."

I run my hands over my face, ashamed now that I've done it. "I can't undo it. How can I fix this?" I whisper. I hear some shuffling behind me, and it's mum. Her eyes are red, and she's stuffing some tissues up her sleeve. "Tabitha hasn't eaten today." I point to the smaller box from the dinner. "We ordered that before I broke the news to her. She walked out before it had arrived."

Mum nods and takes that and the tea up. "Time, Francis. Time," she says as she heads back into the hallway to take food up to Tabitha.

CHAPTER 24

Tabitha

Katie brings me the breakfast from the dinner that Frank ordered for me. I almost don't want to eat it, but it's a waste if I ask her to throw it away, and that's one thing I did learn on the streets. Be grateful for every scrap of food you receive. Surprisingly, even cold, it's tasty, and the maple syrup is in a small pot, so it hasn't spilled out.

"Why would he do that?" I ask, breathing out as I hug my legs a little while later, feeling much better. Katie is sitting next to me on the bed, and she's rubbing my back, again.

"I don't know, sweetheart. You'd need to ask him," she says, sighing heavily. "I'm sorry he's been so inconsiderate, I thought we'd taught him better than that."

There's a knock at my bedroom door, and it's Phil.

"Tea?" he asks, and we nod. I smile warmly at him as he hands me another hot cup of tea, just how I like it.

"He's working out he's done wrong," Phil says as he pulls my dresser stool out to sit on. I shrug. I do care, but I am too angry to do much about it.

"How did the visit to Lee go?" Katie asks, and I sigh.

"He didn't look well, but I told him I was putting a restraining order in place so that he can't contact me at all, never mind Shane. I also enjoyed telling him never to darken our door again. It felt good telling him to stay away." I sip the tea.

We hear a creak outside on the landing, then heavy steps up to the loft. Frank.

"What do I do about..?" I incline my head up to Frank's room. Katie sighs next to me, and she shakes her head.

"I wish we could tell you what to do," she says, her voice low and as gloomy as I feel. The pit in my stomach gets wider.

"You let him apologise," Phil tells me as I look across at him.

I give him a wry smile. "There will come a point he'll expect forgiveness," I state, and Phil nods.

"That's very true, but he'll have to understand that this isn't something he can do time and time again."

"You didn't yell at him?" I ask, surprised I haven't heard raised voices.

Katie smiles in a wicked way, her eyes dancing. "Sometimes, you don't need to. Us conveying our disappointment has told him more than shouting ever would."

I nod, and then I smile, understanding I have just been taught a parenting rule that could be very effective.

"Do you want to come down and join us?" Katie asks as she moves off my bed. I shake my head.

"No thanks. I need to decide what to do." I look up. Katie nods, reaches across and gives me a kiss on my cheek. Phil shuts the door quietly behind him as they leave.

***

The following day, while Frank is out with a client, I call the publishing company in question. He and I haven't spoken since yesterday afternoon and while we ate at the same table and small talk was held between Frank and his parents, I didn't speak to Frank at all. He looked like he wanted to chat with me, but I wasn't in the mood for hearing him.

"Miss Reid, it's lovely to hear from you," the woman on the end of the phone says, enthusiastically.

"Mrs O'Toole, it's nice to speak with you. There are a few things about the book that Mr Allen didn't convey. Have you time to speak now?" I ask, aware that I'm about to burst her bubble.

"Certainly! What things are we not aware of?" she asks, cautiously.

"Well, Mr Allen had no right to act upon my behalf. That book is a personal project to help my brother understand who our mother was and why she is not with us. I'm not sure what Mr Allen conveyed about the circumstance of the creation or need for it."

It takes a moment before she responds to me. "We are aware of your case. We did some research when Mr Allen eluded to it having been created to help your brother. He gave us enough details to find the news reports. The thing is, Miss Reid, may I call you Tabitha?" she asks, and I shrug, then remember this is a phone call.

"You may," I reply, and I can hear her sigh.

"That's great. Tabitha, your book touches upon a very dark subject matter, one a lot of people need but very few actually get, especially if you're a child. Of course, we'd want to change the character names, maybe even create a pen name for you to use, to help protect your brother and yourself."

"I had no intention of having this published, Mrs O'Toole," I begin, and I hear her gasp.

"Oh! I see. Would you consider it? It's a very unique piece of work and brilliantly done."

"I've just started my A-Levels. I wasn't looking to do anything with it beyond creating it for my brother, at least for the next two years. I'm not sure it'll ever be complete. Not totally."

Mrs O'Toole "hmms" again. "We certainly wouldn't want to interfere with your studies. What is it you're studying?" she asks, and I tell her. "Oh, that's fabulous! My name is Sara, by the way," she says, and I grin.

"Well, Sara, I'm sorry to withdraw this from you." I hear her sigh again.

"Is there nothing I can say or do to convince you to finish this and let us publish the manuscript? We have people who take over a year to produce such a piece of work, so I'm sure we can work around your studies and publish it in two years."

I begin to flounder. "I really wasn't expecting this, Sara," I admit, and she chuckles.

"Sometimes, the best things come at us from a totally different direction. Look, how about this? Are there any days you don't have class? Why don't we meet up? We can go through what you want, I can go through what we'd like and maybe we can find some happy ground?"

"And if I still want to walk away?" I ask, not wishing to commit myself.

"Then I'll be gutted, but it's nothing a good bottle of red won't cure." She chuckles at her own joke, but I can't. When I don't respond, Sara changes her tone. "That is, of course, your choice and your right," she affirms.

"Where do you want to meet?" I ask, and the tone of her voice lifts the more we talk.

"How far is Birmingham from you?" she asks.

"Fairly close. A short train ride away. I can meet you a week from Thursday?" I offer. I have no classes then, and I'd be at home, working on pieces as necessary.

"That sounds ideal. There's Whitewall Galleries outside of Snow Hill Station that has a good coffee shop over the road from it. I only know how to get to Snow Hill, you see." She laughs nervously.

"Same here! So, we have a venue and a date. What time?"

"I'll be coming up from London, so the earliest I'd be there is around one pm. Is that okay?"

"Sounds perfect. I'd like to bring a family friend," I say, knowing I don't want to meet her alone.

"Oh, is Mr Allen joining us?" she asks, and I stifle my gut reply.

"No, I'm going to try and arrange for his mother to be with me."

"That sounds like an ideal afternoon. Okay, Tabitha, I look forward to meeting you then. I'll confirm the arrangements by email in a little while. It's been great talking with you, and I look forward to meeting you soon. Take care." She waits until I say goodbye and then she hangs up. Now, I have to go and check my companion's schedule.

***

Katie's in the kitchen preparing dinner. I sit at the breakfast table while she places chicken breasts in a dish and adds cheese, then strips of streaky bacon. On the side is a jar of BBQ sauce.

"What are you making?" I ask, curious.

"Hunter's chicken," she tells me as she places a line of bacon, then cheese on each of the pieces of breast. There are four decent sized ones for us adults, and a small piece for Shane.

"What's in it?" I ask; I've never heard of hunter's chicken.

"Chicken, bacon and cheese, cooked together, then the BBQ sauce is poured on and cooked for fifteen or twenty minutes at the end." She places the chicken in the oven and turns to me. "So, how did the conversation go?" she asks, and I go through how Sara was able to persuade me to at least meet with her.

"She said they can defer things to allow my studies... I really hadn't considered publishing it."

"Your details are on that drawing," she tells me, and I nod.

"Sara did say they'd change the characters, even get me to redraw parts of it, so it's removed from my story. But Shane gets the original version, the one I was always going to make for him."

I pause and watch Frank's mum bustle about and check the time as she sets up the potatoes in a large saucepan.

"The thing is," I say, hesitantly, "I don't want to go alone. Will you come with me?" I ask, the lump in my throat making it hurt to swallow.

"Of course, I will! Tell me when it is while I get these potatoes set up." Once she's got the potatoes into the pot, she's got her phone out, marking the day and time we're meeting Sara. Sara's email pops up, and we put it into our digital diaries.

I reply to Sara, telling her that Mrs Allen will be joining me, and when that's confirmed, I sigh, feeling empowered. I negotiated this. Okay, Frank pushed me in this direction when it wasn't one I was going to go on.

"What do we tell the men folk?" she asks.

"The truth. That doesn't mean I forgive Frank for doing this behind my back." I smile as Katie pops the kettle on. "Oh, let me do that." I volunteer, jumping down off the stool and sorting out the mugs for us. "But, if they can defer for a year, let me build up my skills...," I say and the kettle clicks off just as I'm finishing preparing everything. "I thought it might be another income stream," I state.

Katie nods. "Okay. We need to sit down and decide on what you need from this, so we're both prepared," she grins. I've seen

Katie's negotiation skills. With her by my side, I feel I won't be such a pushover.

We're talking about it all when Frank comes in with Shane.

"Sister!" Shane shouts out, running to me in greeting. I come down to his level so we can hug like always and I pick him up, squeezing him as tightly as I can. Frank stays by the kitchen door, looking sullen.

"I paint," he says, and he goes to his bag to get out a picture he's done at nursery. I look at Katie and smile, but I don't look at Frank. I can make out the sun, the trees and two people who I think are having a picnic.

"That's great! Tell me, what are the people doing?" I ask, and he looks at me with a little scowl on his face.

"Making a book!"

"Ah! I thought they were having a picnic in the park." I can see him think about replying, then he looks at me.

"We can have picnic," he declares, and I chuckle, nodding.

"Not today, but I'd like that." He nods in reply and Katie offers to put it up on the fridge with the magnets she's brought. I clap with Shane when she does, and I give my little brother a huge hug.

"That's brilliant!"

"Book going to be in shops," he declares, and I smile wryly at him.

"Maybe, we'll see. It is going to take even longer to get it into the shops as I have to finish it first!" I laugh, trying to set his expectations.

"When?" he asks, and I grin.

"Well, how old are you?" I ask him, and he holds up three fingers.

"Three," he says, though it sounds more like "free" than "three." And I know he's not quite three yet.

"Okay, well, when you're five," I hold up my hand and spread all my digits wide, "that's when it *might* be ready to be in the shops. But...," I tell him, standing up, "you get the very first version. That one will be very special because that one will never be in the shops," I tell him.

He thinks for a moment, and then he nods. "Okay! Shane hungry," he declares and Katie laughs.

"You can have a banana and some milk, okay?" Katie tells him, and he cheers. Then he is climbing up onto the breakfast bar stools to make himself comfortable as Katie pours him some milk into a straw bottle and hands him a small banana.

He tries to open it, but today he can't, so I do it for him. I still haven't acknowledged Frank.

***

After Shane has had his bath, and he's in bed, I settle into the conservatory with some art supplies. The light is still decent and I begin work on one of my assignments; the human form. I pull up the sketch I've begun of Frank, and I sigh as I look at it.

"Hey, you," he whispers to me from the doorway. I glance up, and I can still see the pain in his eyes.

"Hey," I tell him, not moving my artwork off my lap, but not going back to the "zone" either. The silence between us both is disturbing, I don't want to fight, not with Frank, but he hurt me.

"I'm sorry," he blurts out and comes to sit near me. "It wasn't my call. You were right. I should have asked, encouraged, but not done what I did. I'm sorry. I...," he stops adding to the list.

I pause, waiting for him to continue. When he doesn't, I swallow the fear that's sitting at the back of my throat. "Tell me why," I ask, my voice strained, just audible.

"I believe it's brilliant," he tells me without blinking. "It deserves to be on the shelves in bookstores. Worldwide even."

I blink at him. Worldwide? What?

"But," he continues, "I shouldn't have done it. I hurt you, and I'm sorry. Let me make it up to you?" he asks, and I smile.

"I'd like that... I don't want to fight with you. Not again," I croak out as he becomes blurry. The next thing I know he's kissing me softly on my lips.

"I'm sorry, Tabs!"

"I know," I acknowledge, grateful to have my boyfriend back.

"I brought you something," he tells me as he hands me a tissue. I dry my tears and look at him, then I draw in a breath, wondering what this is now.

"Wait here," he tells me, and I do, putting aside my artwork for a moment. I expect a box of chocolates. The sudden need for chocolate consumes me, but it's not. Instead, he tells me to close my eyes.

"They're closed," I call back.

"No peeking!"

"I won't," I tell him, and I can hear things being pranged and pushed aside. Then, he tells me I can open my eyes.

I blink in the evening sun as it breaks over the fences and into the conservatory. Sitting in the middle of the room is a new easel.

"You brought me an art desk," I state the obvious. I knew my old easel wasn't in the shed, and I hadn't thought about getting one. Why, I had no idea, but this will save my back. This one is far better than the one I had or would have even thought about using back then.

This is metal, like the ones at college, tiltable with more angle settings than I think I'd ever use. The two drawers and the large basket to the side add to its usefulness. I know the rough cost of these. They're not cheap.

"Oh, Frank!" I whisper, in awe at the desk and his thoughtfulness. To say sorry with this? I hear movement near the door, Katie and Phil are there with smiles on their faces.

"Where do I put it?" I ask. There's not enough space in my room, not with the dressing table in there. Phil motions to the shed.

"How about we configure the shed up as a workspace for you?" he asks.

"What?" I blurt out, forgetting my manners. "That's your storage space," I remind him, and he shakes his head.

"Buy it off me for a quid," Phil counters, and I fish into my pocket for a pound. Seconds later, I've paid him for it, though I know it costs far more than the pound he's just charged me for it.

"It's yours, babe," Frank tells me. "It's only even been used to hold your stuff, and we're close to emptying it. Dad knows a sparky," I look at Phil, who nods, "so we can get electricity to it for heat and light. Once that's done, I can insulate it so you can use it in the winter, and we can get that window increased if you want more natural light."

"You'd do that?" I ask, and Frank nods.

"Totally," he tells me, his eyes sincere. I bite my lip, wondering if they'd do something else with it too. "What is it?" Frank asks, his voice low and fearful.

"It's facing the wrong way," I tell him, and he laughs.

"So, we'll get it moved. How do you want it?" He asks, and I tell him. The window to the light, the door on this side, not the other.

"That'll mean dismantling it to rebuild it," Katie says and Frank nods.

"If that's what will make Tabitha happy and forgive me, I'll get it done," he declares.

"You will?" I ask, and he nods. Then he reaches in to kiss me again, but it's not as intense as I want it with his parents watching.

CHAPTER 25

Frank

I organised the art desk from the supplier in Dudley that she went to with me to replace her art stash as the first step of my apology. As good as his word, it was next day pick-up, and I couldn't complain much, even though it was a total pain to assemble, especially without Tabitha finding out. I picked the one I thought she'd like the most, and the cost was secondary.

Then dad had proposed turning the shed into a little studio, and I agree. It'll be perfect. It'll need some work, but when I check with Omar about his cousin doing the window, some of his cousins helping to move and insulating it, he's onboard to help out.

Tabs and I spent that evening talking about a lot of things. Foremost, was her getting her A-Level in art and finishing that book.

"I'm glad your dad is letting me use the shed for a studio," she tells me. "I love the conservatory, but this is your parents' home. I'm sure they'd love to use this room for themselves."

"I'll start making the changes to it when you want," I say to her, not hinting at the plans I have in the works.

"I'm meeting the publishing company next Thursday," she tells me, biting her lower lip. "Your mum is coming with me," she grins. "Best lady for negotiation I've ever met," she declares, and I grin. That she's agreeing to meet them is great!

"That's great news! I'm still sorry I did it, but I'm pleased you're exploring this." I pause, waiting for her to react, and she does, quickly, by hugging me tightly. "So, we can get started then?" I ask, nodding to the shed, and she beams at me when she finally lets me go.

"The quicker it's up, the quicker I can do my coursework, keep things out of Shane's way and tidy this room up for your mum."

"Done," I say, and I pull my phone out, asking Omar about the day Tabs isn't going to be around. He confirms he'll arrange for as many people as he can.

***

We begin sleeping together again from that point onwards. But it's just that, sleeping. Either she's been up for college at the same time I have been up for work, or we're both so tired when we get home, we're asleep before we can do anything. Today, she's meeting the publisher, and mum will be by her side. Dad's booked the day off, so he's watching Shane when he's around or helping us. The first thing we have to do is dismantle the roof and three sides of the shed, then we can rebuild the foundations for the base and turn it. With sand, stones and rubber mats, we get the new ground base assembled and the shed lifted and turned.

Tabs leaves after we've set the floor, and she wishes us all luck. Sheer determination will be what wins things today. With a total of twenty people helping, things don't take long. The sides go back on and the floor is checked to ensure the sand and stone foundation won't shift. With so many people walking over the floor, it's thoroughly tested to ensure it doesn't creak or move, which is going to be perfect for Tabs's art studio.

Liss and Rachel arrive unexpectedly, but their help is most welcome.

When we get the shed reassembled, Omar's cousin who is a glazier, fits in a much bigger window into the front. As he's doing that, the pergola is assembled, the fast setting foundation foam doing its thing.

Everyone scrambles to do what needs to be done. Tabs said she wasn't fussed about the walls being super plaster smooth, just white so that the light was reflected; and plenty of storage. At nearly five pm, with Shane jumping up and down in excitement, Omar and his army move the desk into place as some of his cousins finish assembling the cube storage unit on the far wall.

Another cousin commandeered mum's kitchen and has cooked a huge amount of Indian curry, saving some aside without a lot of spice for Shane, Tabs and mum. We know it's not spicy because the lady got Shane to try some, and he wanted more there and then.

As mum and Tabs come through the door, we've finished washing up so we can eat. Everyone is gathered in the garden, either sitting on the grass, around the table or on chairs they thought to bring.

"Oh my goodness!" Tabs and mum exclaim together as they see how much work has been done.

"It's stunning!" Tabs declares as she walks into her shed studio. One of the younger girls made a sign that hangs on the door. Tabitha grins at it as she turns it to the "Artist in Residence" face. The other side shows "Artist is Recharging", which makes Tabs laugh.

There's a small heater, bright overhead lights and her desk. Tabs purses her lips together, then she bites her lip.

"What needs changing?" I ask, and she looks at me.

"Can we turn the desk around, please? I need my work to be at the window with the light behind me." I nod, calling out to Omar and another guy to give me a hand. We have to walk the desk out and then back in, but then Tabs gives the one word that makes us all happy.

"Perfect!" She makes her way around the group, thanking them with hugs and questions. Liss comes over and hands me a huge bowl of curry, telling me to sit down and eat before I fall. Can't say I want to argue with the southern belle.

***

Hours later, most of Omar's team has gone home after being thanked profusely by Tabitha. There are fairy lights on the pergola, the light from the studio cascading over the whole garden.

"We'll get a blind put up tomorrow," dad tells her. "So that your supplies don't get melted or your work scorched." Tabitha nods in reply. "Are you okay sweetheart?" dad asks her and she nods. It's just us, Omar, Liss and Rachel. Shane is in bed and has been for a while.

"Yeah... I want to tell you all about our discussion with the publisher," she begins and we all sit, rapt. "It's a go! I'm going to get

Mr Carter to check over the legal paperwork, and bar signing it, I'll have my story published in a few years. Of course, I've got to finish it and do my A-Levels first," she grins.

We all cheer and mum hushes us because of Shane. As the champagne is poured out, Tabs goes to shut down her studio, leaving the garden bathed in the many lights from the pergola.

EPILOGUE

Tabitha

(Two Years Later)

Frank, Phil, Katie and Shane hover close by as I am handed my envelope with my results. I only took one course, but with the book being drafted, fashion shoots, social media presence, book marketing and many other things I didn't fully understand I'd need to do for my book, I'm here, collecting the results of my hard work. I hope I've at least achieved a B grade, and as I open my envelope, I stare at the single letter and star.

A*

I got an A* in my A-Level art coursework, and I gasp, forgetting to breathe. College life was... interesting. It certainly made me more of a fighter. Frank takes it from my hand and hands it to his mum to read so she can explain it to Shane. I got higher than I thought I would!

Today is also book launch day, and I'm going to be in Waterstones in the Centre of Birmingham all evening, Frank by my side. My life has changed a lot in two years. From coming back with appendicitis, to facing off my step-dad, launching a fashion career and then becoming an author, as well as being at college on a full-time course, I'm tired.

"Welcome to the first day of the rest of your life, Ms Reid!" The College Dean congratulates me, before being commandeered by a reporter. Mr Carter comes through the doors. He's flustered, but upon seeing me, he smiles broadly. He's also coming with me to tonight's event. His vigilance over the author contract kept me, and my story, safe.

Shane is now five and he has his own private copy of "The Grieving Storyteller". The publishing company's title, not my own. However, Shane has the first-ever copy of that, as well as the one I hand made for him. He keeps it in a small wooden chest that Phil made for him. Volume One releases tonight, Volume Two has been emailed over, and all being well, should be available in about nine months.

With my results in hand, we head home, giddy and happy with the day so far. Omar, Liss and Rachel ask about my results and they get told in the group chat that we have. Lois and Xander ask too, and they send me voice messages of them cheering and whistling.

Back home, we eat a heavy lunch, aware that we won't be eating again until much later in the hotel in Birmingham, something that the publishing company are paying for.

***

I don't expect a large turnout for a children's book about death, and I don't get a huge crowd. What I didn't expect was a lot of children with a parent or parents, to say thank you for giving their child a voice. The emotions my characters go through, the crying, the wondering if you could have done something, the self-blame, the anger. It helped more people understand their grief than I thought possible. If this is the tip of the iceberg, I hope Volume Two is just as powerful.

"Ms Reid!" Sara O'Toole comes over to me with a huge smile and a tray of hot drinks. Katie and Phil have taken Shane back to the hotel room, their adoption process should be complete in a few more weeks. My step-father tried contesting it, but since the State removed his parental rights, his voice wasn't heard. Thankfully!

"How does it feel to be an official storyteller?" Sara asks with a huge grin on her face.

I pause, assessing how I feel. Elated, confused, embarrassed, excited. They're just some of the ones I can name. "Pretty good, thanks, Sara!" is all I can say, pulling Frank close for a hug I so desperately need.

***

Hours later, in our private hotel room, I step out of the heels and change into something floaty. I'm hungry again, too, which doesn't help, but Frank calls for room service and orders me what I'd like; a mushroom omelette with a side of fries.

We celebrate quietly, just us as we eat. I still don't drink. I doubt I ever will.

"So, that's it. You've accomplished your goals. Now what?" Frank asks as he sits back in a chair. He does drink, though not a lot. Tonight, he's let himself have a light beer. He's still as ripped and as fit as ever, but even he takes the odd evening off and indulges in shop bought pizza, burgers and fried chicken.

"Set new goals," I tell him, simply. "There are more stories in this teller yet," I tease with a wink as I drink my lemonade.

THE END

ABOUT LOUISE MURCHIE

Louise lives in the Midlands with her husband and children. Scottish born and bred, alas, she doesn't live in Scotland anymore. Her heart, though, always will be in the mist-covered mountains.

THE DETECTIVE'S FORBIDDEN TEMPTATION

by Melony Ann

CHAPTER ONE

Xavier

"What is this?" my father asks me. I close my eyes and take a deep breath, but don't turn around.

My father. Such a fucking asshole. I'm sure a lot of eighteen-year-old high school students say that, but my father really is an asshole. He's a detective with the Brystone Springs Police Department. Not that he wasn't always a cocky douche, but I think when he became a detective, his arrogance got a lot worse. He turned into an even bigger jerk.

His recent tirade against me, and believe me, there have been many over the years, is that I refuse to choose his beloved university. I don't have any fucking desire to got to Texas A&M, even though I have been recruited by their football team. I'm the best quarterback in the state, rivaling even college quarterbacks with my stats.

I'm good. I know I am. It's the entire reason colleges across the country have offered me full-ride scholarships and a fuck load of perks. One of them even said I'd have off campus housing, all paid for, and be an automatic addition to the most prestigious frat on campus. I looked into the frat. Those that are members get all the pussy they can handle, like I care about that anyway, and literally everything else a person can dream of. They rule the campus.

I don't want any part of them. I chose my college long ago. Much to the dickfuck's dismay. I'm attending Brystone University. It's the second largest school in the State of Texas, and one of A&M's biggest rivals. Choosing them wasn't a coincidence. I like that they're a rival of my dad's fucking college, but I like even more that it's near Brystone. It's just outside of the city, but it's far enough away that I can start my own life while still being a part of the community I've grown to love. Brystone Springs isn't bad. The city can't help that my father is a part of it.

I lean back in my desk chair and rub my head. "What?" I grit out through my teeth.

"What? You know what," he growls. He slams an acceptance letter down on my desk on top of my history book. "What the fuck, Xavier? You're going to A&M."

I sigh. "Dad, we've been through this."

"We have. And I don't give a shit what you want. I worked my ass off to get you into A&M."

I raise an eyebrow as I stand slowly. I face him down. It's not the first time I've stood eye to eye and toe to toe with my father. I'm six feet two. He's the same. We share the same dark hair and silver eyes. We even share the same build. Toned and muscular.

"You didn't do shit. I got myself into every single one of the colleges I've been accepted to. I'm the one who busted my ass getting good grades while leaving it all on the field. Not you."

My dad shoves me backwards onto my bed. "Listen up, you little fucking punk. I'm not paying for you to go to any other fucking college but the one we've worked your whole life. For once, do what you're told."

I just glare. I don't move. I've played this game before. I might match my dad in looks, physical strength, and agility, but there's one thing he will always have on me. His cop training. He knows how to take down even the best fighters and toughest criminals without breaking a sweat.

"I don't want to go to Texas A&M. You can't force me. I'm an adult."

My dad chuckles and looks around my room. "An adult. Who lives under my roof. Drives a car I bought. Has a video and gaming system that came from my pocket. A nice ass TV in his room. Bed. Clothing. Furniture. All because of me. You're an adult? Bullshit you are." I watch as he tears up the acceptance letter that he opened and slammed on my desk. I don't really care where it's from. I already have the acceptance letter from the University I'll be attending.

"Whatever," I grumble. I don't want to fight him today. I just want him gone.

"Whatever?" Before I can react, he backhands me hard enough to knock me flat on my bed. "You best learn manners, boy." He keeps one hand on my chest and slaps me again, harder this time. And it's then I can smell the alcohol on his breath. Of course he's drunk.

"Get the fuck off me!" I shove him back as hard as I can. He stumbles.

"Xavier! You ready for this history test, man?" Brant, my cousin and best friend, says from my bedroom door. He's walked in on my dad and I fighting more than once. Somehow, he always knows how to end it with just words.

My father lets out a low rumble of a growl and leaves the room with the remnants of the letter still in his hand. I lean up on my elbows and watch him leave with fire in my eyes and ice in my veins. One day, I swear to fuck I'll pay him back. For now, I'm just biding my damn time.

I sit up slowly and touch my cheek and lip with hardly a wince. "Motherfucker is going to get what's coming to him one day."

Brant chuckles as he closes my bedroom door. "What was it about this time?"

"Acceptance letter to Ohio State."

He raises an eyebrow as he sits at my desk. "I thought you chose Brystone."

"I did. I already sent them a promise letter. It's confirmed and everything. The coach and administration understand my situation and are happy to call me when they have paperwork. I just drive out there and take care of it."

Brant nods. "Good. I can't wait until we're all there. All of us back on one team. We're gonna miss you next year, man."

This makes me smile. I shrug. "Awe. You'll be okay. You're just as good as I am. And you know I'll put in a good word for you. Coach is already working on a recruitment package for you, Sterling, Kody, and Drake."

Brant, Sterling, Kody, and Drake are all my cousins. My dad has a couple of brothers and a sister. I grew up with their kids. We're all as close as siblings. We also have another cousin, Dylan. We're close to her, maybe even more than to each other, but Dylan's dad is extremely overprotective. He rarely lets her do anything. I'm surprised he let her be a cheerleader. I have a sneaking suspicion it's because we're all on the football team. He knows we'll keep her safe.

I can't really blame the guy. He's nice enough, but he's a State Senator. He gets a lot of fucking attention, and Dylan often catches the brunt of decisions he makes. We've had to step in more times than we can count when other students in school start harassing her for her father's decisions. Dylan takes it all like a goddamn Warrior Princess, though. She never lets any of it get to her.

"Ready to head out? Onyx is waiting. Everyone is already there."

I glance at my clock. It's nearly nine. "Huh. Fucker must have been fucking some bitch behind headquarters again. He's usually home before now."

Brant chuckles. "Unless he's getting his rocks off. Think he's passed out yet?"

"Maybe. He was already swaying when he got up here. The hit wasn't even that strong. I don't think he left a mark on me."

Brant looks over my face. "Just a little red under your eye. Not noticeable."

I stand and glance in the mirror on my door quickly as I grab my belt. "I wonder how many drinks he had before he got home if he was drunk enough to not leave a mark this time." I put my belt on and quickly change into a black t-shirt. I run my fingers through my hair, giving myself the perfect messy look.

"Well, however many it was, it's too bad he didn't crash into a tree on his way home. Do you think your mom is out yet?"

I chuckle. "She mixed her Xanax with Prince Valium long ago. She's out."

"Then let's get the hell out of here. I need a beer. My dad's new wife is driving me fucking crazy."

I laugh. "Driving you crazy by how nice she is? Or how your dick reacts to her?"

He grins and shoves me out of the bedroom door when I open it. "Asshole," he whispers.

We sneak quietly past my parent's bedroom. It's partially ajar, so I peek inside. My dad is sprawled facedown on the bed with his pants still on. No shirt. My mom, just as I predicted, is dead to the world. Neither of them will be moving for the rest of the night.

I chuckle when I see mom's open Valium container on dad's nightstand as I step away from the door. "We could drop a bomb on the house. They wouldn't wake up. He took one of her pills again."

Brant rolls his eyes. "I seriously wonder sometimes if your dad has a drug problem. Like he just goes into the evidence room and takes bricks of cocaine."

I laugh as we walk down the stairs. "Nah. It would be the prescription drugs he'd be into. He loves knocking his ass out with mom's shit. I'm not sure how his drinking and pill taking doesn't affect his job." I lead Brant out the front door.

"Want me to drive?" he asks. "I took my dad's Corvette."

I grin. "His pride and joy."

Brant laughs. "I'm his pride and joy. The car is just a nice perk."

I shake my head as I head for the garage. "I'll drive myself. Might get lucky tonight."

"You need to get your dick sucked. You've been quite the asshole on the field."

I laugh and wink over my shoulder. "Maybe I'll get some guy to loosen me up."

Brant laughs as he ducks in his dad's car and takes off. I jump in my Camaro and follow him to our club. We like it so much because the owner doesn't have a problem serving us. We've always thought it had a little to do with the fact that Dylan has enough money to pay him off. She doesn't get to come out with us all the time, but when she does, she always has the bartender grab the owner before she sits down. They talk for a few moments, and then he walks away while she comes to us.

However it happens, we aren't complaining, and she has more than enough money to slip the guy a few thousand to keep quiet. And she'd tell us if he started making any demands she couldn't handle or didn't want to take part in. She knows we'd deal with it.

After a twenty minute drive, we pull into Onyx and park. It looks a lot busier than usual. The line is even still long. Thank God we have connections. We step out of our car and walk to the bouncer at the front of the line. He lets us right in, despite the grumbles of those in the crowd. We don't get carded or anything.

When we get in, I immediately spot our group. Dylan looks a little distant and upset. Sterling, Drake, and Kody all surround her in our favorite corner booth in the VIP section of the club. We like that we can overlook everything in the club but can't be bothered by people we don't want anything to do with.

A perk of being royalty, to an extent, at our high school is the unlimited admiration and attention we get. It's also one of the downfalls. We always have people sucking up to us and wanting to be a part of our group. While we can basically do and get away with anything we want, our status is coveted by others. It's more an annoyance to me than it is flattery. I'm sure there are a couple in my group who would disagree, though.

Brant and I make our way to our group. I catch the eye of the server in our section. I don't need to say anything. She knows our order. It's a perk I don't mind. I slide in next to Sterling. Brant sits on the other side next to Drake.

"Dylan's asshole biology teacher failed her," Sterling says.

I shake my head and look at her with a raised eyebrow. "What? Why?"

She sniffles and shrugs. "I wouldn't dissect the pig fetus. It made me sick. And not just the smell of formaldehyde. I just couldn't do it. He said if I didn't, he'd fail me. So I walked out of class. He berated me the whole time. Told me some just aren't cut out for doing what it takes. Some of the other students agreed. I heard one of them say that I get special treatment because of who my father is."

"That's bullshit," I growl low. "He can't fail you for that."

She looks at me with watery eyes. "There were other girls in the class who didn't have to. One said it was religious reasons, but I think it's because she sucked his dick or fucked him or something."

"Wouldn't be surprised." I take a long swallow of the cold light beer in my glass. Dark has always tasted like shit to me. Too strong. Not enough taste. I'll take a Coors over an ale any day of the week.

"What are we going to do about this?" Drake asks. "We can't let him fail her. She'll get kicked off the cheerleading squad."

I shrug. I'm the leader on and off the field with my group. "Simple. We use our advantage while systematically destroying the fucker."

Kody grins. "How are we going to destroy him? I'm game. I hate that guy."

"We use her dad. I know you don't like whining to him and being daddy's little girl, but do it in this case," I respond. "As for him? We'll set up Go Pros in the room. We'll catch him doing something we can use against him."

Dylan smiles a little. "Thank you, Xavier. I don't know why I've been so upset about it. I knew you guys would take care of it."

Sterling chuckles. "Not like you wouldn't have figured out some way to get him back. You're not at all innocent."

Dylan laughs. "Only when I get pissed off enough."

I smile as we all start loosening up. One thing I can say for us. Though we may be close and basically the Kings and Queen of our school, we aren't assholes. Not unless we have to be. We don't go around bullying anyone. We all work hard. We're admired. People want to be us. But we certainly don't strike the fear of God into anyone. No one fucks with us, though, because everyone knows we don't and won't take shit from anyone.

I can't wait until we all head off to college and get to be on our own. The only one who won't be with us is Dylan. She has dreams. Big, big dreams. She loves being a cheerleader, but she wants to be a chef and own her own restaurant. She plans on going to some fancy university in Chicago. We'll miss the hell out of her, but no way we won't visit her. She'll do the same.

After a couple of hours, we're all feeling pretty good. But the mood quickly sours when I see a few people from our school at a table near us snorting some white powder off the table they're sitting at. We might drink, but we draw the line at that shit.

"That's fucking brazen," Sterling says quietly.

"No shit," I murmur back.

One of them recognizes us and stands. "Hey, ya'll. Wanna take a few hits with us?" he asks when he reaches our table. "Guaranteed to make your night a blast." He laughs as he hands us a small baggie.

"Are you fucking insane?" I growl, slapping his hand away from us. "Get that shit out of here."

"Come on. Don't be like that, dude. Just trying to share the good time." He actually pouts.

"We aren't interested in you or your brand of fun. Walk away," Kody growls dangerously.

No sooner do the words come out of his mouth, I hear shouts. I glance towards the dance floor and see people running and screaming. They run for exits, but a lot of people in black uniforms that say 'Police' across the chest are converging on them from the very doors they're trying to run out. I usually have inside information of when the cops are planning a raid anywhere in the city. So does Brant. I have no idea why I didn't know about this one.

I don't have time to ponder, though, because we all need to get the hell out of here. I don't want to be caught in a bust with alcohol in my system. I sure as hell don't want anyone at this table to either. I'm the only one who is eighteen. Everyone else here is sixteen or seventeen.

I get up quickly and spring into action. We all duck down as we run behind the bar. Another good thing about whatever Dylan does to make the owner like us is that we know where a lot of escapes are that others don't. Except maybe employees. If we need to make a quick exit and not be seen, we can.

It's happened before. A few of us have had girls all over us who wouldn't give it up. We've used the secret exits to escape without causing a scene. Dylan has had a few guys who wouldn't leave her alone, even after warnings from us. After we've gotten her out, we've taken care of them. They've never bothered her again, but we're grateful for the ability to get her out quietly.

I make sure everyone else gets to the door. Not seeing any cops, I start pushing them all towards it. "Go!" I whisper yell. Dylan looks up at me with terrified eyes. "Go, Dylan! Get out of here!"

"What about you?" she cries.

"I'll be fine! Go! I need to find Brant!"

Brant is the only one who wasn't with us when the raid started. He'd just gone to the bathroom not long before. I duck out of view of the police, but I'm not really sure I'd need to. They all seem pretty occupied with the numerous people in the club on the dancefloor, many of whom are fighting with them.

So, I run towards the bathrooms, praying no one pays me any attention. Hopefully, these guys are as stupid as my father is. He's had his ass saved more than once by one of his partners because he's not observant in the slightest. I'm sure it's because he drinks on the job.

I let out a breath when I reach the bathrooms. They must have checked this hall already because there's no one in it. I duck into the bathroom and look around. There's a window open and no one in any of the stalls.

"Fuck, I hope to hell you got out of here," I whisper.

Not wanting to chance going back out the door, I climb up on a urinal and out the window. I grunt a little because it's not that large. I have to squeeze myself out of it. It's a good thing I chose to go feet first because the ground below would be a hard fall. It's only a few feet down this way. I let go of the window and land in a crouch.

"Nice landing, kid," a deep voice that sends shivers down my spine says from the shadows behind me. "I was wondering how many people would dare come out that window after I saw the first one do it and take off. Didn't catch him, but I've caught six."

Holy fuck, I hope to hell Brant wasn't one of them. I stand slowly as I let out a breath. I'm the son of a cop. One thing I've learned is to not make sudden movements. So, when I turn, I do it just as deliberately as I had when I stood.

I expected a cocky fucker. Most cops I know are. I didn't expect the tall, dark, sexy drink of water standing in front of me with piercing blue eyes I could drown in and die happy. I didn't expect his hard glare to go straight to my cock.

I swallow. Hard. It does nothing to quench my sudden thirst for this man, though. I'm usually the one who commands the boys I'm with in the bedroom. Only those close to me know that secret. The boys I've been with wouldn't dare tell a soul. And that's just what they are compared to the person standing in front of me right now. They are all boys. All of them. They may be my age, but they are nothing compared to him.

Fuck. I'd fall to my knees and do whatever this guy asked me to. I bet he could bring me the kind of pleasure I've longed for but never quite accomplished. I highly doubt I'd have to guide him into position. He'd just know.

I mentally shake myself out of my fantasy. First of all, I doubt he's gay. If he is, I'm far too young for a man like him. Not that I'd care. I'd fall at his feet and kiss the ground he walked on if he asked me to. Second, he's a cop. Who is about to arrest me. And third, there's no way I can flirt my way out of this one. He doesn't look like the type who would fall for it.

"Don't suppose I can talk you into not telling my father about this," I say, hoping I'll at least get that much out of it.

He raises an eyebrow. "Do I look like the type of guy who gives a fuck who your daddy is?"

I shrug. "Nope. But you're a cop. So is he. If I told you he'd probably beat the shit out of me for this, you'd care because it's your job."

"Is he going to beat the shit out of you? Or is that just your way of getting on my good side so I don't tell daddy his precious son is fucking around at a drug party?"

I chuckle and nod. "Fair enough. What if I said I was eighteen?"

He shrugs but doesn't move from his spot against the wall of the club. "Then daddy wouldn't have to know. It would be up to you to tell him so he can come bail your ass out. Turn around."

I have half a mind to run, but I don't doubt he'd be able to keep up. So, I let out a sigh and turn around. When I feel the cold metal of the cuffs hit my wrists, I know it's over for me. I can not only kiss my place on the football team goodbye, but I can also kiss my scholarship goodbye. My entire college career. I'm not even certain I care too much about any of that. Right now, all I can think about is my cousins and wonder if they got out.

And the tingles this cop's hands are shooting through my entire body as he leads me to his squad.

CHAPTER TWO

Colton

I glance in the rearview mirror at the kid I arrested not long ago at the Onyx. Something about him is pulling at places it shouldn't be. Like my heart. And my fucking dick. He's truly gorgeous. Maybe the most handsome guy I've ever seen. The first one to make me feel anything at all for a very long time.

But he's quiet. Too quiet. Xavier Remington hasn't looked up at me since I put him in the car. He's in the backseat looking down at his feet with his legs spread apart to make himself more comfortable. He's tall, and the back seat of a squad car is made to be uncomfortable. Even more so for big guys like me or him.

"Tell me what you were doing at that club," I say after a few more moments of silence. Anything to get him talking again. Something about him makes me want to know everything. Especially what he was doing in a club like Onyx.

He shrugs but doesn't look up. "Don't you have to read me my rights or something? You know. Right to remain silent. Right to not talk to you. Right to an attorney. And then ask me if I'm smart enough to understand what you said. Then if I wish to talk to you."

I can't help the smile that spreads across my face. I chuckle. "Sounds like you already know them."

"My dad's a cop. Remember? They've been ingrained in me ever since I was born."

I chuckle again. "Who is your dad?"

"Buckley Remington. Ace detective extraordinaire," he answers. So much sarcasm laces his voice, though, it makes me raise an eyebrow. "You might have heard him with his whore behind the station," he says low enough I'm sure he doesn't think I can hear.

There are a couple of Remington's who work at the department. I thought he was just being a smartass when he said his dad might beat him. Now, I'm not so sure. Buckley Remington is quite the asshole. I know he has a drinking problem. But he's the higher-up's pet. Getting them to do shit about it is like hitting a target dead center with a Glock from three hundred yards away. If that sounds impossible, it's because it damn well is.

It's also a well-known fact that Buckley Remington likes his girls young. His current fling is one of our newest officers. She's barely twenty-one. She's also not the only one he fucks around with. I'm sure he thinks none of us know, but he's a frequent shopper in our very own red-light district. Most of the time, he's on duty when he goes there. Fucker is his own brand of tool.

I clear my throat. "Your dad isn't all that well-liked around the department."

He lets out something between a chuckle and a grunt. "Nope. He's not all that well-liked anywhere. Except with the command staff. Probably gives them dick or something."

I'm quiet a few moments as I think. Something about all of this just doesn't sit right with me. "So, why were you at a club known for drugs?"

He shifts a little and slumps down in his seat as he leans his head back against the headrest and closes his eyes. "We don't go there for the drugs. We aren't into that shit. We know it happens. We know the owner is lax. We go because he serves us alcohol. It's a nice little reprieve when the day is fucked up. You know. Like, when your mom tells you every day how much you've fucked up her life. Or your dad tries to punch you but only slaps you because he's too fucking drunk to know the difference. Then screams at you about going to the college he's picked for you because your life and choices don't fucking matter."

Now we're getting somewhere. "So, he hit you because you decided you don't want to go to the college he's chosen."

He shrugs, but those silver eyes that mesmerize me stay closed. Probably for the best. What they do to me is probably a crime around the world. "Doesn't matter. I don't need him to pay for college. He knows it. I have my pick of any college in the country. And I'm good enough to get a full scholarship. I only need him until I pack up and leave after I graduate." He opens his eyes then and chuckles. "Ironic, huh? This fuck up will actually be the one that ruins it all."

I keep my eyes on the road because if I look back at him again, I can't be responsible for my actions. He looks so fucking upset that all I want to do is take him in my arms and kiss it all away. I mentally slap myself for the damn thought.

"You went to the club to drink. No drugs. None of that shit."

"Nope. But again. Doesn't matter now, does it? You may as well just put me in a cell and throw away the key because as soon as my dad finds out, he'll kick me out. I could probably stay with a cousin, but my life as I know it is over because no college would accept me with a drinking charge on my record. They expect their quarterbacks to be clean. Lead by example. Probably for the best, right? Maybe this is my wake-up call. Can't be a badass and a good kid. Eventually, the tightrope is going to break. Lines I toe will eventually be crossed."

I glance down at the computer screen all squads are equipped with. His address isn't too far away from here, so I make an executive decision and turn left towards his house instead of continuing to Headquarters. A block away from his house, I pull over and stop. He's closed his eyes again. When we stop, he doesn't move.

I sigh and cut the lights and engine. "Promise me that all you were doing at that club is drinking. That you weren't into the drugs. You're not selling. You aren't part of the illegal underground weapons market I'm positive he has going on." I lean back in my seat and glance at him over my shoulder. He's watching me with wide eyes and a slightly open mouth. I can see how shocked he is, but all I really want to do is plunge my tongue into his mouth just to see how he tastes.

Fuck. What the hell is wrong with me?

I don't even really know why I told him about the drugs and weapons trade. This case is supposed to be top secret. No one knows I'm working it except the Chief of the department. My taskforce, while large, are all cops from other areas that I've pulled in because I suspect that there are some cops in my own department that are a part of what's going on. It's the only way it can stay as secret as it has for so long.

"All I was doing was drinking," he finally says to me after staring at me for a good while.

I nod but say nothing. I get out of the car and make my way to the backdoor. I open it to let him out. He watches me cautiously and confused but eventually slides out. He stands in front of me curiously as I take his arm. I turn him around and unlock the cuffs.

"Who were the friends you were with?" I swallow because touching his skin makes me inadvertently shiver. I let him go.

He turns around slowly and rubs his wrists as he watches me with furrowed brows. "My cousins. Sterling, Dylan, Kody, Brant, and Drake."

I nod and slide back into my driver's seat. I feel his eyes on me. When I glance back, Xavier looks away quickly, but knowing that he was watching me as I was sitting down does things to me I know it shouldn't.

I try to focus on anything else other than him and my reaction. I look up the notes from other officers involved in the raid to see if any of the names he listed show up. They don't. I don't know why I feel relieved to see that, but I am.

"They all got away, it looks like, but I'll keep an eye out."

I can feel his eyes on me. They send delightful shivers down my spine. For the thousandth time in I don't even know how long anymore, I quietly berate myself. My reaction is illogical. He's eighteen. Legal. But he's in high school. Doubtful he's gay. Not like many around here know I am. Just the failed relationships I've left in my wake. I'm not going to waste my time or anyone else's if I don't feel a connection, though.

Like the connection I have with him.

Jesus. What the fuck is wrong with me? He's twenty years younger. I could be his fucking father. I know I need to get a grip. Maybe it's just been too long since I've actually had good sex with anyone other than my hand. I need to go home and release the tension. Maybe then I'll stop thinking very inappropriate thoughts about this young man.

I close my eyes for a moment as I close my screen. I make a mental note to check on his friends later, though I really shouldn't. They were in the club. They were all drinking. They should all, at the very least, get cited for that alone. Instead, I tell myself that they aren't who I was after. They don't deserve to go down in a bust related to drugs if they weren't doing it.

How do I know they weren't? Well, I believe Xavier. I can tell he's had a few, but I've seen far drunker men over the course of my career. I doubt he's had more than a couple. His eyes are still clear. He's not exhibiting any signs of drug use. No. He's not my target. And I believe if he's not taking part in the drug activity, it's unlikely that his friends are. I've been around long enough to know at least a few things.

I take a breath as I get out of my car. "You're free to go."

He gives me a bewildered look that makes him look even more handsome. I try to stop the low groan before it escapes my mouth, but it doesn't work. This is ridiculous. Whatever is happening right now is completely wrong.

Xavier looks at me. "Why are you doing this? You should just take me to jail. Book me. My dad will see the paperwork without me even saying a word to him. He'll get his way. No other college will take me, but he'll pull some strings with Texas A&M. I'll be forced to go there."

I lean against my car and cross my arms over my chest. "You want me to be honest?"

He shrugs. "Yeah."

I look up at the sky before looking straight ahead at the house in front of me. "I don't know. The cop in me wants me to arrest you. Book you for a lot of charges. Fleeing the police. Drinking underage. Drug use. You were in the club. Logic would say you were using. Tests would come back saying you didn't." I shrug. "But that isn't the part of me I'm listening to." I look at him. "I'm giving you a huge break here. You understand that, don't you?"

He nods slowly, still a little confused as to what the hell I'm doing. Fuck, so am I. "Yeah. I get it."

"Don't let me down, Xavier. I mean it." I reach for my wallet and take out one of my business cards. I hand it to him. "Office phone is on the front. Cell is on the back. Call. Day or night. If you need anything."

He looks down at the card. "Colton DeLise. Detective." He looks back at me. "You work with my dad and uncle."

I nod. "I do. Maybe it's why I decided to keep your name out of things." I'm lying. The truth is I can't bring myself to ruin his life. I know this will. Even a drinking charge will fuck him over. That's not even factoring in his dick of a father. "Do we need to go back and get your car?"

He shakes his head with a small smile as he takes out his own wallet. I don't know why it pleases me to see him put my card in his wallet and not toss it on the ground. His eyes meet mine again. Fuck if I don't let myself drown in their depths.

"Nah. One of my cousins would have grabbed it." He grins.

I chuckle. "Good to have a team you can trust on your side."

"We're all pretty close." He shuffles his feet and leans against my car next to me.

It's my turn to give him a confused glance. I figured he would have run home by now. Not be hesitantly leaning against my car like he's testing me to see if I'll tell him to get the fuck home or let him stay and talk to me.

He turns and puts his arms on the roof of my car. He rests his chin on them. I try to stop myself from noticing that tight black shirt of his that leaves nothing to the imagination slide up a little. I can see a little bit of his back, but that's not what draws my attention. It's how muscular he looks. His jeans rest low enough on his hips that I can see the edge of the V-shape leading underneath his waistband. Because that's not going to drive me crazy later. It's driving me fucking insane right now.

"I'm a straight A student," he says after he stands next to me for a while. "He still manages to tell me it's not good enough." He chuckles. "But that doesn't really bother me. It's the team. I'm an All-Star quarterback. I work my ass off. Even during the off season. I stay in shape. I even do a lot of charity shit. It's not good enough for him, though. It used to be. But then he started drinking. The older I get, the worse he gets. He finds things to nitpick. School is just the latest thing."

I don't know why he's telling me all of this, but I don't care. I like his deep, velvety voice. I take a deep breath and take a chance to feel him out. "When I came out to my dad, he very promptly kicked me out. I was sixteen. Lived on the streets a bit. A teacher I liked took me in. I still consider her and her husband more parental units to me than my biological ones. Haven't spoken to my dad since."

He looks at me. Finally. I can't get enough of his silver eyes. I hope I'm not misreading the fire in them as he looks at me. "What about your mom?"

I chuckle. "Couldn't tell you. She left when I was pretty young. I haven't given much of a shit to track her down. Last I knew, she lived with some drug dealer in Montana."

He makes a face and looks away again. I inwardly whimper at the loss. Fucking pathetic of me. "My mom enjoys her Xanax and Valium. It's her escape from my dad. She hates him touching her. Knocks her ass out until late morning. She also loves blaming me for how her life has turned out. If it weren't for me, she would have left. Shit like that. It throws me into a depression that they both just tell me is a phase. I'll be okay." He shrugs. "Probably will when I'm out from under them."

We fall quiet once more. The nice thing about Brystone Springs is that it's small enough to still be able to see the stars in the Texas sky and hear the crickets chirp at night while being large enough to not feel stifling. I sigh a little because I can't help but feel a little bit disappointed that he didn't react a little more to my admission of being gay. I shouldn't fucking care. Dammit. I do, though. Maybe I can feel him out a little more. Would brushing his hand be crossing a line?

"Listen, uh…" I run my fingers through my hair as I stand. If I lean next to him anymore, I'm going to do something stupid. Like kiss him. He's intoxicating. Something about his scent. It's fresh, yet spicy. Unique. I let out a breath and turn to him. He's watching me over his shoulder. "Don't let anyone know about this. Okay? If they find out about me letting you go and erasing anything to do with your group, I could get fired."

He turns and leans against my car as he nods. "I won't. I know you're putting your ass on the line here. Don't really know why, though."

I smile and chuckle. "Because I think you were in the wrong place at the wrong time. I don't think this is something to fuck up your life over. I certainly don't want to be the one who ends your future before it even starts." I shrug with a half-smile. "And maybe I'm secretly hoping you'll come to me before you go out and do something stupid again. Like drink after getting into it with your dad."

He gives me a smile I'm sure melts the panties off any woman he gives it to. It certainly makes mine feel like they're on fire. "Playing the hero here, detective?"

I laugh. "Maybe a little. Complex of being a cop, you know. Always gotta be the hero of the story."

He smiles as he looks down. He looks back up at me after a few moments. "You're a lot different than I thought. You're not as... I don't know. Hard."

"I'm still hard, all right." At least my dick is. "But I'm not a complete asshole. Just... don't... let me catch you in a place like that again. This will probably go in one ear and out the other, but there's a lot of shit going on in this town. This case just landed on my desk a little while ago. Since then, the floodgates have opened. I've found a lot of things out that... well, they're dangerous. I don't want to see you go down for something you're not involved in."

He nods. "Sure thing, detective." He glances towards the direction of his house. "I should probably head home. Not like I'm worried about them waking up, but I do have a test tomorrow." He looks down as he pushes off my car.

I wish I could keep him here all night, but I know that's selfish of me. "Probably a good idea to get home then."

He doesn't move, though. I realize he's waiting for me to get back into my car. The gesture makes me chuckle a little, but it makes me feel a little warm inside that he wants to wait for me to get into my car before he leaves.

So, I do what he silently asks me to. I slide into the driver's seat of my squad. I don't miss the way he watches me do it. Or that he licks his lips when I look back up at him in surprise. But I don't have time to formulate the words my head wants me to before he walks away.

"Goodnight, Detective Sweet Ass."

I blink a few times as if I'm coming out of a stupor and watch him walk down the middle of the street towards his house with his hands in his pockets. A few moments later I force myself to breathe. Apparently, I forgot how.

Holy hell, that did not just happen. It was a figment of my obviously sex-deprived imagination. I need to go home. I need to take a shower and rub one out. When morning comes around I'm positive all of the so far out of line thoughts I'm having will be gone. He didn't just watch me like he was wondering what it would be like on his knees for me.

As I drive away, I know deep down I'm never going to be able to get those eyes out of my head. The way they looked like melting silver when he looked at me. I don't even need to think about it any longer to know just how fucked I am.

CHAPTER THREE

Xavier

"You okay?" Brant asks when I saunter off the field after throwing my second interception of the game.

I throw my helmet on the ground and rub my eyes with a low growl. "Fuck!" I rest my elbows on my knees and drop my head in my hands. "This is the worst game I've ever played. And that counts the one where I played with bruised ribs and could barely breathe."

"What do you want me to do, Remington?" Coach asks as he sits next to me. "Halftime is coming up. You want to take the time to get your head back in the damn game? Or do you want me to throw Brant in there?"

I don't hesitate. I've learned a thing or two over the past couple of years. When to let my backup lead is one of them. I take off my Captain's armband. "Put Brant in. I'm off today. I don't know why." I hand Brant my armband.

He takes it and puts it on, then pats my back. "I got you. I'll bring us back." He jumps up and jogs over to the edge of the field to warm up.

"How pissed is your dad gonna be?" Coach asks.

I shrug and keep my eyes on the field. "Fuck if I know. Don't really care. I'll be out of there soon enough."

"Well, heads up. He's walking this way. Want me to stick around?"

"No." I shake my head and nod to the field. "Team needs you."

He pats my back and stands. He walks towards his assistant. I can't help but smile a little because he's closer than he normally would be. I know he's within earshot in case shit goes down with my dad. It wouldn't be the first time. I'm sure it won't be the last.

My father sits down next to me on the bench and sighs. "What the fuck, Xavier? Where's your head? I don't think you've ever thrown two interceptions in a game."

I don't look at him. "Not feeling good, dad. It's hot. I'm probably thirsty or something."

"Well, get your damn head in the game. Fuck. You're embarrassing me. I talk you up at work all the damn time. I finally get some of my colleagues to come watch my boy play, and this is what you give them? This piss poor performance? This isn't your level. You're playing like a fucking rookie."

I shrug and stand. "Don't worry. I won't be embarrassing you anymore today, pops. Brant is taking over."

I walk away before he can say a word and smile as Coach intercepts him before he can follow me. I beeline for the locker room and lock myself in Coach's office after stopping by my locker and grabbing my gym bag. It's the one place my father not only won't think to look, but couldn't see me in even if he tried. The windows are blacked out and have a black curtain. No one is seeing me in here.

I start taking off my gear. I know exactly what my problem is. It's not my dad. It's not that the team we're playing is just that good. They aren't. My problem is that it's been a week since the raid on the club. A week since we enacted our plan on Dylan's teacher.

And since meeting that sexy as fuck detective. I can't get those eyes out of my head. I can't get him out of my head. The way he filled out those damn jeans and protective vest. How his ass looked as he got into his squad. I've gotten off an embarrassing number of times to images of his face. I've almost texted him just to talk but stopped myself because I don't want to come off as desperate. Though, I'm fucking desperate to see him again.

Not that I feel crazy or anything. I roll my eyes and shake my head. It's definitely insane to be thinking about a guy I know nothing about the way I have been. Especially since he's probably old enough to be my father. I'm sure if I said anything to him about the fantasies he has rolling though my head, he'd probably tell me I have a daddy complex or some shit.

I mentally punch myself and head for the showers to quickly wash the sweat and dirt off me. Hot detective isn't the only thing on my mind. While he's troubling me, he's definitely not the reason I can't fucking concentrate on completing a pass.

Nope.

What's really pissing me off is what we saw on our GoPro cameras. That son of a bitch has a whole group of girls he's getting blowjobs from before classes start. One of them, who Dylan says is a star pupil, fucks him right there on his desk almost every damn day.

Nothing about most of it looks nonconsensual. The girls often start the whole fucking thing. It's bad enough that they are all cheerleaders and all talk shit about Dylan just before the whole sexual encounter starts. I could easily ruin the little bitches. I still might.

The part that makes my stomach churn is what I saw on the cameras this morning. One of the cheerleaders he had giving him a blowjob is barely sixteen fucking years old. She's new to the school and has only just joined the team. The look on her face was pure terror. I don't know what the fucker said to her that our cameras didn't catch, but she definitely didn't want to be sucking his dick.

She hasn't been at the school long enough for it to be going on for long, but I hate the fact that she didn't come to us. She knows that when it comes to what goes on at this school, we have a lot of pull and clout. Everyone knows that. It's unlikely teachers even fuck with us. What's happening with Dylan is so rare it makes me think there's more shit going down that I'm not aware of. I don't like it.

And that all brings me back to Detective Sexy. I finish my shower and grab my towel. The team should be coming in soon, so I quickly dry off on my way back to the office. I start getting dressed and glance at my phone. This is something the police need to be involved in, but his words about shit happening keeps coming back to me. He got cops from other areas to help him with the case he's working on because he can't trust those within the department. I didn't recognize any of the ones I saw.

I've been going back and forth on if I do or don't want to pull him into this. I could just report it to the School Resource Officer. I could make a copy of the video and give him one of the copies. The issue is given what Colton said, I don't know who to trust and who not to. I don't know if anything would get done if I gave it to our SRO.

I grab my phone and leave my gear and gym bag in here. The team should be getting off the field for halftime right now. I sit down on a bench and wait for them as I make my decision. I need to text Colton. I pull up his number that I saved into my phone the very night he gave me his card and send him a text.

Xavier: Hey, Detective. It's Xavier. We met last week. You said if I needed anything to contact you. Well, the time has come, and it's important. I have a game today. I'm not playing, but I'm at the high school. Can you meet me? Text me when you're here.

I let out a breath and put my phone down as the team starts coming in. They're cheering and high-fiving each other, so I assume Brant is doing good at pulling them out of the fucking gutter I led them into. I smile because my cousin is just as good out there as I am. We've worked our whole lives to be the best. The only reason he's not the starting quarterback is because I haven't graduated yet. As soon as I do, Brant will be out there kicking ass each week like I do now.

For now, he's one of our running backs. He doesn't play all the time, just when he's needed, but he's just as good at that as being quarterback. Thankfully, we didn't need him out there playing running back today. He was fresh and ready to go in for me.

"Yeah! Nice throw! I wasn't sure I was going to catch it, but fuck! Dude! Right in my hands! That was like a move right out of Xavier's playbook!" Sterling exclaims as the team seemingly dance into the locker room.

I grin. "I'm sorry I missed it."

"Man, it was incredible!" Drake says as a smiling Brant sits next to me.

"Got us on the board, at least." Brant's eyes twinkle, and I can't help but be proud as hell.

I grin and high-five him. "Nice job!"

"Alright, guys," Coach says as he walks in and stands in the middle of us. His eyes meet mine. "I was going to ask if you wanted to come out after halftime. Looks like you made your decision."

I nod. "Not in the right frame of mind, Coach. Brant has the team. I'll cheer from the sidelines. The team needs someone who can fully focus on the game. I can't. I have some shit that needs to be dealt with. I'll be good next game."

"Okay," Coach says. "It's your team. Your decision." He turns back to the team. "I don't think I need to say much here. We're down by fourteen, but I know we can get it back. Keep playing like you just were. Trust your Quarterback. Keep your eyes on the ball. Adjust out there. Play smart. Defensive line. You're missing blocks out there. Morale was down a bit. But we're on the scoreboard. This game isn't that important, but an undefeated team getting their asses handed to them by a team that hasn't won a game isn't something I want to see. Offense. Remington wasn't the only issue out there. He missed a few passes, threw a couple interceptions, but you guys need to get open. This can't ride on one man's shoulders. Now rehydrate. Catch your breath. Do what you gotta do to right your minds. Let's show this city why the hell we're number one and deserve that championship trophy we're battling towards!"

I smile as the team lets out a resounding cheer. As they all go about their halftime rituals. I turn to Brant. "Nice job out there. Team is fired up."

He grins before sobering quickly. "Did you figure out what we're going to do about the teacher? I know that's why you're off today."

I sigh and nod. "Yeah. Remember the detective I told you about?"

He smiles again. "The one who knocked the great Xavier Remington on his ass? Nope. Don't remember him."

I laugh and playfully shove him. "Asshole. Anyway. I texted him. Asked him to meet me here. I'll turn it over to him, but I need to talk to Rosie. She needs to be prepared for the shitstorm about to come down."

Brant nods. "You do that. I saw her sniffling and walking towards the parking lot. Pretty sure she probably didn't want to be near the girls. Dylan went with her."

"Good." I stand and grab my phone. "Meet you back out there."

Brant grins and joins the team to boost their morale even more. He's learned very well. It makes me feel good about leaving the team to him. I know he'll make them proud, but most of all, I know he'll make himself proud.

I make my way out to the parking lot and look for Dylan and Rosie. It doesn't take me long to spot them. Rosie is sitting on the grass in the shade near the building in tears. Dylan is wrapped around her, rocking her back and forth. When I reach them, I kneel down and raise an eyebrow.

"He's at the game," Dylan whispers.

Rosie, not knowing I'm in front of her, lets out a squeak and wipes her eyes vigorously as her head snaps to me. "Xavier!"

"I haven't told her," Dylan mouths to me.

I nod. "Hey, Rosie. You okay?"

She nods with wide eyes. She looks frantically at Dylan before she looks back at me. "I'm okay! I just… had a hard day." She smiles, but I can see it's faked.

"Rosie, uh…" I take a breath and run my fingers through my still damp hair. "Why didn't you come to one of us? You know if anything is going on with you, we'll help you. Me. Drake. Brant. Sterling. Kody. Hell, even Dylan."

She bites her lip and looks at Dylan again. Dylan smiles softly and runs her fingers through Rosie's disheveled hair. With the tears she'd been crying ruining her make-up, I can see the bags under her eyes. We pulled the footage just before school, but this happened last night. There's no doubt in my mind that she didn't sleep even a second.

"How long has he been forcing you?" Dylan whispers as she hugs her.

Rosie bursts into tears and curls into herself. Dylan looks up when she hears the crowd start roaring with cheers. The teams are running back on the field. She looks at me. She's so obviously torn. She wants to stay with her friend, but she also knows she needs to cover for her.

I jerk my head towards the field as I take Rosie in my arms and hug her tightly while she sobs so hard, my heart feels like it's breaking. "Go. Cover for her."

Dylan nods as she stands. "Okay."

"All the other girls told me that it's what they do," she whispers after several minutes. "That I have to. Or I'll fail his class."

I'm already struggling. I don't understand it. He makes me feel so stupid." She hiccups as she grips my shirt. "He writes comments on my tests. Things like asking me how I could miss such a simple question. And he says things from that movie with Tom Hanks. 'Stupid is as stupid does.' He keeps me after class and berates me while he looks me over. It makes me feel so gross."

"Rosie, we told you that if you ever needed anything to come to us," I whisper as I rub my hand up and down her back.

"They said Dylan did it, too." She sniffles. "I shouldn't have believed them."

"Oh, honey. Don't blame yourself. How long has this been happening?"

She sniffles again as I sway gently with her. "Last night he made me suck him off. A w-week ago h-he…" She trails off, unable to finish. She doesn't need to. I can tell by her sobs what the sick fucker did to her.

All I can do is hug her tighter because I don't want to tell her again that she should have come to us. It will only make her feel like she fucked up and could have stopped it. The truth is, she could have. We would have helped her. But none of what happened to her is her fault. None of it.

"Do you trust me?" I ask her.

She nods. "I trust Dylan. And she trusts you and the guys."

"Then you trust that I'll get this dealt with, but I need your help."

She sniffles and nods again. "I trust you."

"I only have what happened last night on my video. We could have just used the shit from before, but it all looked consensual. Last night was the first time we saw something that will not only get him fired, but thrown in jail for a long time. But I need you to tell a cop I know what happened. The video will corroborate what you say and go a long way in proving that while he did fuck a couple of other cheerleaders who did consent, you didn't."

She nods again but says nothing. After a few moments, she looks up at me and wipes her eyes. "I told my mom." She looks down. "She didn't believe me. She told me not to make waves for her in her new town."

"Then, I'll figure out a way to take her down, too."

She looks up at me with wide eyes. "What?"

"She's part of this. Asking you to stay quiet after a teacher assaulted you?" I shake my head.

She bites her lip again and plays with the grass next to her. "I could live with my grandma and grandpa. And go back home to my old school." She pauses before taking a breath and looking up at me once more. Her green eyes are watery. "You and Dylan and all the guys are really nice, but I hate it here. I love my small town. Everyone knew me there." She shrugs. "Everyone liked me. They knew it wasn't my fault my dad died. They didn't treat me any differently. But everyone knew my mom had a hand in it. Somehow."

I chuckle. I don't know much about Rosie's story, but I do know that she moved here just before school started this year. She hasn't been here long. Only a couple of months. But rumors flew pretty quickly about why she and her mother came here from her small town somewhere near the Eastern border of Texas. Her dad died pretty suspiciously, but the police were never able to pin it on her mom. Even though they tried. Rosie thinks they're still trying. I hope they are.

I look down at my phone I put in the grass beside me and smile when I see Colton's number. My heart starts beating faster as I pick it up. Maybe he'll know or be able to find out about Rosie's case, too. Not that I want to make him feel like I'm using him, but I like the thought of him being able to help her in all the ways she needs to be helped.

Selfishly, though, I also like the thought of him being close.

CHAPTER FOUR

Colton

"Hey, Detective Sweet Ass. You at the school?"

I nearly choke at the nickname because it proves that Xavier was checking out my ass and that I wasn't just imagining him calling me that before. It makes me smile not just at his voice, but also at the fact that I wasn't the only one ogling that night. I may have been hiding it behind an asshole facade, but it's nice to know I wasn't wrong when I noticed him staring at me just as hard as I was him.

It's been a week since I've seen or heard from him. Fuck if I didn't miss him. I can't explain how I feel so drawn to him. I can't stop thinking about him. Which pisses me off because I should not be having feelings about a high school student. It doesn't matter that he's eighteen. He's still a lot younger than me. He lives with his parents. He doesn't even have his diploma. But none of that has stopped me from getting off to thoughts of him. That comment, though, makes me wonder if he has to me, too.

I run a hand down my face and shake my head. I can't think about shit like that right now. "I just got your message. I can be there in a few minutes. I'm not far away. What's going on?" I turn my car towards the school.

"Don't want to discuss it over the phone. We're near the entrance to the football field."

I raise an eyebrow. "Consider my curiosity peaked. I'm a couple blocks away."

"When you get here, you'll see us against the school. A little ways away from the ticket booth."

"Just stay on the phone with me. I'm not far. When you see me, you can direct me. You know what my car looks like." I can't explain the need to keep him on the phone any more than I can the stupid urge I have to kiss him.

"Sure. A black Ford POS."

I chuckle. "Maybe if I crack my case, I'll get one of those new Dodge Chargers."

"Christ. Those are worse." Xavier laughs. "I thought departments were getting rid of those cars because of how much they suck?"

I laugh because he's absolutely correct. "I'll probably get an Impala out of the damn deal."

"Even worse!"

I laugh as I turn into the lot and head towards the football field. "Alright, I'm here."

"I see you. Keep coming this way. We're on the grass by the building. I'm waving."

I look around for him and spot him just where he says he'd be. He's smiling widely and waving erratically, but my attention falls to the girl sitting next to him. His arm is around her, but she's hugging her knees and curled into herself. I don't know what's going on, but cop instincts instantly kick in.

"I see you. Parking now."

I pull up in the fire lane, not really caring that I'd ticket people for doing what I just did. If there's a fire, I'll be a good boy and move. For now, though, the lot is full because of the game. I'm not parking three blocks away and walking when whatever he called me for has to do with that girl.

A cheerleader. She's dressed in uniform. I question why she's not on the field with the rest of her squad. But then I have the same question about Xavier. He's an All-Star Quarterback. I looked up his stats because I'm apparently a stalker now, too, and not just a man who has unexplainable feelings for a guy he doesn't even really know.

Xavier not only leads all high school students in the State as best quarterback, he also rivals college students. Above and beyond that, there are talks he might just be the greatest high school quarterback of all time. He's good. Very good. So, why he's dressed in jeans and a red t-shirt that shows off all of his toned body is something I'm not following. I guess I'm about to find out, though.

"What's going on? How come you're not playing?" I ask as I kneel in front of them.

"Colton, this is Rosie. She's a cheerleader on the Varsity squad. She's really good. She's sixteen."

I raise an eyebrow as Xavier talks, silently questioning where he's going with that lead in, but I focus on Rosie. "Hey, Rosie. I'm Colton DeLise. I'm a detective with BSPD." I speak kindly, keeping my voice low and friendly, and reach out a hand for her to shake.

She doesn't look up at me, but she does take my hand. Hers is trembling as she shakes it lightly and lets it go. "Rosie," she whispers. She goes right back to hugging herself.

Xavier hugs her closer to him and looks at her with a comforting smile. "Colton is a friend. Can I tell him?"

She shrugs and nods slowly. "If you trust him." She sniffles.

"I do." Xavier hands me his phone. "That video is from a Go Pro camera we have set up in a classroom of a teacher."

My eyes widen. "Why would you set a camera up to spy on a teacher?"

He nods to his phone. "Just watch. I have the full video from the past week saved to a couple of flash drives."

I glance at the phone then back up at him. Then I look back down at his phone as I shift and sit down. "What am I about to watch?" I hit play on his screen.

"Something that will shock the ever living fuck out of you. I'll tell you that."

He's not wrong. "Holy... fuck..." My eyes about bulge out of my head, and I have to fight myself to keep my mouth from dropping open. Rosie shifts so she's hiding her face in Xavier's chest. I shake my head. "This is a teacher here?"

Xavier nods. "The first girl is a cheerleader. She's eighteen. You can't hear the audio too well on my phone, but she's talking shit about my cousin, Dylan, who is also a cheerleader. Right after that, she goes down on him."

"In the fucking classroom." I'd growl, but I'm shocked as hell. The video changes to another girl. "This girl is different."

"She's just eighteen. He eats her out right before she blows him."

I glance up at Rosie when she makes a choking sound. Xavier just hugs her tighter. I don't like what I know I'm about to see. "Why did you set this up?" I ask as I look back down at the video.

"Dylan refused to dissect a fetal pig. A few of the other girls refused as well. He let them slide, but not Dylan. She told her dad. He said he'd take care of it. From a grade perspective he did, but Dylan suspected the girls that he allowed to slide and said nothing to were doing favors for him on the side. Or at least one of the girls were. That girl said she had a religious excuse or some shit. But we trust our cousin. While her dad dealt with the grade, we set up a camera to see if we could catch him doing something illegal with that girl. We didn't expect this."

I shake my head as he fucks a third girl. Rather she fucks him. She rides him like a fucking bucking bronco while he's on his desk. "How old is the third girl?" He has no idea how badly I want him to say under eighteen. It makes the case I'm going to file far easier.

"She's eighteen. So is the next girl."

I nod as I watch a fourth girl. I pinch the bridge of my nose. "Fuck."

"When you get to the fifth girl, mute it," He murmurs to me softly. Rosie sobs into his chest as he sways with her. "You can unmute it after her."

"After?" I look up at him. He just nods. I know I'm not going to like what I'm about to see. I already knew, but now I know for certain that whatever it is will make me want to rip the guy's balls off and feed them to him.

As if on cue, Rosie enters his classroom. I watch as she hands him a paper. I couldn't really hear anything before, but I muted this one at Xavier's request, so I really can't hear anything now. Not that I need to. I was trained to read lips a long time ago. It was an extra course I took to expand my police skills. I can't say the angle is great, but I know he's telling her that she's worthless and will never pass his class. Even with the extra credit paper she's handing in.

Of course, that's not all. He almost immediately propositions her by telling her that her grade will improve exponentially if she does a few favors for him. Favors along the lines of what she did for him

Friday. My assumption is that would be last Friday, considering today is Friday and this is timestamped with yesterday's date.

She looks down, so I can't see her lips, but she shakes her head. When she tries to leave, he stops her. She tries to leave several times after shaking her head. I can tell she's crying and upset. When I can catch what she's saying, it's obvious she's telling him to leave her alone. That she never wanted to have sex with him.

The next thing I know, he's shoving her to her knees. Rosie is sobbing as he makes her suck him off. I inadvertently put a hand to my mouth, but I'm glad I've done it because it covers the snarl that escapes my throat. This guy was going down before, but he's absolutely going to face the music for his actions now.

As if that wasn't enough, ten minutes after Rosie flees his classroom, another girl enters. Like the blowjob wasn't enough for him, he has to fuck this girl. Against a wall. The same one who was riding him before.

The video ends there. I shake my head as I hand Xavier back his phone. "Jesus Christ."

"I don't have video of it, but Rosie said something happened last week. It wasn't just that."

"I don't need a video of it." I scoot a little closer to Rosie. "Rosie? That video will go far, but how do you feel about giving me the nail I need to put that son of a bitch away for life?"

She sniffles and nods as she slowly looks at me. "There's more... I told Xavier, but..."

"It's about her mom," he says quietly. "I... guess I'm really hoping you can help her. No one else has."

I hold out my hand for her. It takes her a good minute, but she finally takes mine. "Let's go talk at my office."

She shakes her head. "I... don't... really trust the police here." She glances at Xavier, and I have to wonder if she knows about his dad, or if something has happened to her involving the police here. Whatever it is, I intend to find out.

"Then we'll talk in my mobile office." I tilt my head towards my squad. "It's not very spacious, but it's cool. Maybe we can talk Xavier into coming with us to a park. We'll have a conversation and go from there. What do you think?" I watch Xavier stand out of the corner of my eye, but I stay focused on Rosie.

She smiles softly. "Okay."

"Good. I just need to tell Brant I'm taking off," Xavier says. He quickly jogs towards the field.

I bite my tongue to keep myself from watching his lean muscles move with his effortless motions. My attention needs to be on the terrified girl in front of me. So, I ignore my reaction to him and help her stand. I lead her to my car and wait for Xavier to return. I'm glad he's coming because he seems to be a great comfort to her. She's going to need that.

But secretly, and very selfishly, I'm happy he's coming because it means I'll get to spend more time with him.

***

I sigh and rub my head after we drop Rosie off at Dylan's house. "You think she'll be okay there tonight?" I ask Xavier as my head falls back against the headrest in my car.

"Yeah. Dylan will take care of her. It's better than with her mom."

I chuckle. Not because what he said is funny, but because he's right. Rosie told me a lot of shit that I need to take time to digest before I can even come close to helping her. Just dealing with her sexual assault and the encounters with the other students will tie me up for weeks as I build my case. Adding on what she told me about her father's death, though, is information I don't know how to deal with right now.

Huckleberry Grove, the small town Rosie is from, is nowhere near my district. It's not even in the same county. Hell. Half the town isn't even in Texas. It's in Louisiana. Maybe not half. More like the outskirts of it. Either way, it makes for a very fucked up jurisdiction for law enforcement. If Texas doesn't want to deal with it, they just say it's Louisiana's problem. And vice versa.

Regardless, I have to do something. Cops didn't listen to Rosie when they interviewed her. If they had, her mother would be in prison where she rightfully belongs. I very clearly heard every single word that came out of her mouth. Right down to the part where she said she saw her mother with a shovel that had blood on it and watched her hide it in the barn under bales of hay that they fed to their cows.

But the cops never looked. In fact, they gave the case to Louisiana. Who never did anything with it, according to what I found regarding the case. Rosie believes they are working on it but can't prove her mother did anything. The only thing they've done is rule his death suspicious. Nothing more.

And the reason it was given to Louisiana? Because her house is near the border. She's in the area the two States fight over. Reading over the case notes I was able to access through our databases pisses me off. I can't believe how lazy some cops are. It makes all of us look bad. No wonder we have such a terrible reputation.

I scrub my hands over my face. "Why didn't you tell me what was going on earlier, Xavier?" I look over at him before shifting my car into drive and heading back towards the school so he can grab his car.

He shrugs. "Because I didn't have anything to give you until today. Everyone knows that what Dylan said she thought was happening wouldn't have gotten anywhere. And I didn't know about Rosie until this morning. I've been going back and forth about telling our school officer, but I don't really like him. I guess I just had to think of who I could trust. In the end, I didn't feel like I could trust anyone but you."

I glance at him. He's focusing his attention out the windshield, but I can tell he's exhausted. On a whim, I reach over and squeeze his thigh. It's a way to show him both support and comfort, but I don't miss the quiet sound that comes from his throat and the way his thigh doesn't tense in the slightest under my touch. In fact, it's almost like I can feel him relaxing.

"You can trust me, Xavier."

He nods with a soft smile. "I know. It wasn't a matter of not being able to trust you. It was that I didn't feel like what I had was enough. For anyone. Even if I did take it to the school cop. All of those girls are eighteen. Legal. Except Rosie."

I shake my head and squeeze his thigh again as I drive. Now that I know he'll let me touch him, some fucked up part of me doesn't want to stop. "It doesn't matter if they were nineteen. They're high school students in a school he works at. In the State of Texas, it's still a crime. He's a teacher. It's illegal for him to have a sexual relationship with any of his students unless he's either married to them or less than three years older. Well, it's three years. If he was three years and a day older than them, it would still be a crime."

He looks at me in shock. "Seriously?"

I nod. "He's fucked, Xavier. Your video gives me what I need to go after him just for them. He'd get a lot of time in prison. And I'll charge him with the four counts of statutory rape, but it's Rosie's case that will get the attention from the prosecutor."

He smiles. "Good." He looks back out the window.

After a few moments, I feel his hand on mine. My heart skips a beat at his touch. I glance at him and then our hands. I want to turn my palm so it's facing up. I want to link our fingers, but I can't bring myself to do it.

Maybe it's the logical part of me kicking in for once. The part that is reasonable and understands that I'm playing with fire. Getting involved with a kid twenty years younger than me is dangerous as fuck. But I'm pretty sure it's the terrified part of me. The part that is pretty sure if I move, I'll scare him away.

"What about high school students and cops?" he asks quietly. "Can you get in trouble if..." He trails off and doesn't look at me.

My chest tightens at the prospect of his words. I clear my throat. "Depends on my role in your life. If I were the SRO at your school? I would get in trouble. Doesn't matter your age. If I have anything to do with the school or school district you attend, then yes. I can get into a lot of trouble."

"But... you don't have anything to do with my school. Do you?"

I turn into the parking lot of the high school and park near his car. It's the only one in the lot. "No. I don't."

"So..." He looks over at me a little shyly but still full of a confidence I envy. "I could kiss you right now, and there wouldn't be legal repercussions?"

I look down at his hand. He's started moving his thumb in circles over mine. My throat has suddenly gone dry, and I feel like I'm back in high school and trying to figure out how to kiss my first boyfriend without making it seem like I'm coming on far too strong.

I let my other hand fall between my legs to hopefully hide what he's doing to me, but I don't miss that he's doing exactly the same thing. I force my eyes to slowly rise. His eyes have turned so heated that the reflection of the lights in the parking lot in them make them look like they're on fire.

For me.

Dragging myself away from the cliff edge I'm about to fall off of, I clear my throat. "Not legally." I watch him smile a little more devilishly. "But that doesn't mean you should, Xavier," I nearly whisper. "At least, not right now."

Watching his face fall slightly might damn well be my undoing. Saying those words when all I want to do is taste him is the hardest fucking thing I've ever done. When he nods and opens the door, though, I fight to pull him into me and take what I want.

He's too quick, though. While I'm struggling with myself, he steps out of my car. "See you later, Detective Sexy."

And just like that, he closes the door and is quickly walking to his car. It's not until he ducks inside that I realize what he just called me. Just like that, I'm smiling because it means he heard what I said.

What I didn't mean to say.

The words gave us both hope. While it seems wrong to want an eighteen-year-old high school student, he won't be in high school forever. Until then, we can be friends. If the attraction is still there in a few months when he graduates, then I'm all for exploring it.

Even though it just might kill me.

CHAPTER FIVE

Xavier

(Two Months Later)

I reach for my phone when the alarm goes off and rub my eyes. It takes me a few minutes to sit up, but I finally manage to do it. It's not because I'm tired. It's because last night's playoff game kicked my ass. I took a lot of hits, but we played hard and won. We only have one more game before the championship. We're still undefeated this season, but we face our toughest team and biggest rivals next week.

I yawn and open my eyes as I lean against my headboard. "Dad!" I yell in surprise when I see him sitting on my desk chair staring at me. "Fuck. What the hell?" I rub my chest to assist my heart in resuming its normal rhythm. "What are you doing?"

"The press conference for Texas A&M is today. Imagine my surprise when I found that out and hadn't received a call to set you up attending."

It takes me a full minute to realize what he's saying. The press conference where Texas A&M announces athletes who have signed promise letters to attend their university is today. I scrub my hands over my face because I can't believe we're still having this same conversation. It's been months. We're already almost through the first semester of the school year. In just over three weeks, it will be our winter break.

"Dad. I told you. I'm not attending A&M. I have offers from all over the -"

"The other offers don't fucking matter! Get your ass out of that bed. Get dressed. And meet me downstairs."

I just blink a few times. "Why?"

He stands. "Because I spent all fucking night waking people up all to make sure my son, who forgot completely to commit to A&M, is a part of the conference he's supposed to be a part of! You have five minutes!"

I just stare at him in shock. "What is your problem? Why is A&M so fucking important to you?"

His already bloodshot eyes seem to become impossibly more red. I'd cringe, but I'm not afraid of him at all. "Move!" he screams at me. "I'm not telling you again!"

It's my turn to see red. "No! I'm not going to A&M! I'm going to Brystone Springs! I already committed! Now, get the fuck out!"

I swear to fuck he levitates off the ground, grows horns and a tail, and launches at me without touching the ground. His entire face turns as red as my boxer briefs. I see it coming, though, and dodge the attack. I roll out of bed and hit the ground just as he lands in the bed with his hands around my pillow. My eyes widen when I realize he would have started choking me.

My dad, still quick on his feet, launches again. But this time, he gets tangled in my blankets and crashes into the wall. His hand hits my nightstand, sending books and my lava lamp flying. In his struggle with the blankets, his foot crashes into the nightstand. It topples on top of him.

But it only infuriates him more. "Son of a bitch!" he screams. "When I get my hands on you, I'm going to fucking kill you! Understand me?"

I know I don't have a lot of time to get away from him without getting into a fight. So I grab a pair of jeans and pull them on as he's fighting to stand. I find a t-shirt and grab it, my phone, keys, and wallet.

Just as I reach my door and open it, a hard body shoves me into the wall. "Fuck!" I yell. He spears my hair and shoves my head into the wall. I drop my phone and everything else in my hand as the pain radiates from my temple, through my head, and down my arm and back.

"You think you can just walk out? Huh?" He pushes me harder against the wall. "That you can just leave and go to whatever college you desire? Even though you were already promised to A&M?"

"What?" I shake my head and use all my strength to shove back. His grip loosens, but he just readjusts. One arm is suddenly around my neck. The other is around my torso.

"You think after all I've been through that I'll just let you walk away from A&M? Is that what you think?"

I struggle against his hold. "What the hell are you talking about?"

"You have no choice, you spoiled fucking prick! You have no choice because I don't!"

His words send my mind into a tailspin, but it's the fact that he's cutting off my air supply that really starts to scare me. So, I start fighting back with everything I am. I headbutt him. I elbow his ribs. I wiggle and squirm like my life depends on it because it does.

When I get free, I jump up and turn as quickly as I can, but he's already on his feet. I dodge a hit and shove him backwards. He lands on the bed again. It gives me time to grab the heaviest book that I have, my history book, and swing it as hard as I can at his head just as he stands and lunges again. He immediately slumps to his knees with a groan. I'm about to swing it again, but he falls to his side.

I don't waste a second. I grab my backpack and shove all of my books and school work into it. I find my gym bag with my gear and uniform from last night. He groans a few times while I'm getting my shit together, so at least I know he's not dead. I grab a second gym bag and start throwing clothes into it. I don't know where I'm going, but I'm not staying in this house anymore.

I grab all of my bags and a pair of shoes along with my wallet, keys, and phone I'd dropped just as he's making his way to a sitting position. He gingerly touches the side of his head and looks at his finger to see the blood.

"You just killed me, you know."

I narrow my eyes. "Fuck you. You look just fine to me."

I don't say another word. I walk away as quickly as I can, glancing over my shoulder to make sure he's not following me. I jog down the stairs and through the living room towards the door to the garage. I roll my eyes when I see my mother passed out on the couch.

Same place she was when I got home last night. I'd say I can't believe that she didn't wake up, but I know better.

I hurry to the garage. I don't want to give him a chance to recover enough to come after me. Hopefully, I'll be long gone by then. I throw everything into my car and take off. I don't really know who to go to, though.

After last night's win, Sterling, Drake, Kody, and Brant all went on a camping trip. The only reason I didn't go is because it meant I'd have to drive a very long way to get to Kody's family cabin. The cabin is nearly two hundred miles. And then, because we've never liked staying in the cabin unless we've needed to, we would have had to set up our tents on the property in the dark. I wasn't in the mood.

Dylan has Rosie at her house still. Over the past couple of months, Rosie has basically moved in. Not like her mom gives a fuck. Turns out she has a sexual relationship going on with the teacher who assaulted her daughter. Or so she says. We all question that. Even Rosie, who never saw them together. Whatever her game is, though, it disgusts me. It disgusts us all.

The teacher, though, did get charged with a multitude of crimes. Colton was right. With everything brought against him, I don't think that fucker will see the light of day. I was not happy when the prosecutor dropped the charges against him for the other four girls, but in the end, I understand. He has a strong case with them and the video evidence, but he can get more time if he goes after him for what he did to Rosie. Rosie is being incredible and so strong during all of this.

The girls involved in not only bullying Dylan and Rosie, but also fucking the teacher, all got expelled from school and kicked off the cheerleading squad. Dylan became head cheerleader. There's talks about the team going to Nationals this year. Not only would that look incredible for Dylan, but it makes her happy. Things on that front are coming up roses.

Colton, though, has gotten a lot busier. He wasn't kidding when he said his case was blowing up. There's a lot of shit going on in this city, but he was right about Onyx. The owner was dealing drugs and had an illegal weapons trade going on. Onyx was bought by some hotshot who lives in Chicago and owns a few clubs. Passion projects apparently. The guy is a billionaire in some industry. Cooper Hayden or something.

Colton and I still make time to talk and text. We even hang out a little bit, and he's managed to make it to every game I've played. Including the away ones. We tease each other a lot and flirt even more, but we both agree that until things calm down from the fallout with the school's sex scandal, it would be best to keep our relationship friendly.

Not that that's easy in the slightest. I always have to check myself from letting myself push him too far. I'm not stupid, though. I know he does the same. We've been close to kissing several times. We always manage to stop ourselves, but it's getting a lot more difficult. I want him. I know he wants me. We keep telling each other that it's best to stay friends, but I don't know if that excuse will keep working for much longer.

I smile a little thinking of him. Just his eyes do things to me that no other has. My reaction to him freaks me out while, at the same time, makes me want to explore every inch of it. Which I'm sure is a lot of inches.

I reach down and squeeze my growing cock with a groan. Yeah. Like that's normal. Get into a fight with my dad. Get an erection five minutes later while in the process of trying to figure out where the fuck I'm going to go since I won't be going home. But it's like my dick is trying to tell me what my brain already knows. There is someone that I can reach out to. Someone I know will help me without hesitation.

Colton.

I sigh and pull over into the parking lot of the school. I take out my phone and put it on speaker. I could just use the Bluetooth and keep driving, but I don't know where I'm going. I hate not having a direction. I've been to his place before, but I don't know if he'll welcome me there or not. Maybe he's not there. I don't know.

"Hey, All-Star. What's up?"

I smile at Colton's deep voice and shiver just like I always do when I hear it. "Just fought with my dad. Almost knocked his ass out. I thought I killed him for a minute."

"Whoa. Hold up, cowboy. What the fuck?"

I sigh and rub my head as I close my eyes. "I woke up like I always do on a Saturday morning. I slept an extra hour. You know. Normal shit for me. I was getting up. Just about to get out of bed and grab my workout clothes. Then hit the gym for my workout. My dad was sitting on my desk chair staring at me. It looked like he hadn't slept or was still drunk. I couldn't decide which right away. At least not until he started yelling at me about A&M and how their press conference is today. How he never got a call about me being involved like I was supposed to be."

Colton groans, but it sounds more like a protective growl. I swallow hard and look at my phone as he clears his throat. "He found out about BSU."

"Not exactly." I lean my head back against the headrest and close my eyes as I shake my head. "He attacked me."

"He what?" He makes a dangerous sound. There's no doubting it was a growl, and it makes my eyes snap open. "Where are you? Did you leave?"

"Uh… yeah. I grabbed some of shit and my school stuff. I took off."

"Where are you? Did you go to one of your cousins?"

I sit up a little straighter. There's something about his tone that both turns me on and makes me actually feel how much he cares. "No. They're camping. And with everything going on with Rosie and Dylan, I don't want to go there. Unless it's a last resort. I guess I could drive up to Kody's cabin but it's quite a drive. I could probably stay at one of their houses, but I don't want my dad to show up and fuck with them. He just might. He said a lot of shit that I didn't understand while we were fighting."

"Just… come here. Come to my place. You know the code. It's the same to get into the private garage. Tell me when you're here, and I'll come down. You can't come up without a keycard. It will save you a trip to the lobby. I need to remember to get you a key."

My heart quickens a little. "A key?"

"Well, yeah. You're here enough. Listen, I need to go. I'm home. Just in the middle of something. Call me when you get here." He hangs up.

I sit and blink at the phone a few moments before the mentality to drive the car finally comes back to me. He has my mind racing as fast as my heart. A key? To his penthouse? It's more like a penthouse. I mean, we've become close, and I want things to go further, but the fact that he wants to give me a key, that he trusts me with one, makes me feel like I'm flying.

I smile as I drive to his place. It's not quite downtown, but it's close. It's really nice with a lot of security features. Like I can't access the elevator without a particular keycard. As a guest, the only ones who have that key are security guards or the residents. So, I have to be on an approved list for the guards or have Colton meet me in the lobby. Each keycard is different for each floor, but a code is also needed. If someone loses their keycard, random people can't try to get in without the code.

Which is one of the reasons I'm close to my heart escaping out of my chest. Colton trusting me with his code to get into the building, so I didn't have to wait to be buzzed in was one thing. But wanting to actually give me a keycard is something else entirely. My stomach tightens. My chest feels like it might burst. I can't wait to see him. I just might not be able to resist the urge to kiss him for this.

I wonder if he'd stop me or kiss me back. I've never blushed in my life, but I feel the heat creeping into my cheeks thinking of his tongue. Not that I don't think of what it would be like to kiss him each and every day. Or where that kiss would lead. But something about thinking of actually doing it as soon as I see him makes it all feel different.

More real.

Maybe if I take that step, he'll see that I'm ready. That I've been ready. That there's really no reason to hold back. He doesn't work for the school. I'm eighteen. There's nothing stopping us from giving into the attraction that we both have for each other. What's the point of just teasing each other and testing limits with touches here or there? Or heated gazes while we stare at each other's mouths. I get the reasons we were waiting, but the more I think of them now, the more I'm just sick of waiting.

When I get to Colton's, I've talked myself into kissing him. I'm sick of waiting. He makes me feel like an out of control wildfire. He's the only cure for the inferno he has me in a constant state of. I call him and wait for him to come down. He's deep in conversation on his phone, but he grins when he sees me and waves me in the elevator.

I'm anxious, but I behave. I keep my bags in my grip and lose myself in my thoughts. I don't know what he's discussing, but I know it's important because of the way he's talking. It sounds like some kind of a plan is being set into motion. Cop stuff. He'll tell me later. I love hearing about it and feel pretty good about being the one he can talk to about it all. That he trusts me with it.

Just as the doors open on his floor, he hangs up and smiles at me again. My heart melts. "Good news. I got more outside help to help me clean up the department. People who have done it all over the country. They're good."

I follow him off the elevator. "That's good news."

"Even better, is that they're going to help with Rosie. I've done just about all I can, but they don't have a jurisdiction to worry about."

I raise an eyebrow. "So, the FBI? They don't have jurisdiction, do they?"

He unlocks his door. "Not the FBI. Better. One of the guys on the taskforce I put together recommended them. He works with them. They're..." He trails off and looks down at me. "They're sort of like Black Ops." He pushes the door open.

"Good. We can use all the help we can get for her."

I follow him inside his penthouse and close the door. I drop my bags and, before I lose my courage, grab his arm. When he turns, I kiss him. I crush my lips to his in a kiss that only manages to ignite the fire inside me instead of quenching it in the slightest, even though his lips aren't moving against mine.

Was I wrong?

Did I read his attraction incorrectly?

Did he not admit it?

Did we not talk about it?

Did I imagine it all?

I watch his eyes widen in shock before his hands grip my hips. I think he's about to push me away, but he doesn't. He backs me against the door and moves his mouth against mine hungrily. His tongue slips past my mouth and dives in, tangling with mine. I close my eyes and groan. My arms wrap tighter around his broad shoulders. I didn't even know I'd moved them there.

He pulls me closer to him while simultaneously crushing me against the door behind me. His large hands grip my ass as he angles his head. He presses against me and moans into the kiss as he deepens it further. I can feel his reaction to me grinding against my own hard cock.

Colton pulls away slowly, leaving us both breathless. All doubt I had in my mind about his feelings for me vanishes completely. Reflected in his eyes is the same desire I have for him. The insane attraction I had for him since the second I saw him has grown so much, but right now, it's simmering right below the point of explosion.

I need him.

I need Colton DeLise.

CHAPTER SIX

Colton

Fuck…

Oh, fuck…

I take deep breaths and watch Xavier. Holy fuck. I've never felt like my entire fucking world was exploding around me with just a kiss, but that's exactly what just happened. I've never allowed myself to lose control like that, but I did with him. And I didn't give one single fuck. All I cared about was him. His tongue. His body pressed against me. His hard as hell cock grinding against mine.

"Christ, Colton," Xavier whispers. He runs his thumb over his lip as he grins.

I take a few steps back. "Holy shit," I whisper.

"Colt!" someone yells from somewhere in my penthouse.

"Fuck. Gavin." I shake my head like I'm coming out of a haze.

"Who's Gavin," Xavier asks. I can see the sudden hurt replace the lust that was there moments ago. "A boy-"

"No. No, baby. Not a boyfriend." I scrub my hands down my face at the slip of calling him baby, though it was the most natural fucking thing I've ever done. Second only to kissing him. "Fuck," I groan. I drop my hands to my sides and glance at his bags before looking back at him. Thankfully, the hurt I saw that tore me apart is gone. "Let's… uh… Let's get your stuff to your room."

He watches me as I pick up his bags. I'm pretty sure he's still reeling from the mind-blowing kiss. I know I am. I turn and quickly make my way to my guest bedroom. I open the door and let out a breath as I stride to the bed. I put his stuff down and turn around to face him. That kiss, while absolute fire, can't happen again. At least, not now. He has more important things to worry about.

I mean to tell him that, but when his eyes meet mine and he smiles, I can't find the words. "I probably shouldn't have assumed that when you said to come here, it meant to bring all my shit up here," he says. He tries to portray confidence, but I know him better than that. I can hear how unsure he is.

"I did mean that, Xavier," I say, my voice thick.

I look down because I don't want him to see the war raging in my eyes. I want to kiss him again. I want to do a lot more with him, but it's not the time. We both have a lot going on. I feel like starting a relationship would be a stupid decision, but I also don't care.

When I look back up, he's smiling once more. It strikes me quite suddenly that I'm not the only one of the two of us who is in territory he isn't familiar with or comfortable in. Xavier and I have talked quite a bit about things over the past couple of months. He's usually the one in control. He knows what he wants. He doesn't hold back, but he has with me.

I know how it must make him feel unsure because I feel exactly the same way. I know where I want to go with him, but things are so different with him. He's not just anyone to me. I've had a couple of relationships and fast fucks. He's not a fast fuck or anything like any other man I've been with. He's more.

He's everything.

I clear my throat. "I should probably get back out there." I look back up at him. "We were discussing a few things."

He nods and shoves his hands in his pockets. He rocks back and forth on his heels and looks at the floor. "I'll just hang out in here. Stay out of your way." He's still smiling, but I know he wants to be out there helping. He loves not only hearing about my job, but helping when I get stuck. I like that he brings fresh ideas to the table.

"You don't have to. I'm not hiding anything from you."

"You sure?" He looks at me hopefully with a half-smile.

"I'm positive. Besides, I'm sure you're starving. I was just making breakfast. Should be about done."

His smile brightens. "Okay."

I lead him out to the kitchen. "Take a seat." I nod to the table and head for the oven, where I have bacon, ham, cheese, hashbrowns, and tomatoes baking. "Gavin. This is Xavier Remington. His dad is one of the ones on that list I gave you." I pull the hashbrowns out.

"List?" Xavier asks as he sits down.

"Yeah," I say. I start dishing up the hashbrowns. "We were talking about how we thought a lot of what is going on is suspicious as fuck. Add in your father and how he's the department's golden child, even though none of us like him much. It's got our instincts telling us something just ain't right in this city." I set a plate down in front of him and Gavin. "This is Gavin Vandenberg. The help I was telling you about on the way up."

"The Black Ops guy?" Xavier smiles.

Gavin laughs as I put drinks down for us and sit down. "Sure, kid. Black Ops."

Xavier's eyes narrow slightly as he looks between us. "Why do I feel like I'm missing something? And don't call me kid. I'm eighteen. Not a kid."

I pause with an eyebrow raised and my fork halfway to my mouth. Gavin mimics me as we both stare at Xavier. Gavin might be a little shocked, but I'm in awe. And of course that awe goes directly to my dick. Good thing no one can see how hard that just made me.

"Okay. Not a kid. Xavier. I apologize." Gavin nods his head in both acknowledgement and apology, moving the fork the rest of the way to his mouth. I watch as his face lights up. "Damn. This is good. Might rival my boss. Might not believe it, but Josh Lucinio can cook. Breakfast at least. We're still working on the rest."

Xavier puts his plate fork down. "Lucinio. As in Lucinio Mafia?"

I drop my fork as my eyes snap to his. "You… know who Lucinio Mafia is?"

He looks at me like I'm insane. "My father is a cop. Remember? Besides, I'm not just a stupid kid. I read and watch the news. I know what the Lucinio Mafia does. My laptop has Lucinio Tech antivirus on it. They're the best." He goes back to eating as Gavin and I look at each other.

After a few moments, we both go back to eating, but it's in silence. Maybe I didn't give Xavier as much credit as I should have.

He seems to know quite a lot more about the world than most people his age. Maybe that's where a lot of my hesitation about us has stemmed from. I assumed he was more naive than he actually is for his age. I've been doing him a disservice by thinking that way. Fuck, I've been doing myself a disservice.

When we all finish, Xavier gets up and takes our plates. Why that makes me more attracted to him is far outside my scope of understanding. And something I'll need to figure out later, because I have a lot larger problems on my plate right now that need to be addressed.

"So, Gavin. What do you think?" I ask, attempting to get my mind off how hot Xavier looks washing dishes.

"Well, you have a classic case of police corruption. From what I've seen and had the chance to research, a lot of the cops on this list have huge gambling problems. It doesn't surprise me that they'd be involved in shit to pay off their debts."

"Wait. Debts?" Xavier grabs a towel and turns around, drying his hands. "My dad said something that confused the fuck out of me. But gambling debts. That actually makes sense."

"What did your dad say?" Gavin asks.

"Well, we got into a fight this morning. He wants me to go to Texas A&M. I don't want to. I already signed a promise letter to Brystone Springs University. They hold their press conference next week to announce their recruits. A&M is today. My dad didn't know why he didn't get a letter about it or call to set up my part of it. He said something about me not having a choice because he doesn't. I had no idea what the fuck he meant. Then after I hit him with a book and got my stuff, he told me I just killed him. Do you think my going to A&M had something to do with gambling?"

Gavin leans back in his chair and taps his pen against his notebook as he stares at his laptop. "There's something I remember about A&M. I need to look into it," Gavin finally says after a few moments. "It's possible."

Xavier nods and goes back to the dishes. Fuck me, I'm falling in love with him. I don't have a damn clue how he is taking all of this in stride, but I love all of it. He's showing his true colors. His strength. Maturity. Things I saw already but was afraid to admit to myself.

Things I was using as a barrier to hold me back from our relationship. I was an idiot to do so.

I rub my head as I lean back in the chair. "We know we have a problem with some of the cops. Probably his dad. You think you can help?"

"I know we can. But it's not just the cops in this city. From what I've managed to figure out so far, a lot of the higher ups in this city are on the take, too. With who? I don't know that yet. But given what I do know?" Gavin looks at me seriously. "I need to call in the boss. Because I have a very bad feeling that this is just going to get worse. This entire city is seriously corrupt."

I nod. "I was afraid you'd say that."

Xavier comes back to the table drying his hands. "What about Rosie?" He sits down and looks at Gavin just as seriously as Gavin had me moments ago.

Gavin nods. "Rosie is a whole other aspect to this. A different issue altogether. I already have some people working on that." He looks back at me. "I also want to bring in some men for protection. Going after that teacher has brought attention to you that you didn't need with your current investigation." Gavin's eyes flick to Xavier and back to me. "And considering your connection to Xavier? There's a high chance that he'll have people going after him, too. If not from those with their eyes on you, then from whatever the fuck his dad is neck deep in."

Xavier glances at me and chuckles. "I guess I was right to call you."

"I hope you would have anyway," I say quietly with a soft smile.

Gavin chuckles, bringing us both back to whatever world we sunk into where only each other exists. "I need to make some calls."

"You can use the living room if you want somewhere quiet," I say. I nod to Xavier. "You should probably call Dylan and Rosie."

Xavier watches Gavin stand and head for the semi-closed off living room. "I should call my cousins. All of them. We're all close. They won't want to be kept out of this. If there's going to be some big plan coming together, I'll want them around. Especially with the mafia being involved and potential danger to us."

I nod. "Anything you need." I look up when I hear my buzzer signaling someone is here and head for the intercom.

"That will be Damon and Lance," Gavin says with a chuckle from my couch. "Call them Cute and Quirky when you answer the intercom."

I raise an eyebrow. "That was fucking fast."

He raises his phone slightly. "Boss looked into this a little. He thought we'd need backup. He's finishing a few things in Chicago. Then, he's coming down here. Cleaning up an entire city is going to take time and a fuck lot of work. We might end up calling in the Crane's on this one. Might be an idea to get them down here, too. We'll need all the help we can get."

I nod as I answer the intercom. "Yeah?"

"Mr. DeLise?" one of the two asks.

I glance back towards Gavin. He nods with a smirk. I clear my throat. "Yeah. Cute and Quirky?"

I hear a voice mutter that they're gonna kick Gavin's ass before I hear a response. "That's us."

I laugh. "I'll have security let you up."

"You do that. And tell Vandenberg he's a fucking asshole, and he'd better run."

I laugh as I buzz them in. I quickly call down to security that they're okay to come up, then disappear down the hall where I saw Xavier walk to. I make my way to the guest bedroom. The door is cracked, but I pause just before opening it.

"Yeah," Xavier says. "I don't know, man. I don't know what he'll do. File an assault charge? Sounds like something he'd do. I'll probably be in jail by Monday morning. I need you guys. I'm sorry for pulling you in, but it sounds like this is going to get worse before it gets better. Especially with the mafia involved." He pauses. I peek into the room. He tilts his head as he listens. "No, I don't think you need to pull him into this. Not unless you want him here. Then again, we might need all the help we can get. I don't know. I'll leave that to you." He pauses again.

I push the door open slightly, and lean on the frame. His back is to me. I want him to turn around. Maybe I should make a noise so he doesn't think I'm eavesdropping or something.

He sighs and rubs his head. "I called Dylan. They're on their way. I just need to ask Colton if they can stay. He only has two rooms, and he put me in one of them. The other is his, and I don't think he wants to share it with me."

The fact that he thinks that breaks my heart, but I can't blame him for the thought. I didn't offer it. I haven't told him how I feel about him. It's a situation I need to rectify. Immediately. I can't let him go on thinking I don't want him. I do.

I notice a crumpled piece of paper on the table by the door. I have a random cactus I'm attached to sitting on it. I pick it up and lightly toss it. It hits the back of his head dead center. He jumps and turns to me. I just smile.

"Hey, I gotta go. Colton just threw something at me to get my attention. When you're back, give me a call." He pauses another moment before he says goodbye and hangs up.

I crook my finger at him but stay right where I am. I hear Gavin answer the door and Damon and Lance enter my penthouse, but they aren't what matters to me right now. The sexy guy strutting towards me right now is all that's important.

When he reaches me, I cup his face in my hands. I lean in and kiss him. Slow. Deeply. I pour everything I feel for him into it, so he can't think for one second that I don't want him. I do. I want everything with him. I need him more than the air I breathe. Christ. He is my air. Without him, I don't think I could even manage to get my lungs to inflate; my heart to beat.

And while all of that scares the fuck out of me, at least the part about feeling it for someone half my damn age, there's one thing I'm certain of. Xavier is my person. The only one I want. All I need. I swipe my tongue over his and wrap my arms around him, deepening the kiss even more, because I need to show him that I want him. Only him. No one else in this world can ever fulfill my heart and soul as he does.

I pour all of me into the kiss because it's what we both need. When I pull away, my head feels like it might explode. My heart is beating hard. My entire body has erupted with tingles. My dick is jutting against my zipper. I'm hard as granite.

I take one of the hands Xavier has fisted my shirt in and slowly move it down my body to the waistband of my jeans. "This…" I start moving it lower and grin a little darkly when his eyes widen. "Is what you do to me, baby." I stop moving his hand when we reach my dick.

His gaze drops. "Fuck…," he whispers.

I squeeze his hand over my length just so he has no doubt in his mind what I'm telling him. "I want you, Xavier. Fucking want you. More than I have ever wanted anyone in my life." I squeeze his hand over my dick. I groan low. "Look at me."

His head snaps up. His molten silver eyes meet mine. "Colton…"

"I don't want any doubt in your mind how I feel about you. I put you in this room, baby, because I wasn't sure if we were ready to take that step. I wasn't sure if I was. But I am. I knew the second I saw you that you were it. Scared me to death. The age difference. You being in school. Situations surrounding not only our meeting but our whole goddamn relationship." I release his hand and slowly caress mine up his arm to his bicep until I reach his neck. "I don't care anymore. All I care about is you."

Xavier wraps his arms around my neck and pulls me in to kiss me again. It's slow. Far more heated. I suck on his tongue and nip his lip just before I pull away, but I'm not quite ready to release him. So, I pull him closer and hug him for I don't know how long before I finally let him go. I reach down and grab his bags, still sitting on the floor just inside the room. I bring them to my bedroom and set them inside the door before turning to him again.

His eyes. I could fucking drown in them and die happy. It's a thought I've had so many times, I've lost count. They're bright. Mischievous. Purely Xavier.

And all mine.

CHAPTER SEVEN

Xavier

Fuck... Fuck... Fuck... Fuck... Fuck...

He's... Oh, fuck.

I swallow hard as I watch Colton. He doesn't move, but the way he's looking at me makes me want to spontaneously combust. I can't breathe. I can't think. Well, that's not true. I can think. I can think of his hard cock under my palm. My heart stopped beating in that very moment. I can think of his heated gaze on me right now. And the nice tent my jeans are making right now. Similar to the one his are making, but not as big.

Christ.

I've always thought I was big. Thick. But compared to him? Jesus. He has to be twice my girth. I know he has some length on my almost nine inches. All I want is his cock in my hand again. My mouth. My ass. Anywhere I can get him, I'll gladly take him. I'll even beg for it. And I don't beg. Fucking ever.

Colton stalks towards me as he glances down the hall towards the voices of Gavin and his crew. He must decide they aren't going to bother us because when he reaches me, he takes my hand and tugs me into his bedroom.

Our bedroom?

I'm already fucking thinking about where I'll keep all my stuff. Where I'll park my car. What I'll make him for dinner every night, even though he's a far better cook. I'd do it just to show him how much I care about him.

Love him?

Hell. Maybe.

Probably.

Who am I kidding?

I love him. I really fucking love him.

My throat is so dry that I can't speak. All I can do is watch him and wait for his next move. I'm afraid to even move for fear I'll wake up from whatever dream I just fell into. I don't want it to end. I want to see how far he's going to take this.

He closes the door behind us and walks to his King size bed. The bedspread is dark blue. The accents are wooden and match the dark furniture in the room. My mouth can't decide if it wants to water or feel like I'm swishing sand around in it. He sits down and crooks a finger at me.

I lick my lips. Much like in the guest room, which feels like years ago, my body moves towards him on its own. My heart speeds up. My cock jerks, like it's leading me towards him. A beacon in the turbulent waters that is my life.

I don't know how or why things got so fucked up, but I do know that if they hadn't, I wouldn't have met him. I wouldn't know these feelings I have because no one has come close to giving me them. Only him. I don't want to feel like this about anyone else. I never will.

I stop in front of him, unsure if I should step between his legs like I want to, but he doesn't leave me guessing for long. He grips my ass and pulls me closer. I expect him to drop his hand when he looks up at me, but he doesn't. He leaves it right where it is and grips my ass tighter.

"You drive me crazy," he rasps. "Fucking insane. I can't even think about you without getting hard. I can't sleep without rubbing one out to thoughts of you. Every. Fucking. Night."

My mouth drops a little because I thought I was the only one. Teenage hormones and all that shit. "Really?" I ask, though it sounds a little like a squeak in a tone that's foreign to my ears. I need to get a fucking grip, but the only grip I want is on his dick while he's fucking my mouth.

He starts lightly caressing my ass. "What about you, Xavier? How many times have you thought about riding me while I'm stroking your cock until you come?"

I can feel my eyes widen. My heart accelerates even faster. "How do you... I've never... Fuck, Colt. I've always been top."

His realization knocks the cocky smirk right off his face. "Shit... Xav-"

I don't let him finish. I can't hold back anymore. I need his lips on mine. Anywhere on me will do. I knock him back on the bed and straddle him as I kiss him. Where his kiss was assertive, mine is aggressive. I want him. All of him. I don't even care.

His arms lock around me. He pulls me flat against him, but it's a huge mistake because now we can both feel each other's hard cocks. I kiss him harder and grind against him, getting harder. He matches my tongue stroke for stroke. He counters me moan for moan. When I grind down, he grinds up against me. When I nip, he nips back.

When he's had enough of relinquishing the control he desperately needs, he lets out a low growl and flips me on my back so quickly and effortlessly, it leaves me dazed. For a second, all I can do is blink at him. But then I feel his hand on my jeans. He's ripping open the button as he kisses me. With one hand, he holds my throbbing dick in place. With the other, he yanks my zipper down.

I sit up just enough to tug my shirt over my head and throw it off. My eyes roll back when he tugs my jeans down just enough to free my dick. I sit back up and reach for his jeans, fully planning on pulling them down so I can see what he's packing.

Colton pushes me back down on the bed, though. "Don't you dare."

My dick twitches at his tone, and I narrow my eyes. "Colt, if you don't do something about my hard cock, I'm shoving it in your mouth."

He just gives me a wicked grin as he tugs off his shirt. "Hasn't your mama ever told you that good things come if you wait?"

I laugh as I watch him. Colton is all hard ridges and perfect muscles. "Fuck. My mama barely taught me how to tie my shoelaces. I learned my manners from my imaginary dinosaur friend."

He laughs as he tugs down his jeans. I love his laugh, but holy shit, I love his dick even more. My eyes zero in on it as he fists it in his hand. "Is that why you're so brash?"

I grin but don't get to say anything because his mouth is on mine once more. His kiss is punishing this time, but it's his dick against mine, finally, that sends my head spinning into delicious pleasure. Delirium that only he can give me.

"Oh, fuck…," I moan into his mouth as we grind against each other. I grip his ass, begging for him to get closer. "Fuck, Colt. I'm not going to be able to hold on much longer." The familiar tingle makes its way down my spine. My dick gets harder.

"Not yet, baby," he rumbles against my neck. He reaches between us and grips both of our dicks in his large hand. "I'll make it worth the wait."

I jerk into him. "Colt, good fuck. Oh, shit, I'm gonna come."

"Don't you fucking dare," he pants against my neck as he strokes us both. "Fuck, not yet, baby. Not yet."

I grip his broad shoulders and thrust into his hand. His dick against mine is better than anything I've ever felt with anyone I've ever been with. It's better than my hand and any toy I've experimented with. If his hand gripping us both and his cock sliding against mine feels this good, I wonder what it will feel like when he takes me into his mouth… And deep in his ass.

Our thrusts against each other become more erratic. His kisses along my neck and jaw; more heated. I need my hands all over him all at once, but I'm not sure where to even begin. Everything about him is hard and rough, yet somehow irresistible.

"Now. Come, baby," Colton growls. "Right now." He doesn't stop jerking both of your dicks at the perfect pace and pressure.

I pull him even closer. "Shit… Colton!" I growl into his shoulder as I bite it. I moan and groan. My hips slam up and down as I lose my release all over my stomach and him.

Colton's head falls back. He roars, though quietly. "Oh God, Xavier!" He keeps stroking us both as we thrust into each other, but my name on his lips make me come harder. I feel like my entire body is buzzing. Like a million bees have replaced my bloodstream or something and are flying around.

When we both finally stop making a mess of each other, Colton collapses on his back next to me and rests his hand possessively on my thigh that's covered in his come. We both pant as we come down.

"Fuck, Colton," I finally have the strength to rasp out.

He chuckles. "I needed that." He squeezes my thigh and turns his head towards me with a grin. "Rephrase. I needed you."

I faintly hear the intercom go off over my euphoria. "Sounds like Dylan and Rosie just got here."

"Gavin will take care of it. You and I need to clean up."

I watch his every move as he gets up and pulls me with him. No one has ever owned me like that, and then taken such good care of me afterwards. As he gently cleans me up before he takes care of himself, I'm struck by just how far I've fallen.

I'm never fucking letting him go.

***

Sunday morning, a day I usually lounge around for the morning, is filled with a fuck ton of action I'm not at all prepared to handle before seven in the damn morning. Especially when my night was filled with Colton's mouth around my cock and mine around his.

I smile a little as I sip my coffee. The only good thing about Gavin's boss is that he was nice enough to stop at a local coffee shop and get a variety of it. I think if he arrived any earlier without it, I would have killed him. Maybe not actually killed him. But probably punched him. Maybe.

I growl a little from where I'm perched on the arm of a chair and glare at everyone in the room as they talk. Their boss is helping Colton cook breakfast. It's another point in his favor, but I'm still pissed off at the early wakeup call and ruined morning. I could be playing out more dirty fantasies with Colton.

Instead, though, I'm out here in the living room with my cousins, Rosie, and a few of Josh Lucinio's people. Everyone is having a different conversation, and I want to scream at them all to shut the fuck up until I have enough coffee in my system to think clearly.

Which I do not. Not even close.

"You okay?" Kody asks. "You look like you might actually fuck someone up if they look at you wrong."

I smile a little as I take a drink. "I just might. We didn't go to bed until four in the fucking morning. After you all went to sleep after the movie, we couldn't. So we fucked around. Our own fault. I know. But I'm tired as hell and not in the mood for the amount of people in this penthouse. Even if it is a huge penthouse. Which I don't understand. Cops don't make that much fucking money."

Kody chuckles as he sits in the chair next to me. He rests his elbows on his knees as I look down at him. "Dylan asked him the same thing. I thought I heard something about stocks doing well for him. He invested a lot when he was younger. Smart with his money."

"That doesn't help. Now, I'm pissed off that I never thought to ask him that. Or talk to him about it. Even though I'm curious."

Kody laughs and pats my thigh. "Calm down. Don't be too much of an asshole. I know how you get. And we already have one cranky asshole right now. We don't need two."

Before I can give him some snappy as fuck retort, the intercom goes off. "I might rip the fucking thing off the wall," I growl under my breath. Knowing that Colton is busy, though, I get up to answer. "Yeah."

"Hey. Alec Cassidy for Colton DeLise."

I look for a few moments at the badass biker looking dude. I might tell him to fuck off, but I recognize the guy next to him. I grin and contemplate giving him shit. I know security put them both on the list. I could just let them in. Security will let them up.

But that's not how I roll. "Sorry. Don't recognize you," I say instead.

"If you don't open this door, shitface, the first thing I'm gonna do after greeting my boy, is shave your prized locks." Blade Cruz, the President of the Brystone Springs Viper's Venom Chapter, growls through the intercom. "And you know I fucking will, dickface."

I laugh. "You don't know how much I needed you and your asshole attitude."

"I can guess, doucheball. Now open up." He smirks into the camera. Alec is grinning next to him. I don't recognize all the guys behind them, but I know of them. They're all wearing VV patches. "I miss my boy."

"Yeah, yeah, fucker. Security will let you up." I push the button to open the door and watch as Blade pushes by Alec to get in first. I laugh when I see his hand shoot out and whack Blade on the back of the head for the shove. I turn and almost run into Drake.

"Was that Blade?" he asks hopefully. I don't often see Drake look vulnerable, but he does right now.

I chuckle and push him back in the direction of the living room. "You'll see him in a few moments. But not in the hall. Knowing you fuckers, you'll detour to a bedroom. I know you haven't gone all the way, since he was gone for your birthday, but I know you. You've been apart for at least a month."

"Three months, actually. He's been helping the lead guy in Chicago on something big." Drake grins and winks.

I laugh and shake my head. "If I don't get any action until this is done, you don't either."

Drake gives me a wicked grin. "We'll see about that."

Blade and Drake met about a year ago after Drake was in a car accident. The guy who hit Drake was drunk and fled the scene. Blade was behind him heading to VV's ranch just outside of town when it happened. Lucky for Drake, and all of us, that Blade was around because Drake wouldn't be with us today. Blade saved his life. He pulled him from his burning car just before it exploded. It was because of Blade that the driver was caught. Blade got his plate number, and has been with Drake ever since.

I wait by the door for them to come up and watch as Colton and Josh put breakfast out on the breakfast bar in a buffet style. Everyone else is still talking and laughing. My mood, while improving, still isn't quite there. If I'm being honest, it's not because of the time of morning or even that it was a late night. It's not that I want to be all over Colton right now.

It's because I sense the danger. I know there's far more going on here than I realize. The fact that Gavin called in the big guns and their allies tells me all I need to know. While I understand why when it comes to Rosie and the BSPD, she knows about my relationship with my dad and doesn't trust those he works with, I don't know how I fit into it. I understand my dad is into gambling with some bad people, but I have no idea what it has to do with me and his need to get me into A&M.

It's been his dream since I was a kid. Not mine. But it hasn't been until I started high school that he really started pushing me. A&M. No other option. When I told him about all of the colleges that wanted me, including Notre Dame and Louisiana State, he told me it didn't matter. A&M is where I belonged. His alma mater and that's it. Given the shit he said, I don't fucking understand what it has to do with anything.

When I hear a tap on the door, I look through the peephole. I grin as I open it. "Hey, asshole," I say to Blade.

He laughs as he puts a large hand over my face and pushes me back. He strides past me and down the hall. "Not the face I'm looking for. Drake! Where are you, baby?"

I close the door feeling somehow lighter as Drake takes a running leap into Blade's arms just as he reaches the entrance to the living room. Blade is a big guy. Probably close to six feet five or six feet six. Seeing a guy who is about my height caught in a bear hug and kissed senseless would look comical, and probably does, to a lot of people. But to me? Fucking adorable as hell. Those two were made for each other.

I want that. All of it. The deep kiss when we haven't seen each other for awhile. Though, I hope that's not months like those two. I'd hate that.

As the two kiss like there's no one else in the room, my eyes meet Colton's. He gives me a soft smile that makes me melt a little but also feel like the most cherished person in the room. I smile brighter, and just like that my bad mood dissipates.

I stand straighter as realization hits me.

I have what Blade and Drake have. It's new, but it's still perfect.

Our perfect.

CHAPTER EIGHT

Colton

I've never liked sitting in a room of people being told what to do, where I need to sit, what my role in a raid is going to be. It's part of the reason I worked so fucking hard to get to where I am and be the one leading the raids I go on. While I still have someone to answer to, I am pretty much my own boss. I don't like authority. Never have. Probably never will.

Ironically, this meeting doesn't feel like that. When I took my colleague's advice and called in Lucinio Mafia, I knew I'd be taking a backseat to them and their operation. Everyone knows Josh Lucinio does things his way. And if people don't follow, they're kicked out of the operation, or he walks. His reputation of taking no shit from anyone is well-known. He works from the shadows.

Much like the rest of the people in this room probably do. I know of Viper's Venom, but they keep to themselves. I've never had a problem with them. Even when their rivals have tried to pin shit on them. I know Blade very well because of it. Not really anyone else in his crew.

I didn't know that he was seeing anyone, though. Let alone the high school student, who is curled up in his lap, he likes to call his boy. It sort of makes me wonder if they're into that daddy/boy thing that makes me cringe and chuckle at the same time.

Kody is plastered to Dylan and Rosie. If I didn't know they were related, I'd think he has a thing for Dylan. Hell, maybe Rosie, too. Honestly, though. I think he's just that protective. I learned from

Xavier that while they are all close in age, he's the youngest. A little over a year younger. Just turned seventeen.

Sterling and Brant are both sitting on the floor against the wall near the girls. Alec and a couple of the guys he brought with him are leaning against a wall near the back of the room. Damon is sitting next to Lance, who I found out is Lucinio Mafia's tech guy. Apparently, he's better than the best hackers in the world, except maybe the one with Crane Mafia. I've heard rumors that he once hacked the State Department. Good thing he's on the side of right.

Seth, one of the few people in my life I trust, brings over a kitchen chair, settling it in the space between the couch and oversized chair in my living room, and turns it around so it's backwards. He sits and rests his arms over the back of it as he puts a glass of water on the table near the couch I'm on with Xavier. He's not the one who told me about Josh, but I trust this guy with my life. He's a patrol Sergeant now, but we still work closely. He's one of my best friends. I really only have a couple. They might be the only friends I got. I take the glass and down the water.

Erik, my other best friend, sits down in the oversized chair next to Seth after coming back from the bathroom and quickly takes the glass from me. He puts it on the floor between his feet. He's always been the caretaker of our group. Which some might find surprising, considering he's six feet four and built like a tank. We've been best friends since we were little. I furrow my brows at the look he shoots Seth when he turns his attention from us, but shake it off. He catches Blade's eye before turning back to me and watching me closely.

I'd say something, but I'm too fucking tired and insatiably thirsty. Considering how much I've had to drink in the past couple of hours, since Seth and Erik got here to help me out with setting things up for when everyone else showed up. I've downed a couple of cups of coffee. Water. I shouldn't be tired or thirsty. Don't know why the fuck I am. I guess that's something to think about after this is over.

"Drake, stop snuggling your daddy," Brant says with a smirk and chuckle.

"Shut the fuck up, you little dick squeak," Drake returns with a laugh. "I haven't seen him in months."

"Daddy's not letting him go," Blade says with a teasing grin and a wink at Drake.

Drake cracks up. "I'm not calling you daddy."

Blade hugs him closer and tighter as everyone in the room laughs. "Fuck no. I'm not into that shit." He glances at me. I guess that answered that question.

I grin. "Me neither."

"Thank fuck for that," Xavier says with a chuckle.

"I do love when you call me sir, though," Blade rumbles. I didn't think it was possible, but Drake blushes and hides in his neck.

"Not another dominant," Damon says with a chuckle to Lance. "We have too many of those in this family." He winks at Josh. Josh grins.

When Josh begins talking, everyone falls quiet and listens. He doesn't even need to stand to command a presence. "Lance. You filled me in on what you found, but let's start with you telling everyone else. I don't understand that technical shit."

Xavier chuckles as he cuddles into me. I'm lying on the couch with a massive headache brought on solely from the amount of noise way too early in this house after only getting maybe an hour of sleep. I'd probably be okay if I went to sleep when Xavier did, but I couldn't do it. After finally giving into my feelings for him and not holding back, that's one less thing on my mind. But there are still twenty other problems that need to be dealt with.

So, while Josh leads this massive undertaking, I hold Xavier against my chest and bury my face in his neck as I listen. He doesn't know it, but he's a very calming force and is combating the band of monkeys marching behind my eyes.

"Well, I found a lot of shit. I'll begin with the list of cops and city officials Gavin gave me. They all have extensive gambling debts. All of them. One of them was more than willing to talk when Damon…" He glances at Damon, a dark, muscular, imposing figure who is probably not afraid to spend time in a gym, and grins. "Let's just say when Damon persuaded him a little. He told us that his debt stems from an underground betting ring. You name it, it's going down. Things from pig racing to how long it takes rattlesnake venom to kill the average man."

I raise an eyebrow. "Wait. How the fuck do they figure that out?"

"I'll give you one guess," Damon responds.

I groan and close my eyes. "Jesus fuck."

"Yep," Lance says, confirming everything going on in my head. "They find a couple of homeless men who no one will miss. Lure them with a hot meal and place to stay. After they get them relatively healthy, they send them to their deaths. Only, they don't know it. They're blindfolded and have noise canceling headphones on. They release the snakes and let them bite. Then they watch them until they die."

"I'm going to be fucking sick," Xavier says.

"Not even the worst part," Lance continues. "The worst part is that they aren't only limiting it to money as collateral. They take anything. From your dog to the fucking house. There's even rumors about virginities running around."

Xavier sits up and furrows his eyebrows as they land on Rosie. "Tell me what I'm thinking is wrong."

"Okay," Lance says. "It's wrong. Rosie, as far as I can tell, isn't involved in that aspect of things. At least, not exactly."

My eyes darken as Dylan hugs Rosie tighter. "What do you mean not exactly?" I pull Xavier down next to me again. He's not only calming the headache, he's keeping the demons threatening to surface and tear apart this city from surfacing. Thankfully, Xavier gets the hint and stays put, letting me hug him.

"I'll get to that," Lance responds. "It's a completely separate issue, and one that Alec and Blade will need to deal with. Firstly, this gambling ring. It's not limited to Brystone Springs. The lesser shit is, but this goes beyond that. The deeper people get in debt, the more desperate they become, which the people behind this know very well. College football is a huge thing in Texas."

Xavier tenses. "Mmhmm...," he rumbles on high alert.

Lance pauses before continuing. "The wins and losses are controlled completely by this group of people. And to keep suspicion of wrongdoing to a minimum, they spread out the championships the state wins."

"Texas doesn't win college championships every year," Drake says.

"No, they don't," Damon says. "That's part of the game."

Lance taps a few keys. "It's not just championships. It's game wins and losses. If they want Texas in a big game, they pay a lot of people off. If they want them to lose, they pay off the players. But it's all about what their gamblers are betting. If they have big bets on a Texas team to win…" Lance trails off and looks up at all of us.

I watch Kody sit back on the couch. "They'll pay them off to lose so they don't need to pay out. People end up in huge amounts of debt."

"Correct," Lance says with a smile. "Opposite is also true. If no one thinks the university will win the game and bet on them to lose, they'll pay off the other team to lose so the university will take the win. Again, more people going into debt." He looks up at Xavier. I inadvertently hold him tighter and more protectively. "Your dad figured it out. Texas A&M is one of the two universities in the State who are the biggest players in the scheme. The players take huge amounts of gifts and shit. The coaches take giant payoffs. It all happens at the beginning of the year so they can be controlled the rest of the season."

"Shit…," Xavier whispers. "It all makes sense now."

"Now, I haven't figured out exactly why your dad was pushing A&M. Either he figured you would tell him when you were approached to lose, given you'd be the starting quarterback." Lance shrugs. "Or he figured he could work his way up in this gambling ring by using you as leverage. Say you're his son. You'll do what you're told. Save them money in all of those perks so they'll get more of a profit. Maybe there was another reason. I don't know, but I will. I need to speak with your father. We have some guys bringing him out to Viper's ranch as we speak. As soon as Blade gets the text, Gavin and Damon will be heading out there to get my answers."

Xavier chuckles. "Maybe I won't get a warrant out for my arrest after all."

"About that," Josh says. "You won't. My contacts down here are taking care of it. Besides that, it was self-defense from what I heard."

I close my eyes and smile against Xavier's neck when I feel him relax. He won't admit it, but the thought of being arrested for assault on his dad was terrifying to him. Even though I told him I'd never let anything happen to him, it didn't go very far in easing his fears. Knowing he'll be okay is a giant relief to both of us. I'll have to remember to thank Josh for that.

"Now, as for the meat and potatoes," Josh continues as he stands. "Colton, you mentioned that Rosie's case is going back and forth between Louisiana and Texas. Also, that there are a lot of reports seemingly missing. You're right. Lance found them this morning deep within Texas' system."

"One thing about deleting files," Lance says with a smirk. "They aren't really gone if you know where to look."

Josh chuckles. "There is overwhelming evidence that your father was killed, Rosie." He looks at her as he talks. "But it doesn't look like it was your mother who did it. At least not the actual act. She was there, though." He looks at Blade. "When Ace pulled you into the shit in Chicago, a couple of your guys went rogue."

He raises an eyebrow. "Who?"

Josh shrugs. "Not a hundred percent, but it looks like he wanted power because he went after a few people and got himself involved in the Mexican cartel. Which runs straight through Huckleberry Grove. I sent a couple of guys out there when we kept seeing mentions of Viper's Venom. Apparently, they've been terrorizing the town."

Blade narrows his eyes and growls low. "We don't terrorize towns. We might not be the nicest guys in the world, but we don't fucking hurt people who don't deserve it, or mess shit up if it doesn't need to be done."

"I know," Josh responds and nods to Alec. "VV's President is my best friend. I know how you work. We need to figure out who went rogue on you because according to the reports, Rosie's mom was seen with someone claiming to be the Chapter President."

"Description?" Blade asks.

Josh shakes his head. "Lance hasn't gotten that far. Lots of shit in the reports he did find have been redacted, completely blacked out, or deleted all together. And while those will be able to be retrieved, it'll take time. I might have to pull Robby in to help. I know Lance has taught Damon almost everything he knows, but there is still a lot of information to go through."

Blade looks down at his phone when it goes off. "Time to go. I got the text."

Josh nods at Damon. "Go. Take Gavin."

Alec, or Ace, as I guess he's called, looks at the two bikers against the wall. "Ink. Hawk. Go with them. Whatever our Chapter needs, make sure they get it." He watches them head for the door. "Ink," he calls.

The one I assume is Ink looks back at him. "Yeah?"

"You get that overwhelming feeling, you talk to Hawk. This is your first big assignment since you've been back. Don't hold back if you need him to take over." He watches him with a concerned glint in his eye.

Ink takes a deep breath. "Got it, prez."

I raise an eyebrow but say nothing. I'm not sure what that was about, but I really don't need to. Not so long as whatever it is doesn't affect this operation and keeping Xavier and Rosie safe. Fuck, the whole town by the sounds of it.

Josh crosses his arms over his chest and looks at me. "We'll get the city cleaned up well enough, but you stay out of it. You go about your business. You investigate your cases. The busts we do belong to you. We'll keep you and your taskforce apprised of what we're doing and where. All I want from you is to show up when I tell you to, and keep the cops off my back until we're done. I don't need people I'm not working with showing up while we're in the middle of a raid or clean up. When it's all over, my team will feed you the report you'll hand in. I don't take credit for any of this. You do. By the end of this, you'll be a hero cop whether you want the title or not."

I'm quiet for a few moments before I nudge Xavier so I can sit up. I rest my elbows on my knees and let out a breath. "I'm not going to lie. I want in on the cleanup. But I know how you work." I look up at him. I can feel my eyes darken. "Just clean up my city, Lucinio. I love this place. I'm not about to let it get destroyed by some unknown force of fucking evil. I want them out of my city, and away from the man I gave my heart to. I don't want them touching my family or my people with their dark as fuck ideas."

"I get it. I'll take care of them. Just be where I need you to be. Do what I tell you to do. I know my reputation is of some heartless motherfucker who takes control of everything. I might be all of that. But while I'm cleaning up, I still need to protect you, your family, and the good people who exist in this city. When I go in, I cross lines. I do the shit you can't. And how I do it is my business. I don't want you anywhere near it because when shit goes down, and it will, repercussions of my actions could come back to you. Which makes my job a lot fucking harder because then my attention is split between my job and saving your ass. Got it?"

"Got it. I'm not often the type of guy who allows someone else to lead. I hate authority. But I know how you work. I was prepared for it. I don't give a shit about being a hero cop. I just want my city back. I want it to be a safeplace. Something we can all be proud of again."

"I'll take care of it. I have a couple of my people investigating in Huckleberry Grove. Ace and Blade will be helping with that. I have other guys who will be sticking around here. More flying in." Josh gives me a nod. "We'll take care of it. I'm also leaving a couple of people here for Rosie." He turns to her. "I heard you're not staying at home."

She shakes her head. "No, sir," she whispers.

"She's staying with Dylan," Xavier says.

"My house is Fort Knox," Dylan chuckles with a shrug. "She feels safe there."

Josh nods. "Then you'll stay there. I'll put twenty-four hour security on you. Don't worry. They'll stay discreet. No one will know they're around except you. But until we figure out who the fuck this guy is that it looks like your mother is involved with, it's best to keep you away from her."

"She's sixteen. Can't exactly keep her away if her mom files a missing person's report." I rub my head. The headache is getting exponentially worse.

"Let me take care of that," Josh says to me before turning back to her. "Just trust me. I'll always make sure you know the guys on your security detail. If they tell you that you need to disappear, listen to them. If you don't recognize them, you'll have a panic button. I'll have Lance get you equipped before you leave today."

"I hate to be a dick," I interrupt. "But are you done with me? At the risk of sounding like a whiny toddler, I have a headache that could rival the Texas sky, and I might pass out."

Xavier rubs my thigh and launches into this caring mode I never thought I'd find so sexy. "I'll get you to bed. Josh can fill you in if you need to know anything else."

I'd smile if I didn't think my head might actually explode. I barely register Xavier helping to my feet and asking me if I'm okay before everything goes dark.

CHAPTER NINE

Xavier

"What the fuck?" I scramble to support the sudden dead weight of my boyfriend as he passes out. Just before we hit the ground, I manage to catch us both, but I'm horrified.

Brant is at my side in a flash. "What the hell happened?" He puts Colton's arm over his shoulders and helps me support him.

All I can do is look at him, terrified, because I don't know what's going on. All I know is my heart is beating at a rate that can't be healthy. Colton didn't drink anything last night. He's not drunk. Yeah, we're both a little sleep deprived, but I've never seen anyone pass out because of it.

"He said he had a headache," I wheeze over my sudden hyperventilation. "Can headaches make people pass out like that?" A sudden thought hits me. "Oh, fuck!" I look at Brant. "Remember that kid in the news a couple years ago? He got tackled. Next thing anyone knows, he's dead. Brain aneurysm." The idea doesn't help me calm down. I jump when I feel a hand on my back.

"Get him to the bedroom," Josh says calmly. "Lay him down. I'll call a doctor." He looks over at Lance. "Help them. Make sure he's still breathing."

"On it." Lance shuts his laptop and quickly takes Josh's place. The room is completely chaotic. I can't think. Everyone seems to be running around, but they are all going in super slow motion. Or maybe that's just how it looks to me.

"Blade! Grab him!"

Our heads all snap over to Erik when his voice thunders over the chaos. My eyes widen as I watch Blade drag Seth back into the room from where he was attempting to slide out the door with a huge smirk on his face.

What the hell? Seth? What is he doing?

Seth struggles against him, trying to shove him away, but Blade is a mammoth of a man. He's twice my size. Seth, who doesn't have a lot of muscle and might be five feet ten if he's lucky, has no chance. Especially when Ace and Josh get involved.

Erik strides to their side and grabs Seth by the throat, slamming him back against the wall. "Seriously, motherfucker? You think I didn't fucking have suspicions about you? And you come in here thinking you'll be able to pull the wool over all their eyes? What the fuck did you poison him with? Huh?"

"Poison?" I croak out and look at my unconscious boyfriend. I've surpassed terrified. I might throw up. Going to. I'm going to throw up.

"Lance! Get them to the bedroom!" Josh commands.

I jump but am spurred into action. I practically run. "Shouldn't someone call for help?" I ask. "I'll do it." I reach for my phone, trying to force myself to think clearly.

"Josh has it," Lance says. "Just trust him. Trust me. He's got it."

I nod as we lay Colton on the bed. "Fuck, he doesn't look good." I swallow hard. He's sweating. That has to be good, right? Dead people don't sweat. I mentally slap myself. He's not dead. He can't die. Not like this.

Not fucking like this.

"Go get a bowl with cold water and a cloth," Lance directs. I thank fuck my cousins followed us because I'm not moving.

Kody comes back a few moments later and hands Lance the cloth and bowl. "I got it as cold as I could, but I can get ice."

Lance shakes his head. "No. We're cooling him down. He's burning up. But we can't shock his system like that." He looks up at me. "You need to help me get his clothes off. Pick someone you trust to see him naked because we're going to need help."

I just stare at him. I can't speak. I don't know if I'm breathing or breathing too much, but no words are coming out of my mouth. I trust all of my cousins. There's nothing in this world that I wouldn't trust them with, including my life and Colton's.

"Me," Brant says. He turns to Sterling. "Take the girls to the other bedroom. Kody, go with him to help keep them calm. He'll need the help. Where's Drake?"

"With Blade," Sterling says. "I don't think we'll pry him away even if this shit wasn't going to be his life."

I nod because I can't do anything else and meet Brant's eyes. I'm fucking grateful for him being able to take control and lead the team as well as I can, but I'm even more thankful that he can do the same thing off the field.

I can't breathe.

I can't even think.

Sterling and Kody usher Dylan and Rosie to the other room. Brant helps sit Colton up. I feel tears in my eyes as I wrestle with dead weight to get his clothes off of him while Lance jogs to Colton's private bathroom. I hear water running. It sets off my own waterfall of emotion. I never cry. I've broken bones and not cried.

But holy fuck do I do it now. I swipe at my eyes to get them to stop long enough for me to finish getting Colton's clothes off. His skin is pale. Clammy. He's cold to the touch, but he's sweating so badly that the clothes I just peeled off of him are soaked as badly as the sheets underneath him.

"Pull it together, Cap," Brant says. "He needs that tough as fuck quarterback strength right now. He'll be okay. I feel it."

I take a few deep breaths and help Brant get Colton up. I will the tears to stop as we fight to get him to the bathroom. Colton may be the most ripped man I've ever seen in my life, but all of that muscle on his two-hundred-twenty pound frame isn't easy to carry around. I thought I was strong, but I'm questioning my own strength, physical and otherwise, right now.

As soon as we get him into the bathroom, Lance takes over once more. "We're going to lift him into the tub. It will help him cool down, but we need to make sure he doesn't go under. Best way to do that is someone behind him to hold him up, but we can't do that because we don't need anyone else's body heat affecting his. So, Xavier, You'll have to get behind him the best way you can."

I look at the tub. "It's against the wall. How?"

"On your knees at the side or sit on the edge. However you do it, it needs to be comfortable for you because you might be there for a while." Lance looks around. "Thermometer. Need to keep track of his temp."

"He's really organized. Probably the medicine cabinet," I say with a sniffle.

Lance nods before helping Brant and I lift Colton into the bath. When we have him settled, I make myself comfortable and hold him up. The water doesn't seem to be cold enough, but I trust Lance. I don't know what to do in this situation, so I allow him the lead.

I'm barely aware of Dylan and Rosie entering the room, Kody and Sterling right behind them, with arms full of linens. They head straight for the bed and start stripping it. The four of them work together to remake the bed. Dylan grabs new clothing for Colton while Rosie throws his old ones in a pile with his sheets. Kody picks everything up and moves out of the room while Sterling finishes with the bed. Almost as quickly as they came in, they're gone.

I drop my head to Colton's shoulder. "Come on, baby. You can't leave me like this. I just got you."

Lance pops the thermometer in his mouth and looks up at Brant. "Go get the cloth and bowl. We need to use it on his neck and face."

Brant does as he's told, returning seconds later. Lance pulls the thermometer out of Colton's mouth when it beeps. With a nod, he turns on the cold water and pulls the plug. He lets the water cool more before replacing the plug and letting the level fill slightly. He shuts the cool water off as I look up at him.

"What now?" I ask over the ball forming in my throat.

"We wait," he says.

I nod and kiss Colton's cheek and the corner of his mouth. I hold him close while keeping his head above water. Brant continues using the cloth on his head and face. Lance keeps checking his temperature.

But Colton doesn't wake up.

***

I keep using the cool cloth on Colton's face and checking the ice pack on the back of his neck. I'm being very careful not to get too close to him so my body heat doesn't make his go up, but it's not easy.

I want to hold him close and heal him with all of the love I have for him. I know we technically just began our relationship, but in my eyes I've been falling in love with him for months. Last night was just us admitting what we've both already known, and taking the next step in the relationship we've already established.

I run my fingers through his hair. It's still damp from the sweat, but his fever did break a few hours ago. He still hasn't woken up, though. The doctor said the antidote he gave him to counteract the poison would take a while to really work.

Apparently, it was some kind of venom. Something that Colton couldn't taste or smell. It was colorless. I'm not sure of all of the details, but I really don't care about them. All I care about is how sick he is; if he'll make it through this. The doctor says he'll be fine, but I've refused to allow him to leave this penthouse. If something happens and Colton takes a turn, I want him here.

I look up at the quiet knock on the door. I asked everyone to leave us be when the doctor showed and was done with him. Brant was hesitant, but he listened. I just need to be alone with Colton. They all understood that, as I knew they would. Though, they've all checked in over the day.

"Yeah?" I croak out. I didn't realize how dry my throat was.

Drake pokes his head in with a glass of something cold that's filled with ice. "I brought you a Dew. Thought you could use it. Also, I wanted to let you know what we've found out about what happened."

I take the glass he hands me and take a long drink before handing it back to him. He puts it on the nightstand next to the bed as he sits down. "How is he?"

I look down at Colton. "He's getting his color back. The sweats have stopped. He's breathing just fine, but he's still out."

"He'll wake up, X. I don't know him well, but I know he's fucking stubborn as fuck. Just by what you've told us. He'll want to get his hands on the fucker who did this to him. Though, that's not happening." He chuckles a little darkly. "Blade and Ace took him to Viper's Ranch."

I chuckle, but there's no emotion behind it. The truth is, I really don't give a shit. "All I care about is Colton."

"Fuck, X." He reaches over and squeezes my shoulder. "I know."

I reach over and dip the cloth in the bowl of cold water I just refilled and ring it out. "It's been hours. Scares the fuck out of me. I just got him, Drake." I gently put the cloth on his head.

"Fuck... That's... cold...," Colton murmurs.

I jerk back my arm. My heart leaps into my throat. "Colt?"

He doesn't open his eyes, but a smile slowly turns up one corner of his mouth. "Hey, baby."

"Christ, Colt. I thought I'd lost you."

"That's not happening." He shifts his arms slightly with a groan and wraps it around me. Drake runs out the door calling for the doctor. Colton pulls me into him, but I can feel how weak he is. "I'm still here."

"Barely," I whisper, cuddling into his chest.

The next few minutes are a flurry of motion. The doctor comes in and checks Colton out. Erik comes in to check on his friend. Josh and Lance come in just to make sure things are going smoothly. My cousins come in and make sure we're both doing okay. Erik and I help Colton sit up. The doctor allows him water through a straw. When everything settles, the only ones left in the room are me and Erik, per Colt's request.

I kiss his shoulder as I push his hair back. "I'm so happy you're okay."

"Just a little on the weak side." He turns and kisses the top of my head. I put an arm around his waist. I let myself relax a little and just feel him.

He soothingly runs his fingers through my hair. "What happened?" Colton asks. "Last thing I remember was standing up to go to bed with a massive fucking headache."

Erik nods slowly with a dark glare and chuckles a little. "Fucker came after you. Seth."

Colton raises an eyebrow. "Why?"

"Wasn't sure at first. I got suspicious, though, because he was always around your drinks. Coffee. Water. I didn't see him doing anything, but I did catch him shoving something in his pocket at one point. Didn't know what it was, but that's when I gave you a bottle of water instead of the glass he handed you. Your headache improved a bit. You'd gone to the bathroom a few times. It was like you were coming out of a fog."

He nods slowly and winces a little. "I remember feeling better with the bottled water, but I didn't put two and two together. I thought I just needed water and coffee wasn't agreeing with me or something."

"I kept an eye on you. Especially after I came back from the bathroom and you'd downed another glass of water. It was your second glass. I wanted to see what it did. You started to look more and more tired. I'd already decided to have the glass tested and talk to Seth about what I saw and his fucking attitude about you not drinking from the glasses. I was going to do it as soon as Josh was done talking, but things happened quickly. You were on your feet wanting to go to bed. Then, you passed out."

"All I remember is feeling like I needed to go to the bedroom."

"Well, I wasn't the only one who noticed. Xavier saw a few red flags, but didn't know what to make of them. He thought you were acting a little off. Not as alert. Even though you were tired. He knows you've gone without sleep and weren't affected like that. Josh said he'd started helping you with breakfast because you were stumbling. Blade pulled me aside and asked me if you were okay. You just didn't seem like you."

I shift a little and look at him. "Your skin is returning to a normal color. But if you think I'll stop fussing over you, you'd better think again."

Colton chuckles and pulls me closer until his lips are just brushing mine. "I wouldn't have it any other way. I'll never tell another soul, but I like you taking care of me." He smiles as he kisses me.

Erik chuckles. "You realize there's a witness. Right here." He waves his hand when Colton pulls away with a grin. I laugh. Erik smiles. "See?"

"Yeah, but you'll have my back. Keep my secrets," Colton says.

"Always." Erik pats Colton's leg lightly.

As he continues filling Colton in on everything that went on out there, I can't help but tune it all out. I settle against Colton's chest and close my eyes. His heartbeat, strong and true, along with his hand running up and down my arm calm me more.

It's crazy and far scarier than I'm willing to admit, but I almost lost him today. It's a thought that's run through my mind so many times and chills me to my bones. I'd almost completely forgotten about everything else going on, including my father and how he's in the hands of Viper's Venom.

If I'm being honest with myself, I have no doubts that this is just the beginning. I'm sure all what happened today was just a blip on the highlight reel.

Questions still need to be answered.

People need to be dealt with.

The city is about to go through an intense shake-up.

I just hope to fuck that we all come out on the other side unscathed.

EPILOGUE

Colton

(Three Weeks Later)

I lean against the bleachers at the high school behind where the players sit with a huge smile plastered to my face. Xavier led his team to the championship game. Despite all the shit we've gone through over the past couple of months, and me recovering from being poisoned, Xavier has shined both on and off the field. He's taken care of me, his cousins, and this team. I can see why he's the number one ranked high school quarterback in the state right now. He's broken records, so the talk of him being the best of all time holds a lot of merit. I couldn't be more fucking proud.

I clap and whistle when Xavier throws an ace of a pass that gets the team a first down. Not so sure they need it. It's just coming up on halftime. The Bullhorns are up by twenty-one points. The other team has yet to score. It's a complete slaughter.

I can't believe how much has happened in just three weeks. The Viper's Venom got a lot of information from Xavier's dad about the gambling ring. Turns out, Seth was the head of it. He didn't like that I'd gotten so close to it. He thought if he took me out, that would be the end of it.

But he fucked up.

Twice.

Firstly, he didn't put enough poison in my water. His intention wasn't to make me sick. It was to kill me, but he didn't use the poison correctly. He also didn't count on Erik noticing what was going on and giving me bottles instead of the glasses that he kept putting out for me.

And secondly, he didn't count on me calling in the mafia or a biker's crew to help me out. Even when they showed up, he underestimated them on all levels. He'd heard of the Lucinio Mafia, but he never believed just how powerful they are. And he had no idea how closely they work with Viper's Venom or the police when we ask them for help.

Too bad for him, really. But it doesn't really matter now. He's been taken care of. Cops don't do well in prison. He's still awaiting trial, but I heard he may have had the shit beat out of him, and that the guards stood by and watched it all go down. I don't feel an ounce of sympathy. Not after all the shit he's done. Right up to murder in his sick and twisted snake bite games. Vipers could have finished him off, but we all agreed he'd have a lot more fun with their allies, guards and cons alike, in prison.

We also found out the reason that Xavier was pushed so hard into going to A&M is because his dad made an agreement with Seth and his partners, who Josh and his crew have all so nicely hunted down for me. The deal involved getting all of his debt wiped clean so long as his son played nice and did what he was told.

Xavier was supposed to become the starting quarterback. His dad would tell him to either win or lose the game. In return, Xavier wouldn't have to worry about school in the slightest. His grades and everything would be bought and paid for. Essentially, my theory wasn't that far off. He thought he could make his son do whatever he wanted. I suppose he didn't think Xavier would stand up for himself. What started out simply as a father who wanted his son to follow in his footsteps turned into something far more sinister.

While Seth ended up in prison and his partners won't be heard from again, Xavier's father has to live with the fact that he fucked up so badly that he lost it all. He was fired from the department, along with several other dirty cops, because he was involved in a lot of the gambling. He'll probably spend some time in prison himself because of just how much he let happen, like the murder of innocent men, without saying anything to anyone. Charges of conspiracy and accessory to murder have been filed against him. He's out on bail. He's not only lost his job, but also his entire family, though. Xavier's mother left him. Can't blame her.

I'm a little bit surprised to see her here with Brant's father and step-mother. She's starting life on her own, but she's recovering from a lot of shit from what I understand. Mental abuse, emotional trauma, and a drug and drinking problem. Xavier left just in the nick of time, in my opinion. He avoided the entire implosion. At least most of it.

Josh Lucinio has done a damn good job of cleaning up this city. True to his word, I've gotten all of the credit and will continue to. Command staff in my own department have gone down. City officials, including the Mayor, have been caught up in the chaos. It's only the beginning. He left behind two of his best guys, Lance and Damon, to help with the fallout.

And that's not the only thing that we're caught up in. The teacher who assaulted Rosie may have been caught, but her mother has gone missing over the last three weeks. So has a couple of men from Viper's Venom. It looks like suspicions of them trying to overthrow Blade are correct. What they didn't count on, though, is Blade's close ties to other Chapters of Viper's Venom, including the fucking President of the entire crew himself. Alec, in order to help, has not only left Ink here, but he's also personally flying back and forth from Chicago when he's needed.

With all of the assistance we're getting here, I'm sure it won't be long before the mystery surrounding Rosie's family is solved. Dylan's mom got pretty sick of having Rosie around and complained just enough to make Rosie feel like a burden. Xavier told her she could stay with us, but Damon and Lance offered to keep her with them instead. Rosie agreed because it's more protection for her, even though she's pretty convinced she doesn't need it.

I know she has gotten close to them both. They took the time to make sure she was comfortable and understood everything that has been going on. She didn't say it, but I could see in her body language that she was happy to be living with them. I can't say I'm not relieved about it. With rogue Viper's Venom members involved, she'll need all the protection she can get. She wants to go back to Huckleberry Grove. She misses it.

"Yeah! Go, Xavier!" I yell as he starts running for the end zone instead of passing. I don't see anyone open. The decision to run was a good one.

The crowd erupts in thunderous cheers when he scores the touchdown for his team and brings us into halftime. His teammates hug him as everyone starts jogging off the field. Xavier makes his way straight to me.

"Hey, Detective Fuckable. Did you see that play?"

"Hell yeah, I did." I wrap him in my arms when he reaches me and kiss him long and deeply. One thing I've come to love about him is that he isn't afraid to show us off. He doesn't give a fuck who sees us together. He's just as proud as I am to show us off.

"Damn, you taste good," he says to me when I pull away.

I grin. "So do you." I tap his ass. "Get your ass in the locker room. Your team needs you to rally them to victory."

He laughs. "You seen the scoreboard?" He gives me a quick peck to the lips as he turns and jogs away. "Love you!"

"Love you, too!" I call after him as my heart swells. I really do fucking love him.

I watch him disappear as he makes his way into the school and catch sight of Dylan. I raise an eyebrow. She slowly makes her way behind her squad to their locker room. She looks a little like she wants to cry.

"You okay, sweetie?" I ask her when she walks by me.

She jumps a little as she looks at me and shakes her head. "I heard a weird phone call earlier." She looks down. "I've been obsessing over it."

"What phone call? Who was involved?"

She shrugs. "It was just my dad. He said something like she'll never know. I got the feeling he was talking about me. He just seems so secretive lately." She shakes her head like she's trying to shrug it off. "I'm sure it's nothing."

I hold out my arms and fold her in a hug when she steps into them. "I know you're dad loves the fuck out of you. Maybe whatever it is has nothing to do with you, but I also know you need to follow your instincts, sweetheart." I kiss the top of her head as I release her. "It might be nothing, but it might not be. Just keep your eyes open. Hell, maybe he's planning a surprise party for you."

She giggles and smiles. "Maybe you're right. My birthday is coming up soon."

I smile. "See? You never know."

"Thanks, Colton."

"Anytime, honey."

I smile as she jogs after her squad. I move off to the side more as people start passing me to head for the concession stand. I decide to follow because a Coke and nachos doesn't sound bad at all. Even if the line is long.

"Sloane, wait!"

I turn and see Brant grabbing the arm of a girl who might be half his size. I recognize her as his stepmom. I've only seen her a couple of times. Once was at her wedding. Brant's dad invited the entire department. I hadn't intended to go, but I ended up doing it because a friend needed a date. She didn't want to go alone and get hit on.

Sloane is very petite. She's not all that tall. Her hair is dark. She looks like she's been crying. I know whatever is going on is probably private, but I can't look away. Brant pulls her away from the line a little bit, but they're still close enough to me that I can hear them. Even though they're not talking all that loudly.

"I don't belong here, Brant," she says quietly. She looks past him and shakes her head. "I shouldn't have come."

"Sloane, come on. Don't let him fuck with you like this. This is a huge game for us. I don't get to play running back much because I'm backup for X. To get to play in a game like this is huge. I asked you to come because I want you here. He doesn't matter."

"But he does, Brant. Don't you see? He'll just make things difficult for me if I disobey him and stay. I'm not part of this world." She sniffles. "I never will be." She pulls away from him and runs towards the parking lot.

Brant looks after her sadly but doesn't run after her. I'm just about to ask him what that was all about, but I don't get the opportunity because he turns around with his head down and walks towards the school to join his team. I thought he didn't get along well with his stepmother, but the look he just gave her tells a far different story.

After I finally get my snacks, I make my way back to the field and find a seat this time. Not that I mind standing. It gives me a good view of Xavier. Nothing to be upset about there. I find a seat next to Blade just as they start coming back to the field. I stay standing long enough for Xavier to see where I am.

"Didn't think you were going to get here," Blade says when I sit next to him.

I smile. "I've been here. I was a little late, but I saw the touchdown pass just before Xavier ran for their last touchdown. Fourteen points in like two minutes. Not bad."

Blade laughs. "Drake's catch was something to be proud of. Jerry Rice or Chris Carter shit right there."

I grin. "That catch was fucking phenomenal. One handed. Just plucked out of the fucking air like it was nothing."

"He's a damn good player."

"Probably why all the colleges want him."

He smiles proudly. "Too bad he's already committed to BSU."

"So, it'll be Drake as receiver, Brant as running back and backup QB, and then Sterling and Kody? Fuck. They'll be unstoppable."

"I see a contender for the top spot." Blade steals one of my loaded nachos. "Championships for sure."

I smile widely because I know he's right. These guys are called the Dream Team. Brystone Springs hasn't had a championship team like this. They've won championships, but never with a team this good. They're special.

***

"I think we'll have to turn the guest bedroom into a trophy room," I say with a proud grin as we walk past the room hand in hand.

Xavier laughs. "With the amount of trophies I plan on winning in my life? It won't be big enough. We'll have to move."

"I'd move anywhere you asked me to if it meant you following your dreams and being happy, baby. Except overseas. I'd prefer to keep my feet on United States soil."

He tugs my hand and pushes me against the wall near our bedroom. "My plans don't include overseas football. Do they even call it that?" He presses his body against mine with a wicked grin and glint in his eye.

I groan and wrap my arms around his waist. "Mmhmm. Rugby."

He shakes his head. "Ain't the same. Weird uniforms. Not as popular as soccer."

"Football," I say teasingly, pulling him closer.

He makes a face. "It's soccer. Europeans don't know what football is."

I laugh because I know he's kidding. He'll watch a Chelsea FC game with me all day and love every second. He gets just as into it. Even throws popcorn, chips, or even candy at the screen when there is a foul or a shit call. Penalty shootouts typically have us both clutching our chests and panicking as we wait. Penalties in a normal or championship game are stressful enough. But penalty shootouts at a World Cup game after extra time? Fuck me. Call me a doctor.

Though we may need to find a way to protect the tv when we watch next year's World Cup. Xavier and I invited everyone to our apartment to watch it with us. Somehow, the TV ended up with a smashed screen after Blade threw his glass at it in outrage when the referee made a bad call. Something about how the player had made a dirty tackle. But we all agreed we didn't see any issue with the foul. It looked clean to us.

I let my hands wander under his t-shirt and up his back. "You played a really good game. Kicked ass. I don't think I've ever seen a team obliterate another team in a championship game like that."

If I didn't know Xavier, I'd say he's preening under the praise and blushing. But I don't have much time to really play around with that idea because his lips are crashing into mine in a hungry kiss that leaves me breathless and hard as a steel in seconds.

When his fingertips find the waistband of my jeans, it's all over. I deepen the kiss and grip his ass. I push off the wall and back him into our bedroom without breaking it. At least not until the backs of his knees hit the bed.

I nip his lip as I pull away and push him backwards onto the bed. He looks up at me, a little wide-eyed at the aggression and growl I let out, with a sexy smirk that makes me want to tear his clothes off.

So, I do.

I peel off his shirt, then pants, then boxer briefs until he's bare-ass naked in front of me. I quickly remove mine and crawl into the bed, shifting us so we're both more comfortable. Xavier pushes me on my back with heated lust in his eyes and leans down. He kisses me long and hard, tangling his tongue with mine, as he straddles me.

Xavier has always been a top. He's never taken dick. Always been the one to give it. So, when he allowed me to claim his ass, our relationship catapulted from the just exploring each other stage to the we're each other's person stage.

Xavier is all mine. Just like I'm his.

I let my head fall back with a moan and gasp when he lowers himself over my dick. "Fuck… Xavier."

His ass pulses around my cock. He doesn't even give himself time to adjust to my size before he's moving back and forth on me. I grip his hips as he sits up and rests his hands on my stomach. I'm sure most would have their eyes glued to his dick. Xavier is big. Maybe not my size, but he's big.

His dick, though, isn't what has my attention. It's the fact that his ass is taking all of me. I'm buried balls deep. It's astonishing how well someone who has always done the fucking, never been fucked, can take a guy like me as good as he does.

I start thrusting, but it's not long before Xavier is riding me like a fucking rodeo bull. I always like to be the one in control. It's just not like that with him, though. Neither of us are in control. We just feel and do what's right for us.

Xavier starts clenching around me as he moves back and forth over me while he bounces. He closes his eyes. "Oh fuck. Colt! Don't stop. Don't stop!"

He leans back and grips my thighs. It's my cue that he's done with the ride. So, I give him what he wants. I brace my feet on the bed and grip his hips as I give him the fast, hard, and deep thrusts that he's come to love. I slap his ass with both hands, then grip his hips again, slamming him down so he's meeting my thrusts.

He reaches around to his dick as it slaps up and down. He grips it as I thrust and starts jerking it in time to my punishing pace. I'd stop him and stroke him myself. I love doing that. But one of my favorite things to do is watch him do it while I'm chasing both of our releases. The look of pleasure he gets on his face as I'm thrusting and he's stroking is something I'll never tire of. It makes me harder for him. Thicker.

I thrust faster with a grunt. "Christ, baby. You look so damn good jerking that cock of yours."

He smiles, but doesn't look down on me. "I know you like watching." He clenches around my dick and jerks his hips when I push my cock as deep inside him as I can. "Fuck!"

A shiver goes down my spine. My cock feels like it might break off if I don't come. My stomach clenches in anticipation. His thighs tremble. My fingers grip his flesh tighter. I want so badly to let go, but I'll never do that if he's not there first.

"Come, Xavier," I moan as I give into my temptation. I reach for his balls and roll them in my palm. "Now." I tug on them.

"Oh fuck!" As soon as his release hits my stomach, I thrust hard into him a couple of more times.

"Holy shit… Yes!" I come deep inside him, keeping his ass flush against my hips.

"Colton!" He spasms hard around me as my dick jerks inside him. He releases more onto my stomach, nearly collapsing.

"Xavier!" His balls, hard just moments ago, become putty in my hand as he gives me everything he has. I keep gently massaging them as we both come.

Several minutes later, after we've both come down and cleaned up, I pull Xavier into my side. As I think of how far we've come in such a short amount of time, I run my fingers through his hair. I never really thought I'd be here. I'm not the kind of man who expected to ever have a happily ever after. Especially with a guy who is so much younger than me. He's so far out of my league, it's laughable.

But here I am.

"I love you, Colton," Xavier murmurs as his breathing evens.

"I love you, too, baby," I whisper as I kiss his forehead.

And I do. With all my heart and soul, I love Xavier Remington. Forbidden to me on so many levels. Age. The fact that he's still a high school student. Most of all, because he still has his entire life in front of him. I'm happy to be a part of watching him take the world on.

But it's the fact that he loves me back that's the greatest gift of all.

THE END

ABOUT MELONY ANN

Melony Ann began writing short stories and poetry as a child. She continued honing her craft over the years until she took the plunge and began publishing her work, despite having severe anxiety.

Melony writes contemporary romance stories that are full of suspense and a lot of steam.

When she isn't writing, she is loving her family and working to make her life something she deserves.

Melony believes that if her writing can inspire just one person, then all of her hard work is worth it.

Her hope is that her writing allows each and every one of her readers to escape for a little while. To dive into a different world one book at a time.

TEN DAYS IN HEAVEN

by Samantha Michaels

PROLOGUE

Riley

I still can't believe he did this to me.

I'm Riley Cavanaugh, a pathetic loser who's spending another lonely Friday night in my pajamas. I put the TV on and tune into a marathon of my favorite comfort show, Friends.

I should have been spending tonight making final preparations for my trip to Hawaii. I really need my best friend, but I was too embarrassed to tell her what happened. I kept my time off so I didn't have to explain anything. Plus, it gives me a chance to sit and wallow.

Nights like these remind me of my childhood. I was shy and had very few friends, so I spent most of my time reading. I always imagined myself being in the books I was reading, which helped with my loneliness. Now that I'm older, I've taken up writing as a form of therapy.

I get up and grab my laptop. I open a blank document and sit and stare at it for a few minutes. Suddenly, Ace's handsome face pops into my head. That's all the inspiration I need, and I start typing. Fictional Riley runs into fictional Ace. After she tells him what happened with her trip, he comes to the rescue and gives her ten days she'll never forget.

It takes me a few days to finish the story. After I type 'the end,' I print a copy and read it. I must say, I'm pleased with how it turned out.

I know two things for sure.

First, anyone who reads it is going to need a cold shower.

Second, one of those people can never be Ace!

CHAPTER ONE

Riley

"Earth to Riley. Come in, Riley."

I look up and see my best friend Maddie standing in front of me, I can't help but wonder how long she's been trying to get my attention. "Sorry. My brain already thinks it's in Hawaii."

"Bitch! If you weren't my bestie, I'd hate you."

"But you are, so you have to love me!"

"Can I wait until you're back home?"

"Deal."

"Besides, you'll be making it up to me."

"How?"

"Don't pretend you forgot. Our 30th high school reunion."

"Fine, if you insist." I sigh.

"Damn right I do. I wonder if you-know-who's coming."

"Don't know, don't care."

"Come on, he was your best friend, after me, of course."

"Then he left and forgot all about me."

"Fame will do that to a guy, especially playing lead guitar for one of the top metal bands." She says.

"Big damn deal. Besides, I have Brad."

"Yawn city. Sorry for saying that, but he's no Ace."

"You're right about that. He would never leave me like that."

"I bet Ace is better in bed."

"Brad is just fine in that area."

"Just fine? Oh, that sounds exciting. Guess you keep plenty of batteries around."

"Madison Jane Elliott!" I exclaim.

"Don't pretend you don't. You're not the innocent angel everyone here thinks you are."

"This from the president of the Man of the Month Club."

"I'm not only the president, I'm also a member."

"That's the Hair Club, dingbat!"

Maddie stuck her tongue out at me then headed back to her desk. My mind wanders to thoughts of him. Not the him I should be thinking of, but rather the sexy rock star that used to be my friend. I wish I'd had the guts to tell him how I felt. It's too late now. Plus, I have Brad. But I can't help but wonder what my life would be like if I had told him.

I shake my head and return my attention back to the boring spreadsheet I've been staring at. Most of the time, I enjoy my job. I like researching and resolving problems. Sometimes, though, my boss needs me to perform more tedious tasks, like this report I'm working on. Never have I been happier to see 3:30 than I am today. I'm just finishing shutting down my computer when Maddie stops at my desk.

"Get a move on it, woman. Paradise awaits."

"I have to get home and pack my batteries."

"Ha, ha. Seriously, though, are you all packed?"

"I packed most of my stuff last night. Just need to do my toiletries." I smile.

"That's my predictable friend."

"I am NOT predictable!"

"Yes, you are, but that's why I love you. You keep me grounded."

"Thanks."

When we get down to the parking lot, Maddie gives me a hug. I spend my whole ride home thinking about what she said. Good old boring Riley. Everyone can count on Riley. Just once, I want to be "shocks the shit out of everyone" Riley. But, I can't complain. Tomorrow, I'll be relaxing on a beach in Hawaii. AC/DC's Back in Black takes me out of my reverie. I look at my phone and see Brad's face.

"Hey. Brad. I was just finishing up packing."

"Yeah, well, you can unpack."

"Excuse me?"

"Darcy's coming with me," he states.

"Again, excuse me? I'm your girlfriend."

"You were my girlfriend."

"Excuse me? You're dumping me?"

"Yeah, you're boring as fuck. I'd much rather be with Darcy. Have a nice life." Before I can respond, Brad disconnects the call.

"Asshole! Who the fuck does he think he is?"

I trudge out to the couch, sit down, and grab my Ace London pillow. I clutch it to my chest. Despite him leaving me and our friendship behind, I still support him, regularly shopping in his online merch shop. Holding the pillow tight, I start picturing what my life would be like if he was still in it. He never knew it, but I had a crush on him. I never even told Maddie about that, as she would have just teased me.

I see us in a house by a beach in California. The walls are plastered with platinum and gold records, along with tons of pictures. We have an indoor hot tub, game room and a music room in addition to all the standard rooms. Of course, since he's made it big, I don't have to have a 9-5. Instead, I get to focus on my writing. I'm obsessed with writing and reading smut. I once shared that with Brad and he got offended. I would love to find a man to read dirty stuff to me in bed.

An hour into my self-pity party, I hear my stomach rumble. I head down to Angelo's, my favorite pizza place, might as well drown my misery in some pizza and beer. I jump in my sexy red 1965 convertible Mustang. I pull into the parking lot, and stare at the building for a couple of minutes before I go in. I've been coming here since high school and nothing has changed.

I'm relieved when I see my favorite table is open. I like sitting in the back corner, especially when I'm here alone. I feel a sense of comfort when I look around. The same red and white checkered tablecloths cover each table. The walls are filled with pictures of Angelo and his family. The counter at the front of the restaurant is flanked on each side by a bakery case filled with delicious desserts. Angelo's wife Maria bakes everything from scratch. I plan on putting a dent in one of the chocolate cakes before I leave. Maria stopped by my table to take my order.

"What's troubling you?" she asks me in her thick Italian accent.

"Brad dumped me."

"He's a fool. I can put a curse on him."

I laugh through my tears. "That won't be necessary, but thank you."

"What can I get for you?"

"A man. Seriously, I would like a pizza with pepperoni and extra cheese."

"Anything to drink, honey?"

"A pitcher of beer."

"I can bring you all but the man." She smiles.

A few minutes later, Angelo brings me my beer and two glasses.

"I only need one glass."

He puts both glasses on the table, smiles, and walks away without saying a word. Leave it to Angelo to make it look like I'm not alone. He's the sweetest man. A fresh round of tears fills my green eyes and I look down at my lap, hoping nobody sees me.

"Your pizza, sweetie," Maria says warmly.

"Thank you."

I lower my head back down, still trying to fight the tears that sting my eyes. I hear the door open, looking up to see and my jaw drops. It can't be. I must be hallucinating, but I'm not.

Standing in front of the restaurant, in all his glory, stands Angus 'Ace' London. I haven't seen him in person since the summer after we graduated from high school. Pictures haven't done this man justice.

He's six feet, four inches of chiseled muscles. My fingers ache to get tangled in his golden brown hair, hanging just below his broad shoulders. His day-old beard makes his face even more handsome. And hot damn, the dimples that appear when he smiles are impossible to resist.

I feel a heat spread between my legs. I see him speak to Angelo, who leads him to a table at the other side of the restaurant. I have no idea if he saw me.

CHAPTER TWO

Ace

"Ace Fuckin' London!" Mark yells way too loudly.

He gives me a big "bro" hug. Mark's been my best friend since kindergarten. I can't think of anyone who I'd want to see first. Well, maybe one other person. I wonder what she's up to tonight. I sit down across from Mark. He has a pitcher of beer and two glasses waiting for me. He pours us each a beer.

"To getting old," he jokes as we clink glasses.

I take a sip of beer then ask, "What've you been up to?"

"Jenny and I have been working on the house. Now that we're empty-nesters, we have a couple of spare rooms."

"What are you planning to do with them?"

"One's going to be a home gym. We're still not sure about the other."

"What about a hot tub?"

"I may have to run that by Jenny. How lame are we? Sitting here talking about home improvements."

"Not lame at all. I would trade places with you in a second." I say.

"You're fuckin' crazy. Look at the life you've had. Touring, parties, women."

"Yeah, it was fun. But, there's always been something missing."

"Something or someone?"

"Shut it."

"Hit a nerve, did I?" Mark teases me.

"I fucked up and I know it. It's only ever been her. Now, it's too late."

"Don't be so sure."

"Huh? She's with someone."

"Then why's she sitting at her favorite table alone?"

I stand up and turn where Mark's pointing. I find myself just staring at her. I always thought she was cute in high school. Time has been kind to her and she's moved way beyond cute. This woman is stunning. Her chestnut colored hair begs for my fingers. I see tears staining her cheek and I feel an anger rise up in my gut.

Who the fuck made this woman cry? He better hope I never get my hands on him. She suddenly looks up and her mouth drops. Even with her red puffy eyes, she's still by far the most beautiful woman I've ever seen. I get up and go take a seat across from her.

"Riley Cavanaugh as I live and breathe. Beautiful as ever, love."

"Yeah, right. I must look wonderful,"

"To me you do, but speaking of that, who did this to you?"

"Please, my stupid issues are not your problem."

"Like hell. I want to know who the fuck hurt you." I say angrily. She doesn't respond and I'm afraid I came on too strong.

"Sorry, doll. I just hate that someone upset you. Tell me what happened."

"I guess, but first, would you like a beer and some pizza?"

"I'd love some."

I pour two glasses and give her one. Our hands touch when she takes the glass and I feel electricity course through my body. What the fuck? I can't possibly still have a thing for this woman, can I? I wanted desperately to ask her out in high school, but I was afraid what it might do to our friendship. I've been following her on social media and she's been in relationships, so I thought I missed my shot. Maybe our reunion is exactly what was meant to bring us together.

She sighs and begins, "I was seeing this guy Brad. He was a nice guy, but kinda boring."

"In what way?"

"Well, you know I always had a thing for reading smut? Well, I tried reading him some once and he told me was offended. I thought it would turn him on."

"Uhhh…what the fuck? I'd be hard in two seconds flat." I stifle a laugh as her cheeks turn bright red. Fuck, I feel my dick starting to stir. What the hell is this woman doing to me?

"Well, anyway, he was a decent boyfriend, or so I thought. We were supposed to leave for a ten day vacation tomorrow morning."

"Supposed to?"

"He called me tonight to tell me he was taking his stupid bitch of an assistant instead. Fucker."

"Where does he live?" I growl.

"Why?"

"I'm gonna go kick the shit out of him."

"That's not necessary, but I appreciate the sentiment."

"Fine. So, I know I haven't kept in touch like I should've. Tell me what else has been going on."

"Nothing exciting. My job's okay, and I work with Maddie but she has the habit of telling me that I'm predictable. And sadly, she's not wrong."

"So stop being predictable."

"Easy for you to say. I need to keep a routine. I need to go to my job every day and pay my bills every month. We can't all be badass rock stars who forget their friends." She smiles sadly.

"Ouch, but I do deserve that. I really am sorry, doll."

"Whatever. It's ancient history. Let's just enjoy the rest of this pizza and beer."

I watch more tears form in her eyes and my rage returns. All I can think about is kicking Brad's ass. Well, that and how much I want this woman in my bed. I picture her lying there naked, just waiting for me to give her the pleasure she deserves. How the fuck could anyone think another woman was better than her? I fucked up when I left her. I can't fuck up again.

We enjoy the rest of our meal, while I tell her some of the more horrific stories of being a rock star. Nothing was worse than having women sneak into my hotel room or the tour bus. Most of the other musicians I met over the years loved that but not me. I've always been a relationship guy. Sure, I had my fair share of one night stands, but I only ever wanted her. The beautiful Riley Cavanaugh.

"So, tell me. What do you and Maddie do for fun?" I ask.

"We love hitting the local rock club. Lots of great music plus amazing men to pick from. And it's about to get even better."

"How so?"

"New ownership. Sadly, the previous owner passed away. He left the club to his friend, and she's expanding it to also include a bookstore. That's perfect for me. Alcohol and books are a winning combination."

"Doug passed away? Damn, what happened?"

"You knew him?" She asks.

"Yeah, I played here when his dad was still the owner, and we became friends. Until I left."

"Sounds familiar. He was out for a walk with his wife. They were crossing the road when someone ran a red light. Neither survived."

"That's awful. I'm so sorry to hear. Know anything about the new owner?"

"I know her name's Lexi. She seems cool and she has a rock star for a boyfriend. Ever heard of Damien St. James?"

"Yeah. He's fuckin' amazing. I'd love to meet him."

"I'm friends with the bartender, so might be able to score a meeting."

"Cool. But now back to you, doll. What else have you been up to?"

"Not much besides my job. Even less now that Brad sent me packing. Tomorrow, I would have been in Hawaii for the first time ever. Now I have to spend the next ten days hiding. I don't want anyone to know what he did to me."

Without warning, an idea pops into my head. But, will she go for it? If I play it right, I can meet her needs, and satisfy my anaconda at the same time. I try to imagine what it feels like inside her. I need to find out, but only if she accepts my proposition.

"I have an idea, love."

"Oh, is that so? Judging by the look on your face, I'm intrigued."

"You mentioned everyone thinking you're predictable and that you need to hide. I can help with both."

"How so?"

"Spend those ten days with me. Imagine the fun we could have. And don't tell me that doesn't interest you."

"I can't."

"Give me one good reason," I demand.

"What would people say?"

"Who gives a shit. What do you want to do?"

"Say goodbye to Miss Practicality!"

"Doll, you're in for one hell of a good time!"

"I better be!"

"I'll send a car for you in the morning."

"Can't wait."

We talk a little while longer until Angelo brings the check. It's getting near closing time, so I grab the check.

"What are you doing?" she asks.

"Treating you to dinner, love."

"That's not necessary."

"I want to."

"Thanks."

I walk her to her car. Before she gets in, I grab her hand and kiss the back of it.

"I'll see you in the morning."

Before she can answer, I turn and walk away. I watch her get in her car and head home. I do the same, as I have a lot of plans to make!

CHAPTER THREE

Riley

I'm sitting on my porch, questioning if last night actually happened or if I was dreaming. As if it manifested itself to answer my question, a white limo pulls into my driveway. The driver gets out and approaches my porch.

"Good morning, ma'am. My name is Bruce. Mr. London sent me to pick you up. May I load your luggage?"

"Yes, please."

"Very well."

I watch Bruce load my bags into the trunk. He opens the back door for me. After I climb in, he closes it and gets into the driver seat. He pulls out of my driveway and heads toward what I presume is Ace's home. I'm a bundle of nerves and excitement. It's been too long since I've had sex. Brad had stopped touching me. I thought he was just stressed at work, not that he was fucking that bitch.

To hell with him. I'm going to spend ten days with a hot, sexy rockstar. Someone I always had a crush on. And now I'm going to stay at his house. But do I have the guts to let him see me naked? No way in hell. I'm sure he saw the hottest women on earth during his travels. No way I could compare to any of them. What the hell was I thinking, agreeing to this? I'm about to tell Bruce to take me back home when he pulls into the driveway of the most beautiful home I've ever laid eyes on.

The outside is all freshly painted red brick with black shutters on all the windows. From the outside, it appears the house has three floors. I can't wait to see what's behind the beautiful cedar colored double doors. Each door is carved with a beautiful guitar and features a small stained glass window on top. Bruce opens my door and helps me exit the limo. He grabs my bags out of the trunk. We walk together to the front door, where he rings the bell. My knees go weak when the door opens.

Ace is standing there in tight black leather pants and a black button-down shirt. I love the fact that musicians don't know how to work buttons. I stand there gawking at the sexiest chest I've ever seen. His upper chest is covered with dark hair, just enough to make my panties melt. My eyes follow the trail of hair starting under his navel. I start to picture where that leads and my heart races. And don't get me started on those pants... Holy hell, they leave little to the imagination. Is he smuggling an eggplant in there?

"Thank you, Bruce, for safely delivering this beauty," Ace says.

He flashes that million dollar smile and his dimples appear. I go weak in the knees. He grabs my arm and keeps me from going down. I turn fifteen shades of red when I see Ace and Bruce stifling a laugh. I pretend to be pissed, but secretly, my skin is on fire where he's touching me.

"Is there anything else you need, sir?" Bruce asks.

"No, thank you."

Bruce gets back in his limo and heads out of Ace's horseshoe driveway. Ace picks up my suitcase.

"Shall we go inside, doll?"

"Yes, please."

I follow Ace into the foyer and my jaw drops. The house is stunning. The floor is hardwood with small carpet at the doorway. I look at Ace, who's standing there with a smile on his handsome face.

"Would you like a tour?" he asks.

"Ummm, okay."

What the hell is wrong with me? I'm an intelligent, educated woman and I can barely remember how to speak. To be fair, Ace is the hottest guy on this entire planet. Hell, he might even be the hottest guy in the universe. He takes me into his kitchen, and I'm jealous. I love to cook and would give anything to have that much space. Not to mention what I imagine him doing to me on one of those marble counters. The rest of the first floor has a half-bath, an entertainment room, and an indoor hot tub.

He walks me to the far wall, where I see an elevator. A fucking elevator in his damn house. Holy shit, I could get used to this. He presses the button and we go inside. Again, my mind goes in the gutter. We get to the second floor. I see three doors along the hallway along with sliding glass doors that open to a large balcony. Two of the hallway doors are bedrooms and one is a bathroom. The bathroom includes a walk-in shower and a separate tub for two. Oh, the fun to be had here.

Back inside the elevator, we reach the top floor. He shows me one more bedroom. There's a second door, but we don't go inside. In fact, he doesn't even acknowledge that door. I wonder what's inside. He walks me back to the elevator so we can return to the living room.

Ace walks over to the stereo and puts on some romantic music. He takes me into his arms and I notice how great he smells. Without a word he gently lifts my chin and gives me the sweetest, most passionate kiss I've ever felt. We dance and kiss for several more songs and I'm starting to feel better. I can't believe I'm in Ace's living room, his lips on mine as his tongue dances in my mouth. His words snap me back to reality,

"You're an amazing kisser. I can only imagine what else you're amazing at. I wanna take you to bed and find out." Ace says.

"You could have any woman you want. You don't need someone horrible enough that she was cheated on." I responded.

"You're only partially right, baby. It's true that I've never had a problem finding a woman. But those women were never anything more than a fuck. There's only one woman I've always loved, and that's you. Let me prove it to you."

"Don't waste your time. Brad told me I'm boring. Actually, boring as fuck is what he said."

"Why would he say that?"

"I'm guessing he found me boring in the sack, since he cheated. In all fairness to me, he only had one move and never once gave me an orgasm."

"A beautiful doll like you?"

"Yeah, right."

"By the time this stay-cation ends, I'm going to prove to you that you're stunning. Come with me."

Words escape me, and all I can do is nod yes. Ace holds out his hand, which I take. He leads me to the elevator. The minute we're inside, his hands are all over me. My entire body's on fire and my panties are soaked. He scoops me up in his arms, and when the doors open, he carries me to his bedroom. He puts me down and just stands there, staring at me.

After a few minutes, he grabs me and pulls me in tight, crushing his lips to mine. I feel his tongue eagerly exploring my mouth and I can barely stand. If he wasn't holding me, I'd have hit the floor.

"Babe, I need to ask you something," Ace says.

"Sure."

"Are you comfortable with me telling you what to do?"

"You mean...in here?" I say shyly.

"Yeah, sweetie."

"Ummm...nobody's ever done that. But, okay."

"I promise I won't be mean." he says, reassuring me.

"Okay."

"Good. Now, get that hot little ass on my bed."

His command excites me, and I climb onto the bed. I'm not normally someone who likes being ordered around, but something about him doing it is exciting. Or, maybe it's where he's doing it that's turning me on.

"Eyes on me, woman." he says sternly.

I watch as he slowly strips for me. I've seen him in only swim trunks before, but never completely naked. When he slides his boxers down and kicks them off, my eyes go wide. Holy shit. I could tell it was big when I saw the bulge in his pants, but damn. I suddenly start to panic. What if I can't handle him? I can't take another man making me feel bad about myself. I start to get up, but his sharp command stops me.

"Don't you dare get off that bed." I try to catch my breath, but I can't. I put my hand over my chest, and I see his face soften. "Riley, are you okay?" I nod, unable to form words. He lies down next to me and caresses my cheek. "Tell me what's wrong," he says softly.

"I'm scared."

"Of what?"

"You," I whisper.

"But, you said you were okay with me ordering you around."

"Not that. I'm afraid of your dick."

"Okay, doll, you need to explain. I'm missing something."

"You're so…ummm…massive. What if I can't handle you?" He starts laughing uncontrollably, but he stops when he sees that I'm not laughing with him.

"I'm sorry, doll, I shouldn't have laughed at you. I promise I'll go slow."

I suddenly realize how stupid and inexperienced I sounded and my face turns bright red.

"Babe, don't be embarrassed. Just lie back, relax, and let me work my magic."

He kisses me softly, as his hands slide under my shirt. His hands feel so good on my skin. I'm thankful I chose a front-closure bra today when I feel him open it with ease. His hands massage my boobs and a moan escapes my lips. He slides my shirt off of me, and tosses it along with my bra onto the floor.

"Baby, so beautiful." he murmurs into my ear.

He covers one of my boobs with his mouth, flicking at my hard nipple with his tongue, while teasing the other with his hand. He runs his tongue down to my stomach, setting my skin on fire. He's so close to where I want him most. My breathing shallows as I anticipate feeling his tongue between my thighs.

"Tell me what you want, doll." Ace says.

I'm too embarrassed, so I keep quiet.

"I guess you don't want anything then. If you can't tell me, I can't pleasure you."

I take a deep breath. "I want to feel your tongue."

"Where?"

"You know where."

"Tell me, woman. I wanna hear those filthy words coming out of that pretty mouth."

"I want your tongue on my pussy. Please, Ace," I beg.

"Mmmm, good girl." He rewards me by swiping his tongue between my folds. He slowly drags it over my clit. Damn, it feels so good. I feel my inhibitions slipping away.

"Oh fuck, Ace, suck my clit hard, baby."

What the hell did I just say? Fuck it. He told me he wanted to hear those words. The smile that appears on his face lets me know he likes what he just heard. He responds by doing exactly what I told him to. I quickly explode and my entire body quivers. He keeps sucking on me as wave after wave of glorious pleasure washes over me. He slides up my body, but doesn't enter me. He opens his mouth to say something, but I beat him to it.

"Please, Ace, I need your cock inside me. NOW!"

"Damn, woman, I want you so fucking much."

I feel him enter. He goes slow, allowing me time to adjust to his size. And damn, does it feel good. His dick touches parts of me that none have before. I'm moaning louder than I've ever done, unable to control myself. I've never felt anything like this. Turns out, it's Brad and not me who's the boring one!

"Mmm, Angus, so good."

"Doll, you feel like heaven."

I feel him continue his slow thrusting and I completely come undone again. I scream out a string of obscenities at the top of my lungs as my body bucks off the bed. He must like what he hears as I feel him empty himself inside me. He emits a long, low growl and lies down next to me, pulling me into his muscular arms.

"It feels so right lying in your arms, Ace."

"Did you realize you called me Angus while we were fucking?"

"I did?"

"Yeah. And it was hot."

"What we just did was hot."

"You handled me like a goddess."

Before I can respond, my stomach growls. I'm mortified, especially when I hear Ace laughing.

"I guess you worked up a bit of an appetite, doll. How about we head downstairs and have some lunch?"

"Sounds good."

We get downstairs, and I'm in awe at the appliances he has around his huge kitchen. I zero in on one of my favorites. "How about quesadillas?" I ask.

"I've never made them. I bought the maker but never tried it."

"You're looking at an expert. They're quick and easy, so I make them quite often for myself. Mind if I snoop in your fridge?"

"Snoop away, my sexy doll."

I grab some shredded cheese and bacon. I ask Ace for a skillet so I can cook the bacon then put the quesadilla together. After it's ready, I cut it up and top it with some salsa.

"Damn, a woman who can cook in the kitchen and the bedroom! Might just have to keep you."

"Dickhead!"

"Damn right."

We finish eating and Ace helps me clean up. Such a difference from Brad, who let me do everything.

"So, doll, this is your vacation. What would you like to do next?"

"I would love a soak in your hot tub. Let's get naked again."

"What have you done with Miss Innocent Riley?"

"You've awakened Riley 2.0."

"Finally!" he cheers.

"Could not agree more. I actually feel alive for the first time in quite a while."

We get in the elevator and head to the second floor. Once we're in his bathroom, he pulls me in close. He crushes his lips to mine, and I can feel his erection straining against his pants. Fuck, I wanna taste him. I pull away from him and get on my knees in front of him. I unfasten his pants and slide them down along with his underwear, freeing the beast. I open wide and take his dick into my mouth. I take him all the way down my throat, surprised that I'm not gagging.

"Fuck, baby, nobody's ever been able to handle me like you."

I suck hard and fast until he fills my mouth. I look up at him and swallow every last delicious drop. All he can do is growl. He removes the rest of his clothing and opens the hot tub while I strip. I can see the hunger in his eyes when he looks at me, and I'm instantly wet. I picture sitting in his lap and riding him. That would make a huge mess, but I fully intend to ride that man in bed later.

We end up soaking in the hot tub until near-dinner time. We dry off and head down to the kitchen. This time he cooks for me. I'm impressed as hell when he places a plate of homemade chicken

Parmesan in front of me. He pours two glasses of wine. We sit at his dining room table, eating, drinking, and laughing.

"How about we head to the living room?" Ace asks after we finish cleaning up.

"Okay."

He snakes his arm around my waist and walks me over to his huge sofa. He pats the cushion next to him, but I pick a different seat. I straddle him and his jaw drops. He puts his arms around me, but before he can say a word, I plant a kiss on his sexy mouth. I run my tongue along his lips and he opens for me, so I jam my tongue into his mouth. I break the kiss.

"I want you out of those pants now," I demand.

He stands, and I can see he's ready for me. He removes his clothes and damn, I love seeing him naked. After he sits back down, I give him a naughty striptease. When I'm done, I sit back in his lap, this time, taking his dick inside me. I hold his broad shoulders as I slide up and down on him. I love being in control like this. I position myself for maximum friction. Each time I slide up his dick, my clit rubs against his rock hard erection. He moves his hands to my ass, squeezing as we fuck.

"Oh, fuck, doll. I can't control myself for another second."

I feel him empty inside me, and that sends me over the edge. My body convulses as I finish. I collapse against his chest.

"Have you always secretly been like this?" Ace asks me breathlessly.

"I have, but Brad wanted no part of it. I once tried to read to him from the naughty book I was reading, and he wouldn't let me."

"What the fuck? That would turn me the hell on. I hope you brought one with you."

"I have a few tucked in my suitcase."

A wicked grin spreads across his face, and I know I'm in for one hell of a staycation. After the day we had, we're both completely spent, so we ride the elevator to the second floor. We didn't even bother getting dressed, and even though the elevator's in his house, it still felt naughty. We climb into his bed. He pulls the cover up and pulls me in close. That's the last thing I remember until morning.

CHAPTER FOUR

Ace

The sunlight pouring in my windows awakens me. I reach over and make sure yesterday wasn't a dream. I feel the soft, silky skin of my baby and I can't help but smile. I still can't believe Riley Cavanaugh is naked in my bed. I run my fingers lightly down her back and she stirs. I watch her turn and face me, a sleepy smile on her face.

"Good morning, beautiful." I whisper.

"Mmmm, good morning, sexy." she responds.

"Care to join me for a shower before we have breakfast?"

"Oh, yes. I'd love to."

I watch her get out of bed and grab her toiletry bag. Damn that woman is hot. We walk down to the bathroom and into the shower stall. I turn the water on and pull her in tight. The hot water feels good, but not as good as having her in my arms. I grab her shower gel and squeeze some into my hand, and wash her. I hear her moan softly as my hands explore her skin. I spend some extra time on that hot ass before I rinse her off. I'm aching to run my fingers through her hair, so I grab her shampoo. I inhale the scent of coconut filling my nose.

I would never admit this to the guys, but there's nothing I love more than the scent of women's hair and body care products, especially when that scent lingers on their delicious bodies. I run the shampoo through her hair and massage her scalp. I hear her moan, and my dick stirs. Everything about this woman excites me.

She looks down and smiles. "I guess you really like my hair."

"Baby, I like everything about you."

"Why? I'm boring."

"Doll, you are about as far from boring as anyone I've ever known."

"You're sweet. Now, it's my turn."

I watch her grab my bottle of Bulgari and squeeze some into her hand. She rubs them together and rubs the lather over my body. I notice she spends a bit longer on my dick than anywhere else. I lose the battle, and I'm hard. Fuck, this woman is so damn hot. She washes my hair then rinses me off. I pull her into an embrace and kiss her hard. The feeling of being this close to her with the hot water streaming down our bodies is too much to take. All I think about is being inside her. But, I talk myself down as I have special plans for later.

We get out, get dried off, and get dressed. We head downstairs and I treat her to my famous French toast. After we finish breakfast, we go out to the backyard.

"Babe, I have an idea that I want to run by you."

"Okay, shoot."

"I thought a camping trip would be fun."

"But, I thought the plan was for me to hide out here so nobody knows what happened."

"It is, which is why the camping trip will be right here in my backyard."

"Really?"

"Yeah, I have a tent and sleeping bags in the garage. We can cook out on the grill. Plus I have a fire pit so we can make s'mores. And hey, if we're so inclined, we could have some special fun in the tent." I wink.

"Mmmm…special fun, huh? I have a feeling I'm going to enjoy that."

"So, sound good?"

"Yes it does."

"Cool. For now, how about a dip in the pool?"

"I'd love to. I just need to grab my suit."

"Nah, you don't need it."

"What?"

"Come skinny dipping with me, woman!"

"I can't do that!"

"Why not? I have a privacy fence. Nobody will see us."

"But, I'm not attractive enough." She whispers.

"Doll, you're stunning, I couldn't take my eyes off of you the whole time we were fucking yesterday."

"Still, though…"

"Come on, baby. You said you wanted to be more unpredictable. Get that ass naked and jump in that pool."

"What the hell! Let's go."

I watch Riley run out to the backyard and start stripping. I run out after her just as she jumps in, laughing and splashing around. I love seeing this playful side of her. At that moment, I realize I'm completely in love with this woman, and I always have been. I jump in and swim over to her. I try to grab her but as soon as I get close, she splashes me and swims away. She's in trouble now!

"I'm gonna get you, doll."

"We'll see about that."

She swims away again, but this time I catch her and pull her in close. She tries to pull away but I won't let go. I start tickling her as she laughs hysterically. I've always loved that sound, especially when she does that cute snort. We swim for another hour, then I climb out and grab a couple of towels. I watch Riley climb out of the pool and I'm awestruck by her beauty. I wrap her in a towel, pull her in close, and lay a kiss on her.

"Mmm, I have a feeling I know what's going to happen in that tent tonight." she teases.

"Just you wait, woman."

We get dressed and head to the garage so I can get things set up for later. After we get the tent setup, we head back inside and sit down on the couch, still in our towels. I want this woman so damn bad, I'm not sure I can wait until tonight. And her sitting there in just a towel gives me easy access. I'm craving a taste of that sweet spot between those sexy legs. I stand up, move in front of her, and drop to my knees. I open the towel and admire her sexy curves.

"Spread those beautiful legs, baby. I need to taste you."

She opens her legs for me, and my eyes immediately travel to that sweet pussy.

"I can't believe I'm saying this but I'm turned on by you staring at me like that."

"Is that so, doll? I could sit and look at you all day, but right now, all I want is to take you to heaven with my tongue."

"Yes, please, baby."

I place a hand on each of her shapely thighs and open her legs even wider. I run my tongue up and down her pussy, and fuck, she tastes so damn good. I continue my assault on her until I feel her body quake. I stop and stand up.

"Okay, doll, get on your knees on the couch, facing the back and spread those legs again."

She does as she's told, and after admiring her ass for a few minutes, I lower myself onto the couch and put my head between her thighs. Time to turn this up a notch. I intend to bring out the dirty lioness that lives inside this goddess.

"I wanna watch you get yourself off. Get those hips moving."

I keep my tongue out as she drags that hot pussy back and forth. I watch her tits bouncing as she fucks my tongue and I can barely control myself. I stop her movement and wrap my lips around her swollen clit, sucking hard until she comes hard. I need my dick inside her now.

"Baby, I want you in my lap but with your back against my chest."

"Mmm, Ace." she murmurs as she lowers herself into my lap, taking my dick deep inside. She slides up and down my dick and shit, it feels incredible. I tease her already-sensitive clit with my fingers as she leans back against my chest. I love feeling every part of this woman against me. She quickly sends me over the edge and I empty inside her. She doesn't move off my lap, so I wrap my arms around her, running my hands up and down her body.

"Oh, baby, you truly were made for me. Your body fits mine perfectly, and I can't get enough of you."

I stop short of telling her I love her. I'm not quite ready to say those words yet. But I definitely do. Ten days with this woman is not nearly enough. What if she doesn't feel the same way? I need to find a way to convince her that we belong together. I don't want to be with any other woman, ever.

"Angus, that was incredible. I was satisfied with my sex life before you, but I realize now how much I was missing."

"There's so much more I can show you, baby."

"Oh god, yes please. Teach me everything."

"Damn," is all I can muster. "For now, I think we need to grab a shower. When we're done, are you ready to start our camping adventure?"

"I can't wait. I love…camping."

Holy shit, she almost said it. The thing I most want to hear and the thing I most want to say. I let it go for now, but I will make sure she hears it before these ten days have passed.

After a quick shower, we get in our pajamas and head to the kitchen to grab what we need. She helps me carry everything out while I light the fire pit. We cook hot dogs over the fire pit. After we finish eating, I put some music on, and ask her to dance.

I don't take my eyes off of her beautiful face as we sway together to the music. The warm grass feels good on my bare feet. Suddenly, it hits me that I'm standing in my backyard in pajamas with my best friend and I can't stop myself from laughing.

"What's so funny?" she asks.

"I was just thinking about this whole scenario. The two of us dancing in my backyard in pajamas with a tent set up just reminds me of our youth. All those backyard campouts we had. One thing about having your parents and my parents always going to parties for their job gave us the chance to do anything we wanted. If only they could see us now."

"No thank you. I do just fine without them."

"I hear that. I'm sorry I brought them up."

"It's all good. All I care about is being here right now."

She looks up at the sky and a smile appears on her pretty face.

"Remember laying in the grass looking at the stars?" she asks.

"I sure do. Wanna do that?"

"Yeah."

We lay down next to each other, gazing up at the night sky. The moon is full tonight and looks beautiful. It's beauty, though, pales in comparison to my Riley. I grab her hand and she intertwines her fingers with mine.

"I would always think about what the future held for me when we did this." I say.

"And what did you see?"

"Pretty much the life I ended up with. I always knew I wanted to play music. I used to watch shows like MTV's Cribs, and I was determined I would have that lifestyle someday. And I got it. But, I didn't like it."

"What's not to like?"

"I didn't like the fairness of it all. Don't get me wrong. I love my success but there was always something missing. Even here, having my dream home, it's still not enough."

"What else could you possibly want?"

"Not what, but who. The thing that's always been missing is someone to share it with. Not someone who's here because of the glamor of it all, but someone who loves me for me. Like, someone who knew me before the fame. Someone like the amazing, sexy, smart, talented Riley Cavanaugh."

"I'm really not that special. Just ask Brad."

"The hell you aren't. He's an asshole for not realizing what he had with you."

"Right. If I'm so wonderful, why did he think nothing of throwing me away like a piece of garbage?" She grumbles.

"I honestly have no idea. You're by far the most intriguing woman I've ever known. I thought I knew everything there was to know about you, but I was wrong. The woman who's spent these first two days driving me absolutely wild is something I never expected."

"Well, she's always been there somewhere. Just that nobody ever let her come out and play. Until now."

Before I get a chance to say another word, she's on top of me. I watch, drooling, as she slowly lifts her top off and tosses it aside. Her naked breasts look even more incredible in the moonlight. I want her so damn bad, I can taste it. She quickly strips me naked. My dick's standing at full attention as she runs her hands all over my chest. I slide her bottoms and panties off, loving the feeling of her warm skin.

Still straddling me, she lowers her head and crushes her lips to mine. I feel her tongue in my mouth. All I can think about is having my dick inside her. She moves her lips to my neck then drags her tongue across my throat and down my chest. I'm aching to feel her wrapped around me, but she's still using her tongue on me. I watch her lick down my abs as she moans. I can't take another second of this sweet torture.

"Please, baby, I need to be inside you. NOW!"

"My, my. Eager aren't we."

She ignores my begging and moves down to my inner thighs. She sucks them one at a time and I just about blow my load on the spot. Damn, this woman is trying to kill me. Finally, she slides back up my body and takes me inside her. I watch in awe as she slides up and down my dick, her sexy tits bouncing like crazy. I let out a deep growl when she leans forward and starts sucking my neck. Everything this woman does drives me crazy.

"Oh baby, you feel so good. Ride me hard baby. I love how incredible your pussy feels."

She rides me faster and harder until I fill her. She keeps riding until her body quakes and she screams. She collapses on my chest and kisses me with more passion than anything I've ever felt. That's all it takes and I'm hard again. I'm still inside her, so I roll us over until she's on her back. She wraps her legs around my waist as I fuck her.

"Oh Ace, harder baby. You feel so damn good inside me. Mmmm…baby."

I keep up my hard and fast pace until again I empty inside her. She follows close behind, shaking even harder this time. She screams so loud, I think they heard her in the next county. I lie next to her and pull her close. We're both drenched in sweat, chests heaving from the most incredible sex I've ever had.

"Damn, woman, I think I need a dip in the pool to cool off. Care to join me?"

"Damn right, let's go Mr. Sexy."

We get in the pool and the water feels amazing. She splashes me and takes off, but I quickly catch her and pull her into an embrace. She tries to wiggle away but when she can't, she moves her hands to my ass and squeezes me hard. Damn she's naughty. She starts tickling my sides. We're laughing hysterically, holding each other tight as the water cools our skin.

I lift her up into my arms and she wraps hers around my neck. I kiss her tenderly and sit her down on the edge of the pool. She grabs two towels for us to dry off. I climb out and take one. After we're dry, we get back in our pajamas and again lay in the grass to stargaze. Everything feels different now that we've said those words. Different in a good way, though. She lets out a big yawn. No surprise after the day we had. I get up and help her up. We walk over to the tent. I zip the two sleeping bags together so I can hold her. We kiss goodnight and she quickly falls asleep. I watch her for a few minutes. That's the last thing I remember until the sun lights up our tent the next morning.

CHAPTER FIVE

Riley

I'm awakened by the sound of an acoustic guitar. I sit up and see Ace sitting next to me, quietly strumming. I slide over and lay my head on his shoulder while he continues playing. From the first time he ever picked up a guitar, I knew he was special. The man never took one single lesson. He would listen to a song and just start playing it. We would sit up in his bedroom for hours, me just listening to him play all our favorite songs. I tear up at the memory, still in shock at what these last two days have brought me. I hear him stop playing.

"Doll, is everything okay?"

"Yes, sorry. These are happy tears. I was thinking about how you used to play guitar for me in your room."

He pulls me in close and says, "How are you really, though, after what Brad did?"

"Brad who? Seriously, though, I really am okay and that's all thanks to you. In just two short days, you've reminded me that I'm just as much a person as anyone else. Not to mention the holy-shit-that-was-incredible pleasure you've been giving me. I don't know if you ever knew, but I secretly had a crush on you pretty much from middle school on."

"I had no idea. I must confess something. You weren't the only one hiding their feelings. I was always interested in being more than friends. I never said anything because I didn't know if you felt the same way. I was afraid that if you didn't, it would hurt our friendship. I knew I didn't want you out of my life, so I kept it quiet."

"Then why did you leave me and lose touch?"

"I'm so sorry about that, but I promise it had nothing to do with you. You remember how hard school was for us. My self-worth was at an all-time low by graduation. In my head, the only thing I could think of doing was getting out of here and starting over. I was selfish, never giving any thought to what, or more importantly, who I was leaving behind."

"You weren't selfish. I completely understand. That lack of self-confidence stayed with me. Even though I was successful at my job, I never let myself believe it. It's also why I let Brad treat me the way he did for so long. I should have sent him packing, but in my mind, I was being treated exactly the way I deserved."

"What did he do to you? And if you're not ready to tell me, I understand."

"I've never told anyone. It might help me finally move past it if I do, but I feel bad burdening you with it."

"Don't! I want to listen," he pleads.

"Okay. He never hurt me physically, but in a way, what he did was worse, at least for me. It was constant put-downs and mean-spirited comments. He didn't like the way I did anything. I remember one meal I cooked, and I was so proud of it. He took one bite, spit it on the table, and shoved the plate across the table. Food went everywhere. He screamed at me to clean it up and he stormed out to go get something to eat. He never had one nice word to say about the way I looked or anything. He left me thinking I was this hideous creature."

I pause to take a breath, then continue. "You have no idea how close I came to not getting in that limo. Even as I rode over here, I almost had Bruce take me back home. When you thanked him and called me a beauty, I can tell you that I thought you needed your eyes examined. But you've shown me that I am actually worth something and I don't know how to thank you."

"You already have. For the first time since I left for LA, I don't feel alone. And before you say it, yes, I know I was always surrounded by people, but I was still lonely."

"How could you still feel lonely?"

"Because none of them were you, Riley."

"Oh, Ace." I smile.

"Okay, enough of this mushy stuff. What do you want to do today?"

"I really want to go somewhere. Don't get me wrong, I love your house, I just feel like a change of scenery. But, not somewhere around here."

"I have an idea. Do you trust me enough to keep it a surprise?"

"Absolutely."

"Okay. I'll be back. I need to make a couple of calls."

"I'm so excited."

"Me too, doll!"

I walk over to the bench in Ace's garden while he goes inside. I can't wait to see where he's taking me and what he has in store for me. So far, pretty much all we've done is have sex. I'm certainly not complaining, but I think a certain body part of mine needs a break!

Though I suspect if he flashed me that sexy look, I'd be putty in his oh-so-capable hands. My thoughts totally go on a tangent and I start thinking about the locked door from my tour of the house. I really want to ask him about it, or even better, see it. I'm debating on whether I'm excited or scared to see what's in there. I'm so lost in thought, I don't hear Ace come back outside.

"All set, doll," he announces, as I jump out of my skin.

"I totally did not hear you come back."

"Sorry, babe. But we need to go get ready. Bruce will be here in about half an hour."

"Oh my god, we're taking the limo?"

"Damn right. My girl travels in style! Plus, with the tinted windows, nobody will see you." He winks at me.

"Can we make out while we're riding?"

"Damn, woman, is that all you think about?"

"Hell yeah, sexy."

We head up to his bedroom to pack.

"You'll need enough clothes for three days, babe."

"Okay. I can't wait to find out where we're going."

"You'll know when we get there."

After we pack, we go to Ace's living room to wait for Bruce. He arrives right on time. After he opens the door for us, he puts our bags in the trunk and we head off to our mystery destination.

***

About two hours later, we arrive. Ace and I spent most of the ride kissing, so I never took notice of a single sign. He rolls down the window so I can look out. I squeal with delight when I see where we are.

"Oh my god, Ace, oh my god! I've wanted to come here since it opened, but dick-for-brains wouldn't bring me."

"So that means I get to pop your Hard Rock cherry!"

"Mmmm."

I look and we're sitting outside the VIP entrance. Bruce comes around and opens the door. I get out and Ace follows me. A bellhop comes over and loads our luggage. He waits for us inside. Ace arranges with Bruce when to pick us up. Once he pulls away, we walk inside. The bellhop leads us to the VIP check-in, bypassing the long line of people in the regular check-in. I'm feeling a bit spoiled.

After Ace finishes checking in, the bellhop leads us to the elevator. We're on the 17th floor of the South Tower in a huge suite. My eyes go wide when I walk inside. Ace tips the bellhop then walks over to me and pulls me in close.

"Might this be to your liking, my darling?" he asks.

"Oh yes, good sir. It pleases me greatly."

"And what would my lady like to do?"

I look around. "Sorry, no lady here. Just a horny bitch," I say, laughing.

Before I realize what's happening, I'm over Ace's shoulder and on my way to the suite's bedroom. I bang on his ass like it's a pair of bongos. He puts me down on the bed and lays next to me. We quickly strip each other naked. He fucks me hard and fast, both of us quickly exploding together. I love the long, sexy sessions, but damn, those quickies are hot as hell. We grab a quick shower and get dressed.

"So, what's on the agenda?" I ask.

"I thought we could hit the casino for a while then the boardwalk. I also have something special planned for dinner."

"That sounds perfect."

We're walking around the casino when I see a sign advertising a poker tournament starting tomorrow. A well-kept secret about me is my penchant for playing online. I would really love to enter but I see it's a five-thousand dollar buy-in. I sigh loudly, knowing that's outside what I can safely spend.

"What's Wong, doll?"

Pointing at the sign, I say, "I would love to enter that."

"Wait, you play poker?"

"Yeah, I've been playing online for years. I got hooked after watching a World Series of Poker tournament on TV."

"Damn, girl, any other secrets you've been keeping?"

"That's for me to know and you to try to find out."

"Brat. Now, about the tourney. You should enter."

"I would, but that entry fee is too much for me."

"What if you had a sponsor who paid the fee?"

"A sponsor?"

"Yeah, me."

"I can't ask you to do that."

"You're not asking. Come with me." We walk over to the area where the sign says to register. There's a casino employee named Art sitting at the table.

"May I help you?" Art asks.

"My woman would like to register for the poker tournament," Ace replies.

"Name, please," Art says.

"Riley Cavanaugh. C-a-v-a-n-a-u-g-h."

"I'll need to see your ID, ma'am," Art says. I take out my wallet and show him my license. He nods. "Now, there's just the matter of your entry fee."

"I'll be paying that," Ace answers and hands a credit card to Art.

Art runs the card and once it's approved, he hands a slip to Ace to sign. He then hands me a sheet with the rules and any other information. "Good luck, ma'am," Art says, sneering. We head back towards the casino.

"So, I see he's another asshat who thinks women can't win at poker," I say.

"Are you any good? I didn't mean that the way it sounded, just curious."

"I've won quite a few online tournaments and that's without being able to see my opponents. With this, I'll be able to watch for tells."

"Damn, who are you, Riley?"

"Time changes people." I laugh.

"Definitely for the better in your case, babe."

"You too, Ace. Now, how about some penny slots?"

"Lead the way, beautiful."

We walk around until I see a game that looks fun, called Piggy Bankin'. We sit down at two of the machines and start playing. After only a couple of spins, I hit the bonus game and end up winning a decent amount. Ace has the same good luck and after an hour, we've both got a nice total built up. We decide to cash it out before our luck changes. He puts the tickets in his wallet until we're ready to cash them in.

"What do you say we hit the boardwalk and do some people-watching?" Ace asks.

"Okay. When I was younger and my parents brought me to Ocean City, I would sit on the boardwalk and make up funny stories about all the people."

"You should be writing."

"I wrote some of them down back then, but never did anything with them. I prefer to read, especially all the smutty books."

"I like the sound of that. I'm still waiting for you to read some to me so we can act them out."

"I packed one for our trip here."

"Well, I know one thing we'll be doing then, my naughty woman."

"That bed will never be the same!"

"Who said anything about bed?"

"Oh my, Ace!"

We walk over to a bench and sit down. There's a lot of foot traffic and it's full of some very interesting characters. I feel Ace's arm move around my shoulders, so I lay my head on his shoulder. These last few days have been the happiest I've ever experienced. I can only imagine what the rest of our time together is going to be like. Ace's voice interrupts my daydream.

"Let's head back inside. I have a couple of surprises before dinner." We head back inside and walk over to the South Tower elevators. Ace presses the button for 3 instead of our floor.

"Where are we going?" I ask.

"This is the first of your many surprises, my doll."

We reach the third floor and step out. I see a sign pointing to the hotel spa. Ace takes my hand as we walk to the Rock Spa & Salon. We're immediately greeted by a woman named Jasmine.

"Right this way, Mr. London, Miss Cavanaugh," Jasmine says.

She leads us to a private room with two massage tables next to each other.

"Enjoy your couples' massage. Make yourselves comfortable on the tables. Your masseuses will be in shortly."

Jasmine leaves, closing the door behind her. I've never had a massage before and I'm a little nervous, so I just stand there staring at Ace. He points at the towels hanging on the wall.

"Just strip down, lie face down on the table and cover that sexy ass with the towel," he says, showing me those sexy dimples.

"Thanks. Sorry I'm so dumb."

"Stop that, woman!"

I get comfortable on the table and watch Ace strip down and lie on the table next to me, I need another towel to wipe the drool off my chin. I hear a knock on the door and Ace tells them to come in. A man and woman enter the room to give us our massages. Ace and I hold hands and gaze into each other's eyes the entire time. Once the massages are over, the two employees leave the room so we can get dressed.

"Thank you for this. I really needed it," I say.

"My pleasure, doll."

"It will be later."

"I like the sound of that. Now off to your next surprise. Come with me." Ace walks me to the salon and we're again greeted by Jasmine.

"Our expert Marco will be joining us shortly," she tells us. "Miss Cavanaugh, please have a seat." Jasmine points to the end chair.

I sit down while Ace follows her out of the salon. What else does he have planned for me? I'm sitting for a few minutes when

Marco comes in. He looks at me from several angles before he walks over to the chair.

"Oh yes, I can work with this. You're already beautiful. I'll make you stunning," Marco says.

"Thank you," I respond.

An hour later, I look in the mirror and a new and improved Riley looks back at me. My dark brown hair now has golden highlights and is about six inches shorter. The style really suits my face. For the first time in a long time, I feel good about how I look. A few minutes later, Ace comes back into the salon and I hear a loud whistle escape his lips.

"You're stunning. Marco, wow."

Marco smiles as he walks out of the room. Ace takes my hand and walks me down the hall where Jasmine is standing outside yet another room. She takes me inside and I see a rack of evening gowns and a few closed cases. I can't believe my eyes.

"She's in good hands, Mr. London," Jasmine says as she whisks me into the room and closes the door. "Time to knock that man's pants off," Jasmine says.

I try on several dresses before I find the one. The dress is emerald green satin. The material feels amazing against my skin and I force myself to admit that I look great. The dress shows just enough of my cleavage that Ace is going to drool. The slit in the dress shows off my left leg with each step I take. We settle on black shoes with a low heel.

"Time now for accessories. Mr. London has spared no expense," Jasmine says.

By the time we're done, I have a tiara, emerald earrings and a matching diamond bracelet and necklace. I feel like a princess. All of a sudden a wave of something I can't describe washes over me, and I need to sit down. Jasmine rushes over.

"Are you okay, miss?" she asks.

"I can't do this. I don't deserve to be treated like this."

"If I may, can I offer some advice, ma'am?"

"Please."

"Someone made you feel this way and whoever that someone is, they are dead wrong. No man does all of this for a woman unless she's someone very special. Embrace the woman that you are. I see the way Mr. London looks at you. There's a hunger in his eyes."

"Thank you so much for saying that."

"One more piece of advice. Go commando tonight. He'll worship you for it, if you know what I mean," she says with a wink.

"Oh, I do know. Thank you for everything today."

"It was my pleasure. Now, let's wrap everything up so he's surprised when he sees you tonight."

Jasmine walks me out to the front, where Ace is waiting for me. He takes care of paying for everything and leaves a tip for everyone who helped today. We walk to the elevator to head up to our room. We shower together but I won't allow him to see me get ready. It's my turn to surprise him. I take Jasmine's advice and only put a bra on. The girls are a bit too big to go commando upstairs. Downstairs on the other hand, well, he'll have easy access.

Once I get my dress and shoes on, I put on the tiara and jewelry. I'm starting to feel nervous again, but I take a deep breath and remember what Jasmine said to me. I peek out and see Ace standing there in a white suit with a navy blue shirt and I almost pass out cold. He looks incredible. I can't bring myself to come out of the room. Damn that fuckosaurus rex ex-boyfriend for doing this to me.

"I'm ready," I say quietly.

"Well, then, come out here and let me see you, doll." I walk out and see Ace's jaw drop.

"I look that bad?" I ask.

"You're fucking stunning, woman. Holy shit."

I feel my cheeks get hot as Ace eyes me up and down. He licks his lips and my breath hitches in my throat. I start thinking about his hands on me. Wait until he finds out I'm not wearing panties. But, that will be my secret until later.

"Where are we headed?" I ask.

"You'll find out, baby. Shall we?"

"Yes, please. Are you sure this isn't too much? Jasmine said I needed the accessories."

"Doll, it's perfect."

I smile as Ace holds out his arm. I link my arm through his and we head to the elevators. He leads me across the casino floor to the boardwalk exit. I look out and see a portion of the beach closed off with red velvet ropes. A long red carpet leads to the ropes. I look inside the ropes and see a small iron table and two chairs.

We walk down the beach entrance and cross the carpet. When we get closer, I see a silver bucket with a bottle sticking out and two glasses. A waiter moves the rope aside, allowing us to enter. We sit down at the table and the waiter pours us each a glass of champagne. He lets us know our dinner will be served shortly and heads back inside.

"What's for dinner?" I ask.

"A seafood feast."

"That sounds delicious."

"Not as delicious as you in that dress."

"Thank you."

A few minutes later, a group of waiters comes by with a small table and a couple trays of food. I see shrimp, crab legs, and lobster tails, along with rice and asparagus. My stomach starts growling. I can't wait to dig into some crab legs. One of the waiters hands us bibs with lobsters on them to protect our clothing while we eat. I start with a snow crab cluster, one of my favorites.

"Baby, watching you eat and handle those crab legs is getting me hot."

"Is there anything that doesn't get you hot, Mr. Hornypants?"

He smiles but doesn't say a word. I have a feeling we're gonna have some fun later.

After we finish eating, we clean up our hands with the wipes we were provided. The moon and the sun have swapped places. The night sky is clear so all the stars are visible. The moon's reflection off the ocean is beautiful. The waiters return and clear everything away. They hand a bag to Ace, then return to the hotel.

Ace grabs a blanket out of the bag and spreads it out. "Come lay with me, please, baby." he says.

I lay down and he takes me into his arms, kissing me hard. His tongue in my mouth gets me wet. He runs a hand up my leg and under my dress. When he finds my little surprise, he breaks the kiss and just stares at me.

"My naughty, naughty woman."

I'm about to respond when he moves between my legs. I feel his tongue between my folds, and I moan loudly. He quickly sends me over the edge with his powerful tongue. We spend the next several hours fucking on the beach until we're both completely exhausted. We get dressed and return to our suite. We get undressed and crawl into bed naked. I don't remember much after Ace turned off the light and kissed me goodnight.

CHAPTER SIX

Ace

I wake up in the morning, and I'm alone in bed. I walk out and see Riley sitting at the table in the living room with her laptop open.

"What'cha doin', babe?" I ask her.

"I woke up and couldn't fall back to sleep. I decided to use the time to play some online poker to make sure my skills are sharp for today."

"I can't wait to watch you in action."

"I'm nervous and excited all at the same time. I do have a slight advantage in that men tend not to take women seriously. If they underestimate me, it will work in my favor."

"We need to get you fueled up. Hard Rock Cafe for breakfast?"

"Sounds good!"

I take her hand as we ride down to the casino floor. We walk over to the cafe and get seated. We order breakfast and coffee.

"Still good, doll?"

"I am, but could I ask a favor?"

"Anything, baby."

"After breakfast, can we take a walk on the beach before I have to sign in? The ocean will calm me so I can stay focused for the game."

"Your wish is my command."

She smiles at me and my insides turn to mush. I love this woman more than I ever knew was possible, but I can never tell her.

After we finish breakfast, I pay the check Riley's quiet as we walk to the exit for the beach so I don't say anything. I know she's trying to get herself in the right mindset for the tournament. I put an arm around her as we walk, smiling when I feel her lay her head on my shoulder. After we've walked for a bit, she sits down. I join her and return my arm to her shoulders, as again her head finds my shoulder. I wish I could freeze this moment.

About half an hour before the tournament check in opens, we walk back into the casino and over to the table. I stand in line with Riley and start scoping out her competition. She's the only woman in line so far. I see some of the other men looking at her with smirks on their faces. Little do they know she's no slouch and she certainly isn't stupid. But, like she said, best to let them think she is.

When it's her turn to check in, I see my first glimpse of my woman in action. A casino employee is sitting at the table checking in all the players.

"Name, please," he says to Riley.

"Riley Catacombs." She giggles. "I mean, Riley Cavanaugh. I forgot my last name for a second."

I try my damnedest not to react. I watch everyone else standing in line and most of them are laughing and gesturing at her, She pretends not to notice any of it. I watch her plaster a dopey grin on her face. They point her to the right and she starts to turn left, gives another giggle then heads the right way. I hear one of the men say he hopes he's at her table so he knows he won't be the first one eliminated. Be careful what you wish for, asshole, I think to myself.

We get into the room and there's two signs separated by a rope. One sends spectators to their seating area and the other sends players to the tables. There's a line of competitors waiting so I decide to help her out a bit. Before I head over to the seating area, I give her a quick kiss.

"Good luck, Riley. Don't forget, you're playing poker, not your favorite game, Go Fish," I say.

Not missing a beat, she replies, "I am? Oh no, did I sign up for the wrong tournament again? Oh well, guess I'll play anyway."

She flashes me the slightest smile then heads to the players area, so I lose sight of her. I take a seat in the front row so I have a good view of her while she's playing. I can't wait to see her make an ass out of those jerks. About half an hour later, poker legend Phil Hellmuth walks out to the area where the tables are set up. Riley must be freaking out, as she told me he's the one who got her hooked on Texas Hold 'Em.

"Welcome to today's tournament, everyone. The games will begin shortly. Our players are finding out their table assignments as we speak. As players start to get eliminated, we'll combine tables until we have our final nine players. Those nine players will get a small break then the final table will begin. We'll continue until one player remains. That player will win our grand prize of one hundred thousand dollars. And here come our players now."

Phil stands and waits for everyone to be seated and set their chip stacks how they want them. Once each table has a dealer, he turns his microphone back on.

"Best of luck to all our players. There's only one thing left to say. Shuffle up and deal!"

It doesn't take long for some of the less-skilled players to get eliminated. I watch the big screens set up and see Riley pretend to now know what she was doing for a couple of hands, just to lull her competitors into a false sense of security. Since then, she's already forced two men all-in and eliminated them.

Several hours pass and nine tables have now dwindled down to two. Of course, my woman's still playing, and she's currently sitting in third place in terms of chip count. A couple more hours pass, and the final table is set. Most of the spectators have gone, and I'm guessing those remaining are family and friends of the final nine. Phil again comes to the floor.

"We have our final table. The players will take a 15 minute break, then we'll get started. May the best man or woman win," Phil says to the remaining crowd.

The players return and are assigned seats. Riley has her back to me, which is probably better for her concentration. I sit and watch as player after player eventually busts out and only the top three remain, Riley has moved into second place, only about 1000 chips less than the first place player. The third place player only has about one-quarter the chips of my woman. He only makes it a few hands before Riley puts him all-in and finishes him off with queens full of aces.

Riley's opponent's name is Jason. Riley and Jason are seated at opposite ends of the table, across from the dealer. It only takes a few hands for Riley to overtake the chip lead. From there, she's a force to be reckoned with, and about 90 minutes in, she has Jason all-in. If he pulls this out, it will deliver a serious blow to her chip stack. He turns over kings full of aces and everyone gasps. There's only three hands that beat his. Because of his high cards, she can't tie him. All eyes are on the screen, waiting for Riley to show her hand. I jump out of my seat when I see four queens appear on the screen.

"You did it, baby," I scream out.

Jason walks over and shakes Riley's hand, as Phil returns one more time to wrap things up.

"I'd like to congratulate both players for surviving until the end. But, there can only be one winner. This year's tournament is one for the history books, as we have our first female champion, Riley Cavanaugh," Phil says as he tips the microphone toward my girl.

"Thank you so much. I can't believe this is real."

Phil presents her with her trophy and her prize money as I walk down. I grab her and twirl her around in my arms. There's a small reception in the back of the room, so she and I walk back. This is the most confident I've ever seen her and I couldn't be prouder of my badass woman. We walk over to where Phil is standing.

"I need to give you an extra special thank you for this," she says to him.

"Why is that?"

"You're the reason I got hooked on poker. I was home watching The World Series of Poker back in 1989. After seeing what you did in that tournament, I started playing."

"Thank you for saying that and for watching. That was an amazing year for me."

"I can't even imagine the excitement of winning that level of tourney."

"It's definitely a feeling like no other."

"I hope I'm not overstepping, but would you be willing to sign my registration paper?" she asks.

"My pleasure."

As Phil was signing her paper, a casino employee approaches to grab Phil, Riley, and Jason for a couple of pictures. They take her email address as she'll be sent copies. We will definitely be framing those. After the reception ends, we're given an escort to our room because of the prize money, which we lock in the room safe. It's almost one in the morning when we're finally back in our room.

"Baby, I'm so proud of you. Those dudes never knew what hit 'em. The irony of it wasn't lost on me."

"What do you mean?"

"Babe, you beat his three kings with four queens! Just like my queen beat all those kings."

"In the excitement of it all, I didn't even think about that. Right now, though, all I can think about is my head on that pillow."

"Me too."

We get ready for bed and crawl under the covers together. I pull her in tight and kiss her goodnight. She's quickly sound asleep in my arms, and that's the last thing I remember.

CHAPTER SEVEN

Riley

I'm awakened the next morning by lips sucking on my neck and something hard poking me in the ass.

"Good morning, Mr. Horny," I tease.

"Good morning, poker queen," Ace responds.

Before I realize what's happening I'm somehow out of my pajamas, and he's on top of me. We enjoy a quick, hard fuck then get up and shower. We're heading back home today, but I don't mind. I'm still flying high from my exciting tournament win. We decided to cut the trip a day early before anyone found out what room we were staying in, given the prize money in our safe.

Once we're dressed and packed, Ace calls for a bellhop. The concierge also sends a guard to escort us to the lobby. I see Bruce standing outside the limo when we're escorted outside.

"Congratulations, Miss Cavanaugh," Bruce says once we're inside the car.

"Thank you so much," I respond. He smiles then starts the drive back to Ace's house.

After he drops us off, I ask Ace for a favor, since I don't have my car here. "Would you mind driving me to the bank so I can deposit this?" I ask.

"Of course. I have an idea for today's adventure when we're done. What bank are you with?"

"The one on Main Street."

"My suggestion is we call and make an appointment to handle the deposit privately, given the amount."

"Good idea. Give me a moment to call."

I hang up and let Ace know they have availability now, so we head out to Ace's garage. He hadn't shown me the garage during our tour. My jaw drops when I see what's inside. I gasp when I see it.

"Oh my god! A 1957 Ford Fairlane in official Flame Red. And it's a convertible!" I squeal.

"Wait, you know cars? Where did that come from?"

"My grandpa had one. I absolutely loved it. He taught me to drive in that car."

"You're in luck, as that's what we're taking today."

"Yay!" I exclaim, bouncing and clapping.

Ace puts Sirius XM's Hair Nation on and we start driving to the bank. He parks as close as he can and holds me tight as I clutch the briefcase tight. I let one of the tellers know I have an appointment, so she calls the bank manager and he comes out to get us.

"Good afternoon. My name is William. What can I do for you today?"

I give William a short version of how I got the money and that I wanted to deposit it. We discuss some options. I end up putting half into my savings account and investing the remaining amount. Once we finish all the necessary paperwork, William hands me my receipts and copies of the papers, then walks us back to the lobby.

"Thank you for your business, Miss Cavanaugh. Enjoy the rest of your afternoon." William says.

"Thank you, sir." I respond. We walk out to Ace's car, but he walks to the passenger's side and tosses me the keys. My jaw drops. I can't believe he's letting me drive. "Are you sure?" I ask in disbelief.

"You bet, doll. Let's see what you can do."

"You know I can handle a stick, babe."

"Yes, ma'am, I sure as hell do," he laughs.

I drive us to a diner we used to eat in all the time when we were in high school. After we finish lunch, he takes over driving. He takes us down some country roads and there's no other traffic for miles, so he floors it. The wind blowing through my hair feels amazing, as we both sing at the top of our lungs. We drive for another couple of hours.

"Would you like to stop for some dinner?" Ace asks.

"I'd love to." We drive for another hour when I spot a cute little outdoor café. "Can we stop here?" I ask.

Ace pulls into the parking lot, and we walk inside. We both order a burger, fries, and a chocolate milkshake. We enjoy our dinner and even more, each other's company. We spend a couple of hours at the café, laughing and talking. I'm having some strong feelings for him, but I'm not sure if it's real or just me trying to deal with the pain my ex-fuckface caused me, so I don't say anything.

After we leave the cafe, Ace starts driving back to his house. We're about a half-hour away from his house when he pulls into a scenic overlook and parks the car.

"I thought we could watch the sunset together before we head back to my house," he says.

"That sounds perfect."

"How about we climb into the backseat?"

"Mmmm, naughty..." I tease.

We climb in the backseat. Ace puts his arms around me, and I rest my head on his shoulder as we watch the sun descend. The colors are breathtaking, though not quite as breathtaking as the man holding me. Once the sun was out of sight, we got back into the front seat and finished the drive home.

Once we were inside, Ace asked, "Would you like to get a snack?"

"Yes, I'm hungry."

With the naughty gleam in his eye, he replied, "Me too, baby."

Ace pulled her into his arms again. I could really get used to this man holding me in those sexy, muscular arms. "Baby, we've had some pretty incredible sex so far, but there are some new positions I'd love to try."

"Yes, please, my sexy rock god."

We ride the elevator to his bedroom and we were naked in record speed. We lay down in bed and Ace flashes me the naughtiest smile I've ever seen.

"Did I ever tell you what my favorite number is?" he asked.

"No, but I am curious!"

Not at all surprisingly, Ace responded, "69." I feel a sensation run through my stomach and my heart starts pounding in my chest. "I wanna do that with you. Come sit on my face and wrap that pretty mouth around my cock."

"But..."

"But what, woman?"

"I'm afraid I'll hurt you."

"Stop that, woman. Now get on my face so I can taste that sweet pussy."

I crawl over to Ace and straddle his head. I feel his tongue on my pussy, and I moan. I lower my head and wrap my mouth around his hot dick. Fuck, he tastes so good. I feel his fingers slide in and out of me while he drives me wild with his tongue. I hear him growling as he pleasures me. I tease his balls with my fingers while I suck him hard. My entire body quakes as I start to come undone. He fingers me harder, and I explode on his face.

"Fuck, woman, that was hot," he says as he empties into my mouth.

I climb off and face him so he can see me swallow him. I lick my lips, and he growls again. I've never done that before, and I didn't know what I was missing.

"Now, woman, I wanna be inside you. Get on your knees and lower your chest to the bed." I do as I'm told. "Good girl. Now, get ready for a pounding like you've never felt."

I emit something that sounds like a tigress growling as Ace grabs my waist. I feel his dick slide into my pussy hard and fast. I feel him smack my ass while he fucks me. Feeling bold, I turn things up a notch and tease my clit with my finger.

"Damn, woman, that's fuckin' hot." He quickly empties inside me, groaning loudly. "On your back. NOW!" I lay on my back. "I want to watch you pleasure yourself. Spread those legs and let me see that sweet pussy. Now, get those fingers working."

I keep teasing my clit as I watch Ace licking his lips. He suddenly grabs his dick and starts pumping. Holy shit, he's so turned on watching me that he's hard again. He pulls me on top of him, and I wrap my pussy around his dick. Unlike the hard, fast fuck he gave me, I'm going to make this last. I slide up and down slowly, savoring each stroke. His hands explore my back as we experience the intense passion. This time, we come together as he pulls me down and holds me tight.

He rolls me onto my back and again he enters me. We spend the next hour with our bodies connected in the most intense pleasure I've ever felt. By the time we were done, we were both starving. We didn't even bother to get dressed. We rode the elevator downstairs and went to the kitchen to grab some junk food. I grabbed a box of Lucky Charms while Ace opted for popcorn.

We got into bed and turned on a movie. Ace took one of each marshmallow out of the box and ate them off my stomach, both of us laughing. Once the movie was over, Ace turned everything off and pulled the covers over us. The last thing I remember was him pulling me close and kissing me goodnight.

CHAPTER EIGHT

Ace

"Baby, it's time to wake up."

I watch her sit up slowly and rub her eyes. I'm standing next to the bed, still in my pajamas.

"But Ace, it's still dark outside."

"I know, doll, but I have something special planned for today. We need to hurry though."

She jumps up when I flash her a smile. I take her hand and lead her to the elevator. When we're downstairs, I take her out to the backyard and watch her jaw drop. She does that a lot! I snuck out of bed while she was out cold and set up an open tent. I put an air mattress inside, covered with a large blanket. I also have another blanket on the ground outside of the tent.

"What is all this?" she asks.

"I have a lot in store for you today, but first come lay with me. I want to watch the sunrise with you in my arms."

We lay on the blanket outside the tent and gaze at the sky. I can't get enough of this woman. She feels so right in my arms. I just wish I had the courage to tell her I was falling for her. But, we agreed, this would be a ten-day staycation. I will, however, make sure she forgets all about the ass who put her in this situation. I can't fight the urge to kiss her, so I crush my lips to hers and joined my tongue with hers. I kept her in my arms until the sun had fully risen.

"Go have a seat at the table. Breakfast will be served shortly." I say.

"Mmmm, yummy. I'm starving!" she says, batting her eyes at me. There goes my dick stirring again. Shit, this woman drives me crazy!

I head inside to cook breakfast for us. I return a little while later carrying two plates. I run back inside and grab two cups of coffee then join her at the table. I watch Riley wolf down her food until her plate is clean. I love watching a woman who's not afraid to eat. When we're done, I stand and hold out my hand to her. She takes my hand and stands too. I take her into the tent.

"Baby, get undressed and lie on your front."

I watch as all her sexy flesh appears. I remove my shirt then grab the bag I have in the corner of the tent. I pull out a bottle of edible massage oil.

"Since this is your vacation, you deserve some pampering today. How would you like a sensual massage?" I ask.

"Mmm, yes please. I long to feel your strong hands on me."

I smile as I put a little bit of the oil on her back and start massaging it in. I move to her shoulders and neck, as she emits soft moans. I work my way down to her sexy round ass and spend quite a bit of time there. I run my hands up and down each of her shapely legs and gently spread them. Fuck, this woman is beautiful.

"Lay on your back, doll."

I start my journey back up her incredible body. I massage the insides of her thighs and she starts writhing. I can only imagine the effect this is having on my favorite part of her. But for now, I ignore it. I have plenty in store for that part later. I massage her stomach before moving to her luscious breasts. I can't take it another second, and I lower my mouth on one breast then the other, sucking hard.

I run my tongue between them then down her body, stopping just short of the spot I most want to taste. I can tell she wants it too, the way her body is writhing. I move down and suck the inside of each thigh.

"Oh, fuck, Ace, so good, baby," she cries out.

"Where should I lick next?"

"Please, baby, my pussy. I'm throbbing for you."

I decide to torture her a bit, so I suck her thighs again, harder this time. Her body bucks off the bed. She grabs my hair and tries to pull my mouth up to her pussy.

"Behave, baby, or you won't get what you want."

She lays perfectly still.

"That's my good girl. Get ready for your reward."

I slide my hands under her ass and lift her up to my mouth. I run my tongue slowly between her folds as her fingers run through my hair.

"Doll, I wanna hear you let loose and talk dirty to me while I pleasure you. I better enjoy it or no more tongue inside those sweet folds."

I watch her lock eyes with me. "Oh fuck, Ace. I love the way your hot tongue feels on my pussy. Please, baby, suck my fuckin' clit. Mmmm, yes, like that."

"More baby. Filthier than you've ever talked to anyone. Tell me your secret desires, doll."

"Fuck, Ace, please, spank my pussy. Please, god, make me fuckin' squirt."

"Holy shit, woman."

She takes her fingers and spreads herself wide. Damn, that's the prettiest pussy I've ever seen. I give her a couple light swats on her mound.

"Harder, please, baby."

I spank her a little harder, then slide a couple fingers inside her. I find and stroke her g-spot hard, as she screams. I lower my head and suck her clit hard, while I keep fucking her with my fingers. Her entire body convulses as she comes hard, drenching my hand and my face with her sweet juices. I run my tongue up and down her slit, tasting as much of her orgasm as I can, and fuck, she tastes incredible. My cock is harder than it's ever been.

"Baby, come with me to the hot tub."

Her legs are shaking from her orgasm, so I help her up and carry her. I sit down in the hot tub and motion her to climb onto my lap. She grabs my dick and takes me inside. She bounces up and down on my dick as water splashes everywhere. I cannot get enough of her hot pussy wrapped around me. She feels like heaven. I hold her tight as she moves on top of me until we come together. I have to bite her shoulder to keep from telling her I love her.

Riley climbs off and sits down next to me. I turn on the jets and we sit and relax. I put an arm around her and pull her in close. We sit quietly for a while, basking in the afterglow of more incredible sex while the jets massage our bodies. I hear the softest snores as she falls asleep on my shoulder. I can't stand the thought of ever spending another day without her. I can't believe this is the second half of our time together. What am I going to do without her? I put that aside and just focus on the time we have left.

My mind starts wandering to the room I never showed her. I saw her looking at the door when I was showing her around, but she never said anything. I think I may have to unlock that door on her last day here. I was afraid to show her then, as I wasn't sure how she would react. She has since shown her dirty side, so maybe she can handle it. She stirs awake, snapping me out of my reverie.

"I'm starving after that workout. Mind if I make some lunch for us?" she asks.

"Not at all, under one condition," I reply.

"Oh, and what might that be?"

"I want you to stay naked. I want to watch your sexy body while you cook for me."

"Umm, okay. I guess I won't be cooking bacon, then," I tease.

"How about instead of cooking, we take it back to our youth?"

"Ooh, peanut butter and grape jelly?"

"Yeah, with chips on it!"

"Of course!"

I watch her make the sandwiches. Suddenly, she turns around with a silly look on her face. She points at her naked breasts, and I lose it. She has peanut butter on one and jelly on the other. I walk over and lick each one clean. We both laugh hysterically then grab our lunch and head back out to the tent. After we eat, we hit the pool for a swim. When we're done, we get out and dry off then take a nap inside the tent. We end up sleeping until dinnertime.

Riley is still asleep, so I go inside for a few minutes to order food and dessert for us. When the food arrives, I set things up on the table and wake my woman up. We enjoy a nice meal and dessert together, as we polish off a bottle of wine. After dinner, I turn some music on and we dance naked in the backyard. It's getting hard not to tell Riley that I love her, but I manage to fight it.

We spend the rest of the night having more incredible sex as the sun goes down and the moon replaces it in the night sky. We don't stop until we're both depleted of energy. We lay down on the air mattress, and I cover us with the blanket. I pull her into my arms.

"I hope you enjoyed today's activities." I smile sleepily.

"I enjoyed today more than words could say. Thank you so much."

"It was my pleasure, baby. Or should I say it was our pleasure?"

"Mmm, so much pleasure…," she says as she drifts off to sleep.

CHAPTER NINE

Riley

I stir awake, wrapped in the strong, sexy arms of my man. I can hear him snoring behind me, so I lay there and just listen. I hate the thought that this fantasy has to end. Getting back to my boring reality is going to suck balls. I feel him nuzzle my neck, so I turn to face him.

"Good morning," I whisper.

"Good morning, beautiful. What would you like to do today?"

"I have a few things. Having a hard time picking."

"Tell me."

"I love checking out antique shops, but I also would love to go to Baltimore for the day. I love the aquarium, plus I have a favorite restaurant there."

"Which restaurant?"

"Phillips Seafood."

"You have good taste, woman."

"Thanks. Having a hard time deciding which one I want to do." I sigh.

"Why choose? Let's do both."

"Really? But, that's a lot."

"This is your vacation, and I want you to enjoy it. We can look for antique shops on our drive. Then we can tour the aquarium and have dinner at Phillips."

"I love that idea. Thank you so much for making this so amazing."

"Anything for you, doll. I was thinking we could stay overnight and drive home in the morning."

"Wow, you're really spoiling me."

"It's fun having someone to share all of this with." He smiles.

"Yes it is."

The only difference is, he'll get to keep living like this, while I go back to being boring old Riley. But, I won't let that dampen my mood today. We clean everything up from outside, head up to the shower and get ready for another fun road trip. Ace decides on his brand new red Mustang for this trip. The car is a stunning red, and I love riding with the windows open, wind blowing through my hair.

***

The ride to Baltimore is normally about two hours, but with stopping at several antique shops, we arrive about five hours later. We're staying at the Hilton in the inner harbor, in the Presidential Parlor. The room is stunning and even has a gorgeous view of Camden Yards. I feel like a princess. I have a feeling that the bed is going to see some action later!

After we drop off our luggage, we walk over to the aquarium. The last time we were here was in sixth grade for a school field trip. It was fun touring it with him as adults this time. We held hands the entire time, as if we were two people in love. Thinking about that was making me a little sad, but I couldn't let him know that, so I kept a smile plastered on my face.

We walked around the rest of the inner harbor, checking out shops and other attractions before heading to Phillips. Ace was able to get us the chef's table as the owner was a huge fan of his. I could get used to being a VIP everywhere I went. This is a far cry from the life I've grown accustomed to. We enjoy an indulgent meal and decadent dessert. We decide to take another walk around the harbor before heading back to the hotel.

"I'm gonna go down to the indoor pool and try to swim off some of the calories I consumed at dinner," I say. "Care to join me?"

"I'd love to. I guess we'll actually have to put swimsuits on this time," he laughs.

"Uh, yeah, I don't think they would appreciate us being naked."

"We can do that part later. That bed is going to see some shit tonight!"

I shudder with anticipation of what that sexy man has in store for my body tonight. I'm not sure I'll ever be able to be with another man again, without comparing him to Ace London! I get changed into my swimsuit then pull on a pair of shorts and sneakers. We grab towels then head to the pool. I'm happy to see nobody else is there, so I'll be able to get some good laps in.

We lay our towels on one of the lounge chairs around the pool, along with our shorts and shoes. I climb in the shallow end, and Ace follows. I quickly swim away from him, but he catches me and pulls me into an embrace.

"Behave yourself, dude, or you don't get the goods tonight," I tease.

"Well, well, Miss Feisty!"

I laugh and swim away, but he's hot on my heels. I go underwater and tug his swim shorts down then swim away. He fixes them then comes after me.

"And you told me to behave? What about you, doll? That was naughty!"

"What was naughty?"

"Yanking my trunks down."

"I did no such thing!"

"Doll! You did too!"

"You can't prove it!" I say as I splash him in the face.

"You're in trouble now, woman."

He grabs me, picks me up, and lightly tosses me back into the water. I splash him again and swim away. He catches up, and we start a massive splash fight, both of us laughing until our stomachs hurt. He turns serious, pulls me in close, and lays a kiss on me that I'm surprised didn't cause my swimsuit to fall off.

"Baby, what do you say we go hit a club?" Ace asks.

"I'd love to, but I didn't bring a dress."

"You won't need one. We're going to Angels Rock Bar, so jeans and a t-shirt are perfect."

"I've heard about that place and how awesome it is. I never thought I'd get the chance to actually go."

We get back to the room and start getting ready. We grab quick showers to wash off all the chlorine. I give my hair a quick blow-dry, do my makeup, and get dressed. Once we're both ready, Ace books a rideshare service to take us to the bar. There's a line waiting to get in, so Ace grabs his phone and sends a text. A few minutes later, a man comes out and escorts us inside.

"Ace London! I can't believe you're here!" the man says.

"It's been a long time, dude. Babe, meet Jason Williams, owner of this awesome establishment. We go way back, as my band used to play here when we first started out. Jay, this is my woman, Riley." Ace says.

"Nice to meet you, Jay," I say.

"Likewise," Jay responds. "Now, let me take you to our VIP section."

We follow Jay to a section near the stage and dance floor. He removes the reserved sign from one of the empty tables and motions for us to take a seat. He leaves a menu and lets us know a waitress will be over shortly. We each order a drink and I look around while we wait. I hear some catcalls and whistles on the other side of the dance floor.

I look over and see the three most beautiful women I've ever seen. You can tell right away that they're best friends. Each of them is carrying the same designer bag, in different colors. One of them has a pink bag, one has a yellow bag, and one has a black bag. They're all wearing bikinis that leave very little to the imagination. All eyes are on them as they dance.

Motioning toward the women, I ask Ace, "Wouldn't you rather be with them?"

"Babe, I won't lie, they're pretty, but I only have eyes for my woman. Let's go dance."

We walk to the dance floor. Ace puts his hands on my hips and I sway them. The "fun girls" as I've named them, join us. Ace steps aside as I dance with them, the four of us having a blast together. They told me their names are Sierra, Lacey, and Jazz. We ended up following each other on social media. Everyone should be lucky enough to have those three as friends. When we're done dancing, Ace and I return to the table and down a couple of drinks. We're just finishing another round when Jay drops by our table.

"Could I trouble you to hit the stage for a song or two? It isn't often we get someone your caliber in here," Jay asks.

"It would be my honor," Ace replies.

He follows Jay, so I'm alone at the table. Sierra, Lacey, and Jazz come join me.

"You're so lucky to be here with Ace!" Sierra says.

"I sure am. He's so hot," I reply.

When Ace comes on with the house band, Jazz says, "Come on, girl, get out there and shake your ass for that sexy man."

The girls pull me out to the dance floor. Jay escorts us to the front of the stage so we have the best view. Ace kicks ass up on stage. His voice is still as incredible as the first time I heard him sing. He does three songs with the band before he rejoins me. We end up hanging out until the bar closes at 2 AM. Jay drives us back to the hotel. We're both completely exhausted, so we get ready for bed and don't stir until the following morning.

CHAPTER TEN

Ace

I wake up a little before nine. I roll over and start rubbing Riley's hot little ass. She stirs awake as I run my hand along her side. She moans softly and turns to face me. She kisses me with more of an eagerness than ever before. As her tongue explores my mouth, I feel her hand slip inside my underwear. Her soft skin feels so good stroking my dick. All I can think about is plunging my dick as deep inside her as I can. I tug at her pajama bottoms. She lifts her ass and I pull them off, followed by her shirt. She frees my erection then kicks the covers off.

My eyes travel her body from head to toe. I will never get tired of looking at her, lying there completely naked. She reaches up and pulls me so I'm hovering over her. I feel her legs open. She grabs my hand and guides it to her pussy. I love a woman who knows what she wants and isn't afraid to take it. She's soaking wet and my fingers slide into her with ease. She grabs the extra pillows from the floor and slides them under her ass.

"Fuck me deep," she says in a husky voice.

I position myself completely on top of her, and thrust my dick inside her. The angle of her beautiful body lets me slide all the way in. I fuck her hard as my balls slap her sexy ass. I love everything about sex with this woman. The taste, the sound, the feel, even the way she smells when she's ready for me. Everything is perfection. Listening to her moans as my dick hits her g-spot is the hottest song ever written.

"Oh fuck, Ace, that feels so good," she moans.

I pull the pillows out and lay her flat. I lower myself and kiss her deeply while I slide in and out of her sweet body. There's something different between us this time. Love. Could she be falling for me the way I have for her? I'm still too afraid to say anything, so I keep my lips on hers as our tongues intertwine. I feel her quake as she screams out in pleasure. I feel her release soak my cock as I fill her with my seed.

"Mmm, that was incredible," I whisper as I hold her in my arms.

She sighs and lays her head on my chest. I feel my resistance slipping away. Before I slip and tell her how I really feel, I pull away and get out of bed. I can see the hurt in her eyes, but she doesn't say anything. I spend my entire shower berating myself, but I just can't take the chance of ruining the time we have left. After I'm done, she takes her shower.

I order room service while she's finishing up. We eat breakfast in silence, then get ready to return home. I take Riley to a couple more antique shops on the way home, and she seems to forget how I hurt her feelings earlier. I'm not particularly into this, but seeing the joy on her face as she walks around makes it all worth it. I would do pretty much anything to make this woman happy. If only I could do it for the rest of my life. I think about how this is already our eighth day together and I get sad. I don't want this to end.

"Oh my god, Ace, come look at this!" I hear Riley call from down the aisle.

I walk down and she's holding a record. She hands it to me, and I'm looking at myself twenty years younger. I can't believe she found my band's debut album. I'd almost forgotten how long I used to wear my hair. I definitely couldn't pull off that look anymore. I hand the record back to her, but she doesn't return it to the bin.

"You're not buying that, are you?"

"Damn right I am. I love it!" she responds.

I smile at how excited she is that she found it. We walk around a little more before she heads to the front to pay for her find. After she's done, we drive a little while longer then stop for a quick bite at an outdoor cafe. After we're done eating, I get back on the road, stopping at the same overlook I took her to a few days back. I grab a blanket from the trunk, take Riley's hand and walk her to the same spot. After I spread out the blanket, we lay down together and gaze up at the sky.

I pull her into my arms and crush my lips to hers. We quickly tear each other's clothes off. There's something so primal about fucking in public. I'm not sure if it's the risk of getting caught or what, but I can't feel her skin on mine fast enough.

"Babe, outside is my favorite place to fuck you."

I don't wait for her response. Instead, my mouth covers hers as I get on top of her. She moans into my mouth as my dick enters her wet pussy. Each thrust feels better than the one before. No woman has ever felt this amazing. I truly believe we were put on this earth to be together. Her hands grab my ass and pull me in closer. Every inch of our bodies is pressed together as the world around us disappears. All there is in this moment is me and her. We quickly climax together. I wrap us in the blanket while we come down off of our sexual high. We get dressed before anyone sees us then lay in each other's arms until the sun goes down.

When we finally arrive back at my house, we head up to my bedroom. Within seconds, we're naked and in bed. I just can't get enough of this woman. We fuck for hours until neither of us has anything left to give. She's in my arms, head buried in my chest, and I want to keep her just like this forever.

"I can't believe we only have two days left. I'll have to come up with something epic to finish our staycation."

I'm suddenly overwhelmed by sadness that it will soon be time for this woman to leave my home. But not just my home. She'll be leaving my arms, and that's a level of pain I wasn't prepared for.

CHAPTER ELEVEN

Riley

I wake up and feel an overwhelming sadness. I can't believe it's already my ninth day with Ace. Leaving him after tomorrow is going to be one of the hardest things I've ever had to do. I feel tears forming in my eyes, and quickly wipe them away before Ace wakes up. He stirs a few minutes later and pulls me into his arms.

"Good Morning, baby." he says with a sleepy smile on his gorgeous face.

Forcing a smile, I reply, "Good Morning, Ace."

"Baby, you seem a little down this morning."

"No, I'm fine."

"You don't seem fine. Maybe some of my special brand of lovin' will help."

Before I get a chance to answer, he kisses me hard. I feel that familiar warmth sweep over my body just as it had every time I was in his sexy arms. He quickly gets me out of my pajamas, then slips his boxers off. I'm still impressed by his size and even more so, what he does with it.

"Baby, I never get tired of being naked with you."

"Oh Ace, you always make me feel so good."

He smiles at me, and my insides melt. He moves on top of me and slides inside me, taking my breath away, I moan as his dick moves inside me. There was more of a tenderness from him this time, as if he was making love to me instead of just fucking me. Or, maybe, it was my feelings of sadness that made it seem like something it wasn't. He came hard inside me, then used his magic fingers to send me over the edge. After holding me for a few minutes, Ace got out of bed and pulled his boxers on. I was about to get up when he stopped me.

"Baby, lay back and relax. I'm going to serve you breakfast in bed today."

"That's really not necessary. I can come help you."

"No way, beautiful, this is your vacation, and you deserve to be pampered. In fact, that's what today will be, a full day of me pampering you."

Ace returned a little while later with a tray of food. He made a delicious breakfast of eggs, bacon, and rye toast, all of my favorites. He also had coffee and apple juice for us. He put the tray on the night table and sat down in bed next to me then handed me a plate. After we ate, Ace put the empty plates back on the tray. He got up, walked over to the side of the bed and took my hand to help me up. Such a gentleman!

He led me into the bathroom and to the chair he had moved in there. Once I sat down, Ace poured some bubble bath into the tub and turned the water on. After the tub was full of water and bubbles, Ace helped me up. He walked me over to the tub and helped me get in, then climbed in next to me. He put some romantic music on then moved behind me. I leaned back against his chest and he massaged my shoulders. I felt so relaxed that I fell asleep in his arms. I woke up a while later and sighed with pleasure.

"Baby, we can stay in the tub as long as you want. Once you are ready to get out, I have some more things planned for you."

"As excited as I am to see what else you have in store for me, I want to relax a while longer," I reply.

"Sounds perfect, baby."

He keeps his arms around me as I rest against his sexy chest. I love everything about this man, but I still can't bring myself to tell him. Besides, after tomorrow, he can finally be rid of me and move on to the next one. Even as I think that, I'm not sure I believe it. It sure seems like he has feelings for me too, but who am I kidding? I'm way too plain and boring to be worthy of a hot rockstar like him.

Once I'm done soaking, I say, "I'm ready for what's next."

Ace gets out of the tub and wraps a towel around his waist. He then helps me out of the tub and wraps me in a towel, pulling me into his arms. He leads me over to the walk-in shower so we could rinse the bubbles off. We head back to his bedroom and once we're inside, he lays me down on the bed then removes my towel. He removes his own and joins me in bed.

"Baby, I wanna spend the afternoon in bed, pleasuring each other."

"Oh Ace, that sounds absolutely divine."

He flashes me those sexy dimples before he kisses me. The kiss was more tender and romantic but felt no less amazing. I open for him and our tongues intertwine as his hands caress my skin. Never breaking the kiss, he moves on top of me and gently enters me.

Just like earlier, his thrusting felt different this time, slower and more tender. I moan softly as he slides his arms under me, holding me close. I wrap my arms around him and began rubbing his muscular back and sexy ass. He groans as he continues his slow, rhythmic thrusting.

"Oh Ace, it feels so different this time."

"Is that good or bad?"

"Mmmm…it's sooooo good."

I lose track of how long we stay like this. Ace's slower pace is making it last, and delaying my orgasm. When he finally brings me to orgasm, I have the most powerful release I've ever felt. My body quivered as wave after wave of pleasure courses through my body. I scream in ecstasy as Ace continues moving inside me until I feel him explode. Our bodies are drenched in sweat from that incredible workout. Ace lies down next to me. I nestle into his arms and rest my head on his chest.

"Baby, would you like to go enjoy a picnic dinner? There's a campground not far from here."

"I'd love to. The forest is one of my favorite places…besides your bed of course!"

He smiles and kisses me gently. We get up, grab a hot, steamy shower together then head down to pack what we need. We carry everything out to the garage, load up the trunk of his Mustang and make the short drive to the Country Acres Campground in Gordonville, not too far from my favorite Pennsylvania town name, Bird-In-Hand. He takes us to one of the spots designated for tents. We get our tent setup then put our sleeping bags inside.

Ace builds a campfire and sets up the two chairs he brought. We sit down at the fire to enjoy the picnic he packed us. After we finish eating, Ace puts some music on. He stands and puts his hand out, so I take it. He pulls me into his arms as we sway to the music. We're completely lost in each other. He kisses me and I can tell from the eagerness that our tent is going to be rocking tonight!

When it started to get dark, Ace safely puts out the fire and we clean up the area before we get into the tent. Ace opens up the two sleeping bags so we can lay together. He undresses me then himself and motions for me to lie down.

"Are you ready for more pampering, baby?"

"Oh Ace, you've pampered me enough already."

"There is no such thing as enough when you're on vacation. Now, lay back and let me work my magic."

I do as I'm told. Ace starts kissing my neck to start his journey. He takes each breast in his mouth, licking and sucking gently. I start moaning, thinking about where he will eventually land. He showers my stomach with soft kisses. He runs his tongue down until he reaches my pussy. He runs his tongue between my folds, stopping to tease my clit. I arch my back as my moaning gets louder. Nobody had ever made me feel as good as Ace does.

"Oh baby, your tongue feels so good. Please, baby, go harder. Don't stop, baby."

Ace ignores my pleas and continues his slow and sensual pace. He's driving me wild as the pressure slowly begins. When I finally reach the boiling point, I experience an intense orgasm. Fuck, this man knows what he's doing. He doesn't stop and the pressure quickly builds on my already sensitive clit. He slides a couple of fingers inside me. It only takes a few strokes and my body explodes for a second time. This one was even more intense than the last and I scream. Ace slides back up so we're face to face.

"You taste so damn good, woman. What would you like now?"

"I need to feel you inside me. Please fuck me now."

"In due time. First, will you do something for me?" he asks me with a sly smile.

"That depends on what," I reply.

I watch Ace grab a book and flashlight out of his bag. He hands me the book and I blush when I see what it is. He hands me the latest book by talented local author Eden Davidson. I've seen her at our local rock club with Johnny, the sexy drummer she's married to. If her writing is any indication, Johnny is a very lucky man!

"Will you read a dirty scene to me?"

"Ummm…"

"What, babe? Don't tell me you're embarrassed after everything we did this week."

"Well, I guess not, but I'm a bit nervous."

"Trust me, you want to do this. I promise I'll make it worth your while."

I read him one of her naughtier passages, and I giggle the entire time. I have no idea why I suddenly got so shy. When I finally finish the scene, I look at Ace and see that his dick is hard. Despite my laughing fit, I somehow managed to turn him on.

"Well, I did my part by reading to you. Now, you damn well better do your part inside my part!"

Never one to disappoint, he moves on top of me. That intensity is back, indicative of how much hearing me read aroused him. We fuck like wild animals until the wee hours of the morning. After we're done and drenched in sweat, along with other fluids, we sneak to the campground's pool and take a secret skinny dip. When we're done, we wrap ourselves in towels and run back to our tent before anyone catches us. We cuddle up in our sleeping bags and hold each other close until much later in the morning.

CHAPTER TWELVE

Ace

After we pack up the campground, we drive to one of the local diners and grab some breakfast. I can't believe we've already reached day ten. How the hell am I going to let this woman walk out the door? Once we've unpacked from the camping trip, we sit down on the couch. I turn to her, flash that smile that I've seen melt her, and cause her jaw to drop.

"I can't believe today's our last day together. Just wait until you see what I have in store for you, doll!"

"Sounds like I'm in for quite a day," she says, a bit breathlessly.

"I know you remember when I took you on a tour of the house that there was one room I didn't show you."

"Yes, and honestly, I've wanted to ask, but wasn't sure I should."

"I wouldn't have told you. I was saving that for today. But first, let's shower."

As we ride the elevator upstairs, I think about how this is going to be a shower, and a day she'll never forget. We go into the bedroom and strip down. I watch as she reveals her sexy flesh and I lose control of my dick. I see her look down at my erection and lick her lips. Fuck, she's the sexiest woman I've ever known.

We get into the shower, and I turn the water on, as hot as we can stand it. The hot water and the steam feel amazing. Now, it's time for me to make my woman feel just as amazing.

"Baby, go face the back wall and brace yourself," I say. Once she's in position, I stand behind her. "Spread those legs, woman."

I slide a couple fingers inside her, and fuck, she's already so damn wet. I fuck her with my fingers as she moans into the wall. Unable to wait one more second, I take my fingers out and replace them with my dick. I fuck her slowly, holding her tight so she doesn't slip. The hot water pounding my back while I pound her feels so fucking good that I quickly empty inside her. I slide my dick out of her sweet pussy, and finger her until she comes.

"Holy shit, Ace, that was so fuckin' incredible!" she says.

"That was only a preview of things to come, baby. Now, let's get cleaned up and on to our next adventure."

After our showers, we walk back to my bedroom. "Take a seat on the bed, baby. And stay naked. I'll be back for you when I'm ready."

I walk down the hall to the secret room and grab the key from its hiding spot. I let myself inside and get everything ready. I just hope this won't be too much for her. I pull on my favorite black leather pants and black shirt. I leave half the buttons open to tempt her. I take a deep breath, and return to the bedroom. I keep my eyes locked on her pretty face as I approach the bedroom. Her mouth drops when she sees me.

"Oh my god, you look so damn sexy," she exclaims.

"Come with me," I command.

Like a good girl, she gets up and follows me down the hall. I hesitate for just a second before I unlock the door. Before I open it, I turn to her, and after eyeing her up and down, I put a hand on the doorknob.

"Baby, I want to spend the rest of our last day together in this room. I have to warn you, though, this will be unlike anything we've done so far. I'll need you to tell me if anything makes you uncomfortable."

"Ummm, okay, wow."

"I'm giving you one chance to change your mind. Otherwise, you'll need to be adventurous and willing to trust me."

"No way in hell I'm changing my mind. I want this."

"Then let's go inside and begin our journey."

Riley

I watch Ace's face light up when I agree to go in. He pulls me in tight and kisses me with more aggression than ever before. There's something in his kiss that lets me know I'm in for one hell of a ride inside this room. My heart starts racing and I'm not sure if it's from nerves, excitement, or a bit of both. I feel heat spreading the entire length of my body. Without a word he takes my hand and we walk inside. My eyes go wide when he opens the door and turns the light on.

The walls are painted red and there's a king-sized bed with a beautiful brass headboard in the middle of the room. The only other furniture in the room is a big, red chair, a small dresser and a refrigerator. I'm curious what might be in that fridge. Ace walks over to me and kisses me hard with that same aggression he had in the hallway. Without a word, he removes my clothing and lays me down on the bed. He puts on some sexy music and does a strip tease for me. Once he's naked, he walks over to the fridge.

"Close your eyes, baby, I have a surprise for you," he says in a sexy whisper.

After he returns to the bed and lays down next to me, he tells me to open my eyes. He's holding a can of whipped cream and a bottle of chocolate syrup.

"What are you planning to do with those?" I ask, though I have a feeling I know the answer.

Saying nothing, Ace opens the whipped cream and puts some on my stomach. He does the same with the chocolate syrup. My heart races with anticipation of what he's going to do next. Ace lowers his head and licks. Even after the whipped cream and syrup are gone, he keeps using his tongue on my belly before he moves lower. Damn, I love how his tongue feels on my pussy!

"Mmmm, Ace, so good baby."

He continues until I explode with yet another incredible orgasm. Still not saying a word, just smiling, he gets up and puts the whipped cream and syrup back in the fridge. He again tells me to close my eyes. I hear him open a drawer in the dresser then close it a couple minutes later. I hear him walk back to the bed. This time he stands next to the bed and tells me I can open my eyes. He has two silk scarves, a blindfold and a feather in his hand. My eyes open wide, but I say nothing.

"Baby, do you trust me?"

I nod yes.

"I need to hear you say it, doll."

"Yes, Ace."

I'm a little surprised, but I'm excited by what I think he has in mind for me.

"Good, baby. I'm going to put this blindfold on you then gently tie your wrists to the headboard. If any of this makes you nervous or uncomfortable, please tell me."

Feeling especially naughty, I reply, "Please baby, I want this, too."

He flashes me the naughtiest, sexiest smile I've ever seen. I'm glad that's the last thing I see before he blindfolds me. I feel him take one of my wrists at a time and gently tie them to the headboard with the silk scarves. He puts the music back on so I can't hear where he is. The anticipation of when he'll touch me, where he'll touch me and how he'll touch me excites me like nothing ever has.

Suddenly, I can feel Ace's breath on my skin, so I know he's close to me. I feel the soft feather gently caressing my neck and continuing down my whole body. I'm on fire from head to toe. After he's done with the feather, he lets me lay there for a few minutes. I love not knowing what's coming next.

He lays down next to me and kisses me hard. I feel his tongue in my mouth. I intertwine my tongue with his as I return his kiss. I ache to touch him but I can't, which excites me even more. He continues down my body, showering me with kisses, but this time, he avoids the place I most want him to touch. I had no idea before today how much I would love this mild kink.

Unable to stand it any longer, I cry out, "Please Ace, touch my pussy. I'm throbbing for you."

He doesn't respond, and he also doesn't touch, but I know he's close as again I can feel his breath on my skin. A little while later, I feel his fingers on my pussy, stroking my clit, and I moan loudly.

"Oh baby, you look so sexy tied to my bed. I need my dick inside you now."

"Ace, please baby, fuck me now. My pussy aches for your huge cock."

I feel him move on top of me and thrust his dick inside me hard. He pounds me hard and fast, groaning each time his dick moves inside me. I didn't think it would be possible for him to be any better than the other times we fucked, but holy shit, it was more incredible than anything I've felt so far. He explodes inside me then gets up and I hear the dresser drawer open.

I hear a buzzing sound and without warning, I feel strong vibrations on my clit. The toy is so powerful, it doesn't take me long to explode. Before I've even finished my orgasm, his dick is back inside me. Each time he fucks me and comes inside me, he uses the vibrator on me. Each orgasm comes faster and is more intense than the one before. We continue like this all afternoon and I lose count of how many orgasms we have. My throat's sore from screaming with pleasure all afternoon, but it was so fucking worth it.

"Damn, woman, you've completely worn me out," he says. "Close your eyes. I'm going to remove your blindfold."

When he's done, he unties my wrists. I slowly open my eyes to let them adjust to the light. I look at Ace, and he has the biggest smile on his face. I can't stop smiling as my entire body tingles.

"I've never done anything like that before, Ace. It was the most incredible day yet."

"I had to make sure our last day together would be something you would NEVER forget."

"Oh, baby, you accomplished that."

Both sweaty and sticky from all the sex, not to mention the whipped cream and chocolate syrup, we shower together and get dressed. Ace prepares one last meal for us to enjoy together. Neither of us say much during dinner. After dinner, I help him cleanup then get my stuff together.

Though I don't want to, it's time for me to head home and back to reality. Ace calls Bruce to take me home. He texts Ace when he arrives. I'm about to open the door to leave when he grabs me and kisses me one last time.

"Thank you. I had an amazing time," I say as I fight back tears.

"It was my pleasure, baby."

Bruce drops me off, and I go inside. As soon as I close the door behind me, the tears flow freely. I can't believe I'm never going to see him again.

EPILOGUE

Riley

Monday arrives way too soon. Even though I spent them alone, these two weeks went fast. I've been dreading today, as I know everyone will be asking how my trip was. I can get away with generalities with most of my co-workers, but Maddie is going to want full details. That only leaves me one option. I have to tell her what happened. As if on cue, she appears at my desk, her usual cheerful self.

"Spill it, girl. How was your ten days in heaven?" she asks as she parks her ass on my desk.

I feel tears starting to prick my eyes. I look up at her and the smile disappears from her face. She grabs my arm and says, "Let's take a walk."

We go outside to the break area and sit down at an empty table. I fill her in about what happened and what I spent my time doing, including the story I wrote. She gives me a big hug.

"I'm going to find that fucker and cut his dick off." she shouts.

"No need. I'm over him. I never really loved him, anyway."

"No shit. I know who you love."

I fold my arms and say, "I do not."

"You keep telling yourself that. Now, you know I want to read that story."

"I figured you would. I have a copy in my bag."

We go back inside and stop at my desk so I can give Maddie the story. She takes it and skips away. She updates me each morning that she's still working her way through it and she'll let me know when she's done.

***

The rest of the week drags. When Friday finally arrives, I'm more than ready for the weekend. The weather is gorgeous out and I wish I was anywhere but here. I see Maddie approaching with a big smile on her face.

"Girl, that story was awesome," Maddie says. "Thank you for including me in it."

"You're welcome. If only parts of it could come true," I respond.

"I know. I still follow Ace on social media. Too bad he's not coming to our reunion."

"Me too, but I'm sure he's too busy for that."

"If he saw that fantasy you wrote about him, you can bet he'd be here."

"Yeah right. If only I was how I portrayed myself in that story. But, alas, I'm boring."

"Like hell, woman. Nobody who writes a story like that is boring. Can you imagine what it would feel like to get fucked by that man?" She smiles.

"I bet my story didn't even come close to how incredible he would be."

"Could you imagine if he got his hands on it?"

"I would die of embarrassment if that ever happened!"

"Or, maybe, he would want to start making some of that stuff come true. Especially the sexy stuff." She laughs.

I sigh as I enjoy the rest of my lunch break with my childhood best friend and now co-worker, Maddie Carson. I still remember how we met way back in the first grade. They always seated us alphabetically by last name, so I was right behind her. She turned around and just started talking to me on the first day, and we've been friends ever since. She is the keeper of my deepest secrets, especially the one that has me a mess right now.

I was actually glad to hear through the grapevine that a former classmate turned world-famous rockstar wouldn't be attending our high school reunion. I took a definite chance publishing that story. I made it clear in all disclaimers that it was completely fictitious, but Maddie knows otherwise. Sure, none of the stuff in that book actually happened, but I sure as hell want it to. Especially the naked parts.

Ace didn't join us until we were all in junior high. He just had 'it'." All the girls went crazy when they saw him. For some reason, he chose to befriend Maddie and me. It may have had something to do with the fact that while all the other girls were following the latest pop bands, we came to school in hard rock band t-shirts, just like him. Our lunch break is winding down, so we gather our stuff and head back to our desks.

"Are you ready for tomorrow night?" Maddie asks.

"As much as I can be. I'm just glad I'll be there with you!" I reply.

"We're gonna have a good time. People are going to go crazy when they see the hotties we've become." Maddie says.

I laugh. "Thank you for always helping to build me up. I'd be lost without my bestie."

"You know I love you, girl."

"Love you more."

"I'll pick you up at 6:30 tomorrow!" Maddie says.

"Maybe you should come at 6, in case I need help. You know how bad I am at makeup and picking out outfits," I reply.

"I'm always here to help the beauty-challenged," she teases.

We've reached my desk, so I wave goodbye and she heads off to her work area. I yawn my way through the rest of the day. I'm grateful when 4 o'clock rolls around. I'm in serious need of some sun, so as soon as Maddie reaches my desk, we practically run out the door.

"What do you say to hitting the club tonight? They're having an outdoor night tonight," Maddie says.

"Sounds like fun. I could use a night out." I respond.

"Maybe we'll find hotties to hook up with. I really need some dick."

"Maddie!"

"Oh, don't pretend to be all innocent with me, girl. Remember, I read your story. I know whose dick you want!"

"Shut it, bitch!" I joke.

"How about you head over to my house around 5? I'll pick you out something to wear and get you ready." Maddie says.

"Trying to get me laid, or something?"

"Damn right, girl. We both need the cock!"

"That right there is why I love you, my friend!"

"Dirty girls, at your service!" Maddie jokes.

"Don't you dare use that line at the club!" I joke.

By the time we reach the parking lot, we're both laughing so hard, tears are streaming down our faces. We get in our cars and head home to get ready for tonight. I shower and throw on shorts and a t-shirt, since Maddie's going to give me something to wear. If I know her, she's going to have me showing more skin than I usually do. Fuck it, though, it's been way too long since I've gotten fucked and I'm horny as hell tonight.

***

I pull into Maddie's driveway a little before 5. She's waiting on her porch for me. She drags me right to her bedroom so she can show me the outfits she picked out.

"So, anything you like?" Maddie asks.

"I like the jeans and the black t-shirt," I reply.

"I had a feeling. Just to warn you, the t-shirt is low-cut."

"Maybe I should pick something else."

"No way, the guys will love it. Let's face it, your lady-balls are hot!" she says.

I laugh so hard, I can't respond. I get dressed then Maddie does my hair and makeup. She gets herself ready and we start the drive to the club.

It's still a little on the early side, so the crowd is just starting to gather. We're lucky and we get a decent parking space. We got to the patio area and found a table.

A few minutes later, we have our food and drink order in. I see Maddie scanning the crowd, no doubt looking for some hotties! I start looking around myself when I suddenly spot someone that makes my jaw drop. It couldn't be? I must be imagining him after writing that fantasy about him. I shake my head, trying to clear it when I see Maddie get up and approach two guys. I can tell by her face and body language that she's flirting. Whatever she said to them worked, as the three of them walk to our table.

"Riley, I'd like you to meet Christian and Nathan. Boys, this is my bestie, Riley."

Nathan, who's clearly into Maddie, nods while Christian sits down next to me. He's cute enough, but I find myself comparing him to Ace, and nope, he just doesn't do it for me. But, since Maddie's so into Nathan, I decide to be a polite wingwoman and talk to Christian.. He's a nice enough guy, but that spark just isn't there. Meanwhile, Maddie and Nathan are putting on quite the show on the dance floor.

I'm starting to get bored with Mr. Dull, so I look around, and I see someone looking my way. Holy fucking shit, it is him. I see him headed my way, and every feeling in existence sends my stomach flipping. He's exactly how I remember him, except a little bit older. Time has been kind to him, and he looks even better than he did back in high school. Maddie is so caught up with Nathan, she never notices.

"Hey, girl, there you are. I've been looking everywhere," he says with a slight wink.

Taking his cue, I reply, "This nice guy was keeping me company until you got here."

Christian's face drops, but he accepts his defeat, mumbles something unintelligible and races away from the table.

"You looked like you needed saving," Ace says.

"What the fuck are you doing here? Sorry for being so blunt, but I'm in shock," I say.

"I came back for the reunion," he says matter-of-factly.

"What? I heard you weren't coming."

"That's what I wanted you to think. I wanted to surprise you. I wasn't counting on seeing you here."

"Well you sure as shit surprised me. I thought I was seeing things after writing… never mind."

"No way, you can't start that and not finish. What did you write?"

"Please, forget I said that," I beg.

"Can't. Tell me!"

"I kinda write steamy stories," I say as my cheeks catch fire.

"Is that so? I always knew there was a dirty girl in there somewhere. Dare I ask who you wrote about?"

"I'd really rather you didn't."

"Fine. Have it your way. For now, at least."

He doesn't give me a chance to respond. Without another word, he gets up and disappears into the crowd. I sit there with my mouth hanging open. I'm not entirely sure that just happened, but I know it did. I can't believe Maddie missed the whole thing. I desperately need to talk to her, but I don't have the heart to pull her away from Nathan, especially since his hands are kneading her ass like it's dough.

I can't sit here for one more minute, so I ask the bartender to call me a cab. While I'm waiting, I send a text to Maddie's phone so she doesn't worry. I imagine I'll get one hell of a story at the reunion tomorrow. Wait until she sees who's coming! I just wish I could have read more on his face. I have no clue if he was happy to see me, how he felt about me writing about him, or anything else. I get ready for bed, but sleep is nowhere to be found. I can't turn my brain off and I lay there staring at the ceiling for hours.

***

I'm up around 8 on Saturday morning, I finish up my cleaning and laundry then sit down to read for a bit. Around noon, my cell rings and I see Maddie's face on the screen.

"Hey, girl," I say when I answer.

"What the hell happened last night?" Maddie asks.

"You wouldn't believe me if I told you."

"Christian told Nathan and me that some guy came to the table."

"Not just some guy. It was Ace."

"WHAT. THE. FUCK?"

"I swear."

"What's he doing here?"

"He came for the reunion. He had told his friends to spread the word that he wouldn't be here as he wanted to surprise me."

"I don't understand."

"I'm not sure I do either. Tonight should be, um, interesting."

"No shit, captain obvious." She laughs.

"Enough about Ace. Tell me what happened with Nathan."

"Well, I just got home from his house. And damn did I have one hell of a night. He's an amazing fuck!"

"You gonna see him again?"

"We'll see. He said he would call me, but how often do dudes actually do that?"

"Hey, he could surprise you," I say.

"Not likely." She laughs. "Now, let's get back to Ace."

"I'd rather not. All that will do is freak me out for later. I need to find something to take my mind off of him until it's time to go tonight."

"Okay, are you dressed?"

"Of course. Why?"

"I'm on my way," Maddie says, then disconnects before I can protest. I try to protest when she arrives, but she drags me shopping for something to wear tonight. "Girl, you need to make Ace unable to resist you." Maddie said when she got here.

So, here I am, doing something I hate. I would much rather shop for office supplies or power tools than clothes and shoes any day. But I suffer through and by the time we're done, I do admit I'm going to look damn good tonight. When we're done, Maddie drops me off so I can shower and she lets me know she'll be over early to do my hair and makeup.

***

We get to the banquet hall where the reunion is being held. After we check in and get our ridiculous name tags, we head inside. I quickly scan the room, but there's no sign of Ace. Heads turn when we walk in. When our former classmates, most of whom picked on from K-12, realize it's me, their jaws drop. Good. I hope they're all sorry they never got with this. Assholes.

Maddie and I find an empty table and sit down. I keep an eye on the door, but still no Ace. I guess he's not coming after all. Oh well, even if he did, it's not like I would ever have a chance with him. Once the buffet is open, Maddie and I grab dinner and return to our table. After dinner, a DJ encourages everyone to hit the dance floor. After about five songs, he grabs a microphone.

"Riley Cavanaugh, please come to the dance floor," the DJ says.

I don't move, confused about why I'm being called up. Maddie finally grabs my hand and pulls me up. She drags me up front where I see a chair set up. The DJ points at the chair, so I sit down. Maddie stays nearby to make sure I don't take off. The DJ returns to his booth. I hear Def Leppard's Hysteria start and tears fill my eyes. This was Ace's and my favorite song when we were in high school. I lower my head and stare at my lap, hoping nobody will see my tears.

Suddenly, I feel a hand on mine, and I look up and see Ace. He takes my hand and pulls me up. He walks me to the middle of the dance floor and pulls me in tight. Our bodies start swaying to the music when I feel his breath near my ear.

"Riley, baby, it's always been you," Ace whispers in my ear. "I'm in love with you."

I whisper back, "I'm so in love with you, Ace."

"You just made me the happiest man in the world. Now, let's get out of here and start acting out your fantasies."

Without warning, Ace scoops me up in his arms and carries me out.

Goodbye, boring, predictable Riley Cavanaugh!

THE END

ABOUT SAMANTHA MICHAELS

Samantha Michaels was born in 1973 in the small town of Abington, PA and was raised and still lives in Hatboro, PA (both suburbs of Philadelphia). She is married to her high school sweetheart and they have a rescue dog, a beautiful Black Lab named Holly.

When she's not writing or working at her full-time job, she enjoys watching her Philly sports team (hopefully) win, listening to heavy metal/hard rock music, Texas Hold Em, reading, and spending time with friends and family.

Her love of reading began at a young age, thanks to her mother and Sesame Street. Her mom read to her constantly, and by three years old, she was reading on her own, and hasn't stopped. This eventually turned into a love of writing. She was writing for herself and then for a small group of friends, one of whom told her she should be writing books. She took her friend's advice and has since published several romance books with plenty more on the way.

Made in the USA
Middletown, DE
11 December 2022

17523280R00457